Adored

TILLY BAGSHAWE

ORION

First published in Great Britain in 2005 by Orion,
an imprint of the Orion Publishing Group Ltd.

Copyright © Tilly Bagshawe 2005

The moral right of Tilly Bagshawe to be
identified as the author of this work has been asserted in accordance with the
Copyright, Designs and Patents Act of 1988.

A CIP catalogue record for this book is
available from the British Library.

ISBN 0 75286 743 1 (hardback) 0 75286 744 x (trade paperback)

Typeset by Deltatype Ltd, Birkenhead, Merseyside

Set in Monotype Dante

Printed in Great Britain by
Clays Ltd, St Ives plc

The Orion Publishing Group Ltd
Orion House
5 Upper Saint Martin's Lane
London
WC2H 9EA

www.orionbooks.co.uk

Adored

For Robin.

Through the good times and the bad,
I love you more than words can ever say.

The Major Players

DUKE McMAHON	Legendary Hollywood movie star and Lothario. Autocratic patriarch of the McMahon dynasty.
MINNIE McMAHON	Duke's long-suffering wife.
PETE McMAHON	Their embittered son. A producer.
CLAIRE McMAHON	Pete's quiet, academic wife. Mother of Siena.
LAURIE McMAHON	Duke and Minnie's fat, useless daughter, Pete's sister.
TARA	Pete's spiteful PA.
CAROLINE BERKELEY	Upper-class English gold-digger, Duke's long-term mistress and Hunter's feckless mother.
GEORGE and WILLIAM BERKELEY	Caroline's pompous, bigoted brothers.
SEBASTIAN BERKELEY	Caroline's besotted, elderly father.
HUNTER McMAHON	Gorgeous, sweet-natured but neglected illegitimate son of Duke and Caroline.
SIENA McMAHON	Duke's feisty granddaughter, the only child of Pete and Claire McMahon. A raving beauty.
MAX DE SEVILLE	Childhood best friend of Hunter McMahon. Sexy, blond cad in the finest English tradition.
HENRY ARKELL	Max's beloved half-brother, farmer, family man and all-round good guy.
MUFFY ARKELL	His harassed but devoted, very pretty wife.
BERTIE, CHARLIE and MADDIE ARKELL	Their children.
TITUS and BORIS	Their dogs.
TIFFANY WEDAN	Hunter's actress girlfriend. Like him, beautiful inside and out.

LENNOX	A gay actor/waiter. Tiffany Wedan's loyal best friend.
JACK and	
MARCIE WEDAN	Tiffany's parents, simple folk from Colorado.
RANDALL STEIN	Billionaire producer and biggest Hollywood player since Duke McMahon. A bastard.
SEAMUS	Duke's old childhood friend, now his valet.
GARY ELLIS	Unscrupulous cockney property developer.
CHRISTOPHER	
WELLESLEY	Charming old gentleman farmer, owner of one of the most beautiful estates in the Cotswolds.
MARSHA	Siena's diminutive but powerful modelling agent. A drunken dynamo.
INES PRIETO MORENO	Flame-haired Spanish supermodel.
DIERK MULLER	Charmless but talented German movie director.
HUGH ORCHARD	Highly respected, discreetly gay king of US network television. Writer and creator of a number of hit shows, including *Counsellor* and *UCLA*.
JAMIE SILFEN	The most powerful casting agent in Hollywood.
CAMILLE ANDREWS	Texan model/actress/whore. A Sky Bar bimbo on the make.
MIRIAM STANLEY	LA starlet. Has slept with every successful producer in town.

Prologue

England, 1998

Siena was going back to Hollywood if it killed her.

'So you see, Sister Mark,' she continued, carefully composing her features into an expression she hoped looked both remorseful and resigned, 'I do realise this is an expellable offence. And I just want you to know that I *totally* accept responsibility for my actions.'

God, she almost sounded tearful. But then she always knew she was a terrific actress. The old witch might actually be falling for it.

'I just don't know what made me do it.' She dropped her eyes shamefully to her lap – all nuns, she had learned, were suckers for a bit of humility. 'But I quite understand that I have left you with no choice. I've let St Xavier's down.'

Fabulous. This was working like a charm. Mentally, Siena began calculating how long it would take her to clear out her poky little dorm room. She'd have to say goodbye to the girls, of course, but if she really got her skates on she might make the six o'clock flight to LA. Or maybe there'd be formalities to go through? She'd have to see the Head of Governors perhaps? Even so, an early morning flight out would still get her there in time for a blow-dry at Zapata before she hit the bars on Melrose.

'Miss McMahon.' The headmistress's softly lilting Irish voice belied a firmness of purpose that Siena recognised only too well. She had come to hate the way Sister Mark pronounced her name: 'McMaaarn'. She seemed to stretch the word out, like torture. She wondered what sort of rambling lecture she was in for this time.

Looking around her, Siena took in the familiar surroundings of Sister Mark's office for what she hoped would be the last time. It was simply furnished, as befitted a nun's rooms, but not austere. A full but slightly overblown bunch of peach-coloured roses dominated the desk, and their scent carried all the way to the window seat, which was lined with brightly coloured cushions, the slightly threadbare handiwork of generations of budding seamstresses. An unobtrusive crucifix hung against one of the whitewashed walls, while the others were plastered with photographs of St Xavier's girls past and present, commemorating various sporting or dramatic achievements. Siena, who was not much of a team player, did not feature, other than on the giant whiteboard displaying the detentions received by pupils, where her name made repeated appearances.

It was actually the third time this term that she had been summoned to the headmistress's eyrie of an office above the school chapel. In fact, in the seven years since Siena had first arrived at the school as a frightened ten-year-old, Sister Mark had lost count of the times she had peered across her desk at the beautiful, truculent, scowling little face of this most talented and yet most troublesome of pupils.

No matter how many times she looked at Siena, she never ceased to be struck by the uncanny resemblance: she really was the spitting image of her famous grandfather. As a young girl in Connemara, Sister Mark (or Eileen Dineen as she was then) had always had a bit of a soft spot for Duke McMahon. Well, it was hard not to. *Capri Sunset*, that had been his first big film, with Maureen O'Hara. Eileen and her pals must have seen it, what, nine or ten times? That dark flowing hair, that deep, rich, almost smouldering voice. Oh yes, in his day old Duke's romantic films had been quite an occasion of sin for half the teenage population of Ireland – not to mention the rest of the world. And now here she was, fifty years later, forty years a nun, wondering what in heaven's name to do with his troublesome granddaughter.

Smoothing down her brown Viyella skirt – the nuns at St Xavier's no longer wore the habit, and the only thing that set them apart from the rest of the teaching staff was a plain silver cross worn at the neck – she moved her mahogany chair back a couple of inches and fixed her gaze once again on the enigma that was Siena McMahon.

For some reason, the child had never really settled in at St Xavier's. She was popular enough, that wasn't the problem. There may have been a touch of the green-eyed monster going on with some of the other girls, but as a rule they all wanted to be associated with Siena: granddaughter of a Hollywood legend and daughter of one of the world's most successful movie producers, she represented a glamour and excitement far beyond anything that these well-bred English gentlemen's daughters had ever experienced.

Siena had other advantages as well. She was undoubtedly a beauty, and fifteen years of teaching in a girls' boarding school had taught Sister Mark that this, sadly, was a sure-fire passport to popularity, with or without the McMahon name behind her. And despite her truly appalling lack of discipline and almost pathological aversion to hard work, Siena had sailed through her school career with straight As across the board. On the face of it, she had very little to complain about.

Even so, it didn't take Einstein to work out that, for all her advantages and talents, the girl was deeply unhappy at school.

Her complaint had been the same since the very first week she arrived, a belligerent, feisty little madam even then: she wanted to go home. It was this that Sister Mark found particularly odd, since it was obvious Siena profoundly disliked both her parents. Tragic really. Other than the yearly prize day, which they both religiously attended, Pete and Claire McMahon seemed to spend as little time with their only daughter as was humanly possible. Six weeks in the summer holidays was the only time they spent together at the family compound in Hollywood. Siena never flew home for half-terms or the shorter holidays, spending her breaks instead in the charge of a Spanish housekeeper at her parents' Knightsbridge flat. To be sure, that was no life for a child. But it seemed only to make the girl more wilful, more determined and more desperate than ever to get back home.

Looking across at Siena, Sister Mark noticed she was biting her lower lip, a childish signal of nervousness that looked out of place on the womanly seventeen-year-old she had become. A previous generation would have described Siena as 'buxom', but nowadays the girls seemed to interpret that as 'fat'. In fact she had a small frame, dominated by a very curvaceous bust, to which her blue uniform jumper clung almost obscenely. Her small, rosebud mouth, pale skin and thick cascade of dark curls all belonged to another, more sensuous and feminine era. Only her eyes – two dark blue flashes of ruthless determination – gave her otherwise angelic face its modern, edgy twist. Today they were narrowed in wary anticipation. The headmistress sighed. She was almost as tired of this battle as Siena was.

This time she had been caught red handed smoking marijuana in the prefects' common room. Actually, 'caught' was hardly the right word, as she had made no attempt whatsoever to conceal the offence. Under normal circumstances she should, of course, be expelled. But A-levels were only a few months away, and Siena was expected to do exceptionally well. Besides, after seven long years Sister Mark was damned if she was going to send the little horror home now.

Reluctantly dragging her thoughts from the duty-free Burberry coats at Heathrow – or perhaps a bag, to pacify her mother? – Siena turned to face the elderly nun. Could she just get on with it for once and skip the damn lectures?

'Miss McMahon,' resumed Sister Mark, 'as you rightly say, you have indeed let St Xavier's down.'

Thank God, thought Siena, she's finally going to kick me out of this hellhole.

'However, I feel it would be . . .' A glancing smile flickered across the older woman's lips. '. . . precipitate – or shall we say rash? – to assume that you leave me with "no choice" in terms of your punishment.'

Siena swallowed hard. Fuck. What was she on about now? The spluttering roar of a broken exhaust pipe broke the silence for a moment, and Siena's eyes were drawn down to the rickety old minibus belching its way down the school drive, its chassis seeming to shiver and shake in the biting January wind. It was supposed to be white, but was covered in a layer of grime so thick that it stood out as almost metallic grey against the backdrop of snowy lawns. Inside, giggling groups of girls huddled together, on their way to some hockey match or other. They all looked so fucking happy, so jolly bloody hockey sticks, it made her want to throw up.

'It has not entirely escaped my notice, Siena,' continued Sister Mark as the noise of the failing engine faded into the distance, 'that you harbour a strong desire to leave St Xavier's. Although I will confess I am not quite sure why this should be.'

Not sure why she would want to leave St Xavier's? Jesus Christ, surely the question was why the hell would anybody want to stay? Chapel at 7.30 in the morning, lights out at 10.30, more fucking meaningless rules than the Gestapo? And the worst thing was, most of the girls became totally brainwashed. They actually *looked forward* to coming back to sixth form because they got to have their own toaster in the common room! Toast Privilege, that's what they called it. Was Siena the only one who wanted to scream out loud: *EATING TOAST IS NOT A PRIVILEGE, IT'S A BASIC FUCKING HUMAN RIGHT!*? In LA, seventeen-year-old girls had cars. They wore designer clothes, not some dykey old uniform. They went to parties. They got laid. They had *lives*, for Christ's sake. St Xavier's – in fact the whole of fucking England, grey, freezing, miserable England – was stuck in some kind of nightmare time warp.

'I am not prepared to be manipulated into expelling you when I know full well that this was the response you were hoping for,' announced Sister Mark. Siena glared at her openly now, all pretence at humility gone. The headmistress ploughed on. 'I have, instead, decided to revoke all your sixth-form privileges until the end of the year.'

Oh my God. Siena's stricken face said it all.

'Till the end of the *year*? You can't do that!'

'Oh, I think you'll find I can.' The nun smiled serenely. 'Furthermore, you will be gated for the next four weeks. That means no exeat weekends, no social events, no after-school activities. Other than Mass, of course.'

Oh, of course. Mass. Terrific.

'Siena. Listen to me.' Sister Mark's tone had softened, but Siena was oblivious. If she wasn't going home, then what was the point in listening? What else mattered? The nun reached across the desk for her hand and squeezed it with genuine kindness, ignoring the girl's look of revulsion. 'You are in the home stretch, my dear.'

Siena watched the sunlight glinting off her crucifix and shielded her eyes. She didn't want to hear this.

'It's January now. By July, your A-levels will be over and if you'd only start to apply yourself, well, you've every chance of a place at Oxford. Every chance.' She squeezed her hand again encouragingly, willing the child to look up.

But Siena had tuned out. Sister Mark didn't understand. How could she? Withdrawing her hand, she gazed out of the window, across the frosty convent lawns to the frozen hills of the Gloucester-shire landscape beyond. It was so cold that icicles still clung to the twigs of the sycamores, and she could see the frozen breath of the group of third-years chattering animatedly on their way to class, no doubt excited by the snow and the prospect of tobogganing at the end of the day.

Despite the beauty of the scene, Siena's mind was six thousand miles away. Not in her parents' home in the Hollywood hills but at Grandpa Duke's in Hancock Park, far back into her childhood. Suddenly she was eight years old again, bounding up the steps to the mansion and into his arms. Whenever she closed her eyes, she could feel the warmth and strength of that embrace as though it were yesterday. Sitting in the hard-backed mahogany chair in Sister Mark's under-heated study, she longed for that warmth with every breath in her body.

To her childish mind, it had all seemed so permanent. Grandpa Duke, the house, her happiness. But it had all melted away, all of it, like the Gloucestershire snow. And here she was, as far from that happiness and comfort as it was possible to be.

PART ONE

Chapter One

'Forty-eight, forty-nine . . . fifty! Nice job, Duke, you're looking great.'

Duke McMahon lay back on his workout mat and looked up at his trainer. Jesus Christ, these young guys all looked like shit. Sideburns like a pair of hairy runways, a brown velour jogging suit and more gold jewellery than the fucking Mafia. No wonder so much Hollywood pussy was out there looking for an older man.

Still, Mikey was right about one thing. He was looking great. Duke sat up and took a satisfied look at his reflection in one of the floor-to-ceiling mirrors that plastered the room. At sixty-four, he still had the body of a man twenty years younger, and he didn't owe one inch of it to surgery. He hated working out with a passion, especially the goddam sit-ups, but was infinitely vain. In his six years with Duke, Mikey had never known him cancel a single session.

'You still need to do some more work on your abs, you know,' Mikey chided as he watched the old man untie his sneakers and head towards the shower.

'Yeah, and you still need to do some more work on your fucking wardrobe, man. Not to mention your hair.' Duke held up his hands in mock exasperation. 'I'm telling you, buddy, you look like Cher with a three-day shadow. Get a fucking haircut!'

Mikey laughed and turned down the blaring roar of Mick Jagger on the record player. Duke loved his Stones.

It had been a long time since Mikey had seen him in such a chipper mood. Evidently the new girlfriend was working wonders. He knew he shouldn't really like Duke, but he couldn't help it. Sure, the old man was a bastard. An addictive womaniser, he treated his poor wife Minnie like dirt, and was so right wing – anti-gay, anti-women, anti-blacks, anti-taxes – it was totally outrageous. But he also had this incredible energy, a lust for life that seemed to draw people to him. Mikey had a lot of wealthy, famous clients – although none quite as wealthy or famous as Duke McMahon – and none of them could touch him for raw charisma.

Emerging dripping and naked from the shower, Duke strode over to the window and looked out at the California sunshine. He had had the gym built on the first floor of his sprawling hacienda in Hancock Park, a pale pink, Spanish architectural masterpiece known to the busloads of tourists that hung around outside the gates simply as the McMahon Estate. Although the estate itself had been built in the twenties, when Hancock Park was first starting to become popular with the swelling ranks of movie actors and musicians who had moved west to find fame and fortune, the interior was a bizarre mélange of modern and traditional styles.

Minnie, Duke's long-suffering wife, had impeccable, if rather conservative taste, and many of the public rooms reflected her refined and understated influence.

In striking contrast, Duke's unashamed vulgarity and love affair with all things modern had led to some gruesome decor decisions, of which the gym was only one. The state-of-the-art music centre, complete with eight-track tape deck and stereo speakers, was housed in an immense velvet-lined teak cabinet. A central 'workout' square of polished wood was surrounded by a sea of cream shag-pile carpeting, fitted wall to wall beneath the ubiquitous mirrors, and a disco ball hung in pride of place from the vaulted ceiling.

'For the love of God, Duke, would you put some clothes on?' Seamus, Duke's oldest childhood friend and now his right-hand man, a sort of hybrid manservant, PA and business manager, had stuck his flushed, permanently jovial face round the door, giving a brief nod of acknowledgement to the trainer. 'You have a meeting at eleven, you know. I know the dress code is casual in Hollywood, but I'm sure John McGuire would appreciate a pair of underpants at least.'

Duke looked over his shoulder at his old pal and grinned. They were almost exact contemporaries, but Seamus looked nearly old enough to be his father. His hairline had receded so far that he appeared completely bald from the front, and a lifelong penchant for 'the odd dram', as he put it, had contributed to both his florid complexion and his spreading waistline. In anyone else Duke would have been scathing of such a lack of self-control, but Seamus had always been a special case. Having battled his way through the viper's nest of scheming agents and unscrupulous studios in Hollywood, Duke knew just how rare loyalty and genuine friendship were. Seamus was a gem.

'Go fuck yourself, wouldya?' he replied good-naturedly, scratching his balls for added effect. 'I'm trying to enjoy the view here.'

And quite a view it was. Immaculately manicured lawns rolled down the hill away from the house as far as the eye could see. A blue, Olympic-size pool flashed and shimmered in the morning sunshine, surrounded by a haphazard collection of orange and lemon trees, all groaning with fruit. Tiny hummingbirds, their brilliant streaks of colour clashing with the unbroken blue of the sky, flitted from flower to flower, enjoying the sunshine. It was hard to imagine that such a Garden of Eden could be completely man-made; that without ceaseless irrigation, planting and tending, the whole of Hancock Park would have been nothing more than a lifeless desert swamp. But then that was precisely what Duke loved about LA. It was a place where you could turn a patch of dirt into paradise, if you worked hard and wanted it bad enough.

Any one of the legions of Mexican gardeners and handymen on the lawns below could have glanced up and seen the master of the house stark naked surveying his kingdom from the window, as they had on so many mornings before. Duke didn't care. It was his house. He had worked for every square inch of it and he could shit on the fucking floor if he wanted to. Besides, he liked being naked in front of the staff because it drove Minnie insane with embarrassment. Humiliating his wife was one of Duke's greatest and most enduring pleasures.

'Eleven o'clock.' Seamus raised a reprimanding finger in the general direction of Duke's naked rear view before scurrying off to prepare the paperwork for the day's meetings.

'Look at that, man.' Duke made a sweeping gesture towards the window for Mikey's benefit, once Seamus had gone. 'What a terrific day!'

'We're in California, Duke; every day's a beautiful day.' The trainer zipped up his sports bag and leant back against the mirrored wall. He wasn't in any rush to leave. His next client was a hopelessly overweight Beverly Hills widow who couldn't seem to get enough of his brown velour jogging suit and shoulder-length hair. Chewing the fat with Duke was a whole lot more fun. 'So what's put you in such a great mood all of a sudden? This wouldn't have anything to do with . . . is it Catherine? What's her name, your new girlfriend?'

'Mistress, my new mistress.' Duke grinned. 'I'm a hell of a lot too old for a "girlfriend".' To Mikey's relief, he pulled on a pair of white linen golfing trousers and sat down on the bench, warming to his theme. 'A girlfriend is someone you hold hands with, maybe go to the pictures with,' Duke explained. 'One day, if you find you really like her, then maybe you marry her and she becomes your wife. That's a girlfriend. Now a mistress . . . a mistress is something totally different.' He paused for dramatic effect, a slow smile spreading across his hawk-like, predatory features. 'A mistress is basically pussy that you own.'

'Jesus Christ!' Mikey exploded into laughter, genuinely shocked. 'You can't *say* things like that! Nobody *owns* nobody else, Duke.'

'Ah, kid.' Duke shook his head. 'How little you know.'

Standing up to admire his chosen outfit – white pants, white patent-leather shoes and a tight chocolate-brown turtle-neck that was far too warm for the California climate but which accentuated his chest and biceps – he put an affectionate, paternal arm around his trainer. How come he could never talk like this to his own son, Pete? The boy was always so fucking uptight, a stuck-up little prig like his mother. Duke used to say that Pete Jr was a replica of Minnie, only with balls – but these days he wasn't too sure whether he even had that distinction.

'Anyway, in answer to your question, yes, my mood probably does owe just a little something to Caroline.'

'Sorry, yeah, Caroline, you told me.'

Duke was beaming like a drunk in a liquor store. This must be quite some girl. As if reading his mind, the old man continued.

'Not only is she a world-class fuck . . .' Duke noticed Mikey fighting to stifle a blush. 'Seriously, man, you should see her, she is the sluttiest little whore but she speaks like the fucking Queen. If you haven't screwed an English girl, I'm telling you, you gotta try it.'

'I'll bear that in mind,' said Mikey. 'Thanks.'

'But the best part is . . .' Duke looked at him triumphantly. 'She's agreed to move in with me. Permanently. As of today.'

Had Mikey missed something here?

'What do you mean she's moving in with you?' He knew it was rude to piss on Duke's picnic when he was so patently over the moon. But how could Caroline possibly be moving in? 'What about Minnie? Did you guys, like, separate or get a divorce or something? How come I never heard about this?'

'Nope.' Duke cracked his knuckles and smiled broadly. He was evidently enjoying himself, lapping up the younger man's discomfiture. 'No separation, no divorce. I just told her. This is my house and I want Caroline to live here. Minnie'll do what she's told if she wants to remain a part of this family.'

Mikey winced. Duke's brutality never ceased to shock him, especially where poor Mrs McMahon was concerned. He couldn't understand why on earth she tolerated it. Still, even by Duke's standards this was a bit extreme, moving the girlfriend into the estate right under her nose. He imagined Peter wasn't going to be best pleased either.

'We're having a welcome dinner tonight at eight,' continued Duke, unfazed. 'It's just family: Caroline and me, Laurie, Pete and his wife . . . and *my* wife, of course.' He sneered sadistically. 'But you're more than welcome to join us if you'd like. I'll have Minnie set an extra place.'

Jesus Christ, so Minnie was expected to play hostess at this charade? Suddenly Mikey felt awkward, guilty. He didn't want to be party to any of this.

'I can't,' he said, blushing. 'I'm really sorry, but I can't.'

For all his charm, Duke obviously had a huge hole right where any sense of morality or basic human compassion should be. And when you looked right into that hole, it was black. Frankly, it scared the shit out of him.

Sensing the old man's disappointment, he shrugged apologetically and weakly attempted to lighten the atmosphere. 'Dinner with my girlfriend, you know?'

'Sure. Of course,' said Duke with a mirthless smile. He reminded Mikey of the wolf grinning at Little Red Riding Hood. All of a sudden the room seemed to become terribly cold. 'It's not a problem, kid, really,' said Duke, heading for the door. 'I understand.'

Sitting at her dressing table in the east wing of the house, Minnie fastened the clasp of her pearls with a steady hand. The sweet scent of the cyclamen creepers that grew around her dressing-room window never failed to relax her. She took a deep, calming gulp of the warm morning air and sighed.

Minnie adored her dressing room, her small, private sanctuary filled with the beloved and familiar reminders of a former life: her father's antique English writing table now served as her own bureau, and the richly faded Persian rug on the floor had once been the nursery rug back home in Connecticut, on which she and her brother Austin had crawled and squabbled and built elaborate cities out of bricks. Lavish vases of flowers covered every available surface, and a slightly battered but charming old bookcase beside the door was filled with books, not only collected but read, by generations of Millers. Some had belonged to her great, great-grandfather, and Minnie loved simply to hold them, stroking the spines and thinking of all of her ancestors who had held them and read them before her.

Thirty years in Los Angeles had done nothing to diminish her homesickness for the East Coast. But through her flair for interior design – Minnie had that rare ability to turn a house into a home without diminishing its elegance, with a style that combined traditional conservatism with real warmth – she had created a miniature East Coast oasis inside the estate, which had become a huge comfort to her in her frequent times of trouble.

Having arranged her pearls carefully in the mirror, she picked up the silver-backed clothes brush on the dresser and swept a few stubborn strands of lint from her skirt. Today would be a difficult day. But as her mother had always taught her, a lady never loses her composure, no matter how trying the circumstance. Whatever it took, she must maintain her dignity; draw it like a shield around her in the face of this . . . this . . . unfortunate event.

Ten years younger than Duke, at fifty-four Minnie had embraced middle age as enthusiastically as her husband had fought to keep it at bay. She looked like his mother. That is to say, she dressed like his mother; or like his mother *would* have dressed had she come from an old-money Greenwich family like Minnie's (rather than an impoverished New York Irish tribe of manual labourers and petty thieves). Her daily uniform had barely altered since she and Duke first married over thirty years ago. A khaki linen skirt to the knee, crisp white shirt with jauntily up-turned collar, tan pantyhose (no matter how stiflingly hot the weather, a lady never went bare legged), slightly heeled round-toed pumps and, of course, her grandmother's pearls.

Thanks to a rigorous, no-nonsense daily beauty routine, consisting of soap, water and a good dollop of cold cream at night, her handsome, patrician face was not excessively lined. The years of suffering she had endured through the latter stages of her marriage to Duke had etched themselves only faintly around the eyes, where other, happier women had 'laughter lines'.

Still, Minnie reminded herself grimly, she had a lot to be thankful for. Life as the wife of the world's most famous movie star had brought a lot of material comforts, which had certainly dulled the pain of some of her other marital disappointments. And of course, she had her children. Sweet, reliable Laurie and her beloved son Pete still lived on the Hancock Park estate, and along with Pete's young wife Claire they provided a daily buffer of emotional support against Duke's increasingly open hatred of her.

Her husband might be insisting on moving his cheap little tart into their home. But by God, if he thought he was going to drive her out with his vindictive little games, her or the children, he had another think coming.

'Mother? Oh, Mother, there you are.'

Laurie's forlorn face peered round the doorway. At twenty-eight, Duke and Minnie's younger child had already adopted the appearance of a confirmed spinster. Her full gypsy skirt and loose, shapeless Moroccan blouse did nothing to conceal the rolls of fat acquired through decades of comfort eating. With her greasy brown hair scraped back into a severe ponytail and her face bare of make-up, it was almost impossible to believe that this timid, trembling mouse of a girl could be the natural child of such fine-featured parents. This morning her appearance was further hampered by a bright red shiny nose and eyes dreadfully swollen from crying.

'Well, of course I'm here,' said Minnie, her voice bright and businesslike. 'Where else would I be? We have an awful lot to do today for the dinner, and I'm going to need your help, Laurie-Loo, with the flowers.'

For the last week, Caroline's arrival had been referred to simply as 'the dinner'. No one could bring themselves to utter her name.

'Oh, Mother!' Laurie's swollen, twitching face finally gave way and crumpled into full-throated, childish sobs. 'How can you be so *calm* about it? I mean, how could Daddy *do* this to you, to all of us?'

'For the good Lord's sake, Laurie, pull yourself together,' said Minnie. If there was one thing she would not tolerate it was giving in to one's emotions. It really was disgracefully undignified. 'It's a difficult time for all of us, but we have nothing to be ashamed of, and certainly no reason to cry.'

She handed her daughter a white monogrammed handkerchief and patted the chair beside her. The rosewood creaked as Laurie eased her snivelling bulk into it. Minnie wished her daughter would show just a little more self-discipline when it came to food, but she smiled at her kindly and tried not to show it.

'Really, darling, you mustn't cry.' She stroked her daughter's hair ineffectually, as if she were an obedient dog. 'Believe me, your father will tire of this young woman soon enough. Just as he has of all the others.'

'I hope so, Mother.' Laurie sniffed. 'I really do. But he's never moved any of the others in with us before, has he?' It was a good point. 'I mean, for God's sake, this girl is only twenty-nine. That's even younger than Petey.'

'I can do the math, sweetheart.' Minnie sighed. Squaring her bony shoulders into a stance of unshakeable determination, she squeezed Laurie's hand firmly. 'Try not to worry,' she said. 'It's going to be up to all of us, you, me and Peter, to make sure this young woman *does* go the way of all the rest of them. But I can promise you one thing, darling. I am your father's wife and the mistress of this household. And nothing, Laurie – absolutely nothing – is going to change that.'

Not for the first time, Laurie marvelled at her mother. Pete always insisted that a willingness to accept a lifetime of abuse from Duke was more of a weakness than a strength, but Laurie was in awe of

Minnie's resolute calm in the face of just about any storm. She thought of her mother as some sort of tragic heroine, her unbreakable spirit emerging triumphant through all the batterings that fate and life could throw at her. If only she, Laurie, had inherited some of that spirit, that strength, then perhaps her life wouldn't be in such an unholy mess.

'So . . .' Minnie smiled bravely, anxious to end this emotional interview with her daughter. 'Why don't we start sorting out those flowers for tonight? We want everything to look perfect for Daddy, don't we?'

To everyone who knew them, Duke and Minnie McMahon's marriage was a perpetual mystery.

When they'd first met, back in the late thirties, Minnie was the shy and incredibly beautiful teenage daughter of Pete Miller, the last in a long line of wealthy Connecticut landowners, and his wife Marilyn, a respected society hostess. Duke, who'd been brought by a casual girlfriend to one of Marilyn Miller's charity events, was a recognised young actor, still somewhere between up and coming and a major studio star, and already had something of a reputation as gambler and a womaniser who liked to party hard.

His attraction to the young Minnie Miller was instant and uncomplicated. Standing in the corner of the room, hiding awkwardly in the shadows behind her nerdy elder brother Austin, she seemed to represent everything that had been denied him in his own early life: beauty, fragility, innocence, wealth and breeding. She looked untouched, and untouchable, exactly the sort of virgin, Protestant princess that polite society considered completely out of bounds for a dissolute Irish Catholic boy such as himself.

He had asked her to dance that night – much to his companion's chagrin – and she had declined, blushing furiously and insisting she didn't know how to, clinging on to her brother's hand for dear life. Duke was charmed. He didn't know that such naive girls really still existed within a hundred-mile radius of Manhattan. Certainly he had never met one before. He decided there and then that he had to have Minnie Miller, and for the next nine months he set about the arduous task of seducing her.

For Minnie's own part, she had worshipped Duke from the moment she laid eyes on him. Not only was he breathtakingly good looking, with his hair the same shiny blue-black as a raven's, his firm, jutting jaw and his wonderful, deep, lyrical voice with its lingering hint of Irish brogue. But there was also something dangerous about him, something adult, masculine and forbidden that set him apart from all her brother's preppy Harvard classmates, or the boys she was introduced to at her mother's carefully chaperoned society dances.

Both the strength and nature of her feelings for him frightened her. For her to be courted openly by Duke, a Catholic with no good family and what her mother referred to with shuddering disdain as 'a reputation', was quite inconceivable. On the other hand a secret romance was in Minnie's eyes a step of such seriousness and gravity that for months she could barely sleep for thinking about it, tortured in equal measure by her passionate love and desire for Duke and desperate, all-consuming guilt.

Eventually, as is always the way, love and passion beat guilt hands down. She was still only eighteen when Duke took her virginity, in one of the old boathouses by the lake at her parents' summer house in Maine. For Duke, who was used to the more practised efforts of worldly Hollywood girls, the sex was, technically speaking, dreadful. She had lain rigid and shaking beneath him, her eyes wide open with terror like a rabbit about to be shot. And afterwards she had sobbed in his arms until his shirt was soaked through.

But his sense of triumph and elation, not just of breaking down her defences sexually, but of winning the heart of something so rare and perfect and precious, more than outweighed the disappointment of the event itself. There was something about Minnie that made him want to be a better man, the man she deserved. No one was more surprised than Duke to discover that he had, for the first time in his life, fallen in love.

They were married three months later in a little Catholic church off Broadway. An ashen-faced Pete Miller had led his daughter down the aisle: for Minnie to be marrying a scoundrel like McMahon was bad enough, but a Catholic wedding! His poor father and grandfather would both be turning in their graves.

For Duke, the day was one of unadulterated elation, and he couldn't understand it when, driving his new wife home from their rather subdued reception at the Millers' Manhattan townhouse, she had burst into tears.

'What on earth's the matter?' he'd asked her, handing her his handkerchief with a look of bewilderment and dismay. 'Don't tell me you're regretting it already?'

'Oh, Duke, no,' she insisted between sobs, 'of course I'm not. It's not that. It's just that tomorrow we're going to be leaving for California. I've never been away from Mommy and Daddy before, not for more than a week anyway, and I'm gonna miss them so much. Oh, and Austin!'

At the thought of her brother she began wailing again, and Duke fought down his feelings of annoyance. What the hell did she see in that chinless, judgemental, preppy little son of a bitch anyway?

'Come on now,' he said, reaching over and patting her thigh sympathetically. 'It's not like I'm taking you to Europe or something. Your parents can come visit. I bet you we see them all the time.'

Minnie shook her head sadly. 'I'm not so sure,' she said. 'You know how much they disapproved of us getting married. What if they never forgive me?'

'Sure they will,' said Duke. Although privately he wished his wife didn't already think of their marriage as some sort of sin to be forgiven.

The first year of the marriage was a happy one. Duke had bought them a large house in North Hollywood, back when LA property was still dirt cheap, and Minnie delighted in decorating it and playing house while her new husband was on-set. His career was going from strength to strength, and in 1941 he landed his first leading role, in a farcical comedy called *Check Mate*. The rift with her family remained strong, and she saw her parents only once in that first year, spending an agonisingly awkward long weekend with them at the newly developed resort of Palm Springs. But life with Duke was so blissful, and she was so caught up with establishing herself as a hostess among his new and exciting Hollywood crowd, that she found herself feeling less and less homesick, and less and less guilty, by the day.

Then came the war. And as for so many young couples, overnight it seemed everything changed.

Duke was sent to Asia, where he was to spend the next three and a half years. He was, as he liked to tell people later, one of the lucky ones. He came home. But the home, and the woman he came home to, had changed out of all recognition.

For the first six months after he was conscripted, Minnie remained in Hollywood, trying to make a life for herself among the other army wives there. But loneliness soon overcame her and, encouraged by her mother and brother, she decided to return home to Connecticut. She missed Duke terribly, and wrote to him religiously twice a week. But she also found herself naturally slipping back into the old rhythms of life at home. Soon she was going riding with her father and out to lunches in Manhattan with her mother, just like the old days, and her married life back in California began to feel more and more like a distant dream.

Duke would come home on leave and stay with the Millers. His father-in-law was civil – now that he had seen active service, Duke had apparently become a smidgen more acceptable in the old man's eyes – but still always treated him with a patronising sense of social superiority that Duke bitterly resented.

When he complained to Minnie about it, she dismissed him. He was imagining slights and insults where there were none.

Duke wanted her to move back to LA, but the mere suggestion made her almost hysterical.

'What's the point of me being there when you're away?' she asked. 'I'm isolated and I'm lonely, whereas here I have friends and family to support me. Things are so much better now with Mom and Dad. Please, please don't ruin it all again.'

He couldn't really argue with her. Still, he returned to the front with a gnawing sense that he was somehow losing her. That she was no longer completely on his side.

After the war, they did move back home, and for a while life got back to something approaching normal. Duke went back to work at the studio, and Minnie almost immediately fell pregnant with Peter. The cracks, however, did not take long to start appearing.

Minnie's parents' snobbery and East Coast prejudices seemed to have oozed into her personality in the last three years by osmosis. Whereas before she had been quite happy to have friends over for an impromptu kitchen supper in the evenings, she now insisted on full silver-service dinners every time they entertained, which Duke found pretentious and unnecessary. Worse, she began to show signs of embarrassment at his own social behaviour, reprimanding him in public for excessive drinking, and even on one occasion correcting his grammar in front of the whole crew on-set.

'It's "I should have", darling, not "I should of,"' she'd piped up brightly, overhearing him rehearsing some lines.

Duke was furious.

'Yeah? Well, maybe you should *have* stayed at home and minded your own fuckin' business, Min,' he snapped.

The worst of it was that Minnie herself could not perceive any of the changes Duke accused her of. In her own mind, she was just the same as she had always been, and she still loved her husband desperately.

'Of course I'm on your side, darling,' she'd protest tearfully. 'I love you so much, Duke. You must know that.'

But increasingly, he wasn't sure whether he did know it. With her love and approval, he truly believed he could be a good man, a good husband and father. Without it, there was nothing to stop him from going back to his old ways.

He began an affair with one of his co-stars. It spluttered on for a few months, after which, miserable and guilty, he came home one night and confessed to a distraught Minnie.

'I'm sorry,' he said, 'but I didn't know what to do. I feel like I'm not good enough for you any more.'

'Oh, Duke, that's nonsense! How can you say that?' she cried.

Even in her despair, she seemed to be dismissing him.

'Well, why won't you sleep with me, then? For Christ's sake, Minnie, it's been months and every time I come near you you push me away! You make me feel like some sort of fucking disease.'

'I've told you!' she shouted at him. 'It's because of the baby. I'm just scared, Duke, I want our baby so much, I don't want anything to go wrong.'

'And nothing will,' he said, pulling her to him and holding on to her tightly. What the hell was he doing, cheating on her? God knew he loved her, so much it scared the wits out of him.

That night they had made love, but it was a disaster. Duke, desperate for her love and forgiveness, had tried everything he knew to please her. But she was so terrified of losing the baby she remained rigid with tension throughout, suffering his attentions as a mother must tolerate the needy suckling of her child. The woman who had once filled him with such confidence and made him feel like such a strong, powerful man now made him feel useless, rejected and alone.

Things went from bad to worse. The baby was born, and instantly little Peter became the centre of his mother's world, leaving Duke feeling even more excluded. He began another affair, then another, each time hoping to shock Minnie into realising that he needed her.

She loved him, and was deeply hurt by his infidelities. But as the affairs became more and more frequent, she eventually stopped believing that she had any power to prevent them. Duke was rapidly becoming a huge star, with some of the world's most beautiful women literally throwing themselves at his feet. Obviously, Minnie thought, he no longer loved her. She learned to take comfort and joy in her children instead of her marriage, and cloaked herself defensively in the stoic, reserved conservatism of her upbringing. Slowly but surely, she and Duke grew ever farther and more irreparably apart.

And yet, to the surprise of all who knew them, they never did divorce. In fact, they never even discussed the possibility. Some said it was Duke's almost superstitiously strong Catholicism which held the marriage together. Others saw Minnie as a masochist, who would put up with just about anything for her children's sake and to avoid a society scandal.

The truth, in fact, was much simpler. Somewhere, buried very deep in both their hearts, beneath the hatred, the bitterness and all the many betrayals, a tiny fragment of love survived.

Chapter Two

From Duke's perspective, Caroline's arrival was a huge success.

By eight o'clock the house was looking immaculate. Enormous vases of pink and white lilies jostled for position on the delicate Louis XV walnut tables littering the hacienda's enormous marble entrance hall. Real log fires crackled in the dining room and drawing room (or 'den', as Duke embarrassingly insisted on calling it, despite its palatial proportions), and a festive smell of pine mingled with the sweet, heady scent of the flowers. Two assistants had been hired to help Conchita, the McMahons' cook, ensure that the lobster bisque, monkfish casserole and lemon syllabub were cooked to perfection, much to that formidable Mexican matron's fury. Minnie hated to upset Conchita, but it was imperative that tonight's meal be beyond reproach.

Pete McMahon arrived home from work at six. Although more physically attractive than his younger sister, Pete was certainly no heart-throb and, like Laurie, bore very little resemblance to either of his parents. To begin with, he was ginger haired, although with age his colouring had mercifully faded from the carroty orange of his childhood to a nondescript sandy colour, prematurely flecked with grey. He had his mother's pale complexion, but whereas Minnie's skin was luminous and pure, Pete looked permanently pasty and ill, and had a tendency towards excessive sweating. He was well built, despite being short and physically lazy, and there was a certain bulldog strength about him that some women seemed to find attractive. Nevertheless, he generally made the worst of his looks, such as they were, thanks to a tragic penchant for ill-fitting suits as well as the scowl of resentment that hung almost permanently over his otherwise regular features.

Today he was looking even more bad tempered than usual. What a shitty, shitty day it had been. His long-anticipated meeting with the producer Mort Hanssen had turned out to be a complete waste of time. Pete aspired to produce himself, and had had a couple of vanity credits on some half-decent low-budget pictures. But Mort, like everybody else in Hollywood, clearly still viewed him as Duke McMahon's kid. The fact that at the age of thirty he still lived under his father's roof obviously did nothing to improve his credibility. Man, he really had to do something about that, take the bull by the horns.

He and Claire, his quiet, shy new wife, remained largely financially dependent on Duke and lived in a suite of rooms in the south wing of the main house. Although he had never shown even the most glancing interest in either of his two children, Duke was insistent that his entire extended family should remain living at Hancock Park. Having grown up the youngest of seven children in a vast Irish tribe, sleeping two or three to a bed, Duke liked big families. He also had an almost pathological fear of being alone.

For Pete, living on the estate was like fucking torture. No privacy. No escape. After the day he'd had today, the last thing he needed was to play welcoming committee for some bimbo of his father's.

Walking into the drawing room, he watched Minnie as she darted about tasting the soup or plumping up the already perfect over-stuffed cushions. Pete's heart lurched for her. He felt a sickening combination of love, sympathy and an agonising, impotent rage. Somehow his mother had made it a matter of *pride* to have the house looking wonderful for that little bitch. As if the fucking priest were coming over for Thanksgiving or something. Jesus. Why couldn't she once, just *once*, stand up to him?

But Pete knew, probably better than anybody, that it wasn't that easy to stand up to his father. As a small boy, he had watched helplessly as Duke systematically destroyed his mother's happiness. It wasn't just the other women. In fact, sexual infidelity, Pete reflected, was probably one of the least of his father's crimes. Lust, after all, is instinctive. Whereas vindictiveness, decades of consistent casual cruelty, of emotional torture – now that was something you had to work at.

And boy, Duke had really worked at it. Jealous of his wife's better breeding, her East Coast education and her innate good taste, he had brutally asserted his authority through a combination of economic control – Minnie never had her own bank account, nor did she spend a cent without first having to beg her husband's permission – and sheer force of personality.

It didn't help that for all Pete's life, his father had been a megastar. A matinée idol in the thirties and forties, he had invested his earnings wisely and grown to become a respected Hollywood power broker. People fawned on Duke. People who didn't even know him were mesmerised by him. Men fantasised about being him, women about screwing him. But none of them knew the real Duke McMahon – the vicious husband, the cold, autocratic father. Pete knew him, and for as long as he could remember, he had hated him.

But never more so, he thought, than today. Initially, he had refused to attend 'the dinner', telling his father rather pompously, but with an uncharacteristic display of nerve, that he and Claire would never break bread with his latest whore. In the end it was Minnie who persuaded him to change his mind. She needed him there when Caroline arrived, needed his and Claire's moral support. Reluctantly, he had given in.

By 8.15, Pete was sitting, stony faced, in front of the drawing-room fire, angrily shrugging off his wife's feeble attempts to comfort him. His sister Laurie, still looking tear-stained and lumpen in an utterly unsuitable, over-the-top gold lamé evening dress, was pacing the room anxiously, a habit that failed to improve Pete's foul temper. Why did she always have to look such a fright?

Minnie, calm and regal as ever in a simple black crêpe shift and pearls, sat rigid backed beside the door. Contrary to all outward appearances, her stomach was churning. There had been a time when she believed that no behaviour of her husband's could surprise or hurt her any more. Now for the first time in many years, she did not know what to expect, or how she was supposed to behave. She was in uncharted territory, and Pete's palpable rage was doing as little as Laurie's hysteria to calm her own fraught nerves. What in heaven's name had she ever done to deserve this? She just wanted this evening over with.

All four of them jumped when the doorbell rang.

'Why is he ringing the bell?' snapped Pete. 'He has a key, doesn't he?'

Anxious to diffuse her son's anger, Minnie took charge at once, standing to receive her guests with a serene smile glued to her face.

'Antoine, would you get the door, please?'

The butler glided forward. 'Of course, madam.'

The heavy black door swung slowly open. Duke was nowhere to be seen.

'How do you do?' The accent was cut-glass English. 'I'm Caroline Berkeley. Perhaps you'd be so kind as to take my coat?'

The young woman before her was about as far removed from Minnie's preconceptions as it was possible for her to be. She was beautiful, but certainly not tarty. Her hair, which was either naturally blonde or very expensively dyed, was worn up in a neat chignon, and contrasted dramatically with her flowing, feminine, rainbow-effect

Pucci dress (in fact, wasn't that the dress Minnie had so admired in last month's *Vogue*? It was, she was sure of it). Elegant, strappy Yves St Laurent sandals revealed perfectly pedicured and subtly painted toes. Her make-up was minimal, intended only to heighten her almost neon-blue eyes and surprisingly delicate English complexion. This was no dime-a-dozen playgirl from Venice Beach. Caroline looked, disconcertingly, like a lady.

She was also unusually self-assured. Ignoring the maid, she handed her coat to a bewildered-looking Claire before turning to Minnie.

'So you must be Mrs M?' She smiled, smugly. 'How adorable you look in that dress! My mother has one just like it.'

Minnie failed to suppress a scowl.

'Dukey's told me so much about you.' She winked at Minnie conspiratorially. 'He's just fetching my luggage, by the way, he should be here in a moment. Anyway, I'm sure we'll have simply *tons* to talk about, swapping secrets and all that, but first of all I simply must use your loo. Or perhaps it's my loo now?' Caroline laughed, pleased at her wit, and strode off down the corridor. She evidently knew her way around the house.

Pete exploded. 'Fucking arrogant bitch! And what the hell did you take her coat for?'

He shot an accusatory glance at the terrified Claire, who looked down at the cream Chanel wool in her hands in panic, as though it were about to self-destruct.

'I'm sorry,' she mumbled meekly, 'it just happened so quickly, I didn't really have time to . . . I mean . . .'

'Oh, never mind. My God, that little slut has some nerve, treating my wife like a fucking maid. And the way she spoke to you, Mother. Who the hell does she think she is?'

Before Minnie could respond, Duke came sauntering triumphantly into the hallway, weighed down by two enormous Louis Vuitton suitcases. Taking in his wife's look of shock, Pete's undisguised fury and Laurie and Claire's subdued misery, he laughed out loud.

'So, I guess you met Caroline, huh? Isn't she great? Quite a looker, wouldn't you say, Peter?' he added spitefully to his son.

'Sure.' Pete's tone was utterly dead. 'If you like cheap whores.'

Duke laughed again. Nothing was going to put him out of his good humour tonight, least of all his pussy of a son.

'I'll tell you something, kiddo, she may be a whore but she certainly isn't cheap,' he said. 'I paid five hundred bucks for that dress.'

Minnie felt a small, irrational stab of pain. Even in the early, happy days of their marriage, Duke had never spent anything close to that on her.

'Ask your mother.' He looked at Minnie, his eyes flashing with the excited cruelty of a cat playing with a cornered mouse before the kill. 'She knows all about *class*, don't you, my darling? Wouldn't you say Caroline is elegant? She comes from one of the oldest, most aristocratic families in England. I mean, we're not talking Greenwich here. Caroline's from the *real* upper classes.'

He was hitting Minnie where it hurt and they both knew it.

Right on cue, Caroline sashayed back along the corridor, stilettos clacking painfully loudly on the polished marble, and wrapped herself possessively around Duke. 'Darling,' she stage-whispered into his ear, 'you know, we could always skip supper and just go straight to bed.'

Bitch, bitch, bitch, thought Pete. She's enjoying this.

'Skip dinner?' Duke smiled at her proudly. 'I don't think so. My wife here has gone to a lot of trouble, sweetheart. And we wouldn't want to be rude, now, would we?'

At dinner, the pair of them were insufferable. Duke was deliberately, revoltingly affectionate towards his young mistress, constantly running his roughly wrinkled hand across her cheek or feeding her morsels of monkfish from his fork like a lovesick teenager.

Caroline was also on rare form, and no one was immune from her witheringly bitchy put-downs.

'Gosh, Laurie,' she exclaimed, wide eyed, 'you are brave. I always think gold is *such* a difficult colour to pull off with a fuller figure.'

'Mrs McMahon,' – she seemed to delight in addressing Minnie pseudo-respectfully – 'this food really is delicious. Heavens, if I had a cook as good as Conchita, I don't expect I'd worry about my figure either. Dukey, do you think she'll be able to rustle me up something low-fat for breakfast tomorrow?'

Minnie's self-control in the face of such provocation was quite astounding. Pete, on the other hand, rose like a starving, credulous fish to every piece of bait Caroline threw him.

'Now, Claire,' – she leant forward across the table, giving both Pete and his wife a flash of her small but perfectly rounded porcelain-white breasts – 'I *do* hope that you and I can become friends. It will be so nice to have a girl my own age to play with.'

'Really?' said Pete, stabbing viciously at his syllabub with a teaspoon. 'And here we were all thinking you preferred playing with men old enough to be your grandfather.'

Claire looked miserably from Pete to Minnie. She had dressed particularly conservatively this evening in a long taupe skirt and sweater, perhaps in a subconscious effort to fade into the background. Although undeniably a beautiful woman, with her shoulder-length mane of honey-blonde hair and luminous creamy complexion, her shy looks paled into nothing when set beside Caroline's glamour and electric sexual confidence. Not that it bothered her. Pete's young wife didn't have a vain bone in her body. She just wished that this awful woman who was so upsetting her husband would go away and leave them all alone.

'Peter, that's enough,' said Duke, a razor-sharp edge biting into his famously deep, resonant voice. 'Like it or not, Caroline is a member of this family from now on. I will not have her spoken to in that tone by anyone.'

Father and son glared at one another, their faces eerily illuminated by the candlelight, but Pete dropped his gaze first.

'Least of all you,' added Duke, folding his napkin with a measured finality to indicate that the conversation was now closed.

Laurie, who was suddenly feeling uncomfortable and awkward in what had been her favourite dress, was too choked with self-pity to rally to her brother's support. While poor Claire kept her eyes glued firmly to her plate throughout the whole excruciating ordeal.

Buoyed by Duke's encouragement, and fuelled by more than a few glasses of the vintage champagne Minnie had been told to lay on for the occasion, Caroline allowed her arrogance full rein, rudely snapping her fingers at the staff and generally behaving as though she were the established lady of the house. She had been dreading this evening, the inevitable showdown with the old man's ghastly wife; but now that it had all gone so well, she felt deliriously happy.

All this wealth and privilege were hers for the taking, and she intended to grab them with both hands. How ridiculous to think that she had feared Minnie McMahon so much! The poor old stick was clearly no match for her. Caroline found it almost impossible to imagine the black-clad statue across the table from her, with her drawn features and tight-lipped reserve, as ever having been of sexual interest to Duke. She looked like a relic from another era, one of the many older women for whom the swinging sixties had simply swung right on by, and who woke up in the seventies to find the world they grew up in had disappeared for ever.

As for Pete and Laurie, well, they were even more wet and useless than Duke had hinted. She wondered what possessed him to keep the pair of them under his roof. He had said something about it once – some nostalgic Catholic rubbish about family – but Caroline had been focusing on the divine Cartier necklace they'd been choosing on Rodeo at the time, and hadn't really caught his gist.

27

What had not escaped her notice, however, was that Duke was being extraordinarily tactile this evening. As his hand softly caressed the back of her neck, she wondered whether this meant he would be excessively demanding in bed later, and suppressed a sigh. Humiliating his pathetic wife was obviously turning him on, judging by the size of the erection Caroline had been fondling discreetly for the last hour. You could say a lot of things about Duke, but he certainly still had a very healthy libido.

Her suspicions proved justified that night in bed. Exhilarated by his own demonstration of power and control over Minnie, Duke's eyes were alive with excitement at the prospect of screwing Caroline. Availing himself of her exquisitely ripe, young body would be the perfect end to what had been a thoroughly enjoyable and arousing evening.

He and Minnie had kept separate bedrooms for the last twenty-odd years, and his dark wood-panelled room no longer bore any traces of his wife. Duke had had the exquisite parquet flooring smothered in the ankle-deep cream carpet he so loved, and all the antique furniture replaced with so much chrome and glass that the original walls looked embarrassed and out of place. He loved the modernity of the furniture, and not just because Minnie hated it. It made him feel young somehow. And the thick carpet beneath his bare feet felt wonderfully luxurious to the boy who had grown up running barefoot on the cold, rough wooden floors of a Brooklyn tenement building.

Duke reclined on the enormous, laminated plastic bed, draped in rich purple velvet covers and purple silk pillows fit for a debauched Roman emperor. He felt his cock turn to iron as he watched Caroline start to strip for him.

With one graceful movement she released the clasp at her neck, and $500 worth of Pucci silk slithered to the floor. Staring at her full, high breasts, the pale pink nipples flushing a deeper red with lust, her slender, almost breakable legs looking even longer in those black stilettos, Duke knew he had never wanted a woman more. She gazed wantonly back at him, the dampness from her pussy beginning to show through her minuscule sheer pink panties, and bent down to remove her shoes.

'No. Leave them on.' His voice was rough and brutal with longing, all the faux affection from the dinner table gone. 'Come here.'

Hanging her head submissively, she approached the bed, and climbing up on to it kneeled in front of Duke, awaiting instructions. She was like a doll, he thought joyously; he could do anything he

28

wanted to her, anything. He knew she was only interested in his money, of course. But what did that matter? This was fifty times better than picking up a hooker down on Sunset.

Caroline might be a gold-digger, but she still had social class, something that had always eluded Duke, for all his money and power. That cut-glass English accent, her grand titled friends, it all made her infinitely more exciting in his eyes. He loved to watch her playing the part, acting like the little lady of the manor, and knowing that whenever he snapped his fingers he could have her, naked, compliant, ready to cater to his every whim. His money enabled him to control her, to own her. Mikey was wrong. You *could* own a woman. And Caroline was all his.

'Suck my cock,' he commanded, lying back against the pillows as the small blonde head bobbed up and down in his lap. He had wanted to fuck her tonight, but it had been a long, long day, and the moment he felt her expert tongue rolling itself around his erection, flickering teasingly just beneath its head, he knew he had to come now.

Gripping her tiny, fragile skull with his left hand, he forced her head down farther until his dick was touching the back of her throat. Instinctively she struggled, retching and fighting for breath, legs flailing grotesquely, still in her tight black shoes. The sight was too much for Duke, who cried out as he came, still clamping her head to his cock so that every drop of his semen poured straight down her smooth, white throat before he released her.

Caroline pushed her tangled hair back from her face, gasping for air, and wiped the sweat and saliva from her face. She knew she must look like a first-class whore, and the thought aroused her. Duke was old enough to be her father, if not her grandfather, and she'd be lying if she said that physical attraction was her prime motivation for being in his bed. Even so, she had to admit there was something about him, about the two of them together, which worked. He never, ever gave a thought to her pleasure. But in a perverse way, that pleased her.

Duke looked at her smeared, dishevelled face with satisfaction. He was an old man now and he knew it. Sure, he was in good shape, he took care of himself. But so many of his old buddies were already gone – heart attacks, lung cancer, God only knew what else. He reached over to the bedside table for a Lucky Strike and lit it.

Death did not preoccupy him unduly, although he missed his youth, the adrenalin rush of mass adulation that had fuelled him through his twenties and thirties, already a movie legend.

What an incredible, fantastic life it had been.

With the exception of a few terrible incidents in Japan during the war, and the painful breakdown of his marriage, it had been a life crammed with enjoyment, excitement and excess. Duke had lived it greedily, relishing every second, and he intended to see out the last days of his life with the same energy, the same pursuit of his own pleasure, that he always had.

He had learned long ago to block out the pain of losing Minnie's love. Without her, he had abandoned all hope of becoming a 'better' man and ruthlessly stamped down any finer feelings in himself, of selflessness, honour or decency, whenever they threatened to limit his rampant, hedonistic lifestyle.

He looked at Caroline again and felt a wave of satisfaction flood his senses. How many men in their sixties had mind-blowing sex on tap from a girl as utterly desirable as this? Gazing down at her, inhaling deeply on his cigarette, he felt like a fucking king.

Without taking her eyes from his, she bent her head once again and began slowly licking his balls.

'Good girl,' he purred, stroking her hair more tenderly now. 'That's a good girl.' She wrapped her arms around his thighs, laying her head comfortably between them while her tongue got to work.

'Welcome to the family.'

Chapter Three

In snagging Duke McMahon, Caroline Berkeley felt she had finally achieved her destiny.

The fourth child, and only daughter, of Sebastian and Elizabeth Berkeley of Amhurst Manor, Oxfordshire, she had been born into a world of post-war optimism in 1946. Her privileged parents were still wealthy at that time, although a lot of money had been lost by the previous generation of Berkeleys, grandparents and great-aunts whom Caroline never knew, through alcoholism and heavy gambling debts. After her mother died in Caroline's infancy – Elizabeth had never recovered from the death of her eldest son Peter on the Normandy beaches – the family's financial decline had gone from bad to worse.

Unsurprisingly, Caroline's dissolute grandfather Charles had done nothing to tutor her father in the fine arts of investment or estate management. Sebastian's resulting financial ineptitude, combined with his debilitating grief over the loss of both his wife and son, were to prove fatal to the great old estate.

By the time Caroline turned fifteen, Sebastian had lost Amhurst, along with the bulk of his children's inheritance. This sudden reversal of the family fortunes was the single most formative event in her childhood.

She could remember the day her father had driven to school to break the terrible news to her, could see his ashen face as though it were yesterday. As soon as they sat down on an old stone bench, in the rose garden at Massingham Hall, she had known something was very wrong.

'For heaven's sake, Pa, what is it?' She heard the panic rising in her voice. She had never seen her beloved father in such a state. 'Is it George or William? Are they all right?'

Actually, her elder brothers were the last thing Caroline was concerned about, but she couldn't think of anything else that would make Sebastian look so terrible. If he were ill himself, she was sure, he would tend to make light of it rather than turn up at school with a face like a wet weekend.

When he turned around to face her, tears were pouring down his cheeks.

'Caro, I'm so sorry, so very, very sorry. I've had to sell Amhurst.'

She felt the world spin, and was grateful she was sitting down. She doubted her legs would have supported her if she'd tried to stand up at that moment. Sell Amhurst? What on earth was he talking about?

'Please, darling.' Sebastian had looked at her beseechingly. 'Say something.'

What was there to say? His shame and distress were so obvious, and so acute, she hadn't the heart to reproach him or the energy to throw some sort of tantrum. She had opened her mouth, just to ask him why, *how* could this have happened, but closed it again before the words had even formed on her lips.

What was the point of tormenting herself, or him, with such questions? Amhurst meant the whole world to Sebastian, just as it did to her. If he had sold it, then she knew he must have had absolutely no choice.

For a few fleeting moments, she allowed her mind to fly back there, to linger on each image, on every remembered smell and sound and touch of her home. If she closed her eyes, she could still hear the rooks cawing in the tree-tops of the Great Park, and smell the dampness of the early morning mist, intertwined with the sour smoke of the previous night's bonfire. She could feel the smooth, polished wood of the banisters beneath her hand and see the vast, faded tapestries of hunting scenes that hung, so exquisite and yet almost unnoticed, against the cool stone walls.

She pictured her old Nanny Chapman chasing her out of the cavernous larder, remembered the 'slap, slap' sound of her bare feet as she ran across the cold flagstone floor of the scullery and out into the kitchen garden, with a slice of Cook's apple pie still clenched tightly in her sticky fist.

Her father had sold Amhurst. It was gone.

Silently, lovingly, Caroline folded away each of her precious memories. If she were going to survive this, she knew she could never, ever look back. She also knew, somewhere very deep inside herself, that her childhood had come to an end in that instant.

Getting up slowly, she put her arms around her father's neck and held him while he wept. The rose garden, always such a peaceful place, was racked by the sound of Sebastian's sobbing. Caroline felt she would never be able to set foot there again.

'Don't cry, Daddy,' she whispered. 'It's all right. Really it is. We'll get through it together. We'll find somewhere else to live, maybe a lovely cottage like Granny's or something? It'll be gorgeous and cosy, and I can bring you your pipe and slippers by the fire every night, just like a really old man.'

That, she realised, was exactly what he looked like, slumped and shivering beside her on the cold stone bench. Overnight her strong, invincible father had become a broken old man.

Sebastian stared at his daughter in wonder, deeply touched by her desire to comfort him, overwhelmed with gratitude for her forgiveness.

'I'm afraid it isn't just the house, you know,' he forced himself to continue. 'I'm . . . the thing is, you see . . . well, there are some debts. A lot of debts, in fact.' Her heart felt literally wrenched with love and pity for him as he stared abjectly down at his shoes, all glistening and wet from the dewy grass. 'I can pay them, of course. There's no question of anything not being honoured, of shirking anything.'

'Of course there isn't, Pa,' she assured him. 'I know that.'

'It's just that after everybody's been paid off, well, I'm afraid there's really very little left. A couple of the paintings I should be able to hang on to, and your great-grandfather's Egton chest. But everything else . . . Oh, Caroline, darling.' He was crying again now. 'Your inheritance, and the boys'. It's all gone. All of it. I am so terribly, terribly sorry.'

Caroline was surprised to find herself feeling angry. Not at her father – heaven knows how he had got himself into such a mess, but he had obviously tried his best. He must have been struggling for years, she realised, not wanting to worry any of them with his troubles, hoping against hope that this dreadful day of reckoning would never come.

No, she was angry with fate, angry at whoever it was who had dealt them this card, who had dared to take their beloved Amhurst.

A powerful sense of resolve and of strength surged through her. From now on it would be up to her to make her own way in life. And by God, she was going to do it. Her father was too old and too filled with guilt and shame to do what needed to be done. But Caroline Berkeley was not about to become a common pauper. She would just have to find her own fortune, make her own way as her Berkeley ancestors had done long before her. And she already had a pretty shrewd idea of just how she might do it.

After a horrific, miserable Christmas with her family, Caroline had returned to Massingham and begun, belatedly, to apply herself to her studies.

A private education was, she realised, essential if she were to mix in the sort of moneyed circles that might help to restore her fortunes, and she astounded her family by winning a much-coveted scholarship that would enable her to stay on at school. (The headmaster had generously agreed to give a devastated Sebastian a term's grace in which to make 'alternative arrangements' for his daughter's education. But clearly there was no way he could continue to afford her fees.)

Growing up at Amhurst as the only girl in an otherwise all-male family, Caroline had become exceptionally skilled in the art of manipulating men. This skill, she decided, would be her fastest and surest route back to the lifestyle that she had not only become accustomed to, but considered to be her God-given right.

She would marry money.

She'd thought it all through quite logically. Building a successful career involved a high degree of uncertainty, and she had no real idea of what she wanted to do. Besides, working her way back to wealth would take years and Caroline was not prepared to wait that long. Far better to find herself a rich old man whom she could wrap around her little finger, just as she had always done with her father. With her golden, shoulder-length hair, perfect peaches-and-cream complexion and a body already in full, glorious bloom, at fifteen she was well accustomed to the gratifyingly dramatic effect her looks seemed to have on the opposite sex.

She started to approach her social life as if it were a military campaign, angling for invitations to St Tropez or Sardinia, only ever befriending girls whose parents were rich enough to look indulgently on such blatant free-loading.

Her natural intelligence rapidly helped her to develop finely tuned social antennae. She learned to judge exactly when she was in danger of outstaying her welcome with any particular group, and needed to move on to newer, more fertile pastures. She adroitly avoided ever paying for herself at dinner or on holiday, without ever drawing her companions' attention to the fact. And she perfected using the combination of her aristocratic family name, youth and striking good looks to manipulate potential sugar daddies.

By the time she finished school, Caroline Berkeley reigned supreme among the smart young set as the undisputed brightest star in their social firmament. Penniless or not, she was the queen of 'Swinging London'.

Her twenty-first birthday party was a lavish champagne reception in Eton Square – courtesy of a besotted fifty-four-year-old Greek shipping magnate whom she had 'befriended' the previous summer.

'Spyros, be an angel and do up my zipper, would you?' she asked him, coquettishly, preening herself in front of the bathroom mirror.

She was looking typically foxy that evening, in a bottom-skimming velour mini-dress in baby pink, teamed with spiky black PVC boots. She wore her long blonde hair in schoolgirl bunches, which she knew both her father and her lover would appreciate, although for very different reasons.

'I'll fix your zipper if you'll fix mine.'

Spyros's eyes locked with hers for a moment, and they both looked down at his enormous erection, clearly outlined against his tight brown trousers.

'I'm sorry, baby,' he said. 'That dress is just too much.'

'Darling, I'd love to. Help you, I mean,' said Caroline. 'But there really isn't time.' She finished applying her lipstick. 'People will start arriving any minute.'

'So let them arrive.' He pulled her towards him and placed her hand on his fly, trying to banish the thought that he had a daughter almost exactly Caroline's age. 'Maria can show them in. Besides, I promise you this won't take long.'

He was right, it didn't. Less than a minute after Caroline had sunk to her knees on the cold, blue-tiled floor and got to work on his huge, throbbing dick, he had come gratefully into her mouth. Grimacing slightly, she swallowed, anxious not to smudge her perfect make-up before the party.

Really, she wished Spyros would learn to pick slightly more convenient moments.

Five minutes later, after a brief gargle of mouthwash, she was downstairs greeting her brother George and his wife, Lucy. George was always the first to arrive and the first to leave any party – you could set your watch by him.

'Hello, sweetie, glad you could make it,' she said, and gave him one of her most gracious, hostess-like smiles.

He glared disapprovingly at her dress.

'Happy birthday, Caro. You look . . .' He searched around for an appropriate word. '. . . cold.'

Grumpy bastard. She noticed that his ancient tweed suit was beginning to fray at the cuffs, and wondered why his sour-faced wife never did anything to try to smarten him up. Caroline was not a fan of impoverished gentility.

'Do I?' She forced a smile. 'I expect I need a drink to warm me up. Can I get either of you a glass of champagne?'

'Thank you, I'd love one,' said Lucy. 'George can't, I'm afraid, he's driving.'

George shot his wife a look of annoyance. 'Just an orange juice for me, please, if you've got one,' he said to Caroline, who was glad of an excuse to shimmy off to the bar and leave them.

She badly resented the way both her brothers tried to make her feel guilty all the time. They despised Spyros, and made no secret of their disapproval of her lifestyle. Well, screw the pair of them. If they wanted to spend the rest of their lives in draughty old rooms, nursing single whiskies and crying over Amhurst, that was up to them. Caroline had bigger plans for her life, and no one was going to stand in her way.

At least Pa understood her.

Sebastian, looking very frail and elderly, was the guest of honour at the party, and spent most of the evening chatting animatedly to Spyros about Greek history. She loved the way he could do that, mingle with everybody, try to see the good in people, no matter what their background. He wasn't a small-minded snob, like George or William.

Later, as her huge, pink birthday cake was wheeled into the room, its twenty-one candles flickering merrily, Sebastian cleared his throat ostentatiously and announced that he would like to propose a toast 'to the birthday queen'.

'To my darling Caroline.' He raised his glass, his rheumy old eyes scanning the room full of strangers. He did wish his daughter wouldn't mix with *quite* such a racy crowd. 'You have given me twenty-one years of happiness. Here's to many, many more happy years!'

'To Caroline!' the room erupted in echo.

Two weeks later, Sebastian was dead.

The meagre remnants of the Berkeley estate looked even more pitiful when split three ways. In an uncharacteristic display of generosity, Caroline eschewed her share in favour of her brothers, both of whom had young families to support. Besides, it was 1967. One thousand, three hundred pounds barely amounted to the proverbial drop in the ocean of Caroline's living expenses. She might as well let them have it.

Not that they were remotely grateful.

'I hope, now that dear old Pa is gone, you're finally going to start pulling your finger out and get a job,' said William sanctimoniously over lunch at Rules one Sunday.

It was just the sort of restaurant he *would* like, reflected Caroline bitterly, glancing around at the florid-faced, overweight, Establishment types greedily slurping their port in every corner.

'You can't just keep on sponging off that ghastly Greek fellow, you know,' her brother continued. 'People are starting to talk.'

'Oh, are they?' she bit back angrily, stabbing at her venison with a fork. 'And what have they been saying exactly?'

William removed a piece of steak and kidney pie from between his teeth, and ran his fingers through his thinning sandy hair. God, he was unattractive, a sort of weaker, scrawnier version of George.

'I don't think I really need to spell it out for you, do I?'

'Well, actually, William, yes, I think you probably do,' she said. She was getting thoroughly fed up with his mealy-mouthed insinuations. If he had something to say, why didn't he damn well say it?

'Oh, for Christ's sake, Caroline.' He put down his knife and fork and lowered his voice to what he hoped was a discreet whisper. 'You aren't married. More to the point, he *is* married. Just because you managed to pull the wool over Dad's eyes doesn't mean that the rest of the world doesn't know what you're up to. I'm sorry, but it's just not on.'

Caroline let out a short mirthless laugh, loud enough for the two old buffers at the table next to them to turn and give her a filthy look. She ignored them.

'Just listen to yourself, would you? "It's just not on."' William flushed as she loudly mimicked his hectoring tone. 'Have you any idea how pompous you sound? You're ridiculous, William, quite ridiculous, you and George. It's 1967, in case you haven't noticed, and I'm hardly the first woman to be having an affair. Besides, this has nothing to do with my morality, does it? You just don't like Spyros because he's Greek, and he's older than me, and because he's a self-made man.'

'Nouveau riche, you mean?' William sneered.

'Well, better nouveau riche than stinking bloody poor, William.'

Flinging her napkin down on the table, she got to her feet.

'I'm sorry,' she said. 'I think I need some air.'

And with that she strode out of the restaurant, leaving her brother spluttering with outrage, his full, flabby lips opening and closing wordlessly like a stunned mullet.

Outside, the cool afternoon air hit Caroline's face with a welcome, refreshing blast.

What the hell was wrong with everybody?

Marching down towards the Strand, her face flushed with defiance, blonde hair dancing in the wind behind her, she ignored the wolf whistles of the builders and the stares of the businessmen as she passed.

She felt stung, again, by William's ingratitude. How dare he accept her share of Pa's money with one hand and then try to slap her down with the other, make her feel guilty for enjoying her life, for making her own way?

As it happened, her brothers didn't know the half of it. Spyros, in fact, was only one in a long line of lovers whom Caroline used to support a lifestyle that many a wealthy London housewife would have envied. If William thought she was going to give all that up to become somebody's bloody secretary, and live in some poky flat in Clapham like him and his holier-than-thou friends, he could go to hell.

She did not go back to the restaurant in the end, but hailed a cab and took herself shopping in Knightsbridge instead, with a mental two fingers to William.

As things turned out, she wasn't to see either of her brothers again for a very, very long time.

For six happy years after Sebastian's death and her acrimonious parting from her brothers, Caroline lived a life devoted solely to the pursuit of her own pleasure.

She appeared at all the exclusive society parties, dressed head to toe in the discarded designer clothes of her rich acquaintances, and often dripping in (borrowed) diamonds. She holidayed on friends' yachts off Capri, and spent Christmases with an indulgent former lover on Mustique. If people disapproved of her, she neither knew nor cared. She was young, free and beautiful and having the time of her life – what else mattered?

Her only niggling concern was that she remained utterly bereft of any capital of her own. Sure, she collected the odd gift as she moved like a nomad from one married playboy to the next – Fabien had given her the most *exquisite* Fabergé egg before he broke it off, which even she couldn't bring herself to flog – but ultimately, she knew she needed to actually *marry* money in order to achieve the lasting financial security she craved.

Getting a rich man to fuck you and buy you gifts was a piece of cake. Getting one to marry you, especially if that would embroil him in a costly divorce, was proving altogether more difficult.

At twenty-eight, Caroline still looked fabulous, and every penny she received was spent on maintaining her appearance. But everyone on the scene in London knew her, and knew what her brothers had insisted on calling her 'reputation'. She had heard that Americans were suckers for an upper-class English accent. Perhaps, she wondered, it was time to move on?

Chapter Four

Caroline arrived in Los Angeles in November 1974, in the middle of a blazing winter heatwave, with the addresses of two old schoolfriends and one ex-boyfriend in her Chanel shoulder bag, thirteen hundred dollars in the bank and a pair of the tiniest frayed denim hot pants that the guy at the immigration desk had ever seen.

'How long you stayin' in the States, sugar?' He leered at her appreciatively from behind his bullet-proof plastic screen.

'Well, I'm not too sure,' she replied. 'That sort of depends on how nice people are to me.'

'Baby,' – he stared down blatantly at her crotch, enticingly shrink-wrapped in denim – 'I think there's *a lot* of people gonna be *very* nice to you here in LA.'

'Well, I hope so,' said Caroline, smiling.

Every head turned as she strutted through LAX to baggage reclaim.

'Can I help you with your luggage, miss?' a voice came from behind her. 'That case must be heavier than you are.'

She swung round to find herself face to face with one of the most handsome men she had ever seen. Tall, dark and slightly overly tanned, his white teeth blazed down at her in a wolfish grin as he effortlessly swung her enormous bag off the carousel. He was exactly what she had imagined Californian men to look like: fit, masculine and well groomed.

It was hard, Caroline felt, not to admire a man like that.

'Well, thank you so much, how kind.'

She smiled gratefully up at this plastic Adonis, thinking how much more impressive he looked than most of the chinless wimps who offered her their gentlemanly services back home in London.

'I'm Caroline. Caroline Berkeley.'

She gave him her hand and he crushed it.

'Brad Baxter. It's an absolute pleasure to meet you.'

Meeting Brad turned out to be an extraordinary piece of luck. Over the next six weeks, he helped to introduce Caroline to the myriad pleasures and vices that Hollywood had to offer, none of which were new to her, as well as to many of the movers and shakers in the business, who were. He was, it emerged, a PR whizz-kid from West Hollywood who ran a sideline "talent-spotting" for a soft porn producer in the Valley and was a regular on the starry, decadent social scene that was to become Caroline's natural milieu and favoured hunting ground.

Clearly, she had her sights set a lot higher than porno – although the money Brad was talking about was definitely enough to make your head spin – but she knew a well-connected guy when she saw one. She moved into his apartment immediately, as a stopgap measure while she hunted for a place of her own.

Six weeks, a lot of coke and some mediocre sex later, Brad introduced her to Duke McMahon. The rest, she felt sure, was about to become history.

On the face of it, Duke was not Caroline's ideal catch.

For one thing, he had made it clear that he would not contemplate a divorce from his wife, Minnie, although the marriage was well known in Hollywood to be a complete sham. Duke had had countless mistresses and affairs before her, and his marriage had weathered them all, which was not a good sign.

For another, he was seriously old, even by Caroline's standards. Though he was by no means the least attractive of the many men she had slept with, he was already sixty-four, and physically things could only go downhill from there.

Despite her calculated approach to relationships, Caroline still enjoyed good sex. Brad's ineptly enthusiastic efforts over the past few weeks had been absolute torture. If she were going to devote years of her life to a man, which financially she knew she must, then it had to be someone she could at least tolerate in bed. Duke was a more than adequate lover now – but in five years' time his ancient balls might be flapping against his bony, arthritic knees, and frankly she doubted that she could stomach that.

On the other hand, Duke was rich beyond even Caroline's wildest dreams. On their very first date, he had picked her up in his exquisite blue 1956 Ferrari, and driven her down to his private cove in Malibu.

'Close your eyes,' he said, as he led her, trembling with excitement, down the sandy track that wound from the road to the beach. She could feel the silky dryness of the sand between her toes as she stumbled blindly along in her open-toed stilettos. 'OK. You can open them now. Take a look.'

Caroline gasped with delight. The white sand of the beach was illuminated by a combination of pale, blue-white moonlight and the warmer, rich orange glow of hundreds of candles, some flickering softly in the sand at her feet, others hanging from the boughs of the cedars that grew along the shore.

An over-sized midnight-blue blanket had been spread out at the water's edge. It had been laid with brilliantly polished antique silver and shimmering crystal glasses, as well as a picnic of such delicious-looking food – whole cooked lobsters, tomato and basil salad, peaches in Armagnac, perfect little individual chocolate soufflés – she felt her mouth literally begin watering at the sight of it. Beside the picnic were two large ice buckets half submerged in the sand, each containing two bottles of champagne.

Duke's right-hand man, Seamus, looking half decent for once in a crisp white linen suit, stood at a respectful distance, ready to wait on the two of them hand and foot.

'Do you like it?' asked Duke.

'Do I like it?' She looked at him incredulously. 'Duke, I have never seen anything quite so beautiful, and quite so romantic, in my entire life.'

She meant it, too. She felt like a queen, adored and indulged – and she hadn't so much as kissed him yet. At that moment, she was quite sure that she *could* love Duke McMahon, should she ever find herself called upon to do so.

'Well, I'm glad,' he said, helping her down on to the blanket and signalling to his old friend to crack open the champagne. 'A beautiful girl like you deserves nothing less. In fact . . .' He fumbled in his inside jacket pocket, and produced a long black box. 'I bought you a little something that I thought might complement your beauty this evening. It's just a token. But I hope you like it.'

It was a struggle for her to maintain her composure, to slowly take and open the box rather than snatch it out of his hand like an overexcited kid at Christmas. Inside was an obscenely large diamond-and-platinum necklace.

Caroline, who knew a thing or two about diamonds, could see at a glance that it must be worth upwards of fifteen thousand dollars. Tentatively, lovingly, she stroked the largest of the stones.

'Oh, Duke,' she whispered, her voice hoarse with emotion. 'Oh my God.'

He lifted the necklace, fastening it gently around her neck.

'You like it?'

Caroline kissed him quickly on the mouth.

'I love it.'

'Good. Now take off your dress.'

'I'm sorry?' She'd been so mesmerised by the incredible diamonds, she wondered whether she could have heard him correctly.

'No need to be sorry,' said Duke. 'I want you naked. Please undress. You can keep the necklace on.'

Caroline's eyes narrowed. She was not used to being spoken to like this, and she wasn't at all sure that she liked it.

Who the hell did he think he was?

She wasn't some prostitute, paid to be at his beck and call. Her face flushed with anger and embarrassment. She noticed that Seamus had not moved but stood just a few feet away, impassively watching her reaction.

'How dare you speak to me like that?' she demanded, fumbling angrily at the clasp at her neck and standing up to leave. 'I don't care how fucking famous you are, or how many necklaces you can afford, nobody speaks to. . . .'

'Oh, don't you?' Duke interrupted her mid-flow. 'Don't you care?'

He had grabbed her arm quite forcefully, but Caroline saw with surprise that he was smiling, his eyes full of warmth and mischief. All of a sudden she felt confused. Why was he laughing at her? Was this some kind of joke?

'Well, excuse me, Ms Berkeley, but I happen to think that's a crock of shit.'

'I beg your pardon?' She was doing her best to sound shocked.

'I think you care *very much* how many necklaces I can afford. In fact, Caroline, my darling, I think we both know that's exactly why you're sitting here, about to have dinner with an old man like me.'

'No it isn't. Of course it isn't,' said Caroline.

But she sat back down.

'I didn't mean to offend you,' continued Duke. 'But I also don't intend to be played for a fool. I thought I could save us both a lot of time by laying a few cards on the table right now – so that we can both enjoy the first of what I hope will be many, many pleasant evenings together.'

She looked at him warily. 'Go on.'

'I bought you that necklace because I thought you would look beautiful in it, and you do. And because I knew you would like it.'

'I do like it.' Caroline couldn't resist touching the exquisite stones again as she listened to him. 'Very much.'

'I know you do. And I know there are a lot of other things you would like. Things that I can give you. That I would like to give you.' She smiled at him encouragingly. 'But there is also something that you can give me. Something that I want very badly.'

Caroline's face fell. She drew her cashmere stole tighter around her shoulders.

'Now don't you look at me like that,' said Duke. 'You aren't Pollyanna, and you sure as hell aren't some innocent little virgin either.'

Despite herself, Caroline gave him a conspiratorial smile.

'That's better,' said Duke. 'You're a smart girl, Caroline. You know what you want, and I like that. I like it a lot. We both know I can give you what you want. But I'm not a young man any more, kiddo, and I don't like wasting my time. I didn't bring you here tonight for conversation.'

Without breaking eye contact, he reached out and touched her breast, gently rolling the nipple between his thumb and forefinger through the cotton of her dress.

Caroline thought about it for a split second, but did not protest. Seamus had tactfully withdrawn to the other side of the cedar trees, but she knew he was probably watching them, the dirty old sod. The thought, combined with Duke's practised touch, sent a sudden jolt of lust right through her body.

'Now, please,' he resumed, 'if it isn't too much to ask, I'd like you to take off your dress.'

A couple of weeks later, he had made her a proposal that was too good to refuse, even if it didn't involve matrimony. She was to become his exclusive consort for the rest of his life, in return for which he would not only bankroll her lifestyle but make her a generous provision in his will. That meant a worst-case scenario of a lifetime of financial security as his mistress. Plus, she realised, it would give her ample time to work on undermining Minnie.

After all, if there was one thing Caroline felt secure in, it was her ability to manipulate a besotted old man.

Chapter Five

'Hey, mama, what's goin' on?'

Minnie did a double take. Good God! Perhaps the light was playing tricks on her, but there appeared to be a large semi-naked Negro sprawled out on her antique Italian chaise longue. Other than his state of undress, the young man was remarkable for a huge springy halo of black hair which bobbed up and down as he spoke, and for the long, fat and disintegrating marijuana cigarette which he was holding perilously close to her Chinese silk cushions. But worse even than that, this dreadful, uncouth apparition seemed to be trying to enter into a conversation with her.

'Beautiful place you got here, you know what I'm sayin'?' he continued, littering ash across the furniture and carpet as he attempted an appreciative sweeping gesture with his huge black arm.

'Thank you,' said Minnie, icily. 'We like it. Perhaps you'd be so kind as to tell me who you are, young man, and what you're doing in my drawing room?'

'He's with me.'

A very well-spoken young Englishman had appeared in the doorway, and strode confidently over to Minnie, taking her hand and kissing it before she had a moment to protest. 'Edward Lyle, at your service.'

He couldn't have been much over twenty-one, thought Minnie, but he dressed with an impeccable, gentlemanly English grace that made him seem older. He also had the self-assurance, bordering on arrogance, that so many public-school-educated young people from his country seemed to possess. Minnie hated this in Caroline, but found herself quite prepared to be charmed by it in the case of this handsome young fellow.

'This is Skinny.' He gestured to his friend. 'Stand up, man, show Mrs McMahon some respect.' Skinny looked at him incredulously, but obligingly lifted his massive frame up off the chaise longue. Edward continued. 'We're both old friends of Caroline's. She said it wouldn't be a problem for us to hang out at the pool today, which was damn decent of her.'

Minnie's interested smile evaporated. Any friend of Caroline's was an enemy of hers.

'Please, don't worry, Mrs McMahon,' Edward tried to reassure her. 'We're very self-sufficient, aren't we, Skin? We won't get under your feet.'

At that moment two strikingly beautiful girls, in matching minuscule red Dior bikinis, came skipping into the room, their bare feet still wet from the swimming pool. One of them headed straight to Duke's wet bar, where she proceeded to empty the entire fridge of olives and potato chips, cramming the food into her mouth as though she hadn't eaten for weeks.

'Munchies,' she mumbled at Minnie through a mouthful of chips, before collapsing into a wet heap of giggles all over a pink suede armchair.

Meanwhile her friend had literally flung herself at Skinny, who collapsed back on to the chaise longue so hard that it gave an ominously audible crack.

'Oh no,' said Minnie, flapping her arms frantically in a vain attempt to persuade him to move. 'Get up! You're going to break it!'

But before a disoriented Skinny had a chance to move there was more sickening splintering. Minnie could only look on in horror as one of the legs gave way completely.

Surveying the wreckage, she wanted to scream, but a lifetime of self-control prevented her from doing so. Instead, she addressed herself as calmly as she could to Edward, who seemed to be the only member of the group in something like full command of his senses.

'Well, Mr Lyle, I think it might be better if you and your friends went outside to play, don't you? I'm sure Mr McMahon would appreciate it if at least some of his furniture were still intact by the time he got home.'

'Yes, yes, of course, I'm. . . . we're all terribly sorry, aren't we?'

Skinny looked slightly shamefaced, but both girls had given in to the uncontrollable laughter of the irreparably stoned. None of them looked terribly sorry to Minnie.

'Just go, please,' she said.

Mercifully, they did.

Once the group had shuffled back out to the pool, she sank down wearily to her knees and examined the mahogany shards that were all that was left of the leg. Honestly, this really was the last straw. She would tackle Duke about it tonight, once and for all. Having that dreadful girl here was surely bad enough, without allowing her appalling, insolent, platform-shoe-wearing, drug-taking, long-haired hippy friends to treat the estate like a hotel.

Caroline's first year at Hancock Park had been a living nightmare for Minnie. It was not her husband's infidelity which bothered her so much as Caroline's attempted assumption of the role of lady of the house. Only last week, she had caught her haranguing Conchita in a *most* unladylike manner over some trifling offence or other. (She was sure that Duke must be wrong about Caroline's aristocratic lineage – she had come across hobos in Connecticut with better language.) Day after day, she filled the house with her brash, braying English friends, who thought nothing of eating Minnie out of house and home, or lounging all around the house in their frightful bell-bottoms smoking marijuana. And they didn't just restrict their shocking behaviour to the public rooms either. Heaven alone knew what went on up in the south wing bedrooms, between her beautifully laundered linen sheets.

So far, whenever Minnie had complained to Duke about these riff-raff, he had been non-committal. He had held back from openly supporting his girlfriend over his wife, but neither would he reprimand Caroline, or do anything to ease the almost unbearable tension caused by her increasingly insensitive and tactless behaviour. Minnie suspected, accurately, that he derived a powerful sense of pleasure from watching the friction between the two of them.

Nevertheless, she thought as she grimly swept up the splinters of wood, she would tackle him again about it this evening. It was her fifty-fifth birthday tomorrow and a celebration dinner had been planned for tonight, a long-standing McMahon tradition. Perhaps, on her birthday, he would be in a slightly more receptive mood?

Duke returned home earlier than usual and was relieved to find the house free of hangers-on. He had taken to spending increasing amounts of time away from home recently, either at the country club in Bel Air, or at mysterious 'meetings'. He found Caroline's parasitic social set every bit as grating as his wife did, and intensely disliked returning to a house full of strangers – although he was damned if he was going to give Minnie the satisfaction of admitting as much to her. Despite his lack of solidarity with her over Caroline's friends, his absences nevertheless encouraged Minnie, who hoped he might be beginning a new affair. The sooner he tired of Caroline, the better for all of them.

Strolling into his study, he poured himself three fingers of bourbon and sank into his leather armchair, eyes closed, savouring a rare moment of peace. It was soon to be shattered, however, by the unwelcome arrival of an apoplectic Pete.

'I suppose it's too much to expect that you actually remembered Mother's birthday?' Pete himself was laden with ostentatiously wrapped packages, a walking tower of bright metallic paper and bows.

Duke found few things in life more objectionable than his son's belligerent, whining voice, so full of hatred and yet so utterly lacking the courage to act upon it. He opened one eye momentarily, then closed it again before speaking.

'Well, good evening to you too, Peter.'

'You forgot again, didn't you?'

'I did not forget.' Duke looked his son in the eye. 'I never forget your mother's birthday. I sometimes choose not to celebrate it, which is a different thing.'

A vein in Pete's jaw had begun to twitch, as though his body were barely able to contain the bile and rage within. He only just managed to control himself sufficiently to lay down his presents gently on the desk, rather than hurling them all violently at the old man's face.

'This year, however, I *have* bought a little something for my dear wife.'

Reaching into his jacket pocket, Duke produced a ring box. Pete caught the distinctive Cambridge-blue flash of Tiffany, and watched his father open it to reveal a subtle, delicately crafted band of diamonds and white gold. It was elegant, conservative – exactly to his mother's taste.

'It's an eternity ring. To symbolise the permanence of our joyous union.' Duke snorted mirthlessly. 'For better or worse, kiddo, in sickness and in health. Whaddaya think? Will Mrs McMahon approve?'

What the hell was he playing at? Pete couldn't quite figure out whether it was an act of gross insensitivity, or calculated spite. It didn't occur to him that beneath his father's cynicism and bitterness, he might still harbour feelings of love towards his mother. As far as Pete was concerned, Duke was a monster. Even on Minnie's birthday, he couldn't resist trying to hurt her.

Later that evening, the birthday supper began unusually calmly, with everyone apparently making an effort to suspend hostilities. Duke was oddly quiet, and even asked Minnie quite politely about her birthday plans, much to the astonishment of his children. None of them could remember the last time they had spent so civilised an evening together, and hope that Caroline might finally be on her way out was running high.

Minnie decided to wait until the main course (her favourite, rare roast beef with Yorkshire pudding) before broaching the subject of the chaise longue with Duke. After the best part of four decades together, she knew him well enough to realise that he was far more likely to be responsive to her complaints after a couple of glasses of wine.

'By the way, Duke,' she said, almost casually, once the second bottle of merlot was well under way, 'did you see that we had a small, erm, accident today?'

'Oh yeah?' He looked supremely uninterested. 'What happened?'

'The chaise longue. You know, the Italian one, in . . .' She checked herself. 'In the den? Well, I'm afraid it was broken. The leg's come right off. Seamus had a look at it for me but he says it's quite beyond repair.'

'What the fuck do you mean, it was broken?' This was better than Minnie had expected. He looked extremely irate. 'Who the fuck broke it? I don't believe this. Who broke it?' Duke looked around the table accusingly.

'Some wine, Caroline?' said Pete, who knew what had happened and was beginning to enjoy himself.

'Not for me, thank you,' she replied.

Pete noticed with annoyance that she didn't seem remotely rattled. In fact she seemed, if not quite subdued, then strangely content. It bothered him.

'Is anybody gonna answer me?' Duke's cheeks were reddening, a combination of the wine and his mounting frustration. 'Laurie, was it you? Did you sit your fat ass down on my Italian couch?' He pronounced it 'eye-talian', which had always made Minnie cringe and Caroline laugh.

'Daddy, don't be so horrid,' said Laurie, who was blushing to the roots of her hair. 'I can't help it if I have a problem with my weight.'

'Sure you can,' said Duke, staring at her plate piled high with Yorkshire puddings and gravy. 'Quit eating.'

'Well, it wasn't me,' she said petulantly, pushing her food to the side of her plate and pouting. 'It was some great big black guy, some friend of Caroline's. He's been hanging around the house all week, hasn't he, Mother?'

Minnie knew better than to say anything. She arranged her face into a familiar expression of patient forbearance, and let Duke's rage take its inevitable course.

He looked at Caroline, and when he spoke his voice was ominously quiet.

'Skinny was here today?'

Caroline met his eyes defiantly. She wasn't Minnie, and she wasn't about to let the bastard bully her. 'Yes, Duke, he was. I didn't know he was coming, though. Edward brought him.'

Duke's hand had tightened around his fork. He cleared his throat. 'I see. Caroline, I thought I had made my views patently clear on this point. But perhaps not. So why don't I just restate them for the record. Number one.' He held up one finger. 'I don't want any fucking Negroes in this house.'

'Darling!' Caroline found his racism both objectionable and ridiculous, although she knew Minnie, and probably the children too, shared his prejudices. 'Skinny's a Harvard graduate.'

He raised his hand to stop her.

'Excuse me, I haven't finished. Number two: I will not have my home used as a goddam monkey house for every fucking waif and stray you pick up. Got it?'

At this point Minnie would have backed down completely, but Caroline squared her shoulders at him bravely.

'This is my home too, Duke.'

She was angry, but there were also tears in her eyes. Minnie was taken aback. She had never seen Caroline looking so emotional.

'Yes, honey, it is, it is your home,' said Duke, who had also been surprised by her reaction. He had learned to expect fireworks from Caroline – it was part of the sexual dynamic between them, that she would stand up to him in public, constantly challenging his will, only to be fucked into grovelling, ecstatic submission later in bed. But this evening she looked genuinely upset. 'It is your home. But you did not pay for that couch.'

'Chaise longue,' corrected Minnic.

Duke shot her a withering glance.

'I don't appreciate it when your friends come around here and break valuable shit like that, you know? And I don't like that big black bastard hanging around you all the time.'

Caroline looked up at him and smiled, that same serene smile which Pete had noticed earlier. There was definitely something funny going on between them. Duke took her hand, a gesture that was somehow both possessive and conciliatory.

'I don't like it,' he repeated, softly.

'OK,' said Caroline, suddenly meek again. 'I'll stop seeing him. Promise.' She turned to Minnie. 'And I'm sorry about your couch.'

'Chaise longue!' shouted Laurie and Pete in unison.

'Whatever,' said Caroline.

*

Minnie retired to the drawing room after dinner with the rest of the family, feeling utterly deflated. Listlessly, she picked up one of Pete and Claire's brightly wrapped presents, and sighed as she pulled at its blue silk ribbons. What just happened in there?

For the past two weeks she had become more and more convinced that Duke was cheating on Caroline. First of all there were his unexplained absences, and their increasingly frequent rows about her English friends. And then, last week, he had actually come creeping into her own bed, for the first time since Caroline had moved in.

She had received him wordlessly, without surprise or complaint, and afterwards he had touched her face with a tenderness she had almost forgotten he had ever possessed. Minnie had never really understood the reasons behind Duke's cruelty towards her, and she found his rare bursts of affection equally inexplicable. As his wife, she believed it was her duty to accept both unquestioningly. Duke despised her for her passivity – but deep down, he also recognised her as his moral superior. Whatever had passed between them, however horrifically Duke behaved, both of them knew that the other would never leave. The marriage remained their security, and their prison.

She had been so sure that things were finally about to change, that he was at last getting over this dangerous infatuation with Caroline. But his behaviour tonight at dinner, his tenderness towards her – it just didn't add up. Only a couple of hours earlier, before they sat down to eat, Duke had handed her a tiny black box; pressed it into her hand almost guiltily while Caroline was out of earshot.

'Happy birthday, Min,' he had whispered, and kissed her, just once, on the cheek. She had put the box up in her bedroom, and even in her current state of confusion over Caroline, its presence there warmed her heart more intensely than the roaring log fire in front of her.

Her reverie was shattered by the tinkling of silver on glass. She gave a perfunctory smile and tried to pull herself together. Someone must be about to propose a birthday toast.

'Now that the whole family is together, I have something I would like to say.' Caroline had risen from the couch where she sat beside Duke. She looked happy and relaxed in a creamy white polo-neck and bell-bottom jeans, not at all her usual spiky, confrontational self.

The moment she started to speak, the cosy family atmosphere shattered like a vase in an oven. The group eyed her warily.

'I am so grateful to all of you,' she began, 'for making me feel so welcome here.'

'Oh, for Christ's sake,' mumbled Pete, only to be shot down by a look from his father.

'I know it hasn't been easy for you all, adjusting.' She smiled her most infuriatingly smug smile at Minnie, who was frozen to the spot beside her presents. 'And, well, I just wanted you all to know that I am really proud to be a part of this family.'

'Excuse me.' Pete had got to his feet. 'I think I may need to throw up.'

Laurie, terrified of the imminent confrontation, burst into tears.

'Shut the fuck up, Petey, or get out,' said Duke. He had also stood up, a full six inches taller than his son, the power of his booming voice and huge physical presence instantly filling the room and dwarfing Pete into seething, impotent submission. Pete sat down.

Still smiling sweetly, Caroline continued. 'Well, I'm sorry you feel that way, Pete, really I am. I can only hope that one day you might come to accept me, as the person who has made your father happy. Especially now.'

She paused, mischievously savouring the tension in the room.

'Especially now that I'm going to be giving you a little brother or sister.'

The silence was deafening. Nobody looked more horror stricken than Duke.

'Oh, Duke, darling, isn't it wonderful?' Caroline squealed, flinging herself melodramatically into his arms. 'I'm pregnant! We're going to have a baby!'

For a moment, nobody said anything. Then suddenly Laurie let out a piercing wail, and fled, sobbing, from the room.

'Claire,' said Duke quietly, after extricating himself delicately from Caroline's triumphant embrace, and turning to his daughter-in-law as the calmest, most sensible person in the room. 'Go after her, please.'

'No!' bellowed Pete, as she half started for the door. 'You stay where you are.'

Claire froze.

'I'll go to her.' Minnie heard her own voice sounding oddly detached. For a split second, she caught Duke's eye. There was something in his expression – was it regret? But he quickly turned away and began arguing loudly with Pete, and she slipped silently out of the room.

She found her daughter upstairs in her bedroom, the same baby-pink room she had slept in since childhood, face down on the bed, her shoulders shuddering with grief.

'Why?' she wailed. 'Why is she doing this to us?'

'I don't know, sweetheart,' said Minnie, pushing back a strand of limp, matted hair from Laurie's wet cheek. 'I know it's hard, really I do. But you just have to try and accept it. We all do.'

'No!' Laurie shouted back at her. 'I won't accept it! I'll never accept it and nor will Pete. That child, that *bastard*.' Laurie's fat face was contorted with rage, a hideous contrast to her mother's composed, aquiline features. 'Her kid will *never* be family to me. Or you. I mean, for God's sake, Mother, how do we even know it's Daddy's? She's such a slut, anybody could have fathered that baby. Edward, or . . . or . . . that awful Negro, whatever his name is.'

All of a sudden Minnie felt terribly tired.

'I'm afraid it is your father's child,' she said. 'And don't ask me how I know, because I just know. Now come along, dry those tears.'

Angrily, Laurie shrugged off her hand. She didn't want to be comforted.

Minnie wasn't sure she knew what to say to her anyway. Feeling numb, and faintly dizzy, she closed the door on her daughter's sobs and retreated to the sanctuary of her own bedroom. Wild horses couldn't have got her to go back down those stairs, where she could hear Duke and Peter, still screaming at each other.

Sitting down heavily on her bed, she noticed Duke's birthday gift on her bedside table. She was annoyed to find that her hands were trembling as she opened it. Inside was one of the loveliest diamond rings she had ever laid eyes on. There was also a note, a tiny piece of paper that had been carefully folded and slipped under the velvet of the ring box. Minnie read it:

'To My Wife, On Her Birthday. With Affection. Duke.'

For the first time in many long years, Minnie McMahon gave way to tears.

Chapter Six

They named the baby boy Hunter.

It had been a difficult birth. Caroline, unaccustomed to discomfort, let alone real physical pain, suffered terribly for fourteen hours before Dr Rawley decided the baby was showing signs of distress and performed an emergency Caesarean. She had lost a lot of blood, and for weeks after the birth looked so anaemically pale and vulnerable that Duke hardly knew how to talk to her. For him, Caroline was a purely sexual being. If his mistress had a deeper side – a troubled past or a more complex range of emotions – he neither knew, nor did he want to know, anything about it.

Bizarrely, his physical desire for her had only increased with her pregnancy. As her belly swelled, he felt an intense happiness at this living, growing symbol of his own virility and potency. He loved the shocked, revolted looks of fans on the street, relished their discomfort at seeing such a young and beautiful woman carrying the child of such an old man. The McMahons' living arrangements had become the talk and scandal of Hollywood, and Duke was loving every minute of it.

Even better, Caroline's libido had gone into overdrive. All those fucking pregnancy hormones had made her hornier than ever. When the midwife had suggested that 'aggressive' vaginal sex might not be the best thing for the baby, Duke had happily resorted to sodomising her, and was delighted by her enthusiastic acquiescence. He knew that she had conceived the child deliberately, hoping to cement her place, if not in his affections, then certainly in his will. But if anything, he rather admired her chutzpah. Hunter's arrival had been quite a coup for Caroline.

The baby itself was another matter. Duke's paternal instinct extended no farther than a primitive desire to pass on his genes, and a dimly defined Irish Catholic belief in the importance of 'family'. He had about as little interest in spending time with some puking, shitting little insomniac as in joining the priesthood.

Caroline was smart enough to realise this, and wasted no time in banishing her son to a nursery at the opposite end of the estate, in the care of two full-time nannies. She had also – through gritted teeth – allowed Duke to christen the boy Hunter.

'Honestly, darling,' she had said, when he first suggested it at the hospital. 'Hunter McMahon. It sounds like the name of one of Brad's porn stars. Couldn't we try something a little more traditional? I was thinking maybe Richard or Hugh. Or what about Sebastian?' Her tired face lit up as she thought about dear old Pa and how thrilled he would have been with his grandson. 'That was my father's name.'

'Oh yeah?' said Duke. 'Well, guess what, Peter was the name of Minnie's old man, who was the most miserable, tight-assed son of a bitch to ever walk the planet, by the way. I'm not naming another son of mine after anybody's father, and that's final.'

'But Duke, my father was nothing like that,' she protested. 'He was kind, and honourable, and . . .'

'Caroline.' He put his finger to her lips, not unkindly. 'It ain't happening, OK? And the kid is not getting some fucking English, Lord Rupert the third goddam name either.'

Caroline laughed. She loved Duke's ideas about the English upper classes, largely fed to him over the years by the sycophantically Anglophile Minnie. As far as he was concerned, everybody was called Lord Rupert of the manor and went riding round the countryside wearing coronets.

Still, she was shrewd enough to read between the lines, and knew it was important to Duke that she concede about the naming of the baby. He had never forgiven Minnie, or her family, for the way they patronised him socially. The worst thing she could do would be to appear to be following suit.

'Oh, well, all right, darling,' she said. 'I suppose he *is* going to be an American. And if he has anything like his father's charm I'm sure he'll be able to carry it off. Hunter McMahon it is.'

'Hunter Duke McMahon,' said Duke.

Oh God. In for a penny, in for a pound.

'Absolutely,' agreed Caroline. 'Hunter Duke.'

She made titanic efforts to regain her figure, working out daily with Mikey, and practically starving herself on the new cabbage soup diet that all the Hollywood wives were raving about. A picture of Caroline in a wisp of white chiffon, looking impossibly svelte at the premiere of *Saturday Night Fever* just six weeks after Hunter's birth, made the cover of *People* magazine. Now that she had produced a son, the frosty reception she had been used to among Duke's movie friends was finally beginning to thaw. Caroline Berkeley was here to stay, and anyone who didn't like it was just going to have to lump it.

From the very beginning, Hunter was an angelic baby. His nannies marvelled at his sweet, even temperament, his ability to sleep through the night, and his constant bestowing of smiles on every stranger who so much as looked at him. With his shock of dark hair, tawny brown complexion and huge, midnight-blue eyes, he was the sort of infant that people stopped to admire in the park and queued up to cuddle at cocktail parties.

Ignored by both his parents, and despised by all the other adult members of the household – with the one exception of Claire – Hunter became used to his own company, and could play for hours at a time, quite happily, alone in his nursery. The only time his peaceful, friendly face would cloud over was when he found himself dragged like a pawn into the adults' hostilities. The older he grew, it seemed, the more often this happened.

Shortly after Hunter had turned four, his mother threw an enormous garden party at the estate, to celebrate her fifth 'anniversary' with Duke. *Le tout* Hollywood were invited, and mingled awkwardly with both Minnie and Caroline as each vied for the position of most senior hostess. Minnie, as usual, looked elegant in a beige linen trouser suit, her diamond eternity ring glittering in the California sunshine. Caroline had rather overdone it in a plunging red satin top and matching hot pants – red rags to Minnie's bull.

'I picked it up last week from Valencia in Brentwood,' she was telling an enraptured entertainment lawyer and his disapproving-looking wife as she leant seductively against a huge sycamore. 'Farrah Fawcett came in about two minutes later, *desperate* to get hold of it, but I'd bought the very last one, can you believe it?'

Despite the lawyer's drooling appreciation, she was in fact beginning to regret her choice and wish she had gone for something just slightly less risqué. It was a fine line, dressing to keep Duke happy, whilst also trying to gain acceptance among his friends as what Americans called a 'permanent life partner'. Caroline frequently found herself being outclassed by Minnie, whose conservative, elegant ensembles seemed calculated to paint her as the scarlet woman. It infuriated her.

Oh fuck, what had possessed her to wear red? She'd just have to really play up the whole vamp thing – at least Duke would appreciate it.

While his mother shimmied off into the crowd, gyrating sexily to Neil Diamond as she went, Hunter was discovering the delights of the dessert table, contentedly smearing chocolate gateau all over his face.

'Hunter! What on earth do you think you're doing?'

All of a sudden a furious Minnie was looming over him. Hunter glanced around quickly in panic, looking for a nifty escape route, but none presented itself.

Minnie was beyond exasperation. Not only had she had to put up with watching that little trollop Caroline trying to insinuate herself with all her old friends, but now her hateful little brat had completely destroyed her beautiful chocolate gateau. Why couldn't his slut of a mother ever control him?

'Young man, you are in big trouble,' she whispered ominously at Hunter. 'Just *look* at your face. That's very, very naughty, isn't it?'

The little boy slunk back guiltily behind the tablecloth. Maybe if he shut his eyes very tightly she'd disappear.

'You come with me this instant,' said Minnie briskly, dragging him off in search of Caroline.

She had seized his arm painfully tightly, and this, combined with the harshness of her tone, had frightened him. Wiping the chocolate goo on his sleeve, he began to cry, his fat lower lip trembling pitifully as she dragged him away.

Caroline, as usual, was surrounded by a sycophantic crowd on the other side of the lawn, oblivious to her son's wails. But Claire, who had always had a strong maternal instinct and felt sorry for the boy, caught sight of Minnie pulling him angrily up the steps to the house and hurried over to intervene.

'Come on, Minnie.' She tried to keep her tone respectful. 'You know he didn't mean any harm. He's only four, for heavens' sake.' Stooping down, she wiped away Hunter's tears and the remains of the gateau with her handkerchief and, prising him from her irate mother-in-law, scooped him into her arms.

'How dare you undermine my authority?' said Minnie, glaring at her and further terrifying poor Hunter. She knew it wasn't really the child's fault, or Claire's. It was Caroline she should be angry with. Even so, it was humiliating to be reprimanded by her son's wife in front of so many people. And Minnie had had more than enough humiliation for one day. 'That child is a disgrace!' she fumed. 'He needs a little discipline, although Lord only knows how he's ever going to get it in this madhouse.'

Claire knew better than to argue, but she tightened her grip possessively around Hunter. She hated being in this position, but somebody had to look out for the child. If it were possible, her husband resented his little half-brother even more vehemently than

Minnie did. He flew completely off the handle whenever he caught her defending the boy.

Her heart pounded violently now as she stood on the steps with Hunter in her arms, terrified that Pete might see her and make a scene. Sensing her fear, and acutely aware of the tension coiled within her body, Hunter suddenly lost control of his bladder. A warm yellow stain began to spread slowly across Claire's white muslin blouse.

'I rest my case,' said Minnie, contemptuously, before turning on her heel and descending the steps to rejoin the party.

'Don't you worry, sweetie,' Claire reassured the traumatised child, whose sodden legs remained wrapped firmly around her. 'It was just an accident. Come on, let's go get you cleaned up, shall we?'

She hurried indoors with Hunter, anxious to get both him and herself changed into fresh clothes before Pete found them. Claire had grown to become quite frightened of her husband. More and more these days, Pete seemed to be overwhelmed by some nameless rage that she was powerless to placate. She had thought – well, hoped – that he might mellow once they had a child of their own. But five years of trying had proved painfully fruitless, and Claire felt instinctively that Pete blamed her for their reproductive failure, although there was nothing to suggest that the fault lay on her side.

It didn't help that her father-in-law was so gung-ho about his own virility, showing Hunter off like some sort of fertility trophy, rubbing Pete's nose in it at every opportunity.

She smiled down at Hunter's chubby body as he sat happily in the bath, squirting himself with Matey bubble bath. How could Duke and Caroline just ignore him the way they did? He was such a little angel.

For her part, the longing for a child of her own had become scarcely bearable, a ceaseless drumbeat of yearning pounding away in her head, day after day. How ironic, how cruel it was, that Caroline, who hadn't a shred of maternal feeling in her hard, toned little body, should have conceived so easily; while she, Claire, who would make such a natural, loving mother, seemed destined to remain childless.

'There you go, sweetie.' She wrapped Hunter up in a huge white towel and began rubbing him dry as he wriggled and squealed in delight. How wonderful to be four – the whole Minnie incident already seemed to be quite forgotten.

'I love oo, Claire,' he said, reaching his hands up around her neck and kissing her.

'Oh, honey. I love you too,' she said.

After a lightning change, the pair of them re-emerged into the sunshine. Claire looked beautiful but flustered in a pale yellow sundress. Hunter, already restored to his natural good humour, was beaming in a crisp white sailor suit, tightly clasping her hand.

Pete pounced on them instantly.

'Where the hell have you been?' he demanded. 'I wanted to introduce you to Sheila Peterson, but the moment I turned around you were gone.'

Sheila Peterson was the wife of Anton Peterson, one of the most reclusive and most successful studio bosses in Hollywood history. Pete had been trying for eighteen months to forge an alliance with the famously prickly Anton. The McMahon name still opened a lot of doors in the movie business, and Pete hoped to convince Peterson that he could bring a higher profile and touch of glamour to his thriving but still somewhat low-key business. Today was the first time he'd managed to get him and his wife to accept any sort of social invitation. The least Claire could do was to show him a little support.

'Oh, I'm sorry, honey. Hunter had a little accident, so I just ran in to clean him up.'

The second the words were out of her mouth, she could have bitten her tongue off.

'Jesus fucking *Christ*, Claire.' He seized her by both shoulders and began to shake her hard. 'You are not his mother, OK? When are you going to get that into your stupid head? He isn't your child.'

Suddenly he released her, giving a yelp of pain. The entire party turned to gawp at the scene. Hunter had sunk his teeth into Pete's leg and was screaming at the top of his lungs: 'Oo, stop it! Oo, stop hurtin' her! Leave her 'lone!'

'Excuse me.' Caroline, her face a picture of maternal concern, was pushing her way through the throng towards her son. 'What on *earth* is going on?' she demanded in her best clipped, Mary Poppins voice, looking daggers at Pete. 'What have you done to upset Hunter?'

'What have *I* done?' Pete was spitting blood. 'Your fucking out-of-control son just bit me. Take a look.'

He hitched up the leg of his white linen trousers. A deep purple bruise was already beginning to form around the livid red teeth marks that Hunter had left on his calf. Sheila Peterson winced. Pete looked at Caroline as though she were some particularly repulsive beetle that he was having difficulty in stamping on.

'You know, Caroline,' he said quite calmly, 'if you spent more time giving a shit about your kid, and less time dressing up like some dime-a-dozen hooker . . .' He ran his eyes insultingly up and down her body, lingering with distaste rather than lust on her barely contained breasts as they struggled for release from her red satin halter top. '. . . then maybe – just maybe he wouldn't be such a little savage.'

'How dare you speak to me like that!' said Caroline, indignantly. It didn't occur to her to take any offence on Hunter's behalf. 'Duke, did you hear how that bastard just spoke to me?' Everybody looked around for Duke, but he was nowhere to be seen. Hunter started to cry again.

'On the contrary, Caroline,' said Pete, 'I think you'll find it's *your* child that's the bastard. Now if you'll excuse us, Claire and I would like to get back to the party.'

'You do that,' Caroline spat back, wrenching Hunter's hand from Claire's, to the boy's evident distress. 'And perhaps in future you'll remember that he *is* my child, not yours.' She looked at Pete evilly. 'Poor little Petey, still no luck on the old baby front, eh? What seems to be the problem? Are your swimmers not quite up to it? Or can't you get it up at all? That's certainly not your father's problem, so I don't think it can be genetic, do you?'

A couple of embarrassed titters rose from the crowd.

'Now, if you'll excuse *me* . . .' She addressed herself to Claire, deliberately turning her back on Pete, whose face had turned a livid puce with hatred and was clashing violently with his receding sandy hair. '. . . I think I'll go and get my son a tetanus shot. God knows what evil disease he may have picked up from your poisonous husband.'

And with that she stalked off in search of Duke, her son jogging along reluctantly beside her.

Pete made an effort to collect himself. If that bitch and her son had blown it for him with Peterson, he wasn't going to let her forget it.

'OK, folks, show's over.' He forced a smile and signalled to the DJ to resume the music.

Supertramp came belting out across the lawn as the crowd once again broke off into little groups, all relishing this latest spectacular outburst of the McMahon feud. By Monday the story would be all over the papers. If only old Duke could have been there to witness it.

Standing by his bedroom window, Duke clenched both hands around the model's enormous breasts as he fucked her from behind, gazing down at the spectacle below. Watching Caroline get the better of Pete had excited him more than all the girl's frenzied clenching and moaning, and he found himself coming hard as he thought about what he might do to her later, once all these fucking parasites had gone home. Why the hell did she insist on throwing so many parties, filling the house with these goddam vacuous assholes? Caroline

59

belonged to him – that was their deal – and he was growing increasingly tired of never having her to himself.

Still, he thought complacently as he sent the starlet on her way, he couldn't really complain. He'd had one hell of an anniversary party.

Chapter Seven

It was a year to the day after Duke and Caroline's party, and Pete didn't think he had ever been so happy.

Lying in post-coital bliss with Claire in the honeymoon suite at the Borgo San Felice in Siena, he felt that his life was, at last, starting to come together.

'Mrs McMahon, when was the last time I told you how beautiful you were?'

Claire sighed happily and rolled over on to her stomach.

'Gee, I don't know, Pete,' she mocked him. 'It must have been . . . what? . . . five minutes now?'

He bent his head down and began kissing her spine, his lips brushing each vertebra with infinite tenderness.

'Well, that is terrible,' he said between kisses. 'I don't know what I can have been thinking of for those five minutes. Because you really are . . .' He rolled her over gently and planted another kiss on her left nipple. '. . . incredible.'

Claire was three months pregnant. Just when he had begun to despair of ever fathering a child – for all his bluster and hostility towards his wife, he had long suspected that his sperm count might be less than spectacular, and blamed himself for their childlessness – it had finally happened. After so many months, years, of making ovulation charts, quitting smoking, wearing loose pants, after endless humiliating examinations by a stream of sympathetic but bewildered doctors, they had suddenly hit the jackpot. Just like that.

Pete knew he had not been the greatest of husbands to Claire in their six years together. Things had been so different when they met. A mutual friend had introduced them at some horrific party in the hills. Pete, as usual, was surrounded by a huge crowd of starlets and wannabes, all desperate to ingratiate themselves with the son of the one and only Duke McMahon. He had been on the point of making his excuses and heading home, when a pale, shy-looking girl in the corner of the room caught his eye. She was being aggressively chatted up by Johnny Wright, a loathsome junior VP at Paramount.

'Who is that?' he asked his friend Adam, nominally the host of the evening's bash, although in fact he was only house-sitting and had paid for less than half of the booze being greedily consumed all around them.

'Claire Bryant. Gorgeous, isn't she? But don't go getting any ideas.' He gave Pete a mock-stern look.

'Why not?' Pete asked, knocking back most of his sour apple martini. 'Don't tell me she's with Johnny. That guy is such an ass.'

Adam shook his head. 'No, God no. Look at her, she can't stand the guy.'

Claire had backed so far away from her admirer that her back was now pressed against the wall. She was trying to look at him, not wishing to seem impolite, but couldn't help stealing frantic sideways glances, as if searching for some means of escape.

'Well, what, then?' said Pete. 'Why shouldn't I get any ideas? Not that I am getting any.'

Adam laughed. 'No, of course you aren't! I just mean that she's not like us, man. For one thing, she's smart. She's in her third year of medical school at UCLA. Two more years and you're looking at *Doctor* Bryant.'

'What on earth's she doing here, then?' asked Pete. 'It's hardly the sort of party for an academic girl like that.'

Adam shrugged. 'Danny brought her along, I think. Friend of the family or something. You should talk to her, though. I swear, it's like she's been living under a rock, she knows *nothing* about the business. Seriously, I don't think she'd even know who your old man is.' Pete looked incredulous. 'All she does is, like, read books and shit like that. She's not from this planet, man.'

'Yeah, well.' Pete glanced at the vacant, silicone-enhanced women across the room. 'I'm not so sure I like the women on this planet.' He downed the remnants of his drink and took his friend's arm. 'Introduce me, will you? She looks like she needs rescuing anyway.'

They made their way over to her, battling through the throng, and Adam inserted himself in front of Johnny, much to Claire's evident relief.

'Claire, I'd like you to meet a friend of mine,' he said. 'This is Petey McMahon.'

'How do you do?' said the vision. 'I'm Claire Bryant.'

Close up she was even more beautiful. She was tall, almost as tall as Pete in her flat ballet pumps, and, despite her air of fragility, quite statuesque. He was struck by her long, lean, muscular arms and the womanly curve of her hips. She seemed simultaneously strong and in need of protection.

She smiled at him with such genuine warmth, such femininity, that Pete felt instantly drawn to her. He shook her hand.

'Pete McMahon. A pleasure.'

'He's Duke McMahon's son,' interjected the odious Johnny, on name-drop autopilot.

'Oh,' said Claire, obviously baffled. 'I'm sorry, do I know your father?'

Adam winked at Pete. 'Told you.'

The two of them had hit it off immediately. They talked for hours. Pete had always adored his mother, but Minnie lacked the motherly softness that the lonely, angry little boy had always craved. Even in that very first conversation, Claire had listened to him, comforted him. She invited confidences and inspired total trust in a way that Pete found totally intoxicating.

They began spending more and more time together. He felt he could tell her anything, and found that he became listless and withdrawn whenever he was away from her, as though he had lost his anchor and was suddenly floating out to sea. Importantly, Claire was the first and only woman whom Pete knew for certain was not after either his name or his money. And God knew he was no Marlon Brando, so she sure wasn't with him for his looks. For some inexplicable reason, she actually loved him for himself. He couldn't believe his luck.

Since their marriage, however, his gratitude for her love had gradually been replaced by a bitterness, a hatred of his father that consumed every ounce of his emotional energy. None of it was Claire's fault. He knew that, and cursed himself for the way he treated her, bullying her just as his father had always bullied his mother. But the rage inside him was like a cancer, and ever since Caroline had moved in, and even more so since Hunter was born, he had felt that cancer spread.

Now, though, things would be different. Gazing down at his wife's naked, already swelling body, he felt almost overwhelmed with love for her and remorse at his own behaviour. Now that Claire was pregnant, he could become the husband she had always deserved. And his new partnership with Peterson Studios would finally start to put him on the map as a producer, a success in his own right, not just good ol' Duke McMahon's son. Yeah, it was all coming together, all making sense at last.

'Oh, Pete,' Claire murmured softly as he stroked her hair, 'I really am so happy. With you, with the baby, with everything. I feel like we've been blessed. But don't you wish we could just hide out in Italy for ever, never go back to that house?'

Pete felt the tears stinging the back of his eyes. She was so incredibly forgiving, so easily pleased. After all the pain he'd caused her, she was just happy to be here with him, grateful for one paltry week in Tuscany, their first vacation in over four years.

'I know how you feel, honey.' He stroked her belly lovingly, wondering what he had ever done to deserve such an angel. 'There's something kinda magical about this place.'

'Oh, there is!' said Claire, her eyes alight with enthusiasm. 'Siena's so incredible. The cathedral, the Piazza del Campo, the Palazzo Pubblico – my God, those frescos, I've never seen anything like it. I never dreamed I would actually be here. And that it would all be so perfect, so like I expected, but at the same time, even better than I expected. Sorry, honey, I'm gushing.' She blushed sweetly. 'But do you know what I mean?'

'Absolutely,' said Pete, who had been bored rigid by the frescos and the turgid tour of Siena's famous Gothic cathedral, but was happy just to watch his wife blossoming and in her element.

'But I'm afraid we really do have to go back. You know that, right?'

She sighed, nestling closer. These few days in Siena had been like a dream, her unborn child the magic talisman that had somehow brought her husband back to her. And yet it had all been so sudden. She couldn't help but wonder whether he wasn't going to change back just as suddenly into the withdrawn, aggressive figure she had come to know and dread.

As if reading her thoughts, Pete pulled her close. 'I promise you, Claire,' he whispered, 'you have nothing to fear.' She gazed up at him, her eyes full of trust and hope. 'When we get back home, things are going to be different. Very, very different.'

On 7 December 1981, Claire gave birth to a daughter. Siena McMahon came screaming into the world six days late. Both the screaming and the lateness were rapidly to become two of her trademarks.

'She looks kinda . . . scrunched up,' had been her father's verdict on being presented with a tiny, tightly wrapped white bundle from which Siena's bawling head poked out like a sunburned prune. 'What's she so mad about, anyway?'

'Takes after her father,' said an exhausted Claire. 'Besides, she's had a rough day. It's very traumatic, you know, birth.'

'Yeah, so they tell me. It was pretty hard going out there in the waiting room, I can tell you. We almost ran out of cigars.'

She half-heartedly hurled a pillow in his direction and grinned, stretching out her arms for the baby. 'Here, Pete, give her to me.'

He handed over the bundle with exaggerated care, mingled with a slight sensation of relief, and looked on with pride while his wife unswaddled their daughter and put her to her breast. Instantly the caterwauling stopped, and was replaced by a greedy slurping noise. Pete was mesmerised. After about a minute, her sucking slowed and she literally fell from Claire's breast, mouth open, like a blood-gorged mosquito, into a deep, contented sleep.

'Well, she's not gonna starve to death in a hurry,' said Pete. 'What an appetite!' They both laughed in wonderment at this tiny, greedy little creature they had created. Even in sleep, Pete noticed, her tiny fists were clenched, ready for unseen battles ahead.

Siena was not as beautiful a baby as Hunter had been. They had the same colouring – dark hair contrasting dramatically with striking blue eyes – although Siena's complexion was pure porcelain rather than her uncle's tawny olive, and she lacked his immaculately regular features. She was, however, pronounced by everyone to be 'adorable', and reminded her parents of a fallen cherub. Mischievous eyes twinkled in her soft, chubby face and she had the tiny rosebud mouth of a Tiny-Tears doll, complete with dimples in her cheeks and chin.

If she and Hunter shared some physical characteristics, Siena was about as far removed from him in temperament as anyone could be. Mischievous, confident and the possessor of a truly awesome temper, even as a tiny baby, she ran the entire household ragged with a cry so piercing it could be heard the length and breadth of Hancock Park. The McMahons' two nannies, Leila and Suzanna, thought back with longing to Hunter's peaceful babyhood, and wondered how long they could survive on three hours' sleep a night.

The differences between the two children didn't end there. While his parents' neglect had forced Hunter to develop an independent spirit and maturity beyond his years, it had also made him a reserved and withdrawn child. Siena was the opposite, a noisy, happy, rambunctious little girl who gave out her love readily and without question because, for the first few years of her life anyway, she received nothing but love from everyone around her.

Perhaps a little spoiled by so much constant attention, she developed an early taste for getting her own way and, although she could turn on the charm when she chose to, she could also be as stubborn, wilful and demanding as Hunter was docile and obedient.

On one occasion, when Siena had just turned two, Leila had had to call in the cavalry when she had refused point blank to wear the new Osh Kosh sundress that Claire had picked out for the day.

'She's gone stiff as a board,' the exasperated nanny told Pete. 'Absolutely refuses to bend her arms or legs so I can get the dress on. And the more I try, the more she screams. Just listen to her.'

Siena's yells could clearly be heard from two storeys below in Pete's study, easily out-decibelling the deep, authoritative voice of Suzanna, who had been left in charge while Leila ran down for parental reinforcements.

Pete sighed and put down his paper. 'OK. I'll come up.'

Upstairs, Siena was in the middle of a textbook demonstration of the 'Terrible Twos' – as described by Dr Spock in chapter seven of the parenting guide that Claire and all her friends lived by. She was lying face down on the floor of the nursery, beet red, simultaneously pummelling the carpet with her fists, yelling, and shaking her head manically from side to side. Suzanna had given up trying to get anywhere near her with the hated dress, and was waiting resignedly for the storm to subside.

'Now, Siena, what's all this?' Pete shouted over the din. 'Why won't you let Leila and Suzanna help you with your pretty dress?'

The pummelling stopped for a moment, and a tear-sodden, exhausted face looked up at him. 'Nooooo dress,' sobbed Siena. 'Nooooo!'

'But honey,' said Pete, ignoring all Dr Spock's advice and making the classic mistake of reasoning with an overwrought toddler, 'you'd look so cute in that dress. That's why Mommy picked it out, so you'd look just like a princess. Don't you want to be a princess, Siena?'

With an almighty effort, Siena refilled her lungs and began pummelling again with a vengeance. 'No! Siena not dress!' she screamed.

Pete thought longingly of his paper and the peace and quiet of the study. He looked at his daughter, and then at the offending article, a riot of yellow ribbons and lace. You know what, maybe she had a point? It did look kind of frou-frou.

'Just put her in her dungarees,' he said to Suzanna.

'What? But Mr McMahon,' she remonstrated, 'she's just been told she has to wear the dress. Mrs McMahon specifically requested it. I really don't think it's a good idea to just give in to her like that.'

'I'm sorry, Suzanna,' said Pete coldly, 'but I'm Siena's father and I think I know what's best for her.'

Leila saw Siena give a little smirk of triumph from under her damp curls. Sometimes she could strangle that child.

'Just get her dressed in something else and bring her downstairs,'

Pete snapped. 'My wife is late as it is.' And with that, he turned on his heel and headed for the stairs and the relative calm and safety of the adult world below.

Suzanna looked at her friend in horror and ran an exasperated hand through her hair. 'Can you believe that? What an asshole! Fat lot of good he was.'

'I know,' said Leila. 'If they never stand up to her, she's only going to get worse.'

Siena gave them both the benefit of her most butter-wouldn't-melt smile.

'What an asshole!' she said.

Chapter Eight

Nothing, it seemed, could stand in the way of the entire household's love affair with Siena. Never had so much unceasing affection and attention been heaped on one little girl. Especially not in the McMahon family, who were not renowned for their sentimentality and whose previous generation of children had long been used to playing second fiddle to their larger-than-life parents.

Claire had waited so long for a child, she couldn't help but spoil her. One particular expression of her love – her desire to dress her little daughter like a doll – was a constant source of friction between the two of them. Claire would spend a small fortune on clothes, from tiny, exquisitely embroidered linen dresses to cashmere cardigans and shiny red patent-leather shoes. Siena, who hated to wear anything but her favourite blue corduroy dungarees, fought tooth and nail against her mother over these outfits, and never wore them without a stubborn scowl fixed on her face.

As long as she wasn't being straitjacketed with ribbons and bows, though, Siena loved being with her mother, baking biscuits in the kitchen together or reading her favourite story about the magic porridge pot.

'Stop, little pot, stop!' she would squeal delightedly on cue, while Claire turned the page to reveal the overflowing pot sending magic rivers of porridge down the village street.

'Look, Siena. It *doesn't* stop, does it? The magic pot makes *more* and *more* porridge!'

Siena soon knew the story picture for picture and word for word, but she never tired of listening to her mother tell it.

Not that Claire had an exclusive on her daughter's affections. Laurie, who was still unmarried, also loved her little niece every bit as passionately as she had hated and resented Hunter. She was nervous around children, certainly not a natural like Claire, but despite her awkwardness she made a huge effort to bond with Siena.

One morning, Laurie had waddled into the nursery with a large lollipop – cherry, Siena's favourite – clenched in her clammy palm.

Siena sat contentedly like a little dark-haired Buddha amid a sea of Fisher Price toys. Although it was officially a play room for both the children, most of Hunter's Action Men and Meccano sets had been relegated to the far corner, while the rest of the room had gradually been overwhelmed by a sea of pink plastic, headless Barbies, and other Siena paraphernalia.

'Hey there, sweetie,' Laurie said, in that unfortunate patronising tone that nervous adults use to speak to children, old people and the mentally ill. She squatted down so she was at the child's eye level, and thrust the lollipop out in front of her rather as one would brandish garlic at a vampire. 'Look what your Aunt Laurie brought you!'

With one swift movement, Siena whipped the lolly from her hand and thrust it greedily into her mouth, giving her aunt a sticky kiss before toddling back over to her bricks and hammer. Her number-one game of the moment was building teetering tower blocks and then demolishing them with a little wooden hammer on a string which Hunter had made for her.

'What do you say?' said Laurie, hopefully, but she was met with a blank stare. Being in full possession of the coveted lollipop, Siena's thoughts had now strayed on to other things.

Laurie looked around for a chair, but the entire nursery seemed to have been furnished by midgets, and nothing in the room was going to take her weight. She eventually eased herself down on to the carpet and sat beside her niece.

'What are you playing, honey? Do you want me to play with you?' She picked up a brick and placed it awkwardly on top of the wobbly tower. It collapsed.

'Oh dear,' said Siena, but she flashed her aunt a big grin and seemed unperturbed by her tower-building ineptitude. This child was the one member of the family, thought Laurie sadly, who seemed to accept her for who she was, faults and all.

'Start again.' Siena sighed heavily, doing a good impression of her father after a long day at the office, and began piling up the bricks from scratch, hammer swinging dangerously close to Laurie's face as she worked.

'Oh look,' said Laurie brightly, seeing Duke appear at the nursery door. 'Here comes your grandpa. What do you say he builds your tower with you?'

At the mention of Duke, Siena's eyes lit up. Pushing aside her bricks, she leapt to her feet and raced across the room towards him.

Ignoring Laurie completely, Duke knelt down and opened his arms to his granddaughter. Mirroring him, Siena flung her own chubby little arms wide and hurled herself into his embrace. She was smiling so broadly, her lollipop fell to the floor.

'Whoa there, princess!' Duke grinned. 'Hold your horses! What are you up to in here?' He pulled her up on to his raised knee, and breathed in her sticky, infant smell as she wrapped her arms around him. God, he loved her.

'Bricks!' She beamed at him. 'I doin' my tower, I dot my hammer. Grandpa comin' to play with me?'

'Absolutely,' said Duke, hoisting her up into his arms.

Laurie, who had been watching this loving exchange between grandfather and granddaughter, had decided to slip away and leave them to it. She knew Siena loved her too, and tried not to feel jealous of her special relationship with Duke. But sometimes she wished her father wouldn't show up every time that she and Siena were having some fun together. He sure hadn't been so peachy keen on hanging around the nursery when she and Petey were kids.

'Hey, Laurie.' Duke turned briefly to his daughter, and despite herself she felt her hopes rising that he might ask her to stay and join them. 'D'you wanna get rid of that lollipop? It's gonna stain the carpet if we leave it there.'

Meekly, she picked up her sticky peace offering, now covered with carpet hair. Fighting her sense of dejection and disappointment, she left the two lovebirds to it.

Laurie was as baffled as the rest of the family by Duke's unexpected bond with his granddaughter. The man who had never shown anything other than irritation with children, and especially with babies and toddlers, had suddenly become a tamed tiger in Siena's presence.

The truth was that from the first moment he laid eyes on her grumpy little face, fists flailing in fury, Duke had fallen head over heels in love with his granddaughter.

'That kid is the only one of the lot of you that takes after me,' he would announce proudly.

Siena, in turn, responded to him like no one else, turning off her tears in an instant whenever he picked her up and settling obediently to sleep when he sang her the old Irish folk ballads of his childhood, in that wonderfully deep voice that had so hypnotised women around the world.

'It's the old McMahon magic!' he liked to tell Claire, who often felt powerless to placate her difficult daughter without him. 'She's not the first girl to give up the fight once I start singing to her.'

As the years went by, it was a close-run thing as to who, between

Caroline and Pete, was the more enraged by Duke's blatant adoration of Siena.

'He never gave a damn about any of his own children, and now he wants to monopolise mine. Why can't he just do us all a favour and die?' Pete complained to Claire for the umpteenth time one night, as they lay under the peach duvet in their south wing suite.

These momentary flashes of Pete's old rage rattled Claire greatly. She felt she could bear almost anything rather than lose her husband for a second time. 'I know it bothers you, honey,' she tried to soothe him. 'But he is her grandfather. And, you know, despite all the awful things he's done, I think he really does love her.'

Caroline was less accepting.

'What the fuck is wrong with you?' she screamed one Sunday afternoon, when Duke had returned from Griffith Park with the three-year-old Siena, who was tightly clutching her grandfather's hand and fluttering her eyelashes innocently at Caroline. 'Hunter was waiting all morning for you to come and take him to softball. How could you just disappear like that?'

Duke was unrepentant. 'You're his mother. Why didn't you take him?'

Nothing infuriated Caroline more than being reminded of her own failings as a parent, particularly by Duke.

'I'm taking Siena up for a bath,' he said firmly and, hoisting the child on to his shoulders, he started climbing the stairs. 'Up we go, sweetheart! You stick with your Grandpa Duke.'

'I'm well aware that I'm his mother,' Caroline shouted at his disappearing back. 'But you're his father, Duke, and that's very important to a boy.' Duke continued climbing the stairs. Caroline's histrionics bored him, and he hadn't the slightest interest in talking about Hunter or his ball game. 'You have a son, and he needs you,' she continued, exasperated. 'I can't be expected to do everything with him, for Christ's sake.'

In fact, Caroline would rather have eaten snakes than take Hunter to softball herself and miss her Sunday pedicure with Chantal. Suzanna had taken him, as usual. But that was beside the point, she thought furiously. It wasn't just that Duke ignored the boy. Like her, he had never been interested in children, and until that bloody little girl had arrived in their lives she had never considered his detachment from their son to be an issue. But recently Duke's obsession with Siena was becoming not just unreasonable, but downright dangerous.

She even suspected that he got more pleasure from playing farm animals with his granddaughter than from sex with her, a possibility

71

that made her profoundly uneasy. They still made love with surprising frequency – for a man in his early seventies, Duke had phenomenal energy – and his desire for her remained strong. Caroline knew it was a tactical mistake to go head to head with Duke, and that her attacks on him were almost certainly counter-productive. But she was becoming genuinely fearful for her son's future. After all, she and Duke were not married, and she now accepted that they were never likely to be. She had seen the will, and knew that both she and Hunter were handsomely provided for. But even so, she couldn't shake the lingering doubt over the security of her position. Siena's arrival in their lives had changed everything, and had put paid to any hopes she may have harboured of a conclusive rift between Duke and Petey.

For the first time in her life, Caroline felt at a loss. Duke's love for Siena was getting stronger by the day. It was the one element in his life which was completely out of her control.

Later that evening, eight-year-old Hunter was sitting in the playroom watching *The Muppet Show* with Siena snuggled happily in his lap, smelling of talcum powder and wearing her favourite Snow White pyjamas.

She was kind of subdued this evening, he noticed, probably because his dad had fed her so much ice cream at the park she'd puked up all over Claire, and now it seemed that everybody was mad at everybody else. Sometimes he just couldn't figure out his family. Someone always seemed to be mad, and nine times out of ten it was his fault.

He loved it when they all left him alone, when it was just him and Siena having fun by themselves. It was a testament to Hunter's loving nature and generosity of spirit that he never resented Siena for so effortlessly winning the love that he had consistently been denied. On the contrary, he worshipped his little niece, and never tired of reading to her or crawling down the endless corridors of the estate with her on his back while they played 'horsey'. Most boys in the second grade considered it totally uncool to hang out with a toddler, especially if she was a girl. But those kids all had normal families with brothers and sisters of their own. To Hunter, the experience of having a permanent playmate, another human being who loved him uncondi-tionally, was infinitely more wonderful and more fun than playing the Incredible Hulk with boys his own age. Siena was a little minx, of course – everybody knew that – but he forgave her for it just like everybody else.

'Animal!' Siena squealed in delight as a fuzzy orange Muppet wielding drumsticks came bounding on to the screen, head-banging. 'I wuv dat one! I wuv dat one, Animal!'

'Sure you do!' said Hunter, tickling her. 'You love Animal because he's just like *you*! Noisy and rude and a little *Monster*!' She was terribly ticklish, and after only a few seconds had collapsed into an exhausted, happy heap on the floor. 'Do you surrender?'

She smiled up at him adoringly, her huge eyes alight with mischief, and shook her head no, screaming for all she was worth as he wiggled his fingers mock-menacingly in her direction. 'God, for a baby you sure are stubborn. I hope you're ready for some more tickling?'

At that moment Suzanna came into the nursery and announced that it was Siena's bedtime. The wails of protest were instantaneous.

'Can't she stay up with me just a little bit longer?' pleaded Hunter. 'At least till the end of the Muppets? It's only ten minutes.'

Suzanna was very fond of Hunter and constantly amazed by the way he stuck up for Siena. She had lost count of the times she had seen him meekly take the blame in front of Pete or Minnie when Siena had spilled her juice or carelessly broken one of her grandmother's priceless ornaments, suffering frequent, unjust punishments on Siena's behalf. No matter how vociferously Siena insisted it had been her own fault, none of the adults felt inclined to punish their little cherub when Hunter was so much more satisfying a whipping boy.

'I'm sorry, Hunter, but not tonight,' she said. His face was so pitiful she almost relented, but the only thing worse than Siena's usual behaviour was her behaviour when she was over-tired. Looking at her droopy eyes and enormous dark shadows, Suzanna decided it was definitely bedtime. 'Little madam here has already been thoroughly overexcited today, and her mother wanted her in bed half an hour ago. Come on, you.'

She picked up an irate, struggling Siena and carried her off down the hallway to her bedroom. It made Hunter laugh, the way Siena fought everything all the time. Part of him wished that he could fight the world like that. But another part of him knew it would make no difference how loudly he screamed.

Nobody was going to pay a blind bit of attention.

Chapter Nine

There were two significant male figures in Siena's childhood. And her father wasn't one of them.

It was Duke and Hunter who became, in their very different ways, the foundation stones of her young life, the twin towers of her existence at Hancock Park. Duke was her idol. To her little girl's eyes, he seemed as all-knowing and all-powerful as a god. His huge physical presence both excited and soothed her, and she felt that she could never come to any harm whenever her grandfather was near. Siena didn't draw breath without trying to please him.

Hunter, on the other hand, was more of an equal. She adored him as her big brother, her playmate and her best friend. Being brave as well as kind, he became her constant champion against the traumas and insults of the school playground and, increasingly, her faithful defender against her father's wrath.

When Siena was seven, she came home from school one day in a state of high anxiety. She had totally flunked her spelling test – four out of twenty – and was not looking forward to explaining her failure to Pete.

'Do you think he'd believe me if I told him Mrs Sanders forgot to test us?' she asked Hunter hopefully.

They were sitting at the kitchen table and Hunter was deep into his maths homework, with files and books strewn all around him, but had given up any hope of being able to concentrate thanks to Siena's endless worried chatter. She had perched herself on the opposite end of the table, and was mournfully munching on a chocolate chip cookie while she contemplated her fate.

He sighed. 'Honey, I'm sorry to say it, but I just don't think he's gonna buy that, do you?'

He was right, of course. Pete had to be the strictest dad in second grade when it came to tests and grades and stuff. As soon as he got home he was sure to ask how it went. And there was no point lying about her marks. Her father seemed to have a sixth sense about that sort of thing, and would be bound to check with Mrs Sanders in the morning. Then she'd really be for it.

'Afternoon, Antoine. Is my wife at home?'

Siena froze at the sound of her father's voice. What on earth was he doing home so early? She looked at Hunter in desperation.

'Yes, sir, I believe she's out by the pool,' the butler replied. 'She got back from school with Siena about an hour ago.'

'Now don't panic,' said Hunter, seeing the terrified look on his niece's face. 'Just tell him what happened and get it over with. I'm sure he'll understand.'

'Oh yeah, right,' snapped Siena sarcastically, as Pete strolled into the kitchen looking tired and weighed down by his brown leather briefcase, squash racket and gym bag.

He dropped these burdens unceremoniously on the kitchen floor and, loosening his tie, bent down to kiss his daughter. Not with the slightest gesture or glance did he acknowledge Hunter's presence in the room. Automatically, Hunter started gathering his books together to leave, but Siena's pleading face stopped him in his tracks and he sat back down.

'So, how was your day, baby?' Pete tousled her hair affectionately. 'How'd you go on those spellings?'

Siena felt her stomach give an unpleasant lurch. There was no getting around it.

'Not so good, Daddy,' she mumbled, eyes glued to her lap. She was biting her lower lip, a sure-fire give-away of either nervousness or guilt.

'I see.' Pete's voice sounded suddenly icy. It was amazing, Hunter thought, how quickly his half-brother could switch from friendly to furious. 'And exactly what do you mean by "not so good"?' he asked.

Siena could hear her heart pounding but forced herself to look him in the eye.

'Four out of twenty,' she said. 'I'm sorry, Daddy.'

'Four!' Pete's voice was so loud that both the children jumped. He banged his fist down on the table and sent Hunter's papers flying around the room. 'Siena McMahon, that's an absolute disgrace. Four out of twenty! You can't possibly have studied.'

'I did, Dad, I totally did!' Siena remonstrated on autopilot.

In fact she had stayed up late the night before watching movies with Grandpa, but she wasn't about to pour even more petrol on the flames by telling that to her father. Anyway, she had glanced at her spellings in the car on the way to school, which was sort of studying, so it wasn't *really* a lie.

'Well then, how do you explain your result, young lady?' barked Pete. 'Because you sure as hell aren't that stupid.'

Despite herself, Siena felt her eyes welling up. It was only a stupid old spelling test. Other kids' parents probably wouldn't even ask them how they did, let alone get so het up about it. Why did Daddy have to be so mean about everything?

Peter, in fact, hated these encounters almost as much as she did. But he knew that both Duke and, to a lesser extent, Claire let Siena get away with murder, especially when it came to school work. Someone had to exercise a little control.

'It was my fault, really,' piped up Hunter, unable to bear Siena's wobbling lower lip a moment longer. 'I kept Siena awake last night. We were writing songs on my guitar, and I guess I just lost track of the time. She must have been too tired to sit the test.'

Pete knew he had been thrown a dummy – tiredness alone would not have caused his daughter to tank so spectacularly – but the opportunity to transfer his anger to Hunter was just too good to miss.

'I should have known.' He glared at his little brother. 'Whenever there's any trouble around here, you just have to be at the centre of it, don't you?'

Hunter's twelve-year-old face flushed slightly beneath his thick black hair, but he remained composed. Pete thought bitterly for the hundredth time how incredibly handsome the boy was. He had his mother's wide mouth and high cheekbones, but his colouring and facial expressions were all Duke's. Pete found these physical reminders of his father wholly repellent.

'I'm sorry,' said Hunter quietly, anxious not to enrage his brother any more than necessary. 'But it really wasn't Siena's fault.'

'I'll be the judge of that,' said Pete, who had helped himself to a large glass of the kids' Hershey's chocolate milk from the fridge, into which he was dropping ice cubes from Hunter's Tarzan ice tray. 'But in the meantime, you can stay in your room for the rest of the evening. I don't want to *see* you or *hear* you downstairs at any time, is that clear?'

'Yes, sir.' Hunter nodded respectfully and hurriedly gathered up his books.

'And I'd better not catch you anywhere near Siena on a school night again, understand? You may be too stupid to make it to college, but she isn't, and it's my job to see that she gets there one day.' He took a long gulp of his chocolate milk. 'Writing songs indeed!'

Hunter blushed more deeply before slipping out of the kitchen door. Checking first that Suzanna and Leila were nowhere in sight, he kicked off his sneakers and performed a running skid along the marble hallway, sliding to a halt just short of the front door. He wandered outside shoeless, his files and schoolbooks under one arm, and sat down on the stone steps of the porch. From here he had a clear view down the long driveway to the huge wrought-iron gates that protected the estate from the prying eyes of the outside world. It was a safe bet that a small cluster of diehard fans would be loitering just outside, ever hopeful for a glimpse of his famous father coming or going. He knew what they must all be thinking: that life inside those gates must be perfect, like some kind of paradise.

Well, it sure didn't feel that way to him.

Hunter knew Pete was right, about his being dumb and all that. He had always struggled in class, despite working three times harder at his school work than any of the other kids. His report cards had all been the same since first grade: he was a delight to teach, thoughtful and polite in class, helpful to his teachers and always kind to other children. But academically he just wasn't the sharpest tool in the box. Privately, this sense of failure was a source of deep unhappiness and shame to him.

Meanwhile, back in the kitchen, Siena, who had barely had time to mouth 'thanks' to Hunter before he had scooted off, was left alone with her father.

Now that Pete's rage had somewhat abated, her earlier terror of him had been replaced by righteous indignation on Hunter's behalf.

'Why do you always have to be so mean to him?' She scowled at her father, pushing away her own empty glass in anger. 'He works really hard at school. It's not his fault if he isn't as smart as all the other kids.'

Pete raised his finger at her in warning and fixed her with a threatening 'don't push me, young lady' look that never failed to make her stomach flip over with nerves. But she wasn't going to shut up this time. Hunter was always sticking up for her. The least she could do was repay him in kind.

'No, Dad.' She thrust her dimpled chin forward in a gesture of courage and defiance that was vintage Duke. 'It's not fair. I'm sorry I flunked my test, but it wasn't Hunter's fault. I don't understand why you always want to blame him and put him down all the time.'

'That's enough,' said Pete, wiping a smear of milky chocolate from the corners of his mouth and getting up from the table. He knew there was truth in what she said, but he wasn't about to be given a dressing down by his own daughter. 'Your grandfather might think it's acceptable to talk back to adults like that, but I most certainly do not.'

Siena opened her mouth to say something else, but the look in her father's eyes made her think better of it.

'I want you to go to your room, right this instant, and get on with your homework.' He moved over to the door and held it open, challenging her to defy him. 'The next time you perform that badly on a test, young lady, let me tell you, your feet won't touch the ground.'

With a last defiant toss of her curls, Siena picked up her Snoopy school bag and strode, head held high, out of the kitchen. She wanted to run off straight away and find Hunter, to thank him for going in to bat for her yet again. But she knew her dad would totally lose it if he caught the two of them together now, so she reluctantly made her way up to her own room, her battered old school bag bumping against each stair as she went.

She didn't know what was wrong with her father. He always had to be mad at someone. If it wasn't her, it was Hunter, or Mom. In fact the only person he seemed able to be consistently civil to was Grandma Minnie.

Most of all, though, Siena had begun to notice recently, Pete was mad at Grandpa. Really, really mad. All the time. And try as she might, she just couldn't understand why.

On the first morning of the children's spring break, Duke had promised to take Siena down to the studios to watch the making of the new Mel Gibson movie he was financing. She had spent the previous night in a sleepless frenzy of excitement. Mel Gibson! All the girls at school were, like, totally in love with him, even the sixth-graders. Everyone was gonna think she was the coolest, getting to hang out with him and *loads* of other famous people.

Despite her privileged upbringing, and the ever-present reminders of her family's own fame – the ubiquitous bodyguards, the daily gathering of hard-core fans outside the gates of the estate, all of whom Siena knew by name, having grown up accustomed to their permanent presence – she remained desperately star-struck and enthralled by the glamour of Hollywood. She liked nothing better than to fall asleep in front of one of Grandpa's old black-and-white movies in the huge underground screening room at the estate, dreaming of being one of his beautiful leading ladies.

Hunter felt faintly embarrassed whenever he saw one of Duke's films. His father looked so young and handsome, and always played chivalrous, dashing heroes utterly unrecognisable from the aloof old man that he knew. Kids at school used to tease him about having such an old dad. Whenever he watched those films, which seemed to come from a time so long ago he could scarcely imagine it, Hunter felt he knew what those kids meant.

But to Siena, Duke was still every bit the hero. She knew the lines from every one of his movies by heart.

'Can Hunter come with us, Grandpa?' she pleaded, bouncing up and down excitedly on her chair at breakfast that morning, her bowl of Cheerios untouched. 'Pleeeeease?'

Hunter looked up from his cereal hopefully, but one look at his father's face told him he'd be about as welcome as a fart in a space shuttle.

'Sure,' said Duke, without an iota of enthusiasm.

The kid was OK, he supposed, but he had never had the same passion and love for the movie business that little Siena did. It was another thing that he and his granddaughter had in common, and he'd been looking forward to it being just the two of them today. Still, he could see how much she wanted Hunter to come and he couldn't bear to disappoint her.

'Yay!' Siena clapped her hands excitedly, oblivious to Hunter's look of reticence – he didn't want to come if his dad didn't really want him there.

Caroline was the only other adult who had made it to breakfast. Pete was on business in New York and Minnie, Laurie and Claire had left early that morning for a girls' shopping trip in Palm Desert, from which she had been pointedly excluded.

She had watched the exchange between Duke and her son with dismay, and felt a rare stab of real pity for Hunter. He'd have been happy with a fraction of the love and attention his father gave Siena, but Duke seemed determined to deny him even that. She remembered the close, loving relationship she'd had with her own father and wished her son could have known, if only for one day, what that was like.

'Actually, I'm afraid Hunter can't come, Siena,' she said firmly. 'He has Max coming over today, don't you, darling? That'll be a lot more fun than going to the silly old studios, won't it?'

Hunter rather doubted that it would, but was grateful for his mother's show of support all the same. Max De Seville was probably his closest buddy at school, the son of some old English friends of Caroline's. His mom was right, they did always have a good laugh together, especially when Siena happened not to be around. Max, unfortunately, had a zero-tolerance policy towards little girls in general, and Siena in particular, and had never been able to understand Hunter's enjoyment of her company.

Still, Hunter couldn't help thinking it would have been nice if, just once, his father had actually *wanted* to include him in one of his plans.

'Oh yes,' said Siena churlishly, pushing aside her cereal bowl with an almighty pout. It wasn't *fair* that he couldn't spend the day with her. 'Hunter can stay here and play with pig-face Max. Max the Spax!' The antipathy between Siena and Max was entirely mutual. 'That'll be *much* more fun!' She was a brilliant mimic, and had Caroline's aristocratic English drawl down to a tee.

'Now, honey, you mustn't be rude to Caroline,' said Duke, but he was unable to suppress a grin. The kid really did have talent.

Ignoring this lack of moral support, Caroline got up from the table and sat herself down coquettishly on Duke's lap. At forty-two, she had thickened around the waist and no longer had the perfectly firm breasts and concave belly that had so enthralled and delighted him when they first met, almost fourteen years ago. But she was still, without doubt, an extremely attractive woman. No hint of grey had yet found its way into her sleek blonde bob, and only the faintest of frown lines marred her otherwise strikingly youthful face.

Neither had the years done anything to dull her rampant, wanton sexuality. Duke might not be faithful to her, but he still found her infinitely more desirable and intriguing, sexually, than any of the younger, perter playthings who occasionally made their grasping way into his bed.

Caroline was also not above trying to make a seven-year-old child jealous. Siena glared at her from beneath her tangled mop of curls as she gave Duke a lingering kiss on the mouth, her expert tongue probing hungrily and obscenely for his own, one red-taloned hand burrowing furtively under his shirt, the other dangerously close to his crotch. Duke gave a primitive groan of arousal. Man, she still did it for him.

Hunter squirmed in his seat at this public display of affection between his parents, and wished the ground would open up and swallow him.

'Have a good day, darling,' said Caroline, looking triumphantly over her shoulder at Siena, who was murderously stirring her soggy cereal at the other end of the table. That would teach the spoilt little brat. 'Don't let her tire you out completely before tonight.' Her eyes locked lasciviously with Duke's and he smiled.

'Oh, don't you worry, baby,' he said, as she got up and headed for the door. 'I still have more than enough energy for the both of you.'

Chapter Ten

Fairfax Studios was a ramshackle collection of ugly sixties warehouses and temporary-looking sheds, tucked away off Benedict Canyon in North Hollywood. To call the place unprepossessing would have been a gross understatement, but there was a frenzied flurry of activity around the lot that morning which lent an undeniable air of excitement and glamour to the dull, practical buildings.

Runners scurried to and fro, laden with mysterious boxes, clipboards or armfuls of clothing. Harassed-looking make-up artists dashed between the various trailers, huge silver mobile homes on ugly concrete stilts where the film's principal stars 'rested' between takes. All too often, they 'rested' together, and the entire extended crew were treated to the sight of a ton and a half of aluminium shaking and shuddering while the leading lady 'rehearsed' with various extras. A few jaded-looking journalists, instantly recognisable by their bright green press badges, skulked dejectedly around the set, knowing from bitter experience that they might well have to hang around all day before being granted their promised interview, and that even then the PRs would guard their celebrity charges like Rottweilers, refusing to let them answer any interesting personal questions.

Siena had been to Fairfax only once before, despite repeatedly begging her grandfather to let her tag along. There was nowhere on earth she preferred to be than on a movie set with Duke. It was like Christmas Eve, her birthday and Disneyland all rolled into one. She was excited by every aspect of film-making: the huge furry boom microphones that zoomed backwards and forwards on their enormous cranes, the great coiled firemen's hoses, waiting to pump gallons of foam on to the blazing backs of the stuntmen, resplendent in their red and white flame-retardant suits. Siena was intoxicated by it all.

Most of all, though, she longed to catch a glimpse of the actors themselves: Sylvester Stallone, Sigourney Weaver, Ali Sheedy, Andrew McCarthy, Mel Gibson – they were her idols, her pantheon of gods and goddesses. They all carried with them an almost tangible magic, a glowing, magnetic aura that made the little girl catch her breath in their presence, despite her own long familiarity with fame.

Her whole body would swell with pride as she watched her grandpa mingle with them, being greeted with affection and respect by each of her heroes in turn. Duke was a god among gods, and Siena felt special and uniquely powerful to be his chosen companion as they roamed the set together.

'You've met my granddaughter, Siena?' Duke accosted Mel Gibson as he emerged from his trailer, a battered script in one hand and a huge paper cup of coffee in the other.

Siena's eyes were on stalks as the star squatted down on his haunches so that his eyes were level with hers. His face looked slightly orange under his make-up, but his long, shaggy mane of hair and twinkling blue-green eyes looked just as they did on-screen. Siena felt her heart thump so loudly she feared he might hear it.

'I don't believe I have,' he said in his deep, gravelly Australian voice. 'Hello, Siena. Do you know, you're about the same age as my daughter, Hannah?' Siena shook her head mutely, still gazing at him adoringly. 'So what do you reckon to the set? It's kinda cool, isn't it?'

'I love it!' she said, suddenly emboldened. 'When I grow up, I'm going to be a movie star, just like you and Grandpa!'

Mel Gibson laughed good-naturedly. 'Is that so? Well, I can let you into a secret. Your grandpa here is a much, much bigger star than I'll ever be. You've got a tough act to follow there, Siena.'

Duke lifted her up into his arms, his face alight with love. 'I'm telling you, man, one of these days this girl is gonna be huge. She's got that old McMahon magic in bucketloads, haven't you, princess?'

Siena felt she had never known true happiness until that moment.

The rest of the day passed as if in a dream. Did Grandpa really think that she could make it in the movies, that she had what it took to be like he was? If he did, then there could be no doubt about it. If Grandpa said that something was going to happen, then it did, it always did. Not even the future could defy Duke McMahon.

She followed Duke like an overexcited puppy through the maze of huts, hangars and trailers, while he spoke to the director and various key members of the crew, breaking off frequently to take calls from his lawyer on his state-of-the-art new mobile phone. Siena was incredibly impressed, watching him bellow angrily into what looked like a rather heavy black brick with buttons on it.

'I don't care how you find out, David, just do it. That's what I pay you fuckers for,' he roared.

Siena wondered what he was trying to find out about, but was too enthralled by her surroundings to waste much mental energy on anything else. One of the costume ladies, a laughing Korean woman who wore hundreds of clattering bangles on each arm, gave her a beautiful red satin shawl with a white lace trim for dressing up. Siena wrapped herself in it gleefully and was about to go skipping off after Duke when she suddenly felt a stab of guilt.

'I wonder,' she said, 'do you think you might be able to swap it for something a bit more boyish?'

'Of course.' The costume lady gave her a puzzled smile. 'But why would you want to do that?'

'It's just my Uncle Hunter wasn't able to come today,' explained Siena, 'and I'd really like to bring him something back as a present. To make up for it, you know?'

The woman assured her that she could keep the scarf, but they would find something nice for Hunter as well. After a few minutes of rummaging, she pulled out a futuristic-looking model of a fazer gun from an old plywood crate. It was an exact replica of the ones Siena had seen on Star Trek, and she just knew Hunter would love it.

'How about this?' said the costume lady, and was gratified to see the little girl's eyes light up like fireworks.

'Oh, it's perfect, thank you,' said Siena. She knew that deep down Hunter was disappointed to have missed today. Maybe, in some small way, this would make it up to him.

Running out of the costume trailer, she gazed at the hustle and bustle of the set around her. She was determined to make herself remember every detail of the day, so that she could play it back for herself in bed this evening, and so she could tell Hunter everything after supper, as long as horrible Max had gone home by then.

Siena hated Max De Seville with a passion. He always made out her stories were boring, even when they weren't at all, even when she had met Mel Gibson and Duke had told him that she was going to be famous one day.

She couldn't see what Hunter saw in Max. They weren't a bit alike. Hunter always listened to her. He never said she was lying when she'd only exaggerated just the *tiniest* bit, to make something sound a bit more interesting. And he never laughed at her in the infuriating, patronising way that Max did, treating her like a stupid little kid, even though she was nearly eight and everyone said she was very precocious for her age, which Grandpa had told her meant grown up.

In the end, Duke decided to take her for an In and Out burger after they left the studios, and it was after ten o'clock when they got home, far too late for her to be allowed to see Hunter or Max. Claire and

Suzanna had both swooped on her the moment she walked through the door, complaining that it was way past her bedtime and under no circumstances could she stay up another minute. Even Siena could see resistance was futile. It would have to wait until tomorrow.

Tucked up in bed twenty minutes later, smelling of toothpaste and soap, she gave Duke an ecstatic goodnight kiss. 'Oh, Grandpa, I just had the best day ever. All the kids at school are gonna be *so* totally jealous!'

'I should think they are, sweetheart, and so they should be,' said Duke. 'You're worth a hundred of any of those kids, and don't you ever forget it.'

He kissed her softly on the cheek and turned out her Star Wars night light. She looked so perfect, so innocent and unspoiled, with her thick hair tumbling across the pillow, a ragged old Kermit the Frog clutched tightly to her chest. Duke didn't think he had ever felt so much love for another human being.

'Grandpa?' Her voice was soft and tentative in the darkness. 'Why didn't you want Hunter to come with us today?'

Duke sighed. He hadn't thought that she'd noticed his lack of enthusiasm at breakfast about the boy joining them. She was sharper than he thought.

'Don't you like him?'

It was funny. All of Caroline's ranting at him over the years, pleading with him to show more affection to his son – it hadn't made the slightest bit of difference. He didn't know why he didn't love the boy. He just didn't, and that fact had never troubled his conscience any more than it had done with Peter or Laurie. But being questioned, challenged outright by Siena, his beloved, innocent little girl, made him suddenly feel sorry that he could not be the loving father to Hunter that everyone wanted and expected him to be.

'Of course I like him,' he assured her, the deep cadences of his lingering Irish accent soothing her as always. 'He can come along with us next time, OK? I promise.'

Siena beamed at him happily. He could see her tiny milk teeth glinting at him through the darkness.

'OK.'

'Sleep tight now, Siena,' he whispered as her eyes began to close. 'Don't let the bedbugs bite.'

'Oh, Grandpa,' she murmured drowsily, 'there's no such thing as bedbugs.'

And soon she had drifted into a deep contented sleep.

'Cut it out, Max! Leave her alone!'

It was a month after her triumphant visit to the studios, and Siena, Max and Hunter were out in the tree house 'playing'.

Reluctantly, Max released Siena's arms. She spun around to face him, her eyes blazing with fury, and was about to hurl her little body at him in a second assault when Hunter gently but firmly wrapped his own arms around her.

'Get *off* me!' she screamed at him, still struggling for all she was worth.

'Siena, just calm down and I will.'

'For God's sake hold on to her Hunter, she's a psycho,' said Max.

The tree house had begun to shake ominously. If it broke now, after all Hunter's hard work, he really would murder the pair of them. 'No more fighting, please,' he said, exasperated. 'I'm sick of it, even if you two aren't.'

Hunter had spent the better part of his morning trying and failing to make peace between his niece and his best friend. They were always at each other's throats these days, and both of them expected him to play referee. It drove him nuts. Max really was the worst, forever winding Siena up, teasing her and baiting her until she totally flipped out. The fact that she was only a baby, not even eight years old, seemed to make no difference to his attitude. If anything, Max was tougher on Siena than he was with the kids he didn't like in seventh grade. Hunter found it baffling.

Today it had all started over the tree house he and Max had been building behind the orangery on the estate. They had been working on it for weeks over the long summer, blissfully ignored by their respective parents, who were only too happy to have the boys out of their hair. It became their den, their secret project, and they were both inordinately proud of it.

At first, Siena had been too preoccupied with Duke to pay their little camp much attention. For the last two weeks she and her grandfather had spent almost every day together, either watching old movies at home or hanging out at the studios. When Claire and Pete had insisted on taking her to Santa Barbara the previous weekend to visit some family friends, Siena had screamed the house down and had to be literally prised away from Duke's legs and bundled into Pete's Jaguar. The love affair between grandfather and granddaughter seemed stronger than ever.

Practically the only time the boys saw Siena at all was when she came home triumphant from one of her trips with Duke, bursting excitedly with stories about all the stars she'd seen and how everyone made such a fuss of her.

Max couldn't stomach her when she was in this sort of mood,

yabbering away at high speed like a broken record, and it always ended in a row. Even Hunter had to admit Siena could get pretty tiring, with all her 'Grandpa said this' and 'Grandpa did that'.

But then about a week ago, Duke had decided to take Caroline down to Mexico for a week's vacation.

'Am I coming?' Siena had asked him excitedly when he announced the trip one lunchtime.

'Absolutely not,' said Caroline firmly, and for once Duke backed her up.

'Not this time, princess,' he said to his indignant grandchild. 'It's more of a grown-up thing. Just for adults.'

'That's right,' Caroline couldn't resist adding. 'The focus is going to be very much on adult entertainment.'

Duke grinned.

'But I really want to come!' whined Siena. 'Oh, Grandpa, pleeeease, I'll be so good. I'll be really grown up, I promise. I'll be precocious!'

Duke laughed.

Siena had sulked for three solid days, but eventually resigned herself to the fact that she would be deprived of Duke's company for over a week. It was about this time that she refocused her attention and affection on Hunter, and started taking an interest in the grand tree house project.

'Don't you have some Barbies to go and play with?' Max sneered, as Hunter cautiously released his hold on Siena.

Physical violence having failed her, she decided to give sarcasm a try. 'No, Max, I don't have any *Baaar-bees*,' she parodied his British accent. 'But shouldn't you be orf hunting and fishing in jolly old England? Oh, tally-ho!' She began riding an imaginary horse around the tree house, shaking the fragile structure to its core. 'Look at me, I'm so terribly, terribly English, darling!'

'Shut up!' said Max, who was surprisingly sensitive to taunts about his accent. All the kids at school gave him grief over it, but his parents went ballistic at home whenever the slightest hint of a California twang crept into his voice. He couldn't win.

'Yeah, for God's sake, Siena, pack it in,' said Hunter.

'Tally-ho! Tally-ho!' trumpeted Siena even more loudly, thrilled to have touched a nerve, galloping around Max like a hyperactive maniac.

Before Hunter had a second to react, Max let out an almighty yell and threw himself at Siena, rugby-tackling her to the floor. The tree house gave a final creak, before giving way completely.

Wood, rope and nails flew everywhere as the three children tumbled through the branches of the huge sycamore. Instinctively, Hunter and Max both managed to grab hold of the slippery branches as they fell. But Siena seemed to have lost all co-ordination, flailing wildly for support as branch after branch cracked against her fragile limbs. The two boys watched in horror as she tumbled helplessly to the ground below. Her head hit the earth with a sturdy but muffled thud. She wasn't moving.

For some reason Hunter found himself rooted to the spot. His brain was telling his body to move, but his body didn't seem to be getting the message. It was like one of those dreams where the murderer was chasing you, but every time you tried to run it was as though your legs were knee deep in treacle. He stared in horror at Siena's limp little body.

Oh Jesus, was she dead? How could he have let this happen?

It seemed to Hunter that Max was on the ground in an instant, swinging and jumping from branch to branch like Tarzan, his lithe torso twisting to avoid the worst of the twigs and debris as he made his way down to Siena.

'Siena, wake up,' he said urgently. 'It's me, it's Max. Can you hear me?'

He had bent low over her, and was stroking her forehead with his right hand while his left felt gingerly around her neck and the top of her spine for any breakages. They had done some basic first-aid training at the Santa Monica Lifeguard Cadets, and he knew he must be careful not to move her. There didn't seem to be any serious damage.

'Siena!' he shouted at her sharply, his mouth an inch from her ear.

The suddenness of his voice seemed to jolt her into consciousness. She gave an involuntary kick with her legs, and opened her eyes blearily.

'Well, hello there.' Max grinned, relief and happiness flooding his face. Thank God she was OK. 'You're alive, then?'

Groggily Siena tried to focus. Little by little, his face settled into view. She saw his thin lips splitting into the most enormous smile, revealing two rows of perfectly even white teeth. His eyes had disappeared into tiny twinkling crinkles, and his slightly floppy blond hair had fallen forward over his mud-streaked forehead. Next to Hunter, he had always looked so plain. But just for that moment, their enmity temporarily forgotten, she thought he looked . . . nice.

'Yes, Max, I'm alive,' she said hoarsely. 'No thanks to you.'

But she completely forgot to scowl at him.

Chapter Eleven

Minnie's brow furrowed as she perused the menu for a second time. She was sitting at her favourite table at the Ivy on Robertson, a strategically placed parasol protecting her eyes and delicate skin from the glare of the midday sun.

It was a Thursday in June, three years after Siena's tree house fall, and Minnie had arranged to meet Pete for lunch. He was late, as usual. She knew that her son was working particularly hard at the moment, and had a slew of new movie projects in the pipeline. Only yesterday, she and Claire had had a long conference on the subject of Pete's crazy working hours, and what could be done to persuade him to spend a little more time at home. But as far as Minnie was concerned, there was never any excuse for tardiness.

'Can I get you another drink, Mrs McMahon?' A chiselled but extraordinarily camp waiter had skipped over to her table for the third time in as many minutes, no doubt hoping that Duke would be putting in an appearance.

'No. Thank you,' said Minnie, her lips pursed disdainfully as she took another sip of mineral water. But her face lit up when she saw a harassed-looking Pete making his way through the celebrity-crammed tables towards her.

'Hello, Mother.' He kissed her cheek apologetically. 'I know I'm late and I'm really sorry, but I got stuck in a meeting with Gerry and I just couldn't get away.'

Slipping his Armani jacket on to the back of his chair, he sat down and wearily unfolded his napkin. Minnie noticed that his suit trousers were horribly wrinkled and his paunch was getting more pronounced. 'Evian, big bottle, ice,' he barked at the disappointed waiter.

'Yes, well, never mind,' said Minnie graciously, her previous irritation melting away in the glow of her son's presence. 'You're here now. So what's this 'big news' you wanted to talk about? And why couldn't you tell me at home?'

'Jeez, Mother, what, do I need an excuse to take a beautiful woman out to lunch these days?' Pete reached across the table for her hand

and kissed it. 'You're far too beautiful to spend your life shut up on the estate, you know. You should go out more often.'

Minnie blushed happily and started to fiddle with her pearls, a sure sign of embarrassment. She never had been able to take a compliment. Living with Duke, of course, meant that she was rarely called upon to do so.

'Anyway,' said Pete, slathering butter on to a large hunk of the Ivy's specially baked, sweet brown bread, 'I wanted a chance to talk to you privately. Walls have ears, you know, especially at home. And I'm still at the earliest stages with this, right? I don't have any proof.'

'Proof of what?' asked Minnie. 'I assume we're talking about Caroline, are we?'

Pete nodded with a mouth full of bread.

'So she's definitely having an affair?' Minnie leant forward excitedly. Could this finally be the break they had all been looking for? 'Is it Charles?'

Pete shook his head and swallowed. 'Not definitely. And try to keep your voice down. Like I told you, I don't have proof. I'm just hearing a lot of rumours. And my guess is that Dad must be hearing 'em too.'

Minnie summoned the waiter and ordered her usual stone crab claws. Pete opted for fried chicken, but made a small concession to his arteries by going for the spinach instead of his favourite garlic mashed potatoes.

It was hard to believe that Caroline had hung on to her position as Duke's consort and lived like a viper among them all at Hancock Park for almost fifteen years now. In that time, Minnie had managed to cocoon herself fairly successfully from her husband's second resident family. She spent much of her day in her own private suite of rooms, and usually took her meals in the dining room with Laurie. She found it odd that someone who purported to be aristocratic could prefer to eat in the kitchen with Seamus and the nannies, but at least this enabled her to ignore Caroline almost completely when she was at home. And Minnie had her own friends, of course, and her bridge club in Beverly Hills, and the Church of the Good Shepherd on Santa Monica where she did the flowers twice a week. Between her charities and her children, she had developed a reasonably fulfilling independent life. So much so that a casual observer might well have thought that she had not only accepted her husband's domestic arrangements, but had practically forgotten about their existence altogether.

Nothing could have been farther from the truth. Her silent resentment of Caroline Berkeley and her son had built over the last fifteen years into a violently repressed hatred. Minnie chose never to lash out – at least not until she could be certain that any strike made against her hated rival could be ensured of success. For years she had watched Caroline like a hawk, hunting for irrefutable proof of an affair, or anything else that would bring Duke to his senses. Perhaps, she thought as the waiter refilled her water glass, she had finally found it?

But her adversary was not a fool. Caroline was fully aware how vulnerable her position was as Duke's unmarried mistress. Just one slip could prove fatal to her security and end her pampered lifestyle, and in the past she had always gone to great lengths to maintain the appearance of fidelity and devotion to her aged husband. Even Hunter's existence did not guarantee her a legal share of the McMahon wealth.

Minnie watched disapprovingly as her son gobbled down his lunch at a rate that was bound to exacerbate his heartburn.

She reflected on how much it would have surprised Caroline, and probably Pete too, to discover that she and Duke still talked on a regular basis, about subjects as diverse as their children or his latest business deal. For all the floods of betrayal, cruelty and neglect that had flowed under the bridge of Duke and Minnie's marriage, there remained a bizarrely unbreakable connection between the two of them.

'Has he said anything to you?' asked Pete between mouthfuls of his meltingly tender chicken.

'Your father? No,' said Minnie. 'No, he hasn't. But I'm sure I would be the very last person he'd talk to if he *did* suspect Caroline of anything.'

'Except Caroline herself, of course.' Pete raised one eyebrow enigmatically.

'What do you mean?' asked Minnie.

'Only that if he *does* know something – and let's just say he does – well, it wouldn't be Dad's style to confront her with it.' Pete leant back in his chair and stretched noisily, a habit he had unconsciously picked up from Duke. 'I don't know, Mother. But I'm pretty sure she *is* doing Charlie. And if Dad's heard so much as a whisper of it, then for one thing, he'll be having her followed, and for another, when he finds out the truth, he's going to be ruthless.'

Minnie nodded silently.

'I think he knows,' said Pete. 'And I think he's planning something.'

The restaurant was full to bursting now, and a low hum of Hollywood gossip filled the terrace. On the other side of the white picket fence, harassed-looking valets were fighting their way through a group of paparazzi who had gathered to scoop some shots of Sly

Stallone. He sat two tables away from Minnie and Pete with his very beautiful red-headed manager. Some of the press had mistaken her for a new love interest, and the 'paps', as they were called, had descended on the Ivy like locusts.

'So?' asked Minnie as she polished off the last of her crab meat in one dainty bite, ignoring the undignified scrum of hoi polloi around her. 'What do we do about it?'

'Nothing,' said Pete. 'Not yet anyway. We sit tight. But if either of us hears anything' – he signalled to the waiter for the bill – 'we let each other know right away. OK?'

'Of course, darling, that goes without saying.' Minnie smiled at her only son, always so tense, always in a rush. He and Duke were more alike than either of them cared to admit. 'Won't you stay and have a coffee with me, Petey?'

'Truly, Mother, I'd love to, but I just can't.' He rose from his seat and handed Minnie a sheaf of twenty-dollar bills.

'This could be it, you know.' He smiled, the first genuine smile she had seen on his face in months, and blew her a parting kiss. 'I think we might finally have got her.'

'Oh, please, Charlie, don't! Don't stop yet, I'm so close!'

Charles Murray felt Caroline's marvellously taut thighs tightening around his ears until he could hear his own blood thumping through his brain. He had been licking and nibbling at her swollen clit for the best part of fifteen minutes, and although he always found it exciting watching her writhe with pleasure at his expert ministrations, he was now beginning to get impatient for some pleasure of his own. He was also very aware of how dangerous it was to be doing this in the office. Forcibly prising his head from her vice-like grip he reached for the water bottle on his desk. 'Baby, I'm sorry but I need some air. It's hot down there, you know?'

Caroline was sitting on the desk in Charlie's corner office on the fifth floor of the Beverly Hills attorneys Carter & Rowe. Her demure 1950s-style skirt was rucked up around her hips and her Trashy Lingerie panties had been yanked conveniently to one side. Charlie was kneeling on the carpet, at eye level with her dripping crotch. His boyishly handsome face was so flushed, he looked as if he'd just scored a touchdown.

'Well, all right.' She smiled down at him indulgently while absent-mindedly inserting two fingers into her pussy and rubbing herself gently with the ball of her thumb. 'You can take a "time out". That's what you call it, right, you football-playing types?'

'Right,' said Charlie between gulps of Arrowhead Spring.

'But I *really* need to come, darling.' Caroline looked at him beseechingly. 'Please?' With her free hand she stroked his blond hair, rather as she would a Labrador.

Charlie grinned as he stood up, his six-foot-four frame towering over Caroline like a linebacker. His perfectly toned torso was clearly visible through his tight white shirt, now clinging to the sweat trickling down between his pecs, and his huge, ramrod-straight erection jutted out at an almost perpendicular angle through the open flies of his pinstripe suit trousers. My God, he's a fine figure of a man, thought Caroline longingly. He pushed her back on to the desk, sending notes and papers flying as he clambered on top of her. Supporting himself on his forearms, with his face less than an inch above her own, she felt his quickening breath on her forehead while the tip of his penis nudged teasingly against her labia.

'*You* really need to come?' He laughed. 'How the hell do you think I feel?'

With one swift, delicious motion he slipped inside her, so deep that she could feel his tightened balls pushing up against her bottom with each thrust. For Caroline, at forty-five, to be able to inspire this degree of lust in such an exquisitely beautiful, thirty-year-old man was the biggest aphrodisiac of all.

'Ahhh, lovely,' she sighed as yet another rush of pleasure engulfed her. Within sixty seconds she found herself erupting into a glorious orgasm, tension and frustration flooding joyously out of her body. Charlie closed his eyes and focused on his own pleasure. Caroline gazed up at him, lost in some erotic fantasy of his own as he screwed the life out of her, and felt his cock twitching involuntarily inside her before he finally came, moaning loudly and biting down on her shoulder, so intense was his own release.

'You really are lovely,' she said, as they lay motionless in one another's arms afterwards, amid the wreck of Charlie's office. He kissed her.

'So are you.'

Her relationship with Charles Murray was probably the closest thing to love that Caroline had ever experienced. She wasn't stupid. She knew it was insanely risky, and that it had no future. Charlie was an up-and-coming young litigator at Carter's, whose senior partner, David Rowe, was Duke's personal attorney. The affair was complete madness. But despite herself, Caroline found herself unwilling, or unable, to give him up.

Charlie made her laugh and he made her come, two qualities that Duke had certainly possessed when the two of them first met, but which seemed to have withered with his increasing age. Statistically,

Caroline realised, it was a miracle that a man of almost eighty should be able to make love to her at all. But while she still felt desired by Duke, the thrill of being dominated by such a powerful man had started to wane as the years inevitably caught up with him, and she no longer felt any excitement in his bed. In fact, since the first day she had surrendered to her growing attraction for the young lawyer who had accompanied David Rowe on his trips to the McMahon estate, she had begun to find Duke's sexual attentions actively repellent. Lying beneath him, it was impossible not to compare the sagging skin on his back to Charlie's broad and powerful shoulders, or his liver-spotted, sinewy arms to Charlie's tanned and rounded biceps.

As the months went by, Caroline found herself more and more greedy for both her lover's body and his company. And as the affair developed, she was becoming increasingly reckless.

'We have to start being more careful,' said Charlie as he hastily tucked in his shirt and smoothed down his hair, checking his reflection in the window. Caroline hated the way he could sound so businesslike and brisk almost immediately after they had made love. 'Did David see you come in?'

'No.' Caroline sighed. 'His door was closed. Only Marlene knows I'm here.' Marlene was the litigation department's angel of a receptionist, a skilled keeper of secrets and turner of blind eyes. She had a particular soft spot for Charlie, and would be the last person to breathe a word about their dangerous liaison to anyone. 'Besides . . .' She walked up behind him, pressing her breasts hard against his back and, reaching round, brushed the back of her hand lightly against his crotch. 'Doesn't it excite you just a little bit? Knowing we might get caught?'

Charlie turned and kissed her on the forehead, while gently disengaging himself from her embrace. Of course the secrecy of it all turned him on. Truth to tell, just about everything about Caroline and their affair excited him. Charlie had always been drawn to strong, ballsy women, and Caro was the strongest and ballsiest of them all. It killed him to think of her being pawed over by that revolting old lech McMahon.

But he also understood her. Duke was Caroline's financial security. Charlie's career was his. And both of them were too selfish and hard headed to contemplate throwing that all away for the sake of a few snatched hours of sex, however mind-blowing it might be. Charlie respected Caroline and he liked her – but nothing was worth losing his career over.

Moving away from her, he started tidying the piles of paper and files that littered his desk. This was no time to play games. Without warning he hit the speakerphone. 'Marlene? Charlie. Tell Mr Levy I'll see him in two minutes, I'm just finishing up a call here.'

A pouting Caroline picked up her purse and strode to the door.

'Aw, c'mon, honey,' said Charlie, grabbing her shoulders with his huge hands. 'Don't put this all on me. You don't want to get found out any more than I do, right? Right?'

She nodded grudgingly, but didn't trust herself to turn and look at him.

'I'm not saying it's over.' His voice was softer now, more loving. 'Just that we have to be more careful. The office is too risky, all right? So no more "dropping by".' Caroline laughed. She loved being teased by Charlie. 'Lovely as it was to see you, David's not stupid. And neither is Duke, so no more long lunches up at your place either.' He walked back to his desk and flipped open a brown folder labelled 'Levy'.

Caroline unlocked the door of the office and looked up and down the corridor to make sure the coast was clear before slipping on her dark glasses.

'Trust me,' she whispered to an anxious-looking Charlie. 'We're fine. Duke knows nothing.'

And with that, she closed the door noiselessly behind her.

A few blocks away in one of the wide, tree-lined avenues known collectively as 'the flats', Claire sat behind the wheel of her kingfisher-blue Saab, keeping the engine running in case she needed to make a quick getaway from the jobsworth parking inspectors that always hung around the school gates at going-home time, hoping to catch some poor mother as she dashed in to collect her offspring. Parking in Beverly Hills was always a nightmare, but once the schools got out it was outright war.

She looked at her watch, tapping her manicured fingers impatiently on the tan leather steering wheel. Five after three. The bell should have rung by now.

Normally Leila would pick up both the children after school, although Claire occasionally did one or two of the early morning runs. But Hunter was going over to Max's today and would be dropped back at home later, so she thought it might be nice for her to collect Siena herself, maybe take her for an ice cream or something on the ride home. It was a long time since the two of them had had any fun time alone together.

Claire loved her daughter dearly, but was acutely aware that the two of them had very little in common. Where Claire was thoughtful, patient and calm, Siena was short tempered, feisty and loud. Although she had inherited her mother's intelligence, it was the

McMahon street-smarts and ambition which really formed the core of her emergent personality.

From the day she was born, it was perfectly apparent that Siena was not destined to be a girls' girl. She hated pretty dresses, dolls or any sort of quiet, creative play, always preferring to be outside climbing trees, shouting or – best of all – playing 'war' with Hunter, shooting at any animal, vegetable or mineral that dared to cross her path with the cap gun Duke had insisted on buying for her. Claire never begrudged her these games. But she did begin to feel excluded. And as Siena grew ever closer to Hunter and to Duke, that sense of exclusion and sadness grew.

It didn't upset her in the same way that it upset Pete when people commented on how alike Siena was to Duke. What was the point of getting upset about something that was quite plainly and simply a fact? Siena was like him, frighteningly like him, in so many ways.

But there were also differences. She could be thoughtless, selfish even, and dreadfully spoiled at times. But Claire knew that her daughter was not a cruel child, not vindictive like Duke.

In his own pain at what he perceived as his daughter's rejection of him in favour of his hated father, Pete often lost sight of that crucial distinction. But Claire never did. She wished that she and Siena had a closer relationship, of course she did. But she never blamed the child for loving her grandfather, or for being herself. Besides, hopefully as Siena got older she would develop more of an interest in the feminine things in life that Claire would be able to share with her – simple things like shopping together or getting their hair done. She was really, really looking forward to that.

Suddenly the school doors opened and a scrum of tired, sweaty-looking boys and girls surged out into the school playground. Siena was instantly recognisable as the scruffiest of the lot, hair escaping in corkscrew ringlets from her loosened hair tie, her blue sweater torn at the neck (not again, thought Claire), her battered old Snoopy bag being dragged along the concrete like a sack of coal.

Claire honked her horn loudly, and Siena grinned back at her and waved excitedly, tearing through the gates and across the street without so much as a glance at the oncoming traffic.

'Mom!' she said, leaning forward to give Claire a kiss. 'How come you're here? I thought Leila was getting me.'

Claire was so thrilled by this warm reception that she forgot to tell Siena off for not looking before she crossed the road. 'Well, I thought I'd do it for a change,' she said with a smile. 'If you like, we could stop for an ice cream at Gianni's on the way home?'

'Cool,' said Siena. This was all very out of character. Normally her mom was obsessed with homework and didn't allow any fun at all until all her assignments were done and dusted. Sensing an opportunity, she thought she'd see how far she could push it. 'You picked a good day, actually,' she gabbled on, as nonchalantly as she could, while Claire pulled out on to Santa Monica Boulevard. 'Mr Di Clemente said we all did so well on last week's math assignment that he wouldn't set us any homework for tonight.'

'Really?' Claire was surprised. Not only did her teacher almost never not set homework, but as she remembered it, Siena's math assignment last week had been somewhat less than fabulous.

'Uh-huh.' Siena didn't miss a beat. 'So I was thinking . . .'

'Ye-es?' said Claire warily.

'As I don't have any work to do . . .'

'Ye-es?' She knew exactly where her daughter's wheedling tone was leading.

'Maybe we could go to Tumblorama?'

'Tumblorama' was an indoor kids adventure centre on the borders of Los Feliz, a mile or so north of Hancock Park. It consisted of a maze of multi-coloured plastic tunnels, ladders and slides, all interconnected, through which exhausted parents would chase their overexcited children with a heroic disregard for middle-aged bad backs, aching muscles and bruised limbs. It was Siena's favourite place in the world after the studios, and a popular venue with all the local kids for birthday parties or holiday treats.

It was, needless to say, the sort of place that gave poor Claire nightmares. But Siena sounded so sweet and hopeful. And she had wanted the two of them to have some quality time together . . .

'Oh, all right, then,' she said, with a last lingering look at her freshly manicured nails and her newly pressed Laura Ashley skirt, knowing that neither would survive the dreaded Tumblorama ordeal.

'Really? You'll take me?' Siena couldn't believe her luck and started bouncing up and down on the back seat with excitement like a broken jack-in-the-box. Mom never did stuff like this, especially not on a school night.

'Sure,' said Claire. 'Why not?' She smiled back at her ecstatic daughter indulgently in the rear-view mirror. 'We moms may be old and boring most of the time, but we can still keep a few surprises up our sleeves.'

When they finally got home, three hours later than expected, Pete's first thought was that they must have been in an accident.

Claire's usually immaculate hair was all over the place, standing on end with static as if she'd rubbed it with a balloon. Her face was flushed and red, her nail polish chipped, and her new skirt – one of those dreadful milkmaid, flowery things that he couldn't stand – had thankfully been ripped right along the hem, probably beyond repair.

'What the hell happened to you?' he asked, taking in his wife's dishevelled appearance but also the matching grins that she and Siena wore plastered across their faces, and relaxing slightly.

'Tumblorama,' panted Claire, picking up Siena's school bag on autopilot and extracting the half-eaten remnants of her packed lunch.

'You're kidding?' His tone was quizzical but also amused. It was nice to see his two girls looking so happy together. Particularly to see Siena looking so happy, without Duke or that snotty little brother of his anywhere around. 'You took her to Tumblorama? On a school night?'

'It's OK, Dad,' Siena jumped in quickly, anxious to avert the anger she had come to expect from him. 'I didn't have any homework. Mr D let us off.' She had quite forgotten that this was not, in fact, true, and fluttered her eyelashes at her father like a bona fide innocent.

'Well,' said Pete, still smiling at both of them, 'aren't you the lucky one?'

What, no shouting? What was up with her parents today? Had they both taken a happy pill or something?

Pete moved over to Claire and put his arm around her in a rare display of tenderness. 'Off you go upstairs now and change,' he said to Siena. 'You can tell me all about it at dinner.'

Claire put Siena's lunch box down and reached up with both her arms, wrapping them around his neck and nuzzling against him. They both watched their daughter disappear noisily up the stairs, about as ladylike and graceful as a drunken baby hippo.

'Don't you wish things could always be like this?' Claire sighed, once Siena was out of sight and out of earshot. 'Just the three of us, relaxed and happy, like this?'

He could feel her warm breath against his neck, quickened from the exertion of chasing Siena through endless plastic tunnels. 'Yes,' he said, stroking her hair and smoothing it back into place. 'I do.'

He thought about Caroline. If his suspicions were right – if she was cheating on Duke – then maybe her days at Hancock Park were numbered. What he wouldn't give to be rid of her and her wretched son. 'But you never know, darling, maybe it will be like this one day.'

Claire looked up at him, perplexed. 'What do you mean?'

'Who knows?' said Pete, kissing her gently on the forehead. 'Maybe life around here is about to change for the better.'

Chapter Twelve

'I'm so sorry, Duke. I don't know what to say.'

David Rowe sat awkwardly in the low leather armchair in Duke's study, watching his client flip slowly through eight black-and-white pictures. His face was completely impassive as he studied one image after another, occasionally tracing something on one of the prints with a long bony finger, as though trying to make it out more clearly. But the pictures were already clear as crystal. David knew, because he'd seen them all an hour before he drove over to Hancock Park, and he was still reeling from what he saw.

In the first shot, Caroline was getting into the car with Charles Murray, his young protégé. The next two pictures showed the two of them holding hands, kissing and laughing as they went into what looked like a bungalow at the Bel Air Hotel. After that came six pictures that left nothing to the imagination, two taken at the hotel, and another four in various other locations, including the back seat of Duke's own midnight-blue Bentley. The PI had done a horrifically good job – he'd only been following Caroline for a week.

David felt his chest constricting with stress as he watched his powerful client slowly leafing through this damning evidence. He didn't consider himself a friend of Duke's. In fact, if truth be told, he had never much liked him, but as his contemporary – David himself was a dynamic seventy-seven, a mere two years younger than Duke – he couldn't help but feel sympathy for an old man, betrayed and humiliated by such a beautiful young woman. He was also absolutely livid with Charlie for putting him in such an embarrassing position, and all because he couldn't keep his Johnson in his goddam pants.

'I know what you're thinking,' said Duke, without taking his eyes off a picture of Caroline sitting on a hotel bed, her legs wrapped around the kid's waist and her head thrown back in undisguised delight.

David squirmed in his seat. 'Look, Duke, it's none of my business,' he began, but Duke raised his hand for silence.

'There's no fool like an old fool. That's what you're thinking,

David. Am I right?' He could see his lawyer opening his mouth to protest. 'And no, don't apologise. You're right to think that. You're absolutely right.' He frowned and rubbed at his temples, as though trying to erase the picture of Caroline's betrayal from his memory bank. 'She's played me for a damn fool.'

He finally replaced the photographs in the unmarked brown envelope David had handed him and, unlocking the second drawer of the desk with a miniature key that he produced from his pocket, he slipped the offending package inside, then closed and locked the drawer again, repocketing the key.

David cleared his throat awkwardly. It had to be asked. 'So, what do you want me to do about young Murray?'

Duke stared blankly ahead.

'You're one of the firm's oldest and most valued clients,' David continued. 'We don't want to lose you. Now, if you tell me you want us to let this young man go' – he paused and looked Duke squarely in the eye – 'I want you to know that we wouldn't hesitate.'

Duke stood up and walked slowly over to the window. Outside on the lawn he could see Hunter swinging Siena around by her feet. Her arms were outstretched and her long dark curls were flying in the wind like the tail of a comet. Beautiful.

He noticed that his son was laughing, black hair flopping over his tanned forehead, cheeks glowing with exertion as he spun his niece around and around. Duke felt a slight stabbing sensation in his chest as he looked at Hunter, and raised his hand to his heart. He guessed that the boy must think him a pretty heartless father.

At fifteen, Hunter looked more like him every day. It was funny how none of his genes seemed to have passed themselves on to Pete and Laurie, his legitimate children, while Caroline's son, the little cuckoo in the nest, was every inch his child. Sometimes Duke wished he had been able to connect with the boy, had tried harder to love him. He was such a good-natured kid too. But for some reason he had always felt impelled to keep himself at a distance.

Maybe, deep down, he had always known this day would come with Caroline. After all, he had never intended to start a second family with her. She had never had Minnie's unflinching loyalty. But then why on earth should she?

Duke had hurt Minnie because she let him, and he had always despised her for that weakness. Caroline, on the other hand, had been a breath of fresh air, a kindred spirit. He remembered how much he had once loved her for her independence, for that selfish, ruthless energy that reminded him so much of himself.

The fact was, she was not his wife. He had never wanted her to be. And as a result, he had never really thought of her child as his son.

He turned round and looked at his lawyer's pained, anxious face. 'Don't fire him on my account, David,' he said.

'Really?' The old man looked shocked.

'Really,' said Duke. 'The kid's a good lawyer, isn't he?'

David smiled a little despite himself. 'He's a great lawyer. Most talented guy in a trial situation I've seen in thirty years.'

'Well then.' Duke smiled back. 'It'd be a shame to let him go.' He noted David's look of bewilderment, and opening a battered leather box on the side table, took out two of his finest Cuban cigars and offered him one. 'Look. The way I see it, the boy only did what I would have done myself when I was his age.' He clipped the tip off his own cigar and lit it, inhaling deeply before passing the silver cutters to David. 'She's still a terrific-looking woman. And she fucks like a stoat.'

David wished that Duke wouldn't use such profanities. As a devout Methodist he found his client's brutal language both offensive and unnecessary. Still, he supposed those pictures must have come as a terrible shock to him.

'Well, all right, Duke,' he said. 'I must say I think that's very big of you. And you can rest assured that I will be speaking to Charles in the strongest possible terms about his behaviour. We take breaches of trust very seriously at Carter.'

'Oh, believe me, David,' said Duke ominously, 'I take them very seriously too. Very seriously indeed.'

He looked outside again for the children, but they were gone.

Siena woke up early the next morning to the familiar, blinding glare of sunlight bursting through her window on to walls completely plastered with Mel Gibson posters. She was ten now, and her crush on the rugged Australian had developed into a full-blown obsession. On the back of her bedroom door, the only space not devoted to Mel, hung a framed black-and-white picture of Duke in *Tales of the Desert*, one of his early Westerns. He had worn his hair in a ponytail for the movie, which Siena thought incredibly romantic, and in the poster he was doffing his hat to his crinalined leading lady while his horse reared up, shadow-boxing with its powerful forelegs. She had always loved that picture of her grandfather. He looked so wild and glamorous.

She sat up in bed and rubbed her eyes blearily. Blowing a kiss to Mel, she slipped into yesterday's jeans and T-shirt which she had conveniently left screwed up in a heap on the floor. The school year had ended the week before and months of glorious freedom stretched ahead of both her and Hunter.

Hunter was such a slug in the mornings, though. He was growing so fast, all he ever wanted to do was sleep. Siena, on the other hand, couldn't jump out of bed fast enough. There were bikes to be ridden, pools to be swum in, slumber parties to be arranged – she couldn't wait to get started.

Going over to her desk, she picked up a handful of coloured pencils and the half-finished Get Well Soon card she'd begun making for Aunt Laurie last night. Laurie had twisted her ankle a few days ago while out jogging and was now confined to bed.

Siena didn't always see eye to eye with her aunt, but she had started to feel increasingly sorry for her, especially when Grandpa kept making mean jokes about her being so fat, and how she couldn't even go for a run without falling on her big fat behind. She didn't think that was very nice of him, especially now that Laurie's ankle had swollen up like a big purple-and-black balloon. Anyway, she hoped the card might cheer her up a bit, particularly as it featured the excellent swans that Hunter had recently taught her how to draw by starting with a giant number two and then sketching in the folded wings and beak on top.

Clenching the card and pencils in one hand, she clambered up on to the banister rail in the hallway and slid all the way down the polished wood of the grand staircase.

'Er, excuse me, young lady, but what do you think you're doing?'

Claire was looking immaculate as always in a pale yellow trouser suit and white shirt with fashionably ruffled collar. She had a wicker basket over her arm and Ray-Ban sunglasses on, and was obviously on her way out when her daughter had come hurtling down into the entrance hall and landed with a thud on Minnie's perfectly polished marble.

'Sorry,' said Siena, though she didn't look it.

'Well, so you should be,' chided her mother automatically. 'How many times have I told you not to slide down those darned banisters? It's dangerous, Siena, that must be a forty-foot drop.'

'God,' Siena moaned, the picture of petulance. 'I said I was sorry, didn't I?'

Claire knew she ought to tell her off for using such an impertinent tone, but she was late enough as it was and really didn't have time for a full-blown confrontation now.

'Yes, well,' she said with what she hoped was a stern expression. 'Please try to use the stairs next time like any normal person.' She fumbled in her basket for the keys to the Saab. 'I'm running to the

Beverly Center, and Leila and Suzanna both left early for the beach, so you can ask Conchita to fix you some breakfast if you're hungry.'

'What about Caroline?' asked Siena, trying to provoke her mother and succeeding. 'Couldn't she do it for me?'

'Don't push it, Siena,' said Claire. 'Her car's not here anyway, I guess she must have made an early start too. Now go get some breakfast. And don't forget to clean your teeth afterwards.' She gave her a perfunctory kiss on the top of her head and scurried off to the car. 'And brush your hair!' she called behind her.

Siena wandered into the kitchen.

She was just heading for the fridge when she suddenly stopped dead in her tracks. The coloured pencils she'd been grasping so tightly clattered to the ground, followed by the creased white Get Well Soon card for her aunt. She stared ahead of her in shock.

Duke was lying slumped across the table, still in his dark purple robe. His left arm had been flung wide, and had evidently knocked over a carton of milk, the contents of which had formed a white pool in the centre of the table, with little rivulets trickling out to the edges and dripping on to the floor like anaemic waterfalls. His right hand seemed to be pressed against his chest. It must have been pinned in position there by the table when he fell forward. But it was his face which Siena would never forget, still screwed up as though he were either in severe pain or deep concentration. His skin looked white-blue, like moonlight. She had never seen a corpse before, but she knew immediately that he was dead.

'Mom! Mommy!'

She ran screaming back into the hall and out of the front door, but Claire's dark blue tailgate was already disappearing through the gates. Turning around, her eyes blinded by tears as she stumbled numbly back inside, she ran straight into her grandmother.

'Siena, darling, what on earth is the matter?'

Minnie had heard the child's screams from her dressing room, as had the rest of the household, and had rushed downstairs to see what all the fuss was about. One look at Siena's face told her that this was not just another of her attention-seeking pranks. She was sobbing and shaking as though she'd just stumbled out of a car wreck.

'He's dead.' Siena's voice was almost a whisper.

She wrapped her arms tightly around Minnie's waist and pressed her tear-stained face against her familiar crisp linen shirt.

'Who, darling? Who's dead?' asked Minnie softly.

For one hideous moment she thought it might be Pete. But before she had time to get anything more coherent out of Siena, Seamus,

Duke's assistant and lifelong friend, emerged from the kitchen looking ashen.

'You'd best come in here,' he said. 'It's Duke.'

For an instant, Minnie felt nothing but pure, intense relief. It wasn't Pete. It wasn't her son. Prising herself free from a distraught Siena, she followed Seamus into the kitchen. Her hand flew to her mouth when she saw him.

'Oh my God. Oh God,' she said, collapsing against Seamus as she felt her knees give way. 'Is he . . .?'

Duke's old friend nodded gravely and pulled her close to his chest.

'Definitely. There's no pulse. I'm sorry, Min.'

'But he was fine,' Minnie said absently, unable to tear her eyes away from the body. 'I spoke to him. Last night. About everything. We spoke about everything and he was absolutely fine.'

She looked at Seamus as if imploring him to do something. The whole scene seemed so surreal. She wanted to feel something, other than shock and guilt at her initial relief, but her emotions seemed to be frozen. She wondered whether she might be going to laugh, and the thought appalled her.

Duke had come to see her late last night, after his meeting with David Rowe, and told her everything about Caroline and her affair with the young lawyer. It had taken a lot for him to admit his mistress's betrayal to her, she knew, and sensing his deep sadness and humiliation she had listened as quietly and supportively as she could while he told her what he intended to do.

He hadn't apologised to her, for all the years of misery, for the untold pain he had caused through his own betrayals and by forcing Caroline into their lives in the first place. Apologies weren't Duke's style.

But he had told her it was over. And she had told him she was glad.

Minnie didn't kid herself. It was too late for her and Duke to undo the past and find one another again. She knew that. But she had gone to her bed last night hopeful that at least, with Caroline gone, they could revert to some kind of civility and normality at Hancock Park.

She had waited so very, very long for this moment.

But now he was dead. It just didn't seem real.

At that moment Siena burst into the room and flung herself against Duke's slumped body, frantically kissing his neck and cheek and sobbing uncontrollably.

'He can't be dead,' she wailed, 'he can't be!'

Hunter, who had slipped quietly into the back of the room with the growing crowd of estate servants, stepped forward and put his arm around her. He was still in his boxer shorts and T-shirt, and his hair stood up on the left side of his head like a chimney brush.

'It's all right, baby,' he whispered. 'Come on. Come away now. We can go and sit outside.'

'No!' Siena shrugged him off angrily, lashing out like a surprised rattlesnake. 'You don't understand, do you?' She looked accusingly at everyone in the room, from Hunter to Seamus to Minnie, even at Conchita and Antoine, who were loitering awkwardly by the door in their formal black-and-white liveries. 'You didn't love him like I did. None of you! None of you ever loved him!'

'Go and find Peter and Laurie,' whispered Seamus to Antoine, who slipped noiselessly out of the kitchen.

Minnie stepped forward and, not unkindly, shooed Hunter out of the way. Duke's body lay slumped between her and Siena, and the absurdity of the situation, of his corpse just lying there, struck her again. Somehow it seemed so cruel, so undignified, to have one's heart stop in the middle of a perfectly ordinary breakfast. Not trusting herself to look at the body, she focused on her granddaughter.

'Now, you know that isn't true, Siena. I loved your grandpa. I loved him very much.' And as she said the words, she realised that they were true.

'Not like me,' Siena shot back. 'No one loved him like I did. And you!' Hunter felt like the accused in a murder trial as she pointed at him, still crying and shaking from head to foot. 'You never loved him at all. Did you?'

'Siena, that's enough,' said Seamus sternly, putting a paternal arm around Hunter's frozen shoulders. 'You're upset, sweetheart, all right, and that's fair enough, but we all loved him. Try not to forget that Hunter's just lost his father.'

Hunter drew away from him and stood up tall. At fifteen he was already almost six foot, and even with his tangled hair and cheeks still imprinted with creases from his bed-sheets, there was something noble and dignified about him.

'No, she's right, Seamus,' he said quietly. 'I didn't love him. I didn't love him, and he didn't love me.'

There was a silence in the room you could have cut with a knife. No one contradicted him.

'Are you glad he's dead?' asked Siena. She had stopped crying suddenly.

'No,' said Hunter, shaking his head sadly. 'I'm not. Because I know you loved him. And I love you.'

Like a hurricane, she flew into his arms, the tears flowing again like Niagara. Hunter held her like he would never, ever let her go.

'Don't leave me,' Siena mumbled into his chest. The rise and fall of his breathing relaxed and released her. 'I love you so much.'

'I won't leave you, Siena,' he said, stroking her hair. 'I promise.'

Chapter Thirteen

The first few weeks after Duke's death were a miserable blur to Siena. She felt his absence everywhere. At home on the estate daily life continued, but everything seemed muted, muffled somehow. It was as if the fine tuning of her life had been tampered with and the pictures had gone from colour to black and white, while the soundtrack had turned into white noise, a meaningless, lifeless babble all around her.

Worse still, there was no escape for her at school or in the outside world. Duke McMahon's death had become a huge story around the globe. Every gossip rag in America was running conspiracy theories about what had *really* happened that morning, and Siena could not avoid the relentless images of her grandfather's face that seemed to pour out of every screen and every billboard. She became almost indifferent to the paparazzi, leaping out from behind bushes or ambushing her as she came off the school bus each day, eager for pictures of her grief-stricken face. They loved Siena because she gave them the goods every single day. She was a stunningly photogenic little girl, the spitting image of Duke, and she wore her emotions on her face, unhindered by any adult sense of restraint or reserve. Pictures of poor little Siena, her cheeks a river of tears, were shifting magazines even more effectively than Princess Diana.

Within hours of her discovery in the kitchen, the estate was besieged by the world's press. Hordes of reporters and TV crews gathered outside the gates waiting for a statement, and frantically snapping at the ambulances and LAPD squad cars that forced their way through the crush throughout the morning. Meanwhile, the deafening buzz of helicopter blades grew more and more insistent overhead, circling ever lower over the estate in the hope of a shot of Duke on a stretcher. Dead or alive, the picture would be worth millions.

All the staff, as well as the family, had been told by Pete to stay inside and keep the curtains closed at all times. Various police and other official-looking people had cordoned off the kitchen with bright yellow tape, which Siena thought was odd. It wasn't as if Grandpa had been murdered or anything.

Her parents and grandmother flitted backwards and forwards among these strangers, nodding and whispering. Laurie had retreated to her bedroom in silent shock. They all looked very sombre and serious, but none of them, it seemed to Siena, looked really sad. None of them felt as she did.

She and Hunter, meanwhile, had spent most of the day holed up in their old nursery, now a sort of games room littered with bean bags, cassette tapes and various wires and joysticks connected to Hunter's beloved Atari. There didn't seem much to say, so they mostly sat in silence, eventually deciding to play an extended tournament of Bike Racer 2 to take their minds off what had happened and shut out all the craziness downstairs.

At five o'clock, they had both defied instructions and gone to the window to watch Pete walk down to the gates, flanked by a still-tearful Seamus and a suitably serious-looking David Rowe to confirm to the waiting world what everybody already knew: that Duke McMahon had died of a massive heart attack at approximately 7.15 that morning. That an announcement about funeral arrangements and a memorial service would be made in the coming days. And that the family asked for privacy at this sad and difficult time.

'Anna Vega, *LA Times*!' shouted a brassy-looking blonde in a leopard-print miniskirt at the front of the throng. 'Pete, can you tell us where Caroline is right now? Was she there when it happened?'

It had not escaped the hacks' notice that Caroline's car did not appear to be in its usual spot in front of the house, and that she herself – usually such a glutton for publicity no matter how morbid the circumstances – had not been seen or heard from all day.

'Mr McMahon has no further comment at this time,' said David Rowe firmly.

'Pete! Pete!' screamed a hundred voices as the trio turned to walk back through the gates.

'Pete, Mike O'Mahoney at *The Herald*.' A vastly fat, balding man with a painful Brooklyn accent bellowed through the racket. 'How's your mother taking it? Is she concerned about the will at all?'

Before David could open his mouth, Seamus had launched himself at his fellow New Yorker, knocking him off his feet to the delight of the swarms of photographers who'd been waiting for a half-decent shot all day.

'You bastard!' he roared. 'You disrespectful fuckin' bastard. Is that all you vultures care about, the motherfucking will? He's not even cold, for God's sake.'

The reporter scrambled to his feet, mumbling something about assault and witnesses as he brushed the dirt from his ample backside in a failed attempt to regain some dignity after being floored by a seventy-eight-year-old.

Pete's mouth twitched, an imperceptible hint of a smile dying on his lips. 'My mother, as I'm sure you can imagine, is shocked and saddened by my father's sudden and unexpected death,' he said calmly. 'But I'm sure she appreciates your concern, Mr O'Mahoney.'

The crowd tittered.

'As for my father's will,' Pete continued, 'I understand that it's a matter of legitimate interest.' The fat reporter shrank back nervously behind his fellows as Seamus glared at him murderously. 'Let's just say that my mother and I are not expecting any surprises.'

'What about Caroline and Hunter?' shouted a nameless voice. 'Any surprises for them, do you think?'

Pete paused for a moment. Not by a flicker did he betray the slightest emotion to the waiting press. 'I think we all have a funeral to prepare for. Right now my focus is on that and on supporting my mother and the rest of my family,' he said.

'All right, folks, that's it for today,' said David Rowe, ushering Pete and Seamus firmly back through the gates. 'Let's give the family some privacy now.'

With a general groan, the crowd reluctantly started to down tools. Pete and Seamus walked back up the hill together to the sound of notebooks shutting, tape recorders being clicked off and camera equipment being laboriously dismantled behind them.

'Could you believe that guy, asking you about the will?' said Seamus.

The twilight was playing softly on the lawns, bathing the whole estate in an eerily beautiful cloak of silver. Seamus had known Pete his whole life, but sometimes he still felt as if he knew nothing about him at all. He and his father had always been like chalk and cheese, never got along really, even when Pete was tiny. Seamus had loved Duke so much and understood him so well, but walking along the familiar paths of his house with Pete in the evening light, he almost felt like a stranger. He was a cold fish, young Petey McMahon.

'I don't know,' said Pete, his features impassive. 'I guess it's their job, you know? To ask questions.' He picked up a handful of gravel and started throwing pebbles aimlessly into the rhododendrons that lined the path.

'But surely everyone knows what's in the will by now, do they not?' asked Seamus. 'Caroline gets a chunk of the cash, Minnie gets the house, and you, Laurie and Hunter split the trust three ways. As I remember, that all got leaked to those vultures years ago, right after Hunter was born.'

Pete gave a non-committal grunt that could have been assent, and dropped the rest of the gravel on the ground as he approached the front steps. He wiped his dirty hand on his trousers before offering it to Seamus. 'Goodnight,' he said, 'and thank you for today. I know it must have been very hard for you.'

Christ, he was a stiff, thought Seamus. Did it matter to him at all that his dad was laid out on a slab in the West Hollywood morgue? 'Hard for all of us,' he said, and turned back down the path towards his car, and his own life.

For the first time in almost seventy years, it was a life without Duke.

'Darling, just pick up the phone,' said Charlie. 'Get yourself over there, for Hunter's sake if not your own.'

'I can't. I just can't.'

Caroline sat rigid on the sofa in his Century City penthouse. She and Charlie had not got out of bed until 3.30 in the afternoon, after a marathon sex session that had left both of them happily exhausted. She'd told Duke she was doing a twenty-four-hour detox at the Ocean Spa, so he wouldn't be expecting her back until the evening. Ravenous after her morning's exertions, she had just got the eggs out of the fridge when she flicked on the TV in Charlie's chrome-filled bachelor's kitchen. When she saw the news, she almost had a heart attack herself.

Now huddled in the living room, wearing Charlie's fisherman's sweater and sipping the hot sweet tea he'd made her, she hadn't taken her eyes from the screen in over an hour, even though the ABC7 news team were just replaying the same report over and over again. Duke McMahon found dead at breakfast, apparently having suffered a massive heart attack. LAPD were on the scene, but the death was not being treated as suspicious. Duke's wife of over forty years, Minnie, was being comforted by relatives at the McMahon estate. The whereabouts of Caroline Berkeley, his long-term partner and mother of his fifteen-year-old son, remained a mystery. Then they cut to a well-worn series of clips from Duke's cinematic career, interspersed with more recent footage of him with Caroline arriving at various galas and premieres.

'Wow, old Duke was a big fan of tight pants back then wasn't he?' joked Charlie as a famous still of the young Duke dressed as an outlaw cowboy throwing a lasso popped up on the screen in front of them.

'Oh God, Charlie, don't,' said Caroline, who was wringing her hands nervously as she watched. 'What am I going to do?' She looked at him imploringly.

Charlie sat down beside her and put his strong hands on her shoulders, forcing her to tear her gaze away from the news and face him.

'Caroline, you're going to go home. You have to. People are already wondering where you are, why you haven't rushed straight back. And you know Hunter must be out of his mind with worry.'

'I doubt it,' she replied bitterly, picking at the tassels on the red cashmere throw draped over Charlie's sofa.

'What if he knew something, Charlie? What if he found out about us, and that's what gave him the heart attack? And now the police know, and they're going to want to talk to me. Oh God.' Her voice was rising in panic. 'I can't cope. I mean, he was so fit, he really was.'

'Honey,' said Charlie reasonably, 'the guy was eighty years old. He had a heart attack, baby, it happens. It was nothing to do with you, and nobody's going to think it was. Believe me.'

'Then why are the police there?' asked Caroline, sipping feebly at her tea. 'I mean, what if he *did* know something?'

'He didn't know anything,' said Charlie firmly. 'And even if he did, your having an affair is not a crime, is it? I know the LAPD are a lazy bunch of assholes, but I still think they have better things to do with their time than running around arresting every movie star's wife who has a bit on the side. Just imagine how full the LA jails would be if they did.'

'I'm not his wife,' said Caroline irrationally.

Charlie smiled. His sense of calm was beginning, slowly, to thaw her panic.

'You really think I should go back?'

'I don't think it,' he replied, taking the mug from her hands and placing it on the coffee table beside them, 'I know it. Go home, Caroline. Go comfort your son.'

'But what will I tell people?' she asked him, her voice still quavering. 'Where should I say I've been?'

'God, I don't know,' said Charlie impatiently. 'Tell them you went for a drive up to Santa Barbara. You sat on the beach all day, so you didn't hear the news. I don't know. Tell them whatever you like.'

Caroline nodded uncertainly. She looked so small and vulnerable wrapped up in his huge sweater, her hands lost inside the cavernous sleeves, with her hair still wild and dishevelled from bed. He felt a jolt of longing surge through his body, but suppressed it firmly. This was no time to start fooling around.

For all his reassurances to Caroline, Charlie knew full well that things were about to get complicated. There was a lot of money at stake, and without Duke to protect her, his wife and children would do everything in their power to stop her getting her hands on any of it. Even if her legal rights were watertight, they could still make her life hell once she went home. Pulling her gently to her feet, he wrapped his arms around her.

'You realise that we'll have to be very careful, certainly until after the funeral and the reading of the will.'

Caroline looked up at him aghast.

'I can still see you?' she asked, clasping her hands round his neck. She needed him, now more than ever, and the thought of the next two weeks without him was almost unbearable.

'Not yet. Not until Duke's estate is settled once and for all and that money's in your account.'

She gave him a petulant pout that would have been worthy of Siena.

'Now, come on,' said Charlie. 'You've waited sixteen years for this moment, Caroline. You gave that old bastard the best years of your life.'

'He wasn't always a bastard you know.' Caroline was surprised to hear her own voice close to breaking.

'You've earned that money, every penny of it,' continued Charlie vehemently, his blond hair falling forward in an unruly mop as he spoke. God, he was beautiful. 'Letting that disgusting . . .' He checked himself. 'Letting Duke have whatever he wanted, taking him into your life, your bed, giving him a son.'

'He never wanted a son,' said Caroline.

Charlie ran his hand through his hair, exasperated. She just didn't get it.

'All I'm saying is, don't go taking any silly risks now, all right? You and Hunter need that money. There'll be plenty of time for us later.'

He put his hand against her cheek, slowly tracing one warm, pudgy finger down until it reached her mouth and rested on the plump softness of her lips. They gazed at one another for a moment, each longing to take comfort in the other, before finally releasing themselves to a lingering goodbye kiss.

He smelt so delicious, a heady mix of Givenchy aftershave, sex and sweat that left Caroline reeling with desire for him. Even now, with poor old Duke lying dead and who knew what battles awaiting her when she got back home, she felt that familiar, insistent pounding between her legs. But she knew he was right. She had to go.

'You'll be OK?' he asked, as she finally removed his sweater and pulled on her own to leave.

'Don't worry about me,' said Caroline. 'I'll be absolutely fine.'

Chapter Fourteen

It was about three weeks after Duke's funeral and Pete had summoned Siena to come and see him in his study.

Pacing up and down the starkly functional little room, the sweat trickling down between his shoulder blades under his Brooks Brothers shirt, he felt absurdly jittery. He had barely spoken to his daughter since Duke's death and wasn't sure where to begin.

Unlike his mother Minnie, who for the first time he could remember had really opened up to him in her grief, revealing a depth of feeling for his hated father that Pete struggled to understand, Siena seemed to have retreated into her own silent world. At first, he and Claire had tried to talk to her, sitting patiently with her for hours on end, even bringing in a child psychologist to try to break through the little girl's misery. But Siena had angrily shrugged off their every attempt at comfort, and Pete had quickly given up, not because he didn't want to help her, but because he had no idea where to begin. Thanks to his father, Siena had become a virtual stranger to him.

Claire was more persistent. She longed to comfort her daughter and had hoped, perhaps foolishly, that Duke's death might finally open up the way for the three of them to become a proper family at last. Although Caroline and Hunter were still living on the estate – when she had finally deigned to return home the evening after Duke's death, she had been met by a wall of silence from the rest of the family, but there had been no outright battles, thank God – they had moved into a separate wing, and Minnie and Laurie both kept themselves to themselves. Although she felt badly for poor Hunter, Claire was grateful for the time this allowed her with her own husband and child. For the first time ever, the house had started to feel almost like their own home. But these changes seemed only to deepen Siena's depression.

The psychologist, a kindly, professorial looking man in his mid-sixties who had a soft spot for Claire's fragile beauty, had warned her that Siena was still experiencing profound shock, and she should not expect any miracles overnight.

'You must understand, Mrs McMahon, your daughter has been deeply traumatised, particularly since she was the one who first discovered her grandfather's body,' he had told her, after a two-hour session with Siena up in the old nursery.

'It is not unnatural, even for adults, to experience feelings of guilt and anxiety in these circumstances, and those feelings must be resolved before the true grieving process can begin. Do you understand?'

'I think so,' said Claire, who didn't, but wanted terribly to help Siena.

'Your daughter is only ten,' he continued. 'She feels responsible. She feels to blame. And she may well express those feelings through anger. It is perfectly normal for Siena to feel resentment at losing her grandfather in this way, and she may direct this towards you or your husband, either by withdrawing completely or, as I say, through rage.'

'I see,' said Claire bleakly, sinking down into the same nursery armchair where she used to rock Siena to sleep as a baby. She felt utterly at a loss. 'So what should we do? How can we help?' she asked.

The psychologist gave her an encouraging smile. 'Just be patient. Give her time.'

Patience, unfortunately, had never been one of Pete's strong suits. Nor had he ever had much faith in 'over-priced quacks and their psychobabble'. No, what Siena needed, he had decided, was a complete change. A little discipline might not be a bad thing either. For years, Duke had filled her head with ridiculous ideas about stardom, and turned her into a fearful prima donna. No doubt he'd been hoping to relive his own glory days through Siena. Well, it wasn't going to happen.

'Ah, Siena, honey, sit down,' said Pete as she appeared, scowling and silent, at the door, her whole body coiled in pent-up belligerence.

Siena had perfected a look of vacant hostility whenever in her father's presence which succinctly conveyed her distaste for him without her having to spell it out in words. It both infuriated Pete and disturbed him. It was almost as if she blamed him, in some bizarre way, for Duke's death.

Slumping down sullenly into the only armchair in the study, she swung her legs insolently over one arm and gave him 'that look'. Shit, thought Pete. Just look at that attitude! If she's like this at ten, God help us when she hits sixteen. But he remembered the psychologist's advice about support and encouragement and forced a smile.

'I think we need to talk,' he said, clearing his throat and wishing he didn't sound so damned formal. 'About the future.'

'No we don't,' mumbled Siena obstinately into the sleeve of her new A-Team jacket.

The jacket had been her last present from Duke, and for the last few days she had refused point blank to take it off, even in the sweltering midday heat of the LA summer. Now George Peppard's grinning face, a fat cigar stuffed in his mouth, stared insolently at Pete from his daughter's lapel as she twirled a long black ringlet of hair around her finger and looked pointedly out of the window, very obviously bored.

Pete battled to keep his temper. 'Please don't answer me back like that, Siena.' He sat down himself on the only other chair in the room, an angular, ugly swivel seat upholstered in vile red-and-grey check which his PA, Tara, had picked up from Office Depot. 'And I'd appreciate it if you'd look at me when I'm talking to you.'

At that moment, Claire knocked softly on the door and, seeing Siena, came in and perched herself awkwardly on the other arm of her chair.

'Hey, sweetie.' She kissed her daughter on top of her head. Siena smiled up at her weakly, her first smile in weeks. A breakthrough, thought Claire. At last!

'Hey, Mommy.'

Pete felt a small involuntary stab of envy as he watched mother and daughter clasp hands. What the fuck was wrong with him? First Duke, now Claire. Was he going to resent everyone his daughter loved, just because she refused to love him?

'Claire.' He took a deep breath and made an effort to relax. 'I was just about to talk to Siena about, er, about our plan.'

'What plan?' asked Siena warily, holding her mother's hand more tightly. The cloud of distrust descended over her face again as quickly as it had just lifted.

Damn it, thought Claire. Why did Pete have to bring this up right now? She was still so wounded and so fragile, couldn't he have left it a few more weeks?

'Your mother and I have spoken to Dr Carlson,' Pete continued, not quite meeting Siena's eye. 'We know you're still upset about Grandpa but' – he coughed nervously – 'we think it would be best, better for you, to have a complete change of scene. Take your mind off things.'

'What kind of a change of scene?' Siena glared at him. 'Anyway, I don't want to take my mind off things.'

'That may be,' said Pete, his voice rising in anger despite himself.

'But I'm afraid you've become rather too used to having what you want, young lady, and that's about to change.'

Siena let go of Claire and sat upright, like a bull about to charge.

'Your Grandpa Duke spoiled you,' continued Pete.

'He did not!' Siena shot back angrily, leaping to her feet and accidentally knocking Claire in the ribs with a flying elbow.

'Sit down!' Pete roared, banging both fists down on the desk, which shook as if it had been hit by an earthquake. He had sworn he wouldn't lose his temper, but sometimes Siena pushed him to the limit. If only she wouldn't keep defending Duke. If only she had known him the way Pete had. He was evil. He didn't deserve her loyalty, or her grief.

Siena and Claire both sat, shaken by the violence of his reaction.

'That sort of behaviour is exactly what I mean.' He straightened his tie and cleared his throat, pushing his sandy hair back from his now sweating brow and trying to compose himself again. 'Now Siena, we are all upset about what's happened.'

'Yeah, right,' she muttered under her breath.

'But life goes on,' said Pete, ignoring her. 'And in your case, that means school. I called you in here to tell you that your mother and I have decided to send you away to boarding school in England.'

'No!'

Siena spun round and looked imploringly at Claire. 'Mommy, don't let him! I want to stay here, with you and Hunter. Please, I'll be good, I promise. Please, Mom? Don't make me go away.'

Claire looked helplessly from her daughter to her husband. She knew that Pete's mind was already made up. For the past three days, she'd tried everything to sway him from this decision, using every argument she could think of to convince him that Siena would do better at home, but her pleas had all fallen on deaf ears. Pete was insistent that the discipline and stability of boarding school would, as he put it, 'straighten out' their daughter. Her difficult behaviour in the wake of Duke's death had become a painful daily reminder of his own failings as a father and the distance that had grown up between them. Things would be better all round, he told her, once Siena was sent away to school.

It hadn't helped that Minnie had heartily endorsed the plan of an English education for her only grandchild, not because she didn't love her or wanted to get rid of her, but because she had always been brought up to believe that English boarding schools were the best in the world, both socially and academically.

Claire tried to believe that Pete had Siena's best interests at heart as well, although deep down part of her knew that his own resentment and anger towards his daughter, for loving Duke and Hunter as much as she did, had more than a little to do with it. It was true that Siena *had* become very difficult recently. But was the answer really to wash their hands of the problem? Out of sight, out of mind?

'It's no good appealing to your mother,' said Pete harshly, a livid blue vein throbbing visibly through the sweat on his receding brow. 'She and I are in agreement, as is your grandmother, and the decision has been made. You leave for St Xavier's on Tuesday night.'

'Mom?'

Claire could see Siena fighting back the tears, biting her bottom lip and clutching at the cuffs of her beloved jacket in an effort to hold back the floods. She wanted more than anything to reach out and comfort her. But she was terrified of defying Pete, perhaps damaging their relationship beyond repair. He had not just asked for her support, he had demanded it. Fearful and ashamed, she had given in.

'I'm sorry, sweetheart,' she said, holding out her arms. 'It's for the best.'

'Best for *who*?' screamed Siena, turning helplessly from one parent to the other like a cornered animal. 'I hate you. I hate both of you,' she yelled, and ran sobbing from the room.

'Siena!' Claire got up to follow her.

'Leave her,' said Pete. 'She'll get over it.'

'Will she?' asked Claire angrily, her own despair at the situation now perilously near the surface.

'Of course she will,' he said firmly, but he didn't sound convincing, even to himself.

It was years since he had heard his wife raise her voice to anyone. The strength of her emotion now shocked him. Moving over to her, he drew her towards him and felt the resentful stiffening of her limbs as he held her, gently stroking her hair until she began, reluctantly, to relax.

'Do you love me?' he whispered.

Claire caught the urgency in his voice, the desperate loneliness of a guilt-ridden man. Perhaps they had made the right decision after all? Maybe England would be good for Siena? She certainly wasn't happy at home. And perhaps, in the end, Pete needed her even more than her daughter did.

'Of course I do,' she said, and meant it. 'Of course I love you.'

'Good,' he said. 'Because I need you.' He sighed heavily as he held her tight. 'I need you to be behind me on this, Claire. Please?'

'I am behind you,' she said, returning his embrace. 'I'm just worried about her, that's all.'

*

Hunter didn't think he had ever seen Siena so upset. Her whole tiny frame was so wracked with sobs that she could barely get a sentence out, and it was some minutes before he even understood what she was telling him: that Pete and Claire were going to send her away to school. Away from him.

'I'll never see you again!' she wailed melodramatically through hyperventilating breaths, sitting on her unmade bed with Kermit clasped tightly to her chest between George Peppard and a gold-chain-laden Mr T.

'Of course you will, don't be silly,' said Hunter, who was fighting his own shock at the news.

It was an unspoken rule that he wasn't supposed to hang out in Siena's room any more. Pete didn't want him anywhere near her, and his mother was equally anxious to avoid precipitating any sort of conflict before his dad's will had been settled. But the two children regularly made illicit visits to each other's separate prisons to comfort one another when things got rough.

Life at home had been pretty terrible for Hunter since his dad died. First of all, he felt guilty that he didn't feel more affected by Duke's death. It was as if someone had switched off his emotions at the mains, while Siena's grief poured out uncontrollably like water through a shattered dam, highlighting his own apparent heartlessness.

On top of that, the whole household was acting as if he and his mom didn't exist. If it were possible, his mom was spending even more time away from home than usual, leaving him to cope with Minnie's icy disregard and Pete's aggressive rejection on his own. Claire was too caught up in her own worries over Siena to come to his aid. Even Max had stopped coming over to hang out with him since the atmosphere on the estate had become so tense.

Now, with Siena leaving, Hunter wondered how the hell he was going to get through the days. She was the only person in the world he really loved and now she was being taken away from him.

'There'll be vacations, lots of them, and you can come back home then,' he said, trying to keep his voice bright. 'Besides, now that, you know . . .' He looked at his shoes awkwardly. 'Now that Dad's gone, my mom was talking about spending more time in England anyway. We might be going to visit my Uncle William, she said, so maybe I could come see you at your school as well?'

He sat down on the bed and put his arms around her. Mel Gibson's cheesy grin surrounded him, his famous crinkled blue eyes staring down at him from all four walls, where the peeling, faded posters still jostled with one another for space. 'You just wait. We'll see each other all the time, you'll see. You won't get rid of me that easily.'

'We won't,' Siena sniffled, unwilling to be mollified. 'And I'll never see Max again either.'

'Oh, I see.' Hunter raised his eyebrow at her teasingly. 'It's Max you're really worried about, not me. We've developed a little bit of a soft spot for old Maxy recently, haven't we?'

'Baloney!' Siena pushed him away, unable fully to suppress a sneaking smile. She tried her best to sound dignified. 'I'm just saying, when they send me to England I won't see him again either. But I'm *way* more upset about you. I hate Daddy so much.' She sniffed. 'You were so lucky. I wish I'd had Grandpa Duke for my dad.'

Hunter looked at her knowingly. Siena knew full well that Duke had been less than a perfect father to him.

'Oh, Hunter, what are we going to do?' The tears were back with a vengeance. 'I'm just going to miss you so much.'

'Hey there, come on now.' He passed her a tissue from the pink box Claire had placed on her bedside table, and she blew her nose with a ten-year-old's unselfconscious, noisy abandon. 'It'll be OK. I'm gonna miss you too, you know? Things sure won't be the same round here without you.'

Siena flung her arms around him so tightly he felt he might choke. The age gap between the two of them seemed bigger now than it had ever been. Siena thought of him as almost an adult, and his burgeoning physical 'manliness' – the more pronounced muscles in his arms and chest, the rough, emergent stubble on his cheeks, the smell of deodorant mingling with the sweat and warmth of his adolescent body – made him feel less like her brother and more like the uncle that he was. All the girls at her elementary school were wildly in love with him from afar, but these days he seemed so very *much* older than her and her friends, almost like a creature from another world. Unlike Max, who was going through an unfortunate spotty phase and was still a thorn in her side at times, Hunter seemed only to get more and more beautiful as a teenager. Siena felt immensely proud of him, and was fiercely jealous of his love and attention.

'You have to write to me.' She looked up at him, her face pressed against the faded grey of his T-shirt so closely that she could hear the comforting pounding of his heart. 'Every day.'

'I promise,' said Hunter.

Looking around the familiar little bedroom, he felt suddenly, unaccountably anxious. He seemed to be promising Siena an awful lot these days. Not for the first time, he wondered whether he would actually be able to deliver on this one.

Chapter Fifteen

Charlie Murray looked at his watch. Ten thirty. They'd be starting in ten minutes. Hell, why did he have to be there?

Outside his fourth-floor window, the hustle and bustle of Beverly Hills life continued on the streets below him, and he glanced down absently. Bored, overblown housewives, their once natural beauty long since lost beneath layers of surgery and ghoulish make-up, flitted from store to store with their spookily frozen faces and permanent expressions of surprise.

Maybe they were surprised to wake up one morning and realise they looked like a freakin' experiment?

Charlie couldn't help but compare the women to Caroline, so self-assured in her sexiness, so beautiful still, at least in his eyes. Who cared whether she had a few crow's feet or her breasts didn't explode out of her T-shirt like water balloons? No surgeon could give a woman what Caroline had.

He picked up a bright purple executive stress ball from the desk and gave it a desultory squeeze. Fucking useless.

She was outside right now in Carter & Rowe's conference room, looking suitably demure and grief stricken in a chocolate-brown Dolce and Gabbana suit, along with the rest of the McMahon clan. He'd seen her arrive earlier before making a bolt for the temporary safety of his office. Even here, though, images of her lying naked and lustful, spreadeagled on his desk, lingered like old smoke all around him, and he found it impossible to concentrate.

They'd all arrived for the reading of Duke's will – Caro, Minnie, Pete and Laurie. The atmosphere in the building oscillated between tense and electric, with press gathered outside on the street, all chomping at the bit to find out how the McMahon fortune was to be divided between the old man's wife, mistress and children. The official line was that the will had been settled more than a decade earlier, and there would be no surprises. But a long series of delays, combined with a couple of deliberately cryptic leaked comments from Pete's office, had whetted people's appetite for scandal. A rumour was flying around about a last-minute letter of wishes. Something was up.

Charlie felt it too. He was scared for Caroline and told her so in one of only two furtive phone calls they'd made to each other since Duke's death.

'I just feel uneasy, like Pete's up to something,' he'd told her. 'Watch your back, honey, OK? That's all I'm saying.'

'Honestly, Charlie, you worry too much.' She laughed. 'Everything's going to be fine. You'd have heard something. David would have said something, surely, if there were anything to worry about?'

'He can't,' said Charlie. 'Not until the public reading of the will. It's illegal.'

'Baby, relax,' she reassured him. 'Just think, in two weeks the money will be sitting snugly in my account, and then you and I can finally go public.'

But somehow, he wasn't relaxed. His reverie was broken by Marlene, who stuck her concerned, motherly face around the door.

'Everyone's here,' she told him. 'David wants you in conference room two pronto.'

Charlie groaned. It was perfectly normal for him to attend important client meetings with David, but he wished he could have been spared this one. He knew his boss could have fired him over the Caroline affair, and was grateful that he hadn't, but he still felt the weight of David's disapproval and disappointment whenever they were alone together. That would have made him uncomfortable enough, but now he had to sit through a meeting in front of the whole McMahon clan, and Caroline, who he hadn't seen for almost three weeks. Was this David's idea of a suitable punishment?

'Marlene, can't you tell him I'm sick?'

'Oh, now, come along,' she chided him, 'you'll be fine. And I'm sure Miss Berkeley will be happy to see you,' she added with a knowing smile.

'Ah, Charlie, sit down,' said David Rowe, unsmiling, when he walked into the conference room a few minutes later. 'I think we're ready to begin.'

The one remaining chair was between his boss and Caroline. Talk about the hot seat. Charlie slipped himself quietly into it, briefly acknowledging Caroline and nodding formally to the three black-clad figures on the opposite side of the table.

Pete, whom he'd met once or twice up at the house with David and always found utterly charmless, looked older than he remembered and in need of a good night's sleep. With his spreading paunch, pallid complexion and receding red hair he looked like every middle management heart attack waiting to happen, and absolutely nothing like his father. Laurie, the fat sister, appeared to be on the verge of tears. And on David's left, Minnie McMahon sat as regally elegant as ever in a severely cut black jacket and pillbox hat. Her face was somewhat drawn, but unlike her daughter she appeared completely composed, hands folded together on the table in front of her, ready for business. He didn't dare sneak so much as a glance at Caroline.

'What I am about to read out to you all,' began David, adjusting his reading glasses slightly as he fingered the sheaf of papers in front of him, 'is the last will and testament of Patrick Connor McMahon, otherwise known as "Duke" McMahon, of Hancock Park, Los Angeles.'

'No it isn't,' said Minnie.

Laurie looked up, bewildered. Caroline, forgetting herself, turned to Charlie with a look of pure terror. Pete just smiled.

'I beg your pardon, Mrs McMahon?' said a flustered-looking David.

Minnie carefully removed a slim white envelope from her capacious, worn leather handbag and placed it on the table, smoothing it down almost lovingly with her long, slender fingers.

'I think, after thirty years of acquaintance, David, you might call me Minnie,' she said, allowing herself a small smile.

Caroline squirmed. 'Thirty years of acquaintance' indeed. Who did she think she was, the Duchess of bloody Devonshire?

'I'm sorry, er, Minnie,' said David. 'I don't think I quite understand.'

'Nor do I, Mother. What's going on?' asked Laurie.

Pete opened his mouth to speak but Minnie put her hand on his arm to stop him. She'd waited sixteen long years for this moment, and no one was going to steal her thunder.

'Let me explain.' She smiled graciously around the table, lingering for a moment on Charlie, who was beginning to fear that his heartbeat might be audible. 'The night before Duke died he came to see me. He told me that he had decided to make one or two changes to his previous will.'

The colour drained from Caroline's face as Minnie removed the document from its envelope.

'You see, he had recently come into possession of some information – some rather hurtful and shocking information' – she looked directly at Charlie – 'as I believe you are already aware, Mr Rowe.'

David blushed scarlet. He had no idea that Duke had let his wife, of all people, in on their little secret.

'Mrs McMahon. Minnie,' he said, 'I don't know if this is really the time or the place to talk about this matter.' He laughed weakly. 'I'm afraid that, whatever Duke's intentions might have been, the fact is he did *not* make any formal changes to his will before his death. If he had done, I would have been asked to witness those changes. You see, without an impartial witness – someone who is not a beneficiary – well, any new document would not be legally enforceable. Duke knew that.'

'He did indeed,' said Minnie, passing the document to David. 'As you can see, it was impartially witnessed.'

'By whom?' blurted out Caroline, suddenly indignant.

'By me,' came a voice from the back of the room.

Seamus, Duke's old pal and confidant, must have been standing there all along, leaning against the wall in his slightly crumpled suit. He looked reproachfully at Caroline, and she felt her stomach lurch with guilt, as if someone had just cut the elevator cable. Of all the people in the room, she realised, Seamus may have been the only one who had loved Duke without any of the complications, reservations and self-interest that the rest of them had.

'He loved you, you know,' he said to her, and she was shocked to find her eyes stinging with tears. Charlie gave her hand a surreptitious squeeze under the table.

'Not really, Seamus,' she said sadly. 'Not always.'

'I think you'll find it holds water,' announced Minnie briskly, niftily steering the conversation back to the subject of the will. She was in no mood for Caroline's crocodile tears, or Seamus's sentimentality, for that matter.

'She's right,' piped up Pete, leaning back in his chair and cracking his knuckles gleefully. 'It's valid. So, David, do you want to read it out to us? Or shall I?'

David glanced at Duke's elder son, whose face displayed an ecstasy of spite like some crazed sadist about to begin torturing his victim. He could quite see why the old man had never liked him. 'Very well,' he said. 'As this does appear to be a legitimate revised will, I am obliged to proceed.'

He adjusted his spectacles for a third time, and began reading directly from the paper in front of him. Charlie could make out only two paragraphs of print, followed by a long series of signatures and endorsements. It was going to be brutally brief.

'I, Duke McMahon, wish to make the following changes to my last will and testament. With the exception of the changes and provisions outlined below, my previous will (dated 12 June 1976) shall remain effective in its entirety.

'I hereby revoke any and all gifts, endowments or benefits of any kind previously made to Miss Caroline Berkeley.'

Caroline sat motionless, a brown Dolce and Gabbana mannequin, her face impassive. So he *did* know about her and Charlie, the wily old sod. How could she have expected anything less of Duke? She could feel Pete and Minnie's eyes boring into her, sensed then slavering like wolves for a reaction, but she wasn't going to give them the satisfaction.

'All payments from the Innovation Trust to Miss Berkeley will also cease in the event of my death. All benefits, whether in cash, stock or property, formerly bequeathed to Miss Berkeley are to revert to the Innovation Trust, for the sole and exclusive benefit of my three children, Peter, Laurie and Hunter McMahon.'

Thank God, thought Caroline. If Hunter was still inheriting, she'd be OK. Relief flooded through her veins so violently she thought she might be sick.

'In addition,' David went on in his deep, oddly soothing baritone, 'I hereby appoint my wife, "Minnie" McMahon, as the sole trustee of all trusts benefiting my children.'

He paused, looking across at Caroline.

'Including my younger son, Hunter.'

'What?' She leapt to her feet, unable to contain herself a second longer. *Minnie* was going to have control of Hunter's trust? That meant she would never see a penny. Sixteen years of her life she had given to that bastard. Sixteen years and Duke was leaving her penniless.

'That's not possible.' She looked frantically from David to Charlie for support. 'That's not legal, it can't be.' She waved her arm wildly towards Minnie. 'She despises my son. How can she possibly take legal responsibility for his interests? She'll beggar him, for God's sake, she'll beggar us both! How could Duke do this to us?'

'I'm sorry, Miss Berkeley,' replied David quietly, 'but I'm afraid Duke was quite within his rights to bequeath his estate as he saw fit.'

'It's breach of fucking contract!' Caroline shouted. 'I want to challenge the will. Charlie.' She turned to her lover, who was sitting with his handsome blond head in his hands. 'I want to fight this.'

'Be my guest,' said Minnie, smiling. Pete and Laurie sat beside her like two smug sentries. Even Seamus had walked over to the McMahons' side of the table, his hands placed protectively on Laurie's shoulders. Caroline was on her own. 'But I think you will discover that since you and my husband never married, and given that your bastard child has been *more* than generously provided for, you haven't got a leg to stand on.'

Minnie got to her feet. 'Still, I wouldn't worry too much, if I were you. I'm sure your little toy boy here will be happy to support you, although perhaps not in *quite* the manner you've grown accustomed to.'

Charlie stood up and put his arm around Caroline. God knew he hadn't bargained on playing happy families with her and her son, but he was damned if he was going to let Duke McMahon's frigid crone of a wife dismiss him like that. He was nobody's toy boy.

'Well, ma'am,' – he grinned at Minnie – 'I'll sure do my best.'

'We want you and your son out of the house by tomorrow,' snarled Pete, gathering up his briefcase and jacket.

'Don't be ridiculous,' snapped Caroline. Even from across the table she could smell his fetid breath, like putrefied hatred. 'That house is Hunter's home. He and Siena are like brother and sister, Pete, you know that. You can't just banish him like some sort of outlaw.'

'Just watch me,' said Pete.

'For God's sake, think of the children.' She could hear the desperation in her own voice. 'However much you want to hurt me, you can't seriously want to split up the kids. Think about Siena.'

'Don't you dare talk to me about my daughter,' Pete spat at her. 'Think of the children? When did you ever think about the children? When did you ever think about anyone except yourself? The only reason you gave birth to that little shit in the first place was to get your hands on Dad's money, you fucking whore. Well, guess what? It backfired. I want my daughter as far away from you and that bastard son of yours as possible.'

'Hey, enough,' said Charlie, squaring up to Pete, his powerful football player's shoulders clearly apparent beneath his immaculately cut suit.

While the two men faced each other down, Minnie walked over towards Caroline. Pulling on her black gloves, she looked her former rival in the eye. Sixteen years of enmity and bitterness hung in the air between them. But they had both loved Duke once. For just a moment, the two women stared at one another in silence. Then Minnie broke the spell.

'It killed him, you know. The shock. You two.' She gestured towards Charlie. 'That's what killed him.'

And turning on her heel, she strode out of the room.

PART TWO

Chapter Sixteen

Yorkshire, England, July 1998

'God, he really is gorgeous, isn't he?'

Janey passed the magazine back to Siena, who lay scowling on the library sofa in Janey's parents' house, her long legs draped nonchalantly over Patrick's. Patrick was Janey's older brother and Siena's boyfriend of the moment.

'Hmm,' replied Siena, doing her best to sound bored as she looked at Hunter's face smiling at her from the front of the June issue of *Hello!* All black hair and smouldering blue eyes. 'I guess so.'

Janey Cash was a great schoolfriend of Siena's and had invited her to spend two weeks at her family's tumbledown Georgian rectory in Yorkshire. The girls had sat their last A-level together ten days ago, and waved a joyous goodbye to St Xavier's. They were still recovering from the epic hangover that had followed a drunken week of post-exam celebrations, and Siena decided that two weeks in the peace of the Yorkshire countryside, watching TV and filling up on Mrs Cash's delicious sticky toffee pudding, were exactly what the doctor ordered. Of course, the fact that Patrick would also be there was just an added bonus.

She put the magazine down on the floor, making sure that Hunter's face was floor side down. She was sick of seeing his picture everywhere, sick of all her friends telling her how gorgeous he was. Ever since he'd landed the role of Mike Palumbo in *Counsellor*, the hottest new TV series since *Dynasty*, it was as if she couldn't escape him. The fact that she hadn't laid eyes on him, or even spoken to him, since she was ten years old didn't stop people from asking her endless questions, raking over her memories with razor blades.

What made it worse was that Hunter seemed to be living *her* dream, fulfilling *her* destiny. For as long as she could remember, Siena had wanted to be an actress. Although she knew you weren't supposed to say it, what she longed for above everything else was to be famous. Not just Duke McMahon's granddaughter or Pete

McMahon's little girl – she wanted serious, fuck-off fame, the real deal, in her own right. She wanted the whole world to love her, to have people scream out her name. To be adored, just like Duke had been adored. That was her dream. *She* was the one who ought to have had her face splashed all over the magazines, not Hunter. She knew she shouldn't begrudge him his success, not after everything he'd been through. But it was so hard, being forced to watch him make a name for himself in Hollywood while she was stuck in England, being pushed into seven more long, grindingly dull years of medicine at Oxford. Just because her mom had given up medical school, and now both her parents wanted to live vicariously through her. She didn't *want* to be a goddam doctor!

Patrick picked up one of her bare feet in his hands and gave it a comforting squeeze. She smiled at him. He really was very sweet, and he seemed instinctively to understand that she found it painful to talk about Hunter, or any of her family for that matter. If only everyone else were so tactful.

After Duke died, her father had wasted no time in packing her off to boarding school. By the time she came home for her first long vacation at Christmas, Caroline and Hunter had moved out of Hancock Park into a modest apartment somewhere in Los Feliz. Siena had begged Pete to let her see him, but he wouldn't even give her an address so she could write. She'd pleaded to everyone – Minnie, Aunt Laurie, her mother – but out of either malice or fear, none of them would help her.

Once, when she was back in LA for the summer, she could have sworn she'd seen an envelope with Hunter's handwriting on it at her dad's office. He had the very rounded letters of a young girl, and finished his 'i's with cartoonish circles rather than dots. You could almost smell the effort that went into his spelling and punctuation, poor lamb. But Tara, Pete's vile, anorexic bitch of a PA, had snatched the letter up before Siena could take a closer look and locked it away in her 'confidential' file.

When she'd asked Pete about it later, he'd told her that he'd kept the letter from her for her own protection.

'I'm not letting you read it because it would hurt you to read it,' he said. 'Hunter has decided that he no longer wants to have any contact with our family. He's almost seventeen now, and I think we have to respect his wishes.'

'But he doesn't mean *me*,' Siena insisted. 'He would never say he didn't want to see me any more.'

'I'm sorry, Siena,' said Pete brutally. 'But he would and he has. I think it's best if we don't speak about this again. Hunter has moved on and so must you.'

It was amazing to think that that awful conversation had taken place nearly eight years ago now. And that since then she and Hunter, who had once been so inseparable, had lost each other completely.

'Come on,' said Patrick, extricating himself from Siena's limbs, getting up from the sofa and yawning dramatically. 'I'm bored. Who's up for a spot of corn jumping?'

'What on earth is corn jumping?' asked Siena, admiring the lean, defined muscles on his stomach as he stretched his arms above his head. For a rugby player, Patrick had a slim build, but she loved the smooth lines of his body and the way her own body seemed to bristle with excitement and arousal whenever he came near her.

She was not in love with him – Siena hadn't the slightest intention of falling in love with anybody until she was at least thirty, and rich and famous enough to be happy with or without a man – but she had a genuine soft spot for Patrick. As well as being a complete angel, he was far more talented in bed than any of the other boys she'd been with.

'You've never been corn jumping?' asked Janey, taking her friend's hand and pulling her up from her seat.

'Look, we're not all local yokels, you know.' Siena laughed. 'I have no idea what corn jumping is, but something tells me we don't get to see a whole lot of it in Los Angeles.'

'Well, you're missing out, I can assure you,' said Patrick, in his clipped British accent which reminded her so much of Max De Seville.

Not for the first time she wondered what had become of Max, her old rival, and whether he and Hunter were still in touch.

'Come on,' said Patrick. 'Follow me.'

Siena followed Janey and Patrick as they skipped out into the stable yard, giggling and pushing one another like a couple of kids. It must be lovely, she thought wistfully, to have a family like Janey's. Mr and Mrs Cash were both so cool and laid back. They couldn't give a shit whether Janey got into bloody Oxford. Not that she was very likely to anyway. Poor old Janey. Patrick seemed to have the lion's share of brains and looks in the family.

The three of them clambered over the rotting old yard gate, and ran across the paddock towards the three vast grain silos that marked the entrance to the farm. It was a glorious July day, and the sun beat down on the fields, its warmth intensifying the rich agricultural smells of hay and horses and cow shit that had once been so utterly alien to Siena, but now just smelt of 'England'.

She could never live up here, she thought as she stumbled across the bumpy, irregular field. They were hundreds of miles away from the nearest decent blow-dry, let alone restaurant or club. The Coach and Horses in Farndale was about as close as people got to a good time in Yorkshire as far as Siena could make out. But every now and then it did her good to come and stay with Janey, to soak up the clotted-cream richness of the dale, sheltered beneath the barren, bleak expanse of the moor above. The landscape was breathtaking. It made her feel like Cathy, making wild love to Heathcliff, whenever she and Patrick snuck off to the barn or the stables to fool around. It was another world.

'Move your ass, Siena!' Patrick shouted at her in his appalling attempt at an American accent as she jogged to catch up with them. 'In here.'

Janey opened the door to the silo, and the pungent, overwhelming stench of the grain hit Siena in the face like a Mike Tyson punch.

'Omigod, it reeks!' she squealed, clasping her hand over her nose and mouth.

Inside, the building was like a Tardis, as huge as an aircraft hangar with two enormous mounds of corn, perhaps eighty feet high, shimmering in their own golden dust beneath an industrial lattice-work of metal beams supporting an immense corrugated-iron roof. On the wall to her left, Siena saw two endlessly long ladders bolted together, providing access to a narrow platform at the top of the larger corn pile.

Patrick looked first at the ladder, then at Siena, and nodded evilly.

'Oh no.' She shook her head, laughing, her thick dark curls spilling luxuriously over her INXS T-shirt, eyes flashing the same cobalt blue as her new 501 jeans. Patrick felt his groin stirring as he looked at her. 'I am *not* going up there. Uh-uh, no way, José, ain't happenin'.'

'You sounded *so* like your grandfather when you said that,' said Janey idly, then immediately regretted it. Siena was even more touchy about the late, great Duke McMahon than she was about her divine Uncle Hunter. For once, though, she seemed to take it in good part.

'Thanks,' she smiled, then, turning to Patrick, 'but I'm still not going up there.'

'Oh, don't be such a wuss.' He pulled her towards him and pressed his own wide mouth against her tiny Betty Boop lips. She tasted of black cherry lip balm. 'That's what corn jumping is. You climb all the way up there.' He pointed at the precarious-looking platform. 'And then you jump down into the corn.'

'It's *really* fun,' confirmed Janey, who was already at the foot of the ladder, preparing to climb.

'No way, I can't,' persisted Siena.

'Why on earth not?' asked Patrick.

'I have a job for Ailsa Moran next week,' said Siena. 'What if I bruise myself – I mean, what if I cut my face? I'm supposed to have a "sophisticated forties look", OK? They don't want some scar-faced bungee jumper.'

Ailsa Moran was one of the hot, up-and-coming young fashion designers on the London scene this year. Much to Siena's surprise and delight, Moran had hired her to model some of the more retro pieces from her new collection for a shoot in the *Sunday Times* Style magazine, the first real paying modelling assignment she'd got since signing on with a small London agency in the Easter holidays, two months before her A-levels.

'Oh, well, excuse *me*, little miss supermodel,' Patrick teased her, stroking her cheek affectionately.

Siena knew he felt uncomfortable about her modelling, although he tried hard to be supportive. He didn't understand that she saw it as a way to get herself back to Hollywood, a stepping stone towards launching an acting career that didn't involve her father, or trading on her famous name. She had landed herself an agent and got the Moran job completely off her own bat, and she desperately wanted Patrick to be proud of her for that. But instead he seemed to fear that the whole fashion scene, that superficial London crowd, would pull her farther and farther away from him. Perhaps he was right.

'Fine,' he said, kissing her again. 'You just stay here and be a wet blanket. But I'm afraid you'll have to excuse me. Janey and I have some corn to jump.'

They both looked up as, with an almighty screech, Janey hurled herself from the rafters and landed with a soft thud in the corn below. Siena could hardly see her for dust as she slid down the side of the mound, whooping with adrenalin, her good-natured, ruddy face even more flushed than usual.

'Wow, that was *great!*' she said, scrabbling to her feet and brushing the worst of the prickly corn dust off her yellow-stained jeans. 'Come on, Yasmin bloody Le Bon, don't be so wet. Have a go.'

'Oh, for heaven's sake, all right,' said Siena, shaking her head at her own childishness. She had to admit, it *did* look like fun. 'Pat,' she yelled, racing over to the ladder. 'Hold on, I'm coming up!'

By the time she'd joined him on the little platform, she was already beginning to regret her impulsiveness, and it had nothing to do with her budding modelling career.

'Fucking hell, it's a long way down, isn't it?' she said, biting her lip with nerves.

'To the ground, yes,' said Patrick. 'To the corn, can't be more than twenty or thirty feet, I reckon. You'll be fine.'

'What if I miss it?' wailed Siena, taking another step back from the edge.

Patrick roared with laughter, his gentle, hazel eyes disappearing into creases.

'Darling, even you couldn't miss *that*. It's about the size of fucking Canada.'

Siena didn't look remotely reassured.

'How about we jump together?' He looked her in the eye, inviting her to trust him, and even through her fear she could feel herself melting towards him.

What a sweetheart he was, her little Patricio. A sudden pang of guilt, for the few times she'd been unfaithful to him, stabbed briefly at her heart. She knew it was insecurity which propelled her into other boys' beds, that she was driven by a desperate need to be loved and to have "lifeboats" in case her mother ship – Patrick – should sink. Having lost or been abandoned by everyone she had ever loved, she had learned the hard way never to put all her emotional eggs into one basket, however loyal and lovely that basket might be.

Poor, darling Patrick, he deserved better.

'On three?' she said, reaching for his hand.

'On three.'

'One. Two.'

Siena shut her eyes tight.

'Three!'

With a stomach-splitting whoosh, she felt herself rushing through the air, clinging to the warm, firm grip of Patrick's hand until, what seemed like hours later but could only really have been a second or two, they hit the soft cushion of the corn below.

'We did it!' Siena spluttered euphorically through a mouthful of corn dust. 'That was awesome!' She felt seven years old again, brave, excited and triumphant. Soon she was on her feet, punching the air with her fists and running a victory lap around the corn mound.

Patrick caught his sister's eye and, nodding in Siena's direction, raised his eyebrow at his screeching, circling girlfriend. She seemed to have gone completely barmy. 'American,' he whispered, in explanation.

'Oh yes,' said Janey. 'Very.'

Later that night, after a delicious but enormous meal with Janey's parents, followed by a never-ending game of charades, Siena had sneaked out of the spare bedroom, up the creaky spiral stairs to Patrick's attic room.

Too stuffed with lemon cheesecake to even contemplate sex, she nestled her head against the smooth warmth of his chest and chattered away as he stroked and tickled her bare back.

'Your dad is hysterical,' she said. 'Is he always that competitive?'

'Oh, always,' said Patrick. 'Although charades does rather bring out the worst in him. Normally Ma refuses to play, he's so awful.'

'They're very sweet, though, your parents.' She sighed, wistfully. 'They really seem to love each other, don't they?'

Patrick thought about it for a moment. 'Yes,' he said eventually. 'Yes, I suppose they do. Why? Don't your parents love each other?'

Siena gave a brittle grunt of derision. 'Not so as you'd notice.' She reached up and swept a loose tendril of hair back from her face, snuggling closer in to his body. 'My mom is just totally weak.'

Patrick could hear the bitterness in her voice, and feel her body tensing.

'And my dad . . .'

'I know,' he said gently, 'you don't get on with him.'

'I don't think he cares if I live or die, I really don't,' said Siena blankly.

'Come on now. That's a bit melodramatic, isn't it?'

'I wish it were,' said Siena. 'All he cares about is Oxford and medicine and my goddam reading list. He just wants to be able to go to dinner parties with his Hollywood cronies and their surgically enhanced wives, and say, "My daughter's a doctor, she goes to Oxford, she's been educated with English ladies."'

'What, like Janey, you mean?' he teased her. 'That's considered a selling point?'

'Well, you know what, screw him,' continued Siena, who was on a roll. 'I'm not going. My modelling's going great, although of course Dad doesn't give a shit about *that*. He can shove his reading list up his ass.'

Her voice was rising, and Patrick was worried that his parents might hear them.

'He can shove Oxford up his ass!'

'That might be a bit painful,' he said, trying to diffuse the situation. 'All those dreaming spires look a bit on the sharp side to me.'

Siena didn't smile.

'Sorry. Not funny.'

He sat up in bed and reached over for his Camel Lights. Lighting up, he took a long drag and offered it to Siena, who shook her head.

'Look,' he said, 'you can't just not go to Oxford. You've got a two-E offer, so it doesn't even matter if you've ploughed your A-levels.'

'Which I won't have,' chipped in Siena arrogantly.

'Which you won't have,' agreed Patrick. 'Modelling,' he frowned. 'It's just such a waste. I mean, is that really what you want to be in life, a jumped-up clothes horse?'

Siena gave him a withering look. 'Don't be fatuous,' she snapped. 'I've told you, I'm going to be an actress, and modelling happens to be a very good way into that. My agent says if I do the Paris shows this year I could meet a whole bunch of casting directors. A lot of actresses break into the business that way.'

'Bollocks,' said Patrick, blowing smoke out of his nose like a rather unthreatening dragon. 'Name one.'

'Cameron fucking Diaz, OK, asshole?' He looked blank. 'The girl in *The Mask*?' Furious, she rolled out of his bed and started pulling on her worn, stripy pyjama bottoms. Why couldn't he be supportive about this? Why was he taking her dad's side? 'Marilyn fucking Monroe, ever heard of her?'

'I don't think Marilyn got her big break at Paris fashion week, do you?'

'Right, smartass,' said Siena, who was really in a foul mood now. 'But she was a model first, then an actress. *Model.*' She adopted a patronising tone, as though explaining the alphabet to a four-year-old. '*Actress.* See? You just don't like me modelling because it makes you insecure, thinking about all those guys out there who are gonna see my picture and lust after me.'

'That's not true,' said Patrick, stung because he knew it was.

'You'd prefer I was cooped up with a bunch of nerdy medical students at Oxford. That'd make you feel *much* better, wouldn't it?'

She spat the words out with such vitriol it scared him. How did they ever get into all this?

'You don't care about me, about what I want,' continued Siena, blinded with rage. 'You don't care if I'm happy.' In her haste, she had done up her buttons wrongly, and her irate, contorted little face looked comically incongruous above her lopsided pyjama top. 'You're as bad as my fucking father. Well, let me tell you something: I *am* going to make it as an actress. And when I do it won't be on the back of my name – my *father's* goddam name. It will be because I've made it on my own. Modelling's just the start.'

'Siena,' said Patrick wearily, 'I am nothing like your father.' Even in those ridiculous pyjamas, screaming at him like a banshee, she still looked so sexy it hurt. 'All I meant was that you shouldn't cut off your nose to spite your face,' he said, in a last-ditch effort to calm her down. 'There's no point in missing out on Oxford just for the sake of annoying your dad. I just . . . Look, I just find it hard to believe that modelling is what you really want to do, that's all.' He patted the mattress beside him. 'Come on, come back to bed.'

'Well, it *is* what I want to do,' she barked defensively. 'For now anyway. Until I can get back to Hollywood, until my acting comes together. And as far as I'm concerned I'm not 'missing out' on anything. I hate Oxford. I hate England. If you knew anything about me at all you'd know I've been desperate to get out of this shitty, grey, raining depressing hellhole for the last seven years. Well, modelling's a way out, something that even my father can't control, and I'm taking it. So if that makes you uncomfortable then tough fucking tits!'

With a final defiant flick of her curls and a foundation-shaking slam of the door, she stomped back down the stairs to her own room.

Oh fuck, that was all she needed. Mr Cash, looking like an older Sherlock Holmes in a dark green dressing gown and reading glasses, emerged from the bathroom just as Siena stepped on to the landing.

'Ah, Siena. Just saying goodnight to Pat, were you?' he asked her with a good-natured, conspiratorial wink.

He was such a lovely man, she thought, and so was his son. She didn't know why she was always such a bitch to him.

'Yes, I was, er . . .' She floundered. 'We were just talking about the future actually.' She gestured upstairs. 'You know, career plans. Moving on.'

Jeremy Cash looked at her thoughtfully. He could quite see why his son was crazy about her, but it was as plain as the nose on his face that a girl like Siena was not about to settle down with Patrick. The lad was headed for heartbreak, and Jeremy felt for him, but even so he couldn't quite bring himself to dislike his daughter's feisty best friend. Bending forward, he gave her a paternal kiss on the cheek.

'Goodnight, my dear,' he said.

'Goodnight, Mr C.' Siena beamed back at him.

'Oh, and Siena?' he called after her as he opened the door to his own room. 'Next time you and Patrick discuss your future, you might want to take a trifle longer buttoning up your pyjamas afterwards.'

Siena glanced down in horror at her top and blushed like an overripe tomato.

'Goodnight, young lady,' said Jeremy.

Chapter Seventeen

'I'm sorry, guys, that was my fault,' said Hunter. 'Can we go again?'

The two cameramen rolled their eyes as they prepared for a fourth take, but neither of them could get really mad. It was so unlike Hunter to forget his lines, and he was such a down-to-earth, decent guy, all the crew liked and respected him. They were shooting the second season of *Counsellor* on the back lot at Universal. Despite the show's unexpected worldwide success, Hunter had failed to become the spoilt 'talent' that most young actors transform into the moment they get their big break. So far, there'd been no demands for a massive pay hike, no celebrity tantrums and no ego overload from the scores of hot-looking women that hung around the studio gates night after night, hoping to catch a glimpse of him. To the best of anyone's knowledge, he hadn't ever laid a groupie, and most of his evenings were spent at home, alone, poring over his script. Hell, he even bought the sound guys chocolate muffins from the Coffee Bean most mornings on his way into work. Hunter was the real deal, and the whole set adored him.

'I don't know what's wrong with me today,' he apologised, running his hand through his blue-black hair in frustration. 'I thought I nailed this scene last night, but my mind keeps going blank.'

'Hey, c'mon, forget about it,' said Lanie Armstrong, his stunning blonde co-star, putting a comforting arm around his waist. Like the rest of the cast, Lanie had a thumping crush on her leading man. 'We all have our off days. Why don't you take five and we'll go again.'

Hunter sank down dejectedly into a white canvas chair, and flipped through the day's script for the umpteenth time. Maybe he'd be able to concentrate if it weren't so damn hot. As Mike Palumbo, hot-shot attorney, he spent most of his day wearing a heavy, dark grey wool suit, and sweltering under the punishing glare of the studio lights. Sometimes he would sweat his way through three white Armani shirts in a single morning's shooting. His only respite were the bedroom scenes with Lanie when, to the delight of teenage girls the world over, he got to wander around in only a revealing pair of

Calvin Klein boxer shorts. But that just made him equally hot and bothered with embarrassment.

He tried to concentrate as the familiar lines blurred before his eyes. Man, he wished he didn't find reading and memorising so difficult. Ever since he was a little boy he'd been worse than useless at school work, but it sure wasn't for want of trying. He remembered how Pete used to make fun of him, back when their old man was still alive, looming over him whenever he was trying to revise for a test, constantly telling him what a moron he was.

No, not a moron, a cretin. That was what Pete used to call him, a cretin. Stupid fucking pretentious English word.

In recent weeks, Hunter had been forced to spend a lot of time thinking about his older brother. His inability to concentrate this morning had more than a little to do with Pete's unwelcome reappearance in his life.

If *Counsellor's* overwhelming success had come as a surprise to its young star, Hunter's meteoric rise to prominence had been like a bullet in the heart for Pete.

Since Duke's heart attack, Pete's own career as a producer had blossomed. As the chief executive of McMahon Pictures Worldwide, he was now considered to be among the most influential deal-makers in Hollywood. Regularly fêted in the industry press, and a member of *Forbes'* West Coast rich list, he had finally been able to move out of Duke's long shadow and emerge into the sunlight of his own talent. He might not have had his father's looks, but Pete far outshone the old man when it came to business acumen. With a string of good investments in real estate and technology, as well as three of the four most profitable movies of the nineties to his name, Pete had increased the family fortune almost fivefold in the seven years since Duke had died.

Until recently, he had rarely given Hunter or his mother a second thought. Immediately after the reading of the will, Minnie had banished the pair of them to a decrepit low-rent apartment in Los Feliz, and Pete had been ruthless in severing all contact between Siena and Hunter.

He had lied to his daughter about Hunter's requesting no more contact. In fact, his half-brother had written hundreds of letters, begging to be allowed to see Siena. At first Pete had just ignored them, but when they didn't stop coming he'd been forced to write to Caroline, threatening to invoke some imaginary clause in Duke's trust and rescind Hunter's inheritance altogether if he didn't stop harassing the family. Knowing that losing the money would mean nothing to Hunter in comparison to losing Siena, Caroline had told him that his letters were upsetting Siena, and that the child psychologist had said they were preventing her from moving on and settling into her new life.

Heartbroken, and with enormous reluctance, Hunter had agreed to let her go.

The last Pete had heard of either of them was a year ago, when Hunter turned twenty-one and came into possession of his relatively meagre trust. Under Minnie's well-intentioned but inept stewardship – for all her hatred of Caroline, Minnie was not callous enough to deliberately squander Hunter's wealth – much of the original capital Duke had left the boy had been whittled away; but the remainder had been enough for him to move out of Los Feliz and buy a little beach house in Santa Monica.

Caroline, Pete had heard on the grapevine, had long since returned to England, leaving her son to fend for himself. No doubt she was worming her way into somebody else's family and fortune back in Blighty – *plus ça change* – but Pete didn't care. As far as he was concerned, Caroline and Hunter had been erased from his life, and that was all that mattered.

Until *Counsellor*.

Pete could still remember the sickening lurch he'd felt in his stomach the first time he saw his brother's impossibly handsome face on the screen. As a grown man, Hunter looked painfully like Duke, except that in his dark business suit, with his proud, solid jaw and steady blue-eyed gaze, he radiated an integrity that the old man, for all his charisma, had never had.

Before Pete could catch his breath, it seemed, the world's press were beating a path to Hunter's door, all clamouring for pictures and interviews with television's new wunderkind. If he had to read one more motherfucking journalist going on about how 'sexy, but refreshingly down to earth' his brother was, he was going to fucking implode.

As a TV actor, and of the low-brow variety at that, there was in fact no reason why Hunter's path should have crossed his in any way. Pete moved in a very different league, and could certainly have afforded to be gracious about the kid's fifteen minutes of fame. But just seeing his brother again, looking so happy and handsome and grateful, had reignited all his latent resentment and hatred.

He wanted that boy to suffer, like he and Laurie and Minnie had suffered. And he was determined to do everything in his power to derail his newfound success.

Leaving the script under his chair, Hunter got up and wandered over to the water cooler. Filling a plastic cup with ice-cold water, he gulped it down, hoping to clear his addled brain, but the liquid was so freezing it made his teeth ache. He put his hand to his jaw and winced.

'You OK?'

Hugh Orchard, the show's chief producer, had wandered up behind him. Dressed in his trademark khaki knee-length pants and blue Harvard Business School sweatshirt, his newly wetted hair immaculately parted at the side, Hugh looked more like a Connecticut investment banker on a family picnic than the obsessive, workaholic and famously homosexual king of network television that he actually was.

Orchard had an awesome drive – at fifty-six his ambition was still white hot – and most of the great and the good of the TV world were more than a little afraid of him. Hunter had always liked him, though. As long as you kept your head down and worked hard, he had always found him to be a fair and reasonable boss.

'Oh yeah, I'm fine,' he said, flashing a disarmingly white-toothed smile at Hugh. 'Water's too cold, that's all.'

Hugh suppressed a giant wave of arousal and tried manfully to tear his eyes away from that beautiful body and look Hunter in the eye. He had been with his partner Ryan for almost twelve years now, but it wasn't a crime to indulge in a little wishful thinking every now and then. Hunter tested his professionalism to the limits.

'I saw you were having some trouble with the scene back there,' he said, reaching for a cup himself. 'Anything on your mind?'

Hunter blushed. He looked so adorable, Hugh could have eaten him alive.

'Not really.' He shook his head and looked down at his well-polished lawyer's shoes. 'Well, you know, just this situation with my brother.'

'I thought I told you not to worry about that, Hunter,' said Hugh, flicking the plastic lever on the water barrel and filling his glass. 'I'm not about to give in to blackmail from Pete McMahon, and neither is NBC. He can go jump in a lake as far as I'm concerned. *I* pick the cast of my shows. *I* decide who stays and who goes. Got it?'

Hunter nodded miserably. It was an open secret on the set that Pete had threatened to withdraw McMahon Pictures' funding for two of Hugh Orchard's big-budget miniseries, both of which were due to debut on NBC the following spring, unless Hunter was replaced as *Counsellor*'s male lead. He was very grateful to Hugh for sticking by him, but also embarrassed to have been the cause of so much aggravation in the first place. Thanks to Pete, he was now quite possibly going to be responsible for hundreds of thousands of dollars' worth of lost revenue and production delays.

'I'm just so sorry for all of this, you know?' he mumbled, nervously crushing his empty cup in his hand and not quite meeting his boss's eye. 'You must be sick to death of me and my dysfunctional family.'

Hugh laughed, and clapped both hands on to Hunter's shoulders. 'Dysfunctional? The McMahons? Now that's what I call an understatement. Are you kidding me? You guys are fucking psychotic!'

Hunter's perfect features fractured into a grin. 'Yeah, well,' he conceded, eyes still glued to the ground, 'I guess we have our moments.'

'I'm serious, man,' continued Hugh, who suddenly looked it. 'Look at me.' Reluctantly, Hunter looked up. 'Don't let this shit with Peter throw you. He's not normal, OK? He's psycho, totally whacked. You just get out there, learn those lines, and do what you do best, all right?'

'Yes, sir!' said Hunter, standing to attention and giving Hugh a mock salute before heading back towards the set. Already he felt his spirits lifting a little. Hugh was right. He owed it to everyone to get past this thing with Pete, and do the job he was paid to do.

'Don't you "yes, sir" me, Hunter McMahon!' Hugh yelled after him, unable to resist flirting just a little bit with the heavenly straight boy. 'I don't care if you are *People* magazine's sexiest man of the year. You're not too old for me to put you over my knee, you hear me?'

At home up in the Hollywood hills, Claire McMahon emptied the foul-smelling contents of a tin of dog food into a plastic bowl and set it down on the polished maple of the kitchen floor.

'Zulu!' she called. 'Here, boy!'

Within nanoseconds an excitable white ball of fluff had come hurtling into the room, its eyes almost completely invisible beneath its masses of unkempt fur, and hurled itself head first into the bowl, making appreciative snuffling noises.

Claire laughed. She adored the little bichon frise, whom she'd christened Zulu for a joke because he was just so impossibly fluffy and white. Pete always complained that the dog looked like a pom-pom that had accidentally got plugged into the mains. He pretended not to like him, but Claire had often spied him late at night in his study, surreptitiously feeding the dog smoky bacon crisps.

Pouring herself a glass of Perrier, she wandered out on to the deck by the pool. It was early evening, her favourite time of the day. She loved to sit outside in the warm tranquillity of the fading light, drinking in the spectacular view of the canyon below.

She and Pete had bought the house in Siena's second year at St Xavier's. Claire had had quite a fight on her hands with Minnie at the time, about moving out of Hancock Park, but things had worked out well for everybody in the end.

After so many years of stress and misery with Duke, Minnie discovered to her surprise that she really rather enjoyed living alone. She found it quite therapeutic, ripping out all Duke's revolting cream shag-pile carpeting and slowly, painstakingly redecorating every room to her own impeccable taste. For the first time in her life, she was enjoying some economic, as well as emotional, freedom, and it was wonderful to watch her blossoming as she gradually rediscovered her confidence and love of life. By the time Laurie upped sticks and moved to Atlanta two years later for a job at the university, Minnie was actually rather relieved to have got rid of her.

The move had been wonderful for Claire too. Both she and Pete had fallen in love with their new, sprawling, Nantucket craftsman-style home, with its light, its privacy and its incredible views. They could have afforded something far grander, of course, with all the ludicrous amounts of money Pete was making these days, but neither of them wanted to be rattling around on some huge estate – been there, done that.

Only Siena had never really felt at home in the new house, despite Claire's best efforts to create a beautiful bedroom and bathroom for her, decorated in her favourite indigo blue.

'This isn't home. It'll never be home,' she'd announced flatly, when Claire had excitedly shown it to her at the start of the summer holidays.

'But, darling,' she said, crestfallen. 'You've got all your favourite things in here from Hancock Park. Look, I even saved all your old Mel Gibson posters.'

'I've gone off him,' said Siena harshly, looking at the walls and her mother's efforts to please her with withering disdain. 'Ages ago. You'd know that if you hadn't packed me off to England like an unwanted parcel. And where's my picture of Grandpa, the cowboy one?' She continued accusingly. 'I suppose Dad got rid of it, did he?'

The bitterness in her voice stabbed at Claire's heart like a razor. She knew Siena hated St Xavier's; that her resentment at being sent away to school had only made her *more* spoilt and *more* wilful than ever and pushed her even farther away from both her parents than she had been when Duke was alive. But Pete point blank refused to consider bringing her home.

'It's emotional blackmail,' he insisted, whenever Claire brought it up. 'She thinks that by making our lives a misery, she can get her own way. And we all know who taught her *that*, don't we?'

With Pete, sooner or later, everything came back to Duke.

Siena's hostility and bad behaviour were compounded, Claire felt, by the enforced separation from Hunter. Although she didn't dare say so to Pete, she knew that that boy had never been anything other than a good influence on Siena. Without him, and alienated from both herself and Pete, there was nothing to stop her from running completely wild.

This evening, as she sipped her fizzy water and watched the sun begin its slow descent into the horizon, Claire prayed that Siena would be home soon. Despite all the battles and the tantrums, she missed her daughter terribly.

But it wasn't just that.

Pete was already getting very wound up about her extended stay in England since she'd finished her A-levels in June. He didn't approve at all of his daughter's foray into modelling and had made it patently clear to Siena that he wanted her back at home and studying for Oxford as soon as possible. Despite having no academic background himself – Claire was the only true scholar in the family – he had always expected Siena to excel at school. Her place at Oxford meant the world to him. Subconsciously perhaps, Claire thought, he wanted his daughter to grow up in a world as far removed from Hollywood and Duke's hopes for her as possible.

After all the shenanigans with Hunter and this stupid vendetta with NBC, his temper was already on a knife edge at the moment. Claire prayed that, for once, Siena would do what she was told and not push her father over the edge completely.

Ensconced in the warm comfort of her trailer, in a deserted East London car park, Siena was in a truly foul temper. Sighing and pouting like a five-year-old while she was simultaneously being made up and having her hair pulled, tweaked and pinned into position by an exhausted hairdresser for the Ailsa Moran shoot, she reached down for her cigarette and took in a long-drawn-out lungful of nicotine. Why the fuck couldn't they get a move on?

She'd finally broken things off with Patrick that morning, something she'd been meaning to do for ages, but instead of the relief she'd expected to feel she was overwhelmingly depressed. His words about modelling – that she was just a jumped-up clothes horse, that she ought to take up her place at Keble – kept ringing in her ears like an irksome ghost of Christmas past.

This Moran campaign was a big break for her and she'd been looking forward to it for ages. But now that she was actually here, all the lustre of it seemed to have gone. Whose bloody idea was it to shoot in an 'urban wasteland' setting? Anything less glamorous or fun than mooching about in a cold car park that smelt of tramps' wee would be hard to imagine.

And just to top things off, she'd woken up this morning with a revolting pimple on her chin, and enough PMT to classify her as a one-woman biological weapon.

'Siena, please, keep your head still,' pleaded the exasperated hairdresser through a mouthful of kirby-grips. 'I can't do this if you keep leaning forward.'

'Oh, for fuck's sake,' snapped Siena. She knew she was being a bitch, and it wasn't the hairdresser's fault that she'd broken up with Pat, but she had to take it out on someone. 'I'm just grabbing a magazine. Have you any idea how boring it is, sitting here for hours on end with you lot pulling and prodding at me like a fucking prize cow?'

Prize cow is right, thought the make-up artist, but she doggedly continued brushing Siena's brow with highlighter.

'Don't exaggerate,' said the hairdresser, who was not in the mood to pander to some two-bit model's mood swings. 'You've been in this chair for forty minutes. It's the *rest* of us who have been here for hours.'

Siena mumbled something incoherent and pointedly immersed herself in her magazine.

'Besides, if you want to get out of here, the best thing you can do is sit still. Two more minutes, OK? Just don't move.' She fixed two more pins into the precarious-looking mountain of Medusa-esque curls piled on Siena's head, and covered the elaborate structure with an asphyxiating shower of hairspray.

'Isn't that your brother?' asked the make-up artist in an attempt to change the subject.

Hunter's picture was on the back of Siena's magazine, advertising the new series of *Counsellor*, with a semi-naked Lanie Armstrong wrapped seductively around him.

Siena didn't know what people saw in Lanie. She looked like every other Californian blonde bimbo to her.

'No.' She looked at the hapless woman as if she'd crawled out from under some particularly unpleasant rock. 'He's my uncle. My half-uncle, actually. And words can't describe how fucking bored I am with seeing his inane face or hearing about that bloody awful programme.'

The agony of missing Hunter, combined with the shame and embarrassment of having to admit that she no longer really knew him, or anything about his exciting new life, made her lash out at anyone foolish enough to mention his name. Why couldn't people just shut up about him and leave her alone?

'*Counsellor*? I love it. Never miss an episode.' The hairdresser couldn't resist.

'Me neither,' chimed in the make-up girl, who had also had enough of Siena for one day. 'I think he's got a lovely face, anyway.' She took a clean sponge from her cavernous blue bag and began removing the excess blusher from Siena's cheeks. 'You look like him, don't you?' she went on absently. 'I bet people tell you that all the time.'

'Are you blind?' said Siena rudely, stubbing out her cigarette with such force that the butt snapped. 'He's so dark skinned he practically looks Arab. For all I know he is Arab. His mother was such a slut, Grandpa probably wasn't his father anyway. I'm so pale I'm see-through.'

She looked critically at her complexion in the mirror on the back wall, straining to examine the now invisible spot on her chin.

There was a quick-fire rapping on the trailer door and Marsha, Siena's gushingly enthusiastic agent, came bursting in on the happy trio, waving a piece of paper excitedly. Marsha, who barely scraped the five foot mark even in heels, and was renowned for her questionable business ethics, was universally referred to in the London fashion community as the poison dwarf.

'Darling!' she squealed, arms flapping and face flushed like a munchkin on speed. 'It's confirmed. Confirmed!'

'What is?' asked Siena. 'What on earth are you talking about?'

'What am I talking about?' Marsha was hopping up and down so manically the make-up artist wondered whether she might be about to pee her pants. 'Paris, of course! The October show, McQueen, he loved you. He's confirmed. Paris!'

'Oh,' said Siena weakly, and managed a small smile, her first of the day. 'Good. That's good news.'

'Good news?' shrieked Marsha. '*Good news*? Child, have you gone mad? It's great news. It's fabulous. Do you know how many girls would sell their soul to be doing that show? I'm talking about girls who've been around for years. Have you any idea what it means for a newcomer like you to go from Ailsa Moran to Alexander McQueen overnight?'

Siena did have a pretty shrewd idea.

This was what she'd wanted, what she'd dreamed of and prayed for day and night for the last three months. To be going to the Paris shows at all was a big deal for someone as new to the business as she was. But to be fronting Alexander McQueen's collection? It was unbelievable. A fantasy.

But Paris also meant problems. Marsha did not know that her father had expressly forbidden her to pursue her modelling other than as an occasional hobby. Pete had already refused point blank to sanction her proposed trip to France when she'd floated the idea to him a couple of weeks ago. She would already be three weeks into her first term at Oxford when Paris Fashion Week started, and he expected her to be a hundred and ten per cent focused on her studies by then. As far as Pete was concerned the matter was already closed. But that was before McQueen.

Her hair and make-up finally finished, Siena got up carefully from the chair and admired her reflection in the mirror. The floating, pale green chiffon, Grecian-style dress clung loosely to the voluptuous curves of her body as if held in place by static electricity. One smooth, alabaster-white shoulder rose from the folds of material across her breasts, curving up into her long, fragile neck and finally to the creamy softness of her complexion, subtly heightened by the faint rose glow of her perfectly made-up cheeks. Two gleaming tendrils of jet-black hair tumbled across her face, having struggled free of the immaculate, pearl-and-crystal-studded triumph of coiffure that crowned her head, held in place by a hundred invisible pins.

Siena smiled at the vision she'd been transformed into, suddenly empowered and alive. Just the thought of the cameras waiting outside excited her, and her eyes flashed with an almost sexual rush that would translate into dynamite pictures.

Pete or no Pete, Siena had made her decision. She was not going to Oxford. She was going to be at that McQueen show come hell or high water.

Chapter Eighteen

Curled up on the couch in his Santa Monica beach house, Hunter was deeply engrossed in his script.

'Are you ever going to get your nose out of that bloody thing and get me a whisky? You're not being a terribly good host, you know.'

Max De Seville, his oldest and closest friend, had just flown in from England for a whirlwind week of meetings in Hollywood. Max had sat his last final at Cambridge two weeks ago, and was trying to get his foot on the ladder at one of the studios where, one day, he dreamed of becoming a director.

At twenty-three, Max still looked faintly boyish, with his unruly mop of blond hair and a lingering smattering of childhood freckles across his wide, rugby-broken nose. His body, however, was definitely all man. Six foot four in his socks, and with shoulders like Ben Hur, he strode around Hunter's living room like a clumsy colossus, trying to find a piece of furniture large and solid enough to sit down on.

Max had been there for Hunter in the terrible first few years after Duke died. He had seen him pining hopelessly for Siena, while trying to shore up an emotionally unstable Caroline as she ricocheted from one dead-end job to the next. As his family crumbled around him, Max's friendship soon became one of the only constants in Hunter's life.

Caroline's affair with Charles Murray had fizzled out shortly after their move to Los Feliz, and it was quite plain to the young Max at the time that his friend's once beautiful mother was lonely. He remembered being round at the apartment when Charlie had come to pick up the last of his things, watching with Hunter as his mother tried hard to be brave.

'Look, really, it's OK. We're fine,' Caroline insisted, helping her ex-lover carry a pile of office shirts out to his car. 'You don't owe us anything. You never asked for any of this.'

Charlie threw the shirts on to the back seat of his Porsche and turned to face her. She looked exhausted, worn down by the long, fruitless legal battle with the McMahons and by trying to cope with raising Hunter alone in such hugely straitened circumstances. In baggy jeans and an old sweatshirt, her face bare of make-up, she was still a beautiful woman, all lips and cheekbones. But there was a sadness bordering on despair in her eyes now which had replaced the mischievous sparkle he remembered from the early, crazy days of their affair.

The fact was Charlie simply wasn't ready for marriage and a ready-made family. It would never have worked, and they both knew it. But that didn't stop him caring about her or feeling terrible watching her struggling to keep afloat.

'It's not about owing you anything, Caro,' he said. 'We're friends, aren't we? I want to help.'

Pulling out a cheque from his inside jacket pocket he handed it to her, over-ruling her protests with a firm wave of his hand.

'Take it,' he said. 'I know you need it and it's the least I can do. I want to be there for you and Hunter financially, at least until you get back on your feet. Please.'

Reluctantly, she smiled and pocketed the cheque. He was right, she did need it. Pride, never her strongest suit where money was concerned anyway, had now become a luxury she could not afford. Reaching up on tiptoes, she put her arms around his neck and gave him a kiss on the cheek. She wasn't in love with him any more. In all honesty she probably never had been. But it was still sad, watching him go.

He picked her up in a big bear hug, then set her back down on the pavement as he got into the car. The brilliant LA sunshine and the bright blue sky provided an incongruously cheery backdrop to such a painful parting. Rain, or at least a grey horizon, would have been more appropriate.

'You can always call me, you know that, right?'

Caroline nodded. 'Sure. And vice versa. Take care of yourself, Charlie.'

'You too, babe. You too.'

Max had watched with Hunter from his bedroom window as Charlie pulled away, and seen Caroline wait until the car was out of sight before putting her head in her hands and crying. Until that moment he had always thought of Hunter's mom as hard as nails. Seeing her in tears seemed so wrong somehow, he almost felt guilty having witnessed it. Not that she didn't deserve to suffer, after all the suffering she had put other people through in her selfishness, especially her wholly innocent son. But despite his vehement dislike of her, the scene had stirred some real compassion in Max and the memory of it had stayed with him to this day.

The real tragedy was that, in her own despair, Caroline had been unable to reach out to Hunter. When she finally decided to move back to England, he had been relieved more than anything, and Max had watched him diligently put himself through school and acting classes alone, managing the household budget and bills as if he'd been doing it for years. Which, Max suspected on reflection, he probably had.

Not that Max's own family were exactly the Brady Bunch. In fact, he suspected that Caroline might once have had an affair with his father; but as both his parents seemed to bed-hop among their friends with alarming regularity, it didn't really bother him. At least his parents, unlike Hunter's, still had money. And when the going got really rough, he knew he could always turn to Henry.

Henry was Max's beloved elder brother, his mother's son from her first marriage, who, at ten years older than Max was more of a father to him than his own father had ever been. When he'd decided to apply for Cambridge, it had been Henry who'd driven him to his interview at Trinity, Henry who put up with his unbearable angst and snappiness as he waited for his results, and Henry and his wife Muffy who had taken him out to celebrate when, by some miracle, he got in. Last year, when Max had announced that he wanted to become a film director, Henry had been right behind him, loving, supporting and encouraging him as always. Poor old Hunter had never had anyone in his corner like that. Everything he'd done, he'd done alone.

Hunter put down the script with a sigh and got up to go to the drinks cabinet.

'You're all the same, you goddam directors.' He grinned. 'You think the whole world is at your beck and call.' Max flopped down in Hunter's vacated place on the couch, his long jeans-covered legs sprawled along its full length. He picked up Hunter's script and began to read in a hammed-up falsetto: 'Oh, Mike, Mike! You're so noble and brave, Mike! The way you stood up to that evil conglomerate in court today was just incredible. I'm *hot* for you, Mike!'

'Give that here!' said Hunter, snatching it back from him with one hand and passing him a huge glass of Glenfiddich with the other. 'It does not say that, jerk-off.'

'Practically,' said Max, sipping the warm amber liquid and sighing with contentment.

'Look, I never said it was Shakespeare, OK?' said Hunter, sitting down without complaint on the polished maple floor, his couch having been usurped. 'But it pays the bills. And it's fun, it really is.' His tawny face lit up, cobalt-blue eyes sparkling, and Max saw for the thousandth time exactly why the world's women were all madly in love with him. It was odd that, despite his gorgeous looks, Hunter was the steady, stable one while he, Max, already had a bit of a reputation as a womaniser, or at least as a serial flirt.

'I just wish this thing with Pete would blow over, you know?' Hunter said anxiously. 'Hugh's being great about it, but I can tell he's pissed, and I can't say I blame him.'

Max sat up and took a bigger slug of his drink before passing the glass to Hunter, who shook his head. He was determined to nail this scene tonight, and that meant it was Perrier only.

'If he's pissed, it's with Pete, not you,' Max said firmly. 'Hugh knows how hard you work and how great you've been for the show. Hell, you *are* the show. It's you that gets all the press, you that all those girls are tuning in to see, God help them.'

'Well, I don't know about that,' mumbled Hunter, blushing. Amazing how such a gorgeous, lusted-after guy could have remained so cripplingly shy. 'Anyway, how long are you staying?'

'A week,' said Max.

Hunter rolled his eyes to heaven. 'As long as that?' he said, grinning. The fact was he loved having Max around and they both knew it. 'Seriously, though, what are your plans, long term? I assume you're gonna be spending more time out here, looking for a directing gig?'

Max nodded. 'Yeah, eventually. I'm going back to England first to sort a few things out, and then I guess I'll have to start looking for a place to live.'

'What are you talking about?' Hunter sounded genuinely surprised. 'You can come and live here, with me.'

Max looked doubtful.

'Well, why not?' said Hunter. He waved his arm in the general direction of his three guest bedrooms. 'There's plenty of space.'

'I know,' said Max, draining his whisky and getting up in search of a refill. 'It's not that. The fact is I can't afford it, mate. All I have in the world is a trust from my grandfather so tiny it would barely buy me a deposit on a Mars bar. And last I heard, junior assistant directors aren't exactly the most highly paid blokes in this town.'

'Oh, come on,' said Hunter, laughing with the same warm, infectious laugh that Max remembered growing up with, a laugh that seemed to encapsulate his friendly, open nature. 'Do you think I care? I don't want your rent, I want your company.'

Max still looked doubtful. It was an incredibly generous offer, and he didn't doubt that sharing a house with Hunter would be a blast. But he didn't like the idea of not paying his own way.

'Please,' said Hunter, sensing his hesitation. 'You'd really be doing me a favour. What if some deranged fan tried to break in and attack me one night? You could be my bodyguard.'

Max laughed. 'Yeah, right. Most of your deranged fans are about fourteen and wear miniskirts and too much lipstick.' But he could tell that Hunter really did want him to agree to stay. And the truth was, he *could* do with some help financially, at least for the first few months.

'Well, OK,' he said eventually. 'But only on condition that we keep a track of how much back rent I owe you. And as soon as I'm earning enough to break even, I'll pay you back, every penny.'

'Deal!' said Hunter, delighted.

He hadn't quite realised, until that moment, just how lonely he'd been rattling around the beach house on his own. Living with Max was going to be fantastic. He couldn't wait.

Chapter Nineteen

Siena sipped from her ice-cold flute of champagne, and gazed out of the window contentedly at the carpet of clouds below her. It was October, and she was flying first class to Paris with Marsha, who was supposed to be acting as her chaperone as well as her agent, but was in fact already as drunk as a duchess and snoring loudly in the seat beside her.

Despite being the daughter of one of the richest and most powerful men in Hollywood, Siena was not used to first-class travel. Pete thought the expense wasteful, especially on a short hop like London to Paris. Economy flights were just another part of his on going crusade to prevent Siena from becoming a spoilt monster like Duke, a battle that, so far at least, he appeared to be losing.

'Excuse me.' Siena signalled for the third time in as many minutes to the heroically polite young stewardess. 'I'd like some more champagne, please.'

'Certainly, madam.' The girl smiled, hoping that the forty remaining minutes of the flight would not be long enough for Siena to deteriorate into a Marsha-like state of drunken stupor. She had better things to do than carry some comatose model into the terminal at Charles de Gaulle because she was too far gone to recognise her own Louis Vuitton luggage.

'And these nuts aren't warm. Do you think you could heat them up for me?'

Siena handed her the little porcelain dish of brazil nuts with a smile that would have melted the heart of any heterosexual male. The stewardess, not being male, took it from her with a brisk, professional "of course, madam" and retreated in search of a microwave and some more Moët.

Siena stretched her voluptuous body in the deliciously wide leather seat and purred with pleasure. This was the life! She didn't know what she was enjoying most: travelling first class to France against her father's express wishes, the thought of tomorrow's McQueen show, or the gratifying wave of attention she was receiving from all the rich and famous men on the plane. Mick Jagger, who was sitting just four rows in front of her, had helped her with her hand baggage, and Mario de Luca, Real Madrid's stunning new blond striker, had even asked her for her number and the name of her hotel in Paris.

And it wasn't as if she were the only model on the plane, either. Every other seat was occupied by some identikit, flat-chested, lissom blonde with huge pouty lips, most of them old hands at the Paris shows, some of them known to Siena from the covers of *Marie Claire* and *Vogue*. But it was Siena, all five foot four of her with her long dark hair, and boobs barely contained by a faded lemon-yellow vest, who was getting the lion's share of male attention. And she loved every minute of it.

She looked at her watch, a battered old junk-shop find that had been a gift from Patrick. They'd be on the ground in just over half an hour. Checking that Marsha was still asleep, she reached into the back pocket of her skin-tight Levis, pulled out a small square of paper and began unfolding it.

She'd received Pete's terse note two days ago, while making the final preparations for her trip. Neither of her parents was a big believer in the telephone, although Claire would occasionally brave her daughter's frosty resentment and make a call, invariably finding her attempts at conversation shut down at every turn by Siena.

Pete had long since given up completely, and preferred to communicate with her via Fed Ex. This suited Siena, who was spared the charade of trying to muster up any pretence of daughterly affection, or the futile effort of attempting to reason with her father, whose mind was invariably already made up by the time he put pen to paper.

This last letter, though, had been even stronger and less forgiving in tone than his usual communications. Siena already knew its contents by heart:

Siena,

What the hell are you playing at? I have just had a long and highly embarrassing conversation with the Master of Keble, who is now under the impression that you have been suffering a severe bout of German measles which left you too ill to attend matriculation in September. I have assured him that you will present yourself at college no later than the end of this week. I hope I don't need to spell out for you how lucky you are that he has accepted this version of events and agreed to hold your place.

This stops here, Siena. Under no circumstances are you to go to Paris, for this show or any other. Your mother and I will not allow you to throw away your education and your future through sheer, blind defiance. I am warning you, in the strongest possible terms, that I will deal with any further disobedience on this issue very severely.

I expect you in Oxford within the next five days.

Dad

Claire had followed this up with an emotional and impassioned letter of her own, pleading with Siena to abandon her modelling and get herself up to college, intimating that her father might even go so far as to cut her out of his will if she continued to defy him.

Siena had ripped up her mother's letter in disgust. Claire's weakness revolted her. She had more grudging respect for her father's brutality – at least she knew where she stood with Pete.

She read the letter again, an unpleasant feeling of nerves bubbling up in her stomach along with the champagne. She knew Pete well enough to realise that he rarely made completely idle threats. But cutting her out of the will was a bit over the top, even by her father's deranged standards. Her mother must be exaggerating as usual.

Besides, what choice did she have but to go to France? If she didn't stand up for herself now, she would end up as some bloody provincial GP in England, lancing farmers' boils for the rest of her life. The very thought of it made her shudder.

No, she had to stand her ground. Once she had done the McQueen show, once she could prove to her father that she could earn her own living as a model, that she could be successful at it, he would have to ease up on this Oxford business. Perhaps she could ask him to let her defer her place for a year? By then, hopefully, her modelling would really have taken off – she might even have made the cross-over into acting – and then even Pete would have to admit that she'd been right all along.

Replacing the note carefully in her jeans pocket, Siena took another fortifying slug of champagne. Mario de Luca looked back over his shoulder and raised his glass to her in lascivious salute, the perfectly defined muscles of his tanned forearm flexing slightly as he lifted his hand.

Paris. De Luca. Alexander fucking McQueen. She couldn't remember the last time she'd felt this happy.

Pete would come around eventually. He had to.

Back in the Hollywood hills, Claire was tearing her hair out. She and Pete had been due at Costello's ten minutes ago, but she was still stuck with her fingers down the basin plug hole, trying to prise free her engagement ring, which had somehow managed to slip off her finger as she washed her hands, and was now jammed tightly between two strips of stainless steel.

'Let's just go,' said Pete impatiently. 'It'll still be there when we get back, and we're late enough as it is.'

For the last ten minutes he'd been hovering in the bathroom doorway, hopping from foot to foot like a three-year-old with a weak bladder, which wasn't making Claire's task any easier.

'But what if it's not there, honey?' she pleaded, not looking up from the glinting flash of ruby guiding her fingers. 'If it gets dislodged and falls down that drain, I may never get it back.'

'It's just a ring,' said Pete irritably. 'I'll buy you another one.'

A momentary flash of pain registered on Claire's face. 'It's my engagement ring, Pete,' she said with quiet dignity. 'It can't be replaced.'

Even now, after almost twenty-five years of marriage, she still felt wounded by her husband's frequent insensitivity towards her. As a young wife, she had laid the blame for Pete's bad temper and his mean streak squarely at the door of his father. It was Duke who had made him bitter and angry. Duke who was to blame.

But the real tragedy in their marriage had occurred after the old tyrant had died. Claire remembered how pathetically high her hopes had been that, with Duke gone, Pete might finally relax, might finally become the man she knew he was capable of being.

How wrong she was.

In some ways, of course, he *had* changed. Professionally, his confidence had soared from the moment they lowered the old man into the ground. Success had followed success, and Pete was worth infinitely more now than his father had ever been. But somehow, it was never enough for him. Instead of giving him a sense of self-worth, the money had become a sort of obsession. Some deep but nameless fear drove him ever harder to make more, more, more. Working fourteen-hour days and most weekends, his stress levels seemed to rise rather than fall the more successful he became. And eventually Claire felt cut out completely.

Perhaps things would have been different if Siena had stayed at home? Perhaps between them, Claire sometimes thought, she and Siena could have loved him enough to make him stop, to make him realise that he really had nothing to prove, that they loved him for himself alone.

But Pete had insisted, with the full force of his will, that Siena be sent to England. Even worse, in his blind hatred of a father he was no longer able to hurt, he had separated two innocent children, banishing poor, blameless Hunter from their lives for ever. And Claire had been too weak, too stupidly weak and afraid, to stop him.

How many times had she cursed herself for that decision? So huge a sacrifice, and what had it achieved? The gulf between father and daughter was now wider than ever. Sometimes Claire suspected that Siena actually hated her *more* than she did Pete, for letting it happen. And she didn't blame her daughter for that, not for a second.

With one sudden twist, the ring shifted position and Claire pulled it triumphantly to safety.

'Got it!' She smiled, her face flushed with happiness and relief, Pete's hurtful remark for the moment forgotten.

'At last,' he grunted gracelessly. 'Does this mean we can *finally* get going?'

In the car on the way to the restaurant, Pete's temper deteriorated further. He was, as usual, fixated on the problems with Siena.

'I swear to God, I have had it with her attitude. I don't know where she got the idea that finishing her education was optional. *Fucker!*' He roared at a black SUV that had moved into his lane without signalling, leaning on his horn until Claire had to block her ears. 'Modelling!' He laughed derisively, as if the word itself were a joke. 'What kind of a career is that for a girl with her brains?'

'Honey, I agree with you,' said Claire, in the soothing, quiet voice she would subconsciously adopt to try to calm him down. 'Of course she should be doing more with her life than that, and she will do . . .'

'Damn right she will,' he muttered darkly.

'But you know what Siena is like,' she continued, resting a hand on his knee. 'Stubborn as hell, just like her father.'

She smiled hopefully across at him, but Pete kept his eyes glued to the road and didn't smile back. 'All I'm saying is,' she pushed on, 'that maybe if we let her go to France, let her do this McQueen show she's set her heart on . . .'

'No. No way,' said Pete, swerving off the freeway on to the Third Street Promenade exit with unnecessary violence. He had always been a shocking driver, especially when he was angry. 'She is not having her way this time. She is *not* going to Paris. For once in her life, she's going to do what she's told.'

Claire decided to try a different tack.

'You know, she is seventeen, honey,' she remonstrated mildly. 'In a few months she'll legally be an adult. I don't think it's totally unreasonable that she should want some say in her own future, do you?'

'Ha!' Pete laughed aloud. 'You think she's an adult? You really think Siena has the maturity to make these kinds of decisions?'

Claire sighed. He had a point there.

'She's a kid,' he said firmly, slowing down and pulling in to the valet parking bay in front of Costello's. 'And a damn stupid kid at that.'

A sullen-looking Mexican opened the passenger door for Claire, and the unusually chilly night air burst into the warmth of the car, making the downy hairs on her forearms stand on end. Drawing her grey pashmina more tightly around her shoulders, she stepped on to the pavement, while Pete handed a second Mexican his keys and a five-dollar bill.

'If she wants to be treated like an adult,' he said, putting his arm around her and leading her into the bustling warmth of the restaurant, 'then she'll have to start behaving like one. And that means accepting that her actions carry consequences.

'Hey, Santiago!'

He embraced the maître d' warmly, all smiles suddenly.

'You know my wife, Claire?'

'Sí, sí, of course,' proclaimed the fat, silver-haired little man, stooping to kiss her hand. ''Ow could I forget a face so beautiful?'

As Santiago led them to their table – the best in the house – Pete looked back over his shoulder at his wife.

'I really mean it this time, Claire,' he said, in a tone of voice that left her in no doubt that he did. 'If she defies me on this, she'll live to regret it.'

Siena reached across to her bedside table and fumbled for a cigarette, her last. She wondered whether room service would bring her some more, or if she'd have to send Mario out to the tabac in the morning.

Inhaling that uniquely sweet, rich flavour of her Gitane – there was something so romantic, so Audrey Hepburn about French cigarettes, Siena felt – she admired the taut, smooth lines of the footballer's body as he slept beside her.

Mario de Luca! She'd just fucked Mario de Luca. Or, to put it more accurately, she'd just *been* fucked by him. And how! If only the girls at school could see her now.

He looked exhausted, poor darling, with his arms outstretched and mouth open, dead to the world. But then she had put him through his paces rather, insisting on a second and then a third performance before she finally took pity on him and allowed him some sleep before his big match tomorrow. She chuckled quietly to herself at the thought of him stumbling around the pitch, knackered as a carthorse.

Come to think of it, she might not fare much better herself. She hoped she wouldn't look too puffy eyed and bandy legged on that catwalk tomorrow. Right now, she doubted whether she could even stand.

Holding her cigarette in her left hand, with her right she felt beneath the covers for Mario's dick. Even in its semi-soft state it felt gratifyingly large in her palm, and began to twitch and harden automatically at her touch. Mario groaned in his sleep and pulled her naked body towards him.

It felt so nice to lie in his arms, to feel his comforting strength wrapped around her, and smell that smell of man, a mixture of aftershave and sweat. That smell always triggered her childish sense of security and happiness, and brought back memories of being protected, held and loved.

She sighed drowsily. Disengaging herself gently so as not to wake him, she took a last long drag and stubbed out her cigarette, snuggling down beneath the covers for some sleep of her own. It had been a lovely, magical night. She would never forget it.

But she had already decided. She mustn't become too attached.

She wouldn't be seeing Mario again.

Chapter Twenty

At eleven o'clock the next morning, Siena found herself shivering in a draughty corner of a disused railway station, wearing little more than a red silk scarf, a pair of neon-pink see-through panties and thigh-high silver stiletto boots.

Although it was only October, central and northern France were in the grip of a freak cold spell, just when London looked set for an extended Indian summer – much to the delight of the British papers, which had been revelling in 'Boiling Britain/Freezing France' headlines for the past fortnight. Siena thought longingly of her bottle-green ribbed cashmere jumper, a freebie from the Ailsa Moran shoot, and wondered how badly her nipples were showing through the red silk.

The theme of this year's events, as decreed by the mighty Fédération Française de la Couture, was neo-industrialism. While the PRs and journalists argued over exactly what this might mean in theory, in practice it involved the meticulous construction of catwalks in a series of vast warehouses, factories and 'architecturally signifi-cant' railway stations, all of which were of proportions ill suited to being effectively centrally heated. Thus, while the great and the good of the fashion and media worlds huddled bravely beneath their full-length minks, with cold toes swaddled in cashmere socks and last winter's oh-so-chic sheepskin boots, the models spent most of the day on the brink of hypothermia.

The Paris shows were the culmination of a gruelling worldwide circuit of shows – London, New York and Milan – which had begun with the 'fashion weeks' in early February. This was the last and most important opportunity for designers to show their spring collections for the season ahead. Although perhaps not as prestigious as the spring Fashion Week, the Paris autumn shows were nevertheless considered to be one of the most exciting and dynamic events in the couture calendar, with their distinctive celebratory, 'end-of-term' atmosphere. Paris in October was where every designer, model, stylist, photographer and fashion journalist wanted to be, and competition, in all areas, was extremely fierce. The best or most eagerly anticipated shows were always sold out months in advance, and even A-list movie stars had been known to resort to everything from begging to bribery to secure a coveted front-row seat.

Siena, who had never been known to be on time for any appointment in her eighteen years on the planet, had arrived at the Gare St Michel two hours early, and had already consumed four cups of nuclear-powered espresso at the little café across the street before Marsha had shown up.

Sunglasses and a natty brown beret had done little to hide the older woman's raging hangover as she ushered her young charge into the reception area for the McQueen girls. Siena was feeling none too chipper herself after her previous night's exertions, but a happy combination of youth, cold Parisian air and the hot, strong coffee had already put the colour back in her cheeks.

Once Marsha had scuttled off to find the nearest bar, a thin, brusque young woman named Florence, whose rather pinched features were made worse by the fact that her hair was drawn back too tightly into a bun, handed Siena a time sheet. It outlined each of the outfits she would be wearing, how long she would have to change into each one (in seconds rather than minutes), and what her audio cues would be for every entrance and exit. The show itself would not start until four o'clock, but the girls would be practising their poses and changeovers until they were called for hair and make-up at two.

'Do we get any lunch?' asked Siena, looking faintly ridiculous in her knickers-and-boots ensemble.

She had bolted out of the hotel in such a rush this morning there'd been no time for breakfast, and after her marathon shag-fest with Mario she was starting to feel quite ravenous.

'Zere will be food lat-eur. Now you re-urse,' said Florence disdainfully, staring disapprovingly down at Siena's ample bosom heaving beneath the wisp of red silk.

Stupid French bitch, thought Siena. Who did she think she was talking to?

She glanced round despondently at the waif-like creatures surrounding her. She felt like the one fat pupa in a swarm of stick insects and decided that requests for food at these sorts of event were probably few and far between.

Just then her stomach gave an embarrassingly noisy rumble and a rather gawky but friendly-looking girl with long red hair and a big gap between her two front teeth caught her eye. Wandering over towards her, she handed Siena a fat-looking green pill and a glass of champagne.

'Try zees,' she said in a heavy Spanish accent. 'Ees fabulous, it weel keel your appetite. And your nerves.'

'Thanks,' said Siena, sipping the champagne but eyeing the pill warily. 'What is it?'

'Oh, don't worry.' The girl smiled. 'Ees 'erbal. Ees no drugs. Look, see?' She produced a second pill and swallowed it, knocking it back with the remnants of her own champagne. 'Ees fine.'

Siena followed suit, and soon the two of them were perched on two 'neo-industrial' plastic chairs, chain-smoking and chatting away like old friends. The girl's name, it transpired, was Ines Prieto Moreno. This was her third trip to the Paris shows, but her first time at McQueen, and she was amazed to discover that today was to be Siena's catwalk debut.

'At McQueen?' She raised her eyebrows. 'I don't believe eet. Ees incredible. Your first show? I am so jealous! I waited five years for zees.'

Siena shrugged.

'I have been kinda lucky so far, I guess,' she admitted. 'To be honest, I'm a bit mystified as to why I'm here. I assumed he'd have lots of shorter girls, girls with my kinda look, you know? Old fashioned? I figured maybe it was a forties theme or something. But all the girls here are just regular models.'

'Hey, thanks a lot,' said Ines, trying to look offended.

'Oh, I'm sorry,' said Siena, 'that came out wrong. I didn't mean . . .' She looked so flustered, Ines couldn't help but laugh. 'It's just that you're all so tall. And thin. And blonde.'

'I am not blonde,' said Ines reasonably. 'I 'ave red 'air and funny teeth. I'm deeferent. Like you.'

Siena thought it would be hard to find another human being who looked less like her than Ines, but didn't say so.

'Lots of the girls 'ere are unusual,' Ines continued. 'Take Katya. She 'as a beeg nose.'

Siena looked across at the mighty Russian supermodel and giggled.

'I'm sorry, but she does!' insisted Ines. 'And look. Lisa 'as no teets at all, she is like a leetle girl. And Daria . . .' She pointed to an exquisitely beautiful girl with impossibly high cheekbones reading a novel in the far corner of the room. 'She 'ave no hair at all.'

'What do you mean?' Siena laughed, admiring the girl's sleek white-blonde bob. 'Of course she has hair.'

Ines raised one eyebrow knowingly. 'Not after two o'clock she doesn't,' she said.

At ten to four, Siena was feeling so nervous she thought she might be sick. Thank God for Ines's magic pill. If she'd eaten so much as a vol au vent she was certain it would be making an ignominious reappearance the second she stepped out on that catwalk.

The noisy, excited hum of the audience was clearly audible backstage, not surprisingly as only a giant pair of paper-thin steel screens separated the anxious models from the throbbing crowd of fashionistas in the main body of the room.

Siena, who had a total of five outfits to wear during the show, had spent the past hour desperately attempting to master the art of walking sexily in her ludicrously high boots. Nervousness about her own performance had completely eclipsed all other considerations. Having fantasised for weeks about what she would say when she met McQueen himself, in the event she forgot all her pre-prepared razor-sharp repartee and simply nodded like a dazed rabbit when he approached her to wish her luck.

Now, with ten minutes to go before the show, she was pacing up and down in front of a big whiteboard, on which was scrawled in black marker pen:

> I am Sexy. Powerful. A dominatrix BITCH!!
> I am a lioness. A Warrior Queen.
> But always . . .
> FEMININE.
> Enjoy yourselves out there!!!!

Oh God. She felt her stomach give another hideous lurch – not very warrior queen. Tiny beads of sweat were breaking out on her forehead, no doubt already wreaking havoc with the trowelfuls of dominatrix make-up that caked her face: huge arcs of silver eyeshadow swept above sinister, kohl-blackened eyes, and blood-red, gloss-slicked lips. All the girls were made up the same way, but whereas Ines simply looked bizarre, like an unusually leggy circus clown, Siena looked much more disturbing, a debauched, fallen angel. Instinctively she reached up to wipe the sweat from her forehead.

'No!' yelped a voice from behind her. Davide, the chief make-up artist – known as Camp David to the models for obvious reasons – grabbed both her hands and pinned them behind her back. 'Nevair touch ze face. One smudge, and eet ees ruined!' he wailed.

'God, OK, OK,' Siena snapped. 'I won't touch. It's just so fucking hot in here now with these lights, I'm sweating like a Goddam pig.'

'First you complain ees cold. Now you say ees hot. Let me tell you, eef you wipe your face, you weel *look* like a peeg. Don't touch!'

Davide wagged his finger at Siena like a schoolteacher before darting off to spray some more silver shimmer on one of the German girl's arms.

Ines, who looked a lot more comfortable than Siena in silver flip-flops, combat trousers and a floaty green floral top, came bounding towards her like an overexcited puppy. Siena tried to muster a smile. How could she be so calm? Never mind 'I am a lioness'. She felt as if she were about to be fed to the fucking lions.

'Do you know 'oo is out there?' Ines asked breathlessly.

She was now literally jumping up and down with excitement, two long red plaits flapping behind her like tails on a kite.

'Sure,' said Siena, trying to sound calm and in control. 'I know who's out there. The world's press, a bunch of coked-up, plastic-faced movie actors and every buyer from here to Bangkok. And I gotta tell you, the thought of walking down that runway is scaring me shitless.'

'No, no,' said Ines, grabbing Siena's hands in her own. ''Aven't you 'eard?'

'Heard what?' asked Siena impatiently.

'Jamie Silfen! Ees here!' Ines looked like she might be going to explode.

Siena felt her legs start to give way beneath her. 'No,' she muttered, shell-shocked. 'He can't be. Are you sure? He can't be here.' Ignoring Davide's advice, she began pulling at her elaborately curled hair in despair. 'It's my first show,' she wailed. 'I have no fucking idea what I'm doing out there. Oh shit, Jamie Silfen is gonna see me making an ass of myself. Where is he? I didn't see him out there.'

Ines gestured through the tiny crack in the steel partition wall. 'Third row. Glasses. Beeg sheepskin coat.'

Siena scanned the audience. Holy fucking shit. There he was.

Jamie Silfen, one of the biggest, most powerful casting agents in Hollywood, sitting within a hundred feet of her.

In her more hopeful moments, she had imagined that perhaps some of the lesser-known agents might put in an appearance at the McQueen show. But this was unbelievable.

Even her father was in awe of Silfen. For over fifteen years he had had the Midas touch in the business, and his name had become synonymous with box-office success. If Silfen cast your movie, you could expect to see your profits double. As an actor, even an established box-office draw, you respected Jamie Silfen as a man who could make or break careers with a nod of his shiny bald head.

What the hell was he doing at a fashion show in France?

'I wonder why 'ees 'ere?' said Ines, reading Siena's mind. 'You theenk someone is doing a movie about the catwalks, maybe 'ee wants to see for 'imself? I don't theenk 'ee is eenterested in fashion, you know? Just look at 'ees coat. Eet's revolting!'

But Siena had tuned out. Jamie Silfen. Jamie fucking Silfen was out there, and he was going to be watching *her*. Opportunities like this just didn't come around twice and Siena knew it. She had to seize the moment, to make a real impression on him. This could be it. Her chance.

Almost instantly, she found her nervous energy evaporating, replaced by the familiar pumping adrenalin of raw ambition.

She thought of Duke, and a slow smile spread across her face.

'Lena, Anna Maria, Ines, Siena!'

The stage manager was striding towards them, clapping his hands for action.

'Let's go, ladies. You're first up, in . . .' He looked at his watch. '. . . two minutes exactly. I want everyone in their places. Now, please, girls!'

Ines smiled down at her new friend.

'Nervous?' she asked.

'Not at all,' said Siena, grinning from ear to ear. 'I can hardly wait.'

Chapter Twenty-one

Caroline Berkeley wandered into the dining room of her beautiful Cotswold manor house and checked the place settings for the third and final time.

She didn't want either of her brothers or their ghastly wives anywhere near her at tonight's dinner, but every time she put her head round the door, bloody Christopher had moved everything around, trying to sit himself next to the wholesomely pretty Muffy Arkell. The damn cheek!

Caroline had met and married Christopher Wellesley less than a year after her ignominious return to England. Or rather, she'd met him again. Christopher had been one of the many eligible bachelors on the scene in London, back in her youthful heyday, and although they had never slept with one another back then, they had become firm friends, only losing touch when she settled permanently in Los Angeles.

The general rumour had always been that the gauche, awkward heir to one of the grandest estates in Oxfordshire was secretly gay. This, as Caroline was later to learn, wasn't true. He just rather preferred a quiet day's fishing on the Test, or a nice glass of claret, to sex. Oddly, though, this wasn't a problem for her any more. After everything she'd been through with Duke, she found her new husband's sexual reticence, combined with his uncomplicated loyalty and adoration, to be just what the doctor ordered.

The year after Duke's death had been a living hell for Caroline. Stuck in a tiny apartment with a son who, she soon discovered, she really barely knew, she had thought at first that she might go mad. Her relationship with Charlie had quickly unravelled – not that she really blamed him for that. Setting up home with her and Hunter had never been part of his agenda when they began their affair, and he had continued to provide her with some financial support for two years after they split.

She didn't resent Charlie. But for the first time in her life, Caroline found to her horror that she was unable to land herself a wealthy date. Whether it was her age, or the fact that she had been tainted by her long tenure as Duke's mistress, or a combination of the two, she didn't know. But suddenly it seemed none of the real players in Hollywood would touch her with a ten-foot pole.

At forty-six, having never worked a day in her life, she was ill equipped to begin any sort of proper, paying career. She took on occasional work as a party organiser for friends of friends, and did the odd bit of interior design. But other than that, her time was spent at home in the poky Los Feliz apartment, either alone or with Hunter, nursing her disappointment and a growing sense of depression. She soon started drinking heavily.

In the end it was Hunter himself who had persuaded her to move back home to England. Although she knew he was genuinely concerned for her, she also knew that he was finding her drinking and the accompanying mood swings increasingly difficult to live with.

'I haven't been much of a mother to you, have I?' she observed in a rare moment of honesty when he'd first suggested it.

Hunter shrugged. 'You did your best. I know it's been hard for you.'

'But how will you cope here on your own? I mean, what are you going to do for money and things?'

He didn't like to tell her that he was already living almost entirely on his own earnings from after-school jobs – the trust Duke left him paid for his education, clothes and utilities at the apartment but not much else – and that he could 'cope' a whole lot more easily if he didn't have a drunk, despairing mother to worry about all the time.

'I'll be fine,' he said. 'And you can come visit, you know? Or I could go over there? Let's face it, you're miserable here, Mom. At least in England you have friends and family you can rely on for help.'

Caroline wasn't so sure about that. She'd burned her bridges with most of her so-called friends from the old days, and she'd barely spoken to either George or William in the last decade. But she *was* miserable in LA, so miserable it was slowly killing her. England couldn't be any worse.

As it turned out, thanks to Christopher, it was a whole lot better. When they met up again, the bond between them was stronger than ever. He was fifteen years her senior, but still a spring chicken compared to Duke. He had never married, never wanted children, and the estate was already entailed to his nephew.

'I can't leave you anything,' he'd told her bluntly. 'And I've very little ready cash. No flash cars or holidays in Mauritius or any of that lark. But I think I could give you a pretty decent life here.' He gestured vaguely around his exquisite medieval manor house, Great Thatchers, with its formal gardens and rolling parkland undulating far into the distance. 'And I think we'd have a lot of fun together.'

Caroline thought so too.

She wrote to Hunter and told him she was getting married, and that she had given up drinking for good. 'Christopher's been AA for twenty years, so we're going together,' she'd said brightly.

He was pleased to hear her so happy, and took an instant liking to Christopher when he flew over for their quiet wedding at the village church in Batcombe a few months later.

For the first two years of his mother's marriage he had flown over to visit at Christmas, and they'd all got on happily enough. But gradually the natural distance there had always been between mother and son began to reassert itself. Caroline's visits to LA became less and less frequent, and Hunter had neither the money nor the time to keep making the trip to England to see her.

She was pleased when she heard about *Counsellor*, both happy and frankly surprised at his success, although she never watched the show. 'Absolute drivel,' Christopher called it, and Caroline privately agreed. But she had called to tell him she was proud of him, and she was.

It was enough for both of them to know that the other was happy and settled. They were both wise enough to know that, after all these years, it was too late for them ever to be really close.

'Ah, there you are,' said Christopher, hobbling up behind his wife and wrapping his arms around her.

Now seventy, he suffered occasionally from debilitating attacks of gout, a consequence of his earlier hard-drinking days. For the past two weeks he'd been walking with a stick and grumbling at Caroline that he was in far too much pain to take the rubbish out, walk the dogs, or generally contribute to the running of the household in any way.

'Oi!' he said, seeing that she had rearranged the place cards again. 'That's not fair. I want to sit next to that lovely Arkell woman, not your dreadful sister-in-law.'

'Well, you can't,' said Caroline firmly. 'I want her to sit next to Gary Ellis. Besides . . .' She turned around and kissed him affectionately on the top of his shiny bald head. 'I thought you only had eyes for me?'

'I do, my darling, I do.' He grinned at her. In her blue, stripy Thomas Pink shirtwaister, unbuttoned low enough to reveal just a hint of cleavage, he thought Caroline was looking terrific, as always.

She was nearly fifty-three now, but she could have passed for ten years younger at least. 'I'm just trying to be gentlemanly and rescue her from that creep Ellis. I can't think what possessed you to invite him.'

Gary Ellis was one of Caro's newer 'finds', and was about as popular among the Cotswolds huntin', shootin' and fishin' set as the profiteering Rhett Butler was among the southern gentlemen of Atlanta.

He was a developer, famous for turning some of the most beautiful swathes of English countryside into hideous concrete shopping centres, and he had just bought himself a weekend cottage outside Batcombe. He was also loud, a cockney, and well known for his dodgy business practices, as well as his garish chequered suits and lewd and outrageous sense of humour.

'Don't be such a snob,' said Caroline. 'I like him.'

Christopher gave her a knowing look, the same one she remembered her father Sebastian using whenever he caught her fibbing.

Liking Ellis had nothing to do with it. She had invited him for one reason and one reason only, and they both knew it: he had his eye on a couple of Christopher's lower fields. Christopher had been appalled at the very suggestion of selling one square inch of his estate, but Caroline was unwilling to wave goodbye to the prospect of oodles of ready cash until they'd at least heard what Gary was proposing. He might only want to build a couple of perfectly tasteful houses, and what was so wrong with that? She wouldn't mind having a couple of nearer neighbours, or a bit more money in her pocket.

Besides, having Gary there might distract her other guests from the unremitting tedium of her brothers' company. Despite their bitter resentment that, after all the appalling things she'd done, she had managed once again to land on her feet and had become, for the second time, infinitely more wealthy than either of them, George and William were impressed enough by the Wellesley name and the grandeur of Great Thatchers to continue to pay court to their errant sister and her new husband. And as both lived within fifty miles of Batcombe they became, to Caroline's disappointment, quite regular visitors and dinner party guests.

She knew that they would both vehemently disapprove of Gary Ellis and everything he stood for, but it couldn't be helped. She had not yet completely given up hope of persuading Christopher to change his mind about those fields.

By nine o'clock the party was in full swing. As well as George and William and their wives, dreary Lucy and even drearier Deborah, she had invited a rather eccentric local lesbian in her seventies who was a lifelong friend of Christopher's, plus Gary Ellis and their neighbours, Henry and Muffy Arkell.

Henry owned Manor Farm, a much smaller but some thought even more beautiful little estate about five miles west of Thatchers. He also turned out, to Caroline's amazement and delight, to be the elder son of her one-time great friend from LA, Lulu De Seville.

'I don't believe it,' she said, when they'd first met at last year's hunt ball. 'You're little Max's big brother? He was always great friends with my son, Hunter. What a small world.'

'Yes indeed,' said Henry, who vaguely remembered hearing something from Max about Caroline sleeping with his stepfather, and a God-awful row ensuing as a result. 'Actually, I'm Max's half-brother.' He smiled. 'Different fathers. I believe you knew Max's father better than mine.'

Caroline had the good grace to blush, and Henry instantly warmed towards her. 'And he's not so little these days either. He's just finishing Cambridge, and then he's hoping to go back out to LA, I think. Wants to direct.'

Since that first meeting with Henry, she and Christopher had been invited to dinner at Manor Farm on a couple of occasions, and tonight they were finally returning the favour.

Caroline sat with Gary Ellis on her left and Henry on her right, in seventh heaven. Gary and Millicent, the lesbian, had been making horribly blue jokes all night. The latest involved a farmer's wife performing fellatio on a variety of different livestock. George's po-faced wife Lucy looked as if she might be about to explode with disapproval.

'Did Caroline tell you that Henrietta, our eldest, had a little boy last month?' She was babbling boringly on to poor Christopher in a desperate attempt to rein in the bawdy banter. 'Cosmo. He's really *terribly* sweet,' she gushed. 'Isn't he, George?'

Now a QC in his mid-sixties, Caroline's brother seemed to have become even more small minded and ridiculous with age. He didn't reply, but instead nodded absently at his wife, puffing pretentiously on an in-between-courses cigar.

'I think he's still feeling a *leetle* bit embarrassed about becoming a grandpa,' Lucy simpered in a stage whisper to the hapless, cornered Christopher.

'Fuckin' 'ell!' boomed Gary, from the other end of the table, staring unashamedly at his hostess's breasts. 'What does that make you, Caroline, a great-aunt? I wish I'd 'ad a great-aunt wot looked like that!' He cackled lasciviously, before adding, to Lucy's frank astonishment, 'If your 'enrietta 'as any trouble with the old breast-feedin', I'm sure Great-Aunt Caroline wouldn't mind 'elpin' aht! Eh, love?'

Catching one another's eye, Caroline and Christopher dissolved into giggles, not so much at Ellis's crude humour but at both her brothers' outraged pomposity, and furious, red-faced mutterings of 'well I never'.

''Ow's business?' Ellis had turned to Henry, apparently oblivious to the furore his earlier remark had caused. 'I drove past your place the other day. Lovely bit o' property.'

'Thank you,' said Henry, rather stiffly. From anyone else he would have been pleased at the compliment to his beloved estate. But having seen some of Gary Ellis's monstrosities first hand, hearing *him* admire Manor Farm was rather like hearing a rapist compliment your wife's legs. It made him very uneasy. 'Business is booming, actually. We've just begun diversifying out of dairy for the first time and we're quite excited about it.' He smiled across the table at his wife, who smiled back.

Muffy Arkell was very pretty in a ruddy-cheeked, no-make-up, tomboyish sort of way. Henry liked to boast that she looked just the same now as she had done when he'd met her at sixteen. Looking at her kind, innocent face gazing back at her husband across the table, Caroline could well believe it. The pair of them were obviously still deeply in love.

She knew she wasn't the only one who had noticed how ravishing Muffy was looking this evening, even under-dressed as she was in a pair of grey cords that accentuated her long, slim legs and an arctic-green cashmere jumper that swamped her figure, but brought out the intoxicating green of her eyes.

Christopher had long been an ardently chaste admirer of Mrs Arkell's charms, and had cast the odd longing glance in her direction throughout dinner, much to Caroline's amusement. But Gary, who had none of her husband's gentlemanly scruples, had been positively drooling over the poor girl all evening, pressing his leg against hers under the table when he'd thought no one was looking and taking every opportunity to paw her with his clammy hands when passing food or wine to his fellow guests. Henry seemed to be the only person in the room who hadn't noticed.

It was quite clear from her embarrassed, flushed face that Muffy in no way welcomed his attentions, although she was far too polite to make a scene. Caroline began to wish that she'd listened to Christopher and not sat the two of them together.

Perhaps Gary Ellis wasn't as harmless and amusing as she'd first thought? He'd been boorish, rude and drunk for most of the evening. Not even the amusement factor of her brothers' spluttering outrage had been enough to make up for the burden of his company.

Driving home a few hours later, Muffy was finally free to vent her frustration on a now happily drunk Henry.

'Honestly, that man is really too much,' she said, grinding their ancient Land Rover into first as they chugged up the steep hill towards the village. 'He made my flesh creep.' She shuddered at the memory of Ellis's hot, eager hand lecherously squeezing her knee throughout pudding.

'I know,' said Henry, grimacing. 'Just hearing him talk about Manor Farm – "lovely bit o' property" – made me want to wring his neck. Have you seen that leisure centre he built in that gorgeous valley over in Lechlade? Too vile for words.'

'Bugger the farm,' said Muffy indignantly. 'He was trying to feel me up for most of the night, the disgusting old goat.'

'He what?' spluttered Henry, flabbergasted. 'I never saw anything. Why didn't you say something?'

'Hen*reee*! Honestly. How could you not have noticed? He was pestering me for hours. I think Caroline was mortified.'

'Well, so she bloody should be,' he mumbled grumpily, angry at himself for having missed his chance to play the gallant hero. 'Damn cheek of the man.'

He gazed moodily out of the window at the dim shadows of Batcombe village, its picture-postcard loveliness illuminated only by the pale silver of an almost full moon and the occasional bedroom light still on in one or two of the cottages. Henry never ceased to be amazed by the beauty of the Cotswolds.

'Well,' he muttered darkly, 'he's got about as much chance of scoring with you as he has of ever getting his grubby little hands on my farm, I can tell you that for nothing.'

Muffy rolled her eyes indulgently. She adored her husband. But sometimes she wondered whether Henry actually loved that farm more than he loved her.

Chapter Twenty-two

'For heaven's sake, child, cheer up. You look like you've lost a shilling and found sixpence.'

Marsha and Siena were sitting in a chic little bistro, tucked away in a cobbled street just behind the Champs-Elysées. The weather was still vile so they opted for a table inside by the window. It was blowing an absolute gale outside, and big green leaves from the horse chestnuts swept and tumbled along the winding street, prematurely ripped from the trees before they'd had a chance to turn brown.

Maybe it was the weather which was bringing the girl down? Marsha could not think of any other explanation for Siena's gloomy mood. Yesterday's show had been an unmitigated triumph. From the second she had stepped out on to the catwalk, it was as if some supernatural confidence had possessed her, and she'd come alive. 'Electrifying!' was how the fashion editor of *Le Figaro* had described her in this morning's paper. She had even made it to page three of the *Daily Mail* back home, which had run a magnificent picture of the finale of the show, showing Siena being cheered on by the front row in a pair of lime-green hot pants and a latex dominatrix slashed top, under the headline: 'McMania!'

What more could she possibly want?

Siena prodded morosely at her *croque monsieur* with a fork and looked up at her agent.

'I'm sorry,' she said. 'I just wanted to have a chance to speak with him. He didn't even leave a card, you know? Nothing.'

With her face bare of make-up, except for a slick of Elizabeth Arden Eight Hour Cream on her lips and eyelids, and her hair tied back in a loose ponytail, Siena was unrecognisable from the glamorous, wanton creature in the *Daily Mail* picture. This morning she had opted for comfort clothes: an ancient pair of faded Levis tucked into sheepskin boots with a chunky navy blue sweater from the Gap. She looked about twelve.

Marsha sighed heavily. 'You're not still talking about that Silfen guy, are you?' she asked. 'Sweetie, if he didn't notice you, believe me,

173

he's the only person in that room who didn't. Who cares if he doesn't call? I already had four messages from the agency when I woke up this morning – the phone's been ringing off the hook for you, Siena. Trust me, darling. You are about to become very rich, and very famous, *very* fast.'

Siena couldn't help but cheer up slightly at the sound of the words 'rich' and 'famous' so close to her own name.

'You really think so?' She picked up Marsha's copy of the *Mail* and looked again at her picture and the caption. 'I don't know,' she said gloomily. 'Look at that: McMania. I think people are only interested because of my name. Because of my fucking father.'

Marsha took another sip of her *café au lait*. She had seen these sorts of parent problems before – the resentment, the tantrums, the insecurity – but it usually happened with much younger girls, the fourteen- and fifteen-year-olds who were leaving Mummy and Daddy for the first time. Siena was basically an adult. Her obsession with her parents – her apparent hatred of them – was baffling.

'Look, sweetie, we've talked about this, remember?' she said patiently. '*Of course* people are interested because of your name, your history. Why wouldn't they be? That name is an asset, just like that face and those tits.'

Siena glared at her across the table.

'Oh, come on,' Marsha insisted. 'You know it is. But that doesn't mean those people were cheering you on yesterday just because you're Pete McMahon's daughter.'

'No?' said Siena sulkily.

'No. They loved you because you've got a great look, and because you've got talent.'

'Well, if I've got so much bloody talent, how come Jamie Silfen just buggered off home?' asked Siena.

'Christ, I don't know.' Marsha was starting to get exasperated. She'd taken a huge chance in signing Siena, and quite frankly a little gratitude for her phenomenal, almost instant success might not have gone amiss. 'Maybe he was actually there to see the clothes?' she suggested.

'Oh, please,' said Siena.

'Maybe he was tired. Maybe he had a bad day. Maybe you're just not his type. Who gives a shit?'

Siena pushed her untouched plate aside and lit up another cigarette. That was one good thing about France: at least there weren't tobacco fascists lurking in every corner.

'Look,' said Marsha, already regretting losing her temper with the girl who was now, undoubtedly, one of her most bankable assets. 'I know you don't believe it now. But there is more to life than becoming an actress.'

'Not for me there isn't,' said Siena matter-of-factly.

'Everybody loves to knock modelling,' continued Marsha. 'They make out that all the girls are thick as shit. But the truth is, modelling can be a fantastic career. And for the girls that play their cards right – the really smart ones – it can even be a long career. Look at Cindy Crawford. If she's not still making millions ten years from now' – she threw her arms open melodramatically – 'then I'm Marilyn bloody Monroe.'

Siena laughed.

'Actually, I think you'll find that *I'm* the new Marilyn, darling!' she joked.

'I'll drink to that,' said Marsha, signalling to the waiter to bring them over the wine list. 'Just do me a favour and try not to shag any presidents. Or their brothers.'

'Eeugh,' said Siena, as an image of a naked Bill Clinton loomed into mental view. 'No danger of that. I think I'll stick to footballers.'

'Ah!' Marsha's beady little eyes lit up like Olympic torches. 'The lovely Mario. So, go on, spill the beans. How was he?'

Siena stubbed out her cigarette and smiled wickedly.

'Six out of ten,' she lied.

'No!' whispered Marsha like an overexcited schoolgirl. 'Only six? Really? What was the problem?'

Siena picked up the enormous brown pepper grinder from the centre of the table. 'Let's just say I could have had more fun with this.'

Marsha roared with laughter, a full throated, raucous cackle. 'You know what your problem is, sweetheart? You're too damn spoiled.'

Siena grinned. 'So I've been told. Maybe you and my father should get together some time and compare notes.'

Back in her hotel room two hours later, she could hardly move for flowers and cards as she attempted to pack. A veritable busload of freebies had begun arriving in a steady stream throughout the day: an Hermès scarf, more Chanel scent than you could shake a stick at, even a sterling-silver pair of cufflinks in the shape of the Eiffel Tower, now jostled for position next to Siena's own screwed-up clothes on the elegantly faded antique bedspread. If only Louis Vuitton had sent her a new suitcase to put it all in.

She was scrunching a gorgeous vintage Alaia skirt into a tight ball in a valiant effort to wedge it into her suitcase when she was interrupted by a knock on the door.

'Mademoiselle?'

'Yeah,' Siena grunted between shoves. 'Come on in, it's open.'

Another vast bouquet of lilies entered the room, followed by a sweating bell boy.

'Holy crap, not more?' said Siena, looking round frantically for somewhere he could put them. 'Just lay them on the chair for now.' She pointed to an armchair already piled high with empty gift boxes and wet towels, and the bell boy gingerly set the flowers down and stood hovering for his tip.

'There's a twenty-franc note on that shelf by the door,' said Siena, panting and tugging hopelessly at the zip on her suitcase. 'You can take that, if you like. I'm afraid I don't have any more cash.'

Siena had always been a big tipper, a reaction to her father's legendary meanness with money, and would have liked to have given the boy more.

'Merci, mademoiselle,' he said, apparently more than happy with the twenty. 'I also 'ave two messages for you.'

He held out two small white envelopes embossed with the hotel crest. With a sigh, Siena abandoned her battle with the zipper and took the notes from him.

'Thanks,' she said, catching her breath before strolling over to examine her flowers. 'You can go now.'

The lilies smelled so divine she wished she could take them with her back to London, but the arrangement was so huge it would need a whole seat to itself on the plane. 'Thank you for the most wonderful night,' the card read. 'Call me. Soon. Mario. PS. By the way, we lost, so you owe me dinner next time. xx'

Siena smiled to herself. She shouldn't have been so harsh about him to Marsha. He'd been a lot better than a six. Still, the last thing she needed right now was a serious boyfriend. She'd seen so many women put their lives and their dreams on hold over some guy, not least her own mother and grandmother, and she was certainly not about to join their ranks. Mario would simply have to remain a happy memory.

She looked at her watch.

Five fifteen.

She was supposed to meet Marsha in the lobby at six and then go straight to the airport. It seemed incredible that she had only been in Paris for three days. She felt like a different person. Mario, the show, meeting Ines, all the attention and the press – she had had her first small taste of fame, and after so many years of waiting it had come, quite literally, overnight.

Being overlooked by Jamie Silfen had been the only fly in her ointment. Marsha was right, though. In the grand scheme of things, how much did that really matter?

After yesterday's success there would be other shows, perhaps even international campaigns. Soon, Siena confidently predicted, she would become a household name, one of the girls that her schoolfriends and their little sisters all longed to be like. That had always been her plan anyway – to make a name for herself as a model and then have the casting agents come to her. And she had to admit, despite the fact that she wouldn't trust her as far as she could throw her, Marsha had done an incredible job at catapulting her career into the fast lane, from a (late) standing start.

Silfen could wait. Siena would have him eating out of her palm some day.

But underlying today's elation had been the nagging realisation that some time very soon her parents would get wind of yesterday's events. She tried to convince herself that, once they saw her overwhelmingly positive press, they might, if not change their minds, then at least soften their position and let her delay her place at Oxford for a year. She struggled to picture Pete looking at the *Daily Mail* picture and smiling admiringly at her triumph – but even she had to admit the image wasn't really working.

He'd be mad with her, of course he would.

Nothing new there.

She'd just have to call him when she got back to London and face the music. Still, she felt cautiously optimistic that somehow, perhaps with her mother's help, she would get him to come around eventually. One thing was for sure: nothing on God's earth would persuade her to give up her modelling now.

Standing up, she moved over to the window and gazed out at the dirty Parisian skyline. Today was her last day in Paris, that magical city that had inspired generations of artists and lovers and which seemed, even now, to be looking out for her, protecting her and helping her to realise her long-cherished hopes and dreams. Pete's wrath, his spite and his mean-spiritedness, could not touch her in Paris – she wouldn't allow it.

Bending down, she picked up the two white envelopes that the bell boy had given her, and examined each carefully. Opening the first envelope, she felt a brief stab of what might have been guilt. Janey Cash had called. She and Patrick both wanted to say well done and they couldn't wait to see her when she got home.

England hardly qualified as 'home', thought Siena, although she was no longer certain herself just where home might be.

Darling Janey. She loved her dearly, but part of her wished that her old friend would get angry about the way she'd treated her brother, rather than just carrying on as if nothing had happened. And why was Pat being so bloody big about it? She'd dumped him without any explanation – how could she put into words how frightened she was of allowing herself to love anybody, ever? All Patrick knew was that she'd stopped taking his calls one day. Period. If anyone had treated *her* like that, she wouldn't rest until she'd got good and even. 'You can get mad,' Duke always used to tell her. 'Just make sure you get even as well.'

The memory of her grandfather made her smile.

She scrumpled up the note, threw it into the huge pile of rubbish beside the chair and ripped open the second envelope.

It was from her mother. Could Siena phone home immediately.

Fuck, fuck and double fuck on a stick. How did they know where she was staying? In fact, how did they even know she was in Paris at all? She'd told them last week that she'd agreed not to make the trip, hoping to buy herself a little time at least before breaking the news that her absence from Oxford was to be permanent. How on earth could they possibly have found out so soon?

She began pacing the room like a cornered cat. What time was it in LA? She did a quick calculation: eight in the morning. There was no way they could have seen the papers yet. Not that the show would have made the American press anyway, but her father was a news fiend, and often ordered the English newspapers as well – although not the *Daily Mail*. Pete considered it far too lowbrow.

So how did they know? It simply didn't make sense. Unless . . .

Her heart gave a sudden, sickening lurch. Could it be?

Silfen.

Siena didn't know whether to laugh or cry. It was Jamie bloody Silfen, it had to be. He *had* noticed her after all. He'd seen the show, seen how the audience had loved her, but instead of contacting her directly he'd gone and called her fucking father! The more she thought about it, the more it made sense. Jamie knew Pete, both professionally and socially. In her excitement and surprise at seeing him there, in the audience, she'd completely overlooked the connection with her father. Pete, in fact, was the one person she'd been trying hardest all week to forget.

For almost a minute, she sat motionless on her bed trying to take it all in. Eventually she reached across for the phone and began to dial her parents' number.

'0–0–1 . . .' She pressed each digit with infinite reluctance. '. . . 3–1–0–8–2 . . .'

But it was no good. She couldn't do it. Gently but firmly she replaced the receiver.

Stamping down her anxiety with a supreme effort of will, she returned to her packing. Her father could wait until tomorrow morning. This trip to Paris had been the start of something wonderful for her, a real rite of passage. She couldn't place it exactly, but she felt sure it marked the first step back towards Hollywood, Hollywood on her own terms, and everything that Grandpa Duke had told her she could become.

With her own talent.

In her own right.

No one, least of all Pete, was going to spoil it for her.

At six o'clock that evening in Los Angeles, Pete McMahon signed the bottom of a document and handed it solemnly to his attorney.

He was sitting at his father's old desk, one of the very few artefacts he had requested from Hancock Park after the old man died. The lawyer hastily scribbled his witnessing signature below his client's and scurried out of the room, anxious to leave before the storm brewing between Pete and his wife erupted.

Claire was standing at the window looking out over the lights of West Hollywood below them, with her back to her husband. In her worsted tweed skirt and white polo-neck she looked more like a contemplative nun than a Hollywood mogul's wife. Although Pete couldn't see it, her face was as white as a ghost's.

'Please don't say anything,' said Pete, still seated, so quietly it was almost a whisper. 'Please. It's over.'

Claire turned to look at him, scanning his face for any sort of emotion or weakness, any doubts about this terrible decision that she could cling on to, or use to try to change his mind. But the expression she saw was one she remembered well. It was the same expression he'd had back in the study at Hancock Park, when he'd insisted on sending Siena away to England: desolate, blank, unreachable. She knew in her heart it was hopeless.

'Oh, Pete. What do you mean? How can it ever be over?' Tears streamed down her cheeks, and her hands flew to her hair, distraught. Why was he doing this? What was he trying to prove? 'And what if I said I won't let you do this? She's my child, Peter, my only child.'

He could hear the terrible anguish in her voice and wished he could comfort her. But it was all too late. Siena wasn't their child any more. She had proved that now beyond any doubt.

Duke had stolen her from them, turned her against them for ever.

Even from beyond the grave, he had plunged his hated, destructive hand into the heart of Pete's own family and poisoned it with misery from within.

Claire was shaking.

'What if I said I'd leave you?'

The words hung in the air between them like lead.

Pete put his head in his hands. For almost a minute, neither of them spoke.

'Will you?' he said at last. His right hand, still holding the pen, had started shaking violently, and heavy globules of black ink spilled down on to his white linen cuffs. 'Will you leave me?'

Claire was so overwhelmed with sorrow, she almost felt she might hear her heart cracking open. But even in the depths of her own misery, when she looked at her beloved husband's stricken face, she knew that she could not abandon him.

She realised in that moment, with searing clarity, that she was all he had. And for all the pain he caused her, she loved him.

'No,' she said softly. 'No, Pete. I won't leave you.'

'Never?' he whispered. 'Whatever happens?'

She walked over and put her arms around him.

'Never.'

It was raining in Knightsbridge when Siena finally came to, and the dull, cloudy English light of late morning spluttered rather than streamed through her bedroom window. So much for Boiling Britain. She seemed to be bringing the shitty weather with her wherever she went.

Groggily, she made her way into the kitchen, where she found a note from Isabella, the McMahons' Spanish housekeeper in London, explaining that she had run out to the dry cleaner's but that Siena's breakfast was all laid out and ready for her on the table in the dining room.

Siena wandered through, picking up the Saturday *Times* and a letter addressed to her as she went, and was soon settled down to a feast of freshly ground coffee, wheat toast and her favourite crunchy peanut butter.

The letter was from Oxford, nothing important, just a wadge of information about the freshers' week she had already missed, various college societies and events and a lecture schedule for the Michaelmas term. Siena pushed it all to one side and started skimming the fashion section of the Saturday magazine. She was deeply engrossed in a piece about the revival, yet again, of the micro mini when an overburdened Isabella burst through the door, weighed down with a whopping armful of her dry cleaning.

'Belli, let me help you with that,' she said, jumping up to take the clothes before the housekeeper gave herself a hernia.

Isabella was one of the few people in Siena's life whom she unconditionally adored. Fat and warm and motherly, she had done everything in her power to make the London flat seem like home when, as a lonely little girl, Siena had been abandoned there for endless half-terms and Easter holidays. Not having any children of her own, she found it easy to coddle and indulge Siena in a way that the child's own parents would never have dreamt of. Home cooking, constant physical affection, ceaseless praise for every achievement, no matter how small, and comfort for every setback – these were the things that Siena associated with Isabella.

'Ees OK,' the stocky little woman protested as Siena lifted coat after coat from her arms. 'There ees something else for you. Take these.' She handed her four sheets of A4 which she had carefully stapled together at the top left-hand corner. 'Eet's a fox,' she said gravely.

'Is it?' asked Siena seriously, trying not to laugh. 'From the fox machine? Well, I'd probably better have a look, then.'

Dumping the clothes unceremoniously on the sofa, she returned to the table and her fourth piece of toast. God, she was in demand at the moment! It must be from the agency, hopefully with some decent jobs for next season. Siena started to read.

'Last Will and Testament . . .'

No. Oh, no, no, no. He couldn't be serious.

'My daughter, Siena Claire . . . disinherited . . .'

The words blurred before her eyes.

'Immediate effect . . . to quit the premises, 88 Sloane Gardens, London, SW3 . . . wish no further contact . . .'

Siena put her hand to her mouth. She thought she might be going to throw up, but the feeling passed. Angrily, she hurled the fax on to her pile of Oxford papers. Melodramatic bastard. No further contact indeed. Who did he think he was, Lord fucking Capulet?

She picked up the phone and punched out her parents' number before her rage had time to dissipate into fear. She would not grovel to that bastard. If that was what he was waiting for, he'd be waiting one hell of a long time.

'McMahon residence.'

It was Mary, the stupid pseudo-English housekeeper that Pete had hired two years ago, to howls of derision from Siena, who insisted she must have been born Maria-Elena, her British accent was so terrible.

'Hey, Mary.' She tried to sound cheery. 'It's Siena. Is my mom home?'

'Er . . . Just a moment, please.'

Siena heard the unmistakable frantic scrabbling of someone trying to cover the receiver with one hand while whispering and signalling instructions with the other. Something was definitely up.

'I'm sorry, Siena,' she said after a few long seconds. 'Your mother is unavailable at the moment.'

Siena could feel her hackles rising. Stupid, pretentious little cow. 'What do you mean, unavailable?' she snapped. 'Do you mean she's out?'

Another long pause.

'Yes,' said Mary.

'I see,' said Siena. This was like pulling teeth. 'Well, when will she be back?'

'I'm afraid I can't say. I'm not sure,' answered Mary cautiously.

Siena hung up. This was getting her nowhere. With her heart in her mouth, she dialled the number for Pete's office.

'McMahon Pictures, please hold,' said a voice before she'd had a chance to draw breath.

A rather tinny version of James Taylor's 'Fire and Rain' began playing. James had got as far as 'lonely times when I could not find a friend' before a female voice picked up again.

'Sorry to keep you waiting, this is Mr McMahon's office. How may I help you?'

'Tara?'

'Yes?' The unexpected use of her own name had thrown the girl completely. Her tone instantly became more guarded. 'Who is this?'

'It's Siena.'

More silence. It was the first time Siena could ever remember Pete's poisonous PA being lost for words. It was Tara who had so delighted in keeping Hunter's letters from her when they had first been separated, Tara who had gone out of her way to reinforce Pete's own view of his daughter as spoiled, difficult and in need of a firm hand. Tara enjoyed a place very close to the top of Siena's fantasy hellfire wish list.

'You can't speak to your father, I'm afraid,' she said firmly. It hadn't taken her long to regain her composure. 'He's in a meeting and won't be out till two.'

Siena longed to insist that she interrupt him, but knowing it wouldn't do any good she decided not to give her the satisfaction.

'Fine,' she said curtly. 'I'll call back then.'

'If you like,' said Tara.

'Tell him I called,' said Siena, hanging up before Tara had a chance to sneak in some spiteful last word.

She wondered how much she knew about what had happened. She'd probably sat there and redrafted the will for him, evil little nothing that she was. Siena had never fathomed what it was that made Tara hate her so much. Normally she put down female hostility to envy, of her looks, her wealth and her so-called jet-set lifestyle. But Tara had had it in for her since she was ten years old. This particular hatred evidently ran deeper.

Feeling a little panicked now, she tried calling home again. This time Claire picked up herself.

'Pete?'

Siena heard the apprehension in her mother's voice. She must have called in the middle of a difficult conversation between her parents.

'No, Mom. It's me, Siena.'

Relief at hearing her mother's voice had temporarily eclipsed her usual anger and resentment. It was the first time in years that Claire had heard her daughter sounding so warm towards her.

'Hello, Mom?' she repeated, panic surging up again like lava from her stomach in the face of Claire's silence. 'Are you still there?'

'Yes, Siena, I'm here.' Her voice sounded odd, almost as if it were breaking. When she spoke again, it was barely a whisper. 'What do you want?'

The lava of Siena's fear suddenly erupted into a much more familiar volcano of rage. What kind of a stupid question was that?

'What do I *want*?' she yelled. 'What do you mean, what do I *want*? This is your daughter calling, you know, your daughter, the one you don't give a shit about?'

'Siena . . .'

'What do you think I fucking want? Isabella just gave me Dad's fax. I want to know what the fuck is going on. Did you put him up to this?'

'Oh, Siena, of course I didn't,' pleaded Claire desperately. 'I warned you, darling. I tried to get you to see sense about this McQueen business, to call your father at least . . .' Her voice was breaking with the effort of trying to suppress so much emotion.

'And what?' said Siena. 'I didn't call you back in time, so, hey, guess what, I've been disinherited? You don't have a fucking daughter any more? Is that it?'

The biting sarcasm in her voice failed to conceal her pain. Claire felt for her, but what words of comfort could she possibly offer her now? She'd made her choice and she was just going to have to live with it.

'Do you have any idea how ridiculous that is?' Siena continued. 'How insane? I mean, have you actually read this, Mom?' Claire could hear the pages of Pete's fax rustling six thousand miles away. 'He says he wants me out of the flat. No further contact. He's fucking *evicting* me! Did you know about this?'

'Yes, I knew about it.' Claire sobbed quietly. 'He showed me last night. I'm sorry, Siena.'

'Great.' Siena gave an empty laugh. 'He showed you last night, did he? And what did you say, Mom? Oh, that's nice, dear, go ahead and cut her off like some fucking infected limb?' Claire winced at Siena's temper. It wasn't making this any easier. 'She won't go to Oxford, she won't become the little English lady we all wanted. So why don't we just erase her altogether? Is that it, Mom? Cut your losses and just move on?'

Siena could feel her heart pounding so violently she half expected it to burst through her ribs and land with a thud on the table. The dining room, which only minutes ago had seemed as homely and familiar as an old toy, now looked strange and surreal to her. Was this conversation really happening?

'I'm sorry, darling,' Claire said again hopelessly. Her voice had reverted back to eerie desolation. 'It's not as if we haven't tried. Why did you have to push him? Your father has given you chance after chance.'

'To what?' spat Siena disdainfully. 'To be someone else?'

'I don't know what to say,' said Claire. 'You went to France, you did that show, in absolute defiance of him. You have to take some responsibility for that, Siena.'

'Right,' said Siena, drawing her pride and anger around her like a shield. 'So just let me get this straight. Dad has decided I'm no longer his child. And you agree with him? Is that what you're saying?'

Claire had never hated herself more than she did at that moment. She loved her daughter. But Siena had never understood Pete, or the terrible scars that Duke's behaviour had inflicted on him. She had never seen the ways in which, unwittingly, her rebelliousness and her love for Duke had deepened his pain until it was literally no longer bearable.

'Your father has made his decision,' she said. 'I have to respect that.'

'No, Mom,' said Siena, furious with herself for trembling. 'You don't. You don't *have* to respect it. You *choose* to respect it.'

'Siena . . .'

'So don't lay this all on Dad, OK? *You* chose this, Mom. You chose it.'

Claire was silent. There was nothing else to say.

Siena, feeling strangely empowered suddenly, replaced the receiver. It seemed ludicrous, somehow, to say 'goodbye' to your own mother. She took one deep breath and exhaled slowly, waiting for the enormity of what had just happened to hit her. But the odd thing was she felt fine, she really did.

That was it, then. It was over.

Chapter Twenty-three

Batcombe, England, three years later . . .

'Right, shut up, please, everyone shut up, I've got a joke.'

Henry Arkell was sitting at the head of the table, trying to make himself heard over the excited rabble of his assorted children and dogs. 'Two horses, sitting in the field,' he began, reading from the white slip that had fallen out of his cracker.

'Horses don't sit, Daddy,' piped up a voice to his right, belonging to a child whose entire face appeared to be covered in a combination of chocolate sauce and icing sugar.

'Be quiet, Madeleine,' Henry continued, wiping ineffectually at the goo with his napkin, 'you're putting me off. Right, two horses, sitting in a field, and one of them turns to the other and says . . .'

'Horses don't speak either, Dad,' interrupted another voice from the far end of the table, this time his elder son, Charlie.

'They do if they're Mr Ed,' said Bertie, the six-year-old. 'Can I have some more Coke?'

'Mr Ed isn't real, you doofus,' pronounced Charlie scornfully.

'Well, nor are the horses in Dad's joke, doofazoid.' Bertie hurled a plastic whistle in his brother's direction. 'Are they, Dad? Your horses aren't real, are they?'

Henry opened his mouth to speak, but Madeleine had already begun to wail.

'Horses *are* real! Blackie's definitely real. She's the best pony in the world, and in the universe and in space. You can't say she isn't real, can he, Mummy?'

'I don't think he meant that Blackie wasn't real, darling.' Muffy, nominated family peacekeeper, tried in vain to placate her daughter.

'Space *is* the universe,' said Bertie authoritatively.

'Blackie *is* real!' maintained Madeleine.

'Jesus Christ,' said Henry, who was by now looking rather defeated with his yellow paper crown askew above his springy, light brown hair. 'I'm trying to tell a fucking joke here. Is anyone going to let me finish my bloody joke?'

'I don't think so, darling.' Muffy smiled at him lovingly. 'Why don't you have another glass of claret?'

She handed the decanter to Max, who passed it along to his brother. He loved Christmas lunches at Batcombe.

'Daddy said "fucking",' Charlie pointed out with a grin. 'He has to put a pound in the swearing tin.'

'Two pounds,' said Bertie, watching with delight as his Coke foamed up over the rim of his glass and began to form a pool on the mahogany table. 'He said "bloody" as well. He said no one would let him finish his "bloody" joke. Didn't you, Dad?'

Henry poured himself a glass of claret, and with his best attempt at dignity got up from the table, taking his drink with him.

'I'm going to go and sit in the drawing room,' he announced to the table at large. 'If anybody wants me, I will be sitting in front of the fire with the jumbo *Times* crossword.'

'But what about presents?' protested all three children in unison.

'Anyone who is hoping for presents,' said Henry, holding up his forefinger for silence, 'would be very well advised to leave their father alone for twenty minutes . . .'

'Twenty *minutes!*' they wailed in horror.

'Twenty minutes,' repeated Henry, 'while I finish my glass of wine in peace. Then – and only then – there *may*' – he paused for dramatic effect – 'be some present-opening.'

'But what can we do for twenty minutes?' asked a grief-stricken Bertie. 'That's for ever.'

'You can help Mummy clear the table,' said Max, waving down the howls of protest. 'Come on, Charlie, you can scrape off those plates for Titus and Boris. The sooner we get started, the sooner we can get to those presents.'

Batcombe was Max's sanctuary.

Henry, his much older half-brother and only real family, had inherited Manor Farm from his father, Max's mother's first husband, ten years earlier. It had been in a terribly dilapidated state back then, a picturesque but decaying mess of ancient barns and outbuildings, clustered around a much neglected but nevertheless magnificent sixteenth-century manor house. Henry and his young wife had moved in, full of energy and ambition, determined to revitalise both the house and the business. And revitalise them they had.

From the dining-room window, Max now looked out across a spotless yard to the gleaming rows of snow-covered milking sheds, and beyond them to his brother's three hundred acres of rolling Cotswold countryside. Every hedgerow, wooden fence and dry-stone wall had been painstakingly restored by Henry over the last decade, and the farm was now picture perfect. Max had travelled all over the globe, but he had yet to see anywhere that topped Batcombe for the sheer, heart-lifting beauty of the landscape.

Thanks to years of hard slog by Muffy, the house itself had become as much of a triumph as the farm. Henry's father, who had lived there for most of his life, rarely used any of the larger formal rooms, some of which had mildewed wallpaper hanging from the ceilings when they first moved in. Now, with the wood panelling in the drawing room lovingly restored, and every corner of the house crammed with books, brightly coloured Persian rugs and cushions, and an eclectic mix of objets d'art, ranging from obscure family heirlooms to interesting junk shop finds, the manor was once again a home.

As a teenager, Max had spent a lot of time with Henry and Muffy and his three young nieces and nephews, helping out on the farm. If it hadn't been for the fact that he loved his brother so much, he would certainly have envied him. His home, his rock-solid marriage, his kids, his little kingdom at Batcombe – he really did have it all. But one of the nicest things about Henry was, he knew how lucky he was. Always laughing and joking around, never with a bad word to say about anyone – not even their mother, who had effectively abandoned him when she met Max's father and flitted off to California – Henry was a true hero in his brother's eyes.

Having given up on getting any constructive help from the children, Max and Muffy had cleared the table between them, and Muffy was now extracting fragments of vanilla pods from the sugar bowl so that she could sweeten her own tea, before taking a cup in to Henry.

'D'you think it's been twenty minutes?' she asked, pouring a dash of milk into both Max's and Henry's mugs. 'You did want milk, didn't you?'

Max nodded. 'Even if it hasn't,' he said, 'Bertie's going to explode if you make him wait one more minute for his presents. Anyway, I don't know why you pander to Henry like that. If anyone needs twenty minutes' break today, it's you, not him.'

Muffy sighed and wiped her hands on her apron. 'Tell me about it. Honestly, I know Christmas is always a lot of work but it's been such a struggle this year, especially with money being so tight. I've done all my own baking, and Charlie and I made all those new decorations together, which took an absolute age.'

'Is money tight?' asked Max, taking a tentative sip of his too-hot tea. 'I thought the business was going great guns. Haven't you just diversified?'

'We have,' said Muffy, emptying a packet of Bourbon biscuits on to a plate for the children. 'But it took a lot of investment, and we'd already borrowed quite a bit to revamp the milking sheds and restore the big barn last year. And now we have Bertie's school fees as well as Charlie's to think about. We're definitely a bit pushed.'

'I thought Bertie got a scholarship,' asked Max, risking a second gulp of tea.

Muffy shook her head. 'Flunked it. Look, I wouldn't worry, it isn't like we're stony broke or anything,' she said, catching his concerned expression. 'Just a bit of a cash flow problem. Maddie will just have to wait till next year for the Malibu Barbie mansion, and the boys can jolly well put up with homemade mince pies. Do you know they're over three pounds for a box of six in M&S?'

'Scandalous,' said Max, helping himself to one of Muffy's efforts from the open cake tin on the table. 'Anyway,' he said through a mouthful of crumbs, 'yours are ten times better.'

After the last present had been opened and the drawing-room floor had become a sea of shredded wrapping paper and empty boxes, Henry and Max decided to clear their heads and take the dogs out for a walk.

The winter sky was already darkening, and the cold, crisp bite of the smoky air jolted both brothers out of their drunken Christmas stupor as they strode across the fields, with the two King Charles spaniels, Titus and Boris, running along excitedly at their heels.

'So when are you off back to sunny California?' asked Henry, picking up a stray stick and throwing it for Titus.

'The twenty-eighth,' said Max. 'I'm not looking forward to it, actually.'

'Oh?' said Henry. 'Why not? I thought you had rather a sweet deal living with Hunter McMahon? Did I tell you his mother's married to Christopher Wellesley these days, living over at Thatchers?'

'Yes,' said Max frostily, 'you told me.'

He had not laid eyes on Caroline since he was a teenager, and remembered her only as Hunter's selfish and neglectful mother. It irked him a little that Henry and Muffy seemed to think she was terrific fun, although to be fair Henry's father had been friendly with the Wellesleys for the whole of his life, and Caroline was, apparently, greatly improved as a result of her late marriage to Christopher.

'Never introduce Hunter to my wife, will you?' said Henry, swiftly changing the subject, having remembered that Max had a bee in his bonnet about Caroline. 'She loves that bloody *Counsellor* rubbish. I'm sure she'd swan off into the sunset with him given half a chance.'

Max laughed. 'Don't worry, you're safe there. Hunter's in love. With a very nice girl actually – Tiffany. He met her at an audition for his new show, *UCLA*. It's huge in the States already, but I don't think they're showing it here yet.'

'Tiffany?' Henry raised an eyebrow. 'That doesn't sound like a very nice girl's name to me.'

'I know,' said Max, 'but she really is. Most of the girls in LA are such gold-diggers, especially the ones around Hunter, but she's different.'

'So, why don't you want to go back?' Henry pressed him, as Titus came bounding back with the stick clamped between his jaws.

'I don't know.' Max sighed. 'Living at Hunter's is great, I know I'm very lucky. But sometimes it just gets to me, you know? He's so fucking successful. And rich. Drop, Titus!'

He picked up the stick and threw a dummy for Titus, before hurling it fifty yards in the opposite direction for Boris, who was fatter and slower and needed the odds stacked in his favour when it came to playing fetch. 'Everywhere we go he's mobbed by these incredible women.'

'I thought you said they were all gold-diggers,' said Henry.

'They are,' said Max. 'Which is why none of them are interested in me. I don't *have* any gold. That's the problem. Hunter's been so generous, he's an incredible friend, but he makes me feel like such a fucking failure. I mean, I'm twenty-five years old, and I still live in my buddy's spare room. How tragic is that?'

Henry put a paternal arm around his brother's shoulder. 'Look, Max, twenty-six is young. Take it from me. You still have plenty of time to make money. And you always knew that this directing lark was going to be a bit of a gamble. You can't expect to hit the big time right away.'

That was a bit of an understatement, thought Max bitterly. He'd been out in LA now for three full years and still hadn't earned enough to pay Hunter back a quarter of what he owed him. If it hadn't been for a couple of theatre gigs he'd been offered back in England last year, he wouldn't have been able to afford to stay in America at all, even allowing for his subsidised living arrangements.

'Hunter had the McMahon name behind him,' Henry insisted. 'You've got to do it all yourself, and that takes time and effort and patience. Cut yourself some slack.'

They came to the bottom of the hill and scrambled over a rotting old stile into some woodland. Henry frowned at the state of his fence – he'd have to get that sorted out before spring.

'What about you?' Max asked. 'Muff mentioned something about money being tight. Is everything OK?'

'Oh, yes, yes,' said Henry, waving away the question with a frown and increasing his pace. Max took the hint – whatever was wrong, his brother didn't want to talk about it. 'Don't worry about me. You just concentrate on keeping your own spirits up. The worst thing you could do now would be to lose your confidence.'

Max shrugged gloomily. 'I think I've probably done that already.'

'Nonsense. You're just in a funk, Maxy. Things will look brighter when you get back out there, I'm sure. And if they don't, well, you know you've always got a home with us. The kids would die of happiness if you ever decided to give the old farming a try.'

Max felt quite choked with gratitude. Without Henry's unwavering love and support in his life, God only knew where he'd be.

'Maybe I need a girlfriend,' he said, embarrassed at his emotion and wanting to change the subject.

'Dear God, boy, I hope you aren't going to start complaining about a lack of sex. Because if you are, I'm afraid I may have to hit you,' said Henry. 'Try having three kids and a farm to run. Then you'll discover the meaning of sex-starved.'

'I'm not sex-starved,' said Max, with devastating understatement. 'That's not what I meant.' For all his moping about LA girls' materialism, he still managed to screw more than his fair share of them, and certainly more than the faithfully loved-up Hunter. Still, there was a part of him that envied what Hunter and Tiffany had, or Henry and Muffy for that matter. Recently his litany of casual sexual conquests had begun to seem empty and hollow by comparison.

He quickened his pace as they started up a second hill, determined to work off at least some of Muffy's delicious Christmas cooking.

'I tell you what,' said Henry, warming to his theme of sexual frustration, 'you know who's absolutely bloody gorgeous, but don't tell Muff I said so?'

'No, who?' said Max.

'Hunter's little sister. Siena. Or is it his niece? Did you see those pictures of her in GQ last month? Fucking hell, she's sexy. Why don't you get Hunter to set you up?'

'With Siena?' Max laughed. 'Now that would be a match made in hell. Besides, Hunter hasn't spoken to her in years, not since we were kids.'

In the past two years, Siena had become very well known as a model, and even fashion-phobes like Max couldn't fail to have seen her picture on billboards and TV, advertising everything from Versace couture to shampoo. Out of the 'top ten' girls – the ones whose annual earnings were in seven rather than six figures and whose names appeared as frequently in the gossip columns as the fashion pages – Siena was known as the 'man's woman', sexier, curvier and sassier than any of the other 'supers' – men loved her for her raw sex appeal, and women loved her for the fact that she wore clothes that weren't designed to fit a size-zero giraffe.

'Oh, that's right, I forgot. She was in your gang before you got sent to Ampleforth, wasn't she?' said Henry. 'I tell you what, I wouldn't have minded playing a spot of doctors and nurses with her.'

'God,' said Max, shaking his head, 'that was a long time ago.' Instantly the memories of hanging out at Hancock Park, and particularly all their fights about that tree house, came flooding back to him. 'She was an obnoxious little brat even then. Always had to be the centre of attention. She was the polar opposite of Hunter. Christ knows what she's like now, with half the world's men drooling at her feet.' He rolled his eyes dramatically. 'Spoiled as hell, I expect.'

They had reached the crest of the hill, and emerged from the woodland back on to open fields. The light had almost gone now and it was very cold. Suddenly Max longed to be back at the farm, warming himself with a nice malt whisky in front of the fire.

Thinking back to the Hancock Park days made him feel uneasy, somehow, almost depressed. Siena and Hunter and the tree house reminded him of his childish self – of high hopes, excitement and an unbounded optimism – that was no longer a part of who he was. Back then he'd thought he could do anything, be anything. Now his dreams of making it as a director were already crumbling, before they'd even really begun.

'You're shivering,' said Henry, breaking his reverie. 'Not used to the good old British winter any more, I suspect. Do you want my scarf?'

'No,' said Max. 'No thanks, I'm fine. Let's crack on and get home, though. I could murder a drink.'

Chapter Twenty-four

Tiffany Wedan arched her back and pulled him deeper inside her, closing her eyes as she felt her second orgasm build.

'Hmmmm,' she moaned, 'please.'

Hunter smiled down at the beautiful girl beneath him, her eyes closed, wet strands of long blonde hair clinging to a face flushed with desire, and tried hard to stop himself from coming.

'Please what?' he teased her. 'Please stop?'

'No!' she gasped out, her muscles instinctively gripping his cock tighter as her fingers started stroking and probing for his asshole.

'Ah, no you don't,' whispered Hunter, pulling her hand away. That really would finish him off. He bent lower so that his mouth was right by her ear. The tickling sensation of his breath there always heightened Tiffany's pleasure. 'You're a very naughty little girl,' he whispered, jabbing himself still deeper into her.

'Aaah,' she cried out, climaxing suddenly with such intense force, muscles spasming and arms clenched around him as though her life depended on it, that Hunter felt as if he were being sucked into a warm, wet black hole.

'Fuck! I love you!' he yelled, seconds later, as he finally let himself enjoy the orgasm he'd been trying to suppress for the last twenty minutes, rocking back and forth inside her with delight.

Afterwards, the two of them lay clasped together like exhausted limpets, tired and replete. It was incredible how, after almost three years together, she still made him feel like a fifteen-year-old with his first crush. Ever since he'd walked into that audition room at NBC and seen her looking so adorably shy and flustered, not to mention unbelievably sexy in her cheerleader's outfit, he'd been mesmerised by her. With her slender, coltish legs (she was almost his height) and thick, dark lashes framing deep, green eyes, Tiffany reminded him of a baby racehorse – beautiful but still a little unsure of herself. Her wide, pale pink lips had trembled as she stumbled over her first few lines, and it had been all he could do to tear his eyes away from them and focus on his own lines, so loudly had his heart been pounding.

Tiffany had been auditioning for the part of Kimbo Watson at the time, the darkly psychotic female lead in *UCLA*, a new series that Hugh Orchard had created especially for Hunter to capitalise on the massive success of *Counsellor*. Hunter played Gabe Sanderson, hunky college football captain, and had sat in on all the read-throughs for the Kimbo hopefuls. Tiffany didn't get the part, probably because everything about her radiated sunshine, not inner demons. But she had landed the smaller role of Sarah, the football team's physical therapist, and had been working with Hunter on the show – which was now right up there with *Counsellor* in the ratings – ever since.

Stretching her body upwards to kiss him on the lips again, she wondered in awe for the umpteenth time how she had ever gotten so lucky. She remembered how paralysed with nerves she'd been when she had first laid eyes on Hunter at that very first read-through. He was already an established star thanks to *Counsellor*, while she was still working as a waitress at Benny's Beans and Burgers in West Hollywood. Before *UCLA* she had barely worked in eighteen months, and was spending most of her days in a sweltering kitchen or serving over-priced heart attacks on a plate to revolting, lecherous customers, while wearing a badge that cheerily proclaimed 'I make it happen – Tiffany!' Jeez, how much had she hated that stinking place.

It was all a far cry from the life she'd dreamed of when she first set out from Estes Park, Colorado, to follow her dreams of becoming an actress.

Her parents had been against the idea from the start.

'She graduated magna cum laude, Marcie,' she remembered her normally mild-mannered father yelling at her mom, pointing at Tiffany as though she were an exhibit in a freak show. 'And you want her to throw that all away to become a waitress in Hollywood?'

'She wants to act, Jack,' said her mom, reasonably. 'She's young, and she's following her dream. What's wrong with that?'

'What's wrong with it? I'll tell you what's wrong with it. She'll end up like the rest of those poor suckers, all the small-town girls who grow up being told how pretty and talented they are by all the folks back home, and they head out to LA thinking they're gonna make it. They're gonna be *stars*.' He spat the word out with a bitterness born of his immense fear for his daughter. He loved her so much. Tiffany had never heard her dad speak like that to anyone. It made her feel sick. 'And ten years later,' he raged on, 'they're still serving pancakes at IHOP.'

'Oh, Jack,' said her mother gently, seeing Tiffany's horrified face.

'No, Marcie, I'm right about this and you know it. The waitresses are the lucky ones. Half of those girls end up working the streets. Or in . . .' He could barely bring himself to say it. '. . . in one of those depraved, pornographic films.'

'Jack Wedan!' her mother remonstrated, shocked. 'Don't be ridiculous. Tiffany would never get involved in anything like that.'

'And I won't be working as a waitress for the rest of my life either, Daddy,' Tiffany interjected, her face flushed with anger and disappointment. 'Don't you have any faith in me at all?'

How those words had come back to haunt her as she sweated away in Benny's kitchen alongside her best friend and flatmate, the gorgeously camp Lennox, another struggling actor. She had almost given up hope of ever making it in LA when Lennox had hauled her ass into that *UCLA* audition. And then suddenly, overnight, her life had changed. Just like in the movies.

The role of Sarah may only have been a small part, but it was network television and a regular income, two things she had hitherto barely allowed herself to dream of. Even more incredible, though, had been her blossoming relationship with Hunter. Of all the beautiful girls in the world, Hunter McMahon had chosen her. *Why?* Even now, three years later, she sometimes had to pinch herself when she woke up next to him, in case the whole thing were some sort of heavenly mirage.

For his part, Hunter knew that a lot of women wanted him, whether for his looks, his fame or his money. But he'd never been able to do what Max did, charming his way from one bed to the next, revelling in the fun and excitement of transient, casual flings. Unlike his best friend, Hunter had always been looking for companionship with a lover, and he had nothing in common with ninety per cent of the hot young LA actresses and models who pursued him.

But the way Tiffany wanted him, that was different. The way she clung on to him and screamed his name when they made love, the way her eyes lit up like a little kid at Christmas the moment he walked through the door – that was something else. He had never imagined that a woman so intelligent and talented and good and kind could ever love him the way that she did. She literally filled him with joy, and her love had given him a confidence he had never felt before.

Tiffany was the first woman, the first person in fact, that he had ever opened up to about his childhood. She had made him feel safe, slowly but surely gaining his confidence and trust until he felt able to talk about the loneliness and misery of growing up in Hancock Park, his difficult relationship with his mother and the terrible pain of his enforced separation from Siena.

Privately, Tiffany had always felt that if his supermodel niece was so perfect and had loved him so much, she could have made some sort of an effort to contact him after she became famous. She had never met Siena, of course, but the impression she got from magazine and TV interviews was of rather a spoiled little prima donna, nothing like the angelic figure Hunter so lovingly described. But she knew better than to question or challenge him about his precious memories. She understood that, apart from her, they were all he had.

He rolled on to his side and pulled the covers up over her naked body proprietorially.

'You'll catch cold,' he said, kissing her wet cheeks, which still tasted salty from her sweat.

'You're so sweet,' she whispered, pulling him closer. 'But I'm not staying, baby. I gotta take a shower and get going.'

Hunter pulled away from her. He was so fed up with this.

'For God's sake, Tiffany, why?' he snapped, unable to keep the hurt out of his voice. 'Why can't you just sleep here tonight? I'll set the alarm for six and drive you to the set myself in the morning. You won't be late for anything.'

'Hunter, please,' she said, climbing out of bed and starting to pick up various scattered items of her discarded clothing. 'I've told you before, I need my space.'

'What space?' he shot back at her. 'That rat hole of an apartment you live in is barely big enough to swing a cat in, and Lennox and his buddies are always hanging around like a bad smell. You have more space here.'

Tiffany sighed. It had been such a great night, she hoped he wasn't going to spoil it now. 'Look, can we not make a big deal of this?' she said, scrabbling under the bed for one missing sneaker. 'All my stuff is at home, OK, it's just easier. Besides, I promised Lennox I'd clean the place up a bit before tomorrow.'

She padded into the bathroom and turned on the shower, then came and stood naked in the doorway while she waited for the water to heat up. Looking at her flat, tanned stomach, and neatly trimmed blonde bush, Hunter felt himself starting to get hard again. If only he didn't want her so fucking much.

She walked back over to the bed and sat down beside him. He could still smell the sex on her body, and her closeness made his senses reel. She took his hand in hers and kissed it.

'Look,' she said gently, 'I'm sorry I can't stay tonight. But I'll make it up to you, OK? I promise. If you like, I'll come and spend the whole weekend here. I'll even put up with Max's singing in the mornings. Now how's that for devotion?'

Hunter put his arms around her. Why did he always find it so hard to let her go?

'I'll hold you to that,' he said, kissing her neck and the smooth naked skin of her shoulder. 'I just want us to have more time together.'

'I know,' she said, moving back across towards the bathroom. 'And we will, honey. I promise. We will. Just not tonight.'

Speeding back east on the ten freeway twenty minutes later, with the roar of her Ford jeep's knackered exhaust battering her eardrums, Tiffany punched the dashboard in frustration.

Why, why, why did she always do this? She loved him so much it killed her, so why did she keep on pushing him away?

With the rational part of her brain, of course, she already knew the answer to that question. She was afraid to trust in Hunter, afraid to believe that their love could possibly last. With every woman in the world lusting after him, and stunning models making plays for him night after night, looking right through her as though she were nothing – how could she possibly expect to hold him?

Moving into the beach house, as he was constantly begging her to do, seemed too much like tempting fate. The moment she let him know how hopelessly, desperately in love she was, the spell would be broken and he would leave.

No, the only way to survive was to hold on for dear life to her independence. After three years together, she still lived well within her means, driving her shitty old truck, living with Lennox in their run-down Westwood apartment, never letting Hunter buy her anything beyond dinner and the occasional vacation. She was not about to get used to Hunter's rich, glamorous lifestyle, only to have it all snatched away at a moment's notice.

Back at the beach house, Hunter couldn't sleep. He pulled on a pair of Calvins and a T-shirt and wandered into the kitchen, taking an iced tea out of the fridge and sipping it thoughtfully. He wished Max were here to talk to, but he was still in England with Henry. It must be great to have a family like Max's.

For the first time in months, Hunter found himself thinking about Siena. It was funny – although Pete's machiavellian scheming and attempted sabotage of his career had fixed him as a constant, looming presence in Hunter's life, still he never made the mental association between his brother and Siena, or the rest of the family. He had run into Claire once, about two years ago at Chaya Brasserie, but when he'd asked after Siena he'd been met with a blank wall of silence. If it hadn't been for the ubiquitous billboard pictures of her face – itself only a distant echo of the childish features that Hunter had once known and loved so well – he could almost have believed that she no longer existed.

He knew about the estrangement from her parents, of course – every supermarket tabloid in America had run versions of Siena's *Vanity Fair* interview the previous year, in which she had tearfully recounted Pete and Claire's abandonment. Many of them, in fact, had printed his own picture next to hers, drawing parallels between Pete's vendetta against him and the disinheriting of his only daughter.

As a teenager, he had found the pain of their separation almost unbearable. But now? Well, life had moved on, and life had been pretty damn good to him – to both of them, in fact. He wasn't in any hurry to risk opening up those old wounds all over again.

Still, on nights like tonight, he couldn't help but wonder what Siena would have made of Tiffany. They were the only two people he had ever loved in his life – with the possible exception of Max, but that was different – and they were both so smart, so independent, so fucking difficult!

Tiffany wasn't spoilt or selfish as Siena had been. But then again, she had grown up in a normal, happy home, not the dysfunctional madhouse at Hancock Park. But she had a similar strength about her, something that seemed to tell him 'I don't need you', which reminded him painfully of Siena. He wished he could discover just one ounce of that strength in himself. But the truth was, he needed Tiffany like air. He'd be lost without her.

He broke off his thoughts with a start when the phone rang. The clock on the microwave said it was 2 a.m. No one else would be calling him at that hour. It had to be Tiffany.

Heart thumping with happiness, he sprinted into the bedroom to pick it up.

'Baby?'

'Hunter, I've told you before, I'm very flattered, but I just don't think of you in that way.' Max's deadpan voice was slightly faint on the long-distance line.

'Max' said Hunter, fighting to keep the disappointment out of his voice. 'How are you, man? When are you coming back?'

'Well, that's what I called to tell you,' said Max. 'Oh, fuck, have I just woken you up? What time is it?'

'Two in the morning, but don't worry, I'm up. Tiffany went home to that shit hole she lives in, and now I can't sleep.'

Max was taken aback. He had never heard Hunter sounding so bitter about anything, especially not Tiffany.

'Oh,' he said lamely. 'Well, cheer up, fella, you see the girl every day. I'd make the most of a night off, if I were you. At least you can fart in bed with impunity.'

'Hmmm, I guess,' said Hunter. 'So what's up anyway, did you change your plans?'

'Slightly,' said Max. 'I'm still leaving here on the twenty-eighth, but I'm going to New York for a few days. There's a chance I may have a meeting with Alex McFadden on the twenty-ninth.'

'Max, that's great!' said Hunter, genuinely impressed.

Alex McFadden was a big producer of Broadway musicals, and Max had been angling for a one-on-one meeting with the guy for ever.

'Yeah, well, it hasn't happened yet,' said Max, ever the pessimist. 'But anyway, a couple of mates of mine from school are having a big New Year's Eve bash at this loft in SoHo. Jerry, my mate, just got a whopping great bonus from Goldman, so he's spending a fortune on this thing. It'll be wall to wall beautiful women – and I'm talking New York beautiful, none of your plastic, LA, silicone bullshit. I know you and Tiffany are as good as married, but there's no law against looking. Wanna come?'

Hunter chuckled quietly to himself. Sometimes Max reminded him of nothing so much as an overexcited Labrador. Listening to him gabbling happily away about this party, he could almost hear his tail thumping on the ground.

'Thanks, man, but I can't,' he said, stretching out his arms in a huge, full-bodied yawn and rubbing his head drowsily. 'We're shooting New Year's Eve.'

'You're kidding,' said Max. 'Doesn't that slave driver Orchard ever give you a night off? It's New Year's Eve, for Christ's sake.'

'What can I tell you?' said Hunter. 'He works hard, and that means the rest of us have to keep up. Anyway, I don't mind. Tiffany is working too, so we can maybe have dinner together or something later. To be honest with you, I'm feeling kinda low key right now. And you know how much I hate New York.'

'Suit yourself,' said Max, who considered hating New York to be a form of mental illness. 'I'll see you back in Hell-A on the second or third, then.'

'Oh, get over yourself!' Hunter laughed. 'Don't give me that Hell-A shit. You love it here and you know it. Just wait till you've had three days of sub-zero winds and hail in Manhattan. You'll be *begging* to come back home.'

Taking his drink with him, Hunter climbed back into bed and pulled the covers up around him. The lingering smell of Tiffany's body still clung to his sheets. With all his heart, he wished she were lying there next to him.

Chapter Twenty-five

It had been a bitterly cold winter in New York, one of the worst on record.

Tourists still flocked there in droves, to skate around the Christmas tree at the romantic Rockefeller Center ice rink, to marvel at the snow and the lights on Park Avenue, or to visit Santa's grotto at FAO Schwarz. Ruddy-cheeked families, with Dad in his Brooks Brothers cashmere coat, Mom in full-length mink and the kids in scarves, woolly hats and puffa jackets from the Gap, stamped their feet against the cold on every corner wolfing down cheap hot dogs smothered in fried onions, just so they could feel something warm hitting their stomachs, while passing drivers splashed them with icy spray from the puddles as they honked and swerved their way down Lexington.

The snow had turned to grimy slush on the streets, but it still kept falling, and the taxi drivers came in from New Jersey every morning with six inches of pure white icing on top of their marzipan-yellow cabs. Manhattan was crowded and dirty with a wind-chill factor that could have shamed the North Pole.

But there was nowhere quite like New York at Christmas time.

For just over a year, Siena and Ines had shared a Manhattan apartment, although each spent a good half of their time travelling, doing shows and campaigns around the world. Both the girls had left the city over the holiday; Ines to visit her family in Seville and Siena to stay with a well-known designer and his boyfriend at their weekend retreat in Vermont. But after five days away, they had both found themselves going stir crazy and decided to fly back to New York in time for New Year's Eve.

Sitting in the window seat of their palatial living room overlooking Central Park, with a red-and-green tartan blanket pulled up over her knees and a big glass of cognac in her hands, Siena looked out over the snowy greenery below her.

'So was it lovely in Spain?' she asked Ines, who was busy applying a third coat of purple polish to her toenails. 'You don't look very brown.'

'Ees weenter in Espain, you eediot.' Ines laughed. 'But yes, I 'ad a lovely time. Eet was so long since I saw all my family togethair.' She rolled her eyes to heaven. 'I ate like a peeg, though.'

'Me too,' said Siena, thinking back longingly to the rum-soaked Yule log she'd eaten almost single-handedly at Fabrizio's. 'I'm on champagne and cigarettes only for the rest of the week.'

Ines raised a questioning eyebrow at her friend's half-drunk cognac but said nothing.

'So what are your plans for tomorrow night?' asked Siena. 'Are you going to Matt's New Year thing?'

'No, I don't theenk so,' said Ines, screwing the cap back on her nail polish bottle and blowing gently on her toes. 'I am so tired of heem. I theenk he prefairs you anyway.'

'Oh, baloney,' protested Siena, blushing.

In fact, Ines's most recent boyfriend had already made his feelings towards her perfectly clear at a party a few weeks ago. Fucking slimeball. As if she would do the dirty on her best friend with a scumbag like him. She was glad that Ines was finally seeing the light about Matt.

'I haird about thees party in SoHo,' Ines continued, 'you know, the Eenglish friend of Anya's? A lot of cool people are going to be there. Maybe we should stop by?'

Siena finished her drink and walked over to the fridge, extracting a cold sausage and munching on it contemplatively. She'd start the nicotine diet tomorrow.

'Sure, I don't mind,' she said.

Her own supposed boyfriend, a Brazilian model called Carlo, had been putting pressure on her to join him and his friends at some bash downtown, but Siena's relationship claustrophobia was already starting to kick in. She'd much rather hang with Ines and the girls.

'Those Wall Street guys spend money like water,' she mused, leaning back against the cold fridge door. 'I remember the last banker party I went to, the guy had this fuck-off fountain flowing with Cristal the whole night. He must have spent fifteen thousand on that fountain alone. Totally vulgar, but kinda cool.'

She finished the sausage and started gnawing away at a slightly stale hunk of Cheddar. They really must get around to some grocery shopping. 'So who else is going?'

Ines carefully removed her white foam toe-separators and stood up. She was so tall and thin, with her shock of red hair – she had cut it very short about three months ago – she reminded Siena of an extra-long safety match.

'I don't know exactly,' she said. 'Anya, I theenk Zane and some of the other boys will be there. A lot of bankers.' She wiggled her purple toes admiringly. 'But of course' – she grinned – 'as soon as we arrive, every man in New York weel be banging down that door!'

Siena laughed. Sometimes Ines could be even more of an arrogant bitch than she was.

Max struggled miserably along Fifth Avenue. With his sleet-soaked raincoat clinging like shrink-wrap to his huge shoulders, and trousers splattered from the knee down with filthy spray from the streets, he looked exactly as he felt – utterly dejected.

New York sucked.

His meeting with the great Broadway producer Alex McFadden yesterday had been yet another damp squib. The guy had said some complimentary things about some of Max's English theatre work, and had even admired the short film he'd had at Sundance the year before. But he had been to enough of these 'love your stuff, must get together some time' meetings to know when he was being given the brush-off, however gracefully it was done. Unlike most of the LA producers he dealt with, McFadden had been a gentleman, taking time out of his day to encourage a struggling young director he didn't know from Adam. But the fact remained that Max was no nearer to hitting the big time than he had been last week in Batcombe, and he was starting to feel increasingly hopeless. He couldn't wait for this year to be over.

To cheer himself up, he had run into FAO Schwarz to pick up some presents for the kids. It was Madeleine's birthday on New Year's Day, and he'd promised to track down a Malibu Rollerblading Barbie. Max had spent enough time in New York to know that one's fellow shoppers could be a bit on the pushy side, but he had never seen anything quite like the women in that fucking toy store. They were like drug-crazed prop forwards: grabbing and shoving and wrestling over these Barbie dolls as if they were the last water bottle on a desert island or something. By the time he'd beaten a crowd of them back to secure Madeleine's prize, then gone through the whole ordeal again trying to find something suitable for the two boys, he'd emerged on to the street feeling like a grizzled piece of meat that had just been chewed up and spat out by some giant, man-eating monster.

'Taxi!' he yelled as an apparently empty cab sped straight past him, stopping for a leggy blonde half a block down.

'Fucker,' he mumbled, although he couldn't really blame the driver. He'd have pulled over for the blonde as well. Abandoning hope of finding a cab in such foul weather, and suddenly in desperate need of a restorative drink, he doubled back on himself and nipped into the O'Mahoney's pub on the corner.

Inside, the dingy, dark-wood-panelled bar was almost empty. Thank Christ. He was in no mood to have to wait around for service.

'What can I get you, sir?'

Max looked up from his piles of shopping into the green eyes of a truly stunning girl. She was wearing a tight white T-shirt with the O'Mahoney's logo emblazoned across her quite magnificently ample chest, and her long auburn hair tumbled down around her shoulders, making her look not unlike the storybook pictures of Helen of Troy.

'Fuck me, you're beautiful,' said Max, before realising to his horror that he'd actually spoken the words aloud.

The siren laughed, a deep, mellow sound that Max found quite enchanting. The nightmare of the Barbie department was already fading into the dim recesses of his memory.

'And you're not looking too bad yerself,' she said.

Ah, that Irish accent. It killed him every time.

Max noticed the mischievous way her eyes flickered when she spoke to him and her brazen holding of his gaze. Things were definitely starting to look up.

'I'm sorry,' he said sheepishly, unable to wipe the smile off his face. 'That just slipped out. I didn't mean to be rude. I'm Max, by the way. Max De Seville.'

He offered her his hand and she shook it.

'What, you mean like Bond, James Bond?' she teased him. 'Well, it's a pleasure to meet you, Max. I'm Angela.'

For a few delicious seconds they held on to each other's hands, neither of them saying a word.

'So Max,' said Angela eventually, still looking deep into his eyes. 'What can I get for you?'

'Oh, I don't know,' Max drawled, looking her body up and down as though he were appraising a racehorse. 'But I expect I can think of something.'

He woke up the next morning with a hangover that could have felled an elephant.

'Oh shit,' he whispered, opening one eye and trying to reorient himself to his spinning hotel room. 'I've died and gone to hell.'

'Well, that's just charming, thanks very much.'

Angela was lying above him propped up on her forearms, her big, smooth, rounded breasts spilling down on to his chest, and the tips of her Titian hair softly brushing against his face. Opening his eyes a little farther, Max saw her smudged black eye make-up and lips and chin slightly reddened from kissing, and the previous night's events gradually started coming back to him.

'Not you, angel,' he said, stroking her hair tenderly, but not wanting to risk a kiss with his mouth tasting like a four-day-old ashtray. 'You're heavenly.' She was too. How the hell had he managed to pull a girl like this? 'But unfortunately, I think someone may have broken in here last night and smashed me over the head with an anvil. Oh God.' He groaned, pushing her gently off him. 'Did I miss something, or did you not sink about seven pints last night? How come I'm the only one who feels like a rat's arse this morning?'

She laughed and, whipping the duvet off both of them, straddled him again, this time taking both his arms and pulling them upward so his hands were on her breasts.

'You know what the best cure for a hangover is?' She gave him that mischievous look again.

'Oh please, no, for God's sake, woman, have some compassion for a dying man,' Max whimpered.

Licking her palm, Angela reached down and wrapped her right hand firmly around his dick.

'Just close your eyes,' she whispered. 'I'm about to give you the last rites.'

By the time he arrived at Jerry's loft later that evening for the party, Max's stomach had somewhat stabilised, but he still looked like a man in the final stages of acute liver failure.

'What the fuck happened to you?' asked Jerry, ushering him in from the lobby and relieving him of a bottle of vintage Chablis.

'I had a rough night last night,' said Max, pushing his way through a room full of glamorous-looking New Yorkers and following his old friend into the kitchen, which was crammed with flustered, uniformed serving staff preparing yet more trays of complicated hors d'oeuvres.

'Was she worth it?' asked Jerry, snaking expertly past two waitresses and handing Max a flute of champagne.

'Fuck, yeah,' said Max, shuddering. The faint lemony smell of the fizzing alcohol was making him feel nauseous. He pushed away the glass. 'But I'm never drinking again. Have you got any Coke?'

'Liquid or powder?' Jerry smiled.

'Liquid,' said Max firmly. 'And not Diet. I need the sugar.' He put his hand to his temple. 'That music's fucking loud, mate.'

Jerry produced a Coke from the fridge and passed it over. 'That's the hottest DJ in the city, Max, my friend,' he said. 'He doesn't do quiet. Besides, this is a party, and a shit-hot one at that, in case you hadn't noticed.'

Right on cue, a six-foot brunette with legs up to her armpits sauntered past the kitchen doorway in a skin-tight orange mini-dress and thigh-high boots.

'Hey, Katya.' Jerry nodded at her, acknowledging her smile as she walked past. She blew him a kiss in return and disappeared into the throng.

'So I don't want to hear another word about your bloody hangover, all right?' continued Jerry, slapping Max painfully across the back of the shoulders. 'It's New Year's Eve, mate. Have some hair of the dog, get out there and stop moaning.' He raised his bottle of Beck's to Max's can of Coke in a toast. 'Good to see you.'

Max downed his drink in one almighty gulp. 'Good to see you too, Jerry.'

Wandering back into the main party room, an immense, warehouse-sized living space with panoramic views across the city, Max wished he had made a bit more of an effort. He was not naturally lacking in confidence, but a depressing feeling of inadequacy gripped him as he caught sight of his own reflection in one of the floor-to-ceiling mirrors: pallid, unshaven, wearing a dirty old pair of Diesel jeans and a grey fisherman's jumper of Henry's. He wasn't exactly the epitome of New York chic.

As he approached a low table groaning with more of the hors d'oeuvres he'd admired earlier in the kitchen, and started to swoop in on a caviar and cream cheese blini, he noticed a sea of people parting around him and moving off towards the door. He was starting to wonder whether he still smelt like a rancid skunk and had somehow imagined his earlier shower when he realised that they were not moving away from him, but towards a new arrival.

'She's here,' he heard a fellow next to him whispering to his companion. 'I *told* you she was coming.'

'Who's here?' asked Max, through a mouthful of caviar. He felt ravenously hungry all of a sudden.

'Didn't you see her?' said the man, a trendy advertising executive type wearing orange lenses in his Buddy Holly glasses, and waving in the general direction of the buzzing crowd by the door. 'It's Siena McMahon.'

Max almost choked on his blini.

'And that fit Spanish bird's with her,' piped up the man's English sidekick. Max pushed past them and made his way to a sofa at the back of the room, where two models were deep in conversation. He was very curious to see Siena, but some instinct made him recoil from the idea of battling his way towards her like a besotted fan.

'Mind if I perch here?' he asked the two girls as he eased himself down on to the arm of the sofa.

'Not at all,' said the prettier one, looking at his long legs and huge muscled torso with approval. 'You're a big boy, though. I'm not sure if that armrest can take your weight.'

Max raised one eyebrow at her knowingly. She was a bit standard issue: long blonde hair, very regular features – but she was undeniably an extremely sexy girl. Perhaps his hangover was starting to dissipate after all.

'Anyway, as I was saying,' butted in the girl's friend rudely, pointedly turning her back on Max (like most models, she had no tolerance for flirtation unless it was directed towards herself), 'I've never understood what all the fuss was about. As far as I'm concerned she's short and she's fat. It's a mystery to me what men see in her.'

'I know,' said the blonde. 'Zane says he thinks it's because she looks so slutty and available.'

'Not a bad look,' muttered Max under his breath.

At that moment, a gap appeared in the crowd and he found himself looking, albeit from a fifty-foot distance, directly at Siena.

The first thing he noticed was that she looked nothing like any of the other women in the room. Dressed conservatively in immaculately cut white palazzo pants and a crimson silk shirt, which displayed only the slightest of hints of her famous creamy white cleavage, she radiated confidence and sex appeal, smiling and air-kissing her way through each new group of admirers.

The thick mass of dark curls was exactly as he'd remembered it, as was the pronounced and incongruously demure dimple on her chin, a chin that still jutted arrogantly upwards towards every man who came to worship at the altar of her beauty.

Because whatever other, jealous girls might say, there could be absolutely no doubt that Siena was beautiful. Magnetically, terrifyingly beautiful.

Holy shit, thought Max. She could light up the whole of Park Avenue with that charisma. It was like magic.

Try as he might, he couldn't take his eyes off her.

'I loved your *Vanity Fair* pictures,' a chiselled, Armani-suited clone was gushing as he approached her. 'So brave. So raw.'

Oh please, thought Siena. She hoped Ines was right and there were men other than models at this party. Despite the fact that she had lived and worked among New York's modelling fraternity for the past two years, her inanity threshold remained perilously low. If there was one thing she really had no tolerance for, it was pretty, stupid men.

'You make me sound like a carrot,' she said rudely, looking past him in search of someone, anyone, more interesting.

At first she couldn't quite place him. At the back of the room, an enormous, powerful-looking blond man, dressed like a hobo, was staring straight at her. Siena was used to being looked at, but something about the intensity of this man's gaze left her stomach churning. He was definitely handsome, like a trawlerman who'd got very lost and somehow wound up in a Manhattan loft surrounded by a bunch of spoilt, rich bankers and their beautiful toys.

And yet, he did look familiar.

It was only when she started walking towards him, and he stood up to greet her, that the penny dropped.

No. It couldn't be. Siena froze in her tracks.

'Hello, Siena,' said Max, towering over her like a Roman statue. 'Long time no see.'

She could hear her heart pounding, and a torrent of conflicting emotions raging through her.

Max De Seville! How could Max De Seville be here? Just seeing his face and hearing his voice transported her back in an instant to Hancock Park and the earliest, happiest days of her childhood. Suddenly she was no longer the world-famous model, envied, desired and in control. She was a ten-year-old little girl, being ignored and dismissed by Hunter's fifteen-year-old best friend, and ordered out of their tree house.

Ridiculously, she found her old resentment of Max, always her rival for Hunter's affections, flooding back to her, as though the last eleven years had never happened. But fighting with the resentment was enormous curiosity, combined with another, more unsettling feeling that she couldn't quite put her finger on.

She wished he would stop staring at her like that.

'Max.' She smiled thinly and extended a perfectly manicured hand. 'What a nice surprise.'

Her voice was heavy with sarcasm. Max instantly bristled. So that was the way she wanted to play it. Well, if she thought she was going to come the supermodel diva with him, she had another think coming.

He shook her hand.

'Isn't it? I hardly recognised you at first, actually. Must have been all those clothes you're wearing.'

Despite herself, Siena blushed. That was fifteen love to Max.

'Yes,' she said, 'I have this thing about dressing appropriately for social occasions.' She allowed her eye to wander disapprovingly over his threadbare jumper and dirty jeans. 'But I see that's not one of your priorities.'

Fifteen all.

Max took a deep breath. He was determined not to let the little cow provoke him.

'How are you enjoying the modelling?' he asked.

'Oh, you know.' She waved her hand dismissively. 'It's a means to an end. Of course, the money's fabulous. But I'm going to be doing a lot more acting in future.'

'Oh really?' said Max with a sly smile.

Was the bastard laughing at her?

'What have you done so far?'

'Other than make millions, you mean?' she snapped, wishing he didn't make her feel so defensive. Max raised his eyebrow but said nothing. 'A couple of indie films,' she said eventually, 'some music videos, that kinda thing. I have some very interesting scripts I'm looking at right now, though,' she lied. 'But I can't really talk about it yet. What about you?'

'I'm a director,' said Max, feeling very uncomfortable suddenly.

'Is that so?' said Siena. Like her grandfather, she could smell weakness as a shark smelled blood and instinctively moved in for the kill. 'Of what? How come I've never heard of you?'

For a moment Max struggled to think of a comeback. 'I don't do mainstream, Hollywood shit,' he said lamely.

'Oh, I see,' said Siena. 'Yes, I can tell from your clothes that you must have sacrificed a *lot* for your artistic integrity.'

The fucking snide little bitch. How dare she?

'Well, lovely as it's been Siena,' – he smiled down at her, with a self-control he was justly proud of – 'I don't think I'll be staying to see the New Year in, so I'm afraid you must excuse me.' He put his empty glass down on a side table and turned to go. 'I'll tell Hunter you said hello.'

At the mention of Hunter's name, Siena felt her knees give way and reached out instinctively to the arm of the sofa for support. Her head had started to spin and her mouth went dry with panic. Max was still in touch with Hunter? She watched, paralysed, as his back view receded into the throng. Oh God, she couldn't let him leave.

'Max, wait!' she called out, more loudly and anxiously than she had intended, so that a cluster of revellers near by turned around and stared at her.

Reluctantly, Max stopped and turned.

'Do you . . .' she began, obviously struggling to find the words. If she weren't such a vain, spoilt, selfish little madam, Max thought, he might almost have felt sorry for her. 'I mean, are you and Hunter still friends, then?'

'Of course,' he said harshly. He knew it must hurt her to know that his relationship with Hunter had survived when hers had not. But she was so beautiful and confident and successful, so damn perfect, at that moment he wanted to hurt her. He decided to twist the knife. 'Actually, we live together in Santa Monica. Have done for the last three years.'

'Oh.' She looked completely lost at this piece of news, so much so that he instantly began to regret having told her. He should have just let it lie.

'Look, I should be going.'

'Oh no, Max, please, don't go,' she pleaded, grabbing his arm.

He looked at her panicked face and saw a flicker of vulnerability that instinctively made him want to put his arms around her, as he had done all those years ago when she'd fallen out of the tree house and he'd thought for one awful moment she might have been killed.

But he stopped himself. What was the point? She was clearly so fucked up and emotionally damaged. It would be like trying to pet a porcupine.

'Does he ever talk about me?' she asked.

He knew how much it had cost her to ask the question, and softened slightly.

'He did,' he said, not unkindly. 'But he doesn't any more.'

'Well, sure.' Siena shrugged in a failed attempt at nonchalance, desperately trying to fix her mask of self-confidence back in place. 'I mean, it's been, what, ten years? That's a lot of water under the bridge.'

'Yeah,' said Max. 'I guess it is.'

'Look, I'm sorry,' she said. 'I shouldn't have been so rude before. Just tell Hunter I said hi, or whatever.' She tossed her mane of hair and gave a practised, professional fifty-megawatt smile, a signal, he assumed, that the conversation was over and she was ready to get back to the business of receiving more male attention.

'I will,' said Max.

Suddenly he was longing to get away from her, away from everybody.

He strode through the party without looking back or stopping to say goodbye to any of his friends, even Jerry. Bolting into the elevator as though he were fleeing for his life, he fidgeted impatiently until he reached the lobby and literally ran out into the street.

Leaning back against the cold brickwork of Jerry's building, he paused for a moment to savour the cold night air and the relative quiet and stillness of the city.

Goddam it.

Why had Siena made him feel like such a piece of shit?

Glancing at his watch, he saw that it was only a minute until midnight. Within a few short seconds, he started to hear cheers and shouts, bells ringing and the honking of horns as the city began to welcome in another new year. He thought briefly of Angela, and wondered whether she and her boyfriend were enjoying a lingering New Year's kiss somewhere out there. He guessed they were.

As he mooched off in the direction of his hotel, his sore head still throbbing from a renewed burst of hangover, a wave of loneliness and exhaustion hit him like a ton of lead. He thought of Henry and Muffy back in Batcombe, and of Hunter and Tiffany, no doubt wrapped up in each other's arms at the beach house. He'd never been much of a one for relationships, not really. But suddenly, tonight, he wished to God he had someone to hold on to.

Bitterly, he thought of Siena, still holding court upstairs at the party like the perfect, spoiled goddess she seemed to have become, while he stood knackered, hungover, alone and freezing his ass off out on the street. What was he even doing here? He had no job to speak of, no money and no girlfriend. No wonder Siena had put him down. His life was like one long, bad joke.

Roll on 2002.

Things could only get better.

Chapter Twenty-six

Uptown in Beverly Hills a couple of weeks later, Max and Hunter were tucked away in the prestigious corner table at the Brasserie Blanc. Hunter had already been pestered by three fans before they'd ordered their starters. He refused to wear sunglasses or a baseball cap indoors like so many other celebrities, on the very sensible grounds that it didn't fool anybody anyway and made you look like a self-important jerk. But unfortunately this gave people the impression that he was always approachable.

He put up with the endless intrusions on his privacy with his typical good humour. But Max found going out with him in public increasingly trying.

'So come on then, buddy, spill the beans,' said Hunter after signing his third autograph for a middle-aged tourist from Ohio and sending her joyously on her way with a kiss on the cheek. 'How was New York? Tell me more about your meeting with Alex McFadden.'

'There's nothing more to tell, I'm afraid,' said Max gloomily. 'He was a very nice chap, very complimentary about my film and all that, but he's a Broadway man. I simply don't have enough theatre experience to play in that league.'

'I thought you'd done lots of Shakespeare and all that in London?' said Hunter.

Max loved the way Hunter referred to anything written before 1950 as 'Shakespeare and all that.'

'Some, not lots,' he said. 'Not enough, evidently. But let's not talk about my work, it's too depressing. What's been going on here while I've been gone?'

'Not much,' said Hunter. 'Tiff and I went up to Big Bear, which was pretty cool. Four whole days to ourselves, no work, no distractions, no nothing. I can't remember the last time we had that much time alone.'

'Well, you look well on it,' said Max, smiling at the dopey, besotted expression that had spread across his best friend's face. Just talking about Tiffany sent him ga-ga. It was cute.

They both took a big slug of Californian merlot.

'Never mind about me, though,' said Hunter. 'Fill me in on *your* romantic adventures. How many girls did you sleep with in New York, huh? Three? Four? How long were you there again?' he added with a knowing grin.

'Two weeks,' said Max, pretending to look affronted as he snapped a breadstick in half and began nibbling at it. 'And I only slept with one, thank you very much.' His mind wandered happily back to the night he'd spent with Angela.

'Look at you!' Hunter laughed. 'Like a kid with a fistful of candy. So? Are you gonna see her again?'

'Nope,' said Max, stuffing the rest of the breadstick into his mouth all at once.

The waitress arrived with a plate of carpaccio for Hunter and a big bowl of deep-fried squid for Max, who was starting to feel like the invisible man watching the girl fawning and simpering and fluttering her eyelashes at Hunter, utterly oblivious to his own presence at the table.

'So, what else happened?' asked Hunter after a few mouthfuls of his delicious raw beef. Max normally couldn't stop yabbering on whenever he got back from a trip, regaling Hunter with one funny story after another, never-ending tales of one-night stands, all-night parties and every little step he'd taken towards that ever illusive big break. He was being unusually reticent tonight. 'How was your New Year's Eve?'

It was the question Max had been dreading. He ought to have called Hunter from New York and told him about his encounter with Siena right away. Now, almost two weeks after the event, he found himself unsure where, or even if, to begin.

'It was good,' he said, uncertainly. 'It was fine.'

'What's with all this "good", "fine" shit?' asked Hunter. 'Why do I get the feeling there's something you aren't telling me?'

Max cleared his throat nervously. There was no way around it. 'I ran into someone in New York,' he said at last. 'At Jerry's party.'

'Oh yeah?' asked Hunter. 'Who?'

Max hesitated for a moment, looking from Hunter, to his plate, then back again before blurting it out.

'Siena.'

He hadn't known exactly how Hunter would react to the news; whether he would be shocked and numb or just confused and upset. But nothing had prepared him for the look of pure, unadulterated delight that swept across his friend's face.

'Siena?' He leant forward across the table and grabbed Max by the shoulders, as if he were about to kiss him passionately. 'Are you kidding me? You actually saw her? Did you speak to her?'

'Sure,' said Max. 'Only for a couple of minutes, though. We said hello.'

He wasn't about to let on to Hunter that she'd actually been every bit as self-centred and arrogant as he remembered her, and that he couldn't wait to escape and get away from her.

'Did she ask about me?' asked Hunter.

Max lit up a cigarette, ignoring the loud complaints from nearby diners.

'Yes,' he said, cagily.

'Well, come on, man, don't keep me in suspense,' said Hunter, releasing Max's lapels only when the smoke started getting in his eyes. 'What did she say?'

'Well . . .' Max hesitated, flicking ash awkwardly on to his side plate. 'She asked how you were, and I said you were fine.'

'What else?' demanded Hunter, impatiently.

'She asked if you ever talked about her,' said Max. 'I told her that you used to, after Duke died, but that you didn't any more.'

'Why the fuck did you say that?' Hunter shouted, flinging his napkin down angrily on the table.

The whole restaurant turned round to stare at them.

'Because it's true,' said Max flatly, taking another long drag of his cigarette as if nothing had happened. 'And don't you start shouting at me. I'm just the hapless fucking messenger here, all right?'

Hunter relaxed his shoulders.

'All right. I'm sorry,' he said. 'I just didn't want her to think . . .'

'That you've moved on?' offered Max.

'Exactly.'

'But haven't you, though, mate?' Max persisted, risking a second outburst of Hunter's rarely seen temper. He stubbed out his half-smoked cigarette and looked his best friend in the eye. 'Look, you can tell me this is none of my business if you like.'

'Thanks,' said Hunter, who was already smiling again. 'This is none of your business.'

'But don't you think you might get hurt?' persisted Max.

'By Siena?' Hunter looked genuinely surprised. 'No, of course not. Why would I? Tiffany's always going on about me getting hurt. Says I should 'learn to protect myself'. What neither of you seem to get is that it was being *separated* from Siena that hurt. And that sure as hell wasn't her fault. We were kids, for God's sake.'

'I know, I know,' said Max. 'I was there, remember? I'm not blaming her, Hunter. I'm just saying that it was more than ten years ago, man. She's changed. What if it's not the same between you when you see her again? You don't think that that could hurt you?'

Hunter rubbed his eyes in disbelief. It was all too much for him to take in.

'Look,' he said, 'I appreciate your concern. Really, I do. I know you and Tiffany both care about me. But I think . . .' He struggled to find the words. 'I think that this is fate.'

Max rolled his eyes.

'Seriously,' said Hunter, willing Max to believe him. 'I was just thinking about her in Big Bear only last week – we used to go there sometimes with the nannies when we were kids. It's like she was meant to come back into my life now. Do you know what I mean?'

Max shook his head. 'Not really.'

'I don't expect you to understand,' said Hunter, without bitterness. 'I don't think anyone really understands what Siena meant to me. What she means to me now. Not even Tiffany gets it.' He sighed. 'But Max, I have to see her. Did you get her number?'

'No.' He watched Hunter's face crumble. 'But I have the name and number of her agent.'

He pulled a crumpled piece of paper out of his jacket pocket and handed it to Hunter, who snatched at it greedily, read it, and placed it carefully in his own wallet.

'Thanks,' he said, more calmly, although the excitement in his eyes still gave him away.

'Be careful,' said Max. 'I'm worried about you.'

'I know,' said Hunter. 'But there's no need to be, really. You've just made me the happiest man on this planet.'

'That can't be right.'

Henry Arkell looked up from the piece of paper in front of him and rubbed his temples. He was sitting in the farm office at Batcombe, across the desk from his accountant and old school friend Nicholas Frankel. 'Are you sure?'

Nick shifted uncomfortably in his seat. He always hated having to give bad news to clients, but with Henry, a close personal friend, he felt doubly like the messenger of doom. Avoiding Henry's gaze, he glanced around him. The poky little office in the corner of the farmyard was piled floor to ceiling with clutter. Stacks of old receipts and important legal letters were strewn willy-nilly among photos of Muffy and the children, betting slips and Christmas cards, one of which Nick saw was three years old and covered with a thick layer of grey dust, no doubt unmoved since the day it was opened. Perhaps if Henry made some basic attempt at filing or organisation, his accounts might not be in such a desperate state. He'd been exactly the same since their schooldays, though – energetic, hard working but always terminally scatterbrained.

'Completely sure, I'm afraid, old man.' He sighed. 'It's not looking good.'

'Not good?' said Henry. 'It's bloody catastrophic. According to this, I'm four hundred grand in debt, and that's not including the back taxes. Which are how much again?'

'I don't know exactly,' muttered Nick grimly. 'At least one fifty, possibly quite a bit more.'

Henry winced. What the fuck was he going to do? A big part of him longed to unburden himself to Muffy, for sheer comfort if not for practical advice. But somehow it had never been quite the right time to tell her that the debts were getting on top of him, and now things had got so bad he wouldn't know where to begin. In the past his tax problems had had a happy knack of working themselves out in the wash eventually, and Nick had been a genius at putting the Revenue off until he'd managed to scrape together enough cash to keep the wolf from the door. But this time it wasn't just taxes. What with the cost of diversifying the farm, the lost revenues from the BSE crisis, which had had a knock-on effect on every farmer in England, and a couple of bad investments, his interest payments to the bank alone now came to over forty grand a year. Worst of all, a few months ago he had taken out a small lien against the house itself in an attempt to see off one of his more rabidly litigious creditors – despite having sworn to Muffy long ago that their equity in the manor would always remain sacred. She would absolutely hit the roof if, or he supposed when, she heard about that one.

'Well, there must be something we can do. Some sort of stalling tactic,' he said desperately, getting up from his chair and pacing the box-like room anxiously. It was still bitterly cold outside, but a tiny dilapidated fan heater was belting out heat in the corner, making the office feel like a bread oven. 'Just until we start to see the income back from the arable.'

Nick gave a gloomy shrug, as if to say 'I'm not so sure'. 'Maybe you should talk to Muff?'

'No. No way.' Henry held up his hand and shook his head, blotting out the awful possibility. 'She can't know about this.'

'Well, look,' said Nick, gathering up his papers and slotting them back into his neatly organised briefcase, 'I can probably buy you a bit of time with the Revenue. But the bank's a different story. You're going to have to come up with something concrete, some sort of repayment plan that you can actually deliver, or they're going to start getting nasty.'

'All right, all right,' said Henry, ushering him out into a blast of welcomely cold wind. 'You deal with Johnny taxman and I'll work on pulling something out of the bag for the bank. I'm sure we'll figure it out somehow.'

Nick tried to smile and wished he could share Henry's innate optimism. He didn't know how many other ways to tell him that his financial problems were now beyond pressing and were not going to magically dissolve into the ether, however hard he wished them away. It was a bit like trying to explain to your eight-year-old son that Father Christmas wasn't real. Losing Manor Farm was, for Henry, a literally unthinkable prospect.

'But not a word to Muffy, all right?' Henry whispered, locking the office door behind him. Before Nick had a chance to answer, Muffy herself appeared in the kitchen doorway looking flushed and triumphant, carrying a plate of what looked like freshly baked scones.

'Ready for some tea, you two? Maddie and I just made these from the new Prue Leith cookbook. What do you think?' She walked over to join them, proudly wafting the still-steaming scones under their noses until both men could feel their mouths watering. Looking at his friend's wife, with her pretty unmade-up face, still-girlish blonde hair and trusting, playful green eyes, Nick could quite see why Henry found it hard to confide in her about his money problems. Her trust in him was total and implicit. How could he bear to disappoint someone so utterly loving and loyal, never mind the impact it would have on the children if things got really bad. Nick just prayed that Henry was right and that somehow, between them, they would come up with something.

'Wow. They look bloody amazing,' said Henry, wrapping his arm around his wife's waist and beaming with pride, as though he'd baked the scones himself. 'You'll stay for tea?' he said to Nick.

'No, no.' The accountant shook his head and pulled out his car keys from his inside jacket pocket, blowing on his already frozen fingers for warmth. 'Thanks, but I really must be heading back to London. Lots to do,' he added, with a knowing look at Henry.

'All right, well, look, thanks again for everything,' said Henry. Muffy disappeared back into the kitchen as he said his goodbyes. 'Let's talk next week.'

'Fine,' said Nick. 'I'll get you some exact figures on the back taxes. But in the meantime, you might want to invest in a lottery ticket.'

Reaching into his back pocket, Henry pulled out a scrunched-up piece of pink paper and waved it at him. Nick put his head in his hands. 'That was meant to be a joke.'

'Ah, but you see, I'm way ahead of you, mate.' Henry grinned. 'How's that for financial planning, eh?'

Chapter Twenty-seven

Two weeks later, Siena was contentedly sipping freshly pressed apple juice and looking down at the white sandy beach below her balcony. It was only 9.30 on a Saturday morning, but thanks to the blazing February sunshine, Santa Monica was already starting to look busy.

Serious, professional-looking rollerbladers in tight black spandex whizzed past families poodling along on their hired beach bikes, while buff-looking gay couples jogged through the sand with their dogs. Everyone was in T-shirts and shorts, and the sky was a cloudless California blue. New York, with its freezing winds and urban grime, seemed a million miles away.

Siena was staying at Shutters on the Beach, one of the oldest and most luxurious hotels right on the ocean, adjacent to the gaudy lights of the Santa Monica pier, where Duke used to take her on the Ferris wheel when she was a little girl.

She was back in California for a second audition for *The Prodigal Daughter*, a low-budget but high-profile art-house movie, where she was up for the female lead. It was the first real film role she'd ever been up for which didn't require her either to play herself or to strip, and her screen test had gone extremely well. The producers had told her yesterday that it was between her and one other girl, but that, off the record, they were likely to confirm today that the part was hers. After all the stress and anxiety of the last few weeks – seeing Max again and hearing about Hunter had thrown her more than she cared to admit – Siena had woken up this morning feeling more rested and contented than she had in months.

Her next modelling job wasn't until the twenty-sixth in New York. To Marsha's delight, she had recently won a very lucrative contract as the face of French design house Maginelle's new make-up range, so she could afford to take a bit of time off. If the news today was good, she reckoned she might treat herself to a week or so's break in the West Coast sunshine and recharge her batteries. Perhaps drive up to

Santa Barbara or spend a few nights at the Post Ranch Inn in Big Sur? She couldn't remember the last time she'd taken a real vacation.

'More coffee, Miss McMahon?'

An incredibly good-looking Hispanic waiter hovered over her with a divine-smelling pot of Brazilian roast. The day was just getting better and better.

'Mmmm, thanks,' said Siena drowsily, luxuriating in the long-forgotten feeling of sunshine on her back.

It was funny, after all her fears about coming to LA and the terrible fretting about seeing Hunter again or running into any of the rest of her family, now that she was actually here, she felt more relaxed and happy than she had in ages. Perhaps it was because the audition had gone so well, or maybe it was just the joy of being back in her home city at last. She'd realised on the plane that she hadn't in fact set foot in California since the Christmas before her A-levels, over three years ago.

Back then she was just a schoolgirl, trapped in a life that her father had created for her, with no control over her own destiny. Now here she was, a world-famous model and soon-to-be actress.

It felt good. It felt very, very good.

She was reaching across the table for another freshly baked cinnamon bagel – her third – when she caught sight of a diminutive English woman, dressed for New York in head-to-toe black wool and Gucci sunglasses, pushing her way through the tables and waving at her frantically.

'Hello, Marsha.' She sighed. Just when she'd been feeling so mellow, the hyperactive dwarf had to show up and shatter the mood. 'What's up?'

'Well,' said Marsha, pinching a chair from a neighbouring table without asking and sitting down opposite Siena. 'They called.'

'Already?' Siena choked. A piece of bagel had gone down the wrong way and she took a big gulp of coffee to wash it down, promptly scalding her mouth. Fuck.

She could already tell from her agent's tone that the news wasn't good. No one said 'They called' if the news was good. If the news was good they said 'You got the part!' Goddam it. She'd been so sure this time, as well. What could have gone wrong?

'You got the part,' said Marsha morosely, helping herself to a cup of coffee and a bowlful of Siena's strawberries.

It took a moment to sink in.

'I did?' said Siena, grinning from ear to ear like a little girl on her birthday. 'Shit! Why didn't you say so?'

'I thought I just did,' mumbled Marsha through a mouthful of fruit.

'Well, you might sound a bit more happy about it.'

'What's to be happy about? The movie pays peanuts, and it'll take you four months to shoot,' said Marsha, matter-of-factly. 'Maginelle pay millions for ten days' work. And there's a lot more where that came from if you'd only focus on your modelling. I make no secret of it, Siena. I think you're fucking crazy.'

One thing you could say for Marsha, at least she was up front about what she believed in. The dollar was king, always had been, always would be.

'I can still do Maginelle,' said Siena, trying to mollify her agent, who looked as if Santa had just left the proverbial lump of coal in her Christmas stocking. 'Acting and modelling aren't mutually exclusive, you know. Besides, if I make a name for myself as an actress, my modelling fees will go through the roof.'

'Hmmm.' Marsha sounded unconvinced. 'You should be in New York, honey. Or, if not New York, London. These guys want you here in LA, from March through June, maybe longer. You're going to miss the whole season.'

Siena shrugged. 'So what else did they say? Do they want to see me again? Did they talk to you about a contract?'

'Yeah, yeah, yeah.' Marsha brushed away her questions with a dismissive wave. 'You leave the contract to me.'

'Of course,' said Siena. 'Always.'

If anyone could screw an extra few grand out of the producers, it was Marsha. Despite her desire to act, Siena was far more conscious of her financial interests than Marsha gave her credit for. She had no intention of working on low-budget movies for ever, and saw *The Prodigal Daughter* very much as a means to an end. Until she made it big in Hollywood, she had no intention of giving up her modelling contracts either.

A gentle ocean breeze blew her hair back off her face, and Siena sat back in her chair, indulging for a moment in her triumph.

Her first leading role at last. It had been a long time coming.

'You know what?' She sat forward suddenly and grabbed Marsha's hand, determined to engender some enthusiasm. 'Let's celebrate!'

'Yeah. Sure,' the older woman grumbled.

'Come on! I'm serious,' insisted Siena. 'Let's throw a little party here tonight, just a few people. We can have apple martinis on the beach, do the whole LA thing.'

Marsha still looked nonplussed.

'Oh, come *on!*' Siena coaxed her. 'You know you love a good party. I know you, remember? I'm doing this film, so you might as well get used to it. And who knows? Maybe this will be the start of something big. For both of us.'

'I guess,' conceded Marsha.

Sensing she was weakening, Siena decided to play her trump card.

'I'm paying,' she said, giving her agent the benefit of her million-dollar smile.

'Oh, all right,' said Marsha, giving in with something approaching good grace. 'I guess a *little* party wouldn't hurt.'

By eight o'clock, two hundred and fifty of the LA 'in crowd' were already mingling noisily on the hotel's private beach, getting happily drunk at Siena's expense. She'd say this for Marsha: her organisational skills were nothing short of miraculous. Once she'd got on board with the idea of a party, she'd pulled the whole thing together in a matter of hours.

Siena herself was still upstairs in her room, trying on two different pairs of loaned diamond drop earrings, undecided as to which went best with her floor-length crimson silk halter-neck dress.

She'd really pulled all the stops out tonight, and looked every inch the supermodel that she was, with the halter-neck simultaneously showing off her full, high breasts and a smooth, newly tanned expanse of bare back. Her favourite red Manolos, the only shoes in the world that managed to achieve the double whammy of being both sky high and comfortable, completed her ultra-sexy look. Not many girls could have pulled off something so glamorous and formal at a beach party. But Siena was blessed with enough confidence to turn up naked at the Oscars without looking out of place.

Finally opting for the smaller, subtler earrings, she sprayed herself liberally with Rive Gauche and headed for the elevator. Landing this part had filled her with a wave of confidence that, after a few hours, had translated into a raging libido.

She felt powerful and beautiful tonight. She wanted to be made love to, worshipped and adored.

The instant she appeared on the wooden steps leading down to the beach, an excited throng of people surged towards her. Siena smiled and kissed her way through them on her way to the bar and a pre-cocktail glass of champagne.

She could see Marsha chatting up a well-known director about thirty feet away, and recognised a group of three or four model-cum-actresses from the audition circuit perched at the bar. The trio were being attentively looked after by Jeff Black, a sleazeball real estate developer with a penchant for under-age girls and silicone, but he immediately transferred his attentions to Siena when she arrived at the bar, ordering herself a chilled glass of Moët.

'Let me get that for you.' He leered, ostentatiously pulling out a hundred-dollar bill from his wallet.

'Put your money away, Jeff. It's all paid for already. By me, as I'm sure you know by now,' said Siena bluntly.

A lot of the girls tolerated Jeff, because he never tried to sleep with them or touch them. He was just a rich, middle-aged man who liked the ego boost of being seen surrounded by pretty young things. But Siena found him disgusting. If she wanted a ride in a private jet, she'd get her own.

Turning back to the party, she scanned the beach for familiar faces, but found to her disappointment that, apart from a couple of acquaintances, the whole place was heaving with faceless hangers-on. She wished she'd been able to persuade Ines to come with her to the West Coast, but she'd had a job in Boston and couldn't make it. Suddenly, Siena felt deeply depressed. Here she was in LA, her own home town, celebrating the biggest success of her career – and not a single person she loved was there to share the moment with her. Was this what her life had come to? Was this what success, fame and wealth really meant?

She spent the next two hours dutifully pressing the flesh with the smattering of producers and directors who'd bothered to show up, smiling at everybody Marsha told her to. By eleven she was feeling utterly deflated and decided, despite Marsha's protests, to call it a night. By then the beach was such a crush it took her a further forty minutes to battle her way through all the so-called well-wishers back into the hotel lobby. One tenacious paparazzo who had somehow made it through the manager's elaborate defences thrust a camera in her face just as she gave way to a full-throated yawn while waiting for the elevator. That really was the last fucking straw.

The familiar clicking and whirring won him perhaps six or seven shots of Siena scowling before two of the bell boys manhandled him away and the electric doors mercifully closed and allowed her some peace.

When she eventually made it up to her room, she collapsed on the bed, totally exhausted.

Marsha had been right in the first place. The party had been a stupid idea. What had possessed her to shell out twenty thousand dollars to feed and water a bunch of assholes she had never laid eyes on before, and wind up in bed, alone and miserable, before midnight?

Dropping her dress in a heap on the floor and kicking off her shoes, she padded into the bathroom in just a Trashy Lingerie Gstring and her diamond drop earrings and began running herself a hot bath.

At first the gushing, steaming water was so loud that she didn't hear the knock on the door. When she finally made out the insistent rat-tat-tat, she hurriedly turned off the tap and attempted to cover herself up with the pitifully small hotel bath towel.

'Just a second!' She raced into the bedroom looking for her robe or anything that might do a better job of covering her steam-flushed nakedness, but both bed and floor were covered with evening dresses she had hastily rejected earlier and she couldn't find anything suitable.

Giving up, she ran to the door and opened it – it was probably only room service and they'd seen it all before – still wearing nothing but her tiny towel and the diamonds flashing seductively above her shoulders.

'Jesus, Siena!'

Hunter was standing in the corridor with a huge bouquet of white roses shaking in his right hand. He turned the colour of Siena's discarded dress and clapped his left hand over his eyes in an instant. 'You can't answer the door dressed like that! I mean, undressed like that.'

She screamed and slammed the door in his face.

Oh my God. Hunter. She'd just flashed her tits at Hunter.

Shaking, she sat down on the end of her bed, and pulled a green velvet slip dress mindlessly over her head. After a few seconds, he knocked again.

'Siena?' she heard his sweet, lovely voice enquiring tentatively. 'Are you all right, baby? I didn't mean to scare you. Can I come in?'

Slowly, she went to the door for the second time, pulling it open with infinite trepidation. Was it really him? She'd dreamed about seeing him for so long, it was hard to accept his presence here, now, at this very moment, as a reality.

At first, the two of them stood on the threshold and stared at one another, both unwilling to say or do anything to end this longed-for moment. But then, suddenly, somehow, their bodies moved together and they found themselves clasped tightly in one another's arms.

'How did you find me?' said Siena eventually, once they had finally been able to stop holding each other, as if checking that the other one was real and not some sort of enticing, ghostly projection.

'It wasn't hard,' said Hunter. He was still holding her hand and stroking it as they sat together on the wicker sofa on her balcony. She had finally found her bath robe and was wearing it over the green dress for warmth. 'Half of LA knew you were having this party tonight. Although, to be honest, I'd tracked you down before that. After Max told me he'd seen you, I called your agent in New York.'

'Marsha?' said Siena incredulously. 'And she gave my number out? I'll fucking kill her.'

'You aren't happy I found you?' He looked crestfallen.

'Oh, sweetheart, of course I am,' said Siena, flinging her arms around his neck and squeezing until she almost choked him. 'It's just that the agency isn't supposed to give out our private numbers. To anyone. And I can't believe she didn't *tell* me she'd heard from you, the sly witch.'

'You can't blame her for that, I'm afraid,' he said. 'That was my fault. I swore her to secrecy.' He raised his eyebrow in what he mistakenly believed to be a knowing, clandestine, James Bond sort of way. God, he was so sweet. 'I *can* be pretty persuasive, you know.'

Siena giggled. 'Of course you can, darling,' she said, indulging him. 'That runs in the McMahon family.'

At the mention of the 'f' word, a palpable chill descended on both of them and they fell silent. Siena was the first to speak.

'I read about Dad, you know, trying to screw things up for you on *Counsellor* and everything. I'm sorry.'

Hunter sighed. 'There's nothing for you to be sorry about. It wasn't your fault. Besides, it never got him anywhere in the end. Hugh, my boss, told him to fuck off.'

'Good,' said Siena. 'It's about time someone did.'

'As I remember,' said Hunter, 'you used to make quite a habit of it when we were kids.'

Siena laughed bitterly.

'Yes, I'm told I was a *terrible* daughter,' she said. 'That must be why they cut me off and sent me out to find my own way without so much as a kiss for good luck.'

'I'm so sorry,' said Hunter, stroking her hair with the slow, comforting caress that had always soothed her as a little girl.

'Don't you start,' said Siena. 'There's nothing to be sorry about. My dad always hated my guts, so that was hardly news. And as for the money, well . . .' She shrugged. 'I wasn't doing too badly last time I checked.'

'What about your mom?' asked Hunter. 'Has she been in touch?'

He knew how much Claire had always loved Siena, even when the feeling hadn't been reciprocated. She was frightened of her husband, and weak, but she wasn't a bad person. At least, that wasn't the way he remembered her.

'Are you kidding? She's worse than Pete,' spat Siena with complete contempt. 'She's like Grandma Minnie. No fucking backbone.'

Minnie, like the rest of the family, had done nothing to stand up to Pete when he'd announced he was banishing Siena from their lives, although the press had reported at the time that she'd been devastated by his decision. She had always been fond of her only grandchild.

'I don't suppose you ever hear from Grandma, do you? Or Aunt Laurie?'

Hunter shook his head. 'Hardly. You want to talk about people hating your guts?'

Siena got up from her seat and sat herself down on his lap, snuggling in close to him the way she used to as a kid. He smelt faintly of aftershave, which seemed all wrong somehow. But then she supposed the last time she'd seen him he'd been barely old enough to shave.

'What about *your* mom?' she asked. 'How's she?'

'She's OK,' said Hunter, non-committally. 'She's in England. Remarried to a very nice man called Christopher Wellesley. Given up drinking.'

'And exactly how loaded is Christopher?' Siena couldn't resist. 'Are we talking regular rich, or Bill Gates?'

Luckily Hunter laughed. 'I know,' he said, shaking his head ruefully. 'She's terrible. But she's not such a horrible person deep down. She's improved a lot since she married him. We keep in touch.'

God, thought Siena sadly. That was probably the best family relationship they had between them: Hunter and his mother 'kept in touch'. Other people loved their parents, but Hunter 'kept in touch' with his. And she couldn't even say that about Pete and Claire.

'I've missed you,' he said. 'I'm sorry I didn't find you sooner. But when they told me how upset you were by my letters . . .'

She looked at him blankly.

'What letters?'

Hunter felt a shiver run right through him.

'Siena, please tell me they gave you my letters. I wrote to you every day for almost a year.'

Bewildered, she shook her head.

'Dad told me that you didn't want any more contact with any of us. He said you'd asked to be left alone . . .'

Her voice trailed away as the full enormity of Pete's betrayal began to dawn on her. All these years, Hunter had wanted to find her, had longed for her just as passionately and painfully as she'd longed for him. Not only had her father denied her his own love and robbed her of her mother, he had taken Hunter away from her as well, and in the cruellest way imaginable.

How could she have been so stupid?

Why had she believed him?

Suddenly unable to stop herself, she started to cry.

Hunter pushed his blue-black hair back from his face, and she could see that he was on the brink of tears himself.

'You thought I didn't want to see you again?' he stammered. 'Oh, Siena, I am so sorry. I am so, so sorry. How . . . how could Pete do that to us?'

'You know what?' she said, wiping her eyes and half smiling at the irony of it. 'I really didn't think it was possible for me to hate him any more than I already did.'

Hunter shook his head, still too shell-shocked to know how to react.

'There hasn't been a day when I haven't thought about you,' she said. 'When I haven't wondered where you were or what you were doing. But after so many years . . .' Her voice trailed away. 'I don't know. It just got harder and harder to pick up the phone. I was so scared you might reject me again.'

'I *never* rejected you!' His voice was hot with indignation. How could Pete have told her that? What kind of a sick parent was he?

'I know that now,' she said.

'I'm sorry.'

They both spoke the words together, and immediately burst out laughing, grateful for something, anything, to break the unbearable tension.

'Jinx!' said Siena, just as they used to as little kids when they said the same thing at once. 'I said it first, so you're jinxed!'

'Fine, OK, I'm jinxed.' He beamed at her.

They sat for a while in happy silence, grinning inanely at one another like a couple of loved-up teenagers. What Pete had done was unforgivable and would probably take a while to sink in fully. But the main thing was that they were both here now, together. No regrets or recriminations or what-ifs could extinguish the delight of that one simple fact.

'I have a girlfriend,' Hunter announced, changing the subject abruptly.

'Really?' said Siena, frowning. For some reason she found she didn't want him to elaborate about his love life.

'Yeah, she's called Tiffany. She plays Sarah on the show, if you've seen it. She's the gorgeous blonde one.'

Siena noticed the way his eyes shone and his face cracked into a smile when he said her name. He'd obviously got it bad.

'She's wonderful,' he went on excitedly. 'I can't wait for you to meet her. I know you're gonna love her just as much as I do. You two are so alike.'

Hmmm, thought Siena. We'll see about that.

'What about you?' he asked, once it became clear that she was not about to question him further about Tiffany. 'Are you seeing anybody?'

'No,' she said with a shrug, 'no one serious.'

He looked down at her quizzically.

'And don't you go getting any ideas!' She grinned and prodded him in the chest with an accusatory finger. 'No matchmaking with any of your *Days of Our Lives* friends.'

'Oh, shut *up*,' said Hunter. 'I don't know anyone on that show.'

'I'm not interested. Period,' said Siena. 'My career is the only love of my life right now, and I want it to stay that way.'

'Hey, fine by me,' he said, holding up both hands innocently. 'As far as I'm concerned, no man could ever be good enough for you anyway.'

For a few minutes neither of them said anything. They just sat together under the stars, drinking in the miracle of each other's presence. Siena shifted position on his lap and hugged him tightly round the middle. God, she'd missed him so much.

'So,' said Hunter after a while, 'what happens now? How long are you here in LA?'

She sighed and sat up. She wished she could stay there in his arms for ever.

'Not long, unfortunately. Maybe a week. I have to be back in New York for a shoot by the twenty-sixth, latest.'

Hunter's face fell.

'I'm coming back, though, next month.' She smiled at him. 'We'll be shooting the movie here for four months, maybe longer if there are problems. So we'll be able to see a lot of each other. Catch up, you know? Man . . .' She looked at him in wonder, as though she were seeing his face for the first time. 'I have *so* much I need to tell you.'

'Me too.' He sighed. 'You have no idea.'

It was starting to get uncomfortably chilly out on the balcony. The Pacific coast breezes could take on a bitter bite late in the evenings, and Hunter got up to move indoors, standing back to allow Siena into the warm before him. It was late, and he knew that both Tiffany and Max would be waiting up for him at home, anxious to know how the reunion had gone. Still, he could hardly bear to tear himself away.

He turned around and looked at her: Siena McMahon, the world-famous model, so tiny and vulnerable and sweet in her oversized hotel bath robe. He loved her so much at that moment, he could have burst. And that was when it came to him.

'Move in with me!' he blurted out suddenly, catching her off guard.

Siena looked surprised.

'Really?' she said. 'Do you mean it? I mean, do you think that would be a good idea?'

'Of course,' he said, sounding almost offended. 'Why wouldn't it be?'

She thought about it for a moment. 'What about your girlfriend?' She tried her best not to sound as hostile as she felt about that particular subject. She knew her hostility made no sense – she hadn't even met the girl – but a feeling of resentment at having to share Hunter with anyone was already starting to build to the point where she could feel her chest tightening. 'Wouldn't she mind a complete stranger moving in?'

'You're hardly a stranger,' he said. 'Besides, Tiffany doesn't live with me.'

If Siena hadn't known better, she might almost have thought he sounded resentful. Perhaps things with the perfect Tiffany were not quite so 'wonderful' after all?

'Oh,' was all she said. 'But Max does, right?'

This time she was unable to conceal her dislike. Looking at her frown, Hunter couldn't stop himself from laughing.

'Oh, Siena!' he teased her. 'Don't tell me you're *still* hung up about Max?'

'Don't be ridiculous,' she said indignantly, tossing back her hair for emphasis. 'And for your information, I have never been "hung up" about him, as you put it. I just don't understand what you see in him. He's hung around you like a bad smell for as long as I can remember, and now he seems to be sponging off you permanently. How can you stand it?'

'It's not like that,' said Hunter gently. 'Max has been a wonderful friend to me.'

She gave a brief snort of derision.

'You weren't here, honey,' he said reasonably. 'You don't know the whole story. I'm telling you, I don't think I could have made it through all this stuff without him.'

'Well, fine,' she said grudgingly. 'But won't he have something to say about it if I move in?'

'Noooo,' said Hunter, shaking his head and suppressing a tiny suspicion that perhaps he *should* have run the idea by both Max and Tiffany before making the offer.

'Anyway, it's my house. So stop making excuses and just say yes, damn it.'

Siena jumped up and flung herself against him like a puppy greeting its long-lost master. She couldn't remember the last time she'd felt so deeply and truly happy.

'Yes!' She grinned from ear to ear. 'I will move in with you. Yes, yes, yes!'

Chapter Twenty-eight

Tiffany pulled her battered old truck into the driveway at the beach house, and reached over to the passenger seat for the bag of fresh fruit and bagels that she'd just picked up at the farmers' market. She and her best buddy Lennox both took surfing lessons early on a Sunday morning, and afterwards she would cross the street from ZJ's surf shop to the weekly market and pick up something fresh and delicious for Hunter's breakfast.

It had become one of their favourite little rituals. Hunter loved the way her normally poker-straight hair frizzed up when she'd been in the ocean, and her skin looked tanned and glowing from the early morning workout against the waves. He would brew the coffee while she played house, laying out the bread and fruit in different bowls and filling vases with fresh flowers. Max, if he was up, would walk down to the promenade and buy the papers. The three of them had shared some of their happiest times on those long, lazy Sunday mornings at the beach.

Of course, all that was before Siena arrived.

This Sunday morning, she struggled, laden, up to the house with an anxious and heavy heart. Siena had moved in with Hunter just over four weeks ago now. Some days it felt like four years. For the hundredth time, Tiffany thanked her lucky stars that she herself had never agreed to move in to the beach house permanently. Poor Max had to put up with the she-devil 24/7. She doubted she would have lasted a week in his shoes.

Tiffany's dislike of Siena had developed gradually.

It wasn't so much that she was selfish per se, although there were some teething problems when she first moved in, mainly centred around the late hours she kept. When he was filming, Hunter liked to be in bed by eleven, whereas Siena, accustomed to late Manhattan nights and missing Ines dreadfully, rarely turned in before two, spending literally hours on the phone to New York every night. Then there was the distinct frostiness between Siena and Max, which had sent a chill through the house from the day Little Miss Supermodel first arrived. Not that either of them would admit that they were being off with one another, let alone explain what lay behind their hostility. Hunter had told Tiffany that there had been some rivalry between the two of them when they were children, but that hardly seemed to explain the almost constant sniping now.

But the biggest problem for Tiffany was how possessive Siena could be about Hunter. It was clear from day one that she resented their relationship, and on the rare occasions when the two girls were left alone together, Siena had been far from friendly, always shutting down Tiffany's attempts to open up conversations, particularly if they involved any questioning about her and Hunter's past.

'It must have been so difficult for both of you,' she'd commented one afternoon, after Hunter had told her yet another horrific story about the factionalism and resentment between their respective parents. 'I can imagine how isolated and frightened you must have felt as children.'

'Believe me,' Siena had snapped back frostily. 'You *can't* imagine. Only Hunter and I will ever know what it was like, growing up in that nightmare. That's what's made us as close as we are. *Nobody* can break that bond between us. Nobody.'

When Hunter himself was around, though, abracadabra, Siena was suddenly all sweetness and light, sucking up to Tiffany with a fake, saccharine humility that made her want to scream.

After a few weeks, she had tentatively brought up the subject of Siena's split personality to Hunter, complaining that she was often barely civil unless he happened to be around. But to her horror, Hunter came rushing to Siena's defence.

'She's been through such a lot, honey,' he insisted. 'I'm sure you're just misreading the situation. She's really very sweet and loving when you get to know her.'

'To you she is,' Tiffany replied bitterly. 'Not to me. Or Max for that matter.'

But no matter what she said, or how badly Siena behaved, Hunter seemed to take his niece's side every time. Every fucking time. Even when Max was around to back her up, Tiffany found it increasingly difficult to get him to take any of her concerns or criticisms seriously.

Sticking up for your family was fine. She of all people understood that, what with all the problems they'd been through with their parents, and their disapproval of the relationship. But even so, the situation with Hunter and Siena was really starting to get her down.

Opening the porch door with her key, she was relieved to find that only Max appeared to be up. He was sitting at the kitchen table in just a pair of pyjama bottoms, dividing his attention equally between his laptop and a huge slice of chocolate cake which he had already half demolished. When he saw Tiffany he looked up guiltily and wiped the icing from around his mouth with the back of his hand.

'Ha! Caught in the act, my friend,' she said as she dropped her bags on the counter and swooped down on him, kissing the top of his head and deftly removing the plate with one fluid motion.

'Oi!' said Max, aggrieved. 'I was enjoying that.'

'For breakfast?' She pointedly flipped up the lid of the waste bin and jettisoned what was left of the cake, before burrowing into her bag to produce some fresh walnuts and watermelon slices which she began to unwrap. 'I thought you were trying to get into shape.'

'Ah,' said Max, flipping shut his PC and wandering over to help her. 'But I didn't say *what* shape, did I? Much as I'd love to have a washboard stomach like your boyfriend's, a life of tofu and miso fucking soup just isn't worth it, I'm afraid. Speak of the devil.'

Right on cue, a dishevelled-looking Hunter emerged from his bedroom in his boxers and shuffled over towards Tiffany. Christ, he was handsome. Even first thing in the morning with his black hair standing on end and his mesmerising blue eyes still cloudy with sleep, it was all she could do not to gasp when she caught sight of him.

After all these years she knew every inch of his body, from the supple smoothness of his back to the taut power of his thighs and butt, and the round broad expanse of his shoulders. But she still found his beauty quite incredible. He was like a Michelangelo sculpture – her very own, personal David.

'Hey,' he whispered languidly, enveloping her in his arms and his warmth and his smell until she felt quite dizzy with longing. 'Check out those surfer-girl curls!'

She pulled away from him, embarrassed, and started getting down more plates from the cupboard. Being so tall, she didn't even have to stand on tiptoes to reach them like Siena did. She hated her hair all corkscrewed out from the ocean, and hated it even more when Hunter ruffled it as if she were a pet poodle.

'Yeah, well, I'll blow-dry it after breakfast,' she mumbled awkwardly.

'No! Don't!' said Max and Hunter in unison.

'It looks great like that,' Max assured her.

'Very sexy,' said Hunter, reaching out and cupping a hand over her left breast as she reached up for the glasses. She could feel the beginnings of his erection pressing into the small of her back.

'Hun-*ter*!' She blushed, grinning from ear to ear.

'Oh, get a room, would you?' said Max good-naturedly. He was pleased to see the two of them fooling around and looking so relaxed. Things had been pretty tense around here these last few weeks since Siena's arrival.

'You wanna go for a drive after breakfast?' asked Hunter, still refusing to release a wriggling Tiffany from his embrace.

'Sure.' She beamed at him.

She couldn't remember the last time the two of them had just taken off together on a Sunday. Not since their new year's trip to Big Bear. And that seemed like a lifetime ago already.

'Why don't you head up to Santa Barbara?' suggested Max.

'Ooh, yes,' said Tiffany. 'We could have dinner at that little place in Montecito, the one with all the honeysuckle. You remember, Hunter?'

He did remember. In their first few months of dating, some of the *Counsellor* fans had been getting out of hand, to the point where going out in LA had become a nightmare. Girls would shout insults at Tiffany when they went out as a couple – one silicone-enhanced lovely had even run, naked, into Ivy on the Shore and sat down on his lap as the two of them were having dinner.

Admittedly Tiffany had thought that was hilarious, but Hunter felt desperately embarrassed, and began looking for places out of town to take her on their dates. They had discovered the Montecito restaurant together, and the place would forever remind him of those early days together.

He bent down and kissed her gently on the lips. 'Sounds like a plan.'

Glowing with happiness, she extricated herself from his arms and took an armful of goodies across to the table. She couldn't believe how anxious she'd been driving over this morning. What a fuss she'd been making over nothing. Now they were going to have a lovely, relaxing, romantic day together. She needn't have worried at all.

'Who's going to Montecito?' A sleepy, female voice shattered her reverie. 'Can I come?'

Siena had emerged from her bedroom and sidled straight over to the refrigerator, beaming at Hunter as she went by. The two of them could almost have been twins, Tiffany thought with a pang of annoyance, radiating sexiness with their black bed-hair and blue eyes.

Max glared at Siena and tried not to notice the fact that she was wearing only a pair of semi-sheer nude panties and a child's size Lakers T-shirt that was doing a very inadequate job of containing her braless breasts.

'No,' said Max.

'Yes,' said Hunter simultaneously.

'Hunter and Tiffany want some time on their own,' said Max firmly, before Hunter had a chance to speak again.

'Well, what am *I* going to do?' Siena whined petulantly, pleading with Hunter for support.

Christ, she could be obnoxious when she wanted to, thought Max. 'If you're at a loose end you could always have a crack at that pigsty of a room you live in,' he said, giving her his best patronising smile.

'Don't be ridiculous,' snapped Siena. 'That's what we pay Maria for. Of course, when I say we, I mean Hunter and I. Heaven forbid that the great director should ever make a contribution.'

She knew how easy it was to get Max's hackles to rise by baiting him about not paying his way. What she didn't know was that he kept a meticulous record of the back rent he owed, plus interest, and that absolutely every cent of his meagre income was spent on contributing as far as he could to the household expenses. Nor that he had tried, on numerous occasions, to insist on moving somewhere cheaper but that Hunter had literally begged him to stay, pleading with him until Max felt there was no way out without really hurting and insulting his closest friend, and reluctantly capitulated.

And Max, of course, was far too proud ever to tell her.

'Cut it out, you two,' said Hunter. He was getting sick and tired of the endless bickering between Siena and Max. It had been bad enough when they were kids, but surely they could both let bygones be bygones now?

Sensing his frustration, Siena immediately changed tack. 'Anyway, I'm sure Tiffany wouldn't mind if I tagged along, would you? All girls together? It'd be fun.' She fluttered her eyelashes at a furious Tiffany for Hunter's benefit, and started ostentatiously helping to lay the table, picking up a stack of bowls and putting one by each place. 'I haven't been to Montecito since I was a child. I'd really love to see it again.'

There was a moment's silence, as Tiffany looked at Hunter, willing him just once to stand up to Siena and tell her to take a running jump. But one glance at his pained, torn expression told her it wasn't going to happen.

Tiffany would have loved to tell her to stick Montecito up her perfectly rounded ass, but she was getting better at this game by the day, and knew that outright hostility would play right into the little minx's hands. Instead she took a deep breath and gave Siena a false smile so broad it made her jaw ache, wrapping her arms around Hunter and tossing back her ocean-curled mane of blonde hair in an unmistakable gesture of possession.

'Sure, why not?' she said. 'The more the merrier.'

That'd show the little midget. Two could play at this game.

'Oh, right,' said Max, who could happily have smacked the now triumphant-looking Siena over the head with his PC, which he was clearing off the table. 'Well, if it's the more the merrier, I think I'll join you too. You and Hunter can go in the SL, enjoy the drive on your own. I'll take Siena in my car.'

Siena spun around and gave him a look that could have frozen molten lava. Making sure he was out of Hunter's line of sight, Max stuck his tongue out at her.

Tiffany, who was observing this little exchange as she disengaged herself from Hunter and laid out the fruit plates, felt her heart swell with gratitude. Thank God for Max.

Stuck in traffic on the 101 two hours later, Max was beginning to regret his selfless gesture of support for Tiffany. Siena was being utterly unbearable.

First, she'd delayed them all by insisting on changing her outfit three times before she felt completely comfortable.

'It's Montecito, not Monte fucking Carlo,' he had yelled in exasperation after her third change, into an utterly unsuitable sky-blue linen suit with a pencil skirt and high heels.

Now she was sitting beside him with two bath towels thrown over the passenger seat of his Honda Civic in case she should contaminate her perfect outfit with any dust from the car, her face screwed up like that of a disgusted debutante who had woken up to find herself knee deep in sewage.

For the first half-hour of the journey, neither of them spoke, choosing instead to maintain hostilities via an ongoing battle for control of the stereo: he put on classical, she changed the station to pop, she turned the volume up, he turned it down. But when Max had insisted on taking the faster, less scenic freeway route rather than the coast road, her barely repressed rage had exploded in classic McMahon style.

'Why the fuck are we going this way?' she demanded, as he joined the sluggish-looking lane of northbound traffic. 'I thought this was supposed to be a beautiful Sunday drive, not a freeway crawl.'

'It was,' said Max. 'It was supposed to be a beautiful drive – for Hunter and Tiffany. And I sincerely hope' – he changed lanes suddenly, throwing Siena deliberately against the right side of the car, linen suit and all – 'that they're enjoying themselves. Despite your best efforts.'

'I don't know what you're talking about,' said Siena brusquely, brushing the dirt angrily from her sleeve.

'Oh, pull the other one,' said Max. 'You knew they wanted some time alone today. You only wanted to come so you could mess things up for the two of them. Again.'

Siena drew her shoulders back defensively. She hated it when he was right. 'My, what an active imagination you have!' she sneered. 'I suppose being such an abject, unemployed failure leaves you plenty of time to sit at home and work on your conspiracy theories.'

Max smiled. 'You can say what you like about me, sweetheart. But I've got your number. And so has Tiffany. Believe me, Hunter may be a soft touch, but he's not stupid. Sooner or later he's going to see through you, just like everybody else.'

Siena's eyes flashed with fear and hatred, but for once she managed to control herself. 'Why is it so hard for you to believe that I wanted to come today because I want to see Montecito?' she said. 'And because I like to be with Hunter. And he likes to be with me.'

Max yawned pointedly as Siena drew breath.

'Why can't you and *Tiffany* . . .' She lingered on the word with heavy sarcasm. '. . . just accept that?'

'Because it's crap,' said Max flatly. 'This has nothing to do with Montecito. Or you and Hunter having time together. If you really cared about Hunter, you wouldn't begrudge him and Tiffany their happiness. You'd see that she's the best thing that ever happened to him and stop trying to fuck everything up for him like some sort of neurotic child. You're pathetic.'

'How dare you!' exploded Siena, hitting him hard with both fists on his right arm so that he swerved dangerously towards the central reservation.

'Jesus,' said Max, trying to keep control of the car while shielding himself from her blows. 'Are you trying to kill us or something?'

He pulled unsteadily back across the lanes of traffic towards the hard shoulder, eventually stopping by the side of the road as Siena continued to pummel him.

'You have no fucking clue what you're talking about!' she yelled, losing it completely now. 'What the hell do you know about me and Hunter, about what we've been through? You know nothing about my life, Max, *nothing!* I lost him for eleven years. Eleven fucking years. You were with him for all that time, all that time when I was alone, when I had *no one*. And now, after everything we've been through, we finally find each other again, and there's some stupid damn girl trying to take him away from me all the time. You have no idea what that feels like. I hate her, Max. I fucking hate her. I hate both of you!'

Gently Max took hold of each of her wrists, effortlessly stopping

236

her punches. For a second she struggled against him automatically, but her efforts soon melted into the firm warmth of his grip. She glared up at him defiantly through tears of frustration.

And then, before he knew what he was doing, he found himself pulling her towards him and kissing her passionately on the mouth.

In one confusing moment, he felt the soft, wet skin of her cheeks against his own, and her tongue probing hungrily, almost desperately, for his as their bodies locked together. Then, as suddenly as it had started, it was over.

He let go of her, and sat back, shocked.

'Sorry,' he mumbled, his heart still pounding from the shock of what had just happened.

'Are you?' whispered Siena.

Her voice sounded changed and thick with desire. Max noticed that her left hand was still resting on his thigh.

He gazed across at her. She looked like a clown who'd been left out in the rain – first the tears and then the kiss had played havoc with her make-up. 'I don't know,' he stammered, staring at her hand on his leg, still too shell-shocked to move. 'Are *you?*'

'I don't know,' said Siena miserably. The desire in her voice had already been replaced by something else. It may have been panic.

Oh God. She felt horribly confused. She'd despised and resented Max for as long as she could remember. As a child, he'd always come between her and Hunter, and even now he never failed to take Tiffany's side and to undermine her in Hunter's eyes as much as he could.

When she had got so upset before, all she'd wanted was for him to *understand* for once, to stop preaching for five minutes and tell her that her need for Hunter, her deep, desperate love for him, was OK. She wanted him to tell her that Hunter loved her more than anyone else on the planet. That girlfriends would come and go, but that she, Siena, would never lose his love again.

But he hadn't done that. Instead, he'd told her off for her behaviour, chastised her like a naughty child. And then he'd gone and kissed her.

How was she supposed to react to that?

She toyed with the idea of slapping him round the face, pulling the whole 'how dare you' routine. But unfortunately there was no escaping the fact that she had kissed him back.

For a long time.

Enthusiastically.

In that instant, she had wanted him, and he knew it. There could be no going back.

Oh God. What had possessed her?

Flustered, she pulled her hand off his leg as though she'd just realised it was resting on hot coals, and fumbled in the glove box for some tissues.

'Here, let me,' said Max, reaching over to dab at her smudged cheeks.

Siena flinched. 'It's OK, it's OK,' she said. 'I can do it. You just, er . . .' She waved her hand, signalling him to get going. 'You just drive. We're going to be late otherwise.'

Max's face fell. So that was it, then? They were just going to pretend it had never happened?

Well, maybe it was for the best. Siena was trouble, big, big trouble, and the last thing he needed in his life right now. She was right. It had been a moment of madness, an emotional release for both of them, a stupid mistake that was best forgotten.

So why did he feel so overwhelmed with disappointment?

Reluctantly, he fastened his seat belt and restarted the engine.

'Fine,' he said eventually, not quite suppressing a sigh. 'Fine. Let's go.'

Chapter Twenty-nine

Siena decided that the kiss with Max must have been some sort of evil omen. From that moment on, everything started to go wrong.

The afternoon in Montecito had been complete torture. Hunter and Tiffany were totally wrapped up in one another, endlessly reminiscing about this boring restaurant and that tedious gallery. Siena couldn't have felt more like a gooseberry if she'd painted herself green and hung herself on a bush, and she wished with all her heart that she'd listened to Max in the first place and stayed at home.

'Oh, look, honey, it's that little tea place, you remember?' Tiffany grabbed Hunter's hand and began dragging him across Main Street. 'I wonder if they still do that passion fruit and mango?' She had changed into a clinging white vest and a pair of lemon-yellow shorts for the trip, which even when paired with flat flip-flops emphasised her endless brown legs. That was one area where she definitely trumped the petite Siena, who she was gratified to see looking over-dressed and grumpy, with most of her make-up inexplicably smeared all over her over-priced jacket.

'You coming?' Hunter called over his shoulder to Siena and Max, but they both shook their heads and hung back, looking awkward. He hoped they hadn't had yet another row in the car.

For Siena, the afternoon had gone from bad to worse, with Tiffany scoring point after point and looking radiantly happy with Hunter. Max, meanwhile, had withdrawn into monosyllabic isolation. He didn't make eye contact with her once that afternoon, nor on the long journey back to LA in the evening. Clearly, he regretted what had happened, which only served to heighten Siena's own feelings of embarrassment and confusion.

When they'd finally got back to the beach house, both of them had bolted to their separate rooms and a long-awaited respite from the tension of each other's presence.

What a fucking mess.

Over and over she told herself that she hated Max, that he would stop at nothing to turn Hunter against her, that he was and always had been her enemy. He was a loser, a sponger off her family, a patronising, self-righteous English prig. He was arty and pretentious.

And blond. She hated blonds.

When she thought back to the kiss she felt revolted, ashamed. And yet, however hard she tried to shut it out, the feeling of his body against hers, the power of his arms, the smell of his sweat and the unexpected violence of his kiss, all rushed back to assail her senses with what, despairingly, she could only acknowledge was pure and very intense desire.

For the next week, she threw herself into her work. She would leave the house at seven, before Max and Hunter were up, arriving over an hour early at the set in nearby Venice, where she would pore over her script, making notes and memorising the director's suggestions before rehearsals started.

But not even all her extra diligence could protect her from the wrath of Dierk Muller, the director, when he was less than a hundred and ten per cent happy with a scene.

Muller was a first-generation German immigrant, a charmless little wisp of a man with thinning grey hair, physically striking only for his over-sized Adam's apple, which bobbed up and down grotesquely whenever he spoke. Despite his unprepossessing appearance, he was revered in Hollywood, not only as a brilliant director whose energy, focus and commitment to all his projects were second to none, but as that rarest of things in LA: a true, incorruptible artist. His films were all critical successes, and although he was at best hit and miss at the box office, there was no shortage of top-flight actors, writers and cinematographers queuing up to work with him.

He was not, however, an easy man to work with. Or in Siena's case, to work for.

Dierk knew Siena had talent, but he also recognised her lack of discipline, and her tendency to pull back emotionally in difficult scenes, a self-protective mechanism common in younger, inexperienced actresses. His response was to yell and scream and pour scorn like acid on her performance, bullying her into dropping her inhibitions. It worked, but the process was emotionally exhausting for both of them.

Siena, who was used to being the fashion world's darling, pampered and indulged by designers and photographers at every turn, was in a complete state of shock. At night she would crawl back home feeling worthless and defeated, longing to be left alone with Hunter, the one person who could always make her feel better. But invariably he'd be doing something with Tiffany.

Fucking perfect, sweet, wonderful, always-there Tiffany, who had herself wrapped around his heart like poison ivy.

Embarrassment after their kiss had not stopped Max from continuing to stick up for Tiffany whenever Siena tried to prise her away from Hunter. She was sick of it always being two against one at the beach house, and often her only comfort would be long phone calls to Ines in New York.

Ines, at least, was a true friend, accepting unconditionally that Tiffany was a bitch-cow from hell who must be destroyed and blindly taking Siena's side in everything. At the end of every call, she would beg Siena to come back to Manhattan.

'LA is sheet. Acting is sheet. Teefany is sheet,' she would insist, neatly summarising Siena's own feelings on these three subjects. 'Come back to modelling, honey, we all mees you so much.'

But miserable as she was, Siena knew she couldn't go back. She'd waited too long for this movie, for a real shot at Hollywood, and to be back with Hunter again. She would show Dierk Muller what she was made of. And she'd get the better of Tiffany bloody Wedan as well.

And if Max self-righteous De Seville didn't like it, he could go to hell.

One evening, a few weeks after the fateful Montecito trip, Siena decided she would cook supper for the four of them at home.

One of Tiffany's most irksome attributes was the fact that she effortlessly excelled at all things domestic – cooking, flower arranging, sewing, interior decoration, you name it, she was a right little Martha Stewart. She was one of those infuriating women who only had to rearrange a few cushions to make a room look warm and homely and who whipped up delicious, interesting meals from the few unpromising leftovers she happened to stumble across in the fridge.

Siena knew that Hunter, who had never really had a mother figure in his life, valued such feminine skills very highly, and she was damned if she was going to let Tiffany bask in all the glory. Tonight, she, Siena, would be the angel in the house. Hunter couldn't fail to be delighted.

After two hours alone in the kitchen, however, she was starting to regret the whole domestic escapade.

Her first attempt at winter vegetable soup had ended up a charred and sticky mess, stuck, probably for ever, to the bottom of a giant saucepan. She reckoned she just about had enough ingredients left to attempt a second batch, but that left her very little time to make the rosemary baste for the rack of lamb, not to mention whip up the raspberry pavlova she had rashly already told Max would be on tonight's menu.

Hastily throwing some semi-chopped carrots and parsnips into the blender, she picked up the portable phone and called Ines.

'Lamb,' she shouted over the whirring of the blades. 'How long per pound? And how hot should the oven be?'

'Whaaat?' asked Ines, who had been happily drifting off to sleep on the couch in their apartment with her face caked in a green algae mask. 'Siena? Ees that you?'

Siena turned off the blender. 'How long should I cook this lamb for?' she repeated. 'It's quite big.'

'Ow the fuck should I know?' replied Ines reasonably. 'I'm a model. I don't eat, let alone cook. Why don't you eat out, like normal people.'

'I've told you,' said Siena, wrestling with the lid of the blender which finally came free, spraying vegetable purée into her face and hair. 'I want to cook something for Hunter. I want to show him that I'm better than she is at something.'

'Honey,' Ines reassured her, 'you are bettair than her at everything. Bettair looking, bettair actress, bettair everything. You 'ave nothing to prove to Hunter.'

Siena loved the way that Ines dismissed Tiffany's talents completely, despite the fact that she had never met her, spoken to her or even seen a picture. 'Thanks, babe.'

She wiped the mess from her hair with a tea towel, realising in panic that she would now need to wash and dry her hair before supper as well as finish preparing the food. It was almost half past six now.

'I've got to go,' she told Ines, turning back helplessly towards her pile of carrots.

'Good luck,' said her friend. 'And remembair, ees better to cook it too much than not enough.'

By 7.45, things were beginning to look a little more under control. Siena had washed and changed into a pair of clean chocolate-brown suede trousers and a faded green T-shirt that contrasted beautifully with her blue eyes – she didn't want to look as if she had made too much effort. She hadn't had time to blow-dry her hair, so she'd piled it, still damp, in a messy mop on top of her head, held loosely in place by her favourite silver-and-topaz hair clip.

She never normally wore make-up at home, but this evening she had decided to warm up her porcelain cheeks with a dusting of bronzing powder and to slick some clear gloss over her lips.

'You look lovely,' said Hunter when she emerged into the living room, where he and Tiffany were ensconced on the sofa watching reruns of *Gilligan's Island*.

'Wow, you really do,' added Tiffany graciously. 'And you smell terrific too. What is that?'

'Chanel nineteen,' said Siena. 'You're welcome to borrow some if you'd like.'

Tiffany, who knew this display of sweetness was entirely aimed at Hunter, smiled and declined very politely. 'But I'd be happy to help out in the kitchen, if there's anything you need doing,' she offered.

Two could play at this game.

'No thanks,' muttered Siena. She'd rather die than accept help from Little Miss Perfect this evening. 'I've got it covered.'

'Yeah, honey,' said Hunter, stroking Tiffany's hair in a way that made Siena want to run over there and strangle her. 'Let Siena handle things tonight. You're always slaving away in that kitchen. You deserve a night off.'

Fucking brilliant, thought Siena.

She'd been sweating her guts out since four, and all Hunter could think about was how much *Tiffany* deserved a break.

After twenty more minutes, she was finally ready to roll. The soup was a bit tasteless, but inoffensive and edible, a distinct improvement on her first attempt. The lamb was still roasting away in the oven and the pavlova, if she did say so herself, looked fabulous, if a little unstable; a towering triumph of cream and meringue which she had carefully put in the fridge to chill with an entire shelf to itself.

'Shall we eat?' she announced brightly, standing in the kitchen doorway in Tiffany's apron and looking, she fondly believed, every inch the relaxed and capable hostess.

She'd been so busy in the kitchen, though, that only now did she notice they were a man short. 'Where's Max?'

'Oh, sorry, didn't I mention that?' said Tiffany, scrambling up off the couch. 'He called this afternoon and said he might be late. Something about a meeting at Balboa, I think. He said to start without him. I thought I told you already.'

'No,' said Siena through gritted teeth. 'I guess it must have slipped your mind.'

Well, that was just typical. Max knew how important tonight was to her, how she'd wanted them all there because that was what Hunter would have wanted. But he couldn't be bothered even to show up. And instead of calling her himself, he'd deliberately left a message with Tiffany instead, knowing there was a good chance that she wouldn't pass it on. The pair of them had made her look like a fucking idiot. Again.

'Sorry,' said Tiffany, who was starting to enjoy herself. She'd lost count of the number of times Siena had shown up late, or not at all, for one of her carefully prepared meals. Or the times she had suddenly 'remembered' allergies to this or that, refusing to eat whatever it was that Tiffany had slaved over for hours. Short of grinding arsenic into her cherry crumble, she could think of nothing that would give her more satisfaction than to see Siena fall flat on her face tonight.

Hunter put a comforting arm around Siena. He could see she was upset at Max's defection. 'Hey, never mind,' he said kindly. 'I'm sure he'll show up later if he can.'

'Believe me,' said Siena unconvincingly, 'it couldn't matter less. Now, why don't the two of you sit down and I'll bring you your soup.'

The first course took longer than expected, mainly because Hunter begged for a second and then a third helping, insisting it was absolutely delicious. Meanwhile Tiffany and Siena passed the time by trying to outdo each other conversationally on the nice-as-pie stakes, frenziedly smiling and complimenting one another in a none too subtle attempt to win his approval.

Max eventually fell through the door just as Siena had finished serving the lamb. He looked worn out and stressed, his shoulders hunched and his ancient brown leather briefcase dangling despondently from one hand. It must have been another bad meeting.

But as soon as he saw Siena, looking so adorable, furious and ridiculously out of place wearing Tiffany's apron over her T-shirt, he couldn't help but crack a smile.

Siena McMahon, homemaker?

Arnold Schwarzenegger would have looked more at home in an apron than Siena.

'Sorry I'm late, sweetheart.'

He wandered over and kissed her affectionately on the top of her head. It was the first physical contact of any kind between them since Montecito, and it threw Siena completely.

She looked up at him, her eyes ablaze with hostility. 'Yeah, well. So you fucking should be,' she muttered. Fucking inconsiderate, self-centred asshole. And since when had he ever called her 'sweetheart'?

'I've been trying to escape for the past hour,' Max explained, ignoring her glare. 'Honestly. But I just couldn't shut the guy up.'

He sat down opposite Siena and began helping himself to a huge portion of vegetables before hacking away at the remnants of the small, rather wizened-looking joint. Ines would have been pleased to hear that *no one* could have described it as under-cooked.

'I'm famished.' He grinned at her. 'This looks great.'

Blindsided by what appeared to be a genuine compliment, Siena accidentally smiled back.

Damn it. Why wouldn't he just go away? Or die?

Flustered, she took a bite of her own lamb and nearly choked. It was so over-cooked it was like chewing shoe leather. She glanced across at Hunter, who was manfully ploughing through his own enormous helping, nodding appreciatively at her as though he were savouring the pinnacle of cordon bleu excellence. God, he was an angel. Why did she have to be so fucking incompetent at everything?

While Siena sat gloomily cursing her lack of culinary prowess, Max was regaling the table with wonderfully funny impressions of the producer he'd met earlier, and anecdotes about the most disastrous meetings he'd ever been to. For such a cocky, arrogant guy, he had a surprisingly self-deprecating sense of humour, Siena noticed. Very British, in a way.

Tiffany and Hunter were both roaring with laughter at his tales of woe, with Tiffany trying to outdo him with stories of some of her most excruciating auditions. Having experienced very little failure in her own life, Siena was feeling rather left out of the proceedings.

'Oh, shit, this one guy,' said Tiffany through tears of laughter, 'he actually told me that in order for me to feel empathy with this character – who was meant to be dying from breast cancer, right? – I had to feel "exposed and vulnerable". Well, you can guess what it was he wanted me to expose.'

'No way!' said Max, gulping down a big slug of red wine. 'Does that shit really happen?'

'Omigod, are you kidding me?' Tiffany shrieked, looking to Hunter to back her up. 'It happens all the time. All the fucking time.'

'It's true,' said Hunter. 'Even I've been asked to get naked in auditions before.'

'Really?' Max raised his eyebrow. 'By whom? Not by Orchard?'

'Hugh? Noooo!' Hunter laughed. 'He's far too professional.' He caught Tiffany's adoring eye and started hamming it up, pouting and preening immodestly as if entranced by his own beauty. 'Not that he wouldn't *like* to see me naked, of course.'

'Who wouldn't, baby?' cooed Tiffany, leaning over and kissing him on the mouth.

Siena thought she was going to be sick.

'What about you, Siena?' asked Max playfully. 'Have you ever fallen prey to the lure of the casting couch?'

'Don't be ridiculous,' she snapped. Disheartened by her failure in the kitchen and fed up with being ignored by Hunter, she was having a complete sense of humour failure. 'Directors only pull that shit with sad, desperate unknowns. The sort of girl they know would do anything for a part. I hardly fall into that category.'

'Oh, and I do, I suppose?' challenged Tiffany, whose cheeks had flushed red with anger and embarrassment.

Siena shrugged. 'Not necessarily. But perhaps you give some people the *impression* that you're willing to sleep with someone to get ahead. After all' – she gave an infuriating, smug little laugh – 'hooking up with Hunter hasn't exactly hurt your career, now, has it?'

Tiffany's voice was quiet but she got to her feet, patently furious. 'You fucking bitch.'

'Honey, calm down,' said Hunter. 'I'm sure Siena didn't mean to upset you. It's just that, well, you know what Hollywood's like. People *do* tend to think the worst of someone, if their partner's wealthier or better known or . . .'

'*What?*' Tiffany interrupted him, white lipped and trembling with rage. 'You're telling me you actually *agree* with her?'

'Hey, come on now, Tiffany, calm down,' interjected Max, with a reproachful look at Siena.

'No, no, of course not,' insisted Hunter, who now looked panicked. 'It's not that I agree with her. I only meant . . .' He looked around the table for help. 'Siena,' he said eventually. 'Perhaps you should apologise to Tiffany. I know you weren't intending to upset her.'

Siena failed to suppress a triumphant smile. This was fantastic.

'Of course,' she said graciously. 'I'm *so* sorry if you misunderstood me, Tiffany.'

'Oh, I think I understood you perfectly,' said Tiffany calmly.

She was evidently still livid, but she wasn't going to give Siena the satisfaction of losing her temper. Picking up her jacket from the back of her chair and grabbing her bag, she headed for the front door. She'd had it up to here with Hunter's constant defending of Siena's atrocious behaviour. If he wasn't going to stick up for her when someone called her a whore, he could fucking well sleep alone tonight.

'Where are you going?' asked Hunter desperately, getting up himself to go after her.

'Home,' she said firmly, without breaking stride.

He reached out and put a restraining hand on her shoulder. 'Come on, baby, this is silly. You don't have to go.'

'I *want* to go, Hunter,' she said nastily, inwardly cursing herself for losing it and lashing out at him. She knew this was exactly what Siena had hoped for, that she'd effectively played right into her hands. But she couldn't help it. Sometimes Hunter's blindness and total lack of support were just too much for her to bear.

She stormed out of the door with a look that told him in no uncertain terms that he'd better not even think of following. Miserably, Hunter went back to the table and put his head in his hands.

'Who'd like some pavlova?' asked Siena brightly.

'Shut up,' said Max, before turning sympathetically to Hunter. 'Don't worry, mate. She'll be back.'

'Will she?' asked Hunter. He hated it when he and Tiffany fought, but he hated it even more when she left him. No matter how many times it happened, he couldn't shake the hideous, gnawing anxiety that this might be it, that she might never walk back through that door. 'I don't get it,' he complained in exasperation. 'What am I doing wrong?'

Max poured himself another glass of wine. 'I think it's more a question of what you're *not* doing,' he said. 'Why don't you drive over there right now and tell her you're sorry? Show her you're on her side. I think it would make all the difference.'

Right at that moment, Siena came teetering over to the table with a huge, wobbling tower of raspberries and cream. Max, who had his back to her, suddenly tipped back in his chair and threw out both arms in a full-bodied yawn, catching her by the elbow. Hunter watched horrified as, as if in slow motion, Siena lurched forward desperately trying to regain her balance, before finally dropping the plate with an almighty crash on the maple floor.

She stood there in shock while shards of meringue flew around the room like sugary shrapnel, and tiny drops of cream sprayed everywhere: on the walls, the chairs, the table, some even finding their way into Hunter's hair.

For a moment, nobody made a sound. Then Max burst out laughing.

'I'm sorry, sweetheart,' he said eventually, wiping away tears of mirth and smearing his cheek with raspberry sauce in the process. 'I'm really sorry. But that was pretty fucking spectacular – attack of the killer pudding!'

'It's not funny!' wailed Siena. 'Do you know how long I spent making that damn thing?' She ran her hands through her hair in despair. 'I just wanted tonight to be so perfect for you,' she said, turning to Hunter. 'But first Tiffany goes and has a spac attack about nothing. And then this giant moron . . .' She pointed accusingly at

Max. '. . . goes and destroys my pavlova – which was going to be the best part of the whole fucking meal, by the way.'

'Well, that wouldn't be hard,' muttered Max under his breath, not quite quietly enough.

'Oh, fuck off, would you?' said Siena, with feeling.

She felt as if she was about to cry, which she knew was utterly ridiculous over one stupid dinner.

Hunter, however, had tuned out and was completely oblivious for once to Siena's pouting complaints. He could think only about Tiffany. Maybe Max was right. Maybe he had been unsupportive.

'I'm going over there,' he announced suddenly, getting up and grabbing his car keys from a hook by the door, leaving the house without a word or a backward glance at Siena.

'Can you believe that?' she said as the sound of his engine died away a few seconds later.

Her cheeks were flushed from the evening's trauma and exertions, and unruly tendrils of drying black hair had started to escape from her silver-and-topaz clip. Max could see the faint outline of her nipples through the worn green cotton of her T-shirt, and made a heroic effort to concentrate on her scowling, scrunched-up little face.

'All that work. All that effort,' she moaned. 'And he didn't give a shit. That stupid fucking girl is all he cares about.'

'Would you listen to yourself for one minute?' said Max, squatting down on the floor and scooping handfuls of pavlova into an empty salad bowl. 'Can't you hear how spoiled and selfish you sound?'

'Oh, change the fucking record, would you?' said Siena, kneeling down to help him. 'What is it with you, anyway? If you'd knocked over one of Tiffany's desserts, you'd be all "Omigod, I'm *so* sorry, Tiffany, *poor* you, Tiffany, let me make it up to you, Tiffany."'

She mimicked his English accent the way she used to do when they were kids. Max remembered how much it used to infuriate him back then.

Now it turned him on like hell.

'But of course, because it was *me*,' she ranted on, 'you think it's funny. Fucking hilarious. It's only Siena. Who cares if Siena's evening gets ruined, if all her hard work was for nothing? You don't apologise to *me*.'

'I did apologise,' said Max.

'Do you fancy her or something?' asked Siena bitterly, hurling a handful of pink creamy slop into the bowl.

'Don't be ridiculous,' he replied, rather too defensively. 'She's Hunter's girlfriend. I never think of her in that way.'

But Siena had picked up on his momentary weakness and decided to keep pushing.

'Oh, *I* get it,' she said with a knowing smile. 'You want his house. You want his fame.' She counted them off on her fingers. 'You want his money and his looks. And now you want to screw his girlfriend too. Why not?'

Max could feel his temper building.

'Shut up, Siena.'

'You know, you really want to try and get some kind of life of your own, Max,' she continued mercilessly. 'You're obsessed with Hunter. You always have been. All this envy, all this covetousness, it can't be good for you. It eats you away inside, doesn't it?'

'I mean it, Siena.' He grabbed her by the wrist. 'That's enough.'

Sensing that she had the upper hand, she refused to be intimidated, maintaining her smile and her eye contact.

'You think about fucking her, don't you, Max?' she taunted him. 'Admit it. You'd love to get your desperate little hands on those perky brown tits, wouldn't you? Or see those pretty pink lips wrapped around your cock? Do you think that's what Hunter's getting right now?'

Max felt his stomach churning, as if he were going to be sick. It revolted him to hear her talk so crudely. He wanted to make her stop.

'Shut up! Shut the fuck up!' he snapped, grabbing her other wrist and shaking her violently.

Her head whiplashed backward when he grabbed her, and the rest of her hair burst free from its restraint, tumbling down around her face like a glossy black dam breaking. The cream in his hands felt slippery against the skin of her forearms, and he could feel the soft pressure of her breasts against his chest when he pulled her towards him.

Jesus Christ, he wanted her so much.

Suddenly all the tension, all the longing he'd felt for her since that day at Montecito, came bursting out. He started to kiss her with such force that she slipped backward and clunked the back of her head on the floor.

'Ow,' she said, as Max scrambled to pull up her T-shirt. But she was smiling. 'That hurt.'

'Shut up,' he whispered. He was staring down at her, his face inches above her own, and a look of such desire and love in his eyes that Siena wanted to reach up and stroke him.

So he did want her. He had felt something in Montecito!

She'd been trying to deny it to herself, but she'd known for weeks that her bad mood and frustration had not been down to Tiffany alone, or even to the traumas on-set with Dierk. She'd been trying and failing to stamp down her feelings for Max, so convinced was she that he didn't return them, didn't even like her in fact.

But he did. He wanted her.

She felt deliriously happy.

Max bent his head and softly began kissing her bare breast, his warm tongue circling her nipple. She moaned.

'Tell me you want me,' he whispered, moving with agonising slowness to her other breast, while his hand strayed down to her suede-covered thighs, stroking upward teasingly but always stopping just short of her crotch.

'Please,' she begged him, her voice now thick and groggy with longing, her hands reaching down for his belt. 'Please, Max. Just do it.'

'Just do what?' he teased her, sliding down to undo her zip and slipping her trousers down to her knees, revealing a pair of pale pink silk panties.

Scooping a handful of cream and raspberries from the bowl beside them, he began smearing the sweet mixture on her thighs and stomach, studiously avoiding the one place that she was aching for him to touch.

Siena closed her eyes and allowed the wonderful sensations to flood over her. Max's warm, calloused hands were on her breasts, while he torturously licked the cream from her thighs, inch by inch, the warm wetness of his tongue matching her own juices, which were already beginning to seep through the fabric of her panties. She tried not to think of all the legions of other women he'd done this with before. Judging by how good he was at it, she imagined it must have been quite a few. His hot breath tickled her between her legs, and the roughness of his stubble scraped deliciously against her smooth skin. She felt as if she'd died and gone to heaven.

This wasn't some clumsy, casual lover.

It was Max. Her Max.

At last.

After what seemed like an eternity, having still not laid a finger on her pussy, he finally wriggled out of his own jeans, and she could feel his huge cock nudging against her. Instinctively, she reached down to touch it, but he grabbed her hands and, pulling them back above her head, pinned down her arms so that she could barely move at all.

'So . . .' He grinned down at her. 'Siena. Tell me. What do you want?'

Oh God. She couldn't say it. She wanted him inside her so badly

250

she could cry, but she just could not say the words. Not to Max. Not to him.

'I want you,' she stammered frantically, arching her pelvis up against him. 'I want you, Max. Please.'

He shook his head.

'Sorry, sweetheart,' he whispered right into her ear. 'I'm afraid that's not good enough.'

Siena started to whimper. If he didn't do it soon she was going to come right there, before he'd even touched her.

'Tell me what you want me to do to you. Exactly. I want to hear you say it.'

'Jesus, Max, I can't!' She sounded almost angry. Why wouldn't he just fuck her?

'Really?' he teased her, running the tip of his tongue slowly along her lower lip. 'You can't say it? A few minutes ago you weren't so shy, were you? Or wasn't that you, who said I wanted Tiffany's lips around my cock?'

'God, I'm sorry, OK?' said Siena, who was now squirming as much in embarrassment as excitement.

'Don't apologise,' said Max, releasing her hands and pulling off her underwear with one swift motion. Much as he wanted to hear her beg him for it, he didn't have a second's more self-control left in him. 'You can show me how sorry you are.'

And with that he thrust deeply into her, feeling the strong spasms of her almost immediate orgasm as he did so. Her hands were on his back, in his hair, on his buttocks, pulling and clawing at him, biting into his shoulders in the most totally abandoned display of desire he'd ever felt in a woman. If it were possible, Max thought, she actually wanted this even more than he did.

He tried to hold back his own climax, but it was like swimming against a rip tide. When at last he came, it felt as if a lifetime of tension had been magically, gloriously released.

He wouldn't have traded that moment for all the hit Hollywood movies in history.

Chapter Thirty

Henry Arkell woke up with the sort of hangover he couldn't remember having had since his stag weekend in Dublin twelve years ago.

As soon as he reached consciousness, he got out of bed and staggered into the loo, where he spent the first fifteen minutes of his Sunday morning throwing up.

'Can I get you anything, darling?' shouted Muffy.

She was sitting up in bed with her Rosamund Pilcher novel and a cup of tea, being distracted by the sound of her poor husband's retching.

'Yes. My shotgun,' quipped Henry, who reappeared in the bathroom doorway looking as white as a sheet. He'd tried to take some Alka-Seltzer, but was unable to hold it down. There was nothing to do but go back to bed – preferably for ever.

Crawling back under the duvet, he pulled the covers up over his head and groaned. Just then, Madeleine came bounding into the room clutching her Malibu Barbie and demanding to be allowed into her parents' bed for a snuggle.

'No!' barked Henry, whose head felt as if it was exploding. 'Go and watch cartoons, Maddy. Daddy's not feeling very well.'

'But I always snuggle on Sundays, don't I, Mummy?' she protested.

'You do, darling, yes,' said Muffy, putting down her novel and mug with a sigh and getting up to deal with her daughter. So much for her weekend lie-in. 'But Dad's very tired this morning. Why don't you come downstairs with me and you can help me make some brekka?'

'All right,' said Madeleine, pulling off her pyjama top and scratching her rounded baby's tummy absent-mindedly. 'It's very smelly in here anyway. Poo-eee!' She pinched her nose in disgust. 'Barbie doesn't like it when it's smelly.'

Muffy laughed and shooed her into the children's bathroom to do her teeth, before opening all the casement windows to allow the crisp, fresh April morning air to dispel Henry's alcohol fumes. Maddy was right, the room smelt like an Irish pub on New Year's Day.

She was worried about Henry. He'd gone up to London the night before for some sort of crisis meeting with Nick Frankel. Evidently the crisis had been worse than he'd expected, as he'd arrived home at a quarter to five in the morning, in a black cab, smashed out of his mind.

Muffy had had to get up and empty the petty cash tin from the farm office, as well as her handbag, both swearing tins and Charlie's piggy bank to pay the cabbie his £260 fare, which God knew they could ill afford at the moment, before beginning the arduous task of helping Henry upstairs, out of his suit and into bed.

Normally she would have made him sleep on the sofa and spent the next day furiously ignoring him. But he seemed to have been under so much pressure recently, and his moods had got darker and darker to the point where she was afraid that any show of anger or rejection by her might push him over the edge into real depression.

Tying the belt on her ancient Laura Ashley dressing gown, she went downstairs to start breakfast, knocking on the boys' door as she went past.

'Bertie! Charlie! It's half past eight,' she shouted wearily. 'Up, dressed, teeth.'

With three children, a husband in meltdown and a failing farm to help run, she had long ago abandoned wasting energy on full sentences.

Downstairs, she began frying up a big pan of bacon, eggs and tomatoes, while simultaneously sorting through yesterday's neglected post.

Bills, bills, bills, two brown, three red, a catalogue for new milking products that they couldn't afford, another catalogue for clothes – she should be so lucky! Only one blue, handwritten envelope caught her eye. It was addressed to Henry and postmarked Marbella.

Who on earth did they know in Marbella?

Henry lay under the duvet unable to sleep, or even rest. Unfortunately, the toxic amounts of brandy and champagne he'd downed last night had failed to blot out any part of his nightmare meeting with Nick. Apparently his back tax bill now stood at an incredible two hundred and fifty thousand, not the one hundred and fifty he had originally thought.

A quarter of a million fucking pounds! And that was just the tax, on top of all his other debts, which, Nick was quick to remind him, now ran into many hundreds of thousands. How was it possible?

As far as Henry could remember, he spent every other month filling out tax forms for something or other, and a steady stream of money made its way out of his poor, depleted current account in Bicester into the groaning coffers of the Inland Revenue every year. Nick had spent hours yesterday patiently trying to explain to him exactly how this latest whopper of a bill added up. But even the words 'tax return' caused an impenetrable cloud to form in Henry's brain, intensified in this case by over a dozen brandy and champagne chasers as the grim news had started to sink in.

He couldn't for the life of him work out how he'd allowed things to get quite so appallingly bad.

There was only one salient point that he *had* understood from last night's meeting, and it weighed on his chest this morning like ten tons of lead. With the tax and the debts combined, either he got his hands on three-quarters of a mill within the next six months at the outside or he would lose Manor Farm. Thanks to an ancient clause in the deeds, he wasn't able to sell off small sections of the land piece by piece. The house and land must for ever remain one property, one unit. Bar a few paintings it was his only real asset, all that he had to sell – and short of a miracle, he was about to lose it.

How the hell was he going to tell Muffy?

As if reading his mind, his wife appeared in the doorway, looking as youthful and kind and beautiful as ever, bearing a tray of freshly made bacon sandwiches, a pot of Earl Grey tea and an already wilting bunch of daisies and buttercups in a wineglass.

'The flowers are from Maddy,' she said, setting his breakfast down on the bedside table. 'She's making you a Get Well Soon card downstairs.' She plumped up the pillows behind him and Henry made an effort to sit up without expelling the entire contents of his stomach.

'Thanks,' he said, weakly. 'Let's hope I do. Get well soon, I mean.' He took a tentative sip of the tea. 'Not sure if I can manage the bacon,' he said ruefully. 'It smells fantastic, though.'

'Try,' said Muffy, 'it might help. Oh, this came for you.' She reached into her dressing gown pocket and produced the blue envelope.

Henry took it, but looked as puzzled as she was. 'Marbella? I wonder who on earth that can be from.' He ripped open the envelope with a butter-smeared knife and pulled out a two-page handwritten note. 'Fuck me,' he said, looking at the signature first. 'It's from Ellis.'

'Who?' said Muffy, taking a bite of his sandwich. She was supposed to be on a diet, but it seemed a shame to let it go to waste.

'Your admirer, remember? Gary Ellis?' said Henry, who was reading the letter intently, although the words were still spinning before his eyes. 'He's making me an offer. I think. Wants to fly me out to Spain to discuss it.'

'What sort of offer?' asked Muffy warily.

She had never forgotten the slimy way the developer had tried to paw her at Caroline's dinner party all those years ago. She didn't trust Gary Ellis as far as she could spit. The man was a vulture.

'I don't know. I'm not sure,' said Henry, somewhat shiftily, stuffing the letter hastily into his pyjama pocket. He didn't want to worry Muffy with any of this yet, not until he'd figured out exactly what he was going to do. In fact Ellis had been deliberately vague in his choice of words, expressing little more than a renewed interest in Henry's land. Perhaps word of his debts had started to get out, thought Henry in horror. Nick wouldn't have said anything, but these things always seemed to find their way to the ears of sharks like Ellis. A few days ago, he wouldn't even have entertained the idea of selling up, let alone to some smarmy developer. But all of a sudden his options were looking mighty slim. He'd be a fool not to at least hear what the man had to say.

'Maybe I should fly out there and find out?'

'Don't be silly.' Muff laughed, polishing off the last of the sandwich and taking a long gulp of her own tea. 'What can he possibly have to offer us? All he's interested in is the farm, and we would never sell that to anyone. Oooo' – she raised her eyebrow playfully – 'or d'you think he wants to pay a million dollars to sleep with me, like in that film with Demi Moore?'

'Don't talk rubbish,' snapped Henry. She looked hurt and he felt winded by guilt, as if he'd just been kicked in the stomach. He knew he ought to tell her, come clean about the debts. But when? How? She had trusted him to provide for her and he had let her down, let everyone down horribly. It was all his fault. He'd have to find a way to fly out to Spain and see Ellis without her knowing.

'Sorry,' he said, forcing a smile. 'It's just this bloody hangover. You're right, it's a silly idea. Forget about it.'

'Right, then,' said Muffy. 'Well, I'd better get Charlie ready for riding. You stay here and rest and I'll come up and check on you in a couple of hours, OK?'

'OK. Muffy?' He reached out for her hand and grabbed it as she got up to go. 'You do know I love you, don't you?'

She frowned, puzzled, and bent down to kiss him on the lips. ''Course I do,' she said. 'What a funny question.'

Back in California, blissfully ignorant of his brother's problems, Max lay back on Zuma beach with Siena in his arms. The sun was shining, the surf was absolutely perfect, and the most beautiful girl in the world was curled up and sleeping peacefully on his chest. Life really didn't get much better than this.

It was just over a month since the two of them had got together, and they had yet to spend a night apart. Max had worried that them both living at the beach house might get too claustrophobic, especially at such an early stage in the relationship. But their days were always so hectic and full – Siena's with filming in Venice, and his with rehearsals for a new play he was directing downtown – that they actually found they were glad of one another's company in the evenings.

It helped that the atmosphere at home had improved beyond all recognition since Siena stopped focusing all her emotional energy on Hunter, and since Max had ceased to be the enemy.

She still felt some residual jealousy and resentment towards Tiffany, but her anxiety on that front had considerably eased, and her general behaviour vastly improved as a result.

This weekend Hunter and Tiffany were in Colorado visiting Tiffany's family, so Max and Siena had the whole house to themselves. Having made love in every room, and outside under the cypress tree, and contorted themselves into every possible sexual position, they decided they needed a change of scene and had driven down to Malibu for lunch and a much needed nap on the beach.

Gently, Max rolled Siena off his chest and laid her down on her back in the sand. She started to stir and open her eyes, screwing up her face against the glare of the afternoon sun.

'Wakey-wakey,' he said, straddling her so the dark shadow of his body fell across her face.

Siena looked up and saw him kneeling above her, with his beautiful brown chest and shoulders, and his lovely kind smile beaming down at her from beneath a wall of straw-blond hair. She loved the size and strength of him, the fact that his hands were bigger than her head and that he could lift her up and down with one arm as if she were made of paper. Next to some of the other, super-slim models, she had always felt rather womanly and solid. Max made her feel fragile and delicate, like a priceless china doll. It was a good feeling.

'How long was I asleep?' she murmured, reaching up to run her fingers drowsily through his chest hair.

'Only twenty minutes.' He bent down and kissed her. Her lips still tasted of salt water from her earlier dip in the ocean. 'I'm really thirsty, though, I might go and grab a Coke. Wanna come with me?'

Siena shook her head. Zuma Café was only a couple of hundred yards away, but she felt so warm and comfortable just lying there on the sand, listening to the soporific swooshing of the waves, she couldn't face moving an inch.

'You could bring me a Diet Coke, though.' She smiled up at him imploringly.

'What's the magic word?' he teased her, slowly outlining her nipple with one finger through the stretchy orange fabric of her bikini. Siena watched him do it and gave a sigh of longing. She loved it when he touched her there.

'Please,' she whispered, lifting her leg so that her thigh brushed against his already stiffening cock.

'OK, OK, I'm going.' Max jumped to his feet. A few more seconds of this and he wouldn't be able to walk anywhere. 'One Diet Coke coming up, Your Highness. Don't you go anywhere, now.'

Siena rolled over on to her stomach and let out a purr of pure pleasure.

'No danger of that,' she murmured.

The café, as always on a weekend, was crowded. Hard-core surfers with dreadlocked hair and deep, year-round tans mingled with the rich kids from Beverly Hills, whose Mercedes and BMW convertibles were parked in gleaming black and silver rows along the beach road behind them.

Max joined the 'drinks only' queue behind two preppy-looking guys in their mid-thirties – agents, most probably, judging by their neon-white dentistry, Armani trunks and heavily manicured hands. One of them was reading from a copy of *Variety*, where there was a big piece about Dierk Muller's films, including a paragraph about *The Prodigal Daughter*, accompanied by a picture of Siena in one of her Maginelle adverts.

'You seen this?' said the one holding the paper to his friend.

'The McMahon girl?' said the other one. 'Sure. I'm not usually into models. Too skinny. But that kid has a booty to die for.'

They both chuckled. Max felt his stomach turning to lead and his heart tightening.

'D'you think she can act?' asked the first guy, who was still leering at the picture of Siena draped provocatively over a semi-naked black male model.

'I doubt it,' said his friend. 'I know a guy who's fucked her, though.'

'Seriously?'

'Sure. You know Glen Bodie, the producer? According to him . . . well, let's just say she's not completely without talent.'

They both started to laugh until, without warning, Max grabbed them from behind by the collar, one in each hand, and started dragging them outside into the car park.

'Jeez, man, what's your fucking problem?' yelled the first guy, who had dropped his paper in the scuffle, and was desperately trying to turn around to take a swing at his mystery attacker.

As soon as they were through the door, Max hurled both of them down on to the tarmac with all the ease of a WWF wrestler.

'*You're* my problem, asshole,' he said. 'How dare you talk about Siena like that? You don't know the first thing about her. Where do you get off spreading it around that she's slept with some fucking moronic friend of yours?'

'Yeah, well, what's it to you, buddy?' challenged the second guy, who had got to his feet and was mentally calculating his chances of walking away with both arms and legs if he gave Max the punch he deserved.

'She's a friend of mine,' said Max, defensively. 'I won't have her disrespected.'

'Oh yeah? Well, I don't know how good a "friend" you are. But I'm telling you, she slept with Bodie. That's a fact, whether you wanna believe it or not.'

Max lunged towards him again, but a couple of surf dudes who'd been watching the drama unfold grabbed hold of him and dragged him away.

'Leave it, man,' said one of them, a friendly-looking giant of a teenager who was even bigger than Max and clearly wasn't going to take no for an answer. 'Let it go.'

'And stay the fuck away from me or I'll sue you for assault, you motherfucking psycho!' called the first agent, who was still sitting ignominiously on the ground, rubbing his leg, having grown quite brave now that the danger had passed.

Shaking from head to toe, Max threw off the surfers angrily and started staggering back across the beach. He could see Siena, still laying face down on the white sand, her beautifully curved buttocks rising like two round scoops of ice cream, already tanned to a perfect shade of *café au lait*.

He knew he shouldn't wade right in in anger and confront her, but he couldn't help himself. The thought of what he'd just heard, of some sleazeball producer touching her and bragging about it to all his friends, made him feel physically sick.

'Siena,' he called out gruffly as he came within the last few feet of her.

'Mmmm?' she murmured in reply, semi-comatose with sun.

Rolling over slowly, she failed to notice that she had rucked up her bikini top, leaving her left nipple completely exposed. She gazed up innocently at Max. 'What happened to the drinks?'

'Never mind the fucking drinks,' he barked. 'And cover yourself up, for Christ's sake. Do you want the whole of Malibu to see your tits?'

She blushed and straightened her top. He had never spoken so brutally to her before. It frightened her.

'What's the matter?'

The old Siena would have shouted at him and told him to go fuck himself, but her love for him had done what nothing else had ever been able to achieve – disabled her legendary temper.

'Did you fuck a producer called Glen Bodie?' The anger and hostility in his voice were unmistakable. Siena could feel her heart pounding with fear.

'Did you?' he shouted, when she failed to answer immediately.

'I'm not going to answer you if you keep shouting at me like that,' she said, trying to sound firm, although her voice was still quavering. She drew her knees up to her chest defensively and reached for a beach towel to cover herself with. 'Who told you that, anyway?'

'Never mind who told me it,' snapped Max. He was now crouched down with his face inches from hers. All of a sudden the size and strength that Siena had found so comforting before had become threatening and awful. 'Is it true?'

Instinctively, she recoiled from him, scrambling backward on her hands like a frightened crab.

'Yes,' she blurted out eventually, raising her voice more in fear than in anger. 'Yes, it is true.'

'How could you?' He stood rooted to the spot, looking at her as if she were some sort of scum. It was that look which finally stirred her, despite her terrible fear of losing him, to defend herself.

'What do you mean, "how could I?"' she said. 'How could *you* sleep with all those models and waitresses you used to bring back to the beach house? You're not some saint, you know, Max, and neither am I. Yes, I did sleep with Glen. Yes, I'm an awful, disgusting, terrible, promiscuous person. Is that what you want to hear, Max? Yes, yes, *yes!*'

He looked on horrified as she collapsed into tears, pulling the towel completely over her head in utter misery, her whole body shuddering in a series of terrible lurching sobs.

In an instant he had sat down beside her and pulled her, struggling and crying, into his arms.

'Shhhh. Shhhh, Siena, I'm sorry,' he whispered softly, rocking her in his arms until she stopped resisting, the multi-coloured beach towel still draped over her face. 'I'm sorry, baby. I shouldn't have shouted at you. It's my fault. I don't think you're awful or terrible or any of those things.'

'Or promiscuous?'

She allowed the towel to drop, and looked at him with eyes still welling up with tears, and the wet cheeks and bright red, sniffling nose of a five-year-old. Max felt his anger dissolving. Why was he being such a jealous prick?

'Or that,' he assured her. He tried to explain himself. 'There were these two guys. At the café.' He gestured miserably behind him. 'I overheard them talking.'

'About Glen?' she asked meekly.

Max nodded.

Siena wished the beach could have opened up and swallowed her.

Glen Bodie – to her he had just been an evening's entertainment. Sure, he was a jerk, but he had a great body and a dick like a cruise missile. She hadn't given Bodie a thought before or since.

The fact was, she had always enjoyed sex, and in the past had prided herself on her ability to screw around as and when the fancy took her, without ever becoming emotionally attached to any man. Apart from Patrick Cash – and that had been years ago, a lifetime ago – she had never experienced anything approaching genuine affection, let alone love, for any of her many lovers.

But all that was before Max.

Siena didn't really know how, or why, but Max had broken through to a place in her heart that even she had almost forgotten ever existed. She not only allowed him to see her vulnerability and fear, she *wanted* him to see it, *needed* him to see it. Not even Hunter had got as close to her, in a lifetime, as Max had got in the last four weeks.

Siena knew she could be spoiled and selfish and that she wasn't a millionth of the wonderful, kind, honourable person that Max was. But, by some miracle, he seemed to love her anyway. For the first time in her life, she began to view her past sexual conquests as something less than glorious notches on the bedpost of her invulnerability. She began to view them as mistakes – perhaps terrible mistakes – that meant she could never be the pure, perfect woman that Max wanted and deserved.

'I'm sorry,' she cried despairingly, scanning his face for further imagined signs of disgust. 'It was a one-night thing. A long time ago. Oh, Max, I wish it hadn't happened, I wish a lot of things had never happened, but they did and I can't change them now. And I wish I could tell you that Glen was the only one, but he wasn't. Please. Please don't hate me for it.'

Max squeezed her even tighter. What the fuck was wrong with him?

Here he was with the most incredible, beautiful, loving girl – with Siena, Siena who he'd wanted, deep down, for as long as he could ever remember – and all he seemed to do was make her cry.

He tried to reason with himself. So what if she'd slept with some producer? So what if she'd slept with a whole bunch of them? It had all happened long before they got together. And she was right: he'd certainly been no angel himself in the past, so what right did he have to lay a guilt trip on her?

He was ashamed to admit it, even to himself, but the fact was that he felt scared. Scared that she would wake up one day and realise that she could do a whole lot better than a struggling English director with only a few thousand quid and a battered old Honda to his name.

Everywhere they went together, men stared or swarmed around her. Sometimes it was as if he couldn't hear himself think for the low background hum of industry types taking bets on how long the relationship would last.

It was bad enough being thought of as Hunter's hanger-on. But to be dismissed as Siena's plaything was unbearable, and filled him with a frustration that he couldn't seem to stop taking out on her.

'Angel,' he said, his voice breaking. 'I don't hate you. I could never hate you. If anything it's you who should hate me, for being such a stupid, jealous . . .'

She stopped him with a kiss, a long, lingering embrace charged with love and relief. Sometimes it felt as if the only way they could really communicate was physically. Sex was their safety net.

'Take me home,' said Siena when they finally pulled away from each other. His anger had shaken her more than she wanted to admit. 'Let's go to bed.'

Chapter Thirty-one

Out in Colorado with Tiffany's family, Hunter was anxiously smiling his way through another family meal.

'Thanks, Marcie, honey.' Jack Wedan leaned back in his chair and loosened his belt a notch, patting his groaning paunch appreciatively. 'That was great.'

'Yes, thank you, Mrs Wedan,' said Hunter with a sly wink at a furiously blushing Tiffany, who was clearly mortified by her dad's behaviour. 'It was absolutely delicious.'

Dinner had, in fact, been very good, the highlight of an otherwise rather tense day.

He didn't know what it was about Tiffany's family. They were always gracious hosts and studiously polite, asking him all about his career and his plans, making time to arrange trips or hikes to ensure he wasn't bored during his stay, cooking up a storm.

But still, there was an awkwardness with them that he couldn't seem to crack.

He'd been coming to Estes Park for years as Tiffany's steady boyfriend, and had never done anything to hurt or disrespect her, anything that might cause her parents to distrust him, at least not that he could think of. But for some reason, this undercurrent of something – reticence, suspicion maybe? – hung in the air throughout all his visits. It made it very hard to relax.

'I'm glad you enjoyed it, dear,' said Tiffany's mother kindly, getting up to start clearing the plates.

'Leave it, Mom, Hunter and I can do that, can't we, honey?' said Tiffany, deftly relieving her mother of her plate and stacking it on top of her own.

'Sure, of course,' he agreed, jumping to his feet, ever eager to be helpful. 'You put your feet up, Mrs Wedan, you've done more than enough.'

Tiffany also felt the tension around her parents and was grateful for a few minutes alone in the kitchen with Hunter. Creeping up behind him, she ran her hands over his butt while he was bending down to load the dishwasher.

'Hey, sexy.'

He spun around and grabbed her, burying his face in her neck and kissing her until she broke out in goose pimples.

'Hey, sexy yourself.' He grinned.

She was wearing the pair of black suede hipsters he'd bought her at Fred Segal a few weeks ago, with sleek black ankle boots that made her already long legs look endless. Hunter felt his groin stir. If only her folks hadn't been in the next room, he'd have ripped her clothes off then and there and taken her on the kitchen floor.

'Sorry about my dad,' she said, leaning into his chest and breathing in his musky, familiar smell. 'Sometimes he can be *so* Homer Simpson.'

Hunter laughed. 'Don't worry about it. I love Homer Simpson. Believe me, he's a hell of a lot more functional than my dad ever was.'

He let go of her and went back to rinsing and stacking the washing up. 'How d'you think it's going, though?' he asked, hopefully, scrubbing hard at the inside of a roasting pan. 'I think your mom's starting to like me a little bit.'

'Baby, they both love you,' lied Tiffany, reaching over him to rinse out a wineglass. 'Quit obsessing. Just be yourself.'

Yeah, right. Just being himself hadn't been a roaring success so far. Nearly four years, and he was still waiting for a 'Hey man, call me Jack' from her dad. This weekend was probably the best opportunity Hunter had yet had to try to win over Tiffany's parents, but it was proving to be an uphill struggle. For the last twenty-four hours he'd felt as if he were trying to melt a glacier with a candle.

Once the clearing up was finished they both went through into the family room, where Jack and Marcie were sitting together on the couch, leaving only two armchairs, one on either side of the room, for Tiffany and Hunter. Maybe he was being paranoid, but he couldn't help but feel that the enforced separation was both intentional and symbolic. Reluctantly, he took one of the chairs and watched Tiffany walk over to sit by her father in the other.

Despite the family's inexplicable hostility towards him, Hunter liked the Wedans' house because it felt like a real home. It was built in true Rocky Mountain style, all warm, polished pine with double-height, vaulted ceilings, and antlers on the walls. Every available space was filled with pictures or mementoes of Tiffany, from framed photos of her graduation to an enlarged still of her on *UCLA*, which was perched in pride of place above the fireplace. The refrigerator in the kitchen was still plastered with her early childhood daubs, along with carefully laminated lists of her various phone numbers, addresses and e-mail contacts, held in place by a bunch of multi-coloured magnets.

Hunter couldn't help but contrast it bitterly to the grandeur and sterility of his own childhood home. He was certain that no finger-painting of his had ever made it on to the refrigerator door in Hancock Park.

'So, Hunter.' As usual it was Tiffany's mom who made the stilted effort to kick-start a conversation. 'Have you got any new projects lined up for next year?'

'He's already told you, Mom, no,' snapped Tiffany. She couldn't face any more pseudo chit-chat. She knew that her parents worried about her relationship with Hunter, partly because he was wealthy and well known and they thought she would eventually get hurt. Tiffany, of all people, could understand that. But she still resented their frostiness.

'Don't talk to your mother like that,' said Jack, without ungluing his eyes from the Bobcats game on the local TV station.

'I was only asking,' explained Marcie meekly, 'because Tiffany was telling me that the pilot season has just finished, so I thought, well, perhaps you had something else in the pipeline?'

'That's OK,' said Hunter, with an encouraging smile. If her mom was going to make the effort to express an interest, the least he could do was be nice about it. 'But no, I don't have any new projects,' he explained. 'I'm totally over-stretched as it is. At one point I thought this might be the last season for *Counsellor*. But now we've all signed up again, there's no way I'd have time for a third show, never mind a movie.'

'Mmmm, quite.' Marcie nodded in agreement, with the sage look of someone well versed in the problems of juggling a TV and movie career. 'Well, we're just thrilled that Tiffany's pilot seems to have gone so well, aren't we, Jack?'

Her father grunted non-committally. Tiffany's face went white.

She could have cheerfully strangled her mother.

'What pilot?' Hunter looked across at her, bewildered. 'You never told me you were up for anything.'

'Oh yes,' said Marcie, blissfully unaware of the bomb she had just exploded between the two of them. 'Tiffany called us last week. She did say she wanted to keep it quiet' – she beamed proudly at her daughter – 'but you know, I'm just so excited about it, I don't think I could hold it in a moment longer.'

'The show hasn't been picked up yet,' mumbled Tiffany guiltily, unable to meet Hunter's eye. 'It may still not come to anything, you know? I didn't want to get everybody's hopes up.'

'But you told your mom, right?' Hunter's voice was flat, as if all the emotion had been punched out of him.

'Honey, I was going to tell you, really,' she said, tearing her eyes away from her lap and up to his hurt, disappointed face. 'I just wanted to be sure, to know if we were being picked up or not.'

'If they make the show then she'll have to go up to Vancouver to do the filming,' Marcie ploughed on excitedly. 'I hear it's wonderful up there, although I've never been to Canada myself. Have you, Hunter?'

'Excuse me,' he said suddenly, getting up with a face like thunder and heading for the front door. 'I think I need some air.'

'Take your coat!' Tiffany's father shouted after him, still glued to the game. 'It's cold out there.'

'Oh dear,' said Marcie, taking in her daughter's stricken expression, and registering, finally, that she'd somehow put her foot in it. 'Is there a problem? Was it something I said?'

Tiffany found Hunter outside, shivering in just his sweater, leaning against the gate at the end of the driveway.

It was a beautiful, crisp late April evening, without a single cloud to spoil the blanket of stars above them. Dirty, ice-hardened piles of snow still lay, resolutely unmelting, at the foot of the gate and along the verge of the winding mountain road that led down to Estes Park village. It was warm here during the days in springtime, but the nights could still be bitter right up until early May.

Tiffany breathed in the familiar smell of wood smoke and mountain air and steeled herself to go and talk to him.

'There you are,' she said softly, moving over to stand beside him.

'Yeah,' said Hunter, flicking an imaginary piece of dirt off the gatepost so he wouldn't have to look at her. 'Here I am.'

There was an uncomfortable silence while she struggled to think of what to say or do. She knew she should have told him she'd auditioned for the pilot and that she'd finally got herself a really decent part. Part of her, the better part, had wanted to share her success with him. But another part knew that if the show got picked up in the next few weeks, things would change between them. Difficult questions would have to be faced.

She would, at last, have the means to move out of the crappy old apartment she shared with Lennox, which would inevitably lead to a renewed push by Hunter for her to move in with him, something she felt less inclined than ever to contemplate now that Siena and Max had set themselves up in a permanent love-fest at the beach house.

She would also have to spend a lot of the next year away from home, filming up in Vancouver. Her contract was all but up at NBC, and she would ask them to release her formally before the end of the current series of *UCLA*, so she'd be free to go by mid-June.

She knew that Hunter would react badly to any sort of separation, and she had wanted to come to terms with the idea herself before springing it on him. Besides, maybe the show wouldn't make it, and she wouldn't have had to worry him with it after all. She really could murder her mother – why couldn't she have let her break the news to him in her own time?

'I was gonna tell you,' she said, wrapping her arm around Hunter's waist protectively. 'I was just waiting for the right time.'

He didn't remove her arm but nor did he return the gesture. His awkward, unyielding stance told her he was still angry, but she continued trying to explain.

'What I said in there was the truth. I have no idea if this is even gonna get made yet. I didn't want to get into it all and then have to say 'oops, sorry, ain't happening. Good old Tiffany screws it up again'. Story of my life, you know?'

'That's not true,' said Hunter with feeling. 'You haven't screwed anything up. You're a terrific actress, you always have been. You just needed to get a break, and now you've got one. I just wish . . .' He shook his head in disappointment. 'I just wish you had shared it with me, that's all. I tell you everything.'

'You didn't tell me you were asking Siena to move in.' Tiffany couldn't help herself.

'God, could you *stop* about Siena for five minutes?' said Hunter, exasperated. 'We aren't talking about Siena, we're talking about you. About us. I mean, Vancouver?'

'I know, I know,' she placated him. 'But I can fly back a lot. Or you can come up there. I don't know, we'll figure it out. It might not happen anyway.'

'It'll happen,' he said miserably, still scratching away morosely at the gatepost. 'What's the show anyway? CBS?'

Tiffany nodded. '*Sea Rescue*. You know, the one about the dolphin sanctuary? I'm Barbara, the chief at the rescue station.'

'Great,' said Hunter, without an iota of enthusiasm.

He knew he should be happy for her, be supportive, but all he felt was selfishly, miserably depressed. No sooner had he found Siena and replaced one missing piece in his life than Tiffany was about to leave him.

'It's not like I'm leaving you, honey,' she whispered into his ear, as if reading his mind. 'It's just one season. And it's Canada, not the moon.'

'Yeah, I know,' he said, finally relenting and wrapping his arm around her. He made a supreme effort to smile and try to look pleased. He knew this was a wonderful chance for her. He'd heard all about this particular pilot, and it was a big deal. If it went ahead, and he saw no reason why it shouldn't, she could become a household name overnight.

He was ashamed by how frightening he found that prospect.

Comforted by his embrace, Tiffany heaved a sigh of relief. For the past few weeks this secret had been weighing her down like concrete boots, and it felt good to have everything out in the open at last. She kissed him tenderly on the cheek, and began walking back towards the house. It was bloody freezing out.

Hunter watched her go.

Her long legs were lost in the darkness, but the starlight caught the loose blonde strands of hair that flew around her face, some of them sticking to the lip gloss on her wide, pink, infinitely sensual mouth.

God, he loved her so much.

In that split second he knew, for certain, that he wanted to marry her. He wanted to make her his, keep her safe, have her and hold her for ever, never let her leave. Not for Vancouver, not anywhere without him.

'Tiffany, wait!' he called after her, and she stopped in her tracks. 'Will you . . .' He stammered helplessly, but couldn't seem to get any more words out. She looked so perfect standing there, so beautiful and fearless. What if she said no? What if he ruined everything, what if he lost her for good for the sake of one crazy, impulsive moment?

'Will you promise to tell me this stuff from now on?' he finished lamely. 'No more secrets between us?'

She held out her hand for his, and led him inside.

'I promise,' she told him. 'No more secrets.'

Back in LA the next morning on the *Prodigal Daughter* set, Dierk Muller was watching Siena run through her scene and scowling.

Sometimes, when he watched her act, he could see a raw talent so exciting it made the pale hairs on his arms stand on end. At other times – like this morning – he cursed the day he'd ever been stupid enough to hire a model with next to no dramatic experience, and a seemingly pathological need to hold herself back on camera.

'Cut!' he shouted testily, clicking his fingers at Siena as though summoning a recalcitrant puppy. 'Siena, my dear. What are you doing?'

'Shit, Dierk. *What*?' Siena had had a long night, rowing with Max until two about some stupid little thing or other, then having make-up sex until four. It had been as much as she could do to haul her aching bones out of bed this morning and get to the set on time. She didn't need the cryptic questions. 'I'm doing the scene is what I'm doing. What's wrong? I thought that went great.'

'That, my dear,' he sneered, 'is why *I* am the director, and you are not. It was terrible. I've seen more enjoyable road accidents.'

Siena bit her lower lip hard, and stopped herself from saying what she really wanted to – that Muller was a sad, sadistic old Nazi who got his kicks from terrorising and demoralising whatever hapless actress he happened to be directing.

Some days she longed for the sycophantic photographers of her old modelling days. To think that a few short months ago she'd thought that Michael Murphy, the director of her Maginelle campaign shoots, was a stickler. Dierk could have eaten Michael for breakfast.

'OK,' she said patiently, pulling up a plastic chair and sitting down next to him. For all that she complained and cursed him, Muller was a wonderful director, and Siena wanted to learn from him. 'What do you want me to do?'

The director carefully put his clipboard down on the floor and looked at her. She was dressed for the scene in an immaculately cut chocolate-brown suit, the fitted jacket and tight pencil skirt clinging sexily to her curves, her hair flowing long and loose down her back. He cast a critical eye over her appearance, noting that even after an hour in make-up, the dark shadows under her eyes and the dull pallor of her sleep-deprived skin had not been entirely concealed. Stupid child! She wasn't taking care of herself.

The next thing Siena felt was a sharp, violent slap across her face which sent her reeling back in her chair.

Horrified, she put her hand up to her cheek, which was burning red and tingling from the blow. 'What the fuck did you do that for, asshole!' she screamed at Dierk, her blue eyes glinting with anger.

He watched her, shaking with rage, her picture-perfect, angel's face screwed up into a tight, venomous ball of fury, and a slow smile spread across his pale, Teutonic features.

'For that,' he said pointing at her. 'For that reaction.'

'*What*?' said Siena, still rubbing her throbbing face.

She'd had about as much as she could take of Muller's stupid party tricks.

'Look at yourself!' he babbled on excitedly, leaning forward in his chair and clasping her hands in his. 'Do you see that anger, that emotion? See your arms? They're everywhere, all over the place.

Your eyes, your mouth, your expression, your movements, they're all *real*.'

'Well, of course they're fucking real,' snapped Siena. 'You just whacked me for no reason, you fucking psycho.'

The rest of the cast and crew were glued to the drama unfolding between the director and his leading lady. Most of them had been the victims of Muller's unorthodox motivational techniques at one time or another, and they sympathised with Siena.

'That's what I want to see in your work, Siena,' said Muller. 'That realism, that emotion. Loosen up your body, let go a little bit. You have it in you, sweetheart. You just need to let it out.'

Turning abruptly away from her, he clapped his hands together magisterially for attention. 'OK, guys,' he bellowed to the room at large. 'Next take.'

Siena returned to the set, still clasping her hand to her cheek. Carole, the make-up artist, quickly advanced upon her with some green cream and foundation to tone down the red mark Muller had left.

'Don't worry, honey,' she whispered furtively as she dabbed and blended like a magician. 'He's a real bastard. We all think you're doing a great job.'

'Thanks,' said Siena.

She felt the back of her eyes stinging with tears of gratitude at this small word of encouragement. What with Hunter being so wrapped up in Tiffany, and Max feeling so threatened all the time, heaven knew she'd been getting precious little encouragement at home recently.

Rubbing her eyes and tossing her hair back, she determined to pull herself together. What would Grandpa have thought if he could see her now, practically reduced to tears by some stupid director?

She was Duke McMahon's granddaughter, for Christ's sake. She could handle this.

'OK.' She smiled at the rest of the cast, focused and professional once again. 'I'm ready. Let's do it.'

Chapter Thirty-two

For the next three months, until the end of July, life at the beach house went on more calmly and happily than any of them might have expected.

Siena and Max seemed to grow closer by the day. As the weeks rolled by, and she grew more trusting in his love, she visibly started to relax, and every aspect of her life began to blossom as a result.

Dierk Muller became less and less critical of her work. By the time the film wrapped in late June, Siena knew that she had grown immeasurably as an actress, and Muller was not the only one who was thrilled by her performance. Early screenings of the unedited picture had been greeted with rapturous enthusiasm by one focus group after another, and by mid-July the buzz surrounding *The Prodigal Daughter* was already huge.

Once filming was officially over, Siena spent her days giving interviews or going to photo-shoots, plugging the movie until she was too tired to speak. It didn't hurt that the pre-release PR coincided with the last and most extravagant of her Maginelle commercials, so that by July her face seemed to be, literally, everywhere.

Much to Marsha's delight, the scripts for new projects were already rolling in, and Siena's modelling fees had skyrocketed. The gamble of moving to Hollywood appeared to be paying off in spades.

In the little time she got to spend at home with Max and Hunter, Siena's general behaviour was also much improved. Almost through force of habit, she still tried to pull the occasional fast one on Tiffany. Once she purposely sent her to the wrong restaurant for a date with Hunter, making sure it was far enough up Laurel Canyon that she wouldn't be able to get mobile phone reception, and would think she'd been stood up. But Max had bawled her out so badly afterwards, forcing her to admit what she'd done to both of them and to apologise to Tiffany in Hunter's presence, that she hadn't tried anything like it since.

Everyone who knew Siena could see that Max was a good influence on her. She screamed and yelled, and tried to fight her corner with him. But deep down she respected his opinion, and nothing made her feel worse than the knowledge that she had let him down in any way.

Max was the only person in the world who knew how much Siena had hoped against hope that her parents might have got in touch when they saw all the press surrounding her movie. Every time the phone rang, or flowers arrived at the door, he would watch her spirits soar, then fall each time she realised they were not from Claire. It was painful to watch.

Pete, whose production company, McMahon Pictures Worldwide, had two huge blockbusters pending release at the same time as *The Prodigal Daughter*, had been asked repeatedly by the media about his thoughts on his daughter's first film.

'I'm not going to be making any comments about Siena McMahon,' he'd been quoted as telling *Variety*, referring to his daughter as though she were a total stranger. 'As for the movie, well, what can I say? It's not the sort of picture that MPW would look at, but for an art-house film, I'd say it was perfectly competent.'

In public, Siena maintained a dignified silence. But at night she tossed and turned miserably in Max's arms until he eventually rocked her into a fitful sleep.

In a bizarre twist, the one person from her old life who *had* called to congratulate her was Caroline. In one of her six-monthly calls to Hunter from England, she had actually asked to speak to Siena, and been quite genuinely complimentary about her career.

'Hunter tells me you're going out with darling Max,' she'd gabbled on merrily, as if she and Siena had always been on the best of terms. 'I always did adore that boy. Quite a catch! Seriously, if I were twenty years younger, I'm not at all sure I wouldn't make a play for him myself.'

The thought of Caroline and Max together sent a shiver of revulsion down Siena's spine. In fact, the thought of anyone else with Max made her stomach churn and her chest tighten painfully. As far as she knew, apart from one girlfriend at Cambridge, there had never been anyone really serious in his life before her. Unlike Hunter, who had always been the ultimate steady Eddie when it came to girls, Max had always been, in the nicest possible way, a bit of a cad. Siena remembered how much trouble he'd gotten into in high school when two of the cheerleading squad discovered that neither of them had his exclusive attentions as a boyfriend. Even as a teenager he had always loved women. Like her, he was a natural-born flirt, constantly flitting from one relationship to the next.

Unlike Siena, though, Max had managed to stay friends with most of his lovers. Women seemed to forgive him his roving eye because he was so funny and generous, and because he always treated them with respect. He just wasn't the settling-down type – everybody knew that.

At least, he hadn't been until he fell in love with Siena.

She just prayed that his new-found devotion and commitment to her would turn out to be permanent. She couldn't imagine where she'd be if he ever left her.

One morning in late July, Max was in his room at the beach house, on the phone to Henry in England, when a flustered Siena came rushing in wrapped in a towel, her wet hair leaving puddles of water all over the wooden floor.

'Hairdryer!' She waved her arms at him frantically, rummaging noisily through the chest of drawers and hurling clothes on the floor in her desperate search.

Since they had become lovers, Siena's room, which had the nicer view, had become 'their' bedroom, and Max used his old room as a study and a place to keep his clothes. Every spare inch of the storage space in 'their' bedroom was, naturally, crammed to the gills with Siena's stuff.

'I'm on the phone, darling,' he complained good-naturedly while Siena continued to empty the meagre contents of his wardrobe on to the floor. 'Do you think you could do this later?'

'Fuck, where *is* it?' she wailed, ignoring him. 'My effing hair stylist just called to say her kid's got a temperature of a hundred and five and she can't make it, the photographer was due half an hour ago, and now I can't even dry my own bloody hair because someone's nicked the sodding dryer. *Huuunteeeer!*'

She let out a scream so piercing that Max winced. 'Sorry,' he said to a perplexed Henry on the other end of the line. 'Siena and Hunter have a joint photo-shoot here this morning for *Hello!* The McMahons at home, new generation, all that bollocks. She's a bit stressed out about it.'

'So I hear,' said Henry, who was overloaded with stress of his own and found it hard to muster much sympathy for the pressures of a missing hairdryer. 'What about you? Can I look forward to pictures of my little brother in his gracious drawing room, spouting off about world peace?'

Max laughed. 'They don't have drawing rooms over here, mate. Anyway, since when did you read *Hello!?*'

'Christ, never!' said Henry with feeling. 'Muffy's the gossip fiend in this house, can't get enough of all that drivel.'

Max imagined his poor, beleaguered sister-in-law struggling to find five child-free, farm-free minutes in her day to sit down and read *Hello!* with a cup of tea.

He knew things were tough at Manor Farm, and that Henry's money troubles were escalating, but to be honest he'd been so focused on his own dire financial straits recently, and on Siena, that he hadn't given poor Henry's problems much of a thought.

Finishing the call, he settled down at his desk to make a start on a couple of the scripts he'd been sent last week. Anything to avoid the media circus that was about to get started in the living room.

Max hated photographers and journalists with equal passion. It was hard enough keeping Siena's raging ego and ambition in check without a bunch of sycophantic tossers turning up and telling her how marvellous and talented and beautiful she was all the time.

He picked up the first script, a manky-looking, dog-eared, tea-stained sheaf of paper bound with a cheap black plastic clip. It was the latest play from a very young, critically acclaimed new writer in Oxford who knew of Max's theatre work and wanted him to come and direct in Stratford next year.

He had skipped through it last night, but began reading more carefully now, marking the margins with pencil asterisks and illegible notes as he went along.

No doubt about it, it was good. Fucking good.

The only problem was that this kid, Angus, had had about as much commercial success as Max, i.e. bog all. His plays were considered too dark and depressing to have much mass audience appeal, and the style was too heavy and old fashioned for most London theatre producers to consider.

Max would have loved to do it, but the reality was he'd be lucky if he even got his expenses covered, let alone managed to make money on the thing. Plus it would mean going back to England for a four-month run, leaving Siena alone in LA to be pursued by every playboy producer and director in town.

So that was a definite no-go.

Reluctantly he pushed the manuscript to one side and began reading one of his potential American projects, another bland romantic comedy, gleaming professionally in its bright red CAA dust jacket. Fifteen minutes later he was disturbed by a shout.

'Max!' It was Hunter, calling from the next room where the shoot was obviously already under way. 'Can you come in here for a second, buddy?'

With a sigh, Max got up from his desk and opened the living-room door.

'Sure,' he said, without enthusiasm. 'What's up?'

The house had already been turned into a mini-studio, complete with blazing lights and vast silver reflective parasols to the sides of the sofa and chairs. The living room was full of people, the most visible and self-important of whom were the photographer, an emaciated Karl Lagerfeld wannabe dressed in head to toe black and ludicrously wearing his eighties-style dark glasses indoors, and a fat, garrulous middle-aged woman with a tape recorder whom Max assumed must be the interviewer.

Siena, who had evidently found a hairdryer from somewhere, was curled up on the sofa looking sleek and leaning back against Hunter, who had his arms around her shoulders. They were both smiling and laughing, enjoying the attention and each other's company, like an impossibly glamorous pair of twins.

Max felt his heart tighten.

'This is Johanna,' said Hunter, indicating the middle-aged woman, who obligingly smiled up at him and nodded, her blubbery jowls shaking. 'She was hoping to ask you a few questions, while we're getting the pictures done.'

'Hello, Max,' said Johanna, her fat wet lips issuing a fine mist of saliva as she spoke. 'I wondered if we could have a little chat now, you know, get it out of the way? Siena tells me you've got a lot of work on at the moment, so I promise I won't keep you long.'

Max raised his eyebrow at Siena and gave her a stern look. They had discussed this ad infinitum. No interviews, no pictures. The article was about her and Hunter. He had no desire to go into print as Siena's sad hanger-on of a boyfriend, or Hunter's charity case.

'I appreciate that, Johanna, thank you,' he said politely, forcing himself to give her a friendly smile. He hated journalists, especially fat women journalists. 'But as Siena is very well aware, I'm afraid I don't feel it's either necessary or appropriate for me to be involved in your piece. And I *do* have a lot of work to do. So if you'll excuse me . . .'

'I thought you said it was only pictures he didn't want to do,' said Hunter to Siena, who looked the image of wide-eyed innocence next to him.

'Well,' she said shiftily, 'the pictures were the *main* thing.'

Hunter rolled his eyes. 'Siena?' he pressed her.

'Oh, all right, fine,' she admitted grumpily. 'He did say he didn't want to be interviewed.' She turned to Max, gazing up at him with the pleading look that seemed to work so well with every other man in the universe. 'But I thought you might have changed your mind, darling. I really want you to do it. For me. Please?'

'Well, I haven't changed my mind,' said Max firmly. He wasn't giving in to her this time. 'And I'm not likely to when you try to ambush me like that.'

'But why *not?*' she demanded, screwing her hands into tight little fists and banging them down in frustration on Hunter's thigh. 'You're part of my life, and part of Hunter's, a big part. And you live here. If Tiffany were here, she'd do the interview, wouldn't she, Hunter?'

'Ow,' said Hunter, rubbing his leg.

'She bloody well would not,' said Max, picking his way over boxes of make-up and discarded tripods into the kitchen to grab himself an Oreo from the biscuit tin. Tiffany was away filming in Vancouver – as Hunter had predicted, *Sea Rescue* had been picked up for the full twelve episodes – and Max happened to know for a fact that she'd been relieved to have to fly back up there last week and miss today's shenanigans. 'Besides, that's not the point and you know it. We've already discussed this, sweetheart. We agreed.'

The photographer leered appreciatively at Max as he stumbled clumsily back towards his study, all blond hair, broad shoulders and powerful, tree-trunk thighs. Now there was a real man.

'You agreed, you mean,' said Siena sulkily, as usual becoming unreasonable and moody when she knew she was in the wrong.

'I'm not rowing about it,' said Max, shutting the door firmly behind him.

Why did he always have to be so infuriatingly self-controlled?

For the next two hours, Siena fumed quietly while the photographer shot roll after roll of film.

Why did Max have to be so stupidly proud and stubborn the whole time?

For the first time in her life she was truly, madly in love with someone. And not just someone, but Max, Max who was so gorgeous and sexy and talented and amazing that she woke up every morning wondering how on earth she'd ever won his heart.

She never thought it would happen to her – never thought she was capable of that kind of love. But now she'd found it, she wanted the whole world to know that she and Max were together, that it was real and that it was serious between them.

Was that such a crime?

I mean, what did he have to do today that was so earth-shatteringly important he couldn't spend five minutes talking to that stupid whale of a woman about how happy he was to be with her?

She didn't know why, but somehow Siena felt she would like to see Max's love for her spelt out in black and white, in print, for the whole world to see. It was as if seeing the words written down might magically transform his feelings into something more tangible, more permanent and safe.

It would have meant a lot to her and he knew it.

But oh, no, Mr fucking Integrity, Mr I have my own career and I'm not your sidekick, was too damn insecure to make the effort.

It wasn't until gone two that Max finally emerged from his room to forage for some more food. Things seemed quiet, and indeed, when he opened his study door he could see that the living room was empty.

Moving into the kitchen to grab a cold drink from the fridge, he noticed two empty champagne bottles sitting on the table beside the overflowing ashtray, and followed the distant sound of semi-drunken laughter out through the kitchen door and on to the terrace.

Turning the corner to the western side of the house, he stopped in his tracks in horror.

Siena, topless and giggling, was swinging from one of the low branches of the cypress tree. Admittedly the photographer was shooting only her back view – this was *Hello!*, not *Playboy* – but on the other side of the tree a whole gaggle of assistants and lighting guys were sprawled out on the lawn, mesmerised by her little exhibition. Hunter was nowhere to be seen.

'What the fuck do you think you're doing?' Max roared, dropping his plastic glass of iced tea with a clatter on the ground and vaulting down from the terrace on to the grass below.

Everybody spun around to stare at him, including Siena, who promptly lost her grip and fell with a shriek into the arms of one of the assistants, a boy of about eighteen who could barely breathe with the excitement of having Siena McMahon's bare breasts only inches from his face.

She was laughing so hard at first that she could hardly see her enraged boyfriend, let alone respond. That champagne really had gone straight to her head.

Extricating herself with some difficulty from the dumbstruck boy's lap, she collapsed on the grass, rubbing her ankle and giggling.

'Damn. I think I've twisted my ankle,' she moaned. 'It really kills.'

'Put this on,' Max commanded, pulling his old grey T-shirt off over his head as he advanced furiously towards her. 'You're making a fucking spectacle of yourself as usual. And where the fuck is Hunter?'

Siena took the T-shirt and held it against her chest, but didn't put it on.

'He went out,' she replied flatly. Everybody else had fallen silent. You could have cut the atmosphere with a knife. 'His pictures were all finished.'

'But yours weren't, I see,' snapped Max. 'They just wanted to get a few more shots of you with your tits out for their private collections, I suppose?'

Siena sat rubbing her swelling ankle in shock. She hadn't thought she was doing anything wrong and couldn't understand his sudden outburst of hostility.

'I wanted some shots of her outdoors, looking natural in such wonderful natural surroundings,' interrupted the photographer in a high-pitched, high-camp whine. 'We're only photographing her back, sweetie, no need to blow a gasket.'

'Who the fuck asked you?' said Max rudely. 'Go on,' he shouted, while the nervous group on the ground scrabbled hurriedly to their feet. 'Get out, the lot of you. The shoot's over.'

'No it bloody well isn't!' said Siena, standing up a little unsteadily and flinging Max's T-shirt on the ground defiantly. 'Just who do you think you are, Max, telling everybody else what they can and can't do? Who made you judge and fucking jury?'

Naked except for her skimpy orange bikini bottoms, and less than half his size, Siena nevertheless managed to look very intimidating when she was angry. Sexy, but scary. The crew skulked farther back into the shade.

'You've seen me topless on the beach a hundred times.'

'That's different,' he muttered darkly.

'Why?' she challenged him. She was on a roll now. 'Because this time I'm in a magazine? My fucking *back* will be in a magazine? Because I'm trying to promote my film and my career? Because this is what I do for a living?'

Max stood facing her in uneasy silence.

He knew he was right to be angry – of course he was angry, damn it – but he didn't *exactly* know why. He didn't know how to defend himself when Siena started yelling at him. It was as if she'd turned the tables on him, somehow managed to seize the moral high ground when *she* was the one in the wrong. He felt desperate, trapped.

'Well, *I* think she looks beautiful,' piped up Johanna, the fat journalist, who had a problem with aggressive men and wanted Siena to like her.

'Compared to you, everyone looks beautiful,' whispered one of the lighting guys to his friend, who stifled a giggle.

'Do you?' said Max sarcastically. 'How fascinating.'

Siena felt her eyes welling with tears. Her anger seemed to be spent, and now she just felt miserable.

Max had seen hundreds of topless shots from her modelling days and never batted an eyelid. She couldn't understand why he was being so nasty to her now.

'OK, everyone,' she said eventually, her voice trembling with unhappiness and barely contained emotion. 'He's right, that's enough for today. Thank you all for your time.'

Embarrassed, they all began gathering up their equipment in double-quick time. The fat journalist scowled pointedly at Max in a show of sisterly solidarity and passed Siena her bikini top.

'It's a terrific interview, my dear,' she said in a stage whisper, squeezing Siena's hand encouragingly. 'Don't you worry. You can see the copy before we run it in September, in case you want to make any changes.'

'Thanks,' said Siena weakly.

Max was still just standing there, bare chested, looking at her as though she were the lowest form of life. Of course, it was fine for *him* to stand around with his top off.

After what seemed like for ever, he turned away from her without a word and walked back into the house. Seconds later he was back with a new grey sweatshirt on and his wallet and car keys in hand.

'Where are you going?' asked Siena.

She now felt utterly vulnerable and afraid, unable to recapture the anger and defiance that had protected her before. All she wanted was for Max to turn around and tell her he loved her. He didn't even have to say sorry. Just not to go.

'Out,' he said angrily, without breaking stride.

She tried to run after him as he got into his battered old car, but she was barefoot and nursing her sore ankle and couldn't keep up once she hit the pebbles and shingle of the driveway.

'Out where?' she called desperately after him. 'Max, I'm sorry. Please don't go. Please!'

He seemed to stare right through her, and with one violent rev of his ancient engine, screeched out of the driveway, leaving a distraught Siena standing in a cloud of angry dust.

She was still standing there ten minutes later when Hunter arrived back home, and got out of his Mercedes looking cheerful and relaxed with a bag of Whole Foods groceries under his arm.

'Siena,' he said, his voice all concern as he registered the forlorn, frightened look in her eyes. 'What's wrong, lovely one? What happened?'

Crumpling into tears, she fell gratefully into his arms.

'It's Max,' she sobbed. 'He's gone. Oh, Hunter, I think he's gone for good.'

Chapter Thirty-three

Max drove along the coast road to San Vicente and headed east towards Brentwood, Beverly Hills and, eventually, West Hollywood. Sumptuous homes, in every style from mock Tudor, to Nantucket craftsman to glass-and-concrete modernist boxes, lined the route. The blazing afternoon sun poured down its life-giving energy on the orange and lemon trees that grew in every garden, overflowing with abundance and colour, fruitfulness and life.

But Max barely registered his glorious surroundings as he rattled along in his Honda, the car that Siena had once been too mortified to set foot in, but now loved as a battle-scarred old friend, just as he did.

He felt confused. And angry.

Angry at Siena, and angry at himself.

Fuck.

He banged his fist so hard against the dashboard that the instruments started to spin out of control.

Why. *Why?*

Why had he lost his temper, why did she have to show off in front of all those people, why didn't he know any more whether he was even right or wrong to feel so fucking furious?

His temples were starting to ache from the ceaseless, berating, conflicting voices in his head. He swerved, narrowly missing a huge SUV heading for the beach. He could see the Brentwood housewife in his rear-view mirror shaking her fist at him. Silly cow. He'd had it up to here with rich, spoiled women.

If only he could get a break, he thought bitterly. If he could just have one hit play, or one half-decent film funded – maybe this wouldn't be happening. But that was stupid. What did his fucked-up career have to do with a house full of arse-licking media parasites and Siena exposing herself to half of Santa Monica?

He couldn't think any more. He needed a drink.

Without realising it, he looked up to find that he had already turned on to Wilshire on autopilot, and was now practically at La Cienega. The digital clock in front of him told him it was still only half past three, too early to go to Jones's and hide away in a dingy red booth, unnoticed, to drink himself into oblivion. He'd have to go on up to Sunset and try one of the hotel bars.

Veering sharply left, he found himself looking at a hundred-foot-tall picture of Siena – the face of Maginelle – plastered on to the white west wall of the Mondrian Hotel, and chuckled bitterly to himself.

If that wasn't a sign, he didn't know what was.

Five minutes later, he had left his Honda with a disdainful white-suited valet out front – they were more used to Ferraris and Aston Martins, he supposed – and was making his way through the lobby to the Sky Bar.

By six o'clock, this famous poolside hangout for LA's movers and shakers would be starting to get busy. By eight, big black doormen would be turning away all but the most beautiful women and the most powerful men in Hollywood. But at quarter to four, Max had the place almost to himself, with only a sunburned family from Ohio and a party of German businessmen to prevent the pretty, sarong-clad waitresses from giving him their full, undivided attention.

He sank down exhausted on one of the over-sized cushions underneath the famous potted trees on the deck, and ordered a sour apple martini.

'They're pretty strong, you know,' said one of the dark-haired waitresses, after watching Max guzzle down his fifth drink as though it were Seven-Up.

'So am I.' He grinned at her inanely, plainly already drunk. 'I'll have another, please. May the best man win!'

'Bad day?' she ventured, offering him a bowl of wasabi peas and taking his empty glass.

Max shook his head. 'Not really.' He gave a hollow laugh and flopped back on the cushion. He tried to look up at her face, but it was hard to see because of the sun, so he shut his eyes. 'More like a bad year. Bad life, really.'

'Oh, come on now,' said the girl, with a sceptical raise of the eyebrows. 'I'm sure things aren't that bad. You look fit and healthy to me, and you've obviously got money to burn on these.'

She leaned over and handed him another neon-green martini, which Max grasped with a surprisingly steady hand.

As her shadow fell across his face, he opened his eyes and glanced up at her very flat, brown belly, exposed between the top of her sarong and her tight white T-shirt. He was surprised to find he had an almost overwhelming urge to sit up and lick it.

Fuck. He must be drunker than he'd thought.

'Call me if you need anything else,' she said, and before he had a chance to marshal his incoherent thoughts into any kind of a response, she had shimmied off towards the Germans.

He closed his eyes again for a moment, then opened them to find himself being shaken, gently but firmly, by another saronged nymph, this time a blonde with the most enormous pair of tits Max had ever seen.

'Sir.' She leant down low over his face and shook him again. 'Excuse me, sir,' she said more loudly this time.

Max sat up rather too suddenly and felt a wave of nausea hit him like a punch in the stomach. 'It's six thirty, sir,' the girl was saying. 'You've been out for a couple of hours. I'm afraid I'm going to have to ask you to settle your bill. Unless you wanted something else to drink?'

He rubbed his eyes blearily and tried to focus, but it was no good – the entire bar and pool were spinning around him like horses on a carousel.

Good, he thought. He wasn't hung over yet, he was still drunk. And the only thing to do when drunk, of course, is to keep drinking.

'I'll have another martini, angel,' he said, patting the seat beside him. 'Why don't you sit down for a minute first, though, and tell me your name. I'm Max.'

The girl smiled. He was an attractive guy and she was sure she recognised him from somewhere. An actor, perhaps? Or a producer? Even better. Maybe he could help her out.

'I'm Camille,' she said, extending her hand and looking deep into his eyes. 'But we're not allowed to sit and chat, I'm afraid. I'll get you that drink.'

Max took her hand and held on to it, partly because he wanted her to stay and partly because he hoped it might stop her spinning. She had a beautiful face, but it was hard and, he suspected, lightly surgically enhanced.

When he'd first moved back to California from England, he used to think that all that 'inner beauty' stuff was a load of old bollocks. But the more time he spent in Hollywood, watching pretty young girls rushing out to surgeons to have themselves carved up, then propping up the bar at the Standard or Koi every Friday night, trying to snag some producer or millionaire, sleeping around and wrecking marriages and families wherever they went, the more he had come to recognise a certain inner ugliness that truly revolted him.

Normally he wouldn't have given a girl like Camille a second look. But the combination of the martinis, her incredible breasts and his renewed fury at Siena – how could she have *humiliated* him like that? – all drew him towards her like a moth to a flame.

'I really have to get back to work.' She giggled, trying to remove her hand from Max's bear-like grip.

'You're far too beautiful to be working here,' he slurred, releasing her. 'What are you? Actress? Model?'

'Both,' Camille replied matter-of-factly. She knew she was beautiful and wasn't about to contest his assumptions. 'What about you?'

'I'm a director,' said Max, and even in his drunkenness he clocked the light of interest switching on in her eyes. Poor girl! She probably thought he could help her find work. If she had any idea how broke he was she wouldn't be giving him a second look.

'Listen,' she said in a conspiratorial whisper, 'my shift ends at eleven. If you want' – she bent down and lightly brushed the back of his neck with her long fingers, making his hairs stand on end – 'we could go somewhere afterwards. To talk.'

'Great.' Max smiled wolfishly, throwing caution to the wind.

This was a 'conversation' he was definitely looking forward to.

Back at the beach house, Siena sat miserably on the sofa and scraped out the very last dregs of a huge tub of rum-and-raisin ice cream. She was wearing an old pair of grey tracksuit bottoms, a big Aran sweater of Hunter's and a pair of Max's hiking socks. Her hair was scraped back in a messy bun and what little make-up she'd had on had long since been cried away, leaving her usually porcelain-white complexion red and swollen.

'You look terrible,' said Hunter, not unkindly, emerging from the kitchen still holding the portable phone – he'd been on the line to Vancouver for almost two hours, chatting to Tiffany. 'And what's this crap you're watching?'

Siena budged over on the sofa to make a space for him and he dutifully sat down and put a brotherly arm around her.

'It's not crap, it's HBO,' she said, not taking her eyes off the screen. 'Anyway, *you* can talk about making crappy television!' She instantly regretted the jibe when she saw his face cloud over.

'Sorry, I didn't mean that,' she backtracked. 'I just wanted to try and distract myself, that's all. I mean, it's gone midnight. Wouldn't you have thought he'd be back by now?'

Hunter took the empty ice cream bucket and spoon out of her hands and pulled her tightly into his embrace. He hated seeing her so upset, but it wasn't as if this were the first time Siena and Max had had a humdinger of a row. Every time it happened, she convinced herself that this was it, that it was over – a bit like the way he used to be with Tiffany – and every time she took solace in a vat of Ben and

Jerry's. For someone so crazy and spirited and strong willed, she could be very predictable sometimes.

'Not necessarily.' He tried to sound reassuring. 'You know Max. He's proud and stubborn to a fault. He's probably spending the night holed up in some horrid motel, wishing he hadn't been such an idiot but too pig headed to pick up the phone and call you.'

'I hope so,' said Siena, but she wasn't convinced. Hunter hadn't seen his face when he'd stormed out. He was angrier than she thought she'd ever seen him.

'And I really don't think overdosing on ice cream is gonna make you feel any better.'

Siena managed a weak smile. 'That's because you're a man and don't know anything.'

'Oh,' said Hunter indulgently, stroking back a stray strand of her hair. 'I see.'

'How was Tiffany anyway?' she asked, trying to muster some interest in anything other than bloody Max and his whereabouts. 'Still having fun up there?'

'Yeah,' said Hunter, a huge grin bursting across his face at the mention of Tiffany's name. 'She's loving it. Not so much Vancouver, she says the city's kinda dead. But the show, all the guys she's working with, that's going great.' He sighed. 'I miss her, though.'

'I know you do,' said Siena, who despite herself still wished he didn't.

'I'm off to bed anyway, sweetheart,' he announced. 'I'm beat. And if you've got any sense you'll turn in as well. Trust me, Max will be back with his tail between his legs before you open your eyes.'

He stood up and held out his hand to help pull her to her feet. She let him help her, glad as always of his physical presence and the closeness and comfort it never failed to bring her.

'OK,' she said, pressing the stand-by button on the remote and throwing it down on the couch. 'You're probably right.'

He bent down and kissed her tenderly on her forehead, nose and dimpled chin, just as he used to when they were kids.

'Of course I am,' he said. 'You just wait and see.'

Across town in East Hollywood, Max sat bolt upright in Camille's bed, stone-cold sober.

Jesus Christ. What had he done?

Bleakly, he ran back over the evening's events in his mind. He'd carried on drinking steadily at the Sky Bar until she'd finished her shift. By then he'd been far, far too smashed to drive, which gave him a perfect excuse not to have to show Camille his battered old car.

283

This was particularly important, as by the time they left together he had managed to convince her that he was a super-rich producer and director, and the only reason he didn't want to take her home to his palatial pad was that it was at the far end of Malibu, he needed to pick up his car in the morning, and didn't it make more sense to go back to her place instead?

He didn't know whether he was a frighteningly good liar or whether Camille was just particularly gullible. Either way, he felt an avalanche of guilt crushing him mercilessly when he thought about it.

She lay beside him now, her tousled head resting on a make-up-smeared pillow, her naked body still glistening with sweat and her face flushed with drowsy, post-orgasmic delight. Seeing Max's pained expression, she reached up and rested her hand gently on his bare back.

'What's wrong?' she asked.

'Oh God,' he wailed, staggering out of bed and pulling on his boxer shorts and shirt. 'I'm sorry. I'm really sorry, sweetheart. But I have to go home.'

'Now?' she said, her brow furrowing in disappointment. 'But what about your car? I thought you were going to stay here and pick it up in the morning. You don't want to get a cab all the way to Malibu at this time of night.'

'I'm not going to Malibu,' he said simply, too caught up in his own guilt and panic to spare much of a thought for her feelings.

Buttoning up his jeans, he began scanning the room for his socks and shoes.

'What do you mean?' demanded Camille.

She had sat up in bed now, and Max noticed that her enormous silicone boobs didn't fall so much as a millimetre when she did so, but remained fixed ridiculously in front of her like glued-on beach balls. He thought of Siena's beautiful, natural breasts and wanted to cry. What was he doing here?

'Look, like I said, I'm sorry,' he repeated harshly. 'I lied to you. I'm not a producer or a millionaire, and there is no house in Malibu.'

Camille's mouth dropped open like a stunned fish and she glared at him. That, he supposed, was where the LA girls' 'hard' look came from. From being used and lied to and taken advantage of by guys like him.

'I've been a total jerk, and you didn't deserve it,' he admitted, slipping on his shoes and grabbing his wallet from the bedside table. 'But the truth is I have someone at home. Someone I love more than anything.' He forced himself to look at her. Her eyes were ablaze with hatred. 'I have to go. I'm sorry.'

She looked back at him with utter contempt.

'Fuck you,' she said quietly and, rolling over, she pulled the covers up over her head to block him out.

There were a few seconds of silence, and she heard the door creak open, then close with a soft, guilty click. Under the covers she could feel her rage bubbling up to breaking point, and bit down on her lower lip so hard it bled.

The fucking bastard. The fucking, fucking bastard.

Outside Camille's apartment, the cold night air was like a slap in Max's face, jolting him out of his hangover and any residual drunkenness and bringing starkly home to him the enormity of what he had just done.

He began walking aimlessly down Vine towards Hollywood Boulevard, where he supposed he could get a cab. But to go where? Back to Siena, poor, darling, lovely Siena, who right now was probably lying innocently asleep in their bed, trusting him and loving him and waiting for him to come home?

He couldn't do it. He couldn't pollute her with what had happened tonight. Damn it, he was such a fucking fool! And all because of his stupid pride, his insane jealousy, his terrible, uncontrollable temper.

Why couldn't he be a decent, honest, faithful guy like Henry? No wonder he didn't have a happy family or a successful career. He didn't deserve to. He felt as if he wanted to cry, but he was so out of practice the tears refused to flow. Instead, he looked around for a cab. He wanted to get as far away from Camille as he possibly could.

'Taxi!' he shouted as a weary looking Mexican cabbie slowed down in front of him. Max clambered into the back of the cab, which was filthy and smelt of stale Taco Bell. 'Take me to the beach,' he said. 'Venice.'

He would swim in the icy salt water and scrub himself until all traces of the girl were gone from his body. Then maybe he could sleep down there on the sand for a couple of hours until dawn, clear his head and get his story straight before he went home to face the music.

He had already decided he wasn't going to come clean with Siena. He couldn't face losing her, or hurting her more than he already had. She would never know he had betrayed her. And he swore to himself, by everything he held dear in this life: he would spend the rest of his days making it up to her.

Siena was so deeply asleep she barely registered at first when he slipped into bed beside her. He must have already been to the bathroom and cleaned his teeth, because she could smell mint, combined with sea water, sweat and stale alcohol fumes that no amount of toothpaste could fully disguise. Opening her eyes a fraction, she glanced at the bedside clock. It was 5.30 in the morning.

'I'm sorry,' he whispered, cuddling in to her back and wrapping his arms around her tightly. 'Please forgive me.'

She was so overwhelmed with joy and relief that she swivelled around and smothered his face in kisses. Reaching up to put her hands in his hair she stroked his back lovingly, touching his skin in wonder as though checking he was actually real.

'I'm sorry too,' she said between kisses. 'I love you so much, Max.'

'I know you do, honey,' he said, his voice cracking. 'I know you do.'

Chapter Thirty-four

Henry Arkell had spent the best part of a thoroughly miserable day at Pablo Ruiz Picasso airport in Malaga, where a baggage handlers' strike had left thousands of British tourists stranded after their holidays. The terminal was heaving with exhausted, overweight mothers bawling at their bored and unruly offspring, or struggling to snatch a few hours' kip on the hard red plastic chairs. Henry watched their depressed-looking husbands in silent sympathy as they packed into the one small bar upstairs, a swarm of beer bellies covered in shiny red football shirts, hoping to drown their sorrows with warm Spanish beer.

Like them, he longed to get home, although in his case the marital strife would not begin until he landed in England. There could be no more putting it off now. He'd have to tell Muffy everything.

'Sorry for the wait, sir,' said the briskly polite young stewardess as he handed her his boarding pass, having finally been shown through to the plane. At least he was flying business class at Gary Ellis's expense. 'Would you like me to hang up your jacket for you?'

'Please,' he said, easing his big shoulders out of his ancient tweed. 'Thanks.'

Sinking down into the spacious seat, he accepted an immediately proffered glass of champagne; not that he had the slightest reason to celebrate, but at least he'd be able to get pissed with that bastard Ellis's money.

He'd flown out to Spain yesterday, feeding Muffy an unlikely story about going to some conference on a new EU directive on dairy quotas, and had driven straight up into the hills for a meeting with Gary at his pink monstrosity of a villa.

' 'Enry. Good to see you, mate,' the developer had greeted him warmly, pumping his hand between his own clammy palms and leading him out to the poolside bar.

Gary was topless and barefoot, sporting a lurid lime-green pair of Bermuda shorts over which his big sunburned stomach spilled unashamedly. He had an unlit cigar clamped between his teeth and could not have looked more like a criminal on the run if he'd put on a striped jumper and a mask and thrown a bag marked 'SWAG' over his shoulder. Henry instantly regretted having worn a suit.

''Ere, let me tike your jacket, you must be roasting.' Henry gladly complied, and sat down on one of the bubblegum-pink poolside chairs. A maid immediately arrived with a tray of iced water. The cool liquid tasted delicious, but he couldn't seem to stop the ice from clinking noisily against the side of the glass as his hands shook. He felt guilty, out of place and unaccountably nervous. Gary, on the other hand, looked relaxed and in control.

'So, Mr Ellis,' he began stiffly once he'd finished his drink. 'What was this offer you wanted to discuss with me?'

'Gary, please,' said the developer, with another confident smile.

If Henry had never really liked Ellis, the feeling was entirely mutual. Gary had never forgotten the way in which he had been 'frozen out' by the elitist, upper-class Cotswolds social set in Batcombe when he had first moved into the village. That buffoon Christopher Wellesley and his toffee-nosed cronies had made sure that he was never admitted to their inner circle, that glamorous world of hunt balls and private dinner parties to which he had secretly longed to belong. He remembered the patronising way Henry had looked at him at that dinner party at Thatchers, when he'd first admired the Manor Farm estate. He'd made him feel like a bit of dog shit stuck on the bottom of his green welly, the snooty little wanker. But the boot was well and truly on the other foot now.

He'd first got wind of Henry's financial troubles about a month ago, and had decided to make a move almost immediately. It wasn't just the social slight which had been burned on his memory. He also remembered how prime that land had been, how perfectly ripe for development. And then there was the lovely Mrs Arkell. How satisfying it would be, he thought, to take the bastard's farm *and* his wife, if the opportunity should present itself. Heavy debts, he knew from experience, could put a big strain on a marriage.

Today, however, he hid his inner resentment well and made sure he was charm personified. On his own home ground, and holding all the cards, he could afford to play a waiting game.

'All right, then.' He grinned. 'Let's cut to the chase, shall we? I wanna buy you aht.'

'Buy me out? Do you mean the whole farm?' The colour had drained from Henry's face. Despite the heat he looked as white as a sheet. 'I assumed . . . I mean, when we met before, you'd only seen the lower pastures.'

'Everyfink.' Gary lapped up his discomfiture.

'I'm sorry,' said Henry quietly. 'It's not for sale.'

'No?' Gary raised an eyebrow. 'What are you doing sitting 'ere, then?'

Henry was silent.

'It'd make a lovely golf club,' said Gary viciously. 'Two point six. Tike it or leave it.'

Two point six million. It was more than the farm was worth. A good thirty per cent more. That sort of money would solve all their financial problems in one stroke. But a golf club? His father and grandfather would both be turning in their graves at the very thought of it. Henry could feel himself sweating and looked miserably down at his feet. Why couldn't the slimy bastard have offered less? If he'd come up with some stupidly low figure, it would have been easy to tell him to stick it, to fly back home with a clear conscience, if not a clear balance sheet. But this was a more than generous offer. By any rational standards he'd be crazy to refuse.

'I'll need to talk to my wife.'

'Fair enough,' said Ellis briskly. 'But the offer only stands for forty-eight hours. It's nuffink personal,' he explained, suppressing his inner glee at Henry's panic-stricken features. 'Just business. I'm about to exchange on anuvver bit o' land a coupla valleys over from you. I'd rather 'ave yours, but I need to know.'

That conversation had taken place almost six hours ago. As he sat on the plane, miserably knocking back one drink after another, Henry still had no idea what he was going to do, or how he was going to begin to break the news to Muffy.

She was there to greet him at Luton, looking as adorable as ever in her blue gardening cords and one of his ancient, tattered Guernsey jumpers. She almost never bought anything new for herself – not that she'd ever been terribly into clothes, but since their money troubles she had gone to extra lengths to cut back on even the smallest unnecessary expenditure. Last week she'd proudly told him that she'd started reusing teabags and saving torn wrapping paper. Henry could have wept with guilt.

Looking at her across the arrivals hall, he felt his heart bursting anew with love for her, and with shame at himself. How could he have let her down like this? Mercifully, none of the children were with her. He really couldn't have coped with Maddie's endless questions or the boys' demands for presents all the way home. Not today.

'So how was the conference?' she asked him, ignoring his protests and taking the lighter of his bags from him. 'Was it worth it?' At first, when he didn't answer, she assumed he hadn't heard her. But as soon as she turned and looked at his ashen face, she knew that something was seriously wrong.

'Henry,' she said, her voice full of concern, 'what is it? What on earth's the matter?' And right there in the arrivals hall, he told her.

The drive back to Batcombe was one of the longest of Henry's life. His wife was not given to hysteria, and there had been no screaming fits at the airport as he'd recounted every painful detail of their spiralling debts, his desperate attempts to rectify things with Nick Frankel, and finally Gary Ellis's offer. Muffy, in fact, had listened in complete silence while he miserably unpicked every thread of her security, calmly paying for the parking and loading his bags into the boot without so much as a word of interruption or reproach. It wasn't until they'd been driving for twenty minutes, with Muffy insisting on taking the wheel, and he'd finally come to the end of his desperate stream of explanations and apologies, that she had finally allowed herself any sort of reaction.

'What I don't understand, Henry,' she said quietly, her eyes fixed on the motorway ahead, 'is why you didn't tell me about all this months ago.'

'Oh God, I don't know.' He ground his fists against his temples in frustration, at himself, not her. 'I mean, I *do* know. I should have. But I suppose I hoped you'd never have to know. I thought I'd be able to sort it out on my own.'

'*How?*' Finally her own frustration was starting to find a voice. 'How on *earth* did you think you were going to sort it out?'

'I don't know.' He stared down at his lap, defeated.

'And *why* would you want to do it all alone anyway? I thought we were partners. I thought we trusted each other.'

'We do!' said Henry.

She shook her head angrily. 'Rubbish! You've been lying to me since before Christmas. You obviously don't trust me at all.'

'That's not true. I never lied to you. I was trying to protect you from all this.' He reached out and put a hand on her thigh. She didn't remove it, but still she wouldn't look at him, biting down on her lip to stop herself from crying as she desperately tried to focus on the traffic in front of her.

'Does Max know?' she asked irrationally. She didn't know why, but the only thing that could make this worse would be the thought that Henry had confided in somebody else, but not her.

'No. Of course not,' said Henry. 'Why would you think that? I've hardly spoken to him since Christmas. Besides, he's totally broke himself, and far too wrapped up in Siena McMahon to listen to my problems. Look, I don't know what else to say, Muffy,' he pleaded. 'I love you, and I'm really, truly sorry that I kept all this from you. But, well, you know now. And we have to make a decision.'

'Oh, it's *we* now, is it?' she retorted angrily. She didn't want to lose her temper with him. She could see he felt dreadful and she knew that, however unjustified his deceitfulness may have been, he had never actually intended to hurt her. But it was all too much to take in. Henry had had weeks, months even, to get used to the idea of losing the farm. And now she was expected to say yea or nay to Ellis's offer in a matter of minutes.

For the rest of the drive home they sat in stony silence, Henry too guilty and Muffy too upset to initiate any further conversation. Back at Manor Farm they both did their best to be normal and cheerful at supper for the children's sake. It wasn't until 9.15 that Muffy came downstairs, having finally tucked Charlie into bed, and found Henry staring morosely into a pan of boiling milk on the Aga. She came up behind him and wrapped her arms around his waist, and he turned and hugged her, overwhelmed with relief at this gesture of forgiveness.

'Here, give that to me. It'll burn.' She lifted the milk pan off the hot ring and poured the contents into his waiting mug of hot chocolate.

'Thanks.'

Taking the steaming drink, he sat down at the table, while she automatically squirted some washing-up liquid into the pan and left it in the sink to soak before coming to join him.

'I'm sorry, Muff,' he said again, burying his head in her neck. She stroked his hair and kissed the top of his head. The kitchen was a mess, full of the detritus of the kids' earlier painting play, with half-eaten plates of fish fingers and beans littering the table and worktops. Despite this, or perhaps because of it, Muffy looked around the room and felt her heart swelling with a pride bordering on real love. She had refitted the kitchen herself over many long years, as the first profits from the farm had begun trickling in. She hadn't touched the wonderful, time-buckled flagstone floor and tiny, ill-fitting lead-light windows that had so captivated her when Henry first brought her here, back when his father was still alive. But she had replaced the old man's ancient death trap of a cooker with her beloved Aga, and she and the boys had had great fun helping Henry paint all the cupboards a cheery bright red, now long since faded to the colour of unripe cherries. More than any other room, the kitchen made the manor feel like a home. For the last ten years it had been the living, beating heart of the old house. Sitting there now, with Henry, she knew for certain what their decision must be.

'Stop saying sorry,' she whispered. 'It sounds so defeatist. This isn't over yet, you know.'

He pulled back and looked at her. 'You mean, you think we should turn Ellis down?'

'Of course we're turning him down,' she said sternly. 'That creep will turn this place into a golf course over my dead body. Yours too, I hope.'

Henry put his hand on the back of her neck and pulled her face towards his, kissing her passionately on the mouth. He didn't think he'd ever loved her more than he did at that moment.

'We're running out of options, though, Muff,' he said gravely when he finally released her. 'If we don't find seven hundred and fifty grand in the next few weeks we're going to have to sell to someone. And probably for a hell of a lot less than what Gary's offering.'

'I know,' she said. 'I know. Well, we're just going to have to think of something, then. Aren't we?'

Chapter Thirty-five

Siena was in a fabulous mood.

She stepped out of the Coffee Bean in Brentwood with an iced chai latte in one hand and a freshly baked chocolate muffin in the other, and walked across the road to the news-stand.

It was a baking hot Saturday, and she had a day of pure feminine indulgence planned.

Ines had broken the rule of a lifetime and flown out to LA last night for the long weekend, to a rapturous welcome from Siena, who was so delighted to see her old friend she had even taken pity on her jet lag this morning and allowed her to sleep in while she did the coffee-and-paper run.

As soon as she had stocked up on all the latest mags – Ines was an even bigger gossip fiend than Siena – she would go back to Santa Monica and wake her, then drag her off for a day of massages, facials, a long, late lunch at the Ivy and a *lot* of shopping.

She smiled to herself as she wandered around the news-stand, stocking up on the latest *US Weekly*, *Star* and *National Enquirer* as well as the more upmarket *Hello!* and *OK!* It definitely wouldn't do to see only *one* set of grainy pictures of Tom Cruise's naked butt on a yacht off St Tropez – she and Ines wanted the lot.

But it wasn't just the perfect summer weather or the prospect of spending the day with her best friend which had put her in such high spirits.

The publicity for *Daughter* had been going fantastically, and both Muller and Marsha were glowingly pleased with her. But better even than that had been the almost unbelievable changes for the better in Max.

For the last few weeks he had been an absolute angel to her. It was as if someone had waved a magic wand and all his jealousy and insecurity had disappeared overnight. All of a sudden he was loving and attentive – never in the annoying, lapdog way that her old model boyfriends used to be, though. It seemed funny now to remember how panicked she'd been when he'd stormed out after that awful row on the day of her photo-shoot with Hunter. How sure she had been that this was the last straw and he was leaving her for good.

Maybe that scare was just what they both needed?

Whatever the reason for Max's change of heart towards her, Siena felt deliriously happy and more in love with him than ever as she strolled around Brentwood this morning, oblivious for once to the staring and whispering of her fellow shoppers.

What with things being so great with Max, Ines coming to stay and Tiffany's temporary absence meaning she got Hunter practically all to herself, life at the beach house was like one, long, blissful dream at the moment. She was on a real high.

She paid for the magazines and was heading back to her car when her mobile rang.

She looked at the screen, hoping it might be Max or Ines, but it wasn't. 'Marsha Mob' flashed annoyingly up at her.

It was the second time her agent had called this morning, but 'Marsha Mob' could mean only one thing – work, and she refused to even think about work today. Just the thought of Marsha's insistent, bossy British voice was already causing a small cloud to form on Siena's mental horizon. She switched her phone off. The poison dwarf could bloody well wait.

Clambering up into Hunter's Navigator – her brand-new Mercedes was already in the garage following an encounter with a killer olive tree in Dierk Muller's driveway last week – she pulled out of the Coffee Bean car park and on to San Vicente.

She had the radio tuned to KZLA, Hunter's favourite country station, and Toby Keith was belting out 'Shoulda Been a Cowboy', one of her all-time favourites, in his sexy Southern accent. Siena joined in tunelessly, tapping the steering wheel as she sang along.

She had wound all the windows down, letting the warm summer air rush into the car while the music roared out so loudly that the joggers all turned around to stare. She loved the lyrics, although they described a world she knew nothing about: campfires and six-shooters and cattle drives. The song made her think of Duke, and of the old cowboy poster of him she used to have up in her room at Hancock Park.

She wondered what Grandpa would have made of *The Prodigal Daughter* and Dierk Muller. He probably would have thought both the movie and the director were too arty and pretentious. 'Art' had always been a dirty word to Duke.

But she was sure he would also have been proud of her for what she had achieved. For making her own fame and fortune, for getting back here and into the business and putting one over on her stupid fucking father.

Just remembering Pete's existence caused a tight feeling to start rising in Siena's chest. She wished she didn't care about her parents at all, that she could just block them out, as they seemed to have done so effortlessly with her.

Why was it always when she was at her happiest that the bad memories forced their way back into her consciousness?

Anxious to recapture her good mood of a few moments ago, she reached across to the passenger seat and picked up one of the magazines, glancing at it idly while she drove along. It was the *National Enquirer*, the most sensational gossip rag of them all and Siena's closet favourite. A brand-new issue too, out today, so she and Ines could catch up on all the Hollywood scandal before anyone else.

At first she thought she must have misread the headline. It was above a blurred, slightly grainy photograph that she certainly didn't recognise as herself. Slowing for a red light, she put the car into 'park' and stared at the front page for a closer look.

Oh my God. No.

She felt her heart pounding and the bile rising in her stomach as she saw that the front cover was indeed a picture of her, and not just any picture.

She was hanging topless from the tree at the beach house, with an open-mouthed camera crew at her feet. It had evidently been taken with a long-range paparazzo lens. In the background, the blurred figure of Max, his features barely discernible in the distance, had been circled in red. The headline read:

SIENA MCMAHON: CHEATING LOVER SEES RED OVER TOPLESS PICS.

Numb with shock, Siena flipped through the magazine, looking for the story.

It didn't take her long.

There, on pages four and five, was a full-length photo of an identikit blonde swimsuit model, apparently called Camille Andrews, superimposed next to a picture of Max in black tie, taken at the Emmys two years earlier with Hunter.

Siena started to read, but she could barely take it in:

"'He told me he was a producer,' said stunning Camille from Texas, who works part time at Hollywood's trendy Sky Bar. "It wasn't until after we'd made love twice that I learned he had a girlfriend. I felt so used.'"

She wanted to stop reading, but the words kept drawing her in, like some kind of evil force field, and she couldn't tear her eyes away.

'"Max was only an average lover,"' the girl went on. '"But what he lacked in skill, he certainly made up for in enthusiasm."'

Bitch, thought Siena irrationally. Max could fuck in the Olympics when he was with her. It wasn't any wonder he wasn't inspired by that cheap, hard-faced little whore. She stared at the picture of Max, all messy hair, broken nose and huge, honest smile, his eyes crinkled up into nothing with merriment, as if willing him to jump up off the page and tell her it wasn't true.

It couldn't be true.

Not Max. Not decent, solid, honest, true Max, her rock, her soulmate. He would never do that to her.

He couldn't.

She dimly became aware of horns honking at her from all sides, of angry drivers yelling and overtaking her, flashing their lights and shaking their fists. The light must have gone green. Without thinking, she put the Navigator into 'drive' and lurched forward, the article still clenched tightly in her right hand.

The truck had hit her before she'd had time to blink.

When she came to, her first, awful thought as she re-emerged groggily into consciousness was that she was back at school in England. The stark white walls, the gloomy semi-darkness from the partially drawn curtains and the faint smell of disinfectant all stirred unpleasant memories of St Xavier's.

'Sister Mark?' she mumbled, as a female figure in white uniform loomed into view.

'Well, hello again,' said the figure, smiling broadly.

As she got closer, Siena noticed she was Asian with a lovely, gentle face. Definitely not her old headmistress, then. She was young, probably about her own age, and wore a badge that proclaimed her name to be Joyce Chan.

'Do you know where you are, Siena?'

She tried to nod, but found that her head and neck hurt when she started to move. 'Yeah,' she said. Her voice sounded unusually hoarse and dry. 'Hospital. I guess.'

'That's right,' said Joyce, filling a tumbler of water and holding it to Siena's lips. 'You had a nasty accident, but you were very lucky. You're going to be just fine.'

'Ah, Miss McMahon. Welcome back to the land of the living.'

A strikingly handsome man in his early forties had entered the room and was walking purposefully towards her. He wore a white coat and a stethoscope around his neck, and looked more like a heart-throb soap actor playing a doctor than the real thing, all white teeth and tan.

Joyce stepped back respectfully as he approached the bed.

'How's our patient doing, Nurse Chan?' he asked, picking up the clipboard of notes fastened to the end of Siena's bed.

'She opened her eyes just a few moments ago,' said the nurse, and added with a smile, 'She looks great, though.'

Siena smiled back.

'I'm Dr Delaney,' said the soap star, perching on the edge of her bed and taking her hand in his. For the first time Siena noticed that there was a drip feeding something into her veins. 'Are you up to my asking you a few questions, my dear?'

'Sure,' she said. 'My head hurts a little, but I feel fine. What's this?'

She gestured to the needle protruding from the back of her hand.

'Don't worry about that,' said the doctor briskly. 'It's just a painkiller, for the bruising. I'm more concerned about your head right now. How much do you remember of what happened to you this morning, Siena?'

This morning? So she'd only been out for a few hours. Well, that was good at least; hopefully it meant her injuries couldn't be *too* serious. Thoughts and questions swirled around in her head as she tried to piece together a coherent chain of events from the blurred fragments of her memory. It was difficult.

'Take your time,' said Dr Delaney.

'Well, I was in the car,' she began. He nodded encouragingly. 'I was going home, I think. Yes, that's right, I was going to see Ines – she's here for the weekend.'

The doctor watched his patient smile, pleased and relieved that things were falling back into place. Her right eye, cheek and temple were quite severely bruised and she had cracked two ribs, but she still somehow managed to look incredibly desirable, propped up on the hospital pillows with one smooth white shoulder slipping tantalisingly out of her regulation white nightgown.

Adorable.

If he weren't here in a professional capacity, he would probably have made a play for her himself.

Sadly, though, she was his patient, and a very lucky patient at that. He would run a brain scan on her later, but apart from a mild concussion and the rib injuries, she appeared to be fine. Given that her SUV had been crushed like a Coke can, that was a minor miracle.

'Oh!'

Siena's hand flew to her mouth in shock, and she started trembling.

Here we go, thought the doctor. He squeezed her hand as tightly as professional ethics would allow.

'I remember. I remember what happened now. It was because . . .' Her voice trailed off, and he could see she was fighting back tears and in deep distress.

'I read something,' she said at last. 'It gave me a shock, and . . . and the lights changed.' She was crying openly now, tears streaming down her bruised and swollen cheeks. 'I guess I must have pulled out suddenly or something, I don't know. And that was it.'

'It's all right, my dear,' he said gently, 'you've done very well. It's wonderful that you can remember. Means you're on the mend.'

He already knew what it was that had given Siena the "shock". The paramedics had found her with the paper still clenched in her hands. This being Hollywood, juicy stories had a habit of leaking out, and a growing swarm of journalists and photographers were already gathering outside the hospital gates, hoping for a statement or, better still, a picture of their heartbroken heroine after her brush with death.

Suddenly he felt a wave of compassion for Siena.

Fame and fortune weren't always as great as they were cracked up to be. Poor girl. She was obviously terribly cut up about her boyfriend. Fella must have been mad to cheat on someone so beautiful and vulnerable, and so obviously madly in love with him. With difficulty, he resisted the urge to take Siena in his arms and comfort her.

'Was anyone else hurt?' she asked, dragging her thoughts away for a moment from Max's betrayal and shattering Dr Delaney's lustful reverie. 'Oh God, I didn't kill anyone, did I?' She sounded quite panicked.

'No, no, nothing like that,' he assured her. 'You were lucky you weren't killed yourself, though.' Siena looked dazed. 'Really. Reading and driving at the same time isn't the smartest of ideas,' he chided her gently. 'Your car was totalled.'

'*My* car, you mean.'

Hunter, weighed down with a huge bunch of red and white roses, appeared in the doorway. His beautiful features clouded over when he saw Siena's battered and tear-stained face. Dropping the flowers, he showed none of Dr Delaney's compunction and ran over to her, taking her in his arms and kissing and stroking her tenderly.

'Careful,' said the doctor, who was fighting back an irrational surge of jealousy towards the new arrival, not least because Hunter was even better looking than he was. 'She's got two fractured ribs, you shouldn't squeeze her like that.'

Hunter gave him a "we-need-some-time-alone" stare. He took the hint, and both doctor and nurse made themselves scarce, shutting the door behind them.

'Sorry about the Navigator,' said Siena, when they were alone. She was twirling a loose ringlet round her finger nervously, a sure sign that she was upset.

'Oh, shut up, would you. I couldn't care less about the stupid car,' said Hunter. 'I'm just glad you're OK.'

'Am I?' Her lower lip was trembling. She looked completely lost.

She clung on to him, trying to make herself feel safe and loved and secure, but it wasn't working.

Much as she loved Hunter, she wasn't a child any more.

It was Max's arms she needed.

'Have you . . .' She steeled herself to ask him. 'Have you talked to Max yet? Is it true?'

Hunter gazed out of the window. Siena's pain was palpable, and he couldn't bear to be responsible for making it any worse.

'You should talk to him, angel, not me,' he said.

'Yes, well, *he's* not here, is he?' she shot back angrily, pulling away from him and propping herself up in bed, wincing at the pain in her neck and chest as she moved.

It was a flash of the old, fiery Siena, and it both cheered Hunter and alarmed him to see it now. Anger had always been her natural defence mechanism.

'So I'm asking you,' she said. '*Have* you spoken to him, Hunter?'

He nodded, still looking out of the window rather than at her. 'And?'

'Siena, honey, what do you want me to say?' He was desperate not to have to be the one to confirm her worst fears. But there was no way around it. 'Did it happen? Yes, it happened. And he hates himself for it and he feels terrible about it. It was a stupid, stupid mistake.'

'How long have you known?' she asked.

Hunter sighed. He had known that question was coming. 'I only found out today, sweetheart, I swear,' he said truthfully. 'The police called me when it happened because the car's registered in my name. I guess I'm your next of kin too, right?' Siena nodded. 'They told me about the article, I called Max right away, and . . .'

She held up her hand to stop him. She didn't want to hear any more.

'He had no idea about it,' Hunter went on despite her protestations. 'You know, that the girl had gone to the press, I mean. Honestly, Siena, I was mad at him too, but he sounded so terrible, he regrets it so much, and when he heard about your accident he was crazy, hysterical. He wanted to come and see you right away.'

'How thoughtful of him,' said Siena bitterly.

'But I told him not to risk it,' Hunter doggedly continued. 'There are press everywhere. It was bad enough for me trying to get in.'

She sat quietly and tried to collect her thoughts.

So it was true.

Max, the first and only man she had ever let herself love, had betrayed her. For all she knew, this Camille was probably just the tip of the iceberg, the one who finally went to the papers with her story. There were bound to have been others.

How long had he been making a fool out of her? she wondered.

She was ashamed of herself. How could she have been so stupid?

For her entire life it had always been her worst nightmare to end up like Grandma Minnie, disrespected and humiliated by a man that she was too weak and too desperate to leave. Or like her mother, who may not have been cheated on, but who had been hurt and abandoned emotionally by Pete for years, and who chose to give up her own daughter rather than take a stand and leave the bastard.

She had opened her heart to Max, allowed herself to become vulnerable. And what had happened?

This.

Pain, betrayal, public humiliation. She didn't know who she hated more at that moment, Max or herself.

She raised her hand to her face and felt the swelling around her eye. She must look like shit. So much for her next three weeks of auditions. There weren't many casting agents around desperately seeking girls who looked like they'd come off worst in a bar brawl.

Fucking, fucking Max.

So he was sorry, was he? Well, too fucking bad. She was through trying to change herself for him, trying to be soft and feminine and understanding, all because *he* was too insecure to deal with her fame and success.

Max had made his choice. Now he could damn well live with it.

'Ask the nurse to come in here, would you?' she said to Hunter after what seemed to him like an eternity of silence.

He pressed the call bell and Joyce appeared at the door moments later.

'Can I get you anything?' she asked.

'You can, yes,' said Siena. 'I'd like a phone, please. And some release forms. I'll be leaving in a couple of hours.'

Joyce laughed. 'You can't do that, honey. Dr Delaney will want to have you under observation for a couple more days at least.'

'Then I'm afraid Dr Delaney is going to be disappointed,' said Siena, in a tone that left the flustered nurse in no doubt that she meant business.

'Sweetheart, come on,' Hunter pleaded with her. 'You could have died today. And all this stuff with Max, it hasn't sunk in yet. You guys will work it out, I know you will.'

'I have no intention of *working it out*,' spat Siena sarcastically. 'And I'm not going to hang around here while those paparazzi vultures wait for me outside either.'

'Siena, please, you're not thinking straight,' he insisted. 'Stay here for a couple of nights. Then Ines and I can come and take you home.'

'Home?' she said incredulously. 'What home? You mean the beach house, with you and Max? After the way he's just betrayed me? No, Hunter, no way.'

Her voice was rising and she put a hand to one of her broken ribs – the shouting really hurt, but she couldn't help herself. If she didn't stay mad now, she was sure she'd crumple up and die from the pain.

How could he do this to her?

'I'm sorry, Hunter.' She forced herself to calm down. 'But I've had enough. I need to get away, from Max, from LA, from everyone. My bruises will heal just as well in a hotel as they will here. I need to go somewhere where I can just shut everything out, where I can lose myself. Surely you can understand that?'

Hunter looked stricken.

He could understand, of course he could. He just didn't like it. He wanted to help her, to make everything right again. He wanted her to turn to him in her time of trouble, not run away.

He could have strangled Max for being so fucking stupid and selfish. What had he been thinking?

'Where were you thinking of going?' he asked.

She took his hand and gave him the first smile he had seen since he walked in. It was almost like looking at the old, pre-Max Siena again: tough, determined and wicked.

'Where would I go to lose myself?' she said. The smile broadened into a grin. 'Where else, baby?' And as she said it, she sounded so like Duke it made him shiver.

'Vegas.'

Chapter Thirty-six

It was a hundred and eight degrees outside when Siena woke up in her penthouse suite at the Venetian the following morning. The sort of heat that had chauffeurs opening limousine doors with folded handkerchiefs so as not to burn their fingers, and children wilting like dying flowers, drained of every last ounce of their energy as they wearily traipsed along behind their parents, their usual dreams of chocolate and McDonald's replaced by an even more powerful longing for water, air conditioning and a place to sit down.

High up in the palatial cool of her bedroom, Siena was unaware of the sweltering world outside her window.

She woke up instead to a fleeting feeling of disorientation – where the hell was she? – followed by a searing, throbbing, unbearable pain in her head and chest.

Jesus Christ, that hurt.

She let out a low groan and scrabbled for the painkillers beside her bed.

'One with each meal, maximum four per twenty-four hours,' read the label.

Siena swallowed three with a gulp of tepid water and slumped back on to her white linen pillows. What a mess. What a total fucking mess.

In the end, once he'd realised that she wasn't going to change her mind, Hunter had been very sweet and helpful yesterday, organising her cloak-and-dagger exit from the hospital via one of the service entrances to escape the baying press. Better still, he had called his long-time boss and admirer Hugh Orchard, who had kindly allowed Siena to use his private jet to fly straight up to Vegas from a little-used airfield in Orange County.

When she'd arrived in Vegas last night, the staff at the Venetian had been fantastic. Used to defending the privacy of such famous and reclusive guests as Michael Jackson and Madonna, they did a spectacular job of getting Siena checked in and settled, whisking her up to her suite in the classic Hollywood disguise of dark glasses and full-length fur, an operation that, despite her heartbreak and injuries, she had secretly rather enjoyed for all its clandestine glamour.

Less enjoyable had been Max's attempt to see and speak to her at the airstrip. Despite his promises, Hunter had been too soft hearted to conceal her whereabouts from his distraught best friend, and Max had arrived at speed, his little Honda almost entirely obscured by a cloud of dust, just as she was boarding the plane.

What happened next was already becoming a bit of a blur.

She remembered him crying and pleading with her to forgive him, begging her not to go. And she remembered the look on his face, a combination of terror and fury, as Orchard's security guys forcibly pulled him away from her and she climbed up into the plane.

She'd thought that she would cry, or at least feel something – anger for what he'd done, perhaps some compassion for his all too evident guilt, or even just the lingering force of her love for him.

But she didn't.

Some merciful God seemed to have flicked off the switch that connected her to any deeper emotion at all. The worst she could say was that she felt numb.

Christ, what she wouldn't give to feel numb this morning!

Maybe she had been a bit rash, checking herself out of hospital so soon. Her rib cage was so sore it hurt to breathe in. Hopefully the drugs would start kicking in soon.

Wincing again, she risked another, gentle stretch towards the bedside table and flicked on her mobile phone.

Predictably her inboxes for text and voicemail were both full. After deleting anything from numbers she didn't recognise (bound to be press) and everything from Max, she started to scroll through the remainder.

Three were from Hunter, all imploring her to call him, forgive Max and come home soon. Siena wiped them out with an impatient jab of the thumb – she was not in a forgiving mood this morning. Two were from Marsha, also asking her to make contact. One was from Ines, predictably asserting that all men were bastards, California sucked, and why didn't Siena move back home to New York, where they could go back to partying together again. That one made Siena smile. Darling, darling Ines. If only life were that simple. She scrolled through the list again, checking missed calls as well just for good measure, but there was nothing from her parents or any of the rest of her family.

Angrily, she snapped the phone shut and eased herself out of bed. Why the hell did she still care whether her parents called her or not?

She didn't turn on the TV, for fear that her face, or even worse

Max's or that slutty girl's, might be on it. Instead she showered, changed into a stunning, clingingly low-cut silk jersey dress – her face might be battered, but at least her body would look great for the inevitable paparazzi – and began carefully applying make-up.

She needed enough to restore the natural beauty of her cheeks and bone structure, while being careful not to conceal the bruises and cuts that the press were all longing to see. It might put a hold on her auditions, but she was canny enough to appreciate that, if correctly presented, her swollen face could just turn out to be a PR gold mine.

What with trying to ease her arms into the dress without further damaging her ribs, and painstakingly ensuring that her make-up was done to perfection, it was almost noon before Siena was finally ready to emerge from her suite and face, she assumed, her public.

She took one long last look in the mirror before she opened the door. The dress, now that she'd finally got into it, was flawless, the perfect shade of blue-grey to highlight her fair skin and blue McMahon eyes. Her hair was swept loosely back off her face, so as not to hide any of the bruising around her eye and cheek, and she wore a demure pair of grey kitten heels. Low by Siena's usual standards, they made her look younger and more vulnerable than her normal stilettos.

At the last moment, she noticed she was still wearing the tiny antique silver cross on a chain that Max had given her the week they first got together. She wondered why they hadn't bothered to take it off her at the hospital, after the crash.

Holding it between her thumb and forefinger, she looked at the worn, buckled Moroccan silver, rubbed to a fine sheen from its long and constant contact with her skin. She had loved that cross, because it was beautiful but simple and unpretentious, like Max, and because like him it had always seemed to protect her.

For a few seconds, her cloak of numbness and anger slipped, and she felt the tears welling up in her eyes as she held it.

She missed him so much. What was she even *doing* here on her own?

But she swiftly pulled herself together and, winding the chain tightly around her fingers, she pulled hard, just once, so the necklace snapped around her neck. She looked at the coiled chain in her palm. Broken, just like her and Max. But she was determined not to cry, biting her lower lip for all she was worth.

She couldn't hold on to him, she mustn't. She wouldn't survive.

She was going to throw the cross away, but couldn't quite bring herself to do it, so she slipped it instead into the miniature drawer of the bureau by the door. Perhaps one of the hotel maids would pocket it or sell it, and it could become someone else's treasured possession. It seemed a shame to blame such a beautiful thing for the ugliness of what Max had done.

With one last glance at her complexion, still proudly unstreaked by tears, she walked out of the door, leaving behind the sanctuary of her room and – though she didn't know it – the last moments of peace she was to experience for quite some time.

Sitting in the waiting room at McMahon Pictures outside her husband's office, Claire was growing increasingly frantic. She was dressed in the same khaki skirt and T-shirt she'd had on yesterday, her greying blonde bob looked lank and dishevelled and her usually healthy complexion seemed to have lost every last ounce of colour.

'How much longer, do you think?' she appealed to Tara, Pete's ghastly PA, for the third time in as many minutes.

'Mrs McMahon.' The pinched-faced girl made little effort to conceal her annoyance, tapping her pen on the desk officiously as though some vital work had been disturbed by Claire's question. 'Believe me, if I knew, I'd tell you.'

Tara could imagine what Claire's unexpected visit must be about. The story was all over the papers this morning, about Siena's car crash and the boyfriend screwing around on her.

Serve her right, spoilt little cow.

Tara had always hated and, if truth be known, envied her boss's daughter, and had done everything in her limited power to encourage his estrangement from her. Although there had never been anything sexual between them, she enjoyed what she perceived as her closeness to Pete, and the reflected glory it brought her as one of the great producer's inner circle. As a result, she also resented Claire with an intensity that, had Claire ever bothered to notice it, she would have found unfathomable.

Claire looked at her watch again and sighed. She was desperate to talk to Pete. He'd been away in Reno on business for the last two days, and they had not yet had a chance to discuss what had happened face to face.

It still seemed incredible to her that she, Siena's own mother, knew nothing more about what had happened than what she'd read in the papers, which all had wildly different and speculative reports of yesterday's events. Last night she'd been so frantic with worry she'd even taken her courage in her hands and, praying that Pete didn't find out, called the hospital herself. But as Siena carried a card naming Hunter as her next of kin, and specifically requesting that any information regarding her health be released to him and him alone, she was unable to find out anything about her daughter's condition.

She was just about to try Pete's mobile again when he suddenly emerged from the elevator, looking tired and a little travel weary after his flight, but otherwise unperturbed.

'Hello, honey,' he said, kissing Claire on the cheek and ushering her into his office, while simultaneously signalling to Tara to bring them some coffee, much to her simmering fury. 'What brings you here so early? I thought I was seeing you tonight.'

Claire reached into her bag and, pulling out copies of that morning's *New York* and *LA Times*, thrust them into his hand.

Siena's picture was on page four of the former and the front page of the latter.

'Don't tell me you haven't seen these,' she challenged him. They had spoken yesterday afternoon, but at that point nobody knew how serious the accident had been. 'Look at that.' She gestured to a horrifying picture of the Navigator, smashed into smithereens. 'That's what she was driving, Pete. It says here it was Hunter's car.'

'Hmm,' said Pete, glancing momentarily at the picture before chucking both papers on to a chair in the corner. 'Pity he wasn't driving.'

'Peter!' Claire was genuinely shocked. Even in his most rage-filled moments, she had never heard him suggest that he actually wanted Hunter dead.

'The point is, what are we going to *do*? About Siena, I mean.' She looked at him in desperation.

Slowly, calmly, he put his briefcase on the floor and sat down on the huge black leather sofa next to the window, gesturing for her to sit beside him.

Pete's office was positively palatial, and crammed with trophies of his movie-making triumphs from the past decade. Signed pictures of a host of Hollywood legends who'd worked with him lined the three walls that weren't taken up with window. Just about everyone Claire could ever remember having seen on-screen was up there some-where – Dustin Hoffman, Al Pacino, Nicole Kidman – and all of them had written personal notes of thanks or admiration to her husband, the boy that Duke McMahon had insisted would never amount to anything.

There were very few pictures of Pete himself on the wall. Despite his phenomenal success, he remained deeply insecure about his physical appearance, particularly his red hair. Even though it was now seriously thinning and heavily flecked with grey, Pete couldn't shake the feeling that it lit up his head like a beacon and that it was still the first thing everybody noticed about him.

He preferred to soothe his vanity by prominently displaying his two Best Picture Oscar statuettes, alongside a whole host of other, lesser film awards, at the very front of his desk, right in the immediate line of sight of any visitor who walked through the door.

He picked one of them up now, passing it from hand to hand in his lap, as if weighing up a problem. Then he turned to face his wife, who was sitting, anxiously wringing her cold, slender hands, beside him.

'Nothing,' he said quietly. 'We aren't going to *do* anything about Siena. Nothing has changed, darling. Not really.'

'What do you mean, nothing's changed?' asked Claire, taking the naked golden figure from him and carelessly plonking it back on the desk, ignoring his sharp, worried intake of breath. 'Of course something's changed. She's been seriously hurt, Pete. She needs us.'

He took her hands in his and looked her straight in the eyes.

'Claire,' he whispered. 'How many times are we going to go through this? Siena is no longer a part of this family. And she never will be again. Ever. I thought we'd agreed.'

'But Pete,' she began, although by now she already knew it was hopeless. His eyes had taken on that blank look that meant total emotional shut-down.

He stopped her. 'No. Please, Claire. Are you with me or against me?'

'Oh, for God's *sake!*'

She got up and began pacing back and forth in frustration in front of the window. *Why?* Why did it always have to be this life-or-death battle? Why couldn't he see that she did love him, that she loved them both?

She pressed her face up against the glass and stared down at the tiny, toy-town cars on Century City Boulevard, some thirty storeys below. This being LA, there were no miniature people running around, just traffic, weaving in and out of the various lanes like a confused army of ants on wheels.

It was a very, very long way down. Suddenly Claire felt a lurching sensation of being pulled forward, almost as if the glass might be going to magically disappear or shatter and she would plunge helplessly to her death far, far below.

She shivered and moved back from the window hurriedly.

What had she expected? That just because Siena had had an accident, because her face was in the papers again, Pete was suddenly going to relent and see sense?

She cursed herself for being so naive, for running down here to see him on a stupid impulse. The fact was that no story and no pictures were ever going to make him see Siena for who she really was: a frightened, confused, lost little girl, desperate for her parents' love.

Just then Tara came in with the coffee, without knocking, still boot faced about having been asked to perform such a menial task in front of Claire and having her perceived status so cruelly undermined.

'Leave it on the desk,' said Pete, oblivious to her indignant pout as she did as she was told, then turned on her heel and left.

'So?' he said again, this time to Claire's back.

He'd asked a question, and he wasn't about to let her leave without giving him an answer.

'I'm with you, Pete,' she said wearily.

And kissing him with almost maternal fondness on the cheek, she left him, her cup of coffee still steaming and untouched on the desk behind her.

Las Vegas in the summertime is like nowhere else on earth. Teeming with tourists who don't know any better than to take their holidays in temperatures that could fell cattle, as well as with the lost souls from all across America who come to forget, to try to escape their demons amid the noise and the neon and the relentless clicking and whirring of the slot machines, it's like some bizarre science fiction world of its own.

Siena had first come here as a child with her grandfather.

Duke adored the place. He used to say he and Vegas were made for each other. She remembered watching him and his friends playing poker in one of the private rooms at Caesar's Palace while she had stuffed herself with rum-and-raisin ice cream in the corner. She could only have been about six or seven.

Duke always wore a suit when he played cards, she remembered, and used to look like an even handsomer version of Dean Martin, with his whisky in one hand and his cards in the other, grinning around the big cigar he kept clamped between his teeth. Grandpa had always made Vegas seem so glamorous, and Siena had never quite shaken the feeling that beneath all the tacky freak shows and Siegfried and Roy kitschness, it was still a place where the big players played.

Duke had been a big player back in his heyday, the biggest.

One day, she told herself, she would be too.

As soon as she emerged into the lobby at the Venetian, she was greeted by the blinding flashes of a thousand cameras, and a myriad of strange voices, male and female, calling out her name.

'Siena! Over here!'

'How do you feel, sweetheart? Is it true you broke your ribs?'

'Have you heard from Max? Anything you'd like to say to him?'

Before she had a chance to respond, she found herself being swept up by the hotel manager, whose goons were making a valiant effort to beat back the throng, and bundled into the relative safety of his office.

'Holy shit,' she said, easing herself gingerly down into a chair a few moments later. 'How long have they been here?'

'Since late last night, I'm afraid, Miss McMahon,' said the manager, with a pained, what-can-you-do expression.

He was a very short, very round Italian with a ruddy, drink-ravaged complexion. Siena thought he looked like a human tomato, and suppressed a strong urge to giggle.

'We've done our best to keep them out of the reception area and security has been tightened inside the hotel. But I'm afraid as soon as you step outside . . .'

'I know, I know,' said Siena. 'I'm toast.'

'Excuse me?' The tomato looked bewildered.

'Oh, don't worry about it.' She waved her hand dismissively. 'It's an English expression, something I picked up at school.'

The manager nodded, as though he now understood perfectly, and tried not to stare too openly at Siena's fabulously full breasts, revealingly outlined by the clinging fabric of her dress. He didn't normally go for models, but he thought he could have made an exception in this young lady's case.

'I guess I have to face the music sooner or later,' she said, with a sigh that wasn't a hundred per cent convincing. 'I think I might do a bit of shopping, and they can get their pictures then. Get them out of the way.'

The manager had seen this act before with countless other 'celebrities'. The brave, resigned smile, intended to say: 'All I want is to be alone with my pain, but regrettably I have a public to think about.'

It was all a load of baloney. Sure, the girl was upset, some guy just screwed her over. But she was also loving the attention, every last minute of it.

No one came to Vegas for the privacy.

What he actually said was: 'I know this must be a difficult time for you, Miss McMahon,' tilting his head with practised, professional sympathy. 'If you like I can loan you a couple of my security guys, to come shopping with you? Things could get a bit outta hand.'

'Thank you, but I don't think I'll need them.' Siena got up to go and extended her hand, which he shook politely. 'It *has* been a difficult forty-eight hours, and I appreciate your concern. But I think I can cope on my own.'

'I don't doubt it,' said the manager, admiring her back view as she headed for the door. 'Not for a moment.'

For the first twenty minutes, Siena had a whale of a time. The best, the very best antidote to heartbreak, she decided, was a wave of public adulation.

She strolled along the artificial canals, looking suitably beautiful, victimised and brave, answering two or three questions before diving into Gucci or Prada, where the doors would close firmly behind her, allowing her to shop in peace while reporters pressed their lenses up against the glass. Then she would emerge for another short round of questioning and photographs, before disappearing again.

The slightly surreal atmosphere of the whole exercise was intensified by the seamless artifice that surrounded her: fake gondoliers with fake moustaches waved and shouted out to her in their fake Italian accents, beneath a fake painted sky, peppered with fake, neon-lit white clouds.

It must be incredible to wander through the Venetian on acid, thought Siena. She felt as if she were tripping already.

After twenty minutes, though, she was beginning to understand why they were called 'the press'. So many people were swarming around her it became quite physically intimidating, and before she knew it she seemed to have crossed the line from indulged diva to trapped rat.

The questions were also becoming more personal.

'Do you have any message for Camille Andrews?' asked one wiry little Hispanic woman, who'd got so close to her that her bad breath was making Siena feel sick.

'Not that you can print,' she snapped, her Pollyanna image slipping for an unguarded moment.

A hundred pens began frantically scribbling.

'Do you think you can ever forgive him?' yelled another, male voice.

Siena ignored that one and tried to turn left into a Ferragamo store, but found herself hemmed in by a solid wall of tape recorders and cameras.

Why hadn't she taken the manager up on his offer of some muscle? She started to feel panicked.

'Do you still love him?'

The voice came from about two feet behind her. Siena swung

around and searched for its owner, apparently a middle-aged black reporter, whose badge proclaimed he was from the *LA Times*.

'Do you still love him?' he repeated.

She stood and stared at the man blankly for a moment, while the cameras flashed. Then suddenly, out of nowhere, she burst into tears.

The crowd went wild, pushing even closer around her, raised voices babbling in an indistinguishable roar, photographers punching each other to jostle their way into a more advantageous position for a shot of the unfolding drama.

Oh God. Help.

She was sobbing and spinning around frantically on the spot, desperately looking for a way out. Just then she felt a slight easing of the pressure of bodies to her left, and saw a hand, a man's hand, being held out to her. Instinctively she grabbed it. The hand pulled her swiftly and forcefully through the throng, and she suddenly found herself disoriented and gasping for breath inside Ferragamo, the bloodhounds mercifully shut out on the other side of the door.

Only then did she look up from the hand to acquaint herself with its owner.

She had never met him before, she was sure of that, although something about his face was eerily familiar. She guessed he was in his mid to late fifties, completely bald except for one small strip of closely shaven grey hair that formed a circle at the bottom of his head. He was immaculately dressed in a dark blue suit and white Italian-cut shirt, and he smelled very faintly of some expensive aftershave.

He was overweight – not obese, but heavy – and not at all good looking in any traditional sense. He had a boxer's nose, wide and oddly flattened as if it had been multiply broken, which looked enormous above his small, thin mouth. His eyes were a deep brown, almost black, and were surrounded by symmetrical fans of wrinkles. But despite these rather unprepossessing features, the overwhelming impression he gave was one of power and masculinity.

Her tiny hand lost in his grip, Siena was horrified to find herself thinking simultaneously that he reminded her of Duke, and that she was strongly attracted to him.

'You looked like you could use some help,' he said, smiling down at her. His voice was deep and betrayed only the faintest traces of a long-lost Southern accent. 'I'm Randall Stein.'

Of course! Of course she recognised him. She really must have been on another planet not to have got it right away.

Randall Stein was a legendary producer, bigger even than her own father. He had made his name funding action movies back in the early eighties, and had almost single-handedly created the action comedy genre that went on to dominate the box office in the early nineties. Stein was also well known as a shrewd investor in real estate and on Wall Street. She was sure she'd read something in one of Max's *Forbes* magazines about his having a personal net worth somewhere in the billions.

Holy shit.

Randall Stein.

And here she was looking like something the cat had sicked up, bruised and tear stained and revolting. 'How do you do?' she said, hastily wiping away her running mascara with the back of her right hand.

Randall was still holding her left.

'I'm . . .'

'I know who you are, Siena.'

It was that voice again. Siena felt her knees going weak.

'Really?'

'Of course.' Randall released her hand, and pulled up a chair beside her. The Ferragamo staff, who had all been loitering, gazing at the drama and particularly at Siena – in their world a top model was of infinitely more interest than some dull-as-ditchwater producer – now disappeared to the other end of the store after a meaningful glance from their manager.

'I know your father. In fact I used to know your grandfather as well, for many years.'

'Really?'

She could have smacked herself. Why couldn't she think of anything interesting to say?

Randall smiled again. He seemed to find her embarrassment rather amusing.

'Yes. But that's not why I know you. It may have escaped your notice, my dear, but a lot of people out there seem to recognise your face these days.' He gestured to the paparazzi, who were now being shooed away by some newly arrived police outside the window. 'I enjoy looking at beautiful models as much as the next man. You could say I'm a fan.'

Siena smiled at this. She doubted very much whether Randall Stein was anybody's fan.

'Actually,' she said, finding her voice at last, 'I'm not really modelling much any more. I'm an actress.'

Randall threw his head back and gave a great roar of a laugh. Siena looked offended.

'Oh, I'm sorry. I'm sorry, honey.' He wiped away tears of mirth.

'It's just that I wish I had a dollar for every beautiful young girl who's told me that.'

'I am an actress,' said Siena again. The steeliness in her voice wiped the smile off Randall's face and he looked at her with renewed respect. 'A fucking good one, as it happens.'

'Well,' he said, apparently somewhat chastened. 'You certainly have the genes for it. But never mind all that. You look, if you'll forgive an old man for saying so, terrible.'

'You're not an old man,' said Siena, who hadn't taken offence. 'I know I must look a mess. I've been having a few . . .' She stumbled for the right word. '. . . well, a few problems in the last couple of days.'

'I know,' said Randall. She looked at him questioningly. 'I have a TV.'

'Oh,' said Siena. 'I see. Of course.'

'Look,' said Randall, 'it appears the boys in blue have got your little fan club outside under control.' Siena glanced outside to see the press pack dispersing resentfully under the watchful eye of four heavily armed cops. 'Why don't you let me have one of my guys take you back to your hotel, so you can get some rest. You really shouldn't be out here today, not till things die down.'

'OK.' Siena nodded. 'Thanks.'

'And I'll come and pick you up from the Venetian at around eight,' said Randall firmly, as if referring to a long-standing arrangement the two of them had made.

'Oh. I don't know,' began Siena.

'Eight thirty, then?'

'No, I mean, you've been very kind and everything. But I'm really not looking for . . .' She blushed, trying to think of a way to say this politely. 'I think I'm still in love with someone else. I'm not really ready for, you know, "dating".'

She waited for him to fill the silence, but he didn't let her off the hook. Again, he seemed to be enjoying her awkwardness.

'I'm just not interested in you in that way,' she blurted out eventually.

'Good,' said Randall briskly. 'Because I have absolutely no interest in you romantically.'

'Oh. Right. Good,' said Siena, who felt oddly as if she'd just been punched in the stomach.

'But I'd like to get to know you a little better. As I said, your family and I go back a long way. And you never know, we may even discuss a bit of business.'

He noticed how Siena's eyes lit up at the mention of the magic word business. A girl after his own heart.

'Great,' she said, and flashed him that million-dollar McMahon smile. 'I'm glad we got that straightened out.'

They shook hands again.

'Thank you,' she said sweetly. 'For rescuing me.'

'My pleasure,' said Randall. 'Now go get some rest. I'll see you tonight.'

Chapter Thirty-seven

Back in LA, Max sat on a rock high up in the hills above Will Rogers Park, with his head in his hands.

He'd been having some paparazzi problems of his own.

Ever since the news broke, a posse of press had been camped outside the beach house, waiting for him to emerge like the groundhog. He'd had a hell of a job shaking them off yesterday, on his way to try to see Siena at the airfield.

That was the only small mercy he could think of in this nightmare so far: at least the press hadn't been there to witness Siena dismissing him like some disobedient dog. She wouldn't even look at him, let alone listen to his apology.

He'd been expecting anger, hysterics and tears. Instead he got clinical, almost uninterested rejection. It was far, far worse.

After much pleading by Hunter, the LAPD had finally shown up last night and got rid of the photographers at the house, but by eight this morning they were back in barely depleted force, yelling inane questions at him from the street: had he talked to Siena, did he blame himself for the crash, were he and Camille now a couple?

One cheeky bastard had even had the audacity to stick a note under the front door, offering Max $150,000 for an exclusive on his side of the story, plus more if he was prepared to be filmed flying to Vegas to try to reconcile with Siena.

What sort of tragic gold-digger did these people think he was?

Hunter had suggested that the three of them – Tiffany had flown down from Canada last night to give both the boys some much needed moral support – escape for a long hike in the wilderness to try to talk things through in peace. The atmosphere at home was unbearable, like living through a siege.

So it was that, after some more very nifty driving by Max, they had once again shaken off their pursuers, and were now sitting, exhausted but undisturbed, high up above the canyon.

'If I could just make her see me, *listen* to me,' Max was saying for the umpteenth time that hour. 'I know I can turn this around. I mean, who throws everything away over one stupid mistake? Who does that?'

Tiffany thought privately that a lot of people did that, especially with a 'mistake' as big as Max's, and that she herself would probably be one of them. But she tried to sound encouraging. 'Maybe she just needs some space?' she suggested. 'She hasn't had much time to get her head around it yet, has she?'

Max ran his fingers back and forth despairingly through his hair. 'Oh God, what the hell have I done? How could I have been so *stupid*?'

Hunter sat down beside him and put an arm around his friend's shoulders. 'Come on,' he said, kindly. 'You couldn't have known the girl was going to leap on the phone to the *National Enquirer*.'

'I should have treated her better,' said Max, miserably. 'I was just thinking about myself, and how I'd betrayed Siena, and what a bloody fool I'd been. Maybe if I'd treated Camille with a bit more respect, she wouldn't have done the dirty on me.'

Hunter and Tiffany caught each other's eye. Neither of them contradicted him.

'I can't believe you didn't throw me out of the house and send me packing.' Max looked ruefully at Hunter.

'Come on, man, give me a break.' He squeezed him more tightly around the shoulders to emphasise his point. 'I could never do that to you, and you know it. We all screw up every now and then.'

'You don't,' said Max, honestly.

'Oh, don't you believe it!' Tiffany joked, desperate to lighten things up a bit. She'd never seen Max so down. 'Hunter has his dark side.'

All three of them had to laugh at that. Santa Claus had more of a dark side than Hunter.

'Seriously, though,' said Max, picking up a loose pebble and hurling it violently out across the canyon and into oblivion, 'I know you always thought I wasn't good enough for Siena. No one was good enough for her. And you were right, man. You were totally right.'

'Yeah, well,' Hunter began, 'she is pretty special.'

Tiffany couldn't believe her ears. 'Whoa, whoa, now hold on a minute, honey.'

She knew she was on dangerous ground saying anything against the saintly Miss McMahon, but she couldn't allow Max to shoulder all the blame for the problems in their relationship.

'What Max did was terrible, I think we can all agree on that.' Max looked down at his sneakers and nodded. No one could hate him more than he hated himself right now. 'And I'm not making any excuses for him,' Tiffany went on. 'But Siena was no angel either, so let's not rewrite history here. She could be mean and selfish, she was *always* flying off the handle at you.' She looked at Max. 'It's bullshit to say you didn't deserve her. You have so much to offer, and you put up with a lot of shit from that girl. We all did.'

Hunter was frowning throughout this little speech, and Tiffany waited for the inevitable defence of Siena. Sure enough, it came as soon as she stopped talking.

'I hope you're not implying that Siena *deserved* any of this?' He looked as close as he ever got to angry. 'That she brought it on herself in some way?'

'Of course I'm not saying that,' Tiffany snapped. 'I just don't think we should let Max start to feel that he's somehow not worthy of Siena, like she's some kind of saint. Because she's not, Hunter. She's not, OK?'

Max groaned inwardly. He could see Hunter's face clouding over. That was all he needed, to have him and Tiffany at each other's throats again over Siena.

'Look, this is all beside the point,' he jumped in, before hostilities could escalate any further. 'What we have to figure out is, what am I going to do now? How am I going to get her back?'

Hunter looked at him pityingly. It obviously hadn't sunk in yet.

'Max, I'm not sure there's a whole lot you *can* do, buddy,' he said. 'It's up to Siena to decide if she's going to forgive you, or at least try to work this out. But I gotta tell you, when I saw her yesterday . . .' He paused, looking for the kindest way to phrase it. 'Things didn't look too good. You really hurt her, man.'

Max stood up purposefully.

'I know. I know I did. But I have to see her, I have to at least try and explain.' He turned from Hunter to Tiffany and back again. They both looked highly doubtful. 'Oh, come on, you guys,' he said. 'Have a little faith, would you? Faint heart never won fair lady, right? I don't know how, but I'm telling you, I'm going to do it. I'm going to get her back.'

Later that night, Siena was sitting opposite Randall, gazing out across the Las Vegas skyline and feeling more than slightly drunk.

The view from the roof terrace was quite incredible.

Anxious not to suffer any more unwanted press attention, Randall had taken her to a private apartment – on loan from a friend, he said – where the most incredible table had been laid for two on the fortieth-floor roof garden.

Her initial reaction had been panic: candelabra, white linen, silver service and total privacy were not the usual ingredients of a business dinner. The scent of the bougainvillea alone was enough to make her feel faint, and the illuminated, azure blue of the pool behind them lent the whole place a summery, romantic air.

But Randall seemed so sure and relaxed about it all, she couldn't really say anything. She had already made a fool of herself once today by blatantly accusing him of fancying her. Besides, after he had come to her rescue so effectively this morning, the least she could do was accept his hospitality without being churlish. After all, how many up-and-coming young actresses wouldn't kill to be having dinner with Randall Stein?

Dinner itself had been delicious – lobster tails in garlic butter, wonderfully juicy, rosemary-encrusted lamb and raspberry mousse for pudding. To her surprise, Siena had found she was famished, wolfing down all three courses greedily. She had always read in magazines that men found girls with big appetites a turn-off, but Randall seemed delighted. Judging from his waistline, she assumed him to be another food lover.

She had also been drinking champagne to wash it all down, in blatant disregard of doctor's orders. Apparently alcohol disagreed with her medication or something, but she hadn't had *that* much. In fact she was pretty sure that Randall had drunk the second bottle almost completely by himself.

Pretty sure.

In any event, the ensuing haze of alcohol-induced contentment enabled her to banish all thoughts of Max and that fucking girl from her mind completely. Which, as far as Siena was concerned, was the object of the exercise.

'Coffee?' asked Randall, leaning across the table and taking Siena's hand. She permitted the gesture. All that champagne had really loosened her up. 'Or perhaps you'd like another drink?'

'No, God no.' Siena shook her head. She was very conscious of the warm, slightly rough touch of his fingers, and the unmistakable jolt of desire it triggered in her. Unconsciously, she began stroking the back of his hand with her thumb. 'I think I've had more than enough already. The city's swaying.'

'Coffee, then,' said Randall, pulling his hand away just when she'd hoped he wouldn't and signalling to their private waiter. 'I don't want you to be too far gone. We still have that business to discuss.'

Inexplicably, Siena felt her spirits fall for a second at the mention of business. She gazed dazedly out over the twinkling lights of Vegas, apparently lost in her own thoughts. Randall carried on.

'Perhaps I should start by saying that I know rather more about you than I let on this morning.'

'Oh?' said Siena, woken momentarily from her reverie.

'Yes,' he said enigmatically. 'And this afternoon I had my LA office fly me up a tape of the pre-screen version of *The Prodigal Daughter*. I watched it twice, as a matter of fact.'

'Really?' Siena's face lit up. She was deeply flattered that someone as powerful as Randall Stein should take such an interest in her work, particularly after he'd dismissed her earlier that morning as just another wannabe model. Instinctively she tossed back her hair and pouted at him, giving him the very best angle of the face that had made her a small fortune. Notwithstanding her bruises, she looked breathtakingly sexy. 'What did you think of it?'

Randall took a sip of his freshly poured espresso.

'I thought it was predictable, and a little bit derivative.'

Instantly she flushed with indignation and humiliation. He had set her up for that, the little shit.

'Oh, did you?' she said, standing up unsteadily and retrieving her bag with as much dignity as she could muster. Fucking asshole. If he thought she was sticking around here to be insulted by him, he could stick it up his fat, billionaire ass. 'Well, I'm afraid you're alone in that opinion, *Mister* Stein. The other critics have been universally impressed with my performance. In fact, I've been inundated with scripts already, and *The Prodigal Daughter* doesn't even open for another week. Now, if you'll excuse me . . .' She turned on her heel. 'It's been a long day, so I think I'll get back to my hotel and make a start on some of those scripts before I turn in. Thank you for dinner.'

'Sit down,' said Randall. He took another sip of his coffee, utterly unperturbed. 'Don't be such a spoiled child.'

Siena hesitated for a moment. The only other person who had ever spoken to her like that was Max.

'If you're serious about this business, *Miss* McMahon,' he mimicked her, 'you'll have to learn to listen to criticism without being so damn petulant about it. You didn't let me finish what I was saying.'

Scowling warily, Siena sat back down.

'I did think it was predictable. You're making some silly mistakes.' She opened her mouth to speak again, but he ignored her. 'But I also think you have potential, huge potential. With your looks and your name, you could go a long way.'

It was exactly what Siena didn't want to hear.

'Yeah? Well, fuck my looks!' she said, shaking her head in anger.

'And fuck my stupid name. I'm only interested in making it on the back of my talent.'

Randall smiled. God, he could be patronising, thought Siena.

'I see,' he said. 'Well, unfortunately *I'm* only interested in making money. If we're going to do any sort of business together, you may as well get that straight right now.'

Leaning over the table, he grabbed her by the shoulders and pulled her face close to his. For one awful, confusing moment she thought he might be going to kiss her.

Instead he began talking to her with an urgency and authority that forced her to listen. 'Do you know how many girls out there have "talent", as you call it? And by the way, I hate that word. How much talent does it take to pretend to be someone else? You're an actress, sweetheart, not a rocket scientist.' Siena sat motionless. 'Well, I'll tell you. Thousands. Hundreds of thousands. Maybe even millions of people can do what you do, Siena. And all of them are competing for the attention of guys like me. So how come it's you sitting here, and not them, huh?'

Siena assumed it was a rhetorical question.

'Because you're different, that's why. You're lucky. You have something they haven't got – the McMahon name. And if you don't use it, then you're a bigger fool than you look.' He was holding her so tightly his fingers were leaving livid red imprints on the flesh of her upper arms. 'You need to think long and hard, baby, about what it is you actually want.'

'No I don't,' said Siena, on autopilot. 'I know what I want.'

Although at that moment her statement couldn't have been less true.

She found Randall's physical closeness to her both unnerving and arousing. She had rarely encountered anybody with a stronger will than her own, and she had absolutely no idea how to handle it.

'Do you?' asked Randall. 'Because if you're going to bleat on about talent, you might as well take up a fulfilling career in the theatre in some butt-fuck nowhere little town in the Midwest and be done with it.'

He released her shoulders and sat back in his chair.

'But if you want something more than that . . .' He signalled to the waiter to refill his coffee cup. 'If you want to be a real star, like your grandfather was . . .'

'I do.' Siena's eyes lit up despite herself. 'I do want that.'

'Then you're going to have to make some changes,' said Randall, a new harshness in his tone. 'Big changes.'

'Such as?' She was intrigued again now.

'Such as quit dragging yourself down with some deadbeat loser of a boyfriend.'

'Max isn't a loser,' said Siena, stung. 'He's a director, and he has enormous talent.'

'There you go again, talent, talent, talent. Wake up, kid! The guy's a fucking zero. He's nothing. Nobody.' Each word was like a dagger in Siena's heart, but some force compelled her to keep on listening. 'He cheated on you, didn't he? Went out and had some fun with that dime-a-dozen waitress. Why do you think that was?'

'I . . .' She struggled to hold back her tears. Why was Randall bullying her like this? What did he care about her and Max anyway? 'I don't know,' she stammered. 'I thought he loved me.'

'Jesus, listen to yourself. Would you grow up?' said Randall brutally. 'He did it for two reasons, Siena. One.' He held up his forefinger. 'Because that's what men do. All men. Sooner or later, that's what we do.'

'Including you?' she challenged him.

'Absolutely including me.' He didn't miss a beat. 'And two.' He waved a second finger menacingly in her direction. 'And this is where your boy and I differ. He did it because he's too much of an insecure prick to deal with your success.'

She hated hearing Max's character being shredded by this total stranger. But she had to admit, there was more than a grain of truth in what Randall was saying. Max *had* always been jealous of her success. Besides, she didn't see why she should be defending him, after the way he'd just betrayed her.

'He's holding you back. Get rid of him.' Randall cracked his fingers for good measure, as if he'd just finished wringing something's neck.

'I have got rid of him,' said Siena.

And then she did something she couldn't really explain. She reached across and touched Randall on the cheek.

He didn't smile, or flinch. He simply held her gaze until, what seemed like hours later, he lifted her hand from his face and pressed it to his lips. To her dismay, Siena found herself fervently wishing he would put his lips all over the rest of her body, and the sooner the better.

'I can help you,' he said at last. 'I can give you what you want. But you have to do as I say. No more hanging on to the coat-tails of that soap star uncle of yours.'

'Hunter? Oh, no, you can't say anything against Hunter, he's been wonderful to me,' she protested.

'Fine. Send him a postcard. Spend Thanksgiving with him,' said Randall. 'I don't give a shit about your family life. I'm talking about your image, about the way you want to be perceived. As long as you live with him, as long as you're joined at the hip to a guy at his level, then that's the level people will see you at. Is that all you want to be, some two-bit TV star's sidekick?'

'Of course not,' said Siena.

'I told you,' said Randall, moving his chair closer and placing a warm, proprietorial hand on her thigh, which Siena did nothing to remove. They both knew by now that she was headed for his bed. 'I knew Duke. Pretty well, actually. I think you have a lot of your grandfather in you.'

The hand was moving upwards achingly slowly. Siena felt herself sweating and her mouth parting in longing for him. Her pupils were dilated and her eyelids heavy with lust.

Three days earlier she'd felt as if she would never look at any other man, that she and Max would be together for the rest of her life. Yet now here she was, up on some Las Vegas rooftop with Randall fucking Stein of all people, so horny she thought she might be going to explode.

'I should mention one other thing,' whispered Randall, his face buried in her neck as his fingers deftly pulled aside the cotton fabric of her panties.

'Hmmm?' murmured Siena, dreamily. The pain in her ribs and chest seemed to have magically disappeared.

'I also know your father,' he said, lowering his head to kiss her shoulders and collar bone before moving down to the tops of her beautiful, round, high breasts.

He eased one of them out of her bra and began slowly tracing the outline of her nipple with his tongue, while simultaneously sliding two fingers deliciously slowly in and out of her. Siena moaned with delight, and put a hand on the back of his bald head, pulling his face back up to hers.

'I hate him,' said Randall. Siena opened her eyes and looked at him. 'And he hates me. I hope that won't be a problem?'

She smiled.

Randall was no oil painting. But God, he knew how to turn her on.

'No problem at all,' she said. 'In fact, *Mister* Randall Stein . . . I think I might be starting to like you.'

Chapter Thirty-eight

For the next three months, Siena's feet didn't touch the ground. She never went back to the beach house. After Vegas, she flew back into town with Randall and moved directly into his Malibu estate.

'What about my stuff?' Strapped in beside him in the back of his private G4, she suddenly panicked. 'I have to at least go back and get my things.'

'We'll buy you new stuff.' Randall didn't even glance up from the *Wall Street Journal*. 'Don't worry about it.'

Siena didn't worry about it. After years of battling to make it on her own, first in fashion and then as an actress, it was wonderful to have somebody else make all the decisions, and better still to have them pick up her tab.

Her spirits lifted even farther when she saw the Malibu house. She'd been exposed to more than her fair share of wealth and luxury in her short life, but nothing could have prepared her for the opulence of Randall's mansion.

'Jesus Christ,' she said, clapping her hand over her mouth in awe as he led her into the palatial marble-and-gold atrium.

The walls were hung with enormous medieval tapestries, and priceless gold and silver urns filled with ostrich feathers stood like gleaming sentinels at the foot of the biggest, most dramatic staircase Siena had ever seen. Even Hancock Park couldn't hold a candle to it for sheer grandeur.

'Nice, isn't it?' said Randall, nonchalantly chucking his briefcase on to what looked like a seventeenth-century low table, exquisitely carved with mahogany angels clinging to each of the legs.

'It's incredible,' said Siena truthfully, but not without a twinge of envy.

She wanted to have a house like this. She wanted to be as rich and powerful as he was.

'You want it, don't you?' In their very brief acquaintance, Randall had already developed an uncanny ability to read her thoughts. 'Well, stick with me, sweetheart.' He smiled. 'Anything's possible.'

Siena moved towards him. Standing there, surrounded by all his wealth like a Byzantine emperor, he seemed even more powerful and attractive than he had in Vegas. She stood on her toes to kiss him, but he gently pushed her away.

'Not now, baby. I have a lot of work to do after the trip.' He patted her head, as if he were explaining something very complicated to a small child. 'Why don't you go upstairs and settle in, maybe have a nice hot bath, ease those bruises of yours. Maria Elena can help you.'

Before she could say a word, he had snapped his fingers and a nervous-looking Hispanic maid, in full livery, had appeared at Siena's side, ready to escort her to the bedroom.

It was a wholly new experience for Siena to have one of her sexual advances rebuffed, albeit temporarily, and she wasn't at all sure she liked it. As she was soon to discover, however, life with Randall Stein was to be full of new experiences.

For their first few months together, Siena felt as if she were living in a dream. *The Prodigal Daughter* was released two weeks after she got back from Vegas, and largely thanks to the publicity surrounding her accident and subsequent relationship with Randall, the movie was a huge success, the runaway 'surprise hit' of the autumn.

The ensuing publicity was overwhelming.

Siena, who was used to appearing on *Vogue* covers and to a certain amount of press attention, instantly found herself sucked into a worldwide media feeding frenzy, carefully orchestrated by Randall, who had insisted that poor old Marsha be fired within a week of bringing Siena home and brought in his own promotional team to handle his new girlfriend's image.

Suddenly, pictures of Hollywood's newest golden couple were splashed all over newspapers from LA to London: Randall and Siena at her premiere in Tokyo; arriving in his and hers Armani at the New York premiere for Stein's latest action blockbuster, *Ocean Drive*, arm in arm with Bruce Willis; Siena, looking unfeasibly sexy in hot pants and baseball cap, leaping up and hugging a smug-looking Randall at a Lakers game.

When the news broke in October that Siena had been cast as the heroine in Randall's upcoming Second World War drama, which was shaping up to be the biggest-budget movie of all time, the press went even further into overdrive.

Far from being intimidated, she appeared to thrive on the publicity, drawing energy and life from the flash of the camera bulbs like a pot plant suddenly moved from a dark corner into bright sunlight. Randall also seemed pleased at the success of his promotional efforts with his new protégée, although the 'Beauty and the Beast' headlines irked him more than he cared to show. Siena soon learned that her new lover, manager and mentor, despite all his success and power, was incredibly physically vain. He would typically wake up at five for an hour's gruelling workout with his personal trainer before getting on the phone to his brokers in New York. He was also obsessively careful about what he ate, and almost never drank alcohol, because he didn't like the loss of control.

It was a mystery to Siena why he remained so overweight, while she could sit up in bed munching chocolate bars and still keep her flawless figure.

Which was just as well, as she soon found she needed the chocolate for energy. Randall might be in his fifties and in less than perfect shape, but his sexual appetite nevertheless far exceeded Max's.

For the first time in her life, Siena had found a lover whose libido more than matched her own, and she found his demands quite exhausting. He was also much kinkier than her other lovers, and was especially big on making home porno movies. Despite Siena's frequent misgivings, and occasional protests, he insisted on filming her performing a variety of obscene and degrading acts. Before each performance he would lay out on the bed a spectacular array of sex toys, restraints, vibrators and massive black rubber dildos, like bizarre instruments of torture.

Siena's attraction to him remained intense, although the accessories didn't do a whole lot for her.

Afterwards he would make an attempt to be affectionate, perhaps allowing her to lie on his chest for a few minutes while he stroked her hair. As a rule, though, Randall was not good with any physical contact outside of sex. He did not approve of emotional dependency, either in himself or in others.

Having been burned so badly by Max, Siena was more than happy to embrace this 'every man for himself' philosophy. She enjoyed sex with Randall for what it was – just sex – and she revelled in the fabulous lifestyle he gave her.

Claire McMahon sat in a quiet corner of the car park at Fry's electrical store, out near the airport.

It was 5.30, so the place was fairly busy with after-school shoppers, mostly harassed-looking moms replacing light bulbs or broken fans on their way home to microwave something for their husband and kids. Claire envied them. She would gladly have traded every penny she had for a happy, domestic family life and children.

She readjusted her Chanel sunglasses and glanced around nervously, still scanning the car park for the silver Chevy Suburban she was supposed to be meeting. She knew it was stupid, but her heart was pounding violently and she was gripped by an irrational fear that Pete was going to drive in at any minute and catch her red handed.

This must be what it felt like to have an affair, she thought, and wondered how people ever coped with the stress. But an affair was the last thing on Claire's mind.

For years now she had given in to Pete and cut herself off completely from Siena. Because he needed her, and because she loved him so much, she had put herself through the anguish of having to sit on the sidelines and watch with the rest of the world as her daughter's turbulent life was played out in the media.

But after Siena's accident and her terrible conversation with Pete in his office, everything had changed. It was as if a switch had finally flicked deep inside Claire, and she could see with searing clarity that Pete would never, ever change his mind. That if she didn't do something soon, she really would have lost her daughter for ever.

She knew she couldn't contact her directly. The betrayal might literally kill Peter, and besides, Siena had made it clear in a string of barbed and hurtful articles that she would not have welcomed her mother with open arms should she attempt a reconciliation.

Even so, she had to do something.

There it was. The silver Chevy, a bit on the grimy side, but with the blacked-out windows she'd been told to look for, swept into the Fry's car park and pulled up into a space a few rows behind her.

She stepped out of her own Discovery and, locking the doors with trembling hands, made her way over and rapped lightly on the window of the passenger door, which instantly opened. She climbed inside and shook hands with the man she had met only once before in his grimy office in Compton a few weeks ago.

'Hello, Bill,' she said.

'Claire.'

Bill Jennings was not just black, he was jet black, with that very dark, Sudanese colouring that made his teeth gleam when he smiled, as he did now. 'Don't look so worried.' He chuckled. 'You're not doing anything illegal, you know.'

He handed her a brown envelope, which she immediately began to open. Inside were seven or eight pictures of Siena, as well as a typed and bound document, detailing her daughter's significant movements and news over the past three months.

'Where was this taken?' she asked, pointing to a picture of Siena, her face still looking bruised, outside the gates of a palatial-looking estate.

'That's Randall Stein's place,' said Bill.

Claire frowned. Like everyone else, she had read about Siena's liaison with Stein and the thought of it made her shudder. Claire had met him only once or twice, but she remembered Randall as a thug and a bully, albeit a charming one at times. Pete had always despised the man, and she couldn't help but wonder whether Siena had taken up with Randall as some sort of revenge for her father's abandonment of her. If this was a cry for help, Claire was listening.

'Thanks for these,' she said, gathering up the photographs and putting them carefully back into the envelope. 'I'll wire the money to your account on Monday, then, shall I? And we'll meet again next week?'

He nodded, and she got out of the car.

'Try not to worry,' he said in a kindly tone. He couldn't imagine how he'd feel if his daughter were shacked up with a guy older than he was. 'She seems in good shape right now. And I'll let you know right away if anything significant happens.'

'Thanks.' Claire smiled. Bill was a decent man.

He just didn't know how much of a lifeline he was to her.

One grey morning in November, Siena sat in the conservatory at Malibu, taking a leisurely breakfast on her own.

Since becoming Randall's girlfriend, she had got used to eating in pampered isolation. He was always either in the office or down at the studios long before Siena emerged from bed. Even on weekdays, she didn't have to leave the house until nine, as they rarely started shooting any of her scenes before ten. Working on one of Randall's movies was a whole lot different from working for that slave driver Muller.

But today was a Saturday, so she was looking forward to indulging herself free of guilt and lingering over her blueberry muffin and latte coffee until mid-morning.

'Have you seen-this?'

Randall, looking excited in his weekend uniform of khaki linen pants and black Gucci shirt, his hair still wet from a post-workout shower, burst into the room and slammed the *LA Times* down in front of Siena, scattering muffin crumbs everywhere.

'Seen what?' she asked, unsmiling, annoyed that her peace had been so rudely disturbed. 'Shouldn't you be in the office?'

'Take a look,' said Randall, ignoring her and pouring himself a cup of coffee from the freshly filled cafetière. 'It seems old Minnie McMahon finally gave up the ghost last night.'

Siena picked up the paper, and stared at the headline: MINNIE MCMAHON, WIFE OF LEGENDARY DUKE, DIES AGED EIGHTY.

Below this stark announcement was a picture of Duke and Minnie on their wedding day, looking at each other and laughing. The picture shocked her almost as much as the headline – she couldn't remember her grandparents ever being remotely happy together. How odd to think that they must have been, once.

Putting down her coffee shakily, Siena turned to pages four and five, where a montage of pictures caused her to catch her breath.

There was a small shot of the old Hancock Park house where, it appeared, Grandma Minnie had died peacefully in her sleep. Siena had studiously avoided driving anywhere near the old neighbourhood since moving back to LA, and didn't have any pictures of her own, so this was the first time she'd seen it in years.

She touched the image in wonder, tracing the outline of the house and the big lawn where she and Hunter and Max used to play. It made her want to cry.

Below this were more pictures of Duke and Minnie together at various public functions, as well as one of her parents, sitting smiling on either side of a very frail-looking Minnie. She felt her heart tighten painfully as she looked at her mother's face. It was thinner and slightly more wrinkled than she remembered it, but fundamentally Claire looked the same: kind, nervous and a little bit lost.

Looking at the picture, Siena felt an avalanche of longing and loss hit her in the chest. She was stunned.

'I had no idea the old bat was still going,' said Randall with typical insensitivity. 'There's very little about you in there, unfortunately. Something in the obituary about Hunter and his mother, though – Caroline, isn't it? Couple of the other papers even got on to her in England for a quote. She's married to some lord or something now, I gather.'

'Hmmm?' Siena was miles away, lost in painful memories.

'Anyway, baby, I've been thinking about how we should spin it,' Randall continued, buttering himself a piece of toast and apparently oblivious to her anguish. 'You need to call that dumb-fuck uncle of yours.'

'What?' Siena put the paper down and looked at him, eyes brimming with tears of grief and anger. 'What the hell are you *talking* about, Randall? My grandmother's just died, OK?'

'So?' he said through a mouthful of toast. 'Don't try to tell me you gave a shit about her. When did you last speak to the woman? Five years ago? Ten?'

'That's not the point,' said Siena, crossing her arms and legs defensively against him. 'She's still my family. And my parents . . .' She picked up the picture of Pete and Claire again. 'I wonder how my dad's taking it. They were very close, you know, Dad and Grandma. Grandpa – Duke – he never got along with my father.'

'I'm not surprised,' said Randall bluntly. 'No one gets along with your father. He's a cunt.'

'Randall!' Siena winced at the viciousness of his language.

'Jesus, Siena, *what*?' he snapped back tetchily. 'I've heard you call Pete McMahon a cunt enough times, and worse. You're telling me you suddenly think he's a great guy, just because his mom dropped dead?'

'No,' she mumbled, 'of course not.' She was angry with him for being so insensitive to her feelings, but she supposed he did have a point.

'Why should you care how Daddy dearest is taking it?' Now it was Randall who sounded angry. 'I think I remember you telling me he didn't care too much how you were taking it, when he cut you off without a fucking penny and turned you out on the street.'

'All right, Randall,' said Siena. She was feeling very emotional – it was all too much to take in. She really didn't need a lecture from him right now.

'No, Siena, it's not all right.' Sensing her weakness, he moved in for the kill. 'How many years have you sat around waiting for any of your so-called family to make contact? Huh? When you did your first *Vogue* cover, when you got the lead in *Daughter*, you had the whole world making a fuss of you, telling you how great you were. But did you enjoy it? Hell, no! All you wanted, all you *really* wanted, was for Mommy and Daddy to call and say, 'Well done, honey, we love you.' Wasn't it?'

He was mocking her now, his voice laden with spite, making fun of her weakness, her terrible, shameful need for her parents' love.

'That's not true!' she yelled back at him, willing herself not to give him the satisfaction of tears.

'Yes it is!' Randall banged his fist down on the table with a crash and leaned intimidatingly across the shuddering plates and bowls towards her. Instinctively she shrank back from his temper. 'It *is* true, Siena. You are so fucking weak sometimes, I can't even look at you. Haven't you figured it out yet? They don't love you. They don't want you.' He spoke very slowly, lingering over each word like a sadistic executioner. 'You mean nothing to them.'

'Stop it!' She clamped her hands over her ears, but he grabbed both her wrists and pulled them away, forcing her to hear him.

'When Max screwed you over, when you had that crash and nearly died, where was your father then?' He raised his eyebrows as if expecting an answer, but Siena just shivered in terrified silence. 'Who looked after you then, Siena? Who took care of you and took you in and gave you a home, and a real career, and everything you've ever wanted?'

'You did,' she whispered, defeated and confused.

She just wanted him to stop.

Still clasping her wrists, Randall pulled her into his lap and wrapped his arms around her, kissing her hair and neck and stroking her. It was more tenderness than she had ever experienced from him, and she felt ridiculously grateful and reassured by it. Despite her best efforts, the tears had started to flow.

'I'm sorry,' he whispered, all softness and compassion suddenly. 'I shouldn't have shouted at you. I just can't bear to see you wasting your love and sympathy on people who don't love you back. It's weak.'

Siena looked up searchingly into his inscrutable brown eyes, but drew a complete blank. For months now she'd spent every single day with this man, but she still couldn't figure him out.

She wasn't even sure whether she loved him or hated him. All she knew was they were a team now, a good team in many ways. Randall had picked her up and reinvented her when she was at her lowest ebb. He had showered her with riches, and catapulted her career into the fast lane overnight.

She needed him.

'What do you want me to do?' she asked, drying her tears and wriggling free from his embrace.

'That's better,' said Randall, and smiled at her, evidently pleased to have won her co-operation. 'Well, the first thing I want you to do is call Hunter. Invite him to the Dodgers game with us tonight.'

Siena looked perplexed.

'That's the story here, the spin,' Randall explained. 'You and Hunter've both been abandoned by your family. No one called you to tell you about Minnie's death, and you're really cut up about it. Let the press get some shots of you together, putting on a brave face.'

'It's been done to death, though,' said Siena, apparently happy to talk business now that her tears had dried. 'Me and Hunter, the family outcasts.'

'It's been done badly,' said Randall, 'thanks to your friend Marsha. It's a great card, baby, and I'm going to show you how to play it properly. Besides, things are different now. Your profile is in a whole other league to your pretty-boy uncle's. Your grandmother's death is a gift. Let's make you the star of the show.'

Despite everything, Siena felt a stab of distaste, hearing Minnie's death described as nothing more than a PR opportunity.

She also wasn't crazy about the idea of using Hunter to help promote her image. Things between her and Hunter had been strained to say the least since Randall came on the scene. She couldn't go to the beach house, what with Max still living there and the annoying Tiffany back in almost permanent residence. And Randall had made it quite clear that he disapproved of her closeness with Hunter, or with anyone other than himself, in fact, so she couldn't really ask him out to Malibu either.

What with their geography problems, filming schedules and Siena's constant need to be in the limelight, they had had precious little time together recently. She knew that this had hurt Hunter deeply, and she was ashamed of herself for allowing the rift between them to grow.

'I thought you hated Hunter.' She made a last attempt to stall him. 'Aren't you always telling me not to spend so much time with him, and never to get our picture taken together?'

'This is different,' he repeated, in a tone that was intended to indicate that the matter was now closed. 'Call him, ask him tonight. I'm sure he'll be thrilled.'

'What about the second thing?' said Siena. 'Didn't you say calling Hunter was the first thing you wanted me to do?'

'Ah, yes.' Randall smiled wickedly. 'The second thing.'

Siena gave him an over-the-top look of mock surprise.

She already knew exactly what 'the second thing' would be.

Placing two strong hands on her shoulders, Randall pushed her down on to her knees. Wordlessly, she unzipped his fly and freed his rock-solid erection. Then she looked up at him, smiling. Despite everything, despite all the crudeness, controlling and bullying, Randall's power was still the ultimate turn-on for Siena.

Gently, he lifted her mountain of dark curls and cupped his hand around the back of her neck, pulling her pretty rosebud mouth down on to his cock.

Then he sat back and sighed contentedly as, with consummate skill, she gave him exactly what he wanted.

Chapter Thirty-nine

Across town, Tiffany put the finishing touches to the table with a little sigh of contentment. Grabbing her novel – she was addicted to Patricia Cornwell at the moment – and a chilled glass of Chablis from the fridge, she slipped out on to the front porch and sank down on the wicker sofa to await Hunter's return for lunch.

They had decided to spend the weekend at her newly rented cottage in Venice, a charming, whitewashed 1920s affair on one of the walk streets, with a white picket fence and orange and lemon trees in the front garden.

Tiffany had fallen in love with it the moment she saw it and put down a deposit of three months' rent on the spot, but she hadn't actually moved in until a few weeks ago, when *Sea Rescue* had finally wrapped.

The cottage was a compromise solution. It was only a ten-minute drive along the beach from Hunter's place, which was a lot easier than her old Westwood commute.

She still didn't want to move into the beach house: even with Siena gone, it still felt too much like Hunter's space. But she understood that Hunter felt he couldn't sell up and desert Max in his current hour of need. So they'd agreed to divide their time as equally as possible between the two houses and, unless either of them were away shooting, not to spend a night apart.

She sipped her wine happily and admired her new garden. She was so much happier here, away from the heavy atmosphere over at the beach house.

Ever since Siena had run off with Randall, it was as if a nail bomb had exploded into all of their lives.

Max's initial confidence that he would win her back had soon been replaced by despair. Mercifully, he had finally landed a really decent, paying job directing two short films for a famous Hollywood actor with money to burn who wanted to dabble on the production side. This at least meant he was out of the house and occupied most days.

Even so, he carried his broken heart around with him wherever he went, and Tiffany found it painful to watch. He had lost a shocking amount of weight, and lack of sleep had taken all the mirth and playfulness out of his lovely eyes.

Worst of all, though, was his insistence that he alone was responsible for his misery. Nothing Tiffany or anyone said could change his mind about that.

He was so acutely aware of his own guilt, he refused to hear a bad word said about Siena. The agony of being constantly bombarded with images of her with Randall, rich, famous and utterly beyond his reach, Max thought of as nothing more than just punishment for his betrayal of her and their love.

Hunter was not much better, moping around like a lost puppy, hoping against hope for word from Siena.

It made Tiffany's blood boil, the way that she had dropped him like a hot brick, now that she had her billionaire sugar daddy to take care of her and was a newly minted Hollywood superstar. As far as Tiffany was concerned, Siena had finally shown her true colours and proved once and for all that all she really cared about was fame and money.

But Hunter, as always, point blank refused to see it.

'Have you seen the news?'

Hunter, dripping with sweat from his run along the beach, was clutching a damp copy of the *LA Times*. He bounded over the fence in one giant stride, and sat down on the terrace with his head between his knees, trying to catch his breath.

Tiffany picked up the paper and read the headline.

'Oh, darling, that's terrible,' she said with real sympathy, putting a hand on his sweat-dampened shoulder. 'Are you OK?'

He nodded breathlessly and ran into the kitchen to pour himself a glass of water.

'I'm fine, actually,' he said, wandering back out. Tiffany budged up so he could sit beside her. 'It seems funny to say it, but I never really knew Minnie that well. I mean, I grew up in the same house and all that, but we had very separate lives.'

Tiffany just sat patiently and listened.

'I remember when I was very small, she used to scare me a bit,' he went on. 'Claire, Siena's mother, would always try to stick up for me. I think the problem was, she could never quite forgive me, Minnie I mean, for being my mother's son. Which is understandable, I guess.'

'No it isn't,' said Tiffany bluntly. Sometimes Hunter's turn-the-other-cheek nature could really wind her up. She wished he would stick up for himself a bit more. 'It isn't understandable at all. You were a wholly innocent child. Anyway, I'm sure I remember you or Siena telling me she'd squandered half your inheritance or something.'

'I told you that, but she didn't do it deliberately,' he said. 'She just never had a clue about money. My dad used to handle all that. Anyway. . .' He gave her a kiss, careful not to press his sweaty, salty face against hers and smudge her mascara. 'I'm fine. Must be tough on Pete, though.'

Good, thought Tiffany, but she didn't say anything. Hunter might be able to forgive his mogul brother, but she wasn't about to forget the way that Pete McMahon had tried to destroy his career back in the early days of *Counsellor*.

Hunter picked up the paper again and started to read some of the comment.

'I wonder how Siena is taking it,' he said nervously. He had become very wary of bringing up Siena's name these days, fearful of Tiffany's disapproval. 'Do you think I should call her?'

'No,' said Tiffany, firmly, getting up and leading him into the living room and the delicious-looking lunch she'd prepared. 'She hasn't bothered to call you, has she? She's got your number, darling, if she needs you.'

Hunter looked sad, but he wasn't going to fight about it. 'You're right,' he said.

Tiffany was astonished. She hadn't expected him to let it go so easily. Then again, things *had* been fairly distant between him and Siena this last couple of months.

'I ought to call my mom, though, after lunch. I'm sure she'll have found a few spare moments to talk to the press.'

He rolled his eyes, imagining Christopher's bemused tolerance as his mother lapped up the ever welcome press attention. These days, now that he was so happy and settled with Tiffany, he was inclined to feel much more indulgent towards Caroline's foibles and weaknesses. He viewed her more as a sort of charmingly naughty, overgrown child than the woefully irresponsible parent she actually was.

Tiffany had never met Caroline, although they'd spoken several times on the phone. She knew she ought to dislike her for her horrific neglect when Hunter was growing up. But she was so charming and funny and outrageous whenever they spoke, it was difficult to keep one's anger going.

Plus she seemed to be the only person to have come into close contact with Duke McMahon and emerged, or so it seemed, more or less unscathed. Tiffany couldn't help but admire her for that.

'Just give me five minutes to grab a shower and we can eat,' said Hunter. 'The food looks incredible, by the way.'

'Thank you.' She beamed, throwing back her mane of golden hair, delighted to have pleased him. 'I hope it'll taste OK.'

'You certainly taste OK.'

He leaned forward and kissed her softly on the lips, slipping a hand inside her faded pink shirt to caress her left breast. She was barefoot and wearing a worn pair of old black jeans, but nothing could disguise her beautiful, willowy figure.

As far as Hunter was concerned, she was the sexiest woman in the world.

Before he could get any further in unhooking her bra, his mobile rang. It was on top of the fridge in the kitchen, and he dashed in to answer it, with a 'hold that thought' look at Tiffany.

'Hello?'

She knew what he was going to say before he opened his mouth. His smile said it all.

'It's Siena!' He grinned triumphantly, holding the phone in the air like a trophy. 'She's feeling a bit shell-shocked about the news. Wanted to know if we'd like to join her and Randall at the Dodgers game tonight.'

Tiffany thought that she'd rather chew her own arm off than watch baseball with Siena and her lover, but she knew how much it meant to him for her to be supportive.

'Sure, honey.' She forced a smile. 'Sounds great.'

'What's that?' said Hunter, who was back on the line with Siena already. 'Oh, OK, fine. No, I'm sure it's fine. I'll call you back in five.' He hung up.

'What?' said Tiffany, buttoning up her shirt.

'Well, the thing is,' he began apologetically, 'apparently they only have one spare ticket. And as Siena and I haven't seen each other for ages, I was wondering, you know, if you'd mind . . .'

'Oh, I get it.' Tiffany laughed. Siena was so rude, it was actually funny. 'I'm not invited, right? She only wants you.'

'It's nothing personal,' said Hunter. And the tragedy was, he believed it. 'Honestly. She only has one . . .'

'I know, she only has one spare ticket, you said.' She knew she shouldn't resort to sarcasm, but she couldn't help it. 'And of course, there's no way in the *world* that Randall Stein and Siena McMahon could possibly get hold of another ticket for a baseball game.'

'Please, honey,' he implored her.

He looked so cute and vulnerable with his big, pleading blue eyes, she didn't know how she ever refused him anything. She really did love him so much.

'Fine,' she said at last. 'You go.'

He walked over and picked her up, forgetting about his dirty running clothes, kissing her again and again in gratitude.

'Thank you, baby. I love you. Thank you so much.'

'No problem,' said Tiffany. 'Just don't get your hopes up, Hunter, OK? In my experience, Siena doesn't do anything unless there's something in it for Siena. I don't want you to get hurt.'

'I won't,' he yelled, bounding up the stairs two at a time towards his shower. 'Everything'll be fine, trust me.'

Over at Hancock Park, Tara was thoroughly enjoying herself wandering from room to room with a clipboard, barking orders to three of Pete's gofers while nosily rummaging her way through Minnie's things.

Pete was downstairs, holed up in the drawing room with his lawyers and his wet blanket of a wife. Frankly, she was pleased to get away from him.

Things at the office had been terrible recently, and Tara had been having about as much fun as a germ in a bath of disinfectant. Pete had become even more distant and irritable than usual. Admittedly, McMahon Pictures was in the final stages of production on two hugely costly new movies, which always upped her boss's stress levels. But there were clearly other things on his mind as well.

Although he never spoke about Siena – mentioning her name was strictly *verboten* at work, and more than one of MPW's senior execs had been canned last year for breaking this taboo – Tara could tell that his daughter's relationship with Randall Stein was driving Pete to distraction.

She had managed to glean enough information, largely through the time-honoured method of pressing her ear against Pete's office door, to understand that his problem was not so much with Siena, who by his own admission he no longer thought of as his child, but with Stein. Apparently, Randall had been quite tight with Duke back in the day, and the old man had taken him under his wing as some sort of protégé.

Duke had never recognised his son's formidable business skills, as either a producer or an investor. From what Tara had heard, it was Duke's early admiration for Randall as an up-and-coming producer, over and above his own son, which had started the bad blood between the two of them. The affair with Siena was simply the very bitter icing on an already stale cake of enmity and resentment.

What made matters worse was that Claire had taken to hanging around the office all the time, and she and Pete were constantly fighting. Infuriatingly, her boss's wife was so softly spoken that Tara usually couldn't make out the content of her conversations through the door. But her white, drawn, tight-lipped face as she left spoke volumes, as of course did the foul temper that Pete was plunged into for the rest of the day: Claire had come to plead Siena's case.

Between the spiralling production costs, his marriage problems and his growing obsession with Randall Stein, Pete had been like a bear with a sore head for weeks.

Minnie McMahon suddenly dropping dead yesterday was by far the most interesting thing that had happened at work for ages.

Tara hoped that it might break the deadlock and that, in his grief, her boss might start to lean on her and rely on her again as he had in the old days. He had already put her in charge of organising the mammoth operation of the funeral and memorial service, and this morning had asked her to begin sorting out some of his mother's things.

A whole morning of snooping around the old McMahon mansion! And her own little posse of minions to help her do it! Tara was in seventh heaven.

'You stay in here and start going through the clothes,' she commanded two of the gofers imperiously, leaving them to get started on Minnie's huge private dressing room. 'Alice can come into the study with me to start itemising the jewellery.'

Minnie had long ago taken over what used to be Duke's study, and used the room every afternoon to conduct all her private business, from tracking her investments to managing her formidable charity commitments. It was now painted an airy magnolia yellow, with blue Provençal-style wooden shutters, offset by a large bunch of irises, now peeling slightly at the edges, which Minnie must have bought herself only a few days ago.

Tara, of course, was quite oblivious to her surroundings, and failed to register the poignancy of the wilting flowers, the half-written letter still lying on the desk, or any of the other tiny reminders of a life so suddenly and unexpectedly ended. She made a beeline instead for the jewellery box, which Pete had told her his mother kept in the bottom drawer of her filing cabinet.

'Damn it,' she said, heaving the heavy leather box up on to the desk. It weighed a ton – Minnie must have some pretty incredible pieces locked away in there. 'It's a combination lock.' She rattled the box uselessly, then set it down again on the desk.

'Do you want me to go downstairs and ask Mr McMahon for the

code?' said Alice. She was a very pretty, shy little thing who had only been working at MPW for the last six weeks and was still desperately eager to please.

'No, I'll go,' said Tara. She didn't want Pete distracted by this pretty, blonde child. Hurrying downstairs, anxious to get the code and return to the treasure trove in Minnie's study, she was enjoying the smooth sensation of the polished wooden banisters beneath her fingers when she suddenly stopped in her tracks.

There in the hallway, beneath the shimmering grandeur of the vast chandelier, Pete was standing with his back to her. The lawyers were nowhere to be seen, and he was hugging Claire so tightly that his knees were visibly buckling. She appeared to be literally holding him up.

Neither of them made a sound. But Tara could see Pete's broad back shuddering, rocked with spasms of bottomless grief, as he collapsed into his wife's arms.

She knew how much he had loved and adored his mother.

Suddenly, in that tiny, wizened part of herself that passed for a conscience, she felt a twinge. To her, Minnie's death had been a welcome distraction. To Pete, it was the end of the world.

Quietly, so as not to disturb them, she tiptoed back upstairs to Alice. The jewellery could wait.

Hunter and Siena had agreed to meet outside the stadium at six, so they could be ushered into their VIP front-row seats together a few minutes before the game got under way.

At 6.15, Hunter was still waiting, and his Dodgers baseball cap pulled low over his eyes was doing little to disguise his identity from an ever growing cluster of teenage girls seeking autographs.

While he signed their shirts and programmes and dollar bills good-naturedly, scanning the road for Siena, his heart sank when he noticed a TV crew for the LA 9 News channel advancing towards him. There was no time to escape, so he made the best of it and smiled graciously as Emma Duval, the new and pneumatic face of the seven o'clock news, thrust her prominent double-D assets in his direction.

'Hi, Hunter,' she said, as though they were old friends. She had interviewed him once before for about ten seconds and thought he was a total hottie. 'Got time for a quick word?'

'Very quick,' he said, looking at his watch. 'I'm waiting for someone.'

Classic rookie mistake. He could have bitten his tongue off.

'Oh, really? Who?' Emma tried to smile through a face full of botox. It wasn't a great success.

'No one you know,' said Hunter quickly. 'A friend.'

'Well,' said Emma, with a look that let him know she had a pretty good idea who that 'friend' might be, but wasn't going to say so, 'maybe just a few words then on this morning's news about your stepmother's death.'

'She wasn't really my stepmother,' he began to explain, but Emma had already signalled to her camera and sound guys, and had thrust a microphone under his nose.

'I'm here with Hunter McMahon, who's about to head on in and cheer on those Dodgers!' She punched the air inanely, before switching directly into serious mode. 'Hunter, today's been a sad day for you, with the news of the passing of Minnie McMahon. Can I ask you how you're feeling?'

'I'm, er, I'm fine, really,' he stammered, blinking against the spotlight that some wiseass had decided to shine right into his face. 'I'm sorry for her family, my half-sister Laurie and of course my brother as well. This must be a difficult time for them.'

'Absolutely.' Emma nodded and took a shot at a sympathetic frown, only to be foiled again by her frozen brow. 'Have you spoken to your brother – producer Pete McMahon,' she explained to camera, 'at all since it happened?'

Shit. How had he gotten into this? And where the hell was Siena?

'No,' he said. 'No, unfortunately my brother and I are no longer in contact.'

'Pete McMahon did, in fact, publicly disown you some years ago. That must have been painful.' The woman had all the tact of a stampeding elephant. Hunter didn't respond. 'Will you be attending your stepmother's funeral?' Emma pressed on relentlessly.

'Actually, she wasn't my stepmother. She was my father's wife, but . . .' He looked around despairingly for Siena. If only he had his ticket he could bolt inside the stadium and escape. 'To be honest, I feel a bit awkward discussing it. I'm very sorry for the family, but like I say, we really weren't that close.'

At that moment, as if by magic, every camera swung away from him, and an excited swarm of TV crews, reporters and fans surged towards a black limousine behind him.

Siena and Randall had arrived.

'Siena! Siena! How do you feel?' the voices were yelling. 'Have you spoken to your father, Siena? Will this clear the way for a family reconciliation?'

Hunter watched perplexed as Siena emerged from the back of the car, hand in hand with Randall, and began moving through the crowd towards him, answering questions as she went but pointedly refusing to stop and sign autographs – another of Randall's rules.

If it hadn't been for everybody screaming her name, he wasn't at all sure he would even have recognised her.

First of all, she was dressed head to toe in black, in a fabulously tight-cut skirt and jacket, teamed with sky-high black stilettos and a full-length mink, which she wore open. She looked like a young, sexed-up Elizabeth Taylor in mourning.

Oh my God, he thought, that was it.

She was wearing black in mourning.

For *Minnie*?

It all seemed a bit over the top. Even so, it still made him feel like a heartless jerk for turning up in jeans and a Dodgers T-shirt.

'Hunter, Hunter, darling!' Siena called, fighting her way to his side. Even her voice sounded different, like it was put on. Randall followed behind her in a dark suit, looking, Hunter thought, fat, bald and old. 'How *are* you?'

She held out her arms to him.

He held her, but it didn't feel like her, more like an armful of fur. She kissed him on both cheeks and smiled quite warmly, but something about her still seemed odd. It may have been the trowel-loads of make-up she was wearing, presumably for the cameras' benefit.

'I'm fine, I'm good,' he assured her, wishing he could take her away from the TV crews so they could talk properly. 'I started to think you weren't coming.'

'Oh, are we late?'

Siena looked down at her Cartier watch affectedly, blinding him and everybody else within a twenty-foot radius with a dazzling flash of her diamond-encrusted strap.

Hunter gave her a reproachful look.

'Sorry,' she said, chastened. 'It's really Randall, not me. He's always faffing about what I'm wearing, wanting to change everything at the last minute.' She squeezed Randall's hand affectionately.

'What *are* you wearing?' said Hunter, taking the three tickets silently proffered by Randall, and leading the way through the VIP barriers and into the stadium. 'I mean, you look great. But what's with all the black? This isn't because of Minnie, is it?'

For a split second, he thought he saw her flash him a naughty smile, the kind she used to give as a child when she'd been up to some new mischief or other. He knew Siena didn't care for Minnie any more than he did.

'She *was* Siena's grandmother,' Randall chimed in, as if Hunter needed to have the relationship explained. 'The news of her death came as quite a shock this morning. And of course, it rakes up a lot of old memories, the pain of her parents' abandonment, that sort of thing. Doesn't it, darling? I'm sure you must feel the same.'

Hunter was about to reply that he didn't feel the same, and that he and Siena had each other and didn't need the rest of the family, but was stopped in his tracks when he spun round to find Siena shamelessly hamming it up for the cameras, grasping his arm as if she were about to collapse with grief and holding on to him like a vice as she posed for a final set of pictures.

'Come on, Hunter,' she whispered, between shots. 'You could try to look a little bit unhappy. I mean, we're supposed to be in this together, aren't we, "the poor outcast McMahon children, sticking together through the latest family tragedy".'

She reached into her jacket pocket and pulled out a handkerchief with which to dry her imaginary tears.

It was only then that the penny dropped.

She was using him.

Using him and Minnie's death as a cheap publicity stunt. Like she needed any more publicity.

He felt revolted. Grabbing her by the arm, he pulled her sharply away from the prying cameras. Randall moved forward to follow them, but Hunter glared at him so viciously that he hung back.

'What the hell do you think you're playing at?' he snarled at Siena.

'What do you mean? Let go of my arm, you're hurting me,' she said indignantly.

'Good,' said Hunter. 'Now you know what it feels like.'

Siena was so stunned she was actually speechless.

'Did he put you up to this? Huh? Was it Stein's idea?'

'What?' She sounded frightened. She had never known Hunter to lose his temper with her like this. 'I don't know what you mean. What idea?'

'This.' He pulled at her coat and her jacket, snatching up her handkerchief in disgust. 'These clothes, these fake tears over Minnie, asking me along as some kind of cheap prop. Turning up late, so I'd already have the cameras on me for your grand entrance with lover boy. Jesus, Siena, what's happened to you? I didn't love Minnie any more than you did, but don't you think she deserves a bit more respect than this?'

'No, I fucking don't.' Siena was shaking. She couldn't bear to have Hunter yelling at her like this, knowing that every word he said was true. She was so ashamed, she wished the ground would open up and swallow her, but some instinct urged her to come out fighting. 'I don't think she deserves any respect at all. She was a mean, vindictive old bitch who never gave a shit about me, or you.'

'That's crap, Siena.' For once, Hunter was tired of listening to her shit. For the first time, he'd seen for himself the machiavellian side to her character that Tiffany was always complaining about. And it was ugly. 'Minnie cared for you. She adored you as a child. Everyone did.'

'Yes, well, then I had to go and disappoint everyone by growing up, didn't I?' said Siena, bitterly.

'Don't kid yourself.' He wasn't about to allow her to wallow in self-pity. 'You haven't grown up. Grown-up people don't pull stunts like this. Even if you don't care about Minnie, I'd have thought you'd at least have a bit of respect for me.'

'I do! I do respect you.' Siena looked stricken.

Randall finally stepped forward and put a possessive arm around her shoulders. 'Lighten up, man, you're upsetting her,' he said.

Hunter waved his arm impatiently as if swatting away a fly and ignored him. This had to be said. 'Well, you have a funny way of showing it, Siena. I haven't seen you for months. It's all I can do to get your goddam PA to return my calls these days.'

'I'm sorry, Hunter,' Randall jumped in. 'But you have to understand that Siena's life has changed. She has a very busy schedule now, and a lot of people competing for her time. You can't always expect to be at the front of the queue.'

'Fuck off.' Hunter turned on him. 'No one's talking to you.'

Randall merely raised his eyebrow and gave a smug, patronising little smile, as if to indicate that Hunter was too far beneath him to provoke any deeper response.

Hunter turned back to Siena. 'Then, today, you finally do call.' And you know what? I was so happy to hear your voice. How naive and stupid is that?'

'It isn't stupid,' she pleaded. 'Hunter, please. I was happy too. And I *was* upset this morning, truly. Not about Grandma, maybe. But seeing those pictures of my mom, you know, and the old house. I felt terrible. I wanted to see you so badly.'

'I don't believe you,' said Hunter. He was looking at her with utter disdain, and the anger and disappointment in his voice were unmistakable. 'I don't believe a word that comes out of your mouth any more, Siena. And you know what the irony is?' She stared at him in mute misery, clinging on to Randall as if he were a lifeboat. 'When you stepped out of that car just now, I didn't recognise you. But now? Now I can see it.'

'See what?' she asked, trembling.

'My father,' said Hunter, turning on his heel in disgust. 'That's who you are now, Siena. That's what you've become. You're exactly the same as Duke.'

Chapter Forty

Max lay face down on the bright pink mat on the floor, and tried to clear his head as the Korean girl began expertly pummelling his back.

He'd been coming to the same tiny massage parlour in Korea Town ever since he first moved to LA. It was a bit of a schlep to get out there, but at twenty-five dollars for an hour-long pounding of the muscles – none of this farting about with lavender oil and wind chimes – it was well worth the effort.

Since Siena had left him, his weekly visits to Sun Jhee had become something of a life-saver. Even now, months after it all happened, his sleep patterns were still shot, so the massage provided him with a rare opportunity to relax.

'Breathing out,' the girl commanded, as she pressed down on his lower back with her shoulder. Max felt a satisfying click of the spine. 'Sitting badly,' she diagnosed.

'Probably,' he groaned. 'But I'm afraid poor posture is the least of my worries just now.'

The girl continued pummelling. She obviously didn't understand a word he said, which was good, as the last thing Max wanted was to waste an hour on small talk. He needed to think.

He'd been worrying more and more about Siena in the last couple of days.

Not that he didn't think about her every day – the longing, the nightmares and the dull ache of loss were still his constant companions. But ever since Hunter had had that spectacular row with her at the Dodgers, he'd started to look at things in a different, less selfish light.

He knew he'd lost her. For all the love he still felt, Max wasn't in denial. Every magazine, billboard and TV news show screamed the message home to him, zooming in on her happy, confident face, climbing in and out of limos or waving nonchalantly to fans: she was gone.

But recently, he'd found himself looking up from the depths of his own pain and starting to feel genuinely concerned for Siena's welfare.

It was the rift with Hunter which really did it.

Max had known Hunter since they were little boys. He probably knew him better than anyone else on the planet, with the possible exception of Tiffany. But if he hadn't seen it for himself, he would never have believed that Hunter was capable of turning his back on Siena like this. For three weeks now, he hadn't even mentioned her name.

Whatever had happened at that Dodgers game – and Hunter refused to go into details, so Max and Tiffany were both left to piece events together as best they could – it had alienated him from her in a way that Max would once not have believed possible.

He could arrive at only one conclusion: Randall Stein was poison.

At first he had made heroic efforts to talk himself out of this point of view. He was jealous. He wasn't being objective. He couldn't bear for Siena to find happiness with someone else.

But the more he saw the ways in which Stein had changed her – not just the make-up and the clothes, but the whole diva persona – the more he was convinced that he was right.

He could understand her refusal to speak to him after what he'd done. But poor Ines had called him a few weeks ago in tears. Apparently she'd left dozens of messages with Siena's PA and at the house, none of them returned. It was practically the same story with Hunter. Before the Dodgers debacle, she had seen him only twice since her move to Malibu, both times only for a few snatched minutes on the set of her new film.

Her public behaviour, if anything, was even worse.

Sure, Siena had always been spoiled and attention-seeking. He blamed her parents for that. But she had a good heart, and underneath all her histrionics Max knew her as the most wonderful, loyal and loving woman he had ever met.

With Randall, that whole side of her personality seemed to be disappearing.

She had started treating her fans with disdain, refusing to sign autographs, and reducing one poor little kid to tears by driving away from her own premiere for *Daughter* in a blacked-out limo without so much as a wave.

She had given interviews, arrogantly dismissing Dierk Muller, the man who had gone out on a limb and given her her first break, as a 'second tier' director. And every week, new rumours emerged from the set of *1943*, Randall's big-budget epic in which she starred, of her excessive and outlandish demands for a bigger trailer, shorter hours and a twenty-four-hour on-call masseuse.

Max blamed himself for pushing her over the edge. If only he hadn't been such a selfish, jealous, insecure tosser, none of this would be happening.

But that only meant that it was up to him to put things right. If Siena and Hunter weren't speaking, things really had got serious. Somehow, he had to make her wake up to herself, before Stein destroyed her completely.

About ten days later, on an unseasonably hot December day in Malibu, Siena was pacing the drawing room at Randall's estate, having a massive sense of humour failure.

'I don't fucking believe this!' she roared at Melanie, the hapless party organiser who was overseeing the evening's events. 'The theme is supposed to be winter wonderland. What sort of a winter wonderland is it going to be without snow?'

It was three in the afternoon, but Siena was still in the red silk kimono she'd got up in. She'd been awake since seven, manically trying to finalise the details for Randall's annual pre-Christmas party, and she hadn't yet had a moment to get dressed.

Everybody who was anybody in Hollywood – except her parents, of course – would be pulling up to the gates in four hours' time, and now this muppet of a girl seemed to be telling her that the snow machine had packed up with the rose garden only half covered. The whole thing was a fucking nightmare.

'Sometimes, when the temperature outside rises above twenty,' Melanie unwisely started to explain, 'the machine just sort of shuts down.'

Melanie had a long nose, a slight build and a nervous disposition that lent her the air of a terrified vole. She was not good in a crisis.

'Well, you'd better just "sort of" wake it up. Or get hold of another one,' said Siena murderously. 'Because if that garden doesn't look like Antarctica within the next forty-five minutes, I'm going to sue you for more money than even *I* can imagine. Are we clear?'

'Absolutely, Miss McMahon.' The terrified girl began scuttling away. 'We'll get things under control.'

'In forty-five minutes!' Siena yelled after her retreating back.

She sank down on to the huge William Morris print sofa, utterly exhausted.

Bloody Randall.

He'd disappeared off to play golf with Jamie Silfen early this morning, and Siena hadn't seen hide nor hair of him since. She wondered how on earth he'd pulled off a party this size successfully in previous years, before she came along to do all the work. Then she realised he'd probably had a string of live-in girlfriends on past

Christmases, all more than willing to play at being Mrs Randall Stein for the evening.

The thought made her feel even more pissed. Why did she put herself through it?

She heaved herself reluctantly to her feet. This was no time to be lying around. It would soon be time to start getting ready, and she still had a million and one things to do before Randall got back.

Wandering through into the dining room, she admired the spectacular, festive table.

Snow machines aside, Melanie had done a fantastic job.

Intertwined stems of holly and ivy hung in looped wreaths around all four walls and across the ceiling, dripping at intervals with either bright red berries or tumbling bunches of white mistletoe. Every kind of Christmas delight littered the table, from pecan pies to chocolate Yule logs and imported Carlsbad plums. And in each corner of the room stood twenty-five-foot Christmas trees, decorated only in silver and white, with delicate, hand-painted wooden angels from Sweden perched on top of each one.

Pete and Claire had never been big on Christmas when she was growing up. Even Duke had focused more on buying her expensive presents than on the decorative side of things.

Siena had always dreamed of a house stuffed with Christmas trees, and a magical winter garden smothered in snow. Now she had one, and she had to admit it looked every bit as lovely as she'd imagined.

For a brief moment she felt a pang of loneliness and wished that Hunter or even Ines could be here to share it with her.

She had trained herself never to think of Max.

Ines especially would have been amazed to see her playing at being the accomplished hostess. She remembered that night back at the beach house, when she'd tried to cook a special meal for Hunter, and she'd called Ines for advice.

The night she'd first slept with Max.

That was only eight months ago. Sometimes it felt like eight years, another lifetime.

She missed Ines terribly, her irreverent sense of humour, her unstoppable energy, but most of all she missed the stupid, giggly, girly chats they used to have about everything and nothing.

Randall had been very firm with her about moving on, though. If she wanted to have a new image, a new life, then she had to leave her old crowd behind. Particularly anyone still associated with modelling.

'The last thing you want is to always be thought of as an ex-model,' he'd told her. 'If you want to play in the big league, you have to make sacrifices. There can be no looking back. Think about your grandfather. How many friends from the old days did you see him hanging around with?'

Apart from Seamus, Siena couldn't remember Duke "hanging around" with anyone, at least not with anyone he called a friend, from the old days or otherwise. For the first time ever, she wondered whether Grandpa might have been a bit lonely. The possibility disturbed her more than she cared to admit.

She made a quick pit stop out in the rose garden to check on the lighting, and had a brief word with the official photographer, before disappearing upstairs to have a much needed soak in the bath and begin her grand transformation.

Randall didn't get home until six, and when he did, he disappeared straight into his study to make a couple of business calls, much to Siena's fury. By the time he finally nipped upstairs to change, there was less than half an hour until the guests were due to arrive.

Siena couldn't remember when she had last felt so exhausted. Only nervous energy, and the ceaseless churning of her stomach at the prospect of having to entertain every big-name producer and director in Hollywood, with the exception of her father, kept her eyes from closing.

Mercifully, a new fake snow machine had been unearthed, the ice sculptures and vodka fountain had finally been delivered, and the complicated outdoor lighting system had miraculously decided to work, after four earlier failed attempts.

'The house looks great,' said Randall, kissing the back of her neck as she sat at her dressing table.

She was wearing a midnight-blue silk halter-neck dress, full length but slashed to the thigh, with a sky-high pair of open-toed Manolos in the same blue, laced with criss-crossed ribbon up her calves. She wore her hair up in a loose chignon, with occasional stray curls escaping to frame her face.

As a rule, Siena was not a huge make-up fan. In a town full of surgically enhanced faces and harsh, over-tanned, over-made-up skin, she preferred to let her own natural beauty help her stand out from the crowd.

Tonight, though, she had gone for very dark, dramatic eyes, using a perfectly blended mixture of silver, grey and black shadow, with intensely mascaraed lashes that seemed to go on and on for ever.

'I know the house looks great,' she said ungraciously, pouting at herself in the mirror and applying a second coat of lip gloss. 'I've been working on it flat out since seven this morning, with no help from you. So how *was* golf?'

'Good,' said Randall, not remotely apologetic. He put one warm hand on the back of Siena's neck, then moved it round to caress her smooth creamy chest and the top of her ample cleavage. 'You look very sexy,' he whispered gruffly. 'You don't think it's too much, though? I want these guys to take you seriously. You'll be meeting some very influential people tonight.'

'For Christ's sake, Randall.' She brushed off his hand and stood up, straightening the line of the dress around her ass. She hated it when he patronised her. 'I am well aware of who's coming tonight, and I'm more than capable of handling myself, thank you. Anyway . . .' She admired her reflection in the bedroom mirror. '. . . I think I look great.'

'Hmmmm.' He frowned and slipped his hand around her waist, pulling her very close to him. She could feel the swell of his paunch just below her breasts and his erection pressing against her belly. She tried to pull back.

'Shit, don't muss me up, honey, please. This dress cost sixteen thousand dollars and you haven't even showered.'

Randall looked at her coldly. Despite his hard-on, he was obviously not thinking about screwing her. Siena stared up at his big Roman nose and tiny, impenetrable eyes. Involuntarily, she shivered.

'Just remember,' he said, 'these people have come here tonight because of me, not you.'

Good God, was he jealous? Scared that she might be the centre of attention this evening?

It seemed so unlike him. Randall was never insecure.

'I know that, darling,' she said meekly, anxious not to provoke his temper. 'But you want me to look beautiful for them, don't you?'

His brow knitted instantly into a frown. 'No.' He drew her even closer to him. 'Not for them. For me. I want you to look beautiful for me.'

Before Siena had a chance to move, he plunged his right hand between her legs, through the slit in her dress, pulled her panties aside and thrust three fingers roughly up inside her. She gasped in shock. She was so unprepared, it actually hurt.

He lowered his face to within millimetres of hers, still keeping his hand inside her. 'I made you what you are now, Siena,' he whispered ominously. She could feel his warm breath on her skin, making her hairs stand on end. 'I gave you all this, and I was happy to do it. But don't cross me, sweetheart. Remember: I can take it all away. Like *that*.'

He jabbed deeper inside her, for emphasis.

Then, just as suddenly, he let her go and walked through into the bathroom as if nothing had happened, leaving her shell-shocked and trembling in his wake.

Two hours later and the party was in full, riotous swing.

The A-list had turned out in force, and in even greater number than in previous years. Everyone from the Spielbergs to the Spellings was there, milling around, enjoying the latest Hollywood gossip, washed down with Randall's vintage champagne. Even Mel Gibson, Siena's childhood heart-throb, put in a brief, early appearance, much to her surprise and delight.

In quiet corners all round the estate, diets and discretion were both being thrown to the wind. Guests tucked into huge slices of brandy-soaked Yule log and held hushed conversations about their host and his beautiful young companion.

How long would the relationship last? Did Siena really have the talent to live up to Randall's hype? And did anybody know what Pete McMahon made of his daughter shacking up with a long-term business rival, who also happened to be four years older than Pete himself?

'Do you know, he hasn't seen Siena *once* since she moved out here?' an overexcited young CAA agent was whispering to his boss's enthralled wife.

'I know. Incredible,' she agreed, nodding through a mouthful of pecan pie. 'It's the mother that I can't understand, though. As a mother myself, I don't understand how anyone could just walk away from their children like that. From their *only* child.'

'Pete McMahon's lost the plot,' chipped in her husband, returning from the bar with more champagne. 'He's a virtual recluse nowadays, Claire too. I'm not surprised they haven't seen Siena. As far as I can tell, they haven't seen anybody in the last eighteen months.'

'Look at Stein, though,' said the young man. 'He's besotted.'

The three of them looked over at Randall, who was nodding to the head of merchandising at Paramount and his bimbo wife, pretending to be avidly listening to their conversation, while actually sneaking glances across the room at Siena.

If she was troubled by their little fracas in the bedroom earlier, she didn't show it now. She looked utterly radiant, confident and relaxed, throwing her head back and laughing at some comment of Jamie Silfen's.

Every straight man in the room wanted her, thought Randall with pride. He felt his hard-on reviving and with some effort tore his thoughts back to Mr Paramount and the subject of the Asian distribution rights to *Ocean Drive*.

Siena, meanwhile, was enjoying herself enormously with Silfen.

'I couldn't believe it when I saw you in the front row at the McQueen Show.' She laughingly reminded the great casting agent of their first non-encounter. 'What on earth were you doing there?'

'I like fashion, actually,' Jamie replied with a straight face. 'I follow the trends.'

Siena looked at his portly form squeezed into an ill-fitting tweed suit, his bald head popping out at the top like a giant billiard ball, and found this statement rather hard to believe. If it had been anyone else, she would have laughed out loud, but Jamie was a close associate of Randall's and far too important a person for her to accidentally insult.

'Really?' she said, trying her best to sound convinced.

'Of course not really!' He roared with laughter. 'You didn't think I picked up this little number from Alexander McQueen, did you?' He launched himself into a ridiculous twirl, wiggling his fat bottom in the tight tweed in Siena's direction like Tweedledee. She giggled. 'That's better,' said Jamie. 'I like you better when you laugh. They should have you smiling more in pictures.'

'I know,' said Siena, forgetting for a moment Randall's strict instructions never to talk about modelling with movie people, 'but photographers almost never want the models to smile. We have to look permanently aloof and pissed.'

She struck a regal pose, and now it was Jamie's turn to laugh.

'I enjoyed *The Prodigal Daughter*,' he said, changing the subject suddenly for no apparent reason. 'You were good.'

'Thank you,' said Siena, smiling modestly. She always said she'd have Jamie Silfen eating out of the palm of her hand one day. 'I'm so glad you liked it.'

'Muller was fucking fantastic, though, directing,' Jamie went on. 'You shouldn't have slagged him off in that interview.'

Siena blushed. She'd been feeling guilty about her 'second tier' remark for some time. She knew she owed Dierk a hell of a lot.

'That sort of thing won't help, you know. Getting ahead,' said Silfen. He was deadly serious all of a sudden. 'You might not know it, but loyalty goes a long way in this town. Farther than you'd think.'

'I know,' said Siena humbly, 'you're right. It's just that Randall felt . . .'

'Listen, honey,' Jamie interrupted her, putting a fat, clammy hand on her arm. 'Randall's a brilliant producer. He's made a lot of good decisions, and a lot of money, and all credit to the guy. But trust me, he ain't no life coach. Don't let anyone go putting words in your mouth, Siena. Otherwise who the hell are you anyway?'

She was silently digesting this advice when the whole room turned at the sound of an almighty crash coming from the entrance hall. The crash was followed by raised male voices, one of which Siena thought to her horror she recognised.

'Fuck off! Get the fuck out of my way before I hurt you.'

The clipped English accent was unmistakable.

Suddenly two of Randall's so-called security guys came flying backwards into the room, one after another, smashing a priceless Venetian vase in the process. They were followed by the one person she had hoped she would never come face to face with again.

'Oh my God,' she whispered, barely audibly.

'Someone you know?' asked Silfen.

But Siena just stood and stared at Max in complete horror.

'Stein!' he yelled. 'I want to talk to you. Where are you?'

She wondered for a moment whether he was drunk, but his voice seemed steady, and there was no hint of a stagger as he moved among the stunned guests, like the one moving actor weaving his way through a freeze-frame.

Randall had started to step forward, but as he did so Max caught sight of Siena, staring at him from across the room.

It was the first time he'd seen her since that awful day at the airfield, and he felt afterwards that his heart had literally stopped beating in that instant. She had never looked more beautiful, like some sort of other-worldly dryad in her column of clinging blue silk. Her eyes looked different – stronger, more sultry – but otherwise she looked exactly as she did in his dreams, except that the reality was even more breathtaking.

The miracle wasn't that he'd lost her, thought Max. It was that he'd ever had her in the first place.

Siena gazed back at him dumbstruck. In the months since she'd left, she had trained her mind, with ruthless self-discipline, to banish all thoughts of Max, both good and bad, from her consciousness. She had made a decision, the night she flew to Vegas, never, ever to make the mistake of laying herself open again. She had shut down her heart, with Randall's help, almost completely.

But seeing him now, so lovely, so big, so out of place in his old jeans and Cambridge sweatshirt, standing right there in front of her, she felt all her good work unravelling like a ball of string. She was, momentarily, helpless.

'Siena, I'm sorry,' he began, his voice dry with nerves. 'I'm sorry to burst in on your evening like this. But you won't take my calls – I totally understand that,' he added quickly, before she could release a tirade. 'And this place is always shut up like Fort Knox. This was the only night I had any chance of getting past security, with so many people coming and going. And I had to see you.'

Randall glared at the two security men, who were still reeling from Max's earlier left hook – what the hell was he paying them for? – and made his way slowly to Siena's side.

'I hid in the back of a catering van,' Max explained unnecessarily. He knew he should stop talking, but he felt a need to fill the deafening silence.

The carollers had finally got the message and realised something was up, lamely spluttering to a halt halfway through their rendition of 'Once in Royal David's City', and the rest of the guests maintained a rapt hush, watching him.

Finally, after what seemed like an age, Siena helped him out by speaking, although it was hardly the response he'd been hoping for.

'What do you want, Max? As you can see, I'm busy.' Her voice was as cold as ice.

'I want to take you home,' he said, pushing his hair out of his face and wiping the sweat from his brow. He was still ten feet away from her at least, but didn't want to risk moving any nearer in case she bolted, or Randall took a pop at him before he'd said what he came here to say.

'He's seriously cute, isn't he?' whispered the daughter of a famous director to her girlfriend. 'Who in their right mind would leave *that* for Randall Stein?'

Max cleared his throat and continued. 'Not home to me, though. I know what I did was unforgivable. I know there's no way back for us.'

'Good,' said Siena.

'But to Hunter. He loves you, Siena, and he misses you, even if he is too proud to show it.'

'Are you finished?' she asked.

'No. Not yet.' Max looked her in the eye. Siena was terrified he would bore straight through into her soul and see how frightened and confused she was behind the ice-maiden façade. She willed him to hurry up and get this over with before she cracked.

'I'm worried about you,' he said. 'Everybody is. You've changed, Siena, and not for the better. Stein is poison. He's no good for you. Whether you go back to the beach house or not, you have to get away from him. Please. Not for me, but for yourself. He's fucking evil.'

At this, Randall broke the spell and clapped his hands, signalling to the newly arrived security reinforcements who'd been waiting by the door to make a move on Max.

'No!' said Siena, so loudly and firmly that the goons obeyed her and hung back for a moment. 'I can deal with this, Randall.'

'I don't think so,' he said and, grabbing her quite roughly by the arm, nodded to the men to advance. He had already allowed this little scene to go on too long, and he wasn't about to be overruled in his own house by Siena, or anyone else. It was time to assert a little authority.

'Don't you touch her!'

Before security could lay a finger on him, Max had launched himself across the room at Randall, bringing the older man crashing to the ground in a full-bodied rugby tackle. They came down with such an almighty thud that a huge wreath of holly and ivy, festooned with red berries, swung down from the ceiling and landed right on top of them.

Max pulled back his fist to slam it into Randall's face, but his arm was grabbed from behind and twisted agonisingly behind his back. Before he knew it he was on his feet, tightly restrained by two of the heavier heavies.

He needn't have bothered with the punch anyway. Randall was already out cold.

'See what I mean?' he said passionately to Siena. He was held so firmly that he couldn't even begin to struggle. 'See how he grabbed you like that? He's an arsehole, Siena. He's violent.'

'*He's* violent?' She was so shaken up by what had just happened, she reverted to the safest reaction she knew: white rage. 'Who the fuck do you think you are, Max?' she hissed at him. 'You come in here, shouting the odds, telling me how I've changed, and how Randall's such a terrible influence. Where the hell do you get off?'

Max opened his mouth to speak, but Siena was on a roll.

'You've got a damn nerve, trying to take the moral high ground with me. If memory serves, I think you were the one running around in LA with your dick in every cheap fucking waitress who'd give you the time of day. So don't you *dare* come storming in here and start telling me how to live my life.'

'For God's sake, Siena.' He cried out in pain as the security men pulled so tightly on his shoulder he thought it might be dislocating. 'Can't you see I'm trying to help you? I *know* it's all my fault. I *know* I can never make it up to you. But can't you see what this bastard's doing to you?'

'No, Max,' she said flatly. 'I can't. Other than take me in, and look after me. Randall's a very generous man. And as for me, you know what? You're right, I have changed. I've learned to look out for number one. I've learned that you can't trust anyone except yourself. But it wasn't Randall who taught me that, Max. It was you.'

Between the pain in his shoulder and the pain in his heart, Max was close to tears. He couldn't bear to have to leave her like this. What if he never saw her again?

'I love you,' he said, desperately.

A couple of romantic souls across the room gave an audible sigh.

'That's your problem,' said Siena. 'Unfortunately, I know what your love is, Max. And it isn't worth the paper it's written on. So let me make myself absolutely clear: I never, ever want to see you again.'

He looked at her pleadingly but she turned away, raising her hand imperiously to the security guys.

'Get him out of here.'

In bed later that evening, she lay crying softly to herself, trying not to wake a sleeping Randall.

She'd expected him to be absolutely furious about what had happened, particularly after Max had knocked him out like that. But in fact, almost as soon as he'd come round, he'd been remarkably cheerful, insisting on carrying on until the end of the party and even making jokes about Max's outburst.

'I'm so sorry,' Siena had told him, once the last of the guests had gone. 'You must blame me for all this. The whole party was ruined.'

'Oh, I don't know about that,' said Randall brightly. 'You know Hollywood. People love a good drama.'

Siena looked at him, astonished. 'You mean you're really not mad?'

Randall smiled and took her hand, leading her up to bed.

'No, I'm not mad,' he said. 'Because you know what I realised tonight? He's just a kid. He's a dumb kid, he's nobody.' Siena stared down at the ground and bit her lip. 'He's going to go to sleep tonight in a borrowed room he can't even pay for, in some shitty little house on the beach. And I go to sleep here.' He waved vaguely at the opulence around them. 'With you.'

He stopped to pull Siena towards him and kissed her full on the mouth. His breath smelt of stale champagne, but she tried to appear enthusiastic. She supposed that was the least she owed him after everything that had happened tonight.

Mercifully, once they got into bed he had fallen straight to sleep. She really couldn't have faced sex now. She just wanted to be alone with her thoughts.

Unfortunately those thoughts were not remotely comforting.

For all her bravado, tonight's events had shown her one thing beyond a shadow of a doubt.

She still loved Max.

She wasn't sure whether she could ever bring herself to forgive him for betraying her the way he had. But love him she did.

And yet now, even more than before, she knew that there could be no way back, love or no love. She had told him she never wanted to see him again. He had reached out to her and she had rejected him, brutally and publicly.

One thing Max had never been lacking in was pride. Siena knew him well enough to know that he wouldn't be back for more.

Tears started to flow as she thought back over what felt like a lifetime of lost love: first Grandpa, then Hunter, then her parents. For a brief while there, after she'd found Hunter again, and then Max, she almost felt as if all the wrongs of her childhood had been made right. And for a little while, life had been absolutely perfect.

But now Max and Hunter were both gone. Even Ines had been discarded, in the same way that Siena had discarded Marsha, Patrick and Janey Cash – basically anyone who had ever truly cared about her.

It was as if she couldn't help herself. She had to hit back first, make sure that she abandoned people before they abandoned her.

Hunter was right.

She was like Grandpa Duke.

And tonight, in the vast, opulent emptiness of Randall's bed, that realisation made her want to sob her heart out.

PART THREE

Chapter Forty-one

Max ran down the hill laughing, trying to keep his footing and avoid slipping on the cow pats as he hurtled down towards the stream. Behind him, three screaming children, led by a very determined-looking Charlie, were hot on his trail, brandishing their new pump-action water pistols.

'You'll never catch me alive!' Max yelled over his shoulder, promptly tripping over an unexpected mound of thistle and landing ignominiously, not to mention painfully, on his arse.

The Arkell posse were on top of him in seconds, spraying him mercilessly with water from point-blank range until his entire T-shirt was soaked through.

'Take *that*, Uncle Max,' said Madeleine triumphantly, emptying the last drops from her weapon down the back of his neck.

He flung his arms open wide and lay back on the grass in exhaustion and defeat.

'You win, Maddie.' He smiled at his little niece, and handed over a third pound coin.

The two boys were already racing back up the hill with their own victory spoils, and Maddie scampered off to join them.

Max lay back and enjoyed the warmth of the sun on his face.

It was late June, six months almost to the day since he had stormed into Randall Stein's Malibu mansion, and seen Siena for the last time. Within a week after that fiasco, he had packed up his very paltry possessions, sold his beloved Honda for scrap, said his goodbyes to Hunter and moved back to Batcombe.

He had finished shooting the two shorts for the famous Hollywood actor/would-be producer, so there was no business reason for him to stay on in LA. And living in the same town, even the same country, as Siena was killing him inside.

Hunter had tried to persuade him to stay, of course. But in the end, Max felt his old friend understood his reasons for going.

'Life has changed for all of us,' he'd said to Hunter on the particularly depressing journey out to the airport. 'I need to get over her, get away from all the bad memories and try and make something of myself. And you and Tiffany need some time to be together as well, without me getting under your feet the whole time.'

Hunter had protested that he never got under their feet, that they were both happy to have him, for ever if he wanted. But deep down he knew Max was right. It was time for a change, for all of them.

As soon as he landed at Heathrow, Max had found his spirits lifting slightly. He felt even better when he saw not just Henry but the whole family, hopping up and down with excitement in arrivals, waiting to meet him.

Bertie and Maddie were holding up a homemade cardboard banner with 'Welcum Home Unkel Max' written in multi-coloured felt tip. Charlie, who considered himself too old for such childish activities, merely waved in what he hoped his favourite uncle would recognise as a rather grown-up manner.

Max felt quite choked when Henry stepped forward to help him with his luggage.

'Hello, little brother.' He smiled, patting him warmly on the back. 'Bloody good to see you.'

Henry was shocked by how thin Max looked. He had read the press coverage of his brother's heroic but doomed attempt to rescue Siena. The gossip rags, force-fed by Randall's PR machine, had all crucified him for it, made him out to be some sort of jealous, possessed monster. Even Muffy refused to read the *Enquirer* any more, after seeing the stuff they'd written about poor Max. It wasn't as if he was even famous or courted the publicity.

At first, Max's plan had been to stay for Christmas and the New Year celebrations with Henry, then look around for a place of his own.

He hadn't, in fact, come home solely to escape his demons, or to take solace at Batcombe. There were career reasons as well.

He had belatedly decided to take up the offer from his friend, the young Oxford playwright, to direct his latest work in Stratford. The play was to open in April and run throughout the summer, but rehearsals would start in January.

The money was terrible, but Max loved the dark weirdness of the script, and he was in no urgent need for cash, having just been paid well over the odds for his last two short films. The original plan had been for him to rent a little cottage close to the theatre for six months, popping back to Batcombe for weekends to see Henry and the family. But it hadn't worked out like that.

Understandably, he'd been so caught up in the horrors of his own life back in LA that he hadn't grasped the full extent of Henry's debt problems until he got back home.

Having turned down a huge offer from Gary Ellis last year, his brother had started selling off assets at a rate of knots – everything from artwork and furniture to his cherished vintage MG, a twenty-first birthday present from their mother – just to keep up on the interest payments to the bank. The children had been pulled out of their prep schools and sent to the local village primary, and Muffy had even started taking in commissions as a portrait photographer.

'The fact is,' Henry had told Max despairingly over a whisky one night, soon after he arrived, 'I was a fool not to take up Ellis's offer when I had the chance. He's developing across the valley now, in Swanbrook.'

'You don't mean that, surely,' said Max. 'You couldn't just sell up. Let the place be turned into some Mickey Mouse golf course.'

'We're going to lose the farm anyway, Max.' Henry sounded almost resigned to his fate. He looked older and terribly tired. Over the past six months, he and Muffy had racked their brains day and night trying to come up with something, anything, that would enable them to keep the place going, but it was hopeless. None of their efforts had amounted to more than a drop in the ocean of Henry's debts. The irony was that the farm itself was doing well, with their diversification out of dairy finally starting to pay dividends. But that brought in a steady trickle of income, when what they needed was a tidal wave of cash.

'Barring all my numbers coming up on Saturday's rollover,' Henry sighed, 'I truly don't see a way round it. The only question now is when. How long can we keep the wolf from the door?'

The moment he understood the seriousness of Henry and Muffy's problems, Max had decided to stay. He might not be able to contribute much financially – his director's wages at the theatre barely amounted to a weekly Chinese takeaway – but at least he could help out with the children, and do his best to keep the family's spirits up. Besides, he thought, family life might be just the thing to distract him from his heartbreak.

Taking off his sodden T-shirt and wiping the worst of the cow dung off his tennis shoes with a handful of long grass, he made his way back across the fields towards the house.

It was Sunday, the first full day he'd had off from the theatre in over three weeks.

His play, *Dark Hearts*, had been running for almost three months now, and had won Max some of the best reviews of his career. They were playing nightly to packed houses, which was fantastic, but it did mean he had precious little time to himself to enjoy what was shaping up to be a record-breakingly hot summer.

Walking up the hill, he was struck yet again by the magical view before him. The golden, rose-covered stone of Manor Farm seemed to glow in the late afternoon light, beautiful, like some vision of a lost England.

He couldn't imagine how Henry was going to cope if they did lose it. Despite everything his brother had told him, Max was able to think of the loss of the farm only in terms of an 'if'. He still hoped against hope that it wouldn't come to that, and that some solution would eventually present itself, before it was too late.

Kicking off his dirty shoes outside the kitchen door, he stepped into the pantry wearing only his grass-stained shorts. He had just started to remove them, to throw them into the washing machine along with his sodden T-shirt, when he was startled by a young, female voice behind him.

'Please, monsieur,' said the girl, who couldn't have been much over twenty, in a heavy French accent. 'Don't go any farther. I am 'ere.'

'Jesus Christ,' said Max, spinning round and pulling up his shorts faster than a priest caught trousers down with a choirboy. 'Where the hell did you come from?'

'Toulouse,' said the girl.

They could be damn literal, the French, thought Max. It was hard to tell which of them was blushing more fiercely.

'Yes, OK, I know, Toulouse,' he said, evidently flustered. 'I mean, I don't actually *know* Toulouse. That is, I didn't know you *came* from Toulouse. My point is . . .' He cleared his throat and tried again. 'What I meant was . . .'

'Who on earth are you?' Muffy succinctly finished his question for him. She had just walked into the kitchen carrying a huge pile of children's laundry, looking confused to find a strange woman hovering by the door of her pantry. 'And Max, what on earth are you doing with nearly no clothes on?'

'Washing?' Max gestured lamely towards the open machine.

'Oh. Well, never mind that,' Muffy said, dropping her mountainous load on the kitchen table and turning to smile at the French girl, a pretty, freckled creature with a sleek auburn bob, who seemed to be carrying a suitcase. 'I'm sorry, I must have sounded terribly rude just now. I was just a little surprised to find you standing in my kitchen. Have we met? I'm Muffy Arkell.'

She extended a clean, slightly calloused hand.

'Delighted to meet you, Meesees Arkell,' said the girl, in her stilted, formal English, dropping the suitcase and pumping Muffy's hand enthusiastically. 'I am Frédérique.'

A few long seconds of awkward silence followed this pronouncement. The girl was evidently not about to offer up any further information. She apparently thought that her first name was enough to clear up the mystery of her identity, and presence in the kitchen, entirely.

'I'm sorry, Frédérique who?' said Max eventually.

But before the girl had a chance to answer, Muffy had let out a wail, clapping her hands over her mouth in horror.

'Oh my goodness. Frédérique,' she whispered. 'I thought I cancelled with the agency months ago. It must have slipped my mind. Henry's going to go spare.'

'Have I missed something?' said Max. 'Do you two know each other?'

'Not exactly,' said Muffy. 'Frédérique was going to be our summer au pair.' She looked at the poor girl apologetically. 'But I'm afraid we can't possibly afford you now.'

Once Max had swapped his shorts for a crumpled old pair of Henry's trousers from on top of the tumble-dryer and made both the women a cup of tea, things were fairly swiftly sorted out, to everyone's mutual relief.

Having just come all the way from France, not to mention planned her whole summer, Frédérique was to stay. Max would pay her wages, which were next to nothing anyway, and the extra help with the children would allow Muffy more time to work on her photography commissions.

By the time Henry got home from yet another depressing meeting with his farm manager, Frédérique had already had a bath and unpacked, and was happily playing a game of Monopoly with the children round the kitchen table while Muffy peeled the potatoes for supper.

'Hello, darling,' she said, without looking up. 'How did it go? This is Frédérique, by the way, our new au pair.'

'Hello, Frédérique,' said Henry, waving at her absently and apparently completely unfazed by her arrival. 'Or should I say, *bonjour*.'

'Daddy, your French accent's terrible,' said Charlie. 'Frédérique speaks English anyway, don't you, Freddie?'

'We're allowed to call her Freddie,' Bertie explained to his father. 'She likes it.'

Frédérique, it seemed, was already a hit.

'*Bonjour*, Monsieur Arkell,' she said shyly, standing up to shake Henry's hand. 'I am very 'appy to be working weeth you and all the family. I 'ope we will 'ave a lot of fun togethair.'

'I hope so too, Freddie,' said Henry, slipping his hands round his wife's waist from behind and nuzzling her neck affectionately. 'We've been running a bit low on fun around here lately, I'm afraid. Eh, Muff?'

'Can she stay with us for longer than the summer, Dad?' asked Bertie, who seemed to be particularly smitten with his new playmate.

'Can you stay for ever?' Maddie added her voice to the chorus.

Frédérique laughed. 'Not for ever, no. Anyway, you wait and see. You might be fed up weeth me by tomorrow.'

'We won't,' said Maddie earnestly. 'Do you have a husband? Or a boyfriend?'

'Maddie!' chided her mother, throwing a mountain of peeled potatoes into an industrial-sized saucepan and dropping it with a clatter on to the hot ring of the Aga. 'Leave poor Frédérique alone. That's none of your business.'

'It's OK,' said Freddie. 'No, Madeleine, I don't 'ave a boyfriend. I deed 'ave one, but we broke up.'

'Good.' Maddie grinned. 'Then you can marry my Uncle Max. *He* used to have a girlfriend. But then *they* broke up as well. Grown-ups are always doing that,' she added philosophically.

'Doing what?' said Max, who had wandered in from the kitchen garden to refill his empty Pimms glass. 'Oh, hello, Henry. How'd it go?'

'Shit,' said Henry grimly. 'Things could be looking up for you, though. Your niece here has just been trying to fix you up with our delightful new au pair.'

'See,' said Maddie triumphantly. 'He's very handsome.'

Freddie blushed furiously.

'Apparently the two of you are already altar bound.'

'Oh, Henry, stop teasing them,' said Muffy, who could sense that Max was also feeling awkward, despite his forced smile. 'Give Max another drink, and then why don't you both bugger off out of my kitchen. I'm trying to make supper and it's like Piccadilly bloody Circus in here.'

Out in the kitchen garden, the two brothers sat on the ancient lichened bench sipping their drinks and watching the heavy, blood-red sun beginning to set.

'Did it really go badly today? With Richard?' Max asked.

Richard was Henry's farm manager, really just the chief farm hand, but with responsibility for the other four lads that Henry employed.

He nodded. 'Very. I'm going to have to lay off at least two of them before the end of the summer. If it weren't for the subsidies, I doubt we'd be breaking even at all. I tell you, it's bloody impossible to make a living from farming these days. Unless you're French, of course. Like your beautiful bride to be.'

'Oh, lay off it, would you,' said Max. 'She's hardly my type.'

Henry raised a sceptical eyebrow. 'I don't know. She's very attractive. It wasn't so long ago I remember you saying the same thing to me about Siena. *She* wasn't your type either. "A match made in hell", I believe you once said.'

'Yes, well, that *was* a long time ago,' said Max, with more anger than he'd intended. Seeing his brother's look of surprise, he relented. 'Look, sorry. But d'you mind if we don't talk about Siena?'

'Sure.' Henry could take a hint. He picked a sprig of mint out of his glass and began chewing it thoughtfully. 'Let's talk about your play. That's about the only thing that's going well in this family at the moment.'

Max, who was still thinking about Siena, didn't immediately respond.

'It *is* still going well, isn't it?' asked Henry.

'Oh, yes,' said Max, brightening suddenly. 'We're going great guns. Angus, the guy who wrote it, had a great interview in the *Sunday Times* last week, which means even more exposure for *Dark Hearts*. Not that we need it. We're sold out till September.'

'That's wonderful, Max,' said Henry sincerely.

'As a matter of fact, I have a couple of producers from New York coming to see us in two weeks' time,' Max went on. 'It's the first time that I've actually owned a stake in any of the plays I've done, so it's much more exciting for me.'

'Good man,' said Henry approvingly. 'I've always said you should get some equity in your own work. What's your percentage?'

'Sixty to Angus, forty to me. But I wouldn't get carried away. Chances are they won't go for it – it's a bit bleak for your mainstream theatre audience. Still, it's quite something that they've agreed to come at all. I mean, this is Stratford we're talking about, not the West End.'

'Well, here's to you!' Henry clunked his Pimms glass against Max's and drained what was left of its contents. 'May Lady Luck smile on one of us, at least, for many moons to come.'

Their peace was shattered moments later by an overexcited Charlie.

'Dad! Uncle Max! Come quick,' he called out through the pantry window. '*Sea Rescue*'s gonna start in one minute.'

Max loved the fact that the kids were all such avid fans of Tiffany's show. Charlie, in particular, had a hideous crush on her and was constantly on at his uncle to invite her, without Hunter if possible, to Manor Farm.

'Coming!' Henry shouted back deafeningly. 'Up you get then, Uncle Max,' he joshed his brother. 'It wouldn't do to miss the bit before the music on *Sea Rescue*.'

'Oh, absolutely not,' said Max, following him inside. 'I wouldn't miss it for the world.'

Chapter Forty-two

Randall Stein looked down at the figures in front of him and frowned.

'Nine million?' he said incredulously to the voice on the other end of the phone. 'You didn't think running nine million over budget was something I might, possibly, have been concerned about?'

He reached into his desk drawer and pulled out a bottle of antacid tablets, popping one into his mouth and chewing it grimly while the voice on the speakerphone struggled in vain to explain itself.

Randall was having a bad week.

Production costs on *1943*, his much-hyped Second World War epic in which Siena was starring opposite Jason Reed, Hollywood's latest vaunted successor to Brad Pitt, were spiralling out of control.

The movie had been plagued by bad luck from the start. Freak storms had meant a five-week delay on all the filming on location in Japan at Christmas, which had cost him an absolute fortune. Once they got back to Universal, where the bulk of the film was being made, a general strike by SAG, the powerful actors' union, meant it was another month until they could make any progress, and even then Randall found himself embroiled in distracting lawsuits with more than one of his more minor cast members over the terms of their pre-strike contracts.

Then, having finally got some momentum behind the project in May, Siena and Jason had started giving him headaches.

At first he'd been happy to discover that Siena couldn't stand the sight of her new, Adonis-like co-star. But as the weeks wore on, the director had complained to him repeatedly about the intolerable strains on-set.

Jason, as the bigger, more established star, had taken to lording it over Siena, goading her over everything from her inferior trailer to her relationship with Randall, strongly implying that she had won her part on the casting couch rather than on her own merits.

Siena, stung by this particular criticism because she knew it was true, and desperate to prove herself as a serious actress, met all Jason's taunts with an ever more hysterical torrent of rage. More than once she had stormed off the set screaming, refusing to come back to work until Reed agreed to apologise to her.

Which, of course, he never did.

'She's a great little actress,' the director had told Randall. 'Perfect as Peggy. Always got her scenes down a hundred and ten per cent. But I can't direct her if she isn't there.'

Back home, Randall had torn a strip off her.

'He started it,' protested Siena, after a particularly nasty torrent of abuse. 'Jason's the one you should be screaming at, not me.'

'I don't give a fuck who started it, you dumb bitch.' Randall could be incredibly vindictive when it came to business, totally loveless towards her in his tone, his language, everything. Siena had grown used to it, but it still hurt. 'Jason Reed is a star. No matter how bad it is, people are gonna come and watch this movie because of him. So he's an asshole. So what? You're a professional, Siena. Deal with it.'

'He keeps telling everyone I only got the part because I'm sleeping with you,' she said indignantly.

To her fury, Randall smiled.

'He's right,' he said, adding nastily, 'And if you want to keep sleeping with me – and keep your part – you'd better get your act together. Now.'

Things on-set had improved slightly since then, but the tense atmosphere was still slowing things down.

And now some bozo of an accountant was calling him up to tell him that the problems with the strike had cost 'around' nine million dollars, a figure they'd had since March apparently but only decided to share with Randall today.

'Listen, Bill,' he said, making an effort to keep calm, 'I'm not interested in estimates. If it *is* nine, and quite frankly I find that figure hard to believe, then I want to see that broken down and itemised down to the last fucking quarter. Is that clear?'

The voice on the phone responded with a suitably grovelling affirmative, and Randall hung up and leaned back in his chair, trying to breathe deeply and relax as his therapist had told him to do.

It wasn't really working. But he knew what would.

He pressed the little black button that connected him with his camp but ruthlessly efficient assistant next door. 'Keith.'

'Yes, Mr Stein?'

'Call Becca Williams for me, would you. Tell her I need a girl. Right away.'

The assistant didn't miss a beat. He was used to such requests from his boss. In fact, the madam's number was already programmed into his speed dial.

'Do you want her to come to the office or the apartment?' he asked.

Randall looked at his watch. There was no time to drive over to the Century City apartment where he usually conducted these sorts of assignations.

Fuck it. He could screw her on the desk.

'Send her here,' he said. 'And tell Becca she'd better be good, not like that last anorexic she sent me. I want blonde, and tits like beach balls.'

'I'm on it,' said Keith, ironically for someone who had never been 'on' a blonde who didn't have chest hair and a dick in his life. 'Leave it with me.'

Over on the set at Universal, Siena was sitting in her trailer gloomily playing a game of backgammon with her bodyguard, a 280-pound monster called Big Al.

Contrary to press reports, her trailer was actually rather a modest affair, consisting of two banquettes covered in a revolting seventies-style orange velour fabric that even Duke would have balked at; a noisy and uncomfortable fold-away bed; a minuscule bathroom, comprised of only a toilet and what Siena called her powerless shower, which dripped cold water with a sort of lethargic sneeze; and a little kitchenette, where she and Al had just made themselves some Earl Grey tea, one of the few tastes she had acquired from her long years of exile in England.

'God, I'm bored, aren't you?' She pushed her pieces around the board in a desultory manner.

'Not really.' Al smiled. 'I'm used to it. You need a lot of patience in my job.'

That was the best thing about Al, thought Siena. He was such a cup half full kind of a guy.

She'd been very resistant initially to the idea of having a bodyguard, but Randall had insisted after she'd started getting a string of obscene letters, some of them quite threatening, from an anonymous crazed admirer. Besides, stalkers aside, her fame had grown to such a huge extent in the past six months that she could no longer move about in LA as a free agent without being at best pestered and at worst mobbed by fans and paparazzi alike.

Cut off from her friends and what was left of her family by Randall, unable even to take a stroll along the beach on her own, Siena had discovered that her new-found fame and status could be deeply isolating. There were often days when Al seemed like the only friendly face she saw, and the only person she could really talk to.

She still had Randall, of course. But lately the relationship had been

369

under a lot of strain. She was on the set all day, and he liked to work holed up in his office until very late at night, and typically through most of the weekend as well. In the few snatched hours they did spend together, they argued too much, about everything from the film to his hours to Siena's dress sense.

He was incredibly controlling, and liked to have the final say in every aspect of her life, right down to the colour and size of her T-shirts.

At first Siena had fought him. She remembered Jamie Silfen's advice on the night of the party, and made valiant efforts to preserve her own identity in the face of Randall's formidable will to take over. But her increasing loneliness soon forced her into a state of almost total dependence on him which robbed her of any ability to resist.

It dawned on her that if Randall threw her out, she would lose everything – her career, her fame, her new super-wealthy status, not to mention her home. And despite his constant casual cruelty, she was also afraid of losing Randall himself. He might be a bastard, but he was all she had.

Without her even noticing, he had gradually become the key to her whole world. Siena felt her confidence and self-esteem plummeting as she was forced to give in to him again and again and again.

The only area where the relationship still flourished was in bed.

Randall's desire for her sexually was unabated – if anything it had grown with the shift in the balance of power between them in his direction. He wanted to fuck her every single night, and not infrequently during the day as well. Last week he had even turned up on-set at lunchtime and insisted on taking her back to her trailer for sex.

'Darling, please,' she remonstrated with him. 'It looks so unprofessional, for both of us. You know how these things shake up and down. The whole crew will know what's going on.'

'I know,' said Randall, pushing down her top to reveal a lacy, 1940s-style bra. 'That's what I like about it.'

He left forty-five minutes later looking, as Duke would have said, happier than a pig in shit.

Jason, of course, never let Siena hear the end of it.

Today, she and Al were waiting for Luke, the director, to finish a fight scene between Jason and a young English actor who was playing his co-pilot and love rival. It was taking for ever, and Siena was finding it harder and harder to concentrate on their backgammon game.

'D'you wanna play something else?' said Al, after her third illegal move in a row.

Something was obviously bothering her.

'Oh, sorry,' she said, dragging her attention back to the board. 'I'm not really on the ball this afternoon, am I?'

'It don't matter,' said Al kindly, clearing away the pieces with his giant bear paws. 'We could watch TV if you like?'

Siena picked up the remote and flicked the 'on' switch. Unfortunately, the daytime TV schedules consisted of wall-to-wall soaps, and the very first thing she saw was Hunter's face, looking faintly orange and over-made-up against a cringe-makingly fake background of plywood furniture and wobbly plastic plants.

She switched it off instantly.

'Hey,' said Al. 'That's reruns of *Counsellor*. The first season, that was the best one. Can't we watch that?'

'I'd rather not,' said Siena. She was biting her lower lip and staring resolutely out of the window, evidently quite upset.

'Hey.' Al put a kindly arm around her. He was very fond of Siena and thought Randall Stein was a jerk. 'What's wrong?'

She started to cry. 'Oh, Al, it's nothing, I'm just being silly,' she sobbed.

The big man was not convinced. 'No you're not. Come on, spit it out, girl, what's upset you?'

She wiped her eyes on her sleeve. 'It's me,' she said. 'I've upset myself. I've behaved very badly towards someone I love more than anything. Hunter, my uncle . . .'

'Oh, yeah.' Al nodded understandingly. 'Mike Palumbo.'

'Exactly.' Siena sniffed. 'Well, I really treated him badly, Al. I did.' The big man looked disbelieving. 'I can't bear to watch him on that stupid show. It just reminds me, you know? And I miss him. I miss him so much.'

The tears had started to flow again.

Al, always prepared for such an emergency after long years of working with over-emotional actresses, handed his charge a clean white handkerchief.

'It's never too late,' he said, while Siena blew her nose noisily. 'If you miss him and you think you were wrong, why don't you ring him up and apologise? It's probably just a storm in a teacup. These things usually are.'

She put down the hanky and took his hand. How she wished, with all her heart, that she lived in a world as simple and morally straightforward as his.

'I'm afraid it's not that simple.' She sighed. 'I know it should be, but it isn't. Sometimes . . .' She broke off, unsure of what she was trying to say. 'Sometimes it *is* too late. It just is.'

They were interrupted by a knock on the trailer door. Al lumbered over to answer it and PJ, one of the runners, put his head round the door.

'They're ready for you, Miss McMahon,' he announced breathlessly.

'Thanks,' said Siena. 'Would you tell Luke I need to go back into make-up quickly? Just give me five.'

And leaving Big Al standing there, she was out of the door without another word, dashing across the set towards the make-up trailer and a belated start to her day's work.

Around eight o'clock that evening, she and Randall were in the back of an anonymous-looking, blacked-out limo being driven to an AIDS charity dinner in Beverly Hills.

Siena looked ravishing in a pillar-box-red Versace trouser suit. Randall, by contrast, looked grumpy and exhausted in a dark suit and tie. His heartburn had been playing up dreadfully all day, and every few minutes he put his hand to his chest and groaned as they inched their way along Wilshire.

'Can you believe that schmuck Bill?' he asked Siena for the hundredth time. 'How can you just *forget* to tell someone they're down nine million dollars? What does he think, I'm so loaded that nine million fucking dollars doesn't even matter to me?'

Siena imagined that was exactly what the accountant would have thought, but didn't say so.

'I know, darling,' she said, idly stroking his thigh. 'It must be infuriating.'

'Hmmm,' Randall grunted, moving her hand upward so she could feel his emergent erection through his trousers. The man was a freak of nature – he seemed to have an almost permanent hard-on, at least when Siena was around. 'You look beautiful tonight.'

The compliment was so unexpected she almost choked.

'Thank you,' she said once she'd recovered from the shock, even risking a small smile. 'I'm glad you think so.'

Randall was, in fact, annoyed at himself for having slept with that hooker at lunchtime. It wasn't that he felt guilty as such – he couldn't remember the last time his conscience had been troubled by that particular emotion – but looking at Siena this evening, he was struck again by how mind-blowingly stunning she was.

What was he doing trawling about in the gutter with call girls when he had this kind of welcome waiting for him at home?

'I know I've been a bit tough on you lately,' he went on, to Siena's ill-concealed amazement. 'I'm sorry if I hurt your feelings. But this is a tough business, you know? You need to learn that if you're going to survive.'

'I know,' she said quietly. 'I understand.'

Beneath her calm exterior she felt so relieved she was almost euphoric. In the last few days she'd really been starting to panic that Randall was going off her. Sex was still constant, but otherwise he seemed to be in a permanently bad mood with her, veering from the bad tempered to the totally withdrawn and back again. This sudden show of compassion for her feelings was as wonderful as it was surprising, and she knew better than to question him about what might have caused it.

They arrived at the fund-raiser at the Beverly Hills Hotel in unusually good spirits. The last vestiges of a spectacular LA sunset, a psychadelic melting pot of red and orange, purple, blue and pink, were sinking into the horizon, throwing the famously kitsch pink walls of the hotel and its straight rows of palm trees into dark silhouettes. It looked so breathtaking even Randall was momentarily entranced, not that he was allowed the luxury of time to admire the view. Both he and Siena were mobbed by photographers the moment they set foot out of the car.

'Siena, any comment on the problems you and Jason have been having on 1941?' called out one chancer from the front of the press pack, as she made her way up the pink stone steps.

'What problems?' she called back, giving the reporter a mischievous wink that sent the paparazzi wild.

The whole evening, in fact, was turning into something of a triumph for Siena. Every director in the room seemed to want to talk to her, all drawn to her beauty and confidence like moths to a flame. She'd lost weight, no doubt owing to the combined stresses of dealing with Randall at home and Jason on-set, and her hair had been cut shorter and aggressively sculpted and curled for her role as forties siren Peggy Maples. She was still far too curvy ever to look androgynous, but the shorter hair and trouser suit nevertheless gave her a disturbing, pseudo boyish appeal that wasn't lost on any of the red-blooded males in the room.

Randall was also enjoying himself immensely, contentedly basking in her reflected glory, and being unusually affectionate and relaxed. When he won an antique gold-and-diamond ladies' watch in the raffle, he dragged Siena up on to the podium with him, and made a great show of kissing her hand gallantly while it was clasped around her wrist.

It was the end of the evening, and Siena was happily chatting with a well-known Dutch director, showing off her new watch and wondering whether she had time for one last Kir Royale, when Randall came up to her looking flushed and happy.

'Come on,' he said, taking her arm and pulling her unceremoniously away from the Dutchman. 'We're getting out of here. Johnny Lo Cicero's hired out the Sky Bar for a private party. I said we'd stop by.'

Siena felt a shiver run right through her and a dark cloud descending to smother her happiness.

'No,' she said stiffly. 'I'm not going to the Sky Bar.'

'What?' Randall was still smiling, looking past her and waving to David Geffen as he made his way out. 'Why? What's the problem?'

'That place just gives me bad vibes, that's all.'

An image of Max, lying by the pool, kissing and touching that dreadful girl, rushed unbidden into her mind. She would never set foot in the Sky Bar again as long as she lived. Never. And Randall couldn't make her.

'What vibes?' said Randall, but then it came to him. 'Oh, come on.' He looked at her pityingly. 'Please tell me you're not still hung up about loser boy and the waitress?'

Siena blushed uncomfortably.

'Sweetheart, he's nothing.' Randall was fond of making this observation about Max, and couldn't understand why it didn't seem to comfort her. He pushed her hair back from her face and stroked her neck with unaccustomed tenderness. 'You're playing with the big boys now, baby,' he said. 'That shit doesn't matter any more. You're with me, and I want you to come. It's gonna be a great party.'

Siena hesitated. She desperately wanted to please him. Tonight had gone so well, she really couldn't bear to spoil it.

But it was no good, she couldn't do it. She just couldn't go in there.

'Darling, of course I'm with you, I owe everything to you,' she said, trying to placate him. 'But please understand, I can't face the Sky Bar. I know it seems stupid and superstitious to you, and I know it was all a long time ago. But I really can't go in there. I'm sorry.'

'Fine,' he said coldly, snatching his hand away as though Siena's neck had suddenly transformed into molten lava. 'Do what you want. But I'm taking the car. You'll have to get Al to call Marcel if you want him to come and pick you up.'

Before Siena could say or do anything, an infamous blonde starlet called Miriam Stanley had sidled up to the pair of them. She was wearing a tiny piece of silver thread that barely skimmed her crotch and thigh-high patent-leather boots.

Miriam might be a slut, but she was also gorgeous, thought Siena bitterly.

'Hi, Randall.' She beamed. 'Siena.' She turned to Siena as an afterthought and flashed her the briefest of fake smiles. 'Are you guys coming to Johnny's party?'

'Actually, Miriam, we were just in the middle of something,' began Siena.

'Were we?' said Randall harshly. 'I thought we'd just finished something.'

He pointedly put his arm around a surprised and delighted Miriam. 'Siena is tired, so she's going home. But I'm going over there. If you want I can give you a ride?'

'Well . . .' Miriam flicked back her hair and smiled smugly at a stricken-looking Siena. 'That's really kind of you, Randall. I'd like that.'

Without another word, the two of them headed for the door, leaving Siena standing miserably alone like Cinderella at midnight. Biting down hard on her lower lip, close to tears, she fought her way through the last of the guests out into the lobby. She was looking around desperately for Al, but the big man saw her first and was by her side in seconds.

'Randall's taken the car,' she said, trying to sound as if everything was under control. But her lower lip was going, the classic Siena giveaway.

'Yes,' said Al, giving her a meaningful look. 'I saw Mr Stein leaving. With his companion.' It was quite beyond him why Siena stayed with the bastard. All he ever seemed to do was treat her like dirt. 'I've already called Marcel. He should be here in about ten minutes with the Jag.'

'Thanks.' She smiled at him gratefully, but he could see the tears were about to flow. 'I don't know what I'd do without you, Al. I really don't.'

He put his arms around her and hugged her tightly to his chest, so no one would see her crying. She'd looked like such a vixen earlier in her tight red suit, bursting at the seams with vampy sexual confidence. But all it took was one fight with Randall, and she was suddenly transformed back into a clingy, needy child.

He was bad for her, that man. He really was.

In his modest family house over in Burbank, private detective Bill Jennings was cleaning his teeth, about to get into bed with his wife Denelle for some much needed sleep. It had been a grindingly long week.

'What's this, baby?'

He turned to see Denelle sitting up in bed, looking at a couple of pictures he'd brought home. Damn, she looked hot in that baby-doll nightgown he'd bought her. He hoped the fact that she'd put it on tonight was a good sign. 'Do I know this guy?'

He rinsed out his mouth and climbed into bed beside her.

'Uh-huh.' He nodded, pointing at the naked back view of a man in flagrante with two stunning-looking girls in a hotel room. 'That's Randall Stein. At the Standard, last week.'

'Ooooo,' said Denelle, raising her eyebrows and smiling at her handsome husband. She loved a good bit of gossip, although she had learned to be discreet and never discussed Bill's clients' business with other people. 'And I guess none of those arms, legs or breasts belong to Siena McMahon, right?'

'Right,' said Bill, taking the pictures from her and slipping them both back into the brown envelope on his bedside table.

'What an asshole,' said Denelle, who was always ready to stand up for the sisterhood when a woman was being wronged. Castrate the bastard first, ask questions later, that was her motto.

In this case, though, Bill agreed with her.

'Yeah, he is,' he said. 'He really is.' Leaning over, he gave his wife a lingering kiss on the lips, and slipped one hand under the sheer fabric of her nightdress. 'It's me you should be feeling sorry for, though,' he told her.

'Oh yeah?' She reached down and undid the pink strings confining her beautiful black breasts, without taking her eyes from his. 'Why's that?'

Bill stared down at her cleavage and grinned.

'Because tomorrow,' he whispered, lowering his head and slowly kissing each of her breasts in turn, 'I have to give those pictures to Siena's mother.'

Chapter Forty-three

Max was sitting beside Henry in the passenger seat of his ancient Land Rover, trying to keep his brother's spirits up.

'Just think about that *boeuf Bourgignon* we'll be tucking into at Le Gavroche this evening,' he said, breaking off a few squares of Galaxy chocolate and passing them to Henry. 'You'll be a rich man by then. Well, a rich-*er* man.'

'I bloody won't,' said Henry, chewing the chocolate gloomily. 'I'll be a completely broke man, who may, just *may*, have bought himself a few measly months' leeway to try and hold off his effing creditors.'

'More than a few months, surely?' said Max.

They were driving up to town to try to sell two of Henry's most prized and valuable possessions, a pair of early Turner watercolours. They'd been a christening present from an extraordinarily wealthy godfather, so he had literally grown up with them, and reckoned he must have looked at the pale grey seascapes they depicted almost every day of his life.

He wished he'd looked at them harder now, appreciated them more. But there was no point getting sentimental about it. They had to go.

Freddie had also come along for the ride, and was perched somewhat nervously in the back seat with the grave responsibility of keeping the paintings steady as they jolted and lurched their way down the M40. She had never been to London before, and had also not had a day off since her somewhat unexpected arrival at Manor Farm, so the plan was that they would drop Henry at the art dealer's in Pont Street to sew up the deal while Max took her off for lunch and a spot of sightseeing.

Unfortunately, the traffic was abysmal, and by the time they'd safely delivered Henry and the paintings and agreed to meet back in Pont Street at six, it was already almost lunchtime.

'So,' said Max. 'Any idea where you want to start?'

'Well, I would like to see the 'ouses of Parliament. Big Ben? And I definitely 'ave to go to Buckingham Palace. Do you think there will be time for both?'

Max couldn't help but smile at her enthusiasm and excitement. He remembered the first time he had visited Paris, on a school trip when he was about fourteen, feeling a similar sense of wonder. She was looking up at him, clutching her tatty little London tourist's handbook and a cheap umbrella (just in case), her eyes wide with anticipation.

'Absolutely, buckets of time,' he said, relieving her of both book and umbrella and, to her horror, dropping them in a nearby bin. 'You won't need either of those,' he assured her brightly. 'Just follow me.'

They went to Parliament Square first, and Freddie seemed quite delighted, particularly with the abbey itself. She listened enraptured while Max gave her an impromptu history lesson, pointing out the hallowed resting places of kings, queens and many centuries' worth of the great and the good of England. It was a treat for him too. He loved his history, but since Cambridge had had very little opportunity to indulge his passion.

'You are a wonderful teacher,' Freddie told him afterwards, kissing him on both cheeks in the French style as they emerged into the sunlight of the street.

Max blushed.

'I don't know about that,' he mumbled. 'But it's terrific that you're so interested. A lot of girls your age would rather be whizzing around in the London Eye or something than plodding round a boring old church, listening to me wittering on.'

'What do you mean, "girls my age"?' she teased him, poking him in the ribs in mock indignation. 'You aren't so much older than me, you know.'

He noticed the way she threw her auburn hair back as if in challenge when she said this. Was she flirting with him?

'Well, no,' he said, embarrassed at himself for appearing so flustered. 'No, I suppose I'm not. But you know what I mean.'

By this time they were both starving, so Max made one minor change to their itinerary and took her off to Fortnum and Mason to buy supplies for a picnic in Green Park.

Freddie couldn't believe the prices.

'That's almost fifteen euros for two slices of pâté!' she wailed. 'No wonder your brozzer 'as some problems with money if it costs this much just to eat.'

Max assured her that Henry didn't make a habit of shopping at Fortnum's, but her outrage over the prices soon disappeared anyway once they finally sat down to eat.

'*Mon Dieu*,' she said through a meltingly delicious mouthful of duck's-liver pâté on crusty brown bread. 'Oh my God. That is incredible. *Incroyable*. Amazing. And I thought the English couldn't cook.'

Max laughed. 'Don't let Muffy hear you say that.'

He was surprised by how much he was enjoying himself today. Ever since Siena had left him, but even more so since he'd had to leave LA with his tail between his legs, he'd found it hard to fully relax and be happy.

Henry and Muff had been fantastic, as always, and he adored being at Batcombe. But not even the warmth of Manor Farm, or his unexpected professional success at Stratford, had enabled him to shake a deeper feeling of worthlessness and rejection. Siena was still very much on his mind.

Today, though, for the first time in many months, he felt something that was very close to real happiness. Perhaps it was as simple as lying in the park in London on such a beautiful day. It was also nice to be with Freddie, to be able to show her the sights and talk history with her. She was an attractive girl, and the way she listened to him, and was obviously interested in what he had to say, was pleasantly flattering. It made him feel confident, and Max was grateful to her for that.

Freddie lay back on the grass on her side, propped up on her elbow with her pixie-like head resting on her hand.

'As you English would say' – she patted her non-existent belly and rolled her eyes – 'I'm completely stuffed.'

Max laughed. This was one of Charlie's favourite expressions and it sounded ridiculous coming from her.

'What do you mean, you're stuffed? You've had one slice of bread and pâté and a few cherries! We've hardly started here.' He waved at two more largish Fortnum's bags still crammed with food at their feet. Freddie shook her head.

'I couldn't eat another theeng,' she said. 'Let's just take it 'ome for the children.'

Max noticed the way her tight T-shirt clung to her tiny breasts as she lay down. Other than being short, he reflected, she might well be described as the polar opposite of Siena in terms of looks. But there was nonetheless something sexy about her. Unthreatening, but definitely sexy.

She had the small, toned, compact body of a gymnast, shown off to full advantage in the shorts she was wearing today, the white of the cotton in striking contrast to her tanned, slender legs. And she didn't have any make-up on, something he had always gone for in girls. It showed confidence.

'I suppose we ought to make a move and walk up to the palace in a minute,' he said, somewhat reluctant. 'It's nearly four now, and we need to be back in Belgravia by six.'

'OK,' said Freddie, all energy suddenly, leaping to her feet and standing over him, reaching down for his hands to pull him up.

'I didn't mean *right* now,' Max grumbled.

But he found himself holding on to her small, cold hands anyway, unwilling to let her go. It would have been so simple for him to pull her down on top of him and kiss her. The confident, provocative sparkle in her eyes told him she probably wouldn't protest if he did. But something made him hesitate.

For a moment, they remained frozen in this pose, holding eye contact with one another for just long enough to confirm a flicker of mutual attraction. Then Max let go of her hands and stood up.

'Right, then, you little slave driver,' he said, gathering up the remaining food bags with exaggerated briskness. 'The palace it is.'

By the time they'd 'done' Buckingham Palace, battled their way through central London traffic and finally found a meter in Belgravia, they were fifteen minutes late to meet Henry. He was standing outside the gallery, and from twenty feet away Max could already tell that something was up from his brother's slumped shoulders and hangdog expression.

'Sorry we're late,' he said, shrugging apologetically. 'I couldn't find a meter for love nor money. How did it go?' He looked down questioningly at the two watercolours, which were propped up against the wall at Henry's feet.

Henry looked bleak.

'About as badly as possible, I'm afraid. They're fakes.'

There was a stunned silence.

'What?' said Max, eventually. 'They can't be.'

'Well, they are.' Henry gave a brief, what-can-you-do smile. 'Hamish didn't seem to have any doubts.'

'Christ.' Max shook his head.

He knew how crucial the sale of those paintings had been to Henry. Without that money and the extra months it would have bought him, he would be forced to sell up now.

'Per'aps you need a drink?' suggested Freddie. 'We could find an English pub, before we go to the restaurant, no?'

'I'm afraid I can't,' said Henry, glancing anxiously at his watch. 'You two go and have dinner. Enjoy yourselves. I've got to try and catch Nick Frankel before he leaves the office, sort this business out once and for all.'

Max didn't like his brother's tone. It sounded worryingly final.

'Are you sure?' he pressed him. 'Wouldn't you rather come with us and sort all this out in the morning?'

Henry shook his head. 'Can't, Maxy. There's someone . . .' He hesitated, as if he were about to tell him something but then thought better of it. 'Something I have to try and do tonight, if I can. Really.' He smiled at them both. 'You two go on. I wouldn't be much company for you anyway.'

Max sat at the corner table in Le Gavroche with Freddie, sipping a small glass of vintage port that he really couldn't afford, and worrying about Henry.

'It doesn't make any sense,' he kept repeating through his drunken haze to an equally bleary-eyed Frédérique. 'How can he have had those paintings for all those years, and never known they were dodgy?'

Freddie sipped her own port and said nothing. She was watching the way his blond hair kept flopping forward over his eyes, and longing to reach across the table and push it back for him.

'Sorry,' he said, cutting himself another sliver of Stilton. 'You must be bored silly with all this talk about Henry. So, what do you make of London, then? Was it what you were expecting?'

'I suppose so, in a way,' she said. She didn't seem very interested in reminiscing about their sightseeing trip. 'But I don't find it boring, actually. When you tell me about your brother. It makes me 'appy that you trust me, with your problems, you know?'

Max looked across at her with renewed interest. He hadn't really thought of it like that, in terms of trusting her. But he supposed, in a way, he did.

'I 'ope you don't think I'm being rude,' she continued tentatively, 'but I 'ave noticed that you often seem to be sad. Is it . . .' She twirled her hair in her fingers nervously. 'Is it to do with your girlfriend? With Siena?'

Max bridled for a second at hearing Freddie using her name. One of the worst things about splitting up with someone famous was that everyone you met felt as if they knew the person intimately. Max found people's pseudo-familiarity with Siena hard to take. But he knew Freddie's heart was in the right place, and he tried to answer her honestly.

'Sometimes,' he said. 'I still think about her a lot. Well, all the time, really. But all that stuff people tell you about time healing the wounds – I'm starting to think there might be something in it. I actually had a really nice day today.'

Freddie took this as a compliment and visibly blushed with pleasure.

'Me too,' she said. 'Really nice.'

Emboldened by the wine, she reached across the table, took his hand, put it to her lips and kissed it.

Max felt his heart pounding with nerves.

This wasn't a good idea.

'Look, Freddie,' he began awkwardly.

'What?' she interrupted him, keeping hold of his hand. 'I could 'elp you. I could make you 'appy, Max, I know I could.' She spoke with such urgency, looking him directly in the eyes as if willing him to believe her. It took him aback. 'I also 'ave somebody to forget, remember?'

'I'm just not sure,' he mumbled. 'I don't think I'm over her, not properly. And you're very young. I don't . . .' He found himself unsure of the right words. 'I wouldn't want to hurt you.'

'You won't,' said Freddie. 'I wouldn't let you.'

Before either of them really knew what was happening, they found themselves leaning across the table and kissing one another full on the mouth.

It had been a long time since Max had kissed anyone, and he'd had a lot to drink. Feeling the soft skin of Freddie's lips against his, and the almost forgotten urgency of a woman's desire in her probing tongue and quickened breathing, he found that his physical response was overwhelming. He wanted her to hold him, to come for him, to make him believe that everything was going to be all right. He wanted to take her to bed right now.

'I do hurt people,' he whispered, oblivious of the other diners' stares as he grabbed her hair in his hands desperately, like a drowning man reaching for a buoy, and pressed his forehead against hers. 'I do.'

'Shhh,' said Freddie, stroking his face softly. 'You don't have to worry any more. It's going to be OK.'

The three of them barely spoke on the long journey home. Henry drove with his eyes fixed on the road ahead, consumed with his own worries. Whatever had happened at his accountant's office after he'd left them earlier, he clearly didn't want to talk about it.

Max sat in the front, concerned for his brother, but also agonisingly aware of Freddie's presence behind him, counting the long minutes until he could get home and hopefully sneak her into his bed.

He was too drunk to analyse his feelings in any depth, although part of him knew that starting something with the kids' au pair might not be the smartest move in the world. But a bigger part – the part that had felt so lonely and unloved for a year, the part that wanted to remember what it felt like to be alive, and make love and be happy – could only with an effort be restrained from clambering into the back seat right now and ripping the girl's clothes off.

When they finally did get home, Muffy was waiting up for them.

'Hello, you three,' she said, taking the pictures back from Henry without a word and moving into the kitchen. He would explain it all to her when he was ready. 'You must be exhausted. How was London? Did you have a good day, Frédérique?'

'Yes, I did,' said Freddie, with a meaningful look at Max. 'But I am *very* tired. I theenk I'll go straight up, if you don't mind?'

'Me too,' chimed in Max, rather too quickly.

'Of course.' Muffy smiled, slightly bemused by Max's sudden craving for his beauty sleep. He usually never hit the hay until the small hours.

She was relieved that they were both making themselves scarce. Something had obviously gone wrong if the pictures were back, and she wanted to talk to Henry on his own.

Once Max and Freddie had disappeared upstairs with somewhat indecent haste, Henry walked over to her and gave her a hug. He didn't speak, but just stood there in the kitchen swaying slightly, with his wife in his arms.

'So?' she prompted him gently when he finally let her go and sat down at the table. Henry took a deep breath.

'They were fakes.'

'Worthless?' asked Muffy. She was determined not to look disappointed or shocked. He needed her to be strong, whatever happened.

'Not worthless. But certainly not worth enough. Not even close.' He ran his hands through his greying curls and forced himself to keep talking, before he lost his nerve. 'That money was our last hope, Muff. Without it, we can't pay the back interest on the loans. It's as simple as that. So I went to see Nick this evening.'

She didn't say anything, but nodded for him to go on.

'I said we'd think about putting the farm on the market next week.' He scanned her face anxiously for a reaction, but her mask of calm didn't slip.

'I see,' she said reaching out and laying a hand gently on his shoulder. He pulled out another chair and gestured for her to sit beside him.

'There is another option,' he said.

This time there was no concealing her emotion, and a snapshot of desperate hope flashed across her features at this possibility of a reprieve. Perhaps they wouldn't have to sell after all?

'What? What other option?'

Henry took both her hands between his own and began fiddling with her worn wedding band as he told her. 'It was Nick's suggestion, actually. But I put in a call to Gary Ellis from his office.'

'Why?' Muffy looked shocked. 'I thought we'd agreed, no golf course . . .'

'We have, we have.' He held up his hand to stop her. 'Hear me out. The fact is, as Nick pointed out to me, if we put the place on the open market and sell to someone else, there's nothing to stop Ellis approaching *them* with a fat cheque and developing the land anyway. If he wants it badly enough, that's exactly what he'll do, and then the only difference will be that the money's in someone else's pockets rather than ours.'

'Yes, but *does* he still want it that badly?' said Muff. 'He's gone and ruined Swanbrook now. Does he really want *two* golf courses?'

Henry shrugged.

'He might do. Look, when I called him from Nick's he made me another offer. I think we should consider it.' Muffy opened her mouth to protest. 'Not to buy the place,' Henry continued, heading her off at the pass. 'This time he's talking about a lease agreement.'

'What sort of lease agreement?' she asked warily.

He took a deep breath.

'We would remain the nominal owners of the whole property, with ongoing rights to live in the house, and we could leave those rights to the children. We wouldn't have to sell.'

'I see.' She frowned. 'And what's in it for the ghastly Gary, then?'

'Well . . .' He hesitated momentarily. 'He'd be able to build a golf course and run it without interference for the full term of the lease.'

'Which is?'

Henry winced.

'He's talking about a hundred years.'

'A hundred years?' Muffy laughed, but it really wasn't funny. She got up and started pacing backwards and forwards in front of the Aga. 'For heaven's sake, Henry. Even the kids will be dead by then!'

'I know, I know. But he'd give us enough to clear all our debts up front, plus a chunk left over. We could still live in the house, and so could the children in due course.'

'But they could never sell the house?' asked Muffy, horrified. 'It wouldn't be really *theirs*?'

'Not until the end of the lease agreement, no,' Henry admitted.

'But after that ownership would revert to the family. Whether that's Charlie's children or what have you I don't know, we'd have to sort the details out. They may have to pay some sort of release payment to Ellis's company at that point, it's a bit complicated.'

'Surely you aren't considering saying *yes* to this?' she asked, finally stopping pacing and coming to rest with her back against the warm metal of the oven.

Henry sighed. 'Look, darling, I hate that bastard as much as you do, but he's throwing us a lifeline here. The alternative is that we sell the whole lot to someone else for a shitty price, pay off the fucking debts, and buy ourselves a nice little semi in Swindon with what's left over.'

'Oh, come on. Surely it wouldn't be *that* bad?'

'After we've paid everyone off? I'm afraid it would be,' said Henry. 'At least this way the manor stays in the family. We wouldn't have to move.'

'Yes, but it would be a golf course!' she exclaimed in agony. 'You've seen Ellis's developments. The whole valley would be ruined, completely ruined. I mean, isn't Batcombe supposed to be an area of outstanding natural beauty or something? How does he think he's going to get planning permission?'

Henry rubbed his fingers together to indicate a bribe. 'The man's as bent as a nine-bob note,' he told her. 'He told me and Nick today that he already has preliminary approval for the golf course, *and*, if you can believe it, to build a fucking great clubhouse and "leisure complex" right next to the old barns.'

'I don't know what to believe any more,' said Muffy.

'Look.' He got up to join her by the Aga, wrapping his arm around her shoulders. 'If you don't want to go ahead, you don't have to. This is your decision as much as mine, and if you'd rather sell to someone else, we can sell. But the reality is, he's going to build his bloody golf course anyway eventually, whatever we decide. At least this way, one day, we may have a chance to put things right.'

'You're right,' she said sadly. 'I know you're right. A lease has to be better than an outright sale. I just can't bear the thought of that man, that *awful*, lecherous, predatory man, setting foot on the place.'

'Believe me, darling' – Henry hugged her tightly – 'neither can I. Neither can I.'

Chapter Forty-four

The next few months were a time of both great happiness and great sadness for Max.

Professionally, things were going better than he could ever remember. Not only had *Dark Hearts* proved so successful that they had had to extend their Stratford run, and were even contemplating taking the play on tour to Bristol and London; but one of the short films he'd directed in LA had been nominated for three awards at the Chicago Film Festival, and looked set for even bigger success at Sundance next year. Thanks to the involvement of the big Hollywood star, it had received a disproportionate amount of press.

Ironically, his profile in the States was bigger now than it had been in all the years he'd lived there.

Not that things were remotely slow in England. The name Max De Seville was finally becoming well known in theatre circles, and offers had started to come in from all over the country for Max to direct everything from musicals to 'nihilist Shakespeare', whatever that might be.

Personally, his life had also become more contented, thanks in no small part to his burgeoning relationship with Freddie. After a brief, half-hearted attempt to keep their affair secret, Max had finally decided to be honest about it with Henry and Muffy, as well as with himself.

'I can't imagine why you thought we'd disapprove,' Muff told him, after he'd rather nervously admitted what she had long suspected anyway. 'God knows you deserve a bit of fun, Max. I mean, why not?'

He'd realised then that his sister-in-law was right. He'd been fighting his feelings for Freddie, because he knew that deep down he was still in love with Siena, and probably always would be. But Siena was gone, and there was no point sitting around moping. Freddie was here, and she wanted to make him happy.

Why not?

Set against all these good things, though, was the terrible, ongoing nightmare of life at Manor Farm. Having finally signed the hated lease agreement with Ellis, they were all waiting with a growing sense of despair for the construction work to begin. Awareness that these might be the last days of the estate as a working farm and a tranquil family home made it impossible to enjoy the time they had left together. Henry mooched about the yard and the office like a bear with a sore head, snapping at anyone foolish enough to try to talk to him or commiserate about the golf course.

Meanwhile Muffy tried to maintain some semblance of normality and cheerfulness for the sake of the children, who already had to cope with settling in at the local primary and making new friends, and were soon to have their home life turned upside down as well. Max could see the effort of this pretence was a huge strain for her.

He did his best to keep everyone's spirits up, forcing a reluctant and exhausted Muffy to spend a day at the health spa in Cheltenham, and taking the children on endless exciting outings with Freddie, to such heady destinations as the haunted Minster Lovell and Burford zoo. Mercifully, Bertie and Maddie were both too young to understand the implications of what was about to happen at home, and thought the prospect of construction and activity at the farm was marvellously exciting. But Charlie, who as well as being older was naturally more sensitive to others' feelings, in particular his mother's, knew that the way of life he had grown up with was going to be destroyed for ever and that his parents blamed themselves.

Max spent a lot of time with his nephew, helping him talk through his feelings of sadness, powerlessness and loss. After all he'd been through in the last year, he felt he was now fully equipped to offer advice on all three.

On his way into Stratford one morning, he stopped off at the village shop for a paper and a packet of ten Marlboro Lights – he was half-heartedly smoking again, thanks to all the late nights at the theatre – when he ran into Caroline Wellesley.

Unlike the rest of his family, Max was not a fan of Hunter's mother and was relieved when, despite living within a few miles of her and Christopher, he found that he rarely crossed paths with her socially.

This morning, however, there could be no escape. The shop was far too small for him to pretend not to have seen her.

'Hello, Max,' she said brightly, marching towards him armed with a little green metal basket containing nothing but six packets of chocolate Hob Nobs, Christopher's only real post-alcoholic weakness.

She was dressed in an old pair of canvas gardening trousers and a man's white shirt, and was almost unrecognisable as the former designer-clad nymphette he remembered from his childhood. Fifteen years later, standing in Batcombe Stores dressed like a scarecrow, she *still* had something about her, though. Caroline had the sort of sex appeal and lust for life that barely seemed to dim at all with age. Grudgingly, Max acknowledged what so many men saw in her physically.

'I haven't seen you for ages.' She smiled up at him. 'How are things at Manor Farm?'

He looked at her coldly.

'Bad,' he said, flatly. 'Things are very bad, I'm afraid. But then I expect your friend Gary Ellis will already have told you all about it.'

'Hey, now hang on a minute,' said Caroline, putting down her basket and squaring up to him, all five foot four of her coiled for battle against Max's giant six-and-a-half-foot bulk. He took a step back and very nearly toppled over a giant display case stacked with miniature jars of Marmite. 'That's not fair. He isn't a friend of mine at all. I think it's awful what he's doing to that beautiful valley, everybody does.'

'Really?' said Max, steadying the swaying case behind him before turning to face her again. 'And I thought it was you who introduced him to my brother in the first place and put the whole idea about buying up the farm into his head. You invited him for dinner, when he was leching all over Muffy. Apparently there's nothing of Henry's that that shit doesn't want to get his swindling little hands on.'

'Well, that's hardly my fault, is it?' said Caroline reasonably. 'That dinner was years and years ago, when he first moved here. None of us really knew him then. Muff knows I felt awful about the way Gary behaved towards her that night, but it's all water under the bridge now. We haven't had him back to Thatchers since, anyway. Christopher can't abide him.'

'Good for Christopher,' said Max.

He knew it was childish to lash out at Caroline. The nightmare at home was nothing to do with her, and anyway, as Henry had pointed out, if it hadn't been for Ellis's offer they would have lost Manor Farm completely. Perhaps it was the developer's admiration for Muffy which had kept him coming back for more, even after Henry had walked away from his first offer. Maybe that awful dinner at Caroline's had actually done them all a favour?

'Look, sorry.' He apologised half-heartedly and tried to change the subject. 'How is Christopher anyway? Is he well?'

Caroline smiled. 'Very, thank you. Fighting fit.' It was funny to watch Max trying to be so formal and awkwardly polite towards her. She still remembered him aged nine, chasing Hunter around the house with two stuck-together kitchen-towel tubes, pretending to be Darth Vader. Looking at him now, all broken nose and wounded masculine pride, she thought she wouldn't have minded being chased around the house by him one little bit, and managed to suppress a wistful sigh.

'I spoke to Hunter a few weeks ago,' she said, bringing up the one subject she hoped they still had in common. 'He seemed very happy, very settled with thingumabob.'

She always had been appalling with names.

'Tiffany,' said Max sternly. 'Yes, he is, very happy. I spoke to him myself, as a matter of fact. Yesterday.'

It was a pointed enough remark for even Caroline take the hint: Max spoke to Hunter more frequently than his own mother.

'You think I was a lousy mother, don't you?' she said quietly.

He sighed. He hadn't wanted to get into all this, and he was late for rehearsals as it was. But he supposed he'd brought it on himself.

'You weren't there,' he said, softening his own tone to match hers. 'You didn't see how bad things got for him. I did. Even before Duke died, you were never there for Hunter.'

She looked at him thoughtfully and gave an imperceptible nod, silent and awkward, between the cereal boxes and the breakfast spreads. Then she said cheerfully: 'We might pop in and see Muffy and Henry later. Would you mention it to them if you see them?'

The Hunter subject had apparently been closed.

'Of course,' he said, hastily grabbing a paper and throwing it into his own basket. 'But you'll probably see them before me. I'm expecting to be in Stratford all day working.'

They moved together towards the single till, Max with his *Times* and his fags, Caroline with her biscuits, neither of them speaking until they emerged on to the narrow lane that passed for Batcombe High Street.

'He's happy now, though, you say?' asked Caroline, seemingly out of nowhere.

'Hunter?' Max looked surprised. He hadn't thought she'd bring the subject up again. 'Absolutely. He's blessed.'

'Good,' said Caroline. 'Everything turned out all right in the end, then, didn't it? Even with a *terrible* mother like me.'

And with that she scurried into Christopher's old Range Rover before Max could think of anything else to say to her.

Later that same night, Max sat in his brown leather director's chair, a present from Henry, and ran his hands through his hair in exhaustion.

It was gone 9.30 and he was still at the theatre, going through a couple of scenes with Rhys Bamber, the charming and very hard-working young Welsh actor who played the lead role of Jaspar. But they were both very tired, and weren't really getting anywhere.

'Why don't you come down to the White Hart and have a drink with me?' Max suggested, yawning as he put down the script. 'I could use a pint or two, even if you can't.'

'All right, then,' said Rhys. He was sick of this bloody scene anyway. 'Just a quick one.'

Every female head turned when, fifteen minutes later, the two of them walked into the pub on the high street, but neither Max nor Rhys seemed aware of what an attractive duo they were.

Max was looking unusually brown after a series of weekends spent out in the baking sunshine at Batcombe. Rhys was smaller, slighter and darker, very good looking in a chiselled, almost a Hollywood sort of way, but with the added secret weapon of a divinely lyrical Welsh accent. Girls would walk across broken glass just to hear Rhys say 'hello'. He was Ivor the Engine with sex appeal.

'Thanks for this.' He raised his pint to Max and took a long, refreshing gulp of lager. 'I feel better already.'

'Good,' said Max. 'To be honest, I was glad you had time for a drink. It's a bit sad really, but I'm rather dreading going home.'

He briefly explained the current situation at Batcombe and the strain it was putting on everybody. Rhys listened and nodded sympathetically.

'That's terrible,' he said, when Max had finished. 'I know what it's like to lose a farm. My Uncle Tommy, back in Wales, had to sell up a few years ago, after BSE and all that. It really broke him up. Happened to a lot of the poorer farmers in Wales.'

'And the richer ones in the Cotswolds, I'm afraid,' said Max. 'At least in our case the family get to stay on living there.'

'With their foxy French au pair,' added Rhys, with a naughty wink. 'I think she's lovely, your girlfriend. I love French girls.' He grinned broadly.

Max imagined that French girls probably loved Rhys right back.

'She is,' said Max. 'She is lovely.' He forced a smile.

But inside he felt a creeping unhappiness that he couldn't quite define.

It was still lurking somewhere in his chest as he drove home an hour or so later in the rather nice, souped-up Beetle that the play's producers had loaned him for the duration of its run at Stratford.

He turned on the local radio station, the embarrassingly monikered 'Bard FM', to try to distract himself from his unwanted depression.

After a couple of dreary songs by Dido, Max was relieved to be told it was time for the eleven o'clock news.

'Today in Parliament, the Prime Minister announced that the government has no plans to make any changes to the proposed bill on hunting in response to the massive demonstrations by pro-hunt supporters and other countryside pressure groups last weekend.'

'Twat!' Max shouted at the radio, comforting himself with another square of chocolate from the half-eaten bar on the passenger seat.

More news followed, a whole series of deathly dull items about the findings of the latest rail inquiry and an over-hyped piece about a possible link between alcoholism and colon cancer. He was about to switch over to something more soothing on Classic FM when he heard the West Country presenter say something that made his heart stop.

'And in the entertainment world tonight,' she burred, 'rumours are rife that the producer Randall Stein and his girlfriend, the model and actress Siena McMahon, are soon to be tying the knot.'

Fighting to steady his breathing, Max slowed down and pulled over on the grass verge at the side of the lane. The presenter went on.

'A spokesman for Miss McMahon, who once went to boarding school in England and is the daughter of producer Pete McMahon and granddaughter of Hollywood legend Duke McMahon, has denied there is any truth in the rumours. But Siena was spotted today leaving the set of 1943, Stein's upcoming Second World War blockbuster, wearing a huge diamond-and-ruby ring on her engagement finger and smiling broadly at the waiting press. Miss McMahon and Mr Stein have been living together in Los Angeles for the past year.'

Max turned off the radio and sat for a moment in silence, too shocked to move.

Marrying him! She was marrying that lecherous, twisted old monster? Somehow, even in his most tortured nightmares, he had never considered this horrible possibility. He'd always believed that one day Siena would outgrow Randall. Even if only for reasons of ambition, he thought she would eventually grow up and move on, out from under the old man's wing. But *marry* him?

The thought was too hideous to contemplate.

Perhaps, he began to comfort himself, it wasn't true? Her publicist had denied it, after all. Knowing Siena, it was just as likely to be some stunt designed to whip up a bit more interest in their movie, like the shenanigans she'd pulled with Hunter last year, dragging him to that baseball game to try to make some capital out of Minnie McMahon's death. Even Max, who avoided information about Siena like the plague, knew that 1941 was running into trouble and could have done with some extra press.

Yes. The more he thought about it, the more it made sense. That was what it was. A publicity stunt.

Having steadied his nerves enough to restart the car, he drove the remaining twelve miles to Batcombe with the image of a smiling Siena waving her ring at reporters embedded in his brain like a cancer.

Freddie was running across the yard to meet him before he'd even switched off the engine. It was a bright, moonlit night, and Max could make out her features almost as clearly as if it were daylight.

Her low, smooth brow was furrowed in concern, and her auburn hair, usually so immaculate and sleek, looked oddly dishevelled, as though she'd been running around in very high winds. The shadows under her eyes, the result of a broken night helping Muffy with Madeleine after she'd wet the bed, heightened the overall impression of an under-nourished refugee, as did the baggy pair of dungarees and moth-eaten bottle-green sweater of Muffy's that she'd been wearing to help with milking in what was left of the working farm.

It would be fair to say that she wasn't looking her best.

'Darling.' She pulled open the driver's door and smothered Max with kisses in a Gallic display of affection that, for once, he could have done without. 'I 'eard the news on the radio,' she gabbled. 'When you deedn't come 'ome, I was so worried. I thought you must have 'eard about it and maybe done something stupid. Why didn't you turn your phone on? You 'ave 'eard, 'aven't you? Are you OK?'

The volume and speed of her questions were both too much for Max, who wanted nothing more than a moment's peace with a glass of whisky. Preferably a big one.

'I'm fine, Freddie, really,' he said, trying not to show his irritation. She was only showing concern for him, after all. He mustn't snap at her. 'If you mean the story about Siena's engagement, yes, I have heard, and quite frankly I don't believe a word of it.'

He shut the car door firmly behind him and strode into the house, leaving an agitated Freddie trotting along behind him like a worried terrier.

Marching into the drawing room, he was annoyed to discover that she wasn't the only one who'd waited up. Henry was sitting at the card table with Caroline and Christopher Wellesley, and all three rose to greet him the moment he walked in.

'Hello, old man,' said Henry. 'How were rehearsals?'

Thank God his brother at least had the wisdom to stick to neutral subjects.

'Fine,' he said, a little tensely, extending his hand to their guests. 'Christopher. Caroline. Nice to see you.'

'Hello again, Max,' said Caroline. She was looking at him, if not quite pityingly, then certainly questioningly.

Max felt his hackles rising. Caroline was quite probably the very last person he wanted to see right now. She knew Siena, had known her all her life, and he couldn't stand the thought that this might make her feel involved, connected in some way to his pain. It was hard to explain, but in his mind at least he wanted to keep Siena all to himself. It was the only way he could deal with the horror of her being engaged to Randall, the only way he could begin to control his emotions. Caroline's presence was an intrusion.

'Look,' he said, pointedly moving away from her and addressing them all as a group, 'I know you're all concerned for me after tonight's news, and I appreciate it, really. But as I was just telling Freddie, I'm sure there's no truth in the story. And even if there were, it's nothing to do with me any more.'

He tried to sound upbeat and confident, but it wasn't a huge success. Christopher and Henry exchanged worried glances. It didn't seem to have sunk in yet.

'But Max,' said Henry reasonably, pouring two small whiskies from the decanter on the side table and handing one of them to his brother, 'they showed her on the ten o'clock news, *wearing* the ring.'

'It all looked quite official,' added Freddie, coming up behind him and slipping a comforting arm around his waist.

'So?' Max challenged her. She could sense a formerly unknown belligerence creeping into his voice and instinctively removed her arm, shrinking back a little. 'A ring means nothing at all,' he insisted, once again addressing everyone. 'Believe me, I know Siena. This will be some tacky publicity stunt designed to boost interest in their new film. By all accounts that movie needs all the help it can get.'

He snorted mirthlessly and drained his glass, then walked over to the side table to pour himself another.

'I don't theenk that's the answer, do you?' said Freddie, glancing at the whisky decanter. 'It's late, *chéri*. Why don't you come to bed?'

'Yes, that's a good idea,' Henry chimed in. 'Get some rest, Maxy. We can talk about it all in the morning.'

Their concern was like a red rag to Max's bull. All the repressed tension of the past hour burst out of him, and poor Freddie took the full brunt of it.

'Who the hell do you think you are – my mother?' he snarled at her. 'I'll have a drink if I damn well want to. And as for its being "the answer" . . .' He waved his glass at her aggressively, sloshing a good finger of amber liquid on to Henry's carpet. 'As far as I'm concerned there isn't even a fucking question, all right? There's been some stupid story about Siena, it's been denied, and that's it. It's bullshit. Crap. She would never marry that disgusting old bastard. Never! Can't you get that through your thick head, and stop fussing around me like some melodramatic nursemaid?'

'I say,' said Christopher. 'Steady on, old boy. It isn't Frédérique's fault.'

Freddie, in fact, had kept her cool admirably in the face of Max's onslaught and, politely saying goodnight to Henry and Caroline, and smiling gratefully at Christopher, she turned on her heel to go.

She'd been waiting up all night for Max. She didn't need this shit.

Max made no move to stop her, but she paused at the door anyway and looked at him pityingly. When she spoke, she sounded calm and collected. There wasn't a trace of anger in her voice.

'I don't know 'oo you're trying to convince, darling,' she said. Max looked at her blankly. 'Me or yourself.'

As soon as she'd gone, he turned around to find Henry, Christopher and Caroline all staring at him, mutely appalled.

He felt bad enough as it was, and certainly didn't need a guilt trip from them.

'Oh, for fuck's sake,' he slurred. Those earlier pints with Rhys, now topped up with whisky, were starting to catch up with him. 'Just leave me alone.'

He stomped off in the direction of the kitchen, and Henry got up to follow him, but Caroline put a hand on his arm.

'Leave it,' she said. 'I'll go.' Henry looked doubtful. 'Women are better at these things,' she explained.

Christopher and Henry caught each other's eye. They couldn't argue with that.

Max was sitting in the threadbare armchair next to the Aga. It was known as the dogs' chair, because it was Titus and Boris's favourite spot in the entire house. He stood up defensively when Caroline walked in.

'Look, Caroline, I'm sorry, but I'm really not in the mood, all right?' he snapped. 'I don't want to be rude, but I'd appreciate it if you'd please just take the hint and bugger off. OK?'

Caroline sat down at the table and began nibbling at a chocolate digestive from the open tin.

'You can be as rude as you like, Max,' she said. 'I don't care. And if it makes you feel any better, I am just about to bugger off. Biscuit?'

Still glowering at her, he took a digestive and sat back down. He hoped she meant it, and was going to hurry up and say her piece. 'I only came in here to tell you that you need to let that girl go.'

Great. Another lecture, this time from Miss Morality herself. Honestly, where did this woman get off?

'Siena?' He gave a clipped, joyless laugh and chomped into his biscuit, demolishing three-quarters of it in one bite. 'I have let her go, Caroline,' he said. 'In case you hadn't noticed, she's well and truly gone.'

He dropped the last morsel of chocolate digestive into his open mouth and swallowed, as if illustrating the finality of his loss.

The next thing he knew, Caroline had walked over to him and, leaning down, kissed him on the top of his head, like a child. It was such a gentle, compassionate gesture, he didn't know how to respond.

She put her hand under his chin and slowly lifted his face so that his eyes met hers.

'I wasn't talking about Siena,' she said.

The next morning the story was all over the papers. Even the broadsheets were running pictures of the happy couple.

Max came down to breakfast with a pounding head and a guilty conscience – he had slept fitfully and alone in his own room, unable to face apologising to Freddie – and noticed that the *Telegraph* and the *Mail* had already been tactfully cleared away. He didn't need to look at them – he could imagine the coverage all too well. He sat down and silently poured himself a black coffee from the cafetière.

The children had already finished eating and were upstairs cleaning their teeth and dressing under Freddie's supervision. Henry and Muffy were still halfway through their eggs and bacon, and looked at one another rather anxiously at Max's arrival.

'Are you hungry?' asked Muffy brightly. 'There's still some bacon and mushrooms in the pan. I could do you an egg if you want one.'

Max smiled. His sister-in-law and Hunter were probably the most wholly good people he had ever known. He wished he could be more like them.

'Not for me, thanks,' he said. 'I might do myself a bit of Marmite toast in a minute. I'm feeling a bit ropy.'

'You look it!' said Henry jovially. The more awkward a situation, the more he would try to joke his way out of it.

'I'm sorry about last night,' said Max. 'I was unforgivably rude.'

'Nonsense, forget about it,' said Henry. 'Had a few too many after work, I expect, eh? Drowning the old sorrows? Ow!' He looked reproachfully at his wife, who had just given him a sharp kick on the ankle. 'What was that for?'

'I'm sure Max doesn't want to talk about it,' said Muffy firmly, with what was meant to be a 'meaningful' look at Henry, and involved her opening her blue eyes very wide and raising one eyebrow. She looked like Felicity Kendall from *The Good Life* trying to do a Roger Moore impression.

'Honestly.' Max grinned at them both. 'It's all right. You don't have to tread on eggshells. Siena is getting married. I'm just going to have to deal with it.'

'Oh, good,' said Henry. 'I'm glad you said that. The lovely Frédérique seemed to be worried that you were "in denial", as she puts it. I told her you were just too smashed to take it all in. Have you been teaching her all this Californian psychobabble, Maxy? I do wish you wouldn't, you know, the poor child's here to learn English.'

Muffy's eyebrow had taken on a frenzied life of its own.

'*What?*' said Henry, unable to ignore her any longer. 'Have you got some sort of tic?'

'Poor Freddie,' said Max, who wasn't really focusing on the private battle between husband and wife. He had woken up this morning to the sound of Caroline's words ringing in his ears: 'You need to let that girl go.' 'I'm afraid I was a bit of a shit to her last night. Where is she? I'd better go and build some bridges.'

He found her upstairs in the bathroom, vainly trying to insert a Little Mermaid toothbrush into Madeleine's mouth while giving Bertie detailed instructions on shoelace tying.

'Uncle Max!' squealed Maddie when she saw him, spraying toothpaste foam all over Freddie's sweater. She jumped up and launched herself into his arms.

'Hello, lovely.' He kissed her on the neck, making her giggle. 'How clean are those pegs, then?'

She withdrew the toothbrush from her mouth and grinned at him, proudly revealing a rather gappy row of milk teeth. 'Perfect. I'm finished,' she announced, wriggling free from him and running off down the corridor before Freddie had a chance to stop her.

'Bertie, mate, do you think you could do that in your own room?' Max asked his nephew. 'I'd like to talk to Frédérique on her own.'

'Sure,' said Bertie, beaming. He loved it when his uncle called him 'mate'. It made him feel really grown up. Stamping down the back of his shoes with his heel, he hobbled off after his sister.

Max perched on the edge of the bath next to Freddie and stared down at the floor.

'I'm sorry,' he said. 'I was being a jerk.'

'Yes, you were,' she agreed, to his surprise. But she allowed her hand to brush against his anyway, which Max took as a signal to put his arm around her.

'I didn't mean what I said. I'd had too much to drink. I was upset, but that's no excuse for taking it out on you. Do you forgive me?' He looked up at her and saw, with horror, that there were tears in her eyes. 'Oh God, sweetheart, I'm really sorry,' he said, pulling her to him. 'Please don't cry.'

She wiped her eyes on the back of her hand and looked at him, concentrating on his face in a way that made him feel deeply uncomfortable. It was as if she could see right through him. For a twenty-year-old, thought Max, Freddie could be very old and wise sometimes.

When she finally broke the silence, he wished she hadn't.

'You're still in love with her, aren't you?'

She didn't drop her gaze. Max had no choice but to look right at her when he replied.

'No. No, I'm not,' he said. 'This news, it just took me by surprise, that's all. Knocked me for six.' He tried to sound reassuring.

'Do you love me, Max?'

Freddie wasn't letting this one go. He knew how much it had cost her to ask the question, and he couldn't bear to cause her any more pain. Putting his arms around her again so she couldn't see his face when he spoke, he mumbled the only answer he could.

'Of course,' he said. 'Of course I do.'

But they both knew he was lying.

Chapter Forty-five

As it turned out, Max's suspicions about Siena and Randall's whirlwind engagement had not been entirely groundless.

After the disastrous AIDS benefit at the Beverly Hills Hotel, Siena had gone to bed and waited miserably for Randall to come home. By the time he did roll in, at almost five in the morning, smelling of liquor and women's perfume and with his shirt buttoned up wrong, she was an exhausted, nervous wreck.

'I suppose you've been with Miriam, have you?' she accused him tearfully. 'I just hope for both our sakes she didn't give you anything.'

Randall made no attempt to deny it. 'I'd rather have been with you,' he said, stripping down to his boxer shorts and climbing into bed beside her. 'But you made your feelings pretty clear at the hotel. You preferred to skulk back here and mope about your ex than come to the party with me.'

'That's not true,' she protested, but she was too exhausted to go over it all again. 'It's you I've been thinking about all night, not Max. And I certainly didn't ask you to go and fuck that cheap little slut. How could you, Randall?'

He turned to face her, propping himself up on his elbow.

Her eyes were puffy and red from crying, and her skin looked even paler than usual, washed out with exhaustion. Her new, shorter hair had relaxed from its earlier pinned and hairsprayed solidity, and fell about her face in soft, tangled waves. She looked like a frightened six-year-old who'd just woken up from a nightmare. Except with very big boobs, which she was covering defensively now with both hands, presumably against him.

'Who said I fucked her?' he asked, still gazing at Siena's beautiful naked body.

'You did.' She sounded confused, having been thrown a lifebelt of hope that perhaps, by some miracle, he *had* been faithful to her. 'You said you'd rather have been with me. Which means that you must have been with her, doesn't it?'

'Does it?' said Randall. He was being infuriatingly nonchalant about the whole thing.

'Oh, of course it does!' she cried, hitting him across the chest in frustration as she felt her glimmer of hope disappearing again.

'Well, would you actually care if I had?' he asked calmly, ignoring her near-hysteria. 'Fucked Miriam, I mean.'

'Would I care?' She stared at him incredulously. 'Of course I'd care, Randall. Why do you think I've been lying awake all night, crying my goddam eyes out? Of course I fucking care.'

At which point he had rolled on top of her and made love to her more tenderly than ever before.

For the next three hours, he had gently and expertly licked and teased and caressed her, bringing her to climax again and again, until they were both too exhausted to move. And afterwards, as she was drifting off into a deeply contented, sexually replete sleep, he had asked her to marry him.

By the time Siena woke, it was almost three in the afternoon, and Randall had gone. She leapt out of bed in a panic, terrified that last night's events – the ones at the end, anyway – had been some sort of dream.

But there in the bathroom, propped up on her dresser, was a note from Randall. It said he had gone to the office and wouldn't be back until late – but perhaps tomorrow, if he could get away in time, he would take her out for dinner to celebrate their engagement.

Siena read the note a few times – just to make sure she wasn't seeing things – and sank down on to the toilet seat, weak with relief. He was really going to marry her. It was going to be OK.

Relief was definitely the overwhelming emotion, not joy. She knew she didn't love Randall, or at least, she wasn't in love with him, not with the same blind, trusting passion she'd felt for Max. But she now saw that as a good thing.

As Randall's wife, she would be guaranteed a life of wealth, fame and privilege. She would no longer have to keep looking over her shoulder, waiting for everything she had, all her security, to be snatched away on somebody else's whim. Marriage to Randall meant a safety net, and the only kind of security you could count on – financial.

Her relief that he was finally, and against all the odds, about to make a commitment to her was profound and intense. For the first time since Max had betrayed her, she felt she could breathe easy.

Randall, by contrast, had had a somewhat stressful awakening when he remembered his rash promise of the night before. He'd been so drunk, and so horny, his libido having already been awakened by a truly expert blow job from Miriam at Johnny's party, that he'd got rather carried away.

Siena's extreme vulnerability always turned him on anyway. It made him feel strong. But the real killer last night had been when she'd told him that she actually cared for him. Not for the money, for him.

Since he'd made his fortune, no woman had ever said that to him and meant it, as he was sure Siena did. That made her different, special.

But marriage? What the hell was he thinking?

Randall had already decided long ago that he would never share his life or his fortune with anyone. He didn't want children, and he'd seen too many wealthy guys go bankrupt that way.

His first thought on getting out of bed was that he would have to get out of it as soon as possible. Just tell her he was joking, he was drunk, anything. But as he started to shave and dress, he gradually began to perceive the upside in the situation.

An engagement would be fabulous publicity for the movie, which he desperately, desperately needed. It might also calm Siena down, make her ease up on the histrionics both at home and on-set. Recently she'd been wearing her insecurity on her sleeve to a degree that even Randall had found alarming.

Then there was the other-women factor. Not that he ever had much problem attracting beautiful girls, but there was no doubt that being seen as 'off the market' seemed only to encourage the most rapacious and best-looking gold-diggers. Yes, on second thoughts, a very public engagement would have its advantages.

It wasn't as if he had to go through with the wedding.

As it turned out, his predictions proved completely correct.

Not only did the leaking of the news, and the carefully choreographed denials of an engagement, generate massive world-wide interest in both them as a couple and the film, but Siena also visibly relaxed from the moment she got the ring – an absolutely enormous ruby that had cost more than his entire collection of Bentleys – on her finger.

Her one continuing concern was the question of setting a date. But so far he had been able to wriggle out of that fairly easily by insisting that neither of them would have time to focus on a wedding until after *1943* had wrapped.

One evening in early November, he had come home to find Siena looking unusually morose.

She was curled up on the sofa in the small sitting room next to the kitchen, watching reruns of *I Dream of Jeannie* and smoking. An overflowing ashtray and a large pile of discarded sweet wrappers lay on the table beside her, and there was a bottle of wine, as yet unopened, at her feet.

'What are you doing in here?' he asked, picking up the remote and switching off the TV before removing the lit cigarette from her hand and stubbing it out.

He hated her smoking even though he himself was not averse to the occasional cigar.

'Hey.' She sounded annoyed. 'I was watching that.'

She reached for another cigarette, like a naughty child wilfully defying its parents, seeing how far it could push them. But Randall immediately snatched away the packet, and began drawing back the closed curtains, allowing the early evening sunlight to penetrate the smoky gloom.

'No smoking in this house, Siena.' He crushed the Marlboros in his fat hand and dropped the battered remnants in the waste bin. 'You know that. What's the matter with you this evening?'

He sounded less than sympathetic. Randall found female mood swings supremely boring.

'If I tell you, do you promise you won't get mad?'

'No,' he said, sitting down beside her. He hoped there hadn't been yet another problem on-set.

'It's Hunter,' said Siena, to his initial relief, although he noticed that her bottom lip was already starting to wobble ominously. 'I called him.' Randall looked stony faced. 'I know you said I shouldn't,' she went on nervously. 'But it just seemed so weird that we haven't spoken at all, you know, since it happened.'

'Since what happened?'

Siena frowned, surprised. 'Since we got engaged, of course,' she said. 'Honestly, darling. It's a big thing, you know, agreeing to spend the rest of your life with someone. I wanted him to know.'

'Oh, yeah. Right.' Randall got up and walked over to the bar to fix himself a drink. 'Honey,' he said brusquely, sitting back down with a large iced vodka in his hand, 'you didn't need to call him. He knows. The whole world knows, OK? Hunter may not be the sharpest tool in the box but he can read, right? The engagement's been all over the press from here to Timbuktu.'

'Ha, ha,' said Siena sarcastically. 'Yes, he can read, and yes, I'm sure he's heard about it. But he hasn't heard it from me. We haven't spoken.'

'So?' said Randall. He was getting tired of listening to Siena moaning on about a family that evidently didn't give a shit about her.

'That's his problem, not yours. He's the one who stormed off like a spoilt kid at the Dodgers game. Forget about him, baby. Move on.'

Siena wondered, not for the first time, whether this was what Randall really felt. Could he really not see that they were the ones who had behaved badly at the Dodgers, by setting Hunter up? That she was the one who owed him an apology, not the other way around?

'Well, what did he say anyway?' Randall asked, in a tone that made it clear he had very little interest in Hunter's opinions one way or the other. 'He didn't approve?'

'Nothing,' Siena mumbled miserably. 'He wouldn't take my call. I spoke to that stupid cow Tiffany, and she told me to go to hell.'

For some reason, this seemed to make Randall irate. He stood up and began pacing like a tiger preparing for the kill. 'He wouldn't take your call? *He*, that two-bit little soap queen, wouldn't take *your* call?'

Siena couldn't quite see why this should incense him so much. As upset as she was, she was hardly surprised that Hunter didn't want to speak to her after the way she'd treated him this past year. She'd been so desperate to hold on to Randall and her career, she'd dropped him like a hot brick, for no better reason than that Randall had told her to.

She didn't deserve his blessing, on her engagement or anything else in her life.

'Well, it did hurt me,' she began.

But Randall was still ranting, less concerned about Siena's feelings than with whipping himself up into a fury of indignation. 'How dare he? I mean, who the fuck does he think he is?'

'Look, maybe I shouldn't have mentioned it,' said Siena, who was starting to get concerned by the violence of his reaction.

'Of course you should have mentioned it.' In an instant he turned his displeasure on her. Sitting right in front of him, she made a far more satisfying target than the absent and untouchable Hunter. She shrank back, bewildered, as he glowered down at her angrily, feeling like Jack after he'd just climbed the beanstalk and disturbed the sleeping giant.

'If you ever start keeping secrets from me, Siena, that's it,' he snarled viciously. 'From that moment on, it's over between us. I'll destroy you.'

'Randall, please,' she pleaded, trying to calm him down. 'There's no need to get so upset. I'm not keeping secrets. You asked me what was wrong and I told you.'

The fear in her voice was like petrol on his flames.

'Oh, you told me, did you?' He slammed his drink down on the table and bent his face threateningly low over hers. 'And what about what I told you? I expressly told you never to abase yourself by crawling back to Hunter, or any of the rest of your useless, fucked-up family. And what do you do? The second my back's turned, you're on that phone like a tragic little groupie. And he won't even talk to you!'

Siena shuddered. She could smell Randall's sour breath, like bile pouring out of him. He hadn't flown off the handle at her like this for months, and she had no idea why her call to Hunter should have triggered such a catastrophic relapse.

'You've embarrassed me, and you've embarrassed yourself,' he announced finally, looking at her as though she were something unpleasant he might be forced to disinfect.

'I'm sorry,' said Siena, by now desperate to appease him. 'I was just so happy about us being engaged, and I haven't had anyone to share it with.'

'What do you mean, you haven't had anyone to share it with?' Randall sounded incredulous. 'The whole world's been talking about it. Look!'

He picked up a copy of last week's *New York Times* magazine from the coffee table behind him, still open at the picture of the two of them together at Cannes, and shoved it under Siena's nose.

'I know,' she said, staring at the image. 'But I meant . . .' She was walking on eggshells now, anxious to choose her words carefully and not provoke him any further. 'I meant, I had nobody to share the news with that I love, or that loves me. That's all.'

'Everybody loves you, Siena,' said Randall, pointing to the picture again, more gently this time, and kissing the top of her head, the storm of his anger now apparently subsided. Whether he had wilfully misunderstood her or not, she couldn't tell. She was just relieved the shouting had stopped.

'Now why don't you go upstairs and get changed.' His tone was suddenly brisk and businesslike again. 'I'm taking you to Morton's tonight, remember, with Luke and Sabrina.'

Shit, she'd forgotten. Dinner with her director and his tedious sculptor wife was the last thing she felt like, especially now. Rows with Randall were so terrifying, they always left her utterly emotionally exhausted.

'And don't forget to clean your teeth again, will you?' he added, downing the last of his vodka. 'You know I can't stand the smell of cigarettes on your breath.'

Dinner was every bit as gruesome as Siena had feared.

Luke was a sweetheart – the two of them had been getting on much better now that things had improved on-set – but his wife was terribly pretentious, one of those artistic types who bang on about how much better the Norton Simon is than the Getty, and isn't it a tragedy that they can't move back to New York where the people are so much more *real*?

Sabrina also made the mistake of assuming that because Siena had made her name as a model, she must be stupid.

'I must say, the recent modern American sculpture exhibition at the Getty was a disgrace, wasn't it, Luke? Did you see it, Randall?'

'No, I'm afraid not.' Randall smiled, trying to be polite. He couldn't stomach Sabrina any more than Siena could. 'I don't have a lot of free time for museums and things.'

'Of course you don't,' Sabrina agreed obsequiously, before turning with a patronising smirk to Siena. 'I expect it's not really your sort of thing either, is it, my dear?'

'No, it's not,' said Siena rudely. Unlike Randall, she saw no point in being polite to the hairy-legged old frump, or engaging her in conversation a moment longer than was necessary.

'I expect you're more interested in fashion and things, aren't you? With your modelling background,' Sabrina went on, ignoring the warning glances from her husband.

'Not really,' said Siena. 'Fashion's boring. I was always better at maths and science at school. I had a place at Oxford to read medicine, actually, but I turned it down.'

Sabrina looked suitably amazed.

'My father wanted me to be a doctor, but I wasn't interested. Where did you go to college, by the way?'

Siena watched with satisfaction as Sabrina was forced to mumble, 'Penn State.'

'Oh. Well, that's a good school too,' She smiled. It was her turn to be patronising now. 'I always felt university was a bit of a waste of time, though. I knew I wanted to act from day one, and modelling's a much more effective route into Hollywood than an Oxford degree. At least it was for me.'

She placed her perfectly manicured hand smugly on Randall's arm. That would teach the stupid, bossy cow to put her down.

'I think you would have made it eventually, Siena, with or without the modelling,' said Luke, anxious to get his wife off the hook and change the subject as soon as possible.

Siena beamed with pleasure at the unexpected compliment from her director. 'Do you really?'

'Sure,' Randall answered for him. 'With your surname and my backing, how could you go wrong?'

Bastard, thought Siena. Why could he never admit that she had any talent of her own?

Luke, who could see how wounded she'd been by Randall's comment, decided to risk his producer's wrath still further by saying, 'Actually, I think she'd have made it anyway. Being a McMahon doesn't hurt, but if you couldn't act, you'd never have got this far. Not in one of my movies, anyway. Believe me, I've seen so many stars' kids in Hollywood trying to break into the business, and most of them are terrible.'

Siena could have kissed him. But her elation soon evaporated when she saw Randall's face, and the familiar simmering fury building up inside him as he twisted his napkin round and round, like he was preparing to strangle someone. As far as he was concerned, he had 'created' Siena. No one else, least of all herself, could take any credit for her current achievements.

Watching him, she felt a knot forming in her stomach and realised, almost with shame, that she was afraid of him. She wondered whether this was how Grandma Minnie had felt every time she caved in to Duke. For the first time that she could remember, she felt a stab of real sympathy for her grandmother. Perhaps she and Minnie were more alike than she had liked to believe?

Sabrina, who was also none too thrilled with her husband's impassioned defence of his beautiful leading lady, suddenly stood up and started waving at a party who had just arrived.

'Suzie! Helloooo, over here.' She flapped her arms wildly, as if trying to bring a plane in to land. Siena rolled her eyes at Randall, but he was still too angry to respond.

'Luke, darling, look. It's Suzie Ong. And isn't that your uncle with her, Siena? The actor?'

Siena, who had her back to the door, froze.

She couldn't bring herself to turn around.

'I don't think so,' she muttered desperately.

Please, please, let it not be Hunter, not tonight. That would push Randall right over the edge.

Luke noticed that the blood had drained from Siena's face. She looked like she'd seen a ghost. 'Are you all right?' he whispered.

'It is him, you know, I'm sure of it.' Sabrina's voice was like a foghorn. 'Suzie! Come and say hello! She's *terribly* nice,' she said in an aside to Randall. 'She's a television director over at NBC.'

'I know who she is,' he snapped, glaring at Siena as though she were somehow responsible for Suzie and Hunter's arrival. Suzie was one of Hugh Orchard's protégées, an elegant Singaporean in her mid-thirties who was becoming well known as an up-and-coming director in the TV world. She already had a fistful of hit shows to her name, and had directed Hunter in the last two series of *UCLA*, presiding over the soap's skyrocketing ratings, much to Orchard's and NBC's delight.

A few moments later she appeared at the table, looking rather awkward. Siena didn't know whether Hunter was with her or not. She was too terrified to look up and find out.

'Hello, Sabrina. Luke.' Suzie seemed less than thrilled to see them.

'Suzie, let me introduce you to Randall Stein.' Sabrina was obviously enjoying her role as hostess to Hollywood's elite. Randall gave a grudging nod of acknowledgement, which Suzie returned. 'And Siena McMahon. I imagine you two have already crossed paths?'

'No, actually,' said Suzie, looking at Siena coldly. She knew how the spoiled little brat had treated Hunter and was not one of her biggest fans. 'Hi.'

Siena's head seemed to be magnetically drawn to the table. She still couldn't look up.

'Isn't that Siena's uncle with you?' Sabrina ploughed on, oblivious to the entire table's discomfort. 'Why don't you both come over and join us?'

'I don't think so,' said Suzie and Randall in unison. Their eyes met for a moment, but Suzie dropped hers first. The man looked positively murderous. 'Hunter and I have a lot of business to discuss. Maybe another time. But it was lovely to see you.'

She kissed both Luke and Sabrina perfunctorily on the cheek and disappeared back to Hunter and her table. Siena felt as if she were about to spontaneously combust. She could feel the imagined heat of Hunter's stare on her back and Randall's fury beside her. She dared not look at either of them, but sat twisting her engagement ring round and round on her finger, wishing someone would beam her out of there.

'I wonder what was wrong with her?' said Sabrina to nobody in particular. 'She seemed in a great hurry to get away.'

'Yes,' said Randall nastily. 'Siena sometimes has that effect on people.'

'I'm sorry.' Siena stumbled to her feet. This was all too much for her. Hunter was here, her darling, darling Hunter, and he wouldn't even speak to her. Suddenly she had to get away.

The whole restaurant looked on mesmerised as she stood up and began ricocheting off tables, blinded by tears, running towards the door as if the room were on fire.

'Siena.'

Hunter shot out his arm and grabbed her by the wrist as she

staggered past him. Shaking, she glanced down and saw his sweet, sad, concerned face looking up at her. 'Do you wanna talk?'

She felt as if she were in one of those nightmares where you're trying to run but your legs are stuck in mud. She wanted to fall into his arms, to tell him how much she loved him, how much she'd missed him, to say how sorry she was. But her brain and body both seemed to be frozen, and she just stood there miserably mute. Randall was behind her before she could say a word.

'No, she doesn't want to talk.' He smiled evilly at Hunter. Pulling Siena away from him and putting his arm around her shoulder, he looked more like her jailer than her lover. 'She doesn't ever want to talk to you or hear from you again. It upsets her. Doesn't it, Siena?' He jerked her round to face Hunter, rather as a ventriloquist might jerk his dummy. It was a violent, almost obscene gesture. A few of the women in the room winced. Siena nodded helplessly. 'You see? She doesn't want you,' Randall sneered. Hunter just stared at him, appalled. 'Now if you'll excuse me, I need to take Siena home. Before she gets any more upset.'

With the entire restaurant watching, including a horrified Luke and Sabrina, he bundled Siena outside and straight into their waiting chauffeur-driven Bentley. As soon as they were ensconced behind the darkened glass windows, she broke down in tears.

'I'm sorry, Randall,' she sobbed. She was shaking like a leaf. 'I'm so sorry.'

'You will be,' he said.

And then he punched her so hard in the face she was knocked out cold.

Chapter Forty–six

When she came to, she was sitting up in bed at home in just her underwear. Her hands were tied tightly behind her back, she wasn't sure what with. Randall was sitting in the armchair beside the bed, staring at her, with a half-empty bottle of brandy at his feet.

Siena could smell the stale alcohol fumes from the bed. His voice was badly slurred when he spoke to her.

'You stupid bitch,' he whispered. 'You just had to humiliate me, didn't you? You can't help yourself.'

Siena shifted uneasily from side to side and tried to keep calm. The whole right side of her face felt as if it were exploding, but out of her left eye she could see that the bedside clock said 2.30 a.m. She struggled to get her bearings. The last thing she remembered was Randall hitting her in the car. He hadn't been drunk then – at least, she hadn't thought so. Clearly he was looped up to the eyeballs now.

'Randall, could you please untie my hands. This is ridiculous.'

She tried a firm, confident tone, hoping to jolt him out of this madness. She always knew he could be violent, but he had never pulled anything like this before. Not with her anyway.

'You think you could have got to where you are without me? You and *Luke*. Is that what you think?' He had stood up and was advancing unsteadily towards her, his brandy glass still in his hands.

'Of course not,' said Siena. 'I know how much I owe you.' She tried not to sound as panicked as she felt. 'Luke wasn't trying to insult you.'

'Shut up! I don't want to hear about fucking *Luke*.'

She heard the roar of his voice in her ear, followed by a heavy blow to her left temple. For a moment she felt nothing at all, as if everything were happening in slow motion, or to someone else. Then she became aware of a stream of her own blood flowing down her face, into her eyes and mouth.

He must have smashed the glass into her head.

Her hands were tied, so she couldn't reach up to touch the wound.

Suddenly terror overwhelmed her. She felt like she was drowning in blood.

He hit her again, and this time she felt the jagged glass as it sliced into the flesh around her eye. Everything went red.

'Jesus Christ,' she spluttered, tiny droplets of blood spraying off her lips like a red mist. 'What have you done to me?'

Randall stood stock still and stared at the broken glass in his hand as if he'd never seen it before. Two of his fingers were bleeding slightly.

'Shit, I'm sorry. Oh, shit.' He sounded detached, zombie-like. 'Here, let me help.'

He pulled out a screwed-up handkerchief and moved across the bed towards her. Siena screamed, and kicked out at him as hard as she could, both legs pumping like fury.

'Stay the fuck away from me,' she yelled. 'Stay back!'

Instinctively, Randall fought off her frenzied kicking. One of Siena's feet hit him hard across the bridge of the nose. He yelped in pain and instantly brought his heavy fist down with a crack on her rib cage, right where she'd suffered the fractures after her car crash last year. It was agony. A second punch caught her across the left side of the face, so hard she thought she felt her cheekbone splinter.

Not even the adrenalin pumping violently through her veins could take away the searing pain of Randall's blows. He was a big man, and even with her hands free she would have been powerless against him. She slumped forward, doubled over in pain, the blood from her face cascading on to the white linen sheets.

This time, when he moved towards her, she had not one ounce of energy left with which to fight him. She was only dimly aware of him untying her wrists, and later slipped in and out of consciousness when he brought towels and warm water from the bathroom and pressed them inexpertly to her face, making her cry out in pain. The last thing she remembered was Randall holding a bloodied towel and looking bewildered, asking her over and over again, 'Why, Siena? Why did you make me do it?'

'I'll do what I can, but it won't be easy.'

She awoke disoriented to hear a strange man's voice. She tried to open her eyes to look around her but nothing happened. She whimpered in terror.

'Who's there? I can't see. Why can't I see anything?'

The next voice she heard was Randall's. He sounded sober and in control, almost businesslike. She could tell that he was standing on the far side of the room, and felt relief when he made no move to approach her.

'You're in a private surgery centre, darling, in Beverly Hills,' he told her. 'The doctors are going to take care of you.'

'What do you mean? What doctors?' She was becoming increasingly hysterical. 'I can't open my fucking eyes, Randall! What have you done to me?'

'What have *I* done to you?' He did his best to sound affronted. 'What on earth do you mean?'

'Try to keep calm Siena,' the strange voice said, before she had a chance to respond. It was a soothing, gentle voice, and it was close to her, either sitting on or leaning over the side of her bed. 'I'm going to give you something to help you relax and keep numbing the pain.'

She felt a slight prick in her arm and a quite pleasant, cool sensation as some nameless liquid was pumped into her veins. Instantly her head felt heavy and she slumped back on to the pillows. She could also feel her heart rate dropping, and a surreal mood of calm flooding her senses. It was a quite wonderful, almost blissful peace.

'You've had an accident,' the voice continued. 'I'm Dr Sanford, and I'm going to help you get well.'

'I can't see,' whispered Siena.

Even through her drug-induced stupor, she kept a dogged hold of that one, terrifying fact.

'Randall tells me you fell,' said the doctor. 'Into a glass cabinet. There's been some damage to your eyes, but we won't know how serious it is until we operate. Are you happy for me to operate, Siena?'

She groaned drowsily.

After a long pause, she said, 'I want to see the police. I want . . .' She stopped, apparently exhausted by the effort and concentration involved in speaking. 'I want to report him. Randall. He attacked me.'

The doctor sighed and looked nervously across at his client. This wasn't the first time Randall Stein had brought him a battered girl in the small hours of the morning. But usually they were prostitutes or starlets, whose silence could easily be bought, not world-famous film stars. And in any case, none of them had had injuries even approaching the seriousness of Siena's.

It was a tragedy. The girl's face had been shredded. She would never look the same again.

Both he and Randall had hoped that her concussion would be serious enough for her to have lost her memory of the attack. Clearly, though, this wasn't the case.

'The police? Well, that's your right, of course,' he responded cautiously. 'But I really think we should focus on treating your injuries before anything else. I'll leave you alone for a few minutes to think about it.'

'No!' Siena screamed. She was clearly terrified of being left alone with Randall.

'It's all right,' said Dr Sanford, taking her hand and stroking it until she began to breathe normally. Despite having made vast sums of money over the years thanks to his 'discretion' as Randall's private doctor, even he was disgusted by what he had seen tonight. The girl could have died. If he weren't already so deeply implicated in so many of Randall's past 'accidents', he would have gone to the police himself. 'He won't hurt you, I promise,' he said, with a meaningful look that was not lost on Randall. 'I'll be right outside the door.'

'Stay where you are or I'll scream,' said Siena, the moment she heard the door click shut. Her voice was slurred and drowsy, but Randall could tell she meant what she said and didn't move.

'Fine,' he said calmly. 'But I'd think very carefully before screaming, if I were you. To the police or anyone else.'

He took a small cigarillo from his inside jacket pocket and lit it. Siena could hear this little ritual and smell the sweet tobacco smoke wafting across the room towards her.

'Let's look at your options, shall we?' Randall went on. 'You can tell the police that I attacked you. For which, in any case, they will only have your word against mine.'

'I think,' she said derisively, 'my injuries speak for themselves.'

'Do you?' Randall seemed unconcerned. 'Well, perhaps. Or perhaps the word of a well-respected producer and *very* generous benefactor of the LAPD will count for more than that of a young actress already known to be highly emotionally unstable. Who knows?' Siena opened her mouth to protest, but found that she was overwhelmed with exhaustion. That shot in the arm had really knocked her out. 'In either event, at that point will begin a long, protracted and very expensive legal battle that you are in no financial position to fight.'

'What do you mean?' she challenged him. 'Of course I can fight you. I've got my own money.'

'Two hundred and fifty-eight thousand dollars, to be precise,' said Randall. 'Of the two million you gave me to invest last year, I'm afraid that's all that's left. In your name, that is.'

'Liar!' she snarled. 'That's impossible. You can't have lost that much in a year. And if you have, that's negligence. I'll sue you for every fucking cent.'

'Again, an expensive business, suing people.' He puffed out smoke luxuriously. It was so long since Siena had even attempted to stand up to him, he was quite enjoying the thrill of the fight. 'Particularly when one is being sued oneself.'

'Oh, *you're* going to sue *me* are you?' She wanted to laugh, but even with the painkillers the pain in her chest was too much. 'What for? Damaging your brandy glass? Staining the fucking bedspread with my blood?'

'No,' said Randall, still clinically composed. 'For deliberately delaying production on the movie. For libel, if you try to blame your accidental injuries on me. And for breach of contract. After all, you're hardly able to continue playing Peggy now, are you? After your drunken fall. I'm afraid you've well and truly lost your looks, sweetheart.'

He started to laugh, but Siena wasn't listening. She had no idea whether what he'd said about the money was true, and she wasn't even sure if she cared. Her brain was a fog of anger, drugs and pain. All she knew was that she might never be able to see again. And if she did, would she even recognise herself after what he'd done to her? The thought of her ravaged face suddenly made her feel violently sick.

'Pass me something,' she said, clasping both hands over her mouth.

Randall picked up a steel bowl by the bed, presumably placed there for the purpose, and put it in her hands. He watched while she retched and retched until her stomach was utterly empty. The pain in her ribs and face was so bad, and the effort of throwing up so exhausting, that she fell back against the pillows and began to cry.

That was when he knew he had her.

Silently, he took away the bowl of vomit and put it in the far corner of the room, wrinkling his nose in distaste. When he spoke it was quietly, and with menacing intent.

'If you go after me Siena, believe me, I will crush you.'

She did believe him. Hadn't he crushed her already?

'But if you keep your mouth shut, I'll help you. As much as I can. We'll come up with a convincing story together, and we'll see what can be done about recovering some of your money.'

She didn't trust him for a second. But realistically, what other choice did she have? She had no family, no friends that she could turn to. Even if she had, she'd be too ashamed for anyone to see her like this, to know what she had allowed Randall to do to her. She had, it appeared, very little money and her career was shot to pieces. She had almost certainly lost her looks for ever, and possibly her sight as well.

She was helpless.

'What do you want me to do?' she asked eventually.

The weariness in her voice said it all.

'Nothing,' said Randall. 'Just keep your mouth shut, and I'll do what needs to be done. If you need surgery, we'll do that here, first. Then you disappear somewhere to recuperate. I have a house in Nantucket we could use.' He was thinking aloud. 'It's very private.'

'What about the movie?' she asked, numbly.

'We'll put it on hold for a few weeks, but chances are it's dead. Far too expensive to reshoot the lot now, and I can't see you ...' He hesitated, as if he'd suddenly decided he didn't want to hurt her any further. Taunting her didn't seem quite so much fun any more. 'Let's just say I can't see you getting well enough to go back to work. Not in the time we'd need anyway.'

Stubbing out his cigar, he came and sat down on the bed beside her. Relieved that she hadn't the strength to fight him, he now felt some stirrings of remorse.

It frightened him to think that he was responsible for the terrible wreckage of her face. It was almost more than he could admit, even to himself.

'I am sorry, Siena,' he said, picking up her limp hand in his and squeezing it. 'I didn't mean it, really. I want to take care of you now. If you'll let me.'

She made no response, and the two of them sat silently together for a few minutes until a gentle rap on the door announced that Dr Sanford had returned. He was relieved, and not a little surprised, to see that some sort of rapprochement seemed to have been reached.

'She wants you to operate,' said Randall, looking for all the world like the picture of the concerned fiancé at her bedside. 'As soon as possible.'

'Is that right?' the doctor asked Siena, shooing Randall away and taking her hand himself. 'Will you sign the consents?'

'I can't read the consents,' Siena reminded him. She sounded very weak and drowsy. 'But sure, I'll sign anything. Let's just get this over with.'

The initial operation on Siena's damaged eyes had been touch and go.

The surgeon was certain that she would have some vision in her left eye, where most of the damage had been caused by two burst blood vessels and a shattered socket from a single, powerful punch. But the right eye, which had been extensively scarred with shards of glass and where the cornea had been deeply lacerated, might never recover. Either way, it would be weeks before Siena could remove her dressings and bandages.

By the time the press cottoned on to the fact that she had mysteriously disappeared, Siena was already lying morphined up to the eyeballs, with her head completely bandaged like a mummy's in a guest bedroom in Randall's Nantucket house.

Her whereabouts, as far as Randall knew, were known only to himself, Dr Sanford and Melissa, the private nurse he had hired to care for Siena and escort her, via his private G4 jet, from LA to Boston and then on to the island. He had fed the media a story about Siena suffering some sort of breakdown from nervous exhaustion, and announced that he had suspended production on *1943* indefinitely.

After an initial flurry of interest, other, more exciting stories began to take over the headlines, especially once it became clear that no one knew where Siena was recuperating and there were no pictures to be had.

Hunter had called Randall at the house repeatedly in the first week to try to find out where she was, but had been forced to give up when Randall made public a letter, quite clearly in Siena's hand and signed by her, stating that she wanted time to recuperate in private and did not want her whereabouts to be disclosed to anyone other than her doctor and her boyfriend.

To Randall's surprise and relief, it really had been as simple as that.

As far as the rest of the world was concerned, within about a month it was almost as if Siena McMahon no longer existed.

Chapter Forty-seven

Claire sat in the back of the little plane, looking down at the tiny islands strewn just off the Boston coast.

She was dressed too warmly for the summer's day in a tweed skirt and stiff white linen blouse, with her sleek, grey-blonde hair covered by a blue polka-dot headscarf, and her anxious, worry-lined eyes shielded by big Christian Dior sunglasses.

None of the other passengers in the little pond-hopper of a plane gave her a second glance as they made the twenty-minute flight over to Nantucket. Later, at the airport, she would look like every other well-to-do WASP-y matron, carrying her small suitcase to her nondescript rented Chevrolet, no doubt on her way to join the rest of her family in one of the sprawling Quaker summer homes that littered the island.

Gazing out of the plane window, she sighed.

Deep down, she'd always known that she'd do this eventually. That one day, she'd wake up, walk out of the door and go and find her daughter.

Particularly since she'd hired Bill Jennings to start trailing Siena, Claire felt like her life had become one long emotional roller-coaster. On the one hand there was the torture of feeling so close to her child, and yet being unable to reach out to her or make contact. This pain, combined with the constant terror of Pete finding out and leaving her, or doing something even worse, had frequently pushed her to the point where she had considered calling the whole thing off.

On the other hand, the PI's reports had brought her such exquisite joy. She felt that, on one level, she had been privileged to have a private, personal insight into her daughter's life. Secreted away in her dressing room back home she now had groaning files crammed with pictures of Siena on the set of her movie, as well as even more cherished, if grainier, shots of her relaxing at home alone. In some of these pictures, the earlier ones taken just after her road accident, she seemed happy. And her happiness meant more to Claire than anything else in the world.

But then there were other shots, particularly recently, that had caused her indescribable pain. Pictures Bill had reluctantly given her which no mother should ever have to see.

She had known for months that Siena had become miserable and isolated living with Randall, but still she had prevaricated, hesitating to make contact in case she unwittingly pushed Pete over the edge. Perhaps she had also, subconsciously, been hoping that in her all too evident unhappiness, Siena would take the initiative and reach out to her family herself.

In the end, though, it was Siena's 'disappearance' which had finally convinced her she couldn't afford to wait any longer. Bill had only very incomplete evidence about what might have happened, but he sensed that Siena could be in serious danger. It had taken him an agonising three weeks to track her down to the house on Nantucket, and when he told Claire he'd found her, that was it.

Suddenly, it didn't even seem like a choice any more.

After five long years of separation, wild horses could not have kept her from boarding that plane.

Once they'd landed, she pulled out of the tiny airport and on to the single-track road towards Siasconset and checked her mobile for messages from Pete.

There were none.

Relieved, she began to take in the grey, weather-boarded houses lining the route, their immaculately kept dark green hedges and formal gardens adding splashes of colour to an otherwise flat, marshy landscape.

Although real estate values on the island had skyrocketed since the eighties, so that even fairly modest homes were now worth upward of five million dollars, the plain Quaker architecture ensured that Nantucket retained its essentially humble charm. There were none of the vulgar edifices that defaced LA lining its beautiful beaches, and the villages still had the look and feel of real, working communities, despite the fact that these days even the postman could probably have traded in his home for a cool million, bought himself a Ferrari and moved off-island to Boston in luxurious retirement.

It was amazing really, thought Claire, that more of the locals hadn't cashed in on the property market and made a quick killing, leaving Nantucket exclusively to super-rich tourists like herself. But they hadn't. Some of the old folk loved to tell the wealthy New Yorkers how they had lived in the same house for forty years and seen its value go from two thousand dollars to two million, but that they would never sell.

There was a magic about Nantucket, it seemed, something that you could never put a price tag on. Not in dollars anyway.

As she drew nearer to the village of Siasconset, the large homes were replaced by tiny doll's-house cottages, complete with white picket fences, climbing roses and ornate topiary, many with ornamental hedges cut into the shape of a whale, in tribute to Nantucket's whaling history.

Although she hadn't been to the island since she was a teenager, the strict building regulations meant that Siasconset village had hardly changed at all since the sixties, and Claire found her bearings quite easily.

The Chanticleer restaurant was still there, and still packed with wealthy East Coast honeymooners, sipping champagne and eating lobster salads out on the terrace. The village store on the little triangular green was also just as she remembered it, although perhaps there were even more bicycles parked outside it than in the old days, drawn to the new sandwich-and-picnic shop that had sprung up next door.

Parking her car at the green, she picked up an official-looking sheaf of documents from the passenger seat and, leaving her suitcase in the boot, began walking down the sandy track towards the beach.

The house, unless she was very much mistaken, was only a couple of hundred yards up the track on the right-hand side. Bill had told her that it was entirely concealed from the road behind a massive yew hedge but that, this being Nantucket, there was no security presence or electric gates. She would be able to walk right up to the front door and, she hoped, within a few short minutes would be reunited with her daughter.

Her hands shook so much as she crunched her way along the gravel drive and up to the porch and she fretted that she might drop her papers. Although hot, it was very windy, and if she let them out of her grasp for an instant they'd be snatched up and carried off like Dorothy's house in *The Wizard of Oz*.

Suddenly, standing on the steps, she stopped.

She found herself crippled with fear and self-doubt.

What was she doing here? Would Siena even want to see her? What if she were furious and wanted nothing more to do with her?

Claire could hardly blame her if that were the case.

And then there was Pete. How was he going to react if he found out, or rather *when* he found out, what she was really doing in Nantucket?

She'd told him she was visiting an old school friend, but sensed that he was already becoming suspicious. He'd be angry, of course, when he found out, furious even. But would he understand *why* she'd done it? Would he see that she just couldn't stay away any more, not now, not with Siena seriously ill and alone?

She forced herself to calm down and took two long, deep breaths, pushing the image of an apoplectic, wounded Peter from her mind. She couldn't think about any of that now. All that mattered was getting into that house, and finding her baby.

She pulled back the heavy brass knocker and banged it firmly three times against the wooden door, with a lot more confidence than she felt. After what seemed like decades, a woman about her own age, perhaps a few years younger, opened the door a fraction and glared out at her suspiciously.

'Can I help you?'

She was wearing a formal nurse's uniform and reminded Claire of the terribly strict old matron at her East Coast boarding school. Summoning up all her courage, and helped by a sudden surge of adrenalin, she began her well-rehearsed lines.

'Can you help *me*?' She chuckled, as though the woman had made some inadvertent joke. 'Well, aren't you Melissa Evans?'

Caught off guard, the nurse confirmed it. 'Do I know you?'

'Well, no,' said Claire, smiling broadly. 'You don't. But I hope you're expecting me. I'm Annie Gordon, your relief support.'

Melissa looked blank.

'Hasn't Mr Stein called you?' said Claire, furrowing her brow in surprise. 'Poor man, he must be out of his mind with worry. Here.' She handed over the documents to a wary-looking Melissa, who gave them a cursory read. 'This should explain everything.'

'You're a nurse?' she said eventually, frowning at the last page of Claire's paperwork.

Claire felt her stomach give a nervous lurch. She hoped Bill hadn't made any glaring mistakes on her false résumé and the forged letter of employment from Randall.

'Why else would I be here?' She tried another smile, but Melissa still looked unconvinced. There was nothing for it, Claire decided, but to try to bluff it out. 'Maybe we should give Mr Stein a call?' she suggested. 'I know how important security is to him. Perhaps you'd feel better if you checked things out with him yourself? I'm in no rush, believe me.'

She turned away slightly and moved down a step, a calculated gesture designed to make the other woman feel less threatened.

It worked.

Melissa hesitated. Then, looking at Claire's naturally open and honest face, she smiled herself and said, 'Oh, no, I don't think that'll

418

be necessary, Annie. You must be absolutely exhausted after all that travelling. Come in, come in.'

Claire stepped over the threshold and tried to stifle her sigh of relief.

She'd made it. She was here.

Inside, the house looked elegant but low key, not at all what she had pictured Randall's taste to be, and certainly nothing like the pictures Bill had shown her of his opulent Malibu mansion. Not that she was really concerned with her surroundings. She wondered where Siena was, but didn't want to over-play her hand by asking too many questions too soon.

As it turned out, she didn't have to.

'I'll get you a cup of coffee and show you around in a minute,' said Melissa. Now that Claire had won her trust, it seemed she was glad of someone to talk to after being cooped up in the house, effectively alone, for weeks. The information came pouring out of her like water from a sieve.

'Siena is up there.' She pointed to a room leading directly off the top of the staircase. 'Sleeping. She's still sleeping an awful lot, thanks to the painkillers, up to seventeen, eighteen hours a day.'

That didn't sound good. Claire tried not to look shocked. 'What painkillers is she on?' she asked as nonchalantly as she could.

'Still on the morphine, but Doctor wants us to bring it down in the next few days, move her on to co-proxamol,' said Melissa. 'Don't you have a suitcase, by the way?'

'Oh, yes,' said Claire absently. Morphine? What the hell had happened to her? Bill had told her about the facial bandages, but Claire had assumed they might have been for something cosmetic. You didn't take morphine for a nose job. 'I parked at the green,' she managed to explain. 'Thought I'd walk around a bit, get my bearings.'

'It's beautiful here, don't you think?' Melissa enthused, drawing the reluctant Claire away from the hallway and Siena's room and into the kitchen, where she began reheating the already brewed coffee. Claire sat down at the table and tried to concentrate on what the nurse was saying. 'Although I haven't had much chance to enjoy it yet, as obviously I can't leave her. Milk? Sugar?' Claire nodded. 'Hopefully I'll be able to get out and have a break now that you're here.'

'Hopefully,' said Claire.

The next ten minutes, spent sipping her unwanted coffee and listening to Melissa prattle on about everything from the grocery deliveries to Randall's paranoia about outsiders, and his miserliness as a boss, were sheer torture. It was all she could do to restrain herself from rushing up the stairs two at a time, breaking down the door and taking her daughter in her arms. But she knew it would be wise to bide her time.

At last, though, her patience was rewarded, when Melissa offered to walk down to the green and get her case for her.

'If you give me the keys, I'll drive the car up as well, if you like,' she said helpfully. 'To be honest, I'm longing to get out of this house. You don't mind staying here and holding the fort, do you? We'll sort out a room for you when I get back.' She was already buttoning up her cardigan against the wind and preparing to leave. 'The phone won't ring, but if it does, don't answer it. Randall and Dr Sanford always use the second line, which is in the study. Then they hang up after three rings and call back, so you know it's them. Honestly, it's like working for the CIA around here.' She rolled her eyes heavenward, as if she and Claire were already old friends who regularly shared little jokes about their employer's eccentricities.

Claire assured her that she was more than happy to stay behind and watched as, miracle of miracles, the nurse waddled off down the driveway towards the village, leaving her alone in the house with Siena.

As soon as the heavy old front door had clanked shut, she bolted up the stairs, pausing for a moment outside the door to Siena's room.

She realised that once she opened it and stepped inside there could be no going back, with either her daughter or her husband.

She thought of the loneliness of the past five years; of the countless times she had watched Siena from the shadows, longing with every atom of her being to reach out to her, but never quite finding the courage.

She thought of Pete, of how much she loved him, but also of how futile the sacrifices she had made for him had been. She had lost those years with Siena for his sake, but he remained as paranoid, frightened and embittered against the world as he had ever been. What had it all been for?

And she thought, for a moment, of old Duke McMahon, and how much he had to answer for.

It seemed to Claire that Duke's ambition, his ruthlessness and his casual cruelty, had been passed down through the generations of his family like some inescapable genetic disease. Even his love, the very great love he had had for Siena, had somehow turned into something toxic. And her own love, for both her husband and her child, had been utterly powerless against it.

She would never forgive herself for those terrible, wasted years.

For better or worse, they ended today.

Slowly, she turned the handle, and walked into the room.

Chapter Forty-eight

Inside Siena's room it was very, very dark. There was no natural light at all, only a faint, reddish glow from what looked like a child's night light plugged into the far wall.

Claire could make out her daughter's sleeping figure, but little else. It was only when she moved over to the bed that she saw that the whole upper portion of Siena's face was covered with bandages, leaving only her mouth and chin visible. Her lower lip was split and swollen. She had quite obviously been beaten.

'Oh my God,' she cried out, forgetting all her planned restraint and smothering her child in kisses. 'What has he done to you? Oh, Siena, Siena, darling, I am so sorry.'

At first, Siena thought her mother's voice was part of a dream.

Max no longer haunted her subconscious, but images of both her parents and of Grandpa Duke had begun invading her sleep more and more frequently since the attack. But this time the dream was so vivid she could actually smell her mother, and feel her cool hands stroking the bare skin on her arms and shoulders. She couldn't bear to wake up.

'Angel, can you hear me? Siena, it's Mommy. Can you hear me, darling? Try to wake up. I'm here, Siena. I'm here.'

As she floated up into consciousness, the voice seemed to become louder and more real. But she hardly dared hope it might be true. When she spoke, her voice emerged as a hoarse, tremulous whisper.

'Mom?'

Claire responded with more kisses, allowing Siena to feel her skin and the brush of her hair, and entwining her fingers in her daughter's. Even her hand, she saw in the darkness, looked swollen and bruised.

'Please don't leave me.' She was barely audible, but Siena's words cut through Claire like a knife.

'I won't, my angel,' she promised. 'Never, never again.'

As she spoke, she felt Siena's grip on her hand relax, and watched her tumble back into unconsciousness. A terrible panic flooded her senses.

'Siena! Siena!' she shouted, shaking her by the shoulders.

Why wouldn't she wake up?

'Oh, you mustn't worry about her, Annie.'

Claire spun around to find Melissa standing in the doorway. She wondered how long she'd been there, but her relaxed tone and manner soon convinced her that the nurse could not have overheard anything important.

'That's what she's like with the drugs,' said Melissa. 'Talking one minute, spark out the next. I doubt she'll wake again till supper-time now.'

With Siena in a semi-comatose state, Claire was able to settle into her room for a few hours and try to figure out what to do next.

Her biggest immediate problem was that she didn't know how much time she would have until her cover was blown.

Thanks to her PI's meticulous briefing, she'd been able to plan her arrival in Nantucket to coincide with Randall's trip to the Far East. She also knew that Randall had asked Melissa to notify him of any significant changes in Siena's condition, but that otherwise he was not intending to call, and would not arrive in Nantucket himself to see Siena for almost three weeks.

Dr Sanford was another story, though.

Posing as Randall's new PA, one of Bill's team had informed the doctor that his client had sent a second nurse down to support Melissa, and faxed Claire's forged documentation across to him.

Bill seemed convinced that the doctor had swallowed the story, and that he was unlikely to contact Randall unless something really *did* go wrong with Siena. But Claire remained nervous. One conversation between the two men would blow her cover for sure.

Then there was Pete, who was bound to rumble that something was up sooner or later, probably sooner, and would no doubt storm in, all guns blazing, and undo all her carefully planned work.

She needed to get Siena out of there, to bring her home. But that would take time. Time for her to win back her daughter's trust, and time for Siena to recuperate sufficiently for her to be moved. Right now she had no idea whether she was looking at three weeks or three hours until her cover was blown. The pressure was immense.

Once she'd unpacked her things into the simple Shaker chest of drawers, she sat down on the bed, a heavy, Victorian mahogany affair covered with a white hand-embroidered quilt, and called Pete from her mobile.

He asked after her old school friend, and trotted out a few perfunctory questions about how her trip had been, but generally he seemed distracted by work, which for once Claire was grateful for. With that particular threat neutralised, for the time being at least, she changed into a pair of white flannel trousers and a black sweater and went downstairs to find Melissa.

'I hope it doesn't matter that I'm not in uniform,' she said, finding the nurse peeling three large baking potatoes in the kitchen. 'Mr Stein never mentioned anything.'

'Well, no one's going to see you, are they?' observed Melissa kindly. 'I don't know why I bother with mine really. Force of habit, I suppose. And I like to take it off at night. Gives me the feeling that I've finished work for the day. Even though I haven't! If you know what I mean.'

Lord, did the woman ever stop talking? Still, Claire saw an opportunity in this particular line of conversation and decided to take it.

'Well, at least you can have a night off tonight,' she said brightly. 'I'm more than happy to stay up with Siena, feed her, everything. It'll give me the chance to get to know her a bit. We can sort out our shifts properly in the morning, but you look like you could use a night off.'

Melissa didn't need asking twice.

By seven o'clock she was dressed and ready for a night out in the main town on the other side of the island.

'Now, you're sure you can cope on your own, Annie?' she asked nervously as she bustled out of the door.

'Of course,' said Claire. 'That's what I'm here for.'

Melissa left, and this time Claire bolted the door behind her.

She didn't want to be interrupted a second time. She and Siena had a lot to talk about.

To her amazement, Siena was already awake and sitting up in bed when she came in with the supper tray.

'Melissa?' she said warily. 'Is that you?'

She had woken unsure of whether her earlier, brief encounter with her mother had been real or a figment of her morphine-fuelled imagination, and didn't want to say anything about it to the nurse in either case.

'No,' said Claire softly. 'Melissa's gone out for the night, darling. It's me. It's Mom.'

She put down the tray of food and took Siena's hand again, allowing her daughter to touch and stroke her, to prove to herself for good and all that this was no ghost.

'It is you,' she said at last, and the joy in her voice dispelled Claire's last fears about being rejected. 'Oh my God. It really is you.'

By the time the two women had finished laughing and crying and holding one another, the food had long since gone cold.

It was hard to know where to begin talking about all the years they'd lost. Every time Siena made an effort to start, Claire would be so overwhelmed with guilt and grief that she drowned her out with a torrent of apologies, and the tears began all over again. In the end, they both agreed to postpone these longer conversations and to focus on what to do in the current situation, before Melissa came back and disturbed them.

Siena was able to give her mother a sketchy outline of her life with Randall and what had happened to her. She also told her that it was not yet clear whether she would regain full or only partial sight.

'That's it, then,' Claire announced firmly, once she'd heard the whole sordid tale. 'We have to get you away from here. Right now. Tonight. The man's a maniac. Can you walk, darling? If I help you?'

Wearily, Siena raised a hand for her mother to stop.

'It's not that simple,' she said. 'I can't just leave.'

And she explained, in slightly blurry detail, Randall's threats to destroy her career and reputation, as well as his control of her depleted finances.

'Besides, it's not just that,' Siena finished, as Claire sat reeling from everything she'd just been told. 'What would we be going home *to*? I take it Dad doesn't know you're here?'

'No,' Claire admitted. 'He doesn't. But, Siena, I know your father's always loved you. Deep down, darling, he has. If he knew, if he had any *idea* what this man Stein has put you through . . .'

'He'd what?' asked Siena. But there was less hostility in her voice than there might once have been. On some level, she had come to terms with her relationship with her father, what it was and what it never could be. As overjoyed as she was to see her mother again, she knew it was far too late to talk about building bridges with Pete.

'Be honest, Mom. Dad would probably have done this himself years ago if he'd thought he could have got away with it. He'd have crippled Hunter too if he'd had the chance.'

'Siena!' said Claire, shocked. She wasn't yet ready to admit, even to herself, that her daughter might be right. But she couldn't help remembering Pete's comment about Hunter after Siena's accident: how he wished his brother had been crushed in the wreckage of his SUV. The thought made her shiver.

'He's going to make you make a choice, Mom, just like he did before,' said Siena. 'Me or him. And if you choose me, then we'll both be in the same boat – homeless, penniless and screwed. Oh God, my head.' She fell back hard against the pillow. For a moment Claire thought she'd fainted, but then she spoke again, holding her hand to her shattered left temple. 'Mom, does that bag on my drip need changing? Jesus Christ, it hurts.'

Claire, who had nursed her own mother through terminal cancer and knew a thing or two about pain relief, got swiftly to work. It was comforting to think that the medical training she had abandoned to marry Pete had not gone entirely to waste. Soon Siena was resting more comfortably, conscious but patently exhausted.

They agreed to leave the difficult subjects of Pete and Randall until she was feeling stronger. In the meantime, Claire explained how she had tracked her down to Nantucket, and briefed a drowsy Siena on her cover story.

'So it was *you* who hired that snoop guy?' Siena said incredulously when she had finished. 'Big Al told me he'd seen some black dude hanging around the set trying to get pictures. I thought it was just a super-persistent fan. He came out to Malibu too?'

Claire nodded. 'He's a good man, Bill. And an excellent PI.'

'And you managed to keep it all a secret?' said Siena. 'Wow, Mom. I wouldn't have thought you had it in you.'

'Neither would I, once,' said Claire. 'But it's amazing what resources and what strengths we have, once we get up the courage to use them.'

Siena reached out in the darkness and clasped her hands around her mother's neck, pulling her closer. 'Mom?' she whispered. 'What if I can't see?'

Claire could hear the abject terror in her voice. At that moment, she felt she could have strangled Randall Stein with her bare hands.

'You will see,' she told her daughter firmly. 'Pretty soon, my darling, you're going to see everything much more clearly. And then everything will be all right. Just you wait.'

The gods, it seemed, had decided to smile on Claire.

For the next two weeks, her cover story remained intact, and she was able to nurse Siena back to health and strength with ever decreasing interruptions from Melissa, who seemed more than happy to let her new colleague take on the lion's share of the work. She had almost started to believe that she *was* Nurse Annie, so easy had it been for her to take on that persona and leave the troubles of her life and marriage behind her in Hollywood.

She felt such intense love and pride, watching Siena fighting her way to recovery. When she changed her dressings, she could see that her face, although quite heavily scarred around the eyes and left cheek, was improving visibly by the day. She was starting to look like a battered but recognisable version of her old self.

And it wasn't just her bruises which were healing. Something had changed in Siena since the attack, something quite profound.

Whether it was finding her mother again, losing her money and fame, or the prospect of losing not only her looks but perhaps her sight as well, she had discovered a humility, and with it a bizarre feeling of contentment and calm, that was quite new to her.

For the first time in her life, other things seemed more important than the pursuit of fame and wealth, or even the love of a man. Other people seemed more important than herself.

The future was still a frightening, confusing blur. She couldn't picture life beyond her recuperation, and had no idea how or when she was going to make her escape from Randall.

Yet with others the path seemed clearer.

Hunter, for example, was always on her mind, and she talked about him constantly to Claire.

'The way I behaved, not just to Hunter but to Tiffany as well,' she told her mother through tears of regret, as Claire pushed her in a wheelchair through the rows of sweet peas in the secluded garden. 'I was so horrible and spoilt and selfish. He'll never forgive me. And I love him so much, Mom.'

Claire tried to comfort her and assure her that, in time, Hunter probably would forgive her. 'And so will everybody else who loves you.'

'Ha!' Siena laughed bitterly, snapping the head off a flower and smelling it. She found her sense of smell had become particularly acute since she'd been unable to use her eyes. 'I don't think that's a very long list any more, do you? I've totally lost touch with all my old friends from England and New York. Ines isn't speaking to me.'

'Only because you haven't been speaking to her,' said Claire gently.

'And then there's Max.' Siena went on with her self-flagellation, unable or unwilling to accept her mother's comfort. 'I was so awful to him, Mom, when he showed up in Malibu that Christmas. I was just so hurt and confused and I felt I couldn't forgive him. But I wanted to. I really did.' She was begging Claire to believe her.

'I'm sure you did, sweetheart,' she said. 'I understand.'

'But by then, well, it was complicated. There was Randall, and the film, and . . .' She threw the flower head down on to the ground in despair. 'I couldn't just go back.'

God, sometimes she was so like Duke, thought Claire. Everything was always black and white, right or wrong. And heaven forbid that she should ever go back on a decision. Never look back, never apologise. That was what Duke always used to say.

Poor child. She looked so terribly confused and hurt, with the visible, lower parts of her face all screwed up in misery and anguish. Claire longed to be able to help her, but having lived with Pete for thirty years, she understood a bit about guilt. This was something Siena would have to work through on her own.

'Try not to think about it now,' she would tell her, time after time. 'Concentrate on getting yourself well. That's the only thing that matters.'

Claire was sitting out in the garden reading under the shade of the willow tree, enjoying a brief respite from nursing duties while Siena slept, when she was disturbed by the vibrating of a mobile phone in her pocket.

The screen read 'Home'.

It was Pete.

She glanced nervously around to check that Melissa was nowhere in sight before answering the call.

'Darling!' she said. 'How are you?'

There was a pause on the end of the line.

'Mrs McMahon?' said a familiar female voice. 'Claire? It's not Pete, it's me. Tara.'

The PA sounded distressed. Claire felt her heartbeat quicken. Had Pete finally found out what she'd been up to?

'Is something the matter, Tara?' she asked. 'You sound upset. What's wrong?'

Another pause, which seemed to last for hours.

'I'm sorry, but it's bad news,' the girl stammered. 'It's Pete.'

'What? What about him?' Claire sounded as scared as she felt. It wasn't like Tara to spare anyone's feelings, least of all hers. Why couldn't she spit it out?

'He's had a heart attack.'

It was Tara's voice, but it somehow sounded different.

Tinny and distant.

Unreal.

'I'm sorry, but you have to come home, Claire,' she said. 'Right away.'

Chapter Forty-nine

It took a couple of minutes for the initial shock of Tara's news to sink in. Then she began to think practically.

Her first priority was to get back home. Pete had been taken to Cedars and was apparently in intensive care. She needed to talk to his doctor there and get an update on his condition. But first she had to talk to Siena.

Now that she was on the lower-dosage painkillers and didn't need so much sleep, she'd been moved from the little windowless room at the top of the stairs to a larger, much more cheerful guest bedroom, overlooking the sweeping formal gardens and the ocean beyond. Not that Siena could appreciate the view, of course, but she could now tell the difference between light and darkness, even through her bandages, which everyone took to be a hopeful sign.

Claire rapped gently on the door. 'Hey, sweetie. Only me.'

She hadn't known how she ought to break the news about Pete, what with Siena still being in such a fragile condition. In the end, she just sat down on the end of the bed and told her as calmly and unemotionally as she could.

'I don't know how serious it is yet,' she finished. 'I'm just praying and hoping for the best.'

Siena's only thoughts were of concern for her mother. For all her dad's faults, and despite everything that had happened, she knew that Claire loved him desperately.

'Mom, I'm so sorry,' she said, clasping Claire's hand tightly in her own. 'You must be so worried. And of course you have to go back right away, I totally understand. You mustn't worry about me. I'll be fine.'

'But darling . . .' Claire was taken aback. 'You don't expect me to leave you here, do you?'

Siena's face gave nothing away – there was no tightening of the mouth or furrowing of the brow above her bandages. Evidently she *had* expected it.

'No, no, it's out of the question,' said Claire. 'I'm taking you back with me. We have to get you away from Randall, and besides . . .' She bravely fought back her tears. 'This may be your last chance to see your father, to make things right. You have to come with me, Siena. Today.'

Wearily Siena shook her head. 'I can't, Mom. I can't come with you right now. Randall's going to be here in a few days to see me, and I still have no idea how I'm gonna handle that. He can still do a lot of damage to my career, you know. Not to mention the money. And Dr Sanford's coming with him to take these damn dressings off my eyes and look at the damage. I can't just do a runner.'

'Oh, for heaven's sake.' Claire's exasperation at last began to show. 'What do career and money matter in comparison to your safety? Please, Siena.' She didn't have time to debate the matter. She had to get back to Pete, now, and there was no way she was leaving her daughter to the mercy of that maniac and his private doctors.

'Forget Sanford. There are other doctors, better doctors, eye specialists in LA who could help you. You can't spend another second in the same house as that man after what he's done to you. You can't.'

'Yes I can, Mom.' Siena pulled the quilt up around her shoulders defensively. 'I have to. This is my career we're talking about. It's my life. You don't understand.'

'Oh really?' said Claire. 'Don't I? Well, I'll tell you what. Why don't you let me *show* you what it is that I don't understand, Siena.'

She moved up the bed towards her and gently but firmly began removing her bandages.

'It's OK,' protested Siena. 'The dressings are clean, Melissa already did them.'

But Claire continued unwinding the strips of cotton until her entire bruised and battered face was revealed.

'Now I want you to trust me,' she said, pushing her daughter's shoulders back until she was lying flat on the bed, and leaning over her. Siena could make out the darkening shadow as her mother came closer, blocking out the light from the window.

'I do trust you. But what are you doing?'

'I'm taking off these dressings and I'm taking out your stitches. I want you to see this for yourself.'

Instinctively, Siena stiffened.

'No!' she said.

She sounded desperately afraid. What if she couldn't see? What if the damage was too bad?

Sensing her nerves, Claire took both her hands and squeezed them.

'It's going to be OK,' she said, in a tone of such confidence and serene certainty that even Siena began to feel comforted. 'Trust me.'

She was a deft and practised nurse, and it took only a few uncomfortable minutes for her to complete the entire operation. Siena had been dreading having her stitches removed, but in fact they had come away with such slithering ease that a mild discomfort was all she felt.

That was nothing, though, compared to the inner fear that gripped her.

'Right,' said Claire, wiping firmly across the gluey mass that caked both her lash lines with warm, wet cotton wool. 'Let's do it.'

She unhooked the oval antique mirror from above the washbasin and brought it over to the bed, before propping Siena back up comfortably against the plumped-up pillows. She looked as white as a sheet.

'We'll do your left eye first,' said Claire. She knew from Melissa that this was the eye that had been least damaged by Randall's beating, and that Dr Sanford was optimistic that Siena would regain at least partial sight on that side. 'I'm going to open your eyelid with my fingers now, all right?' Siena managed a tiny nod. 'It'll probably sting a little bit, so try not to panic.'

Siena felt her left lid peel open and instinctively pushed her mother away as a rush of dry, stinging cold air hit her eyeball. It was agony and she was blinking furiously, tears streaming down her cheeks, but in those few split seconds she could make out the contours of the room and Claire's loving, anxious face looking down at her, willing her to be OK.

The relief was so overwhelming, she could hardly breathe.

'I can see!' she said ecstatically, flinging her arms around Claire's neck. 'I can fucking see!'

Her elation was dampened somewhat a few minutes later when they tried her right eye. It wasn't a total loss – she could see shades of light and darkness and, she thought, the occasional recognisable shape. But the damage was still very severe.

Claire was quick to comfort her. 'Eye surgeons can do incredible things these days, you know, honey,' she said, forcing the optimism into her voice. 'As soon as we get you back to LA, I'll take you to see the very best.'

LA. The mere mention of it brought Siena crashing down to earth with a bang. The joy of knowing that she could still see had been indescribable, overwhelming. But her problems were far from over.

Her father was seriously ill, perhaps dying. She was going to have to see him, and that thought alone filled her with emotions so painful and conflicting she couldn't begin to untangle them. And then there was Randall.

She knew her mom was right: she had to get away from him and the sooner the better. But still his words to her at the surgery centre as she'd lain there in agony ran through her brain now like a broken record.

If you go after me Siena, believe me, I will crush you.

He could still destroy her career. He had threatened to ruin her professionally and financially. The thought of losing everything she had worked for filled her with a sickening dread that not even the thrill of being able to see could banish completely.

When Claire's voice cut through her reverie, it was firm and businesslike.

'I said I wanted you to see something for yourself.'

She held up the oval mirror and clasped it against her chest with its worn wooden back facing towards Siena. 'Are you sure you're ready for this?'

Siena nodded mutely. She was frightened, but it had to be faced. She wanted to know what she looked like.

Claire turned the mirror around.

At first, she made no sound at all. She just slumped back against the pillows and lay there like a terrified insect in the presence of a predator, frozen and motionless with shock.

For weeks now, she had probed her wounded skin with her fingers and tried to visualise her facial injuries. But nothing could have prepared her for the reality of what she now saw gazing back at her. A long, livid red scar ran all the way from the corner of her right eye down to just above her mouth in a jagged line where the glass had sliced into the flesh. Although the swellings around both eyes had eased considerably, the bruising was still extensive and disfiguring, and her famous bone structure had been thrown off kilter by a broken cheekbone that made the whole left side of her face look sunken and lopsided. The skin that was stretched like paper over the shattered bones was sickly and preternaturally pale after so many weeks out of any kind of sunlight, and she looked frighteningly gaunt, her hands incongruously over-sized and bony on the ends of her scarred and stick-thin arms.

She felt sick.

Randall had destroyed her.

She had *let* him destroy her.

'I know it's hard,' said Claire softly, seeing the pain in her daughter's face. 'But just now you told me that I didn't understand. That your career was your life. That you couldn't just walk away

431

from here, from that man. And I think . . .' She didn't want to hurt her any more, and struggled for the kindest way to say it. 'I think you needed to see this. To see what he's done. Because it's *you* who doesn't understand, darling. A career is *not* a life. And you *can* just leave him. You can and you must.'

For Siena, it was a moment of revelation. It wasn't just her face which had been battered, she realised. It was her spirit.

For so long she had strived to be like Duke, to live up to all the hopes and dreams he had had for her. Getting back to Hollywood. Making her fortune. Becoming a star. From her earliest childhood, she had craved nothing so desperately and totally as his approval, his admiration and his love. Even after his death, she had carried on her blind pursuit of everything she believed he would have wanted for her.

But at what cost?

How many people had she pushed away? How many people had she hurt as she battled and clawed her way up to become what Duke had wanted her to be? Staring at her shattered face, she realised that the one person she had hurt the most was staring straight back at her.

She loved Duke. She always had and she always would. But she knew now that he had been wrong all along. He was wrong to despise people for being weak. Weakness was what made people human – it was cruelty which was to be despised.

Randall was cruel. And Siena had been weak, holding on to him out of fear and desperation.

Just as Minnie had held on to Duke.

Just as Claire had held on to Pete.

Suddenly she was overwhelmed with a surge of empathy and pity for her mother and grandmother. All these years she had hated them for their weakness. But were they really so different from her? In many ways, they were *better* than her and braver. At least Minnie had loved Duke. And no one could deny that her mother loved her father, despite everything.

She had never loved Randall.

So what had been her excuse for staying with him?

Money? Fame?

Duke had built his emotional security on money and fame. Blindly, stupidly, still desperate to please him even years after his death, Siena had tried to do the same. And look where it had got her.

Duke's blood ran in her veins. She knew that. But so, she now realised, did Claire's. And for the first time in her life, she felt proud of that fact.

A lone ray of bright sunlight had fought its way through the gap in the curtains, and fell in a bright white wedge across the bed and polished wood of the floor, glinting off the mirror into her still-sensitive eyes. She winced.

Claire reached out to take the mirror from her, but she held fast, and for a moment the two women's hands touched in sympathy.

'Would you do me a favour?' Siena asked, still blinking against the sunlight.

'Of course, darling,' said Claire, her voice choked with love. She knew how hard it must be for her daughter to have to see what that bastard had done to her, and she prayed that, in time, she'd find the strength and the courage to come to terms with her injuries. 'Anything you want, my angel. Anything at all.'

Siena let go of the mirror and smiled.

'Pass me my suitcase.'

Chapter Fifty

Max was reading scripts in the little boxroom that served as his study at Batcombe when he heard the news about Pete's heart attack on the radio.

Although the name 'McMahon' always sent a shiver down his spine, he didn't feel any particular emotion about Siena's father being on the way out. From the little he'd known of him, the guy had always been a card-carrying arsehole, just the type of manipulative, megalomaniac wanker that made him glad he no longer lived and worked in LA.

He imagined Siena wouldn't be shedding too many tears either, wherever she was.

Besides, right now he had problems enough of his own to worry about.

Dark Hearts was now definitely moving to New York in the New Year. It was amazing how well they'd done, with what he'd always considered to be rather a brave and uncommercial play, and he thanked his lucky stars that he'd negotiated himself a big slice of the equity early on. No doubt about it, it was a fantastic opportunity, and in theatre terms, great money. But moving back to the States presented other difficulties. He would have to leave Henry just when things at the farm were at their most stressful, with the developers due to arrive any day now.

And then, of course, there was Freddie.

Ever since making up after their titanic row over Siena's engagement, things had been calm between the two of them. But deep down, Max was becoming increasingly unhappy, consumed by a loneliness that he just couldn't shake off. He guessed, correctly, that Freddie sensed this, and his guilt about letting her down made him feel even more depressed.

When Hunter had called him about Siena's reported breakdown, Freddie had tactfully avoided mentioning it, wary of upsetting him further or provoking another crisis in their relationship. Although he was grateful for her sensitivity, the result was that he didn't confide in her about his feelings, and the emotional distance between the two of them widened still further.

At least once a week he steeled himself to talk to her and call it quits. But every time he looked at her kind, loving, trusting face, his nerve failed him.

He hadn't even broached the subject of New York yet. He didn't want to be responsible for yet another woman's unhappiness. Or to explode another misery bomb in the already struggling Arkell household.

Switching off the ancient Roberts radio on the window sill and turning back to his script, he was jolted out of his private thoughts by a loud rumble that seemed to be coming from the bottom of the drive. Moments later the first of the JCBs appeared, roaring and rattling its way towards the farmyard. It was followed by another and another until soon the noise was deafening.

'They're here.'

Muffy had put her head round the door. Her hair was pulled back off her face with one of Henry's spotted handkerchiefs, and Max noticed how pale her skin was looking and how pronounced the dark shadows seemed to be under her eyes. Poor thing. She'd had a terrible time of it these past few months, but Henry had been too caught up in his own guilt and misery about leasing the estate to be able to comfort her. She'd tried to be strong for everybody else's sake. But now that the developers were actually here, she looked as if she was right on the verge of losing it completely.

'They're here! They're here!' Bertie and Maddie ran tearing down the corridor behind her, whooping with excitement at all the commotion.

'I'm going to go in the digger!'

'No, me! I'm going first!'

'Looks like somebody's pleased to see them,' said Max, getting up and putting an affectionate arm around his sister-in-law.

'Come out there with me, Max,' she pleaded. God, she looked miserable, gazing past him to the fleet of trucks that were pulling up, exhausts belching, outside the study window. 'I can't face playing welcoming committee all on my own.'

'Of course,' he said, giving her an encouraging squeeze. 'Don't worry. We can meet and greet in five minutes and then I'll walk the foreman over to the farm office. But where's Henry?'

'Out shooting, over at Millhole Wood. Won't be back till this evening.'

'Well, d'you want me to drive over there and get him? I don't mind.'

'No, no, really,' said Muffy. She was grateful for the offer, grateful for all Max's support in fact. He'd been a rock these last few weeks. But she couldn't drag Henry back from a happy day's shooting to face all this. He'd be living with the horrible reality soon enough. Why begrudge him his last few hours of blissful ignorance. 'I'll be fine. Just stand next to me, all right? And if you see me crying, kick me. As hard as you like.'

Outside, the trucks had parked in a rough semicircle at the entrance to the yard, with their drivers gathered in an awkward-looking huddle to one side. A steady drizzle had been falling throughout the morning, and the heavy tyres had already begun to turn Henry's drive into a quagmire. Behind the fleet of dirty JCBs at the top of the drive, and in striking, shiny contrast, was one spanking-new dark blue Range Rover, of the kind that was clearly more used to cruising around South Kensington than dirtying its wheels on muddy tracks out in the country.

As Max and Muffy came out on to the porch, both the car doors swung open and two men emerged and started walking towards them, their hands extended in greeting. One of them Max instantly recognised from Henry's descriptions as Gary Ellis. He was short and fat, and had made an unfortunate attempt to squeeze his portly form into an ill-fitting checked suit, which gave him the look of a cockney Billy Bunter. A trademark cigar was clamped between his teeth, and he had topped off what he fondly thought of as his 'country gent' look with a flat cap that, like the car, looked as if it had been bought in Bond Street the day before.

''Allo. Muffy, isn't it?' he said, ignoring Max and grabbing and kissing Muffy's hand before she had a chance to protest. Neither she nor Henry had expected Ellis to show up in person at the farm, and certainly not on the first day.

'Hello, Mr Ellis,' she said stiffly, trying to hide her distaste as his wet, flabby lips left their imprint on her skin. He had leased the farm fair and square and had a legitimate right to be there, so it was no good being churlish about it. 'This is my brother-in-law, Max De Seville. And my children . . .' She gestured around vaguely, but was horrified to discover that Bertie and Maddie had run off and were already clambering all over one of the diggers, covered from head to toe in mud.

'Bertie! Madeleine! Get down from there this instant!' she yelled. Two guilty, clay-splattered faces peered back at her from beneath the long neck of the machine.

'Don't worry,' said Gary with a smug, leery grin that made Max want to hit him. Henry had told him the developer had a 'crush' on Muffy, but that seemed like far too innocent a word to describe the blatant, predatory way he looked at her. 'Kids, eh? What can you do?'

The other man from the Range Rover, a tall, diffident-looking fellow who Max guessed must be in his early fifties, had been hanging back behind his boss but now moved forward and introduced himself. 'Ben McIntyre. I'm the foreman here, so I'll be overseeing the construction.' His handshake was dry and firm. He seemed honest. 'Pleased to meet you.'

'And you,' said Max. He didn't know why, but he found himself instantly warming to Ben. He hoped that a decent foreman might help make the nightmare of construction slightly more bearable for poor Henry.

'No point talkin' to 'im,' interrupted Gary rudely, waving a hand dismissively in Max's direction. ''E's just the monkey. 'Is bruvver's the organ grinder, isn't that right, love?' He winked at Muffy. 'So where is the man of the 'ouse anyway?'

Gary had been looking forward to his moment of triumph over Henry, and was put out his rival hadn't been there to witness his grand entrance. Over the years he had nursed his resentment at what he perceived to be Henry's snobbery and stand-offishness into a constantly simmering hatred. Lord Snooty had been quick enough to patronise him when he'd first expressed an interest in Manor Farm all those years ago at Caroline's dinner party. He was so far up his own arse, he'd even turned down the very decent offer Gary had made him last year to buy the place outright. That had annoyed him at the time – given the colossal size of his debts, he'd assumed that Henry would have caved in and sold straight away – but he was pleased that things had worked out the way they had.

He knew when he offered it that the option of a lease would have looked like a lifeline to Henry, so desperate was he not to be forced to sell his ancestral home to a stranger. The stupid, sentimental sod. Gary had no time for whimsical aristocratic notions of heritage when it came to property, and thought Henry an out-and-out fool for agreeing to the deal.

Because the reality was that a lease meant that the Arkells would be shackled to him for the rest of their lives. He could come and go as he pleased, running roughshod through their precious bloody estate whenever, and however, he wanted to.

Just the thought of that made him smile.

He'd have paid twice the value of the lease simply for the pleasure of seeing that stuck-up cunt Henry Arkell cut down to size. And in the meantime, as well as building himself a nice little earner of a golf course, he could amuse himself by making a play for Henry's still very tasty missus.

'He's out,' said Max frostily, moving back to Muffy's side and putting a protective, possessive arm around her shoulder. 'I can show you and Mr McIntyre to the farm office. You'll find everything you need in there.'

By six o'clock it was starting to get dark and Max decided to take a stroll up to the village. He needed to get out of the house. Ellis had been strutting arrogantly around the farm all afternoon, barking instructions at his foreman and arguing loudly with the two terrified-looking local architects who had turned up at lunchtime to go through plans for the new clubhouse.

Muffy had spent the day wandering around the house like an automaton, mindlessly putting on load after load of washing to avoid having to go outside. She was so distracted that she accidentally put one of Maddie's red socks in a white wash and dyed all Max's Calvins a none too subtle shade of pink. She burst into tears when she pulled them out of the machine, despite his protestations that he really quite liked them like that.

Not that he could blame her for being highly strung. The two younger children were in a sulk, having been banned from pestering any of the workmen by their mother and forced to stay indoors until Henry got home. Charlie, the only child old enough to grasp the seriousness of what was happening, had taken up a sentry post by the window on the landing, from which he scowled furiously at everyone who came and went, refusing to be lured downstairs even by Freddie's tempting offer of a slice of Mr Kipling's chocolate fudge cake at tea.

Max wanted to help, but as no one wanted to talk about what was happening it was hard to know where to begin. Besides, he was ashamed to admit that even with the nightmare of Ellis's goons moving in, his mind kept wandering back to Siena. Whether it was the earlier news of Pete McMahon's heart attack which had made it worse he didn't know, but he found himself continually replaying her image in his head, like picking at a mental scab, until it was driving him absolutely insane. Not knowing how she was, or where she was, was killing him.

After a couple of abortive hours of attempted work, he decided a breath of fresh air might help, and set out for the village, with Titus and Boris yapping excitedly at his heels.

They'd barely reached the bottom of the drive when the familiar silhouette of Henry's ancient four-wheel-drive came hurtling round the corner. He pulled over and wound down the window when he saw Max.

'Is that what I think it is?' he said, gesturing to the faint shadows of the lorries in the farmyard. Max nodded. 'How long have they been here? And why the fuck didn't anyone call me?'

'I offered,' said Max, wishing he could take away even an ounce of the pain that was written all over his brother's face. 'But Muffy didn't want to ruin your day's shooting.'

'Jesus Christ.' Henry ran his hands through his hair. 'There's so many of them. It looks like the M1 up there.'

'Oh, it's not so bad,' lied Max. Titus and Boris began jumping up and scrabbling at the side of the car. There were three dead rabbits lying on the passenger seat, and their scent was driving both the dogs crazy. Max grabbed each of them by the collar and pulled them back on to the verge.

'I'd better get up there,' said Henry, grinding the car back into first.

'Oh, and Henry!' shouted Max. He'd been going to warn his brother that Ellis had shown up in person, but his voice was drowned out by the screech of spinning wheels as Henry lurched forward, desperate to get home and see the full extent of the damage for himself.

Never mind. He would find out for himself soon enough.

Henry pulled up in front of the house, and for a few moments he just sat in stunned silence, unable to get out of the car. He had known the construction would be beginning some time this week. Logically, he knew that this would mean months of industrial vehicles and scores of manual workers scurrying all over the farm. But somehow the physical sight of the diggers and skips and cranes, and the strangers hurrying back and forth across his farmyard and in and out of his office, was still a shock. Feeling winded and numb, he eventually managed to open the door, gathering up his gun in one hand and the rabbits in the other, and walked round to the kitchen door – he was too muddy to use the front entrance.

Moving along the path into the kitchen garden, he thought he heard a cry. In a flash he was outside the door, just in time to see Muffy pushing the heavy, insistent form of the loathsome Gary Ellis away from her, sending him stumbling back against the kitchen dresser.

'What the hell do you think you're playing at?' she shouted, her face flushed with the exertion of extricating herself from his unwanted embrace. 'Are you mad?'

Before he had a moment to answer, Henry was through the door like a shot, dropping both gun and rabbits with a clatter as he flew at Ellis, fists flying.

'You fucker.'

'Henry, don't!' pleaded Muffy, as the fat man hit the ground, his head grinding against the corner of the dresser with a sickening crunch as he fell. 'It's all right. It was nothing. Please!'

Gary whimpered in pain and brought his arms up to his head as he lay on the floor, trying to shield himself from further blows. Henry dropped to his knees and, grabbing the gibbering developer by his collar, pulled back his arm for one final punch before apparently thinking better of it and letting his head drop back on to the flagstone floor.

'You're not fucking worth it,' he spat, standing up and turning to Muffy, who was shaking with shock by the sink. 'You OK?'

She nodded mutely. She'd been peeling the potatoes and crying when Gary had wandered in and surprised her. At first he'd seemed to be genuinely offering comfort, saying how it must have been a huge shock for her, them all arriving like this and having to deal with it all on her own. But then, almost before she knew what was happening, he had started pressing himself against her until she could feel his hot, excited breath on her neck and his fat, rubbery hands reaching round for her bottom. Eeeugh. Thinking about it again now made her shudder.

'That wasn't a very smart fing to do.' Gary had staggered to his feet, and was wiping away a small trickle of blood from his lip with a handkerchief. A swelling was already beginning to form around his mouth and chin where Henry's punch had hit home. He was going to look terrible in the morning. 'I could sue you for assault.'

'Not before I sue you for indecent assault, you little toerag.' Henry's eyes had narrowed to small, murderous slits. Instinctively, Gary took a step backward. But he was still smiling that smug, confident smile – the smile of a man who knew he held all the cards.

'It's only assault if she didn't like it. Isn't that right, darlin'?' He leered at Muffy. Very slowly, Henry bent down and picked up his gun, which he proceeded to point at Gary. For one brief but glorious moment, the smile withered on the fat man's lips.

'Get out of my house.'

'Now now, 'Enry,' said Gary, still eyeing the gun warily. He didn't think Henry would have the balls to actually use it, but you could never be a hundred per cent sure. 'Is that any way to talk to your new landlord?'

'GET OUT!' Henry roared. This time Gary didn't hang about but bolted straight out of the door, leaving his jacket and mobile phone on the table in his ignominious haste to get out of there. Henry put down the gun and shut and bolted the door behind him. He was surprised to find that his own hands were shaking.

'Oh, Henry,' said Muffy, giving way to tears at last. 'What if he does sue? We haven't got a bean to fight him with.'

Henry walked over and hugged her tightly to his chest. 'He won't,' he said. 'He wouldn't dare, not after trying it on with you like that.'

She held on to him for a moment or two, allowing herself to be comforted, pleased that he was home, that they were in this together. Then she dried her tears and, pulling away from him, said what they had both been thinking. 'This is it, though, isn't it? This is what life's going to be like. You can punch him as much as you like. But he *is* our landlord. And nothing we say or do can ever change that.'

Henry frowned but didn't contradict her.

'We're stuck with him, aren't we?' she said. 'We're stuck with him for ever.'

By the time Max got back home it was almost midnight and Henry and Muffy had long since gone up to bed. His walk to the village had led him, inevitably, to the King's Arms, where he'd been persuaded to stay for a great many more pints than was probably advisable. By closing time he was quite unsteady on his feet, and if it hadn't been for his trusty canine companions, Boris and Titus, he doubted he would have found his way home at all.

After two minutes of abortive and increasingly noisy fumbling at the front door with his keys, Freddie had finally let him in with a face like fury.

Oh fuck, he remembered through his alcoholic haze. He had promised yesterday that he would take her out to dinner in Stroud this evening. He'd just stood the poor girl up.

'Where the 'ell 'ave you been?' she demanded. 'We were supposed to go out hours ago.'

Instead of apologising as he should have, he flew completely off the handle, his anger fuelled by guilt about his own behaviour as well as by almost a gallon of bitter. 'Mind your own damn business,' he bellowed at her.

To her credit, Freddie was not about to be bullied into silence.

'Well, I'm sorry, but I theenk it ees my business, when you stand me up, and you can't even be bozzered to call.'

Max stepped inside and she closed the door behind him. Only her concern not to wake the entire household after their harrowing day prevented her from slamming it violently.

'It wasn't a question of not being bothered,' he snapped back unsympathetically. 'I forgot, OK?'

'Oh, really?' she scoffed. 'And that's supposed to make eet OK, is it?'

She was looking particularly foxy tonight in a tight black cashmere jumper that must have cost her a whole month's wages, teamed with her favourite red suede miniskirt and boots. She had obviously made an effort to look her best for their date.

The red of the skirt clashed adorably with her auburn hair and with cheeks now flushed and rosy with anger. But Max was too guilt-blinded to be distracted by her beauty.

'I had more important things on my mind,' he said savagely, staggering into the hallway and collapsing against the wall. He noticed his name on a bright pink Post-it note stuck on the message pad by the phone and bent down to read the note. His agent in LA had called three more times, and could Max please call him back as soon as possible. It was urgent.

Not to me it isn't, thought Max bitterly, screwing up the note and dropping it in the bin.

He knew why the agent was calling. Miramax had apparently shown some interest in buying the film rights to *Dark Hearts*. Max had been in the game long enough to realise that 'shown some interest' almost never translated into 'paid good money for', and he wasn't about to get his hopes up this time. He'd ridden the hope-and-despair roller-coaster for three painful years in LA, as studios sniffed agonisingly around one after another of his projects but never quite came through in the end. Hollywood was an all-or-nothing town, and ninety-nine times out of a hundred, that meant you longed for it all but got nothing.

For all his cynicism, though, he knew that six months ago he would have been excited about the big-studio interest and rushed to return his agent's call. But now? He didn't know what was wrong with him. Nothing seemed urgent, or even important, any more.

He knew he was behaving appallingly towards Freddie. He had not, in fact, completely forgotten about their plans. The truth was that, subconsciously, he had known he couldn't face sitting through an overtly 'romantic' evening with her and had been glad of the chance to run away to the pub and escape.

'You 'ad more important things on your mind, did you? Like what?' she challenged him. Max could hear the despair and bitterness in her voice. He didn't look up at her. 'Just what were zose ozzer things, Max? 'Enry's troubles? All zees people at the farm? Or Siena McMahon?'

Max winced.

'You can't forget 'er, can you?' Her fear was making her spiteful. 'Which is funny. Because she seems to 'ave no trouble forgetting about you.'

Max felt his heart fall into his stomach like a medicine ball, and his head began to throb. He swayed unsteadily as he tried to move away from the wall.

It was as if all the suppressed grief and longing of the past year were about to burst physically free from his body. The hall had started to spin.

'You don't know what you're talking about!' he shouted at Freddie. Pushing past her, he pulled open the front door again and fled into the garden, clutching his head and running for all he was worth.

'Max!' she called after him. 'Max! I'm sorry. Come back!'

But he had already disappeared into the gloom.

He ran through the darkness, across the dew-wet lawn until he reached the firmer, concrete ground of the old farmyard. There, he sank to his knees and, pressing his palms down hard on the cold ground for support, began throwing up, retching and retching until it felt as if not just his stomach but his soul was empty.

Then he started to cry.

Oh God.

What was he going to do? What the hell was he going to do?

Chapter Fifty-one

Melissa didn't think she had ever seen anyone so angry.

When Randall arrived in Nantucket to discover that Siena had packed her things and gone, he turned on the nurse in a blind fury, face flushed, eyes bulging, and demanded to know what had happened.

'Please, Mr Stein, there's no need for that sort of language,' she muttered, blushing as one obscenity after another tumbled from his thin, angry lips. 'Annie took her back to Los Angeles on Wednesday, just as you instructed.'

'Instructed?' He was apoplectic, and his cheeks had gone such an intense shade of puce that Melissa genuinely started to worry that he might be about to have a heart attack. 'I never instructed anything! And who the fuck is Annie?'

It took almost twenty minutes for him to rein in his temper sufficiently to allow a gibbering Melissa to fill him in on what had actually happened. Frankly it beggared belief, how easily the stupid woman had been duped, allowing a complete stranger into the house after everything he'd told her about security, on the strength of a few forged papers.

Glancing through the false résumé and letter of employment a few minutes later, though, he was impressed by how much this mystery woman had managed to find out about him: she had known not just about the Nantucket house, but clearly also had access to all sorts of other information about his employees in LA, his business trip to Asia and, most worryingly of all, his relationship with Daniel Sanford. His initial assumption – that *Annie* was an undercover journalist – had been wide of the mark. This was not the work of some amateurish, snoopy hack. It was a meticulously planned sting, presumably orchestrated by someone close to Siena.

A woman.

He thought for a moment of Ines, but dismissed the idea almost immediately. She wouldn't have had the time or the money for such a thing, and as she hadn't heard a word from Siena in months he doubted she would have had the inclination either. Besides, Melissa had told him that Annie was blonde and older. No amount of disguising could make Ines look fifty.

That was when it came to him.

'Would you recognise her?' he asked Melissa. 'Annie, I mean. If I showed you a picture?'

The nurse nodded furiously, relieved to be able to give him at least one of the answers he wanted. She scurried after him into the study and watched him boot up his computer, tapping impatiently on the desk with his fat fingers until he could bring up the Google home page, then finally clicking on 'image search' and typing in just two words.

Claire McMahon.

'Oh yes, there she is,' trilled Melissa happily, as an image of Claire, looking awkward and formal in a blue suit at a cancer research gala, filled the screen. 'That's her all right. That's Annie.'

Dr Daniel Sanford was out in the garden playing baseball with his two young sons when his wife called him in to take the phone call.

'It's Randall Stein, calling from the East Coast,' she yelled out at him through the patio doors that led from the palatial living room of their Beverly Hills home out on to the rolling, manicured lawn.

Frowning, he dropped the wiffle ball and stomped back into the house. He was flying out to Nantucket tomorrow to check up on Siena, and didn't appreciate Randall bugging him on a weekend.

'Yeah, this is Dan,' he said grumpily, taking the call in the relative privacy of his home office and closing the door behind him. 'What's up?'

'She's gone.' Randall's voice was controlled, but the fear was still unmistakable. 'Her mother came down here, pretending to be a nurse or something, and took her back to LA. You know anything about this?'

'Of course not,' Sanford snapped, although his heart sank as he immediately thought of the letter he'd received last month, about that 'relief nurse' for Melissa.

He'd thought it was a bit odd at the time, but he found dealing with Randall so unpleasant, and the whole business with Siena so troubling to his conscience, that he hadn't bothered to call him and double-check.

Shit. This wasn't good news.

'We need to talk,' said Randall. 'Figure out what we're gonna do. If she goes to the press . . .'

The doctor could hear his client's teeth grinding with stress on the

445

other end of the line and tried to marshal his own thoughts. His wife Cora knew nothing about his 'work' with Randall. He badly wanted to keep it that way, but that might not be possible now.

He wondered how hard it would be to wash his hands of Stein, even at this late stage.

'It could get very bad,' said Randall. 'We need to work out our stories, make sure there are no loose ends. I've got Dean Reid, my attorney, flying down here as we speak.'

'Good,' said Daniel, deciding on his strategy on the spur of the moment. 'You're gonna need him.'

'What do you mean, *I'm* gonna need him?' asked Randall, his nerves betraying themselves now in barely controlled spleen. 'You're in this up to your neck, my friend, and don't you forget it. You treated her and you didn't report it. And I don't need to remind you that this wasn't the first favour you've done me in return for a nice fat cheque. You could be struck off.'

He hissed out each word like venom. Daniel's heart was pounding – he knew there was some truth in what Randall was saying, but his only hope was to bluff it out and stand his ground.

'Bullshit,' he whispered, cupping his hand around the receiver. He didn't want his wife listening in. 'Siena gave me permission to operate. She signed the consents. It's up to her if she wants to go to the police, not me. I'm just the doctor. You've got nothing on me, Randall.'

'Listen, you piece of shit.' The cool façade had completely crumbled. Like most bullies, Randall seemed utterly thrown to find himself being stood up to for once. 'I'm nine million dollars in the red on this fucking movie. If Siena goes to the press, if she pins this on me, I'm gonna lose my financing.'

'How?' Daniel sounded maddeningly unconcerned.

'There's a morality clause in the contract,' said Randall. 'Basically if I do or say anything that might reflect badly on the movie's backers, they have the right to pull out. And as exec producer, I've underwritten the whole thing.'

'Hmmm.' Sanford paused to take in exactly what Stein was saying. 'So you mean if Siena can prove you beat her to a pulp, you'll have to pay the nine million yourself? Out of your own pocket?'

'Exactly,' said Randall. At last, Sanford seemed to be grasping the seriousness of the situation, the slimy little shit. 'So you'd better get your ass on a plane tonight. Because if I go down, you're going down with me. We need to shut her up, and we need to do it fast. For both our sakes.'

There was a long pause. This last rant smacked of desperation. Empty threats.

Finally, Daniel said: 'I don't think so, Randall. You know what? I hope that young lady *does* go to the press – and frankly, I can't see how you think you're going to stop her.'

There was some apoplectic wheezing from Randall's end, but the doctor showed no mercy.

'With any luck some of the other girls will come forward as well, and show the world what a twisted, arrogant, dangerous little son of a bitch you really are.'

'You'll regret this,' snarled Randall. 'I promise you. Your career will be *over*.'

Daniel ignored him.

'And as for losing the nine million dollars . . .' He paused, savouring the moment. Randall had had a hold over him for years. It felt wonderful to finally be free – whatever the ultimate cost turned out to be. 'What can I say? It couldn't happen to a nicer guy.'

He hung up, took a deep, satisfying breath and opened the study door, running straight into his wife. She had obviously been straining to hear the conversation, and her cheeks flushed red with embarrassment as he caught her in the act.

'Everything OK?' she asked anxiously. 'You sounded stressed.'

He smiled and put his arm around her.

'Absolutely,' he said. 'Everything's just fine, honey. Just fine.'

Siena had felt her first misgivings the moment her plane took off from Boston.

Not about leaving Randall. She had never made a decision she was more sure of in her entire life. But about the future. Clasping Claire's hand as the American Airlines jet roared shakily upward, the euphoria she'd felt about her sight and about finally breaking free had started to dissipate, and the precarious reality of her situation began to reassert itself.

Thanks to her bruises, dark glasses and a baseball cap, no one had given her a second glance as her mother paid for both their last-minute first-class tickets, and the two of them had shuffled on to the plane unnoticed by the other weary commuters.

After living and breathing for public adulation for so long, she was amazed by how liberating it felt not to be stared at. She was also grateful for her mother's silence.

Having called the hospital and ascertained that Pete's condition was serious but stable – as the specialist had put it, 'He's not going anywhere, Mrs McMahon. No need to bust a gut to get here' – Claire

447

had relaxed a little, and was able to focus on helping Siena. Sensing that her daughter needed to be alone with her thoughts, and craving her own distraction, she had immersed herself in a novel as soon as they took their seats, leaving Siena to stare out of the window and try to make sense of everything that had happened in the last twenty-four hours.

She wanted to make the bastard pay.

You can get mad, Duke used to tell her, *just as long as you get even*.

But that wasn't going to be easy. Randall was a formidable adversary, and he had a lot of power and influence in LA. Police, lawyers, movie studios, press – they could all be bought, or pressured by him into taking sides and twisting the truth. He would portray her as unstable, desperate, a liar.

If you go after me, Siena, I will crush you.

He was right about one thing. She would never work again in Hollywood. Not with her ruined face and only partial sight. To that extent, he had already crushed her.

Running her index finger along the groove of her long scar, she felt her resolve hardening. Somehow she would make him pay. But the next few months were going to be tough.

Hatred and rage against Randall gave way to sadness. She leaned her head against the plastic window and began, quietly, to cry. But her tears were not for her lost beauty, wealth and fame. Nor were they for all the lost time with the people she loved – her mother, Hunter, Ines. They were not even for her father, lying critically ill in his hospital bed, and the love it was too late for her to find with him.

She was crying for one person only.

And he was thousands of miles away in England, crying for her.

In Manhattan a week later, Max dragged himself up off the hard hotel bed and wearily began taking off his clothes. Perhaps a nice long bath would help.

He was actually becoming quite worried about himself. It wasn't normal for a man his age to keep crying. Some days the sadness was so overwhelming he was frightened to go out in public at all, in case he should suddenly burst into tears. Maybe he needed a shrink.

Lying back while the piping-hot water eased the stress and tension from his muscles, he tried to think positively about the future. After that terrible day when the developers had arrived at Batcombe, he had finally realised that there was no way he could go on trying to make things work with Freddie.

'You deserve better,' he told her. 'You deserve a man who still has his heart to give you.'

Closing his eyes now, he could picture her brave, heartbroken face, and almost started crying again. Why did he always have to hurt people?

'I don't want better,' she said. 'I want you.'

But they had both known there was nothing he could do.

After that, he'd had no real choice but to accept the offer to move to New York with the play, and had flown out two days earlier to begin an initial recce looking for an apartment.

He realised that he'd been kidding himself that Henry and Muff needed him at Manor Farm. The truth was that he had needed them. He couldn't bear to be alone with his grief, and his longing for Siena.

He had thought that Batcombe, the only place other than the beach house where he had ever really been happy, might ease some of the pain. But it hadn't. And now even that safe haven was being destroyed, turned into a battleground between Henry and Gary Ellis.

He had to get out.

Rising up out of the bath, he dried himself on one of the fluffy white hotel towels, sat down on the bed and flicked on his mobile to check for messages. There were two, and despite the absurdity of it he still felt a sharp pang of hope that perhaps one of them might be from Siena.

The first was from Muffy, just 'checking up' on him, as she put it.

He knew that she and Henry were concerned about him, and he felt guilty about adding to their worries. But he was grateful for her message all the same.

The second message was from Dorian Klein, his agent.

Shit. He'd forgotten to call the guy back again. What with the move and the play, and all the shit going on in his personal life, he just hadn't got around to it.

Punching out the number, he hoped that Dorian wasn't going to ask him to fly out to LA for some pointless meeting. To have to be that close to Siena and all his memories would be totally unbearable.

'Klein.'

Shit. He was answering his own phone now? Times must be tough.

'Hello, Dorian, it's Max De Seville. I'm sorry I didn't get back to you sooner.'

'Max? Jesus, man, where the fuck have you been?' He sounded genuinely stressed out, nothing like his usual slick, imperturbable self. 'Angus and I have been trying to reach you for weeks.'

Oh Christ, Angus. Now he came to think of it, he *did* remember getting a couple of calls from *Dark Heart*'s writer back in Batcombe, which he'd failed to return. Angus was on holiday in the Highlands, supposedly working on his new play, and Max had assumed he was

449

calling about that. He liked Angus a lot, but he just hadn't had the energy to provide any sort of artistic encouragement while his own world was caving in on him.

'Sorry,' he said sheepishly to Dorian. 'I've had a lot going on at home. Anyway, I'm here now. So what's up?'

The agent laughed.

'What's up, my friend, is that we've done the deal without you. I tried everything to get hold of you, but in the end Angus flew out here last night and signed on the dotted line himself. And before you start screaming at me, Max, he's perfectly legally entitled, it's still sixty per cent his baby . . .'

'Dorian.' Max interrupted him mid-flow. 'Slow down. I have no idea what you're talking about.'

The agent laughed again, and Max wondered what joke it was that was going over his head so completely.

'Let me give you a clue.' Dorian chuckled. 'Miramax.'

Max felt his heartbeat creeping upward. To be honest, he'd pushed the studio's supposed interest in the play to the back of his mind weeks ago. It had all seemed so unlikely – there was nothing Hollywood about *Dark Hearts* – whereas the move to Broadway was something real and tangible that he could focus on.

'You're not serious,' he said, once his breath had returned. 'You mean, they actually want it?'

'Forget "want it",' said Dorian. Max could hear him grinning down the phone. 'They bought it. Two days ago. For six million dollars.'

The ensuing silence was so long, Dorian began to worry that his client might have passed out.

'Max? Buddy? Are you there?'

Like an idiot, Max sat in his towel, nodding at the phone. He tried to speak but no sound came out.

'Look, if you're pissed about Angus signing,' said Dorian anxiously, 'you shouldn't be. We were under pressure to make a deal and if I do say so myself I think we got a great price.'

'No, no. It's not that. Sorry.' He was able to force some words out at last. 'It's fantastic. I'm just in shock. I think.'

Six million dollars.

What was forty per cent of six million? Two point four?

Holy shit.

He was rich.

'Look, Dorian,' he managed eventually after another long, shell-shocked silence. 'Do you mind if I call you back? I think I need to lie down.'

'Sure.' The agent laughed, delighted. 'You finally made me some money, Max. You can lie down for as long as you want.'

Max put down his mobile and lay back, slowly, on to the bed, staring up at the swirly patterns etched into the white ceiling. He tried to take it all in.

Two point four million dollars.

He was a rich man.

A success.

How very odd.

He waited for a rush of happiness to overtake him, but it didn't. Instead horrible tendrils of depression began tightening themselves painfully around his heart.

After all, without Siena to share it with, what did the money matter? What did anything matter? The money should have come to someone who could appreciate it, someone who deserved it, not to him.

But then, almost immediately, another thought occurred to him. And for the first time that day he felt almost happy.

Picking up the hotel phone this time – what the heck, he could afford it – he began to punch out the well-worn number. It rang twelve or thirteen times before a sleepy female voice answered.

'Muffy?' he said excitedly. 'It's me, Max. Look, I'm sorry to wake you up sweetheart. But I've got some good news for you. Some very, very good news.'

Chapter Fifty-two

After Minnie had died, Pete and Claire had moved back into the old mansion in Hancock Park to begin the process of sorting through her estate. The house held unhappy memories for both of them, but it was part of Pete's history, not to mention Hollywood history, and he hadn't immediately been sure what he wanted to do with it. Moving in temporarily seemed like the best way to make up their minds.

So it was to Siena's childhood home that mother and daughter returned when they came back from Nantucket.

Siena felt a strange mix of emotions as she stepped through the heavy wooden front door – the same door with its brass bolts and neo-Gothic panels. How many times had she fantasised about walking into this marble hallway, with its curling, sweeping staircase, the banisters worn to a sheen by generations of sliding children? She couldn't possibly count.

But somehow, now she was actually here, the joy she had anticipated for so long failed to materialise. The Hancock Park she had clung to in her dreams for so many years was the buzzing, vibrant home she remembered from her childhood. To her child's eye it had been a magnificent palace, a living presence, almost, which had absorbed her grandfather's energy and spirit until every wall, every staircase, felt alive. Now she was returning to the reality – a lonely, empty shell of a house, shrouded with all the betrayals and disappointments of her grandmother's life.

It wasn't just that Minnie had redecorated, eradicating all of Duke's vulgarity. By any rational, adult standards, Siena recognised, those changes constituted a dramatic improvement. It was more than that.

It was as if the house she remembered had died all those years ago, along with her childhood and her happiness. Looking around her now, she couldn't help but mourn for it.

Claire took one look at her pale, shaken face and put her straight to bed with a cup of hot chocolate into which she had crushed two Rohypnol. It had been a long and difficult journey for Siena and she was still very weak physically.

She protested, but her mother was firm.

They would talk in the morning.

The next day, Siena had been so frail she couldn't get out of bed. Claire could hardly bear to leave her for a second, but she had to go to the hospital and see Pete.

'Are you sure you'll be all right, darling?' she asked anxiously, plumping up Siena's pillows as she prepared to leave. 'I spoke to Dr Davis last night and he'll be in to see you at ten.' Dr Davis had been the McMahon family doctor since Siena was knee high. Just hearing his name reassured her. 'He can talk to you about eye specialists, and sort out some pain relief. And I'll be home as soon as I can.'

'Really, Mom, I'm fine.' She smiled weakly through her exhaustion. The long journey, combined with all the emotional stress of the last twenty-four hours, was really starting to catch up with her. 'You just focus on Dad.'

Seeing Pete was a shock.

'He looks terrible,' Claire said frankly to the senior consultant, looking at his pale, apparently lifeless body rigged up to a horrible-looking mesh of wires and machinery. 'Are you sure he's stable?'

The consultant had explained, kindly but very clearly, that 'stable' meant nothing more than that his heart was not expected to stop again imminently. It didn't mean that he would not have another attack in the future. And it didn't mean that he would ever regain consciousness.

He might. But as of today, no one could say for sure which way things would go. Nor could they tell her how long it would be before his condition changed, for better or worse.

For the next week, Claire made the daily trip into Cedars alone. She longed to bring Siena with her, but Dr Davis had warned her not to rush things.

'Give her time,' he'd said. 'She'll be fine, but she needs to regain her strength.'

About ten days after their return home, Siena was finally well enough to make it downstairs for breakfast. She still looked terrible, although she insisted she had slept well and Claire was greatly encouraged to see her smiling for the first time in weeks when a totally hyperactive Zulu, her beloved bichon frise, launched himself into Siena's lap like a rocket-propelled pom-pom and began frenziedly licking her face.

She laughed. 'Nice to see that someone still appreciates me.'

Claire clucked around her like a mother hen in her old white dressing gown – she had had the same one since Siena was little – making toast and coffee and signalling for Siena to sit still and be waited on.

'It feels funny, being here. In this kitchen,' said Siena. 'Sitting at this table. This is where Grandpa died, right here.'

She stretched out her fingers and swept them in an arc across the worn wood of the table, lost in the awful memory. Whatever his failings, as a father, a husband, a man, Siena had loved her grandfather with the pure, uncomplicated adoration of a child. Duke's death had marked the end of her childhood and the beginning of a long and painful journey. But the irony was that it was a journey that had ultimately led her back to Hancock Park, to this same table. She had come full circle.

'I know, honey.' Claire placed a steaming mug of milky coffee in front of her daughter. 'But we had a lot of good times at this table as well.' When Siena didn't say anything, she went on, 'I think your grandfather would be pleased to see you back home.'

That made Siena smile and, while she petted Zulu and nibbled at the peanut-butter toast that Claire had piled high in front of her, she found herself starting to talk about Randall. It was the first time she had admitted to anyone, perhaps even to herself, just *how* controlling and abusive he had been. The first time she had said the words out loud, anyway.

Claire let her finish without interruption. She wasn't about to pass judgement, or even offer advice. It was up to Siena what she wanted to do now. And whether she decided to risk going after him through the courts or the press, or just walked away and let it go, this time she was going to be there for her daughter one hundred per cent.

'Well,' she said at last, once Siena's stream of consciousness had come to a natural end, 'that's all in the past now, my angel. I'm just glad you're here.'

'Me too.' Siena smiled at her, pushing all thoughts of Randall from her mind for the time being.

'So,' said Claire, kissing the top of her head and clearing away her empty plate, 'I guess we should think about heading for the hospital.'

'Oh, I don't know, Mom.' Siena frowned nervously. 'I'm not sure that's such a good idea.'

'What do you mean?' asked Claire. 'You want to see your father, don't you?'

Siena felt torn. The truth was, she was terrified of seeing Pete and had no idea how she was going to react once she got into that hospital room. On the other hand, she knew how desperate her mother was to be at his bedside, and to have her support. It was almost obscene to sit here worrying about herself when her dad might be dying, whatever she did or didn't feel for him. But she couldn't seem to help it.

'Well, what if the press see me?' she heard herself saying, knowing how selfish she must sound and cursing herself inside. 'They'll go beserk.'

'No they won't,' said Claire reasonably. 'No one recognised you on the plane from Boston, did they? Besides, so what if they do see you? It's hardly a crime to visit your own father when he's d . . .' She only just stopped herself from saying it. 'When he's seriously ill.'

Siena thought about it.

'Did you speak to his doctor today?' she asked. Claire nodded. She looked terribly anxious suddenly. She must have aged years in the last few days. 'Is he conscious?'

'He hasn't been. Not for the last forty-eight hours.'

'All right, then,' said Siena. She was scared shitless, but so what? It was time to put her mother first for once. 'In that case, I'll come with you.'

Kenneth Sams was starting to get pissed off.

He'd been over the moon when he heard that he was going to get the bulk of the shifts taking care of Pete McMahon. All the other nurses had been *sooo* jealous.

'You're bound to meet loads of celebrities coming to visit,' they said.

'Hunter world's-most-beautiful-man McMahon is sure to come see his brother,' they said.

That was over a week ago. And how many famous movie stars had he met? How many gorgeous, tight-assed TV hunks had stopped by to patch things up with their only brother before he croaked?

None.

Nothing. *Nada*. Zip.

Only the old boy's wife, who was a nice enough lady and all, and occasionally his blubbering lump of a sister. For a guy who had practically ruled Hollywood for the last fifteen years, Pete McMahon sure didn't seem to have a lot of friends.

This morning, Kenny had checked on his patient as usual – still no change – and was heading back to the staff room for a slug of coffee when he saw Mrs McMahon arriving. Only this time, she wasn't alone.

All he could make out of her companion as they approached was that she was small and female, but he noticed she was wearing big dark glasses and a scarf – the classic celeb disguise!

'Hello, Mrs McMahon.' He minced over to them excitedly, staring without restraint at Siena's scar and collapsed cheek. 'He's still sleeping, I'm afraid. And are you, er, another friend of the family?' He cocked his head curiously at her.

'No,' said Siena rudely. She was in no mood to pander to some nosy queen of a nurse. 'Did you mean asleep, or is he unconscious?'

Kenny paused. She didn't look much like her, but then they could do incredible retouches these days on some of those magazine pictures. And he was sure he recognised the voice.

'Unconscious,' he said. 'He's still unconscious.'

'Fine,' said Siena. 'Well, we'd like to see him now, please.'

She swept into the private room regally, with Claire following anxiously behind.

'Did you really have to be so rude to him?' she said once the door was safely closed behind them. 'Kenny's your father's nurse and he's always been really helpful and supportive.'

'Sorry,' said Siena, although privately she thought 'Kenny' looked like a classic star-fucker and could imagine exactly what had inspired his 'support' towards her mom. 'I just don't want people asking too many questions, you know?'

Down the hall, Kenny pumped three quarters into the nurses' payphone and tried to stop his heart from pounding.

'Hello?' he stammered breathlessly. '*LA Times*? Yeah, put me through to the news desk, please. Uh-huh. Yeah, my name's Kenneth. Kenneth Sams.'

Staring at her father, Siena tried to feel something, anything. But it was as if she had no emotion left at all.

He was naked from the waist up and fatter than she remembered, with his sandy red chest hair shaved to allow six round pads trailing wires to be stuck to his rib cage, as though somebody might be planning to electrocute him. His face looked unusually placid – he didn't appear to be in any pain – and his breathing was deep and regular.

Claire pulled up a chair and positioned herself beside him, taking his limp hand in hers and stroking it as she spoke to him.

'Siena is here, honey,' she said. 'She's come to visit you. She's come back home.'

Pete made not the slightest flicker of recognition and Siena relaxed slightly. At least he wasn't going to wake up and start screaming at her. Unfortunately, she did not share her mother's belief that he

456

would feel anything other than anger should he wake and find the prodigal daughter returned.

The room was cold and clinical and smelt sterilised. It made Siena shudder. She'd seen more than her fair share of hospitals recently. The only noise was a dull, constant hum from the high-tech-looking machine next to Pete's bed, which she assumed was some sort of heart monitor, although it didn't have one of those green, blippy screens with a squiggly line like they had in all the TV shows.

The thought occurred to her that if Pete had had his way, she would have gone to Oxford and become a fully fledged doctor by now, and would no doubt understand the significance of every blip and whirr.

On the table next to the machine, two huge vases of pale yellow roses, Claire's favourite flowers, defiantly attempted to inject some colour and natural beauty into the sterile room. But even they, Siena noticed, had started to brown and fray at the tips of the petals, as if contaminated by the artificial atmosphere all around them.

'Are you OK, Mom?' she asked, trying to smile for Claire's sake. 'You want me to go get you anything from the canteen? Some coffee or something?'

Claire shook her head. 'No, darling. I have everything I ever wanted right here.'

She took hold of Siena's hand and placed it on top of Pete's and between her own. Siena closed her eyes and tried with all her might to feel something.

It was no good. She was still numb.

What kind of heartless monster was she?

As if reading her mind, Claire said gently, 'It's all right, darling, it's not your fault. You haven't seen him in a long time.'

'I'm sorry,' Siena whispered in reply. Then she blurted it out. 'I don't think I love him, Mom. I really don't.'

'Shhh,' said Claire, placing two fingers gently over Siena's lips to silence her. 'It doesn't matter. You're here, darling. That's all that matters. Why don't you try talking to him? Tell him how you feel.'

Tell him how she felt? She very much doubted whether he or her mother would be ready to hear the truth, even if she knew what to say, where to begin. But she could tell from Claire's anxious, desperately hopeful face that she was longing for her to make some sort of gesture of reconciliation.

She knew in her heart she couldn't forgive him. It was too late for that. But she could do this one small thing for her mother. She had to do it.

Taking Pete's hand in hers, she cleared her throat awkwardly.

'Hello, Dad,' she said, blushing self-consciously as she spoke. 'It's me, Siena. I . . .' She stumbled, unsure of what her mother would want her to say. In the end, she decided to keep it simple. 'I want you to know that I love you, and I forgive you. For everything.'

Suddenly, she let out a little scream of shock and jumped back from the bed, as if a snake had bitten her.

'What is it?' asked Claire in panic. 'What's the matter?'

'Holy shit,' said Siena, whose heart was beating like a rapid-fire machine gun. 'He squeezed my hand. Jesus, Mom. I think he heard me.'

They stayed for almost two more hours, Claire talking almost constantly to Pete and Siena doing her best to make some further show of affection for her mother's sake, holding his hand and at one point wiping the sweat from his forehead with a flannel – but to Claire's dismay he made no further noise or movement whatsoever.

She started to wonder whether Siena had imagined the squeeze. But Siena knew for certain it had happened. It had scared the hell out of her.

During the long, awkward silences, Siena was ashamed to find her mind wandering to other things.

She thought about her sight and whether it would ever fully recover. She'd seen the eye specialist at home yesterday for an initial consultation, and he'd been guardedly encouraging, but by no means certain he could put things right.

She thought a lot about Hunter too, and everything that had happened between them. She longed to go and see him, to tell him how sorry she was for everything. But when she pictured herself walking up to his door and pressing the buzzer, she found she was frozen with terror.

What if he didn't forgive her? What if Tiffany refused to even give her the time of day, refused to let her in? She didn't think she could bear it if Hunter were to reject her now.

Most of all, though, she thought about Max.

It was funny how, after ruthlessly blocking out all her feelings for him for over a year, she now seemed incapable of going a minute without images of his face popping up unbidden in her mind. After he cheated on her, she'd been so hurt, so blinded with misery, that it had seemed easy, cathartic even, to blame him for everything. She'd nursed her anger like a mother nursing her child, egged on of course by Randall, until it had hardened into a safe protective shell around her heart. She had remembered nothing good about him.

But now, she felt as if the dam was breaking, and all those good and happy memories were flooding out, assaulting her senses, cracking what was left of her weakened self-defences. And for the first time, she realised that perhaps it wasn't all his fault. That perhaps, in the months they were together, she might have said or done things to push him away.

She missed him so much. She wanted to say sorry, for the way she'd treated him when he gatecrashed the party at Malibu and tried to help her. She wanted to say sorry for everything.

The thought of never seeing him again was infinitely more painful to her than any of her injuries, but she didn't even know where he lived any more. Besides, even if she tracked him down, she could hardly expect him to want her now, with her shattered face and her scars. She was practically a cripple. The whole thing was utterly hopeless.

Finally, Claire agreed that they should take a break and go and get some lunch.

'Do you mind if we get out of the hospital?' Siena asked her. 'I really need some air. We could grab a bite up on Melrose or something, sit inside at Le Pain. No one will recognise us there.'

'Sure, honey,' said Claire.

She could tell that Siena felt ill at ease and had been itching to escape ever since they got there. She had also noticed her scratching and worrying at her right eye, constantly taking off her dark glasses to touch the still-red scars. She prayed that the new specialist would be able to help her. God only knew what a hatchet job Randall's doctors might have done on her.

Mother and daughter walked hand in hand to the elevator and shot down the seventeen floors to the lobby in just a few seconds. Scarf and shades firmly in place, and with her head down, Siena walked across the polished marble floor to the electric double doors, which opened as they approached to let them out into the December sunshine.

She winced as a flashbulb erupted in her face.

The noise was deafening.

'Siena! Is it true that you had a breakdown?'

'Siena, what does Randall Stein think about your reconciliation with your family?'

'How do you feel? Can you tell us anything about your father's condition?'

'Mrs McMahon, what's it like to be reunited with your daughter after all these years?'

Siena tried in vain to shield her face with her hands, but the cameras kept rolling, their flashes blinding her sensitive eyes so she had to cling to her mother helplessly for support.

'Leave us alone!' shouted Claire, but she was barely audible over the frenzied pushing and shouting of the press pack that now surrounded them. 'We have nothing to say.'

She looked back longingly over her shoulder at the hospital doors, but at least two TV crews stood between her and safety. She was conscious of Siena shivering like a frightened fawn beside her, clinging on to her sleeve for dear life. How on earth were they going to get out of here?

Suddenly she heard a male voice piercing the racket. She couldn't quite place it at first, although she was sure she recognised it from somewhere.

'Excuse me. Out of my way, please. Coming through.'

The voice was calm but forceful, and the scrum of reporters audibly quietened and backed away slightly to allow its owner to move forward. When he appeared beside her, Claire didn't think she had ever been so pleased to see anyone in her life.

'Come on,' said Hunter. 'Let's get you two inside.'

He scooped Siena up into his arms – Jesus Christ, she was thin, she weighed almost nothing – and ushered Claire towards the hospital doors, elbowing aside journalists and cameramen effortlessly as he strode forward.

'Hunter!' came the yells from behind them.

'Are you here to see your brother?'

'Can you tell us about Siena's breakdown? When did you two last see each other?'

'Has your brother's heart attack brought the family back together? Hunter!'

As they approached the doors, hospital security surged forward to let them through and keep the cameras back. Claire glanced back to see a crowd of faces pressed up against the glass at the sides, and where the doors stood open in the middle hundreds of arms were blindly thrusting tape recorders and cameras into the lobby, desperate for one last comment or shot.

How could Siena, or anyone, ever have *chosen* to live like this?

Hunter carried Siena, who was still shaking, into the elevator, and she let out a loud sigh of relief as the doors closed behind them.

'What floor?' he asked.

He looked enormous in the confined space of the elevator, and Siena seemed little more than a limp rag doll, pressed against the broad white-shirted expanse of his chest.

Claire hadn't seen him since he was a teenager, although she'd seen pictures. He'd grown into quite a man. He looked frighteningly like a young Duke.

She stood there, gazing at him blankly, and said nothing.

'What button should I press?' he asked again.

'Seventeen,' said Claire.

And to her own surprise, as the elevator lurched upward with a stomach-churning whoosh, she suddenly burst into tears.

Upstairs, the three of them filed back into Pete's room. Hunter set Siena down gently on the softer of the two chairs, and tried not to look at the pitiful spectacle of his brother, while Claire perched on the edge of the bed.

'Thank you,' she said. 'I don't know what we'd have done without you down there.'

Siena seemed to have been struck dumb. She was overjoyed to see Hunter, but what was she supposed to say? 'Thanks for saving my ass again, sorry for being such a manipulative bitch, and by the way, did you notice I now look like a freak?'

'Hey, c'mon, it was nothing,' he mumbled awkwardly to Claire. 'I just stopped by . . . you know. I thought maybe I'd just ask how he was doing. I mean, I wasn't meaning to intrude or anything. I wouldn't even have come up to the room.'

'It's wonderful you're here,' said Claire.

He would never know how incredibly touched she was that he had cared enough to come and see Pete. Hunter, of all people, owed him absolutely nothing.

'I wanna go back out there.' Both Hunter and Claire were startled to hear Siena speak. It took a moment for them to take in what she was saying. 'I want them to see what Randall did to me. This is as good a time as any.'

Hunter tried not to show how shocked he was by the damage to her face. He had caught a glimpse of her injuries downstairs, but she was so well wrapped up, and he'd been so focused on getting her out of the scrum of reporters, that this was the first time he'd had a chance to take in the full extent of her scars.

He felt physically sick, not because of how she looked but because of Stein's unimaginable, bestial savagery. And because he hadn't been there to save her when she needed him. Now it was his turn to be struck dumb with guilt.

It was Claire who spoke first. 'Are you sure, Siena? This morning you were worried about seeing any press at all. There are so many of them down there, darling. Are you sure you can handle it?'

Siena nodded grimly. 'I've handled worse.'

'And you've really thought this through, have you?'

Claire wanted Randall to suffer for what he'd done more than anybody, but she was still scared of what all the publicity and perhaps a protracted, expensive lawsuit might do to Siena. She had almost hoped that her daughter would decide just to let the whole thing drop. That way, they could all move on with their lives as if Randall Stein had never existed.

'I've thought about nothing else for the last two weeks,' said Siena. Despite her bruises, Hunter could see the flash of strength and determination he remembered so well lighting up her eyes. He felt immensely proud of her. 'I'm gonna get that fucker.'

Emerging through the front doors a few minutes later, supported by Hunter, she was greeted by a second furore of flashbulbs and shouted questions. But this time she was ready for them.

Slowly, as if savouring the moment, she removed her dark glasses and scarf, allowing the astounded photographers and film crews a full minute to capture every angle of her ravaged face.

She had thought her strategy through carefully. She wasn't going to explicitly accuse Randall and open herself up to a lawsuit and police investigation. This was a town where might was right, and she knew that there was a solid chance, despite the evidence of her injuries, that Randall could defeat her in court and quite possibly bankrupt her into the bargain.

She would be silent, let the pictures speak for themselves, and damn him by implication. That should easily generate enough negative publicity to destroy his career, and reveal him to the world as the monster he truly was, without allowing him the opportunity of a legal defence.

Why should Siena need to accuse him herself, when she could get the rest of the world to do it for her?

After a decent interval, and once she was pretty sure that they all had the shots they needed, she held up her hand for quiet and announced that she wanted to make a statement. It took a further minute or so for the crowd to quieten down sufficiently to allow her to speak.

'As you can appreciate,' she began in a quiet but steady voice, 'this is a very difficult and emotional time for me and for my family.' Hunter squeezed her hand and she squeezed back. 'My father is very ill. And I am also in the process of recovering from a violent attack.'

A murmur of questions began building, but she held up her hand for silence before continuing.

'I will not be making any comment today, or at any other time, about the circumstances of that attack. Or . . .'

She paused dramatically.

'Or disclosing who did this to me. For personal reasons, I don't wish to press charges against that individual, or to involve the police. However, I would like to take this opportunity to correct an earlier statement by Mr Randall Stein – that's S-T-E-I-N.' The reporters laughed at that, and Siena couldn't help but smile back. She was still the media's darling. 'Implying that I had been suffering from a nervous or emotional breakdown. The only sign of mental illness I've shown in the last year was moving in with Mr Stein in the first place.'

More laughter.

'Thank you all for your support. That's all I have to say.'

She turned to go back into the building with the deafening shout of more questions ringing in her ears.

'Why aren't you pressing charges?'

'Have you seen or spoken to Randall since the attack?'

'Will Stein be making a statement, Siena? Siena!'

With some difficulty, Hunter ushered her back into the elevator.

'You OK?' he asked as the doors closed.

But it was a stupid question. Her face was flushed with triumph. She'd just pulled the pin out and lobbed a hand grenade right into Randall's life.

What could be better than that?

'I'm fine,' was all she said. 'I'm sorry, Hunter. For everything.'

'Me too,' he said, and pressed her fragile body into his chest as if trying to prove it. 'I'm sorry I wasn't there to stop him.'

Randall's financial backers heard the news before he did.

He took the call in the car.

'Listen, John, it's all bullshit, OK? She can't prove a thing. I'll be talking to my attorney about it within the hour; this has to be libellous.'

But they weren't interested in listening to his bluster.

'That's your problem, Randall. Look at your contract. It's very clear. The morality clause says we pull out if continued association with the project can be shown to reflect detrimentally on Orion Enterprises, *for any reason.*'

'But, John, these are just rumours. Come on. You can't seriously expect me to fall on my sword to the tune of nine million dollars on the basis of some unsubstantiated, malicious gossip. I'm telling you, she's unstable. John? Hello? Hello?'

But the line had already gone dead.

Chapter Fifty-three

The next few weeks were a roller-coaster of emotions for Siena.

The pictures of her battered face outside the hospital made the front pages all across America, and speculation about her injuries was rife. The accusations against Randall were all made indirectly with cautiously worded caveats and lots of 'allegedly's sprinkled around for good measure – the papers didn't want to get sued any more than she did – but the damage was done. Both his main backers had pulled out of 1943 and he'd taken a huge financial bath on the failed movie. What no one could put a price on, though, was the damage to his reputation.

Randall Stein's Hollywood glory days were well and truly over.

He made only one public comment on the matter, telling a journalist as he emerged from his limo at a charity gala that he and Siena remained friends and that he wished her well and categorically denying any involvement in her injuries.

Siena noticed with a wry smile that he was accompanied to the event by none other than Miriam Stanley, the starlet who'd been so desperate to get her money-grabbing claws into him that night at the Beverly Hills Hotel.

Good luck to her!

Now that she'd had her revenge she felt nothing, nothing at all for Randall. She couldn't even muster much anger any more. He existed for her only in a past life, a life that was now gone for ever.

It wasn't all good news, though. Some of the comments about her scars were hurtful, although Siena found herself feeling more resilient than she'd thought she would be. Now that she had her family back, she no longer felt defined by her beauty, or her fame, in the way that she had before, and the barbs about her lost looks mostly felt more like nettle stings than piercing arrows.

Mercifully, the media had begun to lose interest in Pete's illness as the weeks went by without any noticeable change in his condition. The doctors had told them that he might never regain consciousness,

464

but Claire refused to give up hope. She continued to visit him every day, and Siena accompanied her occasionally, mostly without overt harassment from the press.

Hunter began spending a lot of time at Hancock Park, at both Siena and Claire's request.

Tiffany was very wary at first about him building bridges with Siena yet again.

'I just don't want to see you hurt again,' she'd told him, when he'd first suggested it one weekend at their little house in Venice. 'Every time she's down, she needs you, but as soon as she gets her strength back she forgets all about you and moves on.'

They were sitting on the sofa together in front of the fire, watching the unexpected rain outside as it hammered mercilessly against the window panes and gushed along the walk streets in torrents, like some biblical flood. In LA, rain was an event, and Tiffany had been quite happy just to sit and watch it with Hunter, until Siena's name, as usual, shattered her peace and contentment.

Inevitably, he insisted that this time was different, that she really had changed, and pleaded with her to come with him over to Hancock Park for dinner. Tiffany remained sceptical.

'Just one dinner, baby. Please?' he persisted. 'And if you never want to see her again after that, I swear to God, I'll understand.'

'*One* dinner?' She was weakening.

'One, I promise you.' He beamed at her. 'Only one. I just want you to see her, that's all.'

The evening marked a turning point for all of them.

Tiffany didn't know what was more shocking, Siena's ravaged appearance or her obviously genuine remorse for her past behaviour.

'I was jealous of you,' Siena had admitted, when the two of them took a private walk in the moonlit grounds after dinner. For Tiffany, who had never been to Hancock Park before, the whole experience was surreal. She'd heard so much about the unhappiness of Hunter's childhood here, and the emotional torture he'd been put through by just about every adult member of his family, that in her mind she'd built the place up as some sort of House of Horrors. But now that she was actually here, walking round the orangery with Siena, the reality of the estate in all its beauty and opulence took her breath away.

'Jealous of *me*?' She sounded incredulous. 'Why?'

'Because you had Hunter's love,' said Siena. 'Because you deserved it.'

She still walked slowly, owing to the recurrent pain in her ribs, and Tiffany had to make a conscious effort to slow down her own pace in sympathy. When they came to the rose garden and an old wooden bench, Siena eased herself down on to it to catch her breath and Tiffany sat beside her.

'He always loved you too, you know,' she said. 'Always.'

Siena nodded weakly. She looked so fragile, as if the slightest gust of wind might pick her up and blow her away.

'I know,' she said. 'It's hard to explain. But I always felt . . . I always *knew* that I didn't deserve it. I didn't deserve his love. I was scared that if he knew what I was really like, what a selfish, horrible person I was, he'd run away from me like everyone else. He's so perfect, you know?'

'I know.' Tiffany couldn't help but grin. 'He really is. Did, er, did he tell you our news?'

She'd sworn to Hunter that she wouldn't say anything, but somehow the time felt right. Siena shook her head and looked up at her inquisitively.

'I'm not supposed to tell you yet.' She smiled. 'So you have to promise not to say anything. But, well, I'm pregnant.'

'Oh! Oh, how wonderful!' Siena stumbled shakily to her feet and threw her arms around her in genuine affection and excitement. 'A baby! Oh, I hope it looks like Hunter.' She immediately clapped her hand over her mouth, realising that what she'd just said might be considered rude. 'I didn't mean . . .' she began, but Tiffany just laughed.

'That's OK,' she said. 'I hope it looks like him too.' She took Siena's arm in hers and they began walking back towards the house. Bathed in silver moonlight, it looked incredibly romantic, like some medieval Spanish castle. No wonder the whole world had envied Hunter for growing up here. If only they knew . . .

'You realise,' she said as they approached the steps to the huge oak front door, 'that this baby is going to be your cousin?'

'Holy shit!' said Siena, now laughing herself. 'Really? How fucked up is that?'

At least her bad language was still intact. Tiffany had begun to worry that the real Siena had been abducted by aliens and she was talking to a sweet and charming impostor.

It wasn't until after Christmas, and some two weeks after this conversation with Tiffany, that Siena finally summoned up the courage to ask Hunter about Max.

She had been hoping that he or Tiffany might offer up some information voluntarily, or at least casually mention Max's name in passing so that she could raise the subject naturally. But whether it was out of sensitivity to her own feelings or for some other reason, neither of them had said a word. In the end she could bear it no longer and tackled Hunter about it one morning at breakfast.

She put down her newspaper and smiled at him across the table. The bruising around her eyes was finally starting to fade, he noticed, and thanks to a recent visit to Claire's doctor her broken cheekbone had been reset correctly, making her look more like a bashed-up version of the old Siena than the stranger he'd taken in his arms at the hospital. She still had almost no vision in her right eye, but she was definitely on the mend.

He smiled back.

'Do you . . .' She cleared her throat. Her heart was pounding violently, but she made herself go on. 'Do you ever hear from Max any more?'

'Sometimes,' said Hunter warily. He had been anticipating this question and also dreading it. He didn't want Siena to have to go through any more pain.

'Only sometimes? You used to be so close.'

'Well, he moved back to England a while ago. We are close but, you know, we don't speak as much as we used to. Life moves on.'

'Yes, it does,' said Siena sadly, retreating behind her paper again.

Hunter could tell that her thoughts were already miles away. He didn't want her to pin her hopes on a reconciliation with Max, only to be disappointed. He wanted her to look forward, not back.

'Listen, sweetheart,' he said. 'I'm not sure things would ever have worked out between the two of you in the long run. Even if he hadn't . . .' He paused, not wanting to rake up any more unhappy memories for her. 'Even if things hadn't happened the way they did. You're very different people.'

'Is he still in England?' Siena couldn't help but ask. She knew Hunter was right, she should let it go. But she had to know where he was, where she should picture him in her thoughts and dreams.

'No,' he said brusquely. 'He moved to New York. He's directing a play there, I think.'

'Oh.' She digested this information silently for a moment. 'Does he have a girlfriend?'

'Siena.' Hunter frowned. 'You have to move on, honey. Forget about Max. He's part of the past, remember? You have a whole new life now. One day, you're going to meet someone else, someone who's going to be wonderful to you and love you and give you all the happiness and stability you need. Trust me. I know you don't believe it now, but it's true.'

'Does he?' she insisted.

She had to know.

Goddam. He was clearly never going to get her to drop it. So he took a deep breath and did something that he couldn't remember ever having done before. He lied to her.

'Yes,' he said, picking at a crumb on the table and not meeting Siena's eye. 'A French girl. I think it's fairly serious.'

He hated himself for saying it, as he knew full well that Max had ended things with Freddie before he moved. But it was the only way he could think of to make Siena let go. The only way to protect her.

Every word knifed into Siena's heart like a razor, but not by a flicker did she betray her emotions. She was scared that once she gave in to that pain, once she let it show, she might never be able to stop crying.

With every last ounce of her will-power, she held back the tears, and even managed a weak smile.

'I'm happy for him,' she said. Hunter looked at her doubtfully. 'Really, I am. He deserves it. He deserves to be happy.'

'I think I need help. I know it's ridiculous and self-indulgent and, well, damn stupid after everything that's happened. But I'm still so unhappy. Some days I feel like I can barely breathe.'

The elderly doctor looked at Max and smiled reassuringly.

It wasn't every day that a young, talented, newly minted millionaire walked into his surgery with glaring symptoms of depression: sleeplessness, uncontrolled crying, loss of energy, inability to concentrate; this guy had the lot.

'You *are* showing signs of mild clinical depression,' he announced, trying to be gentle. Max looked shocked. 'I can refer you to a psychiatrist, who may be able to prescribe something.'

'What, like Prozac?' said Max, aghast. 'I'm not sure I'm ready for all that.'

The doctor smiled again. 'You could try counselling of some sort. A lot of people find cognitive behavioural therapy to be useful in combating emotional or mood disorders. You'd probably have to do it privately, though, if you wanted to start soon. It's about fifty pounds a session, I believe.'

Max grinned. 'Yeah, well. I guess I can afford it.'

He was back at Batcombe after an extended Christmas vacation, and decided on a whim to pop into the doctor's surgery in the village while out for one of his many solitary walks.

Having given Henry and Muffy a huge injection of cash with which to buy off the odious Ellis and reclaim the farm, he'd been guest of honour at Christmas. The last of the trucks and building equipment had gone by early December, and all that was left to remind them of the whole sorry nightmare was a muddy drive and a couple of big piles of bricks in the corner of the old farmyard.

'I'll pay you back. I'll make good every penny,' Henry had assured him, endlessly, although Max had no intention of letting him do any such thing.

'Pay me back for what? For giving you some money that I did nothing to earn and certainly don't need? Behave yourself.'

'It's not just *some money*, Max,' said Muffy, who was busily putting the last of the children's presents around the Christmas tree. 'It's a bloody fortune.'

'Believe me,' he told them both. 'I'm doing this as much for myself as for you. Manor Farm has always been like home to me. I'm as happy to be rid of that bastard as you are.'

Ellis, as it turned out, had proved a lot easier to buy off than they had feared.

The golf course was already running behind schedule and way over budget, and the bad feeling on-site after Gary's ill-advised lunge at Muffy had caused him no end of trouble with his foreman. Along with most of the men, Ben McIntyre had developed a lot of sympathy for the Arkells, and disapproved of the way his boss had maliciously taunted and harassed them for months on end.

'I want a damn sight more than I paid for it,' Gary had told Max gruffly when he first floated the idea of a buy-back on the lease. 'I've lost a small bleedin' fortune on that place so far, and I'm sure as 'ell not leaving while I'm down on the deal.'

But despite his bravado, he'd agreed on a fair price. Now that the new section of the M40 was no longer being routed via Witney, Batcombe was not quite the ultra-desirable site it had once been. That, combined with the fact that he was clearly never going to get anywhere with Muffy, made him glad to be rid of the place.

Max knew he ought to have felt happy.

Happy for Henry and Muff about the farm, happy at his own unexpected good fortune. He had never dreamed that *Dark Hearts* would come good in such spectacular style. And it wasn't just the money he had to be thankful for. There was the opening of the play and his new life in New York to look forward to as well.

Plus, he was finally free of the stifling relationship with Freddie which had caused him such torments of guilt for so long. Darling Freddie, she had even sent him a Christmas card from France, full of kindness and without any bitterness or reproach, telling him all about her new life and friends back in Toulouse. Oh, to be so young and resilient, thought Max.

Christmas came and went, and he did his best to smile through it all and join in the festivities. But even the children could see that something was wrong. When Maddie had asked him one night at supper why he only smiled with his lips – 'You've switched your eyes off,' as she put it – he'd had to leave the table and bolt upstairs to his room to cry.

Thanking the GP, he walked out of the surgery and into the cold drizzle of the village. Perhaps things would improve when he got back to New York.

He trudged down the hill towards the farm, willing himself to believe that work and the non-stop, sleepless energy of the city might jolt him out of his stupor. Only three more days until he went back. Rehearsals started in earnest next week.

As he passed the village school, he took out of his Barbour pocket the piece of paper that the doctor had given him, with the name and number of a local psychiatrist and a depression helpline. He let a few stray droplets of rain fall on it, smudging the ink, before screwing it up into a tight ball and dropping it into the bin.

He didn't need a psychiatrist.

He needed Siena.

It was New Year's Eve in Los Angeles, and Siena and Claire were enjoying a low-key celebratory dinner in Hancock Park, each wanting nothing more than the other's company.

Hunter and Tiffany had gone to Colorado to see her parents and tell them all about the baby. Siena wondered how they were going to take the news. She supposed that even the Wedans would have to bestow their blessing now that their daughter and Hunter were starting a family together.

The evening had been so incredibly peaceful that both women were startled when the phone started ringing at eleven o'clock.

Siena was in her pyjamas, curled up with a book by the fire in the room that Grandpa used to call the den, while Claire composed a letter to one of her college girlfriends.

'It's probably just Aunt Laurie, getting confused with the time zones,' said Siena, as her mother walked into the hallway to answer it. 'Just say "Happy New Year" now, so she doesn't call back.'

Claire gave her daughter a reprimanding frown. Poor Laurie, she was harmless really, although she *could* be a nuisance at times. She was with friends in New York tonight, so at least she wouldn't be lonely.

Siena, who went straight back to her book and forgot all about the call, didn't notice Claire replace the receiver, white faced, and come back into the room. She started and turned around when she heard her mother speak.

'That was the hospital,' said Claire. 'There was no time to call us, apparently. It all happened very quickly.'

'Oh, Mom.' She ran up to her shivering mother and hugged her tightly. 'I'm so sorry.'

'So am I, my darling,' said Claire. One heavy, solitary tear rolled down her cheek and splashed down on to Siena's shoulder. 'I'm sorry for so many things.'

Pete's funeral was small and private. Only Siena, Claire, Tiffany, Hunter and Laurie attended.

Laurie wept openly and profusely. She and Pete had never been close, but she had never married, and he was the only other person in the world who had shared her childhood memories, as painful as they were.

Siena hadn't seen her aunt since her early teens, but she was shocked at how badly she'd aged. She was only in her mid fifties, but looked twenty years older at least, with her completely grey hair worn in a severe bun that made her look like the granny from the Tweety Pie cartoons.

Claire's grief was more dignified and controlled. Whatever regrets she may have had about her marriage and the choices she had made, she kept them to herself. She knew that Pete had loved her, and she had loved him. In a strange sort of way, that was enough.

So much of her past she had devoted to the man she now saw buried beside his beloved mother in the old cemetery in Pasadena.

Her future was going to be for herself, and for her daughter.

A week or so after the funeral, a huge, very public memorial service was held at the Good Shepherd Catholic church in Beverly Hills. Most of the great and the good from the movie business, past and present, were there to pay their respects to the man that few of them had really known and even fewer liked, but who had been as much a part of Hollywood as the famous sign itself.

Afterwards, a number of people had come up to Siena, ostensibly to offer their condolences but really to check out for themselves the damage that, it was now an open secret in industry circles, Randall Stein had done to her legendary looks.

She was starting to get exhausted, and had signalled to Hunter that she was just about ready to go home, when another gawper tapped her on the shoulder.

'Look,' she said, swinging round, 'I'm sorry, but it's been a really long day for me. I . . .' She stopped, and immediately smiled when she recognised Dierk Muller, her old director, the man who had given her her first break, and about whom she had once been so poisonously ungrateful in print. 'Dierk!' She blushed. 'What are you doing here? I didn't know you knew my father.'

'I didn't,' he said, honestly. His clipped German accent was just as she remembered it. 'I came here to see you.'

Siena's face fell.

'Look, I'm sorry for all those things I said about you, truly I am,' she stammered.

'About me being "second tier", you mean? Or are we talking about a different article?'

'Oh God,' she blurted out. 'I really am sorry. But I'm not sure if I can deal with another telling off today. So if you've come here to tell me how selfish I've been, you needn't bother, I already know. My dad just died, I'm supposed to feel awful about that but I don't, and people keep coming up to me and staring at my face like I'm some kind of fucking circus freak. I just want to go home and die.'

When she looked up, she saw that Dierk was smiling at her.

'Well, that's a shame,' he said brightly. 'Because I actually came here – and I know it's probably terribly inappropriate to intrude on your grief . . .' Siena shook her head and smiled at him reassuringly. 'But I wanted you to come and do a screen test for my new project. It's a bit off the wall. But I think the part would be perfect for you. I can messenger the script over to you in the morning, if you like.'

A screen test? She was so amazed, she stood there opening and closing her mouth wordlessly, like a wooden puppet.

'Well?' he said. 'Are you interested or not?'

'I thought you hated me,' she mumbled.

'Did you?' Dierk seemed to find that amusing.

'What about my face? My eyes?' she said. 'I have almost no vision in my right eye now, you know. I'm officially partially blind.'

'I didn't know that,' he said, nodding slowly and thoughtfully. 'But I don't see that it matters so terribly much. You can see, can't you?'

His confidence in her was infectious. If he could see past her scars and her damaged sight, perhaps other people would too, eventually.

She could have reached up and kissed him.

'Look, Siena,' he said, taking her by the shoulders to drive his point home, a habit she remembered from torturous hours on *The Prodigal Daughter*. 'I'm not interested in your face. I never was. I didn't cast you last time because you were some great big model.'

'You didn't?' She looked up at him hopefully.

'No,' he said, almost angrily. 'I cast you because you have talent.

472

Shitloads of it. It's in your soul and it's in your blood. Whatever that psychopath Stein may have told you, you've always been more than a pretty face. So.' He released her shoulders and reverted to his usual, even Teutonic tone. 'Do you want the script, or not?'

'Yes,' said Siena, and she flashed him the smile that no amount of battering could extinguish.

'Yes, I do. I want it. I want the script.'

Chapter Fifty-four

Eight months later . . .

Tiffany ripped the flower out of her hair and threw up her hands in exasperation.

'Lennox, honey,' she moaned, 'can you do this for me? I can't seem to get the stupid thing centred.'

'You know your problem, don't you?' said her old friend, sashaying over to her in his very expensive, slightly too tightly cut suit and deftly pinning the wayward white rose into place. 'No feminine skills. No feminine skills at all.'

It was the morning of her wedding day, and she was sitting in Laurie's old room at Hancock Park in a silk nightdress, practising her hair for this afternoon.

The wedding wasn't until three, and she'd rather hoped for a long lie-in, but unfortunately little Theo Wedan McMahon had had other ideas and had noisily demanded a feed at 5 a.m.

Any other day and Hunter would have given him his bottle, but of course it was bad luck to sleep together the night before your wedding, so he'd stayed across town in Venice with Max, who'd flown in from England to act as best man. Not that she really minded. Tiffany enjoyed the early morning feeds with her son, the feel of his tiny stroking fingers against her breast and the way he gazed directly up at her with his father's beautiful, deep blue eyes.

The baby had been born two months ago, and much to the disgust of her girlfriends Tiffany had already regained her slim, willowy figure, although now she had the added bonus of truly enormous breasts. Hunter told her she had the face of an angel and the body of a porn star – but then again, he was probably slightly biased.

It was he who had pushed for them to get married so soon after Theo's arrival. At first Tiffany had been opposed to a wedding. Neither of them was especially religious, after all, and she was frightened that the whole thing would turn into another McMahon media circus.

But now that the day had arrived, she was pleased she'd let him talk her into it. Claire had hired top-of-the-range security to protect their privacy as much as possible. But anyway, press or no press, she knew she shouldn't let a few paparazzi stop her from becoming Mrs Hunter McMahon. She did love him so utterly and completely.

'Hey there, the bride, can I help?'

Siena had mooched in and stood behind Lennox, admiring his handiwork.

She was looking so much better these days, thought Tiffany. Months of Claire's delicious food had helped her to regain her former curvaceous figure. Gone was the deathly pale, gaunt look she had had when she'd first left Randall. Her hair had grown back to its full length, and this morning it tumbled long and loose down her back in gorgeous Pre-Raphaelite waves. The scar on the right side of her face remained, and her left cheekbone now sat permanently lower than her right. Her face was no longer perfect. But Tiffany, at least, felt that it had gained something for that, a more real, approachable beauty that somehow sat better with the happier, kinder and more confident person she had become.

She had never regained the sight of her right eye, although to look at her you couldn't tell. And Siena herself had come to terms with her damaged sight with such an easy grace, laughingly displaying a prominent 'partially sighted' sticker on her jeep, that people often forgot she had any disability at all.

This morning she was wearing faded jeans and an old shirt of Hunter's, tied loosely under her breasts to reveal a smooth expanse of midriff. For the first time in her life, she was properly tanned after a week's break surfing in Maui, and the brown glow of her skin added to her general aura of well-being.

'I think we're OK here actually,' said Tiffany. 'Lennox has things under control, don't you, babe?'

'You better believe it,' he mumbled, through a mouthful of hairpins.

'I'm so tired, though. Theo was up half the night, bawling his little head off.'

'You should have called me,' said Siena, swiping a tortoiseshell clip from the dressing table and pinning up her own hair in a loose bun. 'I was up at four rereading that damn script. Dierk's such a fucking slave driver. Theo could have kept me company.'

She was four months into filming on Muller's new movie, and despite her frequent complaints, everyone could tell she was in seventh heaven about it. For all her braggadocio, in the past she had always been deeply insecure about her own talent. Now, for the first time, she felt she was being genuinely valued as an actress, not just Randall's girlfriend, Pete's daughter or a chip off the old Duke McMahon block. It was liberating.

'Hunter called earlier, by the way,' she said, a shadow falling across her face which Tiffany couldn't help but notice. 'He said he . . .' She paused for a split second. 'He and Max were going for a run, so you weren't to worry if you called and he wasn't there.'

'Oh, OK. Thanks.'

Tiffany was fully aware what an agony it was for Siena to be seeing Max again. Hunter had offered not to invite him if she thought she couldn't cope with it, but Siena wouldn't hear of such a thing. 'Don't be ridiculous!' she'd insisted. 'It's your wedding. You can't possibly not invite Max. How could you even think of having another best man?'

But inside, Tiffany knew that it was killing her. She had not enquired again about his life, or his supposed girlfriend. Tiffany was not at all sure that Hunter had done the right thing by lying to Siena about this, but she had to admit that she did seem happier and more stable as a result. So perhaps it *had* been for the best.

As far as Tiffany knew, Siena hadn't heard about Max's film deal and his new-found wealth, nor did she even know the name of his Broadway play. Today was bound to be difficult for her.

'Are you sure you're OK?' she asked, swinging round on her chair, to Lennox's annoyance as the rose slipped out of place yet again. 'About Max, I mean.'

'Oh, sure,' said Siena unconvincingly, waving her hand casually in an 'it's nothing' gesture. 'You know, I've known Max since I was a little kid, don't forget. It's not such a big deal. And it's not like we have to spend the whole evening together or anything. All I have to do is say hi to him, right? I mean, come on. How hard can it be?'

A few hours later, Hunter stood by the altar, shaking like a whippet.

Just when nobody thought he could get any handsomer, he'd gone and put on his morning dress for the wedding and outdone himself once again. He looked so divine, with the perfectly cut dark wool of his jacket offsetting his olive skin and the brilliant blue of his eyes, it would be a miracle if anyone even noticed the bride.

'She said she wouldn't do this,' he said in panic to Max, who was standing beside him in his own, slightly more threadbare version of the formal dress theme. In an ancient morning coat of his father's that had seen him through scores of rainy English weddings and which despite being a good two sizes too small for him, he considered 'lucky' and therefore indispensable, he looked more like Hunter's impoverished bodyguard than his best man. 'She swore to me she wouldn't make me wait. Where the fuck is she?'

'Mate.' Max laid a comforting hand on his friend's shoulder. 'Just relax. She's *not* late. It's only five to three.' He turned and gave a small smile to a beautiful red-headed girl in the second row, who returned his smile and added a small conspiratorial wink of encouragement.

'What's her name again?' asked Hunter. Max had brought the girl over with him from England, but between all the last-minute organisation for the wedding and his general state of heightened anxiety, Hunter had had little time to be sociable.

'Helen,' said Max.

'Pretty,' said Hunter.

'Hmm.' Max smiled. 'Yes. She is.'

The church was packed to the gills, with a congregation that looked alarmingly like a Who's Who of American television. Hugh Orchard was there with his partner, a small part of him dying inside to be watching Hunter finally getting married, in silent sympathy with teenage girls all across the country, and Tiffany's buxom cast-mates from *Sea Rescue* flashed white-toothed smiles across the aisle at the various perma-tanned hunks from *Counsellor*. On Hunter's side of the church, Caroline sat looking glamorous if somewhat under-dressed in a bottle-green halter-neck Armani dress that showed off rather a lot of her still-excellent cleavage, bottle-feeding a beautifully behaved Theo. Beside her sat an obviously dreadfully jet-lagged Christopher, who kept falling asleep and then waking himself up with a particularly violent snore, asking people in a loud, very British accent where on earth he was, much to the amusement of Claire, who sat on his other side.

'That's my son,' Caroline was whispering proudly to anyone who would listen, gesturing towards the altar. 'Isn't he handsome? Tiffany is a very lucky girl. Of course, Hunter and I have always been *terribly* close.'

Outside, kept back twenty feet from the church steps by solid steel fencing and six burly security guys, a growing crowd of fans and photographers jostled for position, trying to catch a glimpse of the famous guests as they arrived. Emma Duval, the frozen-featured face of LA-9 news, who had cornered Hunter at the now infamous Dodgers game with Siena and Randall, was engaged in a frantic battle with the bimbo from E! as to which of them had the right to the spot closest to the steps.

'I was here first, Tanisha,' she pouted, as the Amazonian, black goddess pushed past her.

'What*ever*, Emma,' replied her rival. 'I'm sure there's room for both of us.'

Meanwhile, the latest of the stragglers dashed past them into the church, the actors stopping for a few seconds of courtesy poses, everybody else darting inside as quickly as possible in the hope of bagging a late seat. The atmosphere, both inside the church and out, was electric.

After what seemed like an eternity to Hunter, the organ finally started playing the Trumpet Voluntary, and the entire church let out a collective gasp as Tiffany appeared on her father's arm and began her slow procession up the aisle.

She looked lovelier than even Hunter had imagined, in a simple, bias-cut cream silk dress and full-length veil that somehow made her look both demure and sexy. She was gazing directly at him and smiling, that same loving, serene smile that he had fallen in love with the very first day he saw her in the studios, when he'd helped her with her audition.

Suddenly, everyone else in the room seemed to melt away. He felt as though he might burst with pride and happiness as she drew nearer and nearer. What had he ever, ever done in life to deserve a girl so truly beautiful, inside and out?

Max, standing beside him, was probably the only man in the church not mesmerised by the bride.

He had sworn he wouldn't do it, he wouldn't stare at her or make an idiot of himself the moment she walked through the door. But he couldn't seem to help himself.

His eyes were drawn like magnets to Siena.

She was walking sedately behind Tiffany, in a full-length, pale gold dress, its subtle colour glinting seductively against the unusually bronzed glow of her skin, and its slick folds clinging to her beautiful body as though she had been poured into it.

He felt his chest tighten, and made a conscious effort to breathe.

Her hair was loose, her face . . . different, although nothing like some of the terrible photographs he'd seen in the New York press. Not that he would have cared how bad her scars were. She would always be infinitely beautiful to him.

Oh God, thought Siena, don't look, don't look, don't look!

She could feel Max's eyes boring into her like lasers. He must be shocked by her face. Revolted, probably.

The last time he'd seen her she'd been at the height of her beauty. Now look at her. He must be thanking his lucky stars that he had his beautiful French girlfriend here with him, instead of a washed-up freak like her. Siena had seen her the moment she arrived, standing in the second row, just behind Caroline. She'd only been able to catch a quick glimpse from the back, but it was enough to reveal the girl's elegant figure, tiny waisted in a fitted pink silk dress, and her mane of shining Titian hair.

Then she'd seen Max turn and smile at her, and felt her own heart shatter, like an egg in a microwave. There could be no more hope. They might be in the same room. But Max was lost to her. He was somebody else's now.

Somehow, she had to find the strength to walk down the aisle. She knew it was ungenerous and selfish, but she found herself wishing that Tiffany weren't looking quite so stunning. By comparison, she thought miserably, her eyes fixed to the gleaming parquet floor of the church, she must appear even uglier than ever.

Christ, thought Max. She can't even look at me.

Does she really still hate me that much?

Somehow they both made it through the service.

Siena was sitting next to a hugely pregnant Ines, who looked like a flame-haired stork with a giant beer belly. The father, apparently some feckless Argentine model she'd met on a shoot in Buenos Aires, was nowhere to be seen, but Ines seemed blissfully unconcerned.

'I 'ave 'is genes already,' she told Siena happily. 'What else do I need 'im for?' The two girls had become friends again in recent months, and Ines tried to cheer her up and distract her from Max and pink-dress girl during the wedding by making rude comments about all the *Sea Rescue* bimbos. 'Look at that one,' she whispered, pointing to a ludicrously 'enhanced' bottle blonde opposite. 'What deed she play – the inflatable safety ring?'

Siena smiled dutifully, but inside she felt utterly devastated.

How was she going to get through a whole evening, knowing he was only feet away from her? Watching him laughing and kissing and dancing with his stunning French girlfriend? The whole thing was unbearable. He was going to have to make a speech! She hadn't even *thought* about that. What if he started talking about the old days with Hunter? Would he mention her? He would have to, wouldn't he? And then everyone would be turning around to look at her, remembering that the two of them used to be together, back when she'd still had her looks, thinking how much better off he was now with Mademoiselle Perfect Body.

Oh God. She couldn't do it, she couldn't! Why hadn't she told Hunter not to invite him when she'd had the chance?

Once the torturous service was finally over, all the key players were ushered out on to the steps for formal photographs. As best man, Max was standing within a few feet of the bridesmaids, so it was impossible for Siena to keep ignoring him completely.

He glanced across at her and gave a tentative nod of acknowledgement. She nodded back, before hurriedly turning her attention to the photographer. Please God, just get this over with.

'Right.' Caroline's cut-glass English accent pierced the excited hum like a dart from a blow-pipe. Everybody turned to listen. 'I'd like a picture of the bridesmaids, please. Oh, and Maxy, darling, you too. Chop, chop! The bridesmaids and the best man.'

Like two zombies, Max and Siena edged reluctantly closer together. Max, his heart pounding, frantically scanned the crowd for Helen, but couldn't see her anywhere. Meanwhile Siena practically hurled Liza, the only other adult bridesmaid, between herself and Max. But Caroline, never famed for her sensitivity, intervened. 'No, no, no,' she said bossily. 'Max in the middle, big girls on either side, little girls at the front. Come on, you lot!'

Stupid cow, thought Siena. Stupid, stupid cow. She hadn't seen Hunter in donkey's years and now she was acting like the star of the fucking show. Why couldn't she just fuck off back to England and leave them all alone?

Max, who knew Caroline a little better, suspected that her rearrangement of their places was entirely deliberate. She'd made it clear at Batcombe that she was fully aware of his feelings for Siena, the meddlesome old witch. Unfortunately he was also in no position to argue with the mother of the groom, and shuffled around Liza to do as he was told.

He and Siena were now side by side. He could feel her bare arm brushing against the dark wool of his suit, and could have fainted with longing. Where the fuck was Helen when he needed her? She was supposed to be protecting him from this. That was why he'd brought her with him, for God's sake. Even now, despite their physical closeness, or perhaps because of it, Siena refused to look at him. He could feel himself sweating beneath his too-tight morning coat. Evidently its lucky properties had run out.

This was torture. He wanted to reach out and pull her to him, never, ever let her go again.

'Say cheese!' said Caroline brightly.

The camera flashed, and caught for posterity the image of four smiling girls, and two wretched souls, gazing in miserable desperation into the distance.

'Oh, Max, there you are.' Siena's heart leapt into her mouth and stayed there. It was the girl. She was even more stunning close up,

480

with her creamy white cheeks and watery blue eyes which made her hair look even more goddess-like than it had from a distance, and her clinging, raw-silk dress showing off her tall, lean body in all the right places. Siena didn't think she had ever felt so much hatred for another human being.

'Are you done with the pictures?'

She didn't sound very French.

'Yes, yes, I think so.' Max sounded relieved, thought Siena. Probably pleased to be able to get away from her at last.

'Helen, this is Siena,' he mumbled, somehow managing to introduce the two of them without making any eye contact. 'Siena, Helen.'

Siena opened her mouth to say something. How do you do, pleased to meet you, anything. But suddenly, as if an elastic band had just snapped inside her, she found the words had stuck in her throat and the tears that she had been holding back for so long began pouring out of her in an uncontrollable flood. Oh Jesus. What must she look like?

She looked from the girl to Max and back again and was horrified to hear herself emit a sort of howl, like a dying animal.

She had to get out of there. But there was nowhere to go. A solid wall of photographers hemmed her in on all sides.

Pushing her way past Caroline and the other bridesmaids, she turned and ran, sobbing, back into the empty church, slamming the heavy wooden door behind her. It was her only chance of escape.

'Siena!' Hunter started after her, followed by a concerned-looking Tiffany.

'Oh my goodness,' said Helen. 'D'you think she's all right?'

But Max was too quick for all of them.

'No, leave it,' he said, pushing past Hunter and barring his way. 'This is between me and Siena. I'll go.'

He stepped inside. Immediately the cool, dank air of the church, smelling faintly of extinguished candles, incense and the lingering miasma of a hundred different perfumes, assailed his senses. For some reason the smell reminded him of England, of home.

At first he couldn't see her. It was gloomy with the doors shut and all the lights out, and his eyes took a moment to adjust from the glaring sunshine outside. But then he heard a stifled sob, and saw a tiny figure curled up in a ball at the foot of the pulpit, half hidden by a vast spray of white bridal lilies.

'Go away!' she wailed, as she heard footsteps approaching. 'Please. I just want to be alone.'

The footsteps kept coming, louder and louder, with a firm, male tread. When she looked up and saw it was Max, she put her head in her hands and moaned even louder. He squatted down on his haunches beside her and waited for her to look up at him. When she did her beautiful, dark blue eyes were still wet and glistening with tears, and she was biting down on her lower lip to prevent it from trembling. She looked ten years old again.

'I'm sorry,' he whispered. 'I didn't mean to upset you.'

Siena sniffed, wiping her eyes briskly with the back of her hand. 'You didn't,' she said quickly. 'It was . . . something else that upset me. Really, I'm fine.'

'Oh.'

He frowned, disappointed. How arrogant she must think him, for assuming her tears would be over him. After all, she had hundreds of reasons to be feeling over-emotional on Hunter's wedding day. 'OK,' he said awkwardly. 'Well, er, do you want to talk about it? Can I help?'

He noticed that she had pulled her mane of hair forward to cover the scars on the left side of her face. Without thinking, he reached his hand towards her and pushed it back again.

'Don't,' she said, hurriedly placing her hand over his.

She felt the familiar warm roughness of the back of his hand. The physical sensation of his skin against hers was so powerful she almost stopped breathing.

Oh God, what was she going to do? She loved him so much.

Neither of them released the other's hand.

'Why not?' His voice was deep and gentle, like a caress, and when he spoke he never took his eyes from hers. 'You look beautiful. So beautiful.'

'Please.' She pulled away from him, with another involuntary sob, and cringed back behind the lilies like a frightened fawn. Max sat down on the cold stone of the altar steps beside her. 'I don't look beautiful.' He could hear the anguish in her voice. 'I look horrific.'

'That's not true,' said Max.

'It is!' she insisted. 'You know it is!'

'Siena . . .' he began, his own voice breaking. How could she possibly think she looked anything other than perfect to him?

'Max, no,' she said desperately, putting her hand across his mouth.

His kindness – his sympathy – was more than she could bear. Especially with his girlfriend waiting outside for him. At last all pretence of self-control went out of the window.

'Please don't say any more,' she implored him. 'I don't want your pity! I know what I look like now and I know who I am, all right?

482

And, and . . .' she stammered. 'Whatever has happened between us in the past, however awfully I've behaved . . .' She wrung her hands together desperately, unable to look at him. 'We loved each other once.'

Max felt the tears stinging his own eyes.

'Oh, darling,' he began, but she wouldn't allow him to speak.

'And I want to remember that the way it was. The way I was. I know that you're happy and settled with someone else now.' A solitary fat tear rolled off her cheek and splashed noiselessly down on to the gold silk of her dress, spreading into a dark, round patch across the top of her thigh. 'And she's beautiful, absolutely beautiful, and she seems very nice and everything as well . . .'

'Siena . . .' He tried to interrupt her, but she knew if she didn't say this now she would never find the strength again.

'And her English accent is really good for a French girl,' she found herself adding irrationally, unable to stop the words from coming now that they had started.

So *that* was it, thought Max. She thought Helen was Freddie. But how did she even know about Freddie?

'I'm happy for you, Max, truly I am,' she wittered on. 'Hunter's already told me all about her – Helen, is it? You deserve someone decent and kind, someone who loves you and will treat you . . .'

'*Siena!*'

He bellowed the word so loudly that it echoed around the empty church, bouncing off the walls like the booming voice of God. She looked up at him, startled.

'I don't know what Hunter has told you,' he said. 'But Helen is not my girlfriend. She's just a friend I've known for years. I brought her here because . . .' He hesitated. 'Well, because I thought I might need a shoulder to cry on. Moral support. Or something.' Clearly he was having difficulty getting the words out. 'Because I knew I'd be seeing you again. And I didn't know if I could handle it.'

She looked at him blankly. She'd heard what he said, but she couldn't quite take it in.

'There is no one else, Siena. There was someone for a while, but it ended. Months and months ago.'

For a moment she couldn't speak at all. When she did, her voice was so hoarse it was almost a whisper.

'Why?'

'Because I love you,' he said quietly, reaching down for her hands and pressing them both in his. What was the point of denying it now? 'Because I never stopped loving you. And I know I behaved appallingly, and there's no reason why you should ever, ever forgive me, for Camille or anything else, let alone love me again. But I need you to know.' He gazed at her solemnly. 'That I'll always love you, Siena. And I'll always be here for you, whenever you need me. Even if it's only as a friend. I just want to be near you.'

Could it really be true?

Did he really still love her? Even now, after everything?

She looked across at his beautiful face. The blond floppy hair, the broken nose with its perpetual smattering of freckles, the soft, loving eyes, searching her own anxiously for a response.

'Max,' she whispered, almost to herself.

'Siena,' he said. 'My darling, darling Siena.'

And before she knew quite how it was happening, she found herself leaning in towards him, her fingers wrapping themselves around the back of his neck, her lips locking with his in the kiss that both had fantasised about for so, so long.

When they finally, reluctantly released one another, Max sighed and slowly allowed his face to relax into an enormous, boyish grin.

'I want to pinch myself,' he said. 'I can't quite believe this is real.'

'I know,' said Siena, leaning forward to kiss him again, this time on his forehead, eyes, nose and chin. She needed to remember every inch of him. To never, ever let him out of her sight, or her arms, again.

Just then, the huge oak door of the church creaked open, and a shaft of brilliant, blinding sunshine burst in on them, lighting up their embrace like a theatre spotlight on Romeo and Juliet.

'Oh sorry.' It was Hunter, silhouetted awkwardly in the glowing doorway. 'I thought I'd come and see if Siena was OK. But, er, I see things are, er, are all fine. So, I guess I'll just leave you guys to it.'

The door swung shut again with a clunk, plunging them back into welcome darkness. Max wrapped his arm around Siena's waist and pulled her even closer to him.

'Do you think it would be *terribly* wrong . . .' he began.

'What, in a church, you mean?' she said, allowing her hand to slip joyfully beneath the waistband of his suit trousers in response to his embrace, feeling his desire for her as strong and powerful as her own. 'Oh, yes.' She smiled. '*Terribly* wrong. Unforgivable, really. Especially for a good Catholic girl like me.'

'Yes, I thought so,' said Max, easing her gently down on to the cool stone floor and positioning himself above her, face to face. 'Shame.'

For a moment she felt a stab of disappointment. Surely, after so long, he wasn't going to make her wait? But she relaxed when she looked up and saw him gazing wickedly down at her.

Now *that* was a look she remembered.

Painfully slowly, he began peeling the gold silk dress from each of her shoulders in turn.

'Still,' he said, kissing her softly on the mouth and feeling her squirming beneath him with pleasure, 'there's always confession, isn't there?'

Siena grinned.

'Confession? Oh absolutely,' she said, kissing him back for all she was worth. 'Absolutely.'

Acknowledgements

Thanks first and foremost to my family: my parents, for their bottomless love and support; my brother James, and my sisters, Louise and Alice; my lovely husband Robin; and last but not least, my beautiful daughter Sefi. I am so proud of you, darling, my wonderful, wonderful girl.

Thanks to all the writers who helped and encouraged me, not only to start but to finish this book. Especially Louise, my sister; Fred – you can do it, Tills – Metcalf: I'm proud to be a mentee; Lydia Slater, who took a chance on a totally unknown writer at the *Sunday Times* and was the first person to pay actual money for something I wrote – thank you so much; and the uniquely gorgeous Chris Manby, my lifeboat in LA.

Unfairly, for someone with the world's best family, I also have the world's best friends. I owe so much to all of you, but must specially mention a few: Zanna Hooper, the kindest woman in England, for her endless hospitality and for being a shoulder to cry on; also Soph, Scorbs and all the Cambridge girls. Rupert Channing, my former partner in crime, for Pimms and champagne chasers in Boisdale and for making the city so much fun. Katrina Mayson, Claire Depke and Belen Hormaeche, my fellow Wolditz survivors, I love you all. Christian Brun, Jamie Griffith, Rutts, Sparky, Mambly and all the boys in my life. Special thanks also to Dominique Rawley, whose kindness and compassion through my *annus horribilis* will never be forgotten. You are a friend indeed.

Finally, many thanks to my editors, Kate Mills at Orion and Jamie Raab at Warner, for all your patience, help and good advice, and to everyone at Janklow & Nesbit; especially Luke Janklow for believing in me, and this book, from the beginning; and the lovely Christelle Chamouton.

But the last word on this page must go to my incredible agent and very dear friend, Tif Loehnis, without whom this book would never have been written, let alone published. Who'd have thought, Tif, when I first saw you across second court all those years ago in your multi-coloured, stripy jeans, that it would ever come to this? For once, words fail me. But from the bottom of my heart, thank you. For everything.